I0746964

SHADOWLANCER

HEART OF A DARKDANCER #1

RAMÓN TERRELL

TAL PUBLISHING

Shadowlancer
Heart of a Darkdancer #1
Ramón Terrell
Copyright © 2022 Ramon Terrell
1st Edition 2022
All Rights Reserved
Tal Publishing

All rights reserved. No part of this book may be reproduced or transmitted in any form or by any electronic or mechanical means, including photocopying, recording or by any information storage and retrieval system, without the express written permission of the copyright holder, except where permitted by law. This novel is a work of fiction. Names, characters, places and incidents are either the product of the author's imagination, or, if real, used fictitiously.

ISBN: 978-1-7778964-5-4 (Paperback)

Edited by: Michelle Dunbar

Cover artwork by: Nick Deligaris

Tal Publishing

SPECIAL THANKS

A special THANK YOU you to my dear friends, Michelle Corsillo, Katie J Cross, and Greg Vose. You are amazing friends who always grab my arms when I stumble and start flailing.

A special THANK YOU to Cat Lee, Karen Pellet, Jessica Springer Guernsey, and Flora Samuelson. I don't know what I'd do if I couldn't count on you. You rock.

Another very special THANK YOU to Alexander Tyler, Dai Dao, and Arthur Carnevale. Your contributions to Shadowlancer have meant a great deal.

And a very special THANK YOU to Robin Hobb, Brandon Sanderson, Dan Wells, Sherrilyn Kenyon, Diane Salvatore, R. A. Salvatore, Dean Wesley Smith, Kristine Kathryn Rusch, and James Artemis Owen for believing in Shadowlancer, spreading the word, and helping me where I needed it.

ACKNOWLEDGMENTS

This book is special in a number of ways, one of which is how so many of you graciously entered my universe to help bring Shadowlancer to life. My sincere thank you to all of the amazing people who backed the kickstarter that brought Shadowlancer to reality. Every single one of you are amazing, and I'm honored and humbled to have you as part of this book.

My heartfelt thank you to Steven Scott, Stone Sanchez, Charles Beeghly, Tam Quach, Dayron Lee Colon Centeno, Mike Thompson, Cody Allen, Sam Fishbeck, Noah Gustafson, Danielle Wolf, Alex Serrano, Kirk Tinsley, Dave Fonville, Jacob Malevich, Matthew Murphy, Megyn MacDougall, David Hankerson, Chris Arnold, Joshua P. Earl, Tyler Barnwell, Lisa Barracato, Brandon Tupper, Jordan Green, Gabriel Ouellette, Keegan Spillane, Nicholas Olinger, Vennessa Moon, Jonathan Hamm, Erika Kuta Marler, Amélie Bouvier, Gerald P. McDaniel, Chrissandra Porter, Sarah L. Stevenson, Michaël Gibbons, Dominic Kotwica, Breanna Martinez, Jason Bowden, Michael B. Mitchell, Julio A. Paul, Ty Fortenberry, Dylon Kiley, Dave and Rose Fonville, Collin Bartley, Breanna Martinez, Michael Sugarman, Rob Martineau, Michael Scott Boone, Ryan James, Tyler Hise, Jennifer Huckabay, Kelvin Golden, Gareth Edwards, Caleb Christensen, Adam Cole, Caitlin Northcutt, Deborah Hedges, Eric Cabral, Brian Bauer, Neil Trotman, Sam Fischbeck, Erik Foxvog, Kristen Roskob, Dirk Rasmussen, Ellisha Holliman, Liam Fischback, Robert Kennedy, Matthew E Adcock, Austin Kile, Alicia T Stoesser, Taylor Pope, Timothy Maynard, Jonathan Bloom, Michael Gibbons, Sarah Stevenson, Marc Berry, Nathan J. Sulger, Joshua Kurtz, Mike Goins, Dustin Thatcher, Broderick Dicken, Andrew Scott, Carolynn Steele-Law, Christopher Manley, Karissa Wahl, Michael Mitchell, Sarah Phillips, Carson Leeney, Sean, Alan Smith, Samuel Taylor, Trazon, Darin Hoover, Travis Condo, Lincoln Rose, and Dragonsteel Entertainment.

And once again, thanks to ALL of you who backed this project in Kickstarter. This book is here because you believed in it, and I am forever humbled by your generous contributions.

1

Blood in the sand—a coppery smell mingled with a baking, dusty odor that Zaiyera hated. When the wind shifted, betraying the presence of raiders hiding on the other side of the towering dunes ahead, she knew she'd soon be surrounded by that smell.

The few black braids hanging out of her keffiyeh fell over her face as she leaned forward to give her camel a pat on the neck. "Be ready, my friend. There will be death today." She straightened again and touched the small, red four-point flower tattoo on her forehead, then the two identical ones on each cheek.

Another camel appeared beside her, ridden by a man built like a wedge of muscle. A sturdy northerner. Zaiyera regarded him as he pulled up beside her. Barum, he'd said his name was? He'd had a thick black beard when she had met him at the beginning of this journey. The heat had persuaded him to cut it off. "You talk to that thing like it understands you," Barum said. "Can't deny you southern folk're different, but you're a little further different than any I've met."

Zaiyera returned her gaze to the approaching dunes as they slowly made their way forward, several hundred yards ahead of the main caravan. A breeze dragged its warm fingers through her hair and across her face, further infecting her nostrils with the scent of sweat and the arrogant confidence of their future attackers.

"You don't talk much, do you?" Barum said after the silence endured. "Didn't mean offense, miss my lady."

"No offense taken," Zaiyera replied, scanning the peaks of both sand dunes towering over the trail between them. The raiders she smelled were on the other side of the dune on the right, but it would be foolish not to assume there would be an attack from the other side as well. The whole scene looked like a set of jaws waiting to clamp shut as soon as they were fully inside the waiting maw.

Barum followed her gaze. "You see something I don't? Other than an ocean of sand sprinkled with dunes and rocks, that is."

"Prepare the caravan for attack." Zaiyera jerked her chin in the direction of the dunes ahead. "It will come from both sides as soon as we're completely between them."

Barum grunted. "Does seem a perfect spot for an ambush. Why not just go around?"

Another camel arrived on Zaiyera's left side, ridden by a man with the tell-tale beauty of a Viriksani. Jaide Amadi nodded in greeting, his green eyes sparkling like the Great Sea to the east. "Because, good Barum, the sand on the other side of those dunes is too thick for wagon wheels. If we travel far enough around to avoid *that*, we will be well away from the trail, and the raiders would attack us anyway, yes? The only advantage would be the possibility of running them off or killing them before their friends arrive. Either way, it's a fight."

He was right, of course. There would be no avoiding a fight this day. Zaiyera just hoped, as always, that there would be no casualties among the people she and these two men guarded. "Warn the caravan and prepare the guards for attack."

"You're the boss," Barum replied, and turned his mount away.

The Viriksani offered a half smile and held his hand to his heart with a bow in the saddle. "It will be done." He wheeled his mount away, the straps at the back of his brown turban flapping as he set his camel into a long-legged gallop.

Ten guards, including Barum and Jaide, were divided in half and positioned on either side of the wagons by the time they reached the halfway point between the dunes. The looming slopes cast a welcome shade from the blazing sun, complemented by the soft breeze that drifted by. While the caravanners—almost all foreigners—complained that even the breeze felt like it came from a kiln, the Samharan people native to these lands closed their eyes and breathed a contented sigh.

Then the attack came.

* * *

The raiders spilled over the side of the dunes in a cacophony of shouting, whooping, and hollering. They waved scimitars and machetes with jagged edges designed to break an adversary's weapon.

"*Soo loonah,*" Zaiyera cooed into Sadiq's ear. The camel's furry ear twitched and some of his tension released beneath her.

She looked over her shoulder to the caravan where the guards waited on mounts. Two raiders broke off from the main band and sped her way, having noticed the distance between Zaiyera and the caravan. They

"*Heyup!*" Zaiyera barked. Sadiq lurched into motion. The camel's run was swift, blowing the few exposed braids from underneath Zaiyera's purple keffiyeh away from her face. She guided Sadiq to the right of the approaching trio and the marauders angled with her. Zaiyera drew Shatr, her magnificent blue-steel scimitar.

After so many years together, Sadiq knew her intention, and the camel continued his arcing direction, just managing to get Zaiyera to the outside raider while avoiding the other two. The woman closest to Zaiyera looked at her with murderous brown eyes that widened in surprise upon their first clash.

Zaiyera flipped her scimitar over her head and caught it with her left hand. She swung the blade into the raider's weapon with such force, she nearly disarmed her opponent. As soon as the blades disengaged, Zaiyera cut down and back. The maneuver missed, but she hadn't intended to score a hit. The true blow came to the raider's confidence. As Zaiyera turned Sadiq, she saw the other woman's realization that her intended prey was stronger and quicker than she.

"Ip yip!" Zaiyera chirped. Sadiq surged forward.

The raider shouted to her companions and pointed her scimitar at Zaiyera. They had been forced around the far side of the duel, but now were headed straight for Zaiyera. With a squeeze of her knees to his sides, she guided Sadiq to veer to the right. The raiders adjusted with her, but they wouldn't be able to come at her from both sides.

One of the raiders slowed, while the other continued toward Zaiyera, angling to the side to get behind her.

"Ip yip!" she said to Sadiq, who stretched his neck out as he burst into a full run.

Zaiyera guided Sadiq toward the raider coming up beside her. As he drew the blade back to sweep at her head, Zaiyera snapped her hands to the back of the camel's hump. The raider's triumphant grin disappeared when Zaiyera, with her weight on her hands, tucked her feet in and leapt toward the raider from Sadiq's back.

Shatr flashed in her left hand. Zaiyera blocked the raider's blade while curling her body midair. She snapped her foot into the attacker's nose. It shattered in a spray of blood while Zaiyera drew her foot back and collided with his chest, knees leading.

Her opponent hit the ground head first with a sickening crunch, while Zaiyera landed in a roll. As soon as her feet were under her, she spun in a crouch with Shatr held in a defensive angle, the raider with the broken neck dying behind her.

The second rider turned his camel and was heading straight for her.

Zaiyera stole a quick glance over her shoulder. The woman she'd first clashed with was bearing down on her from behind. She sprinted toward the closer woman.

The raider veered to the left to line up Zaiyera for a swing of her blade.

Having seen enough of the woman's actions to know that she was right-handed, Zaiyera guessed the raider's move and started in that direction. The woman pulled her camel farther to the left, but they were too close. Zaiyera gave a shout and leapt at the camel, feigning a jab at its head.

The frightened camel groaned and lurched away, causing the rider to overbalance toward Zaiyera.

Shatr flashed out toward the top of the woman's head. The raider screamed as the scimitar dug into her scalp. Zaiyera gritted her teeth as she slid the blade free. The woman tumbled from the saddle while her camel angled toward the other riderless animal shambling away from the battle.

Back down the trail, the other raiders had reached the base of the enclosing sand dunes and had engaged the caravan guards. Clanging steel and battle cries shattered the serenity of the desert, while the coppery smell of blood leaking into the sand assaulted her nostrils. Blood in the sand.

The ground vibrated beneath her feet. Zaiyera instinctively dove to the side just as a scimitar whipped overhead. She came to her feet in a crouch as the third raider came around. *That was stupid, Zaiyera,* she chastised herself for forgetting the other attacker.

She held Shatr at her side, waiting as the raider turned and moved his camel to the left to get a clear swing at her.

Zaiyera drew a dagger from its sheath on her leg.

The raider saw her draw the weapon but was moving too fast. He pulled on the reins and the camel grunted as it turned aside. Zaiyera let fly the dagger. The throw had been to distract, which worked, as the rider flinched away, causing his camel to slow to a trot to keep from stumbling. Zaiyera sprinted after the slowing animal as the raider struggled to get it under control. When he turned, Zaiyera cut Shatr at him in a sideways arc.

The blade bit deeply into his arm, and Zaiyera slid it free. The man screamed as he tumbled from the saddle. His screams died abruptly when Shatr opened his throat.

Doing her best to ignore the horrible smell of death, Zaiyera called to Sadiq. *"Kaya yip!"* she called. Waiting patiently, if nervously, a dozen feet away, Zaiyera's groaning companion trotted toward her.

She jogged to Sadiq as the woman Zaiyera had felled struggling to stand. She held one hand to her profusely bleeding scalp, while her other hand moved in a pattern in the air. Her shaking hands began to move more smoothly, and a faint golden glow trailed her gestures.

Zaiyera changed direction and sprinted for the woman, Shatr at her side. The raider completed her gesture and a three-foot tall glowing green disk appeared in front of her. More than a dozen spheres opened in the disk and launched razor-like shards. Zaiyera sliced Shatr upward and dove aside. The shards zipped past her.

The raider's mouth fell open when the green disk fell apart in the air. The hesitation cost her.

Zaiyera came to her feet in a run, quickly closed the distance between herself and the other woman and ran the blue-steel scimitar through her stomach. The impaled raider bent forward with a gurgling grunt. Zaiyera snatched her blade free, and the woman crumbled to the ground. More blood flowed into the once pure sand.

She wiped blood off the scimitar on the raider's clothes, sheathed it, then turned and cupped her hands to her mouth. "Lancers!" she shouted, using the northern term for those who danced the stream.

If anyone heard, they didn't have time to respond. All the caravan guards were fully embroiled in battle. One was down, his body lying at an awkward angle, and the rest were outnumbered two to one.

Sadiq trotted up beside her, and Zaiyera crouched, swung her arms, and leapt with all her strength. She reached up and grabbed hold of the saddle and swung her leg over. *"Hey yup!"* she yelled. Sadiq groaned and broke into a run.

As she drew near the embattled caravan, Zaiyera saw that the big Dor'haighener, Barum, and one of the other guards had taken a back-to-back position. On the other side of the caravan, Jaide Amadi battled two men at once. The Viriksani danced beautifully between his adversaries, keeping them at bay with slices and parries, stabs and feints. He seemed hardly to tire at all.

A man and woman appeared at the top of another dune. They made their way down to the middle of the mountain of sand and began to dance the stream. Their gestures were wide and sweeping, with golden light trailing their movements. If those two weren't trying to kill the people Zaiyera was defending, she'd have thought their dance beautiful. The way their movements complemented each other, how the man swept his arms in a wide, upward arc, while the woman swept her leg into the air, then arced both her hands in a downward sweep.

The beautiful dance turned deadly as the streamdancers finished their movements and released the flow they'd drawn.

A disk larger than one of the caravan wagons materialized in the air as if sliding out of a running stream of water. The warping image continued to slide upright seemingly out of an invisible slit in the air, until it finally became solid.

Zaiyera felt the stream from even this far away. She imagined the pure bliss of touching it, swirling it, and drawing the flow into herself and projecting it outward. Zaiyera clenched her teeth and shook herself out of the distraction. *Never. Never again.* She changed course and charged straight for the two streamdancers.

The translucent blue disk pulsated, then rotated. The disk turned sideways, spinning faster and faster. Bolts of electricity streaked across the disk while it spun faster still. Now a blur, the disk shot across the distance between the streamdancers and two of the caravan guards. It blasted one unfortunate man apart and sliced cleanly through the nearest guard. She hit the ground in two parts and lay on her back, staring sightlessly at the burning sun.

Zaiyera drew her scimitar in frustration, but she could do nothing. *Too far away.* She urged Sadiq to run faster, and her laboring companion stretched his neck out, moving as fast as his long, knobby-kneed legs could take them.

The disk spat streaks of electricity that struck several nearby caravanners. They collapsed, twitching and spasming on the ground. The disk shot across the air again. Three caravan guards in its path dropped to their stomachs at the last moment. The disk whizzed over their heads, missing by inches.

The disk stopped several feet in front of the streamdancers again, and both made complementing gestures drawing from the stream once more and adding it to the disk. It grew larger as it spun in place before them.

Zaiyera sheathed Shatr and placed her hands in the middle of Sadiq's hump. She leaned forward, placed all her weight on her hands, and lifted herself up. Placing her feet just behind her hands and at the back of the hump, Zaiyera slowly uncurled her body, holding her hands out for balance atop the running camel.

One of the streamdancers made a short, snapping gesture toward Zaiyera. A tiny disk appeared in front of him, elongated into a spear, and shot toward her.

Zaiyera drew Shatr and sliced it apart before it got close.

The dancer's eyes widened and he said something to the woman beside him. She made a gesture, and the spinning disk turned horizontal again.

Zaiyera crouched and tapped Sadiq on his right side. The camel veered in that direction. She leapt from his back.

The disk shot forward.

The bolt of raw power shot underneath Zaiyera as she glided into a forward flip over it. As she continued her flip, the disk streaked toward a crowd of caravanners.

Zaiyera sliced Shatr in an upward arc as she came upright in her flip. It was a blind strike, and she prayed to the Goddess Shakimah that her blade struck true.

She hit the ground in a roll and sprawled onto her side amidst a shower of electric sparks. Zaiyera forced herself up, spitting sand and grit. Without looking, she swiped Shatr upwards in front of herself.

The scimitar cut through a speeding disk of blue light coming straight for her face. Zaiyera sprinted for the two streamdancers, grinning at the look of disbelief on their faces.

They began their movements again, their gestures coordinated, each sweep of a hand or swipe of a foot complementing the other. They were working as one to share the lifeprice. *Smart.*

Two small rotating disks appeared in the air and flew towards her.

Zaiyera skidded to a stop and sheared through the disk with an outward cut, then brought the hilt of the scimitar up, the blade pointing down across her body. The disk collided with the blade and sliced in half around it. Both pieces fizzled into nothingness in the air.

By the time the two streamdancers could process the what had happened, Zaiyera closed the distance and ran the woman through before she could touch the stream again. In one motion, Zaiyera turned from the dying woman while pulling her scimitar free. The remaining streamdancer fumbled to draw his rusty scimitar.

He'd barely gotten half the blade free by the time Shatr took his hand. The sword slipped back in its sheath as the raider's hand tumbled into the sand. The man gave one brief holler of agony before Zaiyera silenced him forever.

She lowered the lifeless body to rest against the dune and pulled her weapon free. A quick survey of the area told her that the battle had mostly been won. With all three of their streamdancers dead, and the remaining guards bolstered by a handful of caravanners, the raiders had no hope of victory.

Zaiyera started toward the caravan as the attackers began their retreat. The defenders gave chase until one of the last of the fleeing bandits turned and made a quick gesture. Zaiyera growled. She'd thought only three streamdancers were with this band.

The woman stabbed her hand into the air and drew back. A whip that looked like it was made of air came into form, and she lashed it at the pursuing guards.

The air-whip struck the two leading guards as though it were a physical weapon. The whip cut through robes and tore flesh open. The pursuing guards fell mid-stride, grabbing at bleeding wounds. Another guard got close and drew her scimitar. The streamdancer flicked the whip at her, and the guard chopped in a downward stroke.

Zaiyera looked on with a mental sigh. It must have been a reflexive action. The guard knew better than that, surely? The whip passed right through the sword and slashed the woman's sleeve, ripping open an angry gash in her arm.

She sprinted toward the conflict and finally got herself between the streamdancer and the remaining guards. The raider lashed her air-whip at Zaiyera, who brought Shatr up. With a flick of the scimitar, she sliced cleanly through the whip. It dissipated in a puff of air before the shocked woman.

With a quick circular gesture, the raider touched the stream and blasted sand into the air.

The defenders guarded their eyes against the assault. When Zaiyera looked up again, the woman was halfway up the dune. She gave chase, high-stepping up the shifting mound. By the time she reached the crest, the woman had nearly reached the base of the dune. The rest of the raiders had already mounted their camels and taken flight.

Zaiyera half ran half leapt down the other side of the dune. She clenched her eyes and mouth shut when she lost her balance and tumbled. Sand found its way into every space in her clothes, grinding on her skin.

Halfway down, she regained her feet and opened her eyes in time to see the woman well away from the base. She moved in rhythmic patterns, golden sheets of light trailing her sweeping gestures. A giant glowing blue disk wavered in the air and became solid, almost twice the woman's size. Patterns mirroring the gestures the raider had made filled the disk as it flared to life.

To pay such a lifeprice *she must be really afraid.* Zaiyera tried to sit back into the soft slope and stop herself before that thing discharged. She finally managed to stop and crouched on the side of the dune. She held Shatr in front of her, hilt up, blade pointed down diagonally.

The giant disk pulsated with energy, then burst into hundreds of shards. The shards elongated downward and plunged into the ground.

Zaiyera held her stance while she scanned the area. Those shards went into the ground, which meant …

She took off down the dune, hardly caring if she fell again and tumbled all the way to the base. A section of dune exploded behind her in a giant funnel.

Her braids whipped about her head as the funnel passed overhead. She kept Shatr in a white-knuckled grip, her lifeline against this massive display of power.

The funnel sucked her up into its middle. Zaiyera squinted through the blowing sand. If she lost her orientation, this thing could spit her out headfirst into the ground.

Another blast knocked her sideways, and through the tempest,

Zaiyera saw a second woman gesturing in her direction. She must have been hidden to the side of the dune.

Zaiyera couldn't stop her body from turning and tumbling in the funnel, but she managed to keep mental stock of her enemies' positions. A barrage of glowing shards pierced the tempest.

Her back almost parallel to the ground, Zaiyera swept Shatr over her body and down. The scimitar cut through the stream powering the shards, and most of them burst to pieces. Her counter had come late, however. Some shards slipped through and dealt her stinging cuts. If not for her robes and her body tumbling, they might have struck vital areas.

The funnel moved away from the dune, carrying her dangerously high in the air. If Zaiyera severed the stream powering the funnel now, she would fall more than twenty feet. She tried to keep from getting dizzy in the endless turning and flipping, side to side, head over heels.

One of the women on the ground touched the stream again, sending wave after wave of glowing blue shards speeding into the funnel.

Struggling to see through the haze, Zaiyera sliced in the general direction of the streamdancers. She cut through the flow of one, then another of the women's efforts. Most of the shards dissipated in the air, but some reached her before Zaiyera severed the flow powering them.

Zaiyera grunted when another handful of shards sliced across her skin. She clenched her teeth. The blowing sand all around her worsened the sting, but she dare not cry out, lest she breathe it in.

Two more assaults came. Another slipped through her defense; this one in the form of a blue spear that nearly ran her through. At the last moment, Zaiyera swept Shatr in a downward arc. The spear grazed her side just before she cut through the flow. Searing pain shot through her side, and she almost lost her grip on the scimitar.

The ground was less than ten feet below. It would have to do. Zaiyera focused on the funnel, feeling the force powering it. The flow, drawn from the stream of power itself, kept the funnel alive, kept Zaiyera spinning aloft inside of it. With a swing of her scimitar, she cut through it. Like a rock causing a river to sweep around its sides, Shatr sliced through the middle of the flow and cut it off from the stream.

The funnel evaporated and Zaiyera twisted herself around as she fell. Her feet had barely touched the ground when she threw her shoulder forward and rolled with the momentum. Despite the softness of the sand-covered ground, the landing lit a flaming pain in her right ankle, and another twinge of pain when her hand banged the ground as she rolled.

Zaiyera ignored the pain and regained her feet. She held Shatr in her left hand, shifting most of her weight to her left foot.

Both streamdancers advanced, their faces twisted with anger.

"Your right hand is hurt, then?" one of the women said in a Shanhazian accent. "How long you think you can last with that fancy sword without your dominant hand, then?"

"Give us that blade and we let you live, then," the other woman said. "There's two of us and one of you. And we're both dancers. You have no chance."

They were almost close enough to engage, just another ten feet. Zaiyera could feel her ankle swelling. She would have to take them both in one try.

As the women drew closer, Zaiyera saw their faces. Gray streaked their black hair, and faint wrinkles formed on their cheeks. Crow's feet creased the corners of youthful eyes. These women had likely seen little more than two decades each of life. Zaiyera continued her exaggerated limp forward. The heavy lifeprice these women had paid this day would mean nothing, shortly. Just a few more feet.

"Stop where you are," the woman on the left said. She'd been the one trying to cover her and her comrades' retreat. Or perhaps, her comrades had simply benefitted from her trying to cover her own retreat.

The hot, still air held the scent of sweat and dust. The dune at Zaiyera's back insulated them from any sounds from the caravan on the other side. While the overconfident women moved closer, Zaiyera thought she heard faint moaning and coughing. She tuned it out. She couldn't afford to take her eyes off these women for an instant.

Zaiyera stumbled the last few feet she needed, then stopped. The one on the left had joined her power to the woman Zaiyera had been chasing, thus she showed less of the aging the lifeprice induced. She'd need to take that one first. Zaiyera held Shatr sideways in front of her, the tip of the blade pointing right.

The woman on the left licked her lips. It reminded Zaiyera of the sand and grit she'd eaten several times during the attack. She could still taste it, the tiny granules mixed in her saliva and grinding along her teeth.

"Drop it to the ground," the woman said. "Maybe this strange weapon give me back the lifeprice, then?"

"Not how it works." Zaiyera leapt forward, scimitar sweeping to the left. She gritted her teeth through a fresh burst of pain in her ankle, but the effort succeeded. The streamdancer on the left hadn't expected Zaiyera to be ambidextrous, which led to her disembowelment.

The second woman fell back and threw herself into the Dance. After cutting the first woman across the stomach, Zaiyera hopped into a sideways spin, switched the sword to her right hand, and thrust sideways.

The attack missed, but it was enough to distract the woman from touching the stream. Zaiyera collapsed into a roll as soon as her bad foot touched the ground. She came into a partial kneeling position and stabbed out again. This time, she caught the woman in the hip.

Her focus broken, the streamdancer cried out and grabbed at the wound.

Zaiyera pulled the blade free so quickly, her enemy had little time to register the movement before the blade flashed across her hand. Three fingers thumped into the sand. The woman's horrified scream ended in a gurgle as Shatr drove through her midsection to the hilt.

The dead dancer slumped forward and Zaiyera pushed her aside. The body fell over in a heap.

Zaiyera rolled over onto her back, heaving. She needed to treat her wrist and ankle before they swelled further and she couldn't walk or use her hand. That required getting back to the caravan before they presumed her dead and left her behind.

With a grimace, she curled up into a sitting position. The dune she'd climbed sat several dozen feet away. Given the pain in her ankle, it looked like a mountain. She looked in the direction of the second dead streamdancer and saw where the woman had come from. A couple of desert shrubs stood sentry in front of a makeshift shelter. In it lay three men, their arms bound.

With effort, she climbed to her feet. Northerners, and surely dead in this heat, shelter or not. She started toward the dune, dreading the climb, when she heard a groan.

2

Zaiyera turned back toward the three unmoving figures lying in the shade of the sagging lean-to. One of them spasmed as he went into a fit of coughing.

She made her way back, stepping lightly on her tender ankle. One of the men raised his head and cracked his eyes open when she drew near. His sunburnt lips moved, but barely more than a whisper came out.

Zaiyera froze when she saw the image of a golden fist encased in black flames emblazoned on the scabbard of a sword. It lay atop three others piled in a corner nearby. She looked from the sword to the men several times, then stepped back. She should leave immediately. The man who'd moved was practically dead anyway, as the other two appeared to be. There was nothing she could do for them.

She took another step away, then started to turn when the man moaned again and lifted his icy blue gaze to meet hers. Comprehension filled his weak eyes. "Please," he whispered. "Must … help."

Zaiyera stared at him for several heartbeats. Only shydon hunters bore that insignia. A tainted streamdancer must be somewhere near, for those were the people they hunted. *Just turn around and walk away. He*

15

can barely raise his head. He'll go to sleep and Sun Dancer will deliver him into Shakimah's embrace.

The man mumbled something again and lifted his bound hands. His glazed eyes bore into her; pleading.

Zaiyera absently rubbed her fingers together. The worst place she could be was in the presence of shydon hunters. Nothing but trouble could come of it, yet she couldn't leave the man to die.

With a sigh, she walked over and knelt in front of him. The chains binding his wrists were held by a lock with a small keyhole. "I'll be back." She left them and went back to the dead women. Zaiyera searched the streamdancers and found a little key in an inner pocket of one of their cloaks.

She returned and unlocked the man's shackles, then looked him over, trying to figure out how to help him to his feet with her own ankle injured. "Help me help you up," she said. He looked at her without comprehension, and Zaiyera remembered he wasn't Samharan. She repeated her words in the common tradetongue.

This time, the man nodded and braced himself with one hand, while lifting his other for her to grab.

Using the strength in her left leg, Zaiyera gritted her teeth and pulled the heavier man by the arm as he pushed himself up. Once he was up, she stumbled away, hopping to avoid putting weight on her right ankle. The man held on to keep her upright, and they both almost fell.

He stood and breathed for a few moments before turning on stiff legs toward the man lying closest to the weapons. His legs shook as he lowered himself beside his fallen comrade and turned him onto his back. After listening to his chest, then placing his ear over the man's mouth, he sighed and climbed back to his feet.

He did the same with the other man who looked to be the youngest of the three. After a few moments, the man's eyes widened and he waved her over. They lifted the young man into a sitting position and Zaiyera held his head to keep it from falling backwards. She lifted his eyelid and saw his eye move.

"You both need water," she said to the older man.

He nodded and pointed toward the swords strewn about the ground. Behind them lay a waterskin.

Zaiyera retrieved the water and helped the hunter drink. Once he'd had his fill, she poured a little bit on the younger man's chapped lips. His tongue slid weakly over his lips. He opened his mouth to speak, but only a strained grunt came out. Zaiyera held the skin to his lips again. "Drink," she said. The young man said nothing, but opened his mouth a bit more and received the water. Once he finished, Zaiyera handed the waterskin to the older man.

She tried not to sigh again while she surveyed the scene. One dead shydon hunter and two nearly so. From what she knew of the organization, a typical team consisted of five, with a larger team numbering eight. If she assumed only five of these hunters traveled, either they had encountered more than one darkdancer, or had come upon a full *kivuli dayasa.*

The latter seemed unlikely, but where were their companions? It was highly doubtful a band of raiders could dispatch a team of shydon hunters, even if every one of them were dancers. Too many questions she didn't want the answers to. Better to be as far away from these men as possible.

"My thanks to you," a raspy voice said.

Zaiyera turned back to see the older man, the sides of his blond hair streaked with grey, take another careful draw from the waterskin.

"You surely saved our lives, my lady miss."

A Dor'haighener accent.

"We … stand in your debt."

"You're not standing yet," Zaiyera replied. "But you must help me get him standing, quickly." She lifted the young man's arm and slipped under his shoulder. "You must summon whatever strength you have to help me. I can hardly walk myself, but we must climb the dune to get back to the caravan before they figure me for dead and leave."

The shydon hunter groaned as he climbed to his feet. "Surely they wouldn't abandon you."

"They know not my fate," Zaiyera replied. "We were attacked by what I suspect are the same raiders who captured you. They may think me dead."

"Then we make haste." He inclined his head, fist to his heart. "I am Malker Argen, of Dor'haighen." He stretched his neck forward as he swallowed, the pain of a parched throat still apparent. "Let's move."

"Are you strong enough?" Zaiyera asked.

Malker moved to the other side and draped the young man's arm over his shoulders. "I'll have to be. Come, Dyren. Let's get you out of here."

They lifted him up and made their way out of the shelter. The shydon named Malker gasped as they stepped into the sun. A hot breeze sighed through the shelter behind, stirring Zaiyera's braided hair and sliding across their faces.

"Even … the wind … feels like it comes from an … oven," Malker said between breaths.

Zaiyera focused on the ground in front of her, concentrating on putting as little weight on her ankle while holding up her half of their burden. "It is the sigh of Sun Dancer, Malker Argen of Dor'haighen. Her breath upon the land keeps the air moving, and so too, the life upon it."

"Feels like hot death," came the reply.

Zaiyera glanced at him. Northerners. "Don't talk. Save your strength."

They stopped at the base of the dune to catch their breath and craned their necks to look up to the top.

"I'm not looking forward to this," the shydon hunter said.

Zaiyera didn't disagree. It would have been hard enough climbing the dune on her own. She didn't know how she'd do it half carrying a full-grown man.

She was about to suggest Malker climb the dune alone and signal for help when a figure in light brown robes emerged over the top of the dune and waved.

3

"You have wandered a long way, *niyima*!" the robed figure called down in *Soloush*. "We thought you'd gotten bored and gone home. I convinced them to let me look here for you!"

Zaiyera responded with a conservative smile as Jaide made his way down.

"What did he say?" Malker asked.

"He's here to help," Zaiyera replied. "He's one of the caravan guards I'm working with."

"I heard him say something about *niyima*? Is that your name?"

Good ear. "No, Malker Argen," Zaiyera said. "That is a term of respect for a lady. My name is Zaiyera Tuneesh, of Kushtanja."

"Kushtanja," Malker said thoughtfully. "You are a nomadic people, are you not?"

"We are."

Jaide Amadi finally reached them and moved to relieve Zaiyera of her burden. "You must excuse me for not aiding you instead, northerner," Jaide said to Malker, switching to tradetongue. "This damsel you travel with is in much need of my masculine assistance, lest she break and collapse to the ground in all her fragile glory."

Malker frowned, but Zaiyera replied with another restrained grin. "You've truly saved me, Jaide Amadi."

Jaide smiled and bowed at the waist—as much of a bow as he could, under his half of the burden. "At your service, *niyima*."

With the help of the Viriksani warrior, they helped the young shydon hunter over the dune and down the other side to the waiting caravan.

A short and sturdy man with an even sturdier beard met them halfway to the assembled wagons. As with every northerner Zaiyera had ever met, the man's gait was more of a forward-leaning stomp. She wondered if these people developed joint problems later in life, heavy-stepping around like that.

"Mr. Jaide Amadi," the man said, throwing a curious look at the man he helped to support. "I'm Greg Vose. You have the situation in hand, I see. But …"

"Your questions are best directed at my superior, my friend," Jaide interrupted, chuckling. "She's just there." He jerked his chin at Zaiyera.

"Oh. I … apologies, my lady Zyera," Greg said. "I didn't … I mean …"

"Mr. Vose?" Zaiyera replied, having long gotten used to the mangling of her name. "What is it?"

Greg looked from Malker to the semiconscious shydon, then to Jaide. He rubbed his hands together. "Uh, looks like you've acquired a couple extra people."

"It's possible the same bandits who attacked your caravan attacked these men," Zaiyera said, nodding to Malker. "They would have perished had I not happened upon them."

"Of course," Greg said. "Our supplies are rationed, but I'm sure we can make do."

"We who light the shadow appreciate your kindness, Mr. Vose," Malker said.

Greg's eyes looked like they would bulge out of his head. "I … you're shadow hunters? My apologies." He bobbed into several bows. "I didn't see …"

Lines creased Malker's face. He held up a hand. "It is fine, good sir. If you could find a place that we might shelter from the sun and recover, it would be most appreciated."

"Of course," Greg replied. "You don't even need to ask. Let me help." The stocky man relieved Malker of his burden. "What's his name, if you don't mind my asking?"

"Dyren Faust," Malker replied.

"Ah, fine name. Strong name." Greg grunted as he shifted Dyren's weight on his shoulders. "All right then, Mr. Faust. Let's get you to a wagon and on the mend." He waved a hand at a brown and white wagon a hundred yards ahead. "Marys has a wagon filled with cloths and other woven types of stuff. She can make a cot for him."

They took the semiconscious Dyren to the wagon and soon the young man was fast asleep under the watchful eye of mother hen Marys.

"There's plenty of wagons for you to find a place to ride, sir," Greg said.

Malker nodded. "My thanks, but if you've a camel to spare, I would ride."

Greg tilted his head. "You've the accent of a Nanshaighaner."

"You've a good ear. I am Malker Argen, and I do indeed hail from Nanshaigha."

Once again Greg's eyes bulged, giving Zaiyera the impression of a species of nocturnal monkey from the jungles far south. She bit back her snicker.

"Malker Argen as in … Master Shadow Hunter Malker Argen?" He removed his cap and bobbed several bows again. Now he looked like a Narobaub bird in a mating dance. "My apologies, sir. I didn't recognize you."

Malker patted the air in front of him. "You've no need to apologize and I do not rank as Master Shadow Hunter, Mr. Vosc."

"Beggin' your pardon, sir," Greg said, "but far as anyone else knows, the only person whose skill matches yours is Commander Durst, sir."

"I appreciate your words," Malker replied, "but I fear tales of my skill are greatly exaggerated. And skill level does not equal rank."

"Oh, begging your pardon again, Master … uh … Sir Malker Argen."

"I am no knight, my good man."

"I … uh … of course…"

"Perhaps that camel?" Malker asked.

"Oh yes! Of course."

"You seem in good hands, now," Zaiyera said. "I must find my friend."

"You lost someone during your skirmish?" Malker asked. "Perhaps I can help once I've a mount. We can both ride."

"Thank you, Malker Argen of Nanshaigha," Zaiyera replied. "But I will find him, or he, me."

She left before the shydon could say anything more. With luck he would want to ride near his companion and leave her in peace at the front of the caravan.

The luck of the Domahir spirit must be with these traders, for some of the wagons bore only superficial damage. Sadly, that luck didn't extend to everyone. A few solemn faces rose from their prone comrades to meet her gaze, their sorrowful eyes bloodshot from weeping.

Zaiyera dipped her head in respect for their loss. It was a meager gesture that belied the twisting anguish in the pit of her stomach. She and the other guards were supposed to protect these people, and their trust—some of them, at least—had been misplaced.

She cupped her hands over her mouth and shouted. "Sadiq, my friend. *Kaya yip! Kaya yip!*"

Several more times she called, ignoring the chill settling in her heart that her camel friend might have been killed or stolen away. She almost shed tears of relief upon hearing a series of long groans in the distance. She half trotted half limped to the lead wagon and rounded it to see her dear friend trotting toward her.

He lowered his head and gave her a headbutt. Zaiyera laughed quietly, careful not to mock the grief of others. "Of course they could not take you, my friend," she said. Sadiq blinked his long thick eyelashes at her, his huge lips flapping as he regurgitated and began chewing his cud.

"I cannot leap onto your back right now, my friend," Zaiyera continued. "Will you kneel for me?" She gave him a friendly rub along his side, then two quick pats as high up to his hump as she could reach.

His mouth still moving side to side, Sadiq lazily swung his head around to look at her, then crouched, folding his legs underneath himself until he was sitting. Careful of her tender ankle, Zaiyera limped around to his left side so that she could shift her weight on her good foot. She swung into the saddle and held on as he stood again.

Fortune followed their resumed journey, as no further attacks came. Occasionally Zaiyera would look back over her shoulder to check on the procession. As she'd hoped, the shydon named Malker Argen remained beside the wagon bearing his comrade. She wondered just how old the man was. His blue eyes shone with the light of youth despite the gray at his temples, and the weathered look upon his face that spoke of at least five decades of life.

As Sun Dancer's influence waned and Moon Dancer held sway, Greg Vose insisted the caravan was unanimous in their desire to push on. After a raider attack, foreign caravans usually became more agreeable to longer hours of travel.

Zaiyera recognized the shydon hunter's voice from behind as he called her name. She sighed, not bothering to look back, as the man's camel trotted to catch up.

"Zaiyera, my lady miss," he called again.

She raised her hand in greeting.

"Might I have a word, if you please?" At Zaiyera's nod, he went on. "I was hoping to get some information from you about this region."

"That is many more words than one, Malker Argen."

The creases at the corners of his eyes deepened with his grin. "Very well, I wish many words with you, if you please?"

Zaiyera offered a polite smile as she willed her heartbeat to slow.

"My thanks," Malker said. "Have you any unusual news of this region?"

"Unusual news?" Zaiyera asked.

"Have you heard news of any conflict in these lands? Has anyone spoken of a suspicious man able to lance the stream?" Malker added. "He wears layered black robes and a wrapping about his head and around his face from the nose down. His robes are light brown, the form of dress common to these lands."

"I'm afraid I cannot help you," Zaiyera said. "I have heard of no such man." He'd piqued her curiosity, but she stifled any question before it reached her lips.

"I see," came Malker's response.

They rode in silence for a time, Malker casually scanning the desert landscape sprinkled with hardy grasses, shrubs, and trees, as well as the occasional niyabi tree with its green-leaved branches reaching toward the sky. The light brown landscape stretched as far as the eye could see, the rippled sand sheets slithering away into the distance like a great flat serpent.

Beside Zaiyera, the northerner wiped sweat from his face and gazed at the sun, his mouth hanging open. What was placid unsullied beauty of the grandest scale to her, was hot suffering to those from the cold north.

She flinched as she rotated her foot, working the sore ankle. She did the same with her left hand. Hopefully the remainder of their journey would be uneventful.

"Your injuries aren't serious, I hope?" Malker said.

"Sprains only. I will be fine so long as we reach our destination without another fight."

"And where might that destination be, may I ask?"

More questions.

"Burkiba."

Malker rubbed his chin. "I know that name." His face brightened. "Ah, the land of delicious cactus beer. Your beer is known to every major city of Dor'haighen, and likely the small towns as well. If you've never had it chilled, I would recommend it."

"I've only sampled it once," Zaiyera replied. "The cactus from which the beer is made grows only in that region. I'm from farther south. You likely know more about it than I."

Silence stretched again, and Zaiyera was happy to let it continue. She'd only met one shydon in her life before Malker, and that woman had been the definition of intimidating. Every word she'd said, every question she'd asked, felt like an effort to dig into Zaiyera's life for incriminating information. This man was pleasant, at least on the surface, but she had no illusions as to what he was. Even the most lawful of streamdancers—lancers, as they were called in the north— were uneasy around shydon hunters, and with good reason.

"I haven't traveled to this land often," Malker finally said. "Are all Samhari so aloof?"

Zaiyera opened her mouth to reply, then thought about it. "Excuse me, Malker Argen. I've a lot on my mind."

Malker looked on her with friendly pale blue eyes that carried a hardness to them. She knew that look. It spoke of adversity, friends lost, pain, and death. He sat his camel with the erect posture of a disciplined warrior from the north. The youthful way he moved despite his past middle-aged appearance, made Zaiyera wonder what could have driven the man to trade so many years of his life to touch the stream so deeply.

He faced forward again and nodded. "Seems like every year we live, there's a little more to think about. How long till we reach Burkiba?"

"Two days or less," Zaiyera replied. "If the caravan can continue at its current pace, perhaps a day and a half."

"What will you do after you've delivered these people to their destination   "

"How fairs your companion?" Zaiyera interrupted. "Was he conscious when you left him?"

Malker glanced over his shoulder at the procession behind. "He still sleeps, but his pulse and breathing are stable."

"Still," Zaiyera said, "you should check on him. For those unaccustomed to the heat, an unhealthy person can easily slip away in their sleep."

While he weighed her words, it looked as though he might ignore Zaiyera's advice and continue prying at her life. Eventually, though, he agreed.

"I suppose you would know best, in this regard. Part of your job as a caravan guard?"

"Somewhat."

"Very well. I hope to speak again, my lady miss."

Once Malker was well on his way back to the caravan, Zaiyera spared a look back. Jaide and Barum galloped past the shydon as though they'd been waiting for the man to finally leave her. She sighed. She would have no peace with her thoughts today.

"How's it go?" Barum said once they came up on either side of her.

"As well as one could hope, Barum Hurst."

He squinted at her. "You know, miss milady … you've got to be the most formal person I've ever met outside the hoity halls of Nanshaigha palace. Not to say you're the snobbish type, but that look of yours could make a glacier cringe."

The silence stretched while he waited in vain for her response. The northerner leaned forward and looked around Zaiyera at Jaide, who shrugged.

"Please excuse my mood," Zaiyera finally replied. "I've killed several people today and it's dampened my spirits."

Barum snorted. "They'd have killed us all and took everything they could off our corpses."

"True," Zaiyera replied. "But that fact does nothing to dull the sensation of my blade entering their bodies, their death shudders, or the sound of them choking on their own blood."

Barum's mouth worked silently.

"You've gone and done it, *niyima*," Jaide said. "You've made the burly northerner resort to mimicking a drowning fish for your amusement." He winked.

Zaiyera chuckled and offered a friendly nod at the northerner. "Please excuse my … glacier-cringing mood."

"You're also thinking about those who were lost," Jaide surmised, his tone sober for the first time since she'd met him on this expedition. "Their loved ones grieve, but each of them knew the risks of traveling this route. Either take the longer route and risk harsher elements that could ruin some or all of their wares or brave the less traveled routes across northern Samhar and risk the raiders. You cannot always save everyone, *niyima*, though I know it weighs no less on your shoulders."

Zaiyera smiled politely. This was but another weight to add, but she had no right to do anything but shoulder it without complaint. "Did the two of you come to check on my mental state, or is there another reason you're here?"

That question sobered the mood quickly.

"You know who them folks are with?" Barum asked. "The ones you picked up earlier today?"

Zaiyera nodded. "They're shydon hunters, or rather, shadow hunters, as you call them in the north."

Barum grunted. "Overheard the older one talking to the guy you dumped in that wagon."

A constant breeze swept through like the sigh of an oven, ushering in a canopy of gray clouds gliding in from the west. A nearby niyabi tree swayed lazily in the strengthening wind, waiting patiently as the earthy wet smell of rain settled heavily in the air like a promise.

"I don't know what you did on the other side of that dune," Barum continued, "but it's got that man interested in you."

Zaiyera's heart skipped. How much had Malker Argen seen? What could he determine from what he *had* seen?

"I didn't think much about it, being honest," Barum continued. "Shadow hunter's ain't much concern up in the north, long as you're not doing things you shouldn't be. You folk in the south though, seem to have an aversion to them, so our buddy Jaide informs me."

"From what I gathered," Jaide said, "the man who just left you had been barely conscious, but he saw your battle. Bits of it, at least."

"Which means," Zaiyera said, a sinking feeling settling in her stomach," that he probably thinks I'm a streamdancer."

Barum frowned at her obvious discomfort. "I can't see why that'd be a problem. It's not like you're goin' around syphoning people to death. And you saved them, to boot. Being a lancer ain't a crime in our land. Is it here in the south?"

"It isn't," Zaiyera answered.

"Sounds simple to me, then," Barum said.

"Cultural differences ensure nothing is simple, Barum Hurst of Dor'haighen."

"Definitely the most formal woman I've ever met outside the courts," Barum said. He moved his camel closer, his northerner scent drifting into her nostrils. They smelled different than Samharans. It was a scent she couldn't exactly describe, but if her eyes were covered she would be able to tell Barum and Jaide apart with ease.

"Don't know how much experience you have with shadow hunters," Barum said, glancing over his shoulder. "But they travel in teams of five or seven. If they've crossed into another land, it's probably in pursuit of a major threat. You might wanna ask that fellow some questions. Whoever they were chasing might not be far from us, or they might be between us and Burkiba. That would be a real problem. You saw how much damage a few lancers among those raiders could do. Imagine if they're chasing darklancers."

Zaiyera bit her bottom lip. So much of the stream had flowed on that battlefield around her when she'd fought those two women, before discovering Malker and his companion. So much of the stream, that sweet, fulfilling, enveloping stream of life, creation, and destruction.

She shoved down the tiny hunger inside her until it was no more than a dot, a tiny pinprick in her otherwise solid will. Zaiyera gazed at the sky. Night would be upon them soon, but those clouds looked ominous. *Moon and stars, this couldn't be worse timing.* She needed to dance the stream tonight, to taste it, or at least feel it around her, even if she could never again touch the flow directly.

"Our chances are improved by the path we take, *niyima*," Jaide Amadi said, misunderstanding her strained expression. "A tainted one would not take this route. Not enough travelers to feed their addiction. I believe good fortune favors our odds."

"Hopefully you're right," Zaiyera replied.

"You know," Barum said. "I saw you at work with that blade of yours. I don't know how it works and it's no business of mine to ask, but you could find a bit of extra pay with those shadow hunters. After we reach Burkiba and they've rested, they'll need a guide. All the better that you can fight."

"Thank you for the suggestion," Zaiyera said.

Thunder crackled in the distance like a great beast awakening to a hibernation-long hunger. The wind howled over the surrounding dunes, gradually picking up strength until it chased the heat away. Despite the refreshing turn in the weather, it held an energy that made Zaiyera uneasy.

After once again sitting in silence for a response that didn't come, Barum finally gave up. "Anyway, thought we'd just warn you what the deal is." He turned his camel about. "I'll keep my ears open," he called over his shoulder.

"That northerner is a good man," Jaide said. "Smells like animal leather even though he's wearing none, but a good man nonetheless."

"We probably smell just as odd to him," Zaiyera replied.

Jaide shrugged. "I doubt you haven't thought of it already, *niyima*," he said, reverting to their native tongue of *Soloush*. Like Barum earlier, he too glanced over his shoulder. When his brow creased, Zaiyera guessed Malker must be approaching.

"Your scimitar," Jaide continued, speaking quickly. "Please excuse my bluntness, but it is obviously dancecraft. Northerners do not think favorably of such items. Please be careful with these men."

"Thank you for the warning," Zaiyera replied.

Jaide gave a polite smile and nodded, then repeated the gesture when Malker arrived. "Good day to you, sir," he greeted, reverting back to tradetongue.

"Good day to you as well, friend," Malker replied.

The trio rode in silence, though Zaiyera could practically feel the northerner's desire to speak with her alone. She threw Jaide a quick nod of appreciation. The Viriksani winked.

Malker finally gave up all pretense. "I must ask your pardon for my rudeness, sir," he said to Jaide. "But I would speak with the lady about an important matter in confidence."

Thunder crackled again, and a gust of wind blew across the open land. Rippled sandy sheets blew away in clouds.

Jaide lifted part of the keffiyeh wrapped around his neck over his nose, so that only a tiny slit was visible for his eyes.

Zaiyera did the same and pointed ahead. "Our conversation will have to wait, Malker Argen," she said, her voice muffled.

Malker looked in the direction she indicated and frowned. "It's just a storm, isn't it? Does this area flood?"

Lightning split the distant sky and its thunderous voice rumbled shortly after. The first drops of rain thumped into the sandy ground. Zaiyera breathed in the invigorating smell of dampness. The air was always richer with the first drops of rain after a drought. Lightning shouted down from the heavens again, illuminating the sky.

Thick black clouds rolled in fast, bringing with them harsh gales blasting across the landscape. The clouds flickered as lightning streaked through them, and thunder rumbled in its wake. The ground itself vibrated.

"That isn't a regular storm," Jaide shouted above the howling winds. "It's a grinder!"

Malker shielded his eyes against the stirring dust and sand. "What's a grinder?"

"A more violent kind of sandstorm," Jaide answered. "If you get caught in it, the combination of sand blasting you and the powerful wind rolling you across the ground will literally grind the skin off your bones." He looked to Zaiyera. "We need to circle the wagons!"

"Yes!" Zaiyera called back.

A sheet of rain blasted against them and the camels groaned in protest. Zaiyera squinted as she looked into the distance, to where a brownish-red wall of rain and sand rolled in from the east.

"That's a wet grinder—look!" She pointed, and Jaide held his hand over his brow.

"Moon and stars. You're right!" He wheeled his camel around and sped back to the caravan.

"Do I need to ask how much worse a wet grinder is from a regular one?" Malker said.

They turned their camels and galloped after Jaide.

"One is clouds and whirling sand," Zaiyera said. "This is speeding clumps of it, solidified by the water in the air. I hope the wagons are well constructed."

Fortunately, the other Samharan guards had already begun organizing the caravan. In the time it took Zaiyera and Malker to return, the wagons had begun to form a circle.

"What are they doing?" Zaiyera muttered to herself.

The first row of wagons had created a tight circle, but the outer wagons had stopped in a semicircle. At the opening, a group of people were arguing. Arguing!

"Dija," she said. Sadiq's furry ears twitched back in her direction and he slowed to a stop in front of the caravanners. "Why are you not trying to live?" she asked them. That got a round of puzzled expressions until she half turned in the saddle and jabbed a not too patient finger in the direction of the storm.

"It's not fair," one of the caravanners said, her Dor'haighen accent thick in the tradetongue. "Why do we have to risk our property while their stuff is safe?" She waved irritably at several caravanners whose wagons made up the inner portion of the circle.

Zaiyera's light brown gaze settled on each of them from within the slit of her keffiyeh. "Carry on." She started away from the protesting caravanners, gesturing for the rest of the caravan guards to follow.

Malker trotted his camel to catch up. "You'll leave them to die out here? Are you not their protector?"

"We are," Zaiyera replied. "But we cannot protect those who will not allow us to. We lead and try to advise. They follow our instruction or not. We do not hold a blade to their necks force cooperation, and we'll not die over their quibbling."

They reached a group of caravanners in the midst of completing the circle, and a few of the wagons whose owners hadn't hesitated to form the outer layer of protection.

"It doesn't seem fair," Malker said. "But neither is life, I suppose."

"We all take risks," was all Zaiyera said.

After helping the remaining caravanners position their wagons,

Zaiyera turned to two of the guards. "Remind them one last time that they will die without shelter," she jerked her head toward the still protesting group. "If they choose to take cover, help them organize their wagons. Do not risk your lives for those who care more for their possessions than their lives."

The guards nodded and rode off while Zaiyera and Malker rode their camels through a gap between the wagons and dismounted. Zaiyera led Sadiq to where a group of nervous camels stood. She rubbed her companion on the neck, then behind his ears. "Be their rock, my friend. Your calm will calm them."

She stepped back, and Sadiq gave a short groan, then settled to the ground. The other camels shuffled about, but some wandered over and sat beside him. Camels were normally calm in a sandstorm, but they knew better than any human how dangerous a grinder could be. Zaiyera hoped the rest would eventually sit. The lower to the ground they were, the better.

The wind screamed, stirring up clouds of dust and sand. Zaiyera thought she heard something else in the sudden burst. She strained to listen but heard nothing but the steady cacophony of the gale.

A crouching figure holding a staff trotted across the central space of the encircling wagons, making a path straight for Zaiyera and Malker. When he finally straightened, he stood only a bit taller than she, and considerably shorter than Malker. He looked to each of them in turn with concerned, almond-shaped brown eyes.

The man executed a quick bow. "Please excuse me," he shouted over the wail of the storm. He pointed at a wagon from the direction he'd come from. "Can you help me secure that man's wagon? The wind is strong and we are but two people."

They followed him across the middle of the circle to where the owner struggled in vain to pull his wagon closer to the one in front of it.

"I'll push from the back!" Malker said, and made his way into position. The short man and Zaiyera followed. The three of them put their backs against the rear of the wagon and pushed.

The wagon was heavy, and it took several moments to get it

moving. They growled and pushed, while the owner guided the wagon into the curve. When the call came from the front for them to stop, the trio leaned against the back to catch their breath.

They left the owner to secure the wagons together and searched for anyone else in need of help. From between the gaps, Zaiyera saw wagons moving around each side of the circle. The storm must have aided the stubborn caravanners in choosing survival over temporary losses.

"By Fu Mei's fiery gaze," the foreigner said, his accented voice muffled behind the strip of his keffiyeh covering his mouth. "How long will this beautiful destruction endure?"

What an odd description. "It could last an hour or the entire night," Zaiyera shouted back, barely able to hear herself over the cacophony. "Pray this intensifies no further, or it will carry the wagons and all of us away."

"What is that?" Malker asked.

Zaiyera had almost forgotten about the shydon hunter. "What?"

"Listen."

Zaiyera stared at the ground as she concentrated. Her heart nearly stopped when she finally heard it.

"Against the wagons! NOW!"

"What is it?" Malker asked again.

"I ask the same," the foreigner said. "It sounds as if the storm itself screams as it descends on us."

"Screamers!" Zaiyera ran toward Sadiq and the gathered camels. They must have heard the sound as well, for they had grown more agitated.

"Smart thinking," Malker commented once they reached the animals. "If something comes, they will provide a larger target than us."

Zaiyera leveled a narrow-eyed glare on him. "He is my companion and friend for many years, Malker Argen, not my shield."

That drew a puzzled look from the northerner, which only irritated her further. Rationally, she knew it was a difference in culture. Northerners viewed animals more as property and tools than equal sharers of the world. It didn't lessen her distaste for such a primitive view.

"Lady of Samhar," the short foreigner said. "Please tell me of this screamer, that we may know what to expect."

Zaiyera held her keffiyeh in place and hunkered down beside the nervous Sadiq. "They are a large bird of prey that use powerful sand-storms to travel distances that would otherwise take them days or weeks of flight."

A wooden groan sounded above the storm. The trio looked across the opening in the circle to a leaning wagon. Three people held tried to pull it back down, but the wind simply blew it and them over. Zaiyera started to go to help but settled back when a group of caravanners ran to their aid. They left the wagon as it was and helped the other two people to find better shelter.

A shrill chorus split the noise of the storm and froze everyone in the midst of their labors. *Sheeeeeeeeeeeeeeeeeeee.* Guards and caravanners alike covered their ears against the ear-splitting sound.

"They do not stop for breath, ah?" the foreigner said. "It's one continuous song of horror!"

"Stay low," Zaiyera said. "Their eyesight is sharp, even in a storm like this. When they spot their prey, they tuck their wings in and shoot through the sky like an …"

The side of a wagon exploded, and a woman flew out from the side. She screamed in agony while pulling at a long bolt embedded in her abdomen. As she pulled at it, the black and brown bolt suddenly opened its wings and lowered its legs. Those legs were as big around as a man's arms, with a wingspan comparable to the length of the wagon it had passed through.

The screamer planted its taloned feet on the ground and rose to its full height, lifting the woman with it. The poor woman wasn't much taller than five feet, but the predatory bird stood taller yet.

Wings half extended at its side, the giant bird spread its feet and threw its head sideways, dislodging the woman from its long, spear-like beak.

"Tears of the Ancients," the foreigner said.

Several more crashes. Several more giant birds blasting through wagons.

One bird crashed through a wagon near where three men crouched. The hollering men scampered away from their hiding spot and out into the circle.

"No!" Zaiyera stood and tried to wave them back. "Stay out of the open—"

A screamer shot through the air like a giant arrow. It hit one of the men in the back with such force, it punched through and came out his chest.

"Jakta skree," Malker swore. "Those things are evil."

The giant bird rolled across the ground and spread its wings to stop. It stood and shook off bits of bone and gore from its feathers, then turned on the other two men, now falling over themselves in retreat. Three more screamers hit the ground in a roll and came upright. They surrounded the two men, opening their wings and flexing scaly claws at the shoulders of each wing.

Zaiyera drew Shatr. She ignored the protest of her freshly wrapped ankle and sprinted for the men. She heard a scream to her left and ducked backwards on instinct, and dropped to her knees. A long feathered missile whipped overhead. Zaiyera untucked her legs, rolled sideways, and got back to her feet. She nearly fell over when a stab of pain shot through her ankle.

Three more screamers tumbled across the ground and rose. Zaiyera took the head from the nearest bird. She spun with the motion and stabbed a second before it fully gained its feet. From her periphery, she saw the shydon hunter Malker cut a bird in half with a downward chop of his sword.

A screamer turned toward her. A full head taller, it croaked and stabbed its sharp beak toward her face. Zaiyera recoiled, then threw her hips back as it retracted and stabbed for her abdomen. It stepped forward, stabbing that lethal beak high and low.

Zaiyera swept Shatr in an upward ark and parried the beak aside, then kicked it in the chest. She instantly regretted the reflexive counter.

A fresh wave of pain washed over her ankle and she and the bird stumbled back, the latter flapping its wings to regain balance.

Zaiyera let herself fall and roll. She came back to her feet, placing most of her weight on her good foot, then shifted her stance. Good foot leading, she lunged, fully extending her arm in a forward stab. The scimitar took the bird in the chest and it croaked and screamed as it stumbled sideways.

Monstrous birds hit the ground everywhere, like bolts of black lightning striking the sandy ground. *Shreeeeeeee*. The screamers spread their wings and shrieked. The sound buzzed inside Zaiyera's head, but she dare not drop her weapon to cover her ears.

A screamer to her right side fell silent. She looked to see the short foreigner battering the giant bird with a flurry of well-placed blows with his staff. The weapon moved so fast in his hands that she could barely see it. Another bird shot out of the darkness of the storm, speeding straight for him.

Zaiyera shouted a warning, but the bird had already reached him. She thought it would be his death, but the man spun sideways and whipped his staff up. Whether it was skill or luck, she couldn't be sure, but the staff hit the bird in the neck with an awful crunch. The bird hit the ground in a tangled heap of wings and feathers and didn't rise.

The three warriors fought in a triangle formation; Zaiyera at the front, Malker and the foreigner with the staff behind her at either side. The screamers turned their attention from the unarmed caravanners to the approaching threat. The man who'd almost been killed by the nearest bird looked this way and that, his eyes frantic as he searched for a place to hide. He scooted backwards, then scrambled to his feet and ran.

"Don't move!" Zaiyera shouted just as another incoming screamer blasted into him. Both hit the ground in a tumble of limbs, wings, and flashing talons. The man screamed and kicked, blood pouring from his side. The bird ignored his thrashing and leaped on top of him. Razor sharp talons bit into his flesh while it folded its wings and grabbed him with the claws at its shoulders. Once it had him restrained, the screamer stabbed its long spear-like beak through his chest, then lifted him from the ground. It spread its wings, took several strides, and lifted into the air. Zaiyera could barely glance in regret in the direction of the large bird as it disappeared into the storm.

"That was horrible," the foreigner said. "Let us save the rest of these people and get to shelter, ah?"

They burst into action, a trio of death plowing through the predatory birds.

By far the fastest of them, the short foreigner with the staff dove right into the middle of the winged predators, his staff little more than a circular blur as it cracked skulls, broke necks and legs, and knocked beaks aside. Two screamers limped away and took wing while three more lay battered on the ground.

Several more screamers pierced the storm and hit the ground around them. The birds tumbled to their feet, while several unlucky ones rolled too close. Malker and Zaiyera stabbed them before they could rise.

"Will this ever stop?" Malker said.

"As long as they see us out here in the open," Zaiyera said, "no."

"Then let us move to cover, ah?" the foreigner said.

More of the birds "landed" around them, slowing their progress.

From behind several birds between her and the wagons, Zaiyera saw a figure sprinting toward them. He drew his sword, leapt, and drove it into the nearest bird's back. It let out a gurgling squawk and fell convulsing to the ground, but the man was already on the move.

He moved with a similar style to Malker, but with obviously superior skill. The second shydon hunter.

With their newest ally, the group of four worked their way across the circle, grabbing the surviving caravanner who'd had the presence of mind to stay low to the ground and keep close.

Zaiyera surveyed the situation when they finally reached shelter. Several wagons were overturned, their contents blowing away in the wind. Most of the wagons outside the circle had been positioned to bolster the inner circle, providing more protection from the storm. Guards and caravanners alike huddled against the shelter of the wagons, waiting out the storm.

The sound of metal sliding against a scabbard drew her attention. Zaiyera looked past Malker to see the other shydon hunter sliding his sword in its sheath. He stared out at the pounding, sideways rain. Those glacial blue eyes calmly searched for any threat that might appear. He glanced Zaiyera's way and gave a curt nod, then returned his attention to the storm.

The short foreigner crept around Malker, careful to stay low and close to the wagon. He smiled at the shydon, who shuffled sideways to make room.

"Usually one knows the name of the person they fight beside, *ixu*?" He bowed his head. "I am Xaiylin Zhuyun. Though you on this side of the Great Sea prefer the given name first, ah? So that means you would call me Zhuyun Xaiylin, or simply Zhuyun." The short man smirked. "Of course, if you were to read my name, you would likely call me Zooyoon, but that is wrong. So please, if I'm killed in this insanity and you see my name in writing, read it as Joouyun and press the corners of your tongue to the top of your mouth. This will be as close to correct as you can get when speaking of my bravery."

The corner of Zaiyera's mouth twitched. "I will remember, Xaiylin Zhuyun. I am Zaiyera Tuneesh of Kushtanja."

The storm ceaselessly battered the wagon circle, but it didn't intensify. Wagons outside the circle rocked sideways. Nearby caravanners scrambled over to steady them, taking great care to keep as low to the ground as possible.

Zhuyun whistled through his teeth. "This is quite a homeland of yours, ah?" He indicated the storm with an open hand. "Warm and welcoming."

4

"That … is a truly powerful smell."

Zaiyera cracked her eyes open, then shielded them from the bright sun. She stretched, feeling a large furry body behind her. With a contented smile, she gave Sadiq a friendly rub.

"I'm surprised that animal's odor didn't wake you earlier," Malker said. He, too, stretched, having slept with his back against the wagon.

"Actually, it was your complaint that woke me, Malker Argen." Zaiyera rose and gave Sadiq another pat on the side. The camel gave a friendly groan as he stood. "We all have a scent, don't we?" She indicated the Dor'haighen warrior. "Your scent is foreign to me, while Sadiq's is familiar and comforting."

Several feet away, Zhuyun laughed. "I think she means you *smell*, Dor'haighener. Surely you've not had an opportunity to bathe in days, ah?"

"Have you?" Malker countered.

A voice from several feet away cut through the humor. "When does the caravan resume?"

Zaiyera lifted her gaze to Dyren, who stood looking to the west. It seemed odd to see him not only conscious, but fully recovered from having looked to be near death just yesterday. He stood tall and erect, those hard blue eyes staring intently into a distance much farther away than what was in front of him.

"I assume as soon as their property can be readied for travel," Zaiyera replied, "we will be away. After all that's happened these past seven days, I doubt these people want to delay any more than need be."

Dyren responded with the same curt nod as last night. "How far is our destination?"

Zaiyera glanced from Dyren to Malker. Despite appearances showing otherwise, the former seemed to be the one in charge. "If we encounter no further difficulties, we will reach Burkiba today."

The shydon hunter gave yet another curt nod, then started away.

Zaiyera stared at the man's back. "You're welcome."

* * *

The desert of Samhar stretched into infinity from horizon to horizon, its mighty dunes sitting placid, as though a terrible storm carrying murderous predators hadn't ravaged the previous night.

Zaiyera closed her eyes and took a deep breath. The fresh, hot morning air felt good. She enjoyed riding out front, away from the frequent murmurs of complaint about the heat and terrain. Samhar was a harsh place, undeniably. But it was also quiet, peaceful, and majestic. She looked forward to a cloudless sky tonight, that she might dance the stream while the stars gazed down on her. Every night she wondered if their gaze was of appreciation or judgement. Did she deserve aught but the latter?

The sound of approaching camels dissolved her solitary peace. "Might we have a word?" Malker asked.

"Only one?"

The shydon hunter frowned, then smirked. "Very well. Might we have a conversation?"

"As you wish," Zaiyera replied.

"Your skill with the blade is formidable," Dyren said in heavily accented tradetongue. "Malker spoke of how you defeated two lancers to free us. I offer my thanks. We would have perished, had you not arrived."

That last bit was forced, though Zaiyera didn't blame him. Who would want to admit they would have died if not being rescued? This man seemed the prideful sort. She imagined the admission doubly difficult for him. "I'm sorry about your companion."

Dyren's visage actually softened at that. "Javick was his name. He was a good soldier and a good hunter. We will complete this mission in his name, as well as the others who fell."

The following silence grew heavier by the moment. "Malker … spoke to you about the man we hunt."

"Some," Zaiyera replied. "Unfortunately, as I told him, I've little to offer you in the way of assistance. I know nothing of this man, nor where he might be going."

"That is understood," Dyren said. "However, we'd like to employ your services once your contract is fulfilled with this caravan."

There it was. Zaiyera refrained from sighing. "Your faith in my abilities is flattering, but I must decline."

"You have another job after this one?" Malker asked.

"I … do not find the thought of hunting down a fallen streamdancer enticing."

"Fallen," Malker said. "As if they've fallen from grace? Pardon, Zaiyera of Kushtanja, but the addicted were never in grace to begin with. Anyone possessed of a heart to kill and syphon another's lifestream has nowhere to fall to. Such a person is without morals, much less the concept of honor—"

Dyren held up a hand and Malker bit off his rant. "My apologies, Zaiyera my lady miss," Malker said.

"Your apology is not needed, Malker Argen of Dor'haighen," Zaiyera replied. "Your feelings are your own, and you have every right to them."

"It's a subject close to the heart," Dyren said."

"Revenge?" Zaiyera asked.

"To protect," Dyren corrected. "No man or woman is raised to become a shadow hunter carrying a personal goal of vengeance. That is not who we are." He looked out at the serene expanse.

Zaiyera suspected he saw little more than a desert wasteland littered with unattractive plant life and teeming with hidden dangerous animals. Foreigners rarely saw beyond that. They were blind to the way the wind swiped its ethereal hands across the sand, swirling it into wavy designs. The dunes, both small and towering, were a testament to that graceful hand. The sun, while hot and constant, gave life even in its harshness, and the life that did thrive here was strong and sure and beautiful. Every waterhole, every oasis, was a treasure to human and animal alike. Samhar was a work of art.

"We are here to neutralize a threat to every living thing in this land," Dyren continued. "An addicted lancer is a danger to everyone around them. We must find him as soon as possible. Surely you understand that."

So that you can kill him. "I understand your purpose," Zaiyera said.

"You're hesitant about us, about what we are. Many share your feelings. That is their burden. We have no business with any who have not succumbed to addiction to the stream."

"Has there ever been an effort to cure the addiction, or help someone to cope with it?" As soon as the question left her lips Zaiyera regretted it.

"Impossible," came Dyren's predictable reply. "The addiction is incurable and cannot be endured without syphoning more lifestream. Death is the only cure." He looked directly at her, and she returned his hard cold gaze. Stubble populated his sunburned face. His equally sun-damaged hair hung in a slight frizz down to his ears.

"Many, perhaps most, even, think us monsters for carrying out the tasks we do," Dyren continued. "They think we fashion ourselves judges and executioners. Whatever they think, they are alive to think it. That might not be the case if darklancers, or worse, shadowlancers, roamed the land unchecked."

"You don't seem the type to offer much in the way of explanation," Zaiyera said. "Why tell me all of this?"

"Respect, Zaiyera of Kushtanja." Dyren placed his fist over his heart, then opened it toward her. "Respect not only from one warrior to another, but from one who is himself in your debt. Information is the least we can offer."

On Dyren's other side, Malker made the same gesture.

"Thank you," Zaiyera said. "But any debt owed to me was paid the moment I aided you in your time of need. Goddess Shakimah smiles upon her children who are kind."

Dyren's nod was not the curt, precise one of before, but softer. "Perhaps the smile of your Goddess would broaden, should you aid us once more?" He held up a hand when she opened her mouth to respond. "I ask for no answer now, just that you at least consider it. From what Malker has told me of what he saw, and from what I witnessed with my own eyes, your skill added to ours would be a great boon. The faster we catch up with the darklancer, the more lives will be spared."

They turned their camels away, leaving Zaiyera with dark thoughts. More caravanners had been lost in the storm on her watch, and now these shydon hunters. She gave Sadiq a pat on the neck. "Maybe I should take up another profession, my friend." The camel grunted in response, foamy lips flapping as he blissfully chewed his cud.

The addicted. Darklancers. Shadowlancers. All names that made them into monsters. Those who'd committed the most unforgivable offense. Did they know the torment a person addicted to the stream endured? Had they talked with a so-called darklancer? Did they take the time to understand what could happen to take a person down such a terrible path? Or was the only answer to put them down as quickly as possible because the addiction could not be managed? "Impossible", Dyren had said.

Not at all.

* * *

A ragged cheer of relief rolled through the caravan as word spread that Burkiba was in sight. The appearance of ogko trees drew a smile from the Samharan guards, Zaiyera included. The short, sturdy trees with their thick gray bark heralded the beginnings of green life in the region. Sand sheets and dunes gave way to thick patches of vegetation which noticeably cooled the air. Just outside the town border, knee-high straw grass swayed lazily in the late afternoon breeze.

"Ah!" Zhuyun said, smiling at the green trees and plants, the distant mountainous plateaus and the rocky hills. "And here I thought this was only a place of heat death. Many years of my life have I traveled to distant lands, but never have I seen such extremes."

"There is no place like Samhar, good traveler," Jaide said. "It is as diverse as its people. Or rather, the people are as diverse as the land."

"Seems you're the mystery man of the bunch," Barum rumbled. Of all the riders, the thickly muscled Dor'haighener looked the least comfortable. He'd wanted the biggest camel he could find, being such a big man. Unfortunately, two-humped camels weren't suitable for speed and endurance like the single-humped ones.

"Then allow me to demystify myself," Zhuyun said. "I am from the land of Yuntai, across the Great Sea to the west. Now, if you were to read the name of my homeland on parchment, you would feel compelled to pronounce it as if there is a 'Y' in front of the word 'untie'." He waggled a finger. "Do not fall victim to this compulsion. My homeland is not called 'untie' with a 'Y'. It is pronounced Yooooontaaaai, with the corners of your tongue pressed to the roof of your mouth." He said it slowly once more, drawing amused expressions from the rest of the group.

"Do all of the people of Yooooontaaaai," Jaide asked, "walk foreigners through the pronunciation of their names?"

"Only those of us who travel a lot," Zhuyun replied. "Hearing one's name, or the name of one's homeland being mangled by foreigners can become torturous. Better to get you pronouncing it correctly right from the start, *ixu*?"

"Sounds like a lovely place," Jaide said.

"Lovely?" Zhuyun replied. "How could that be, as I have not described it to you, Samhar man."

Jaide grinned. "I was using my clever subtlety to nudge you out of your very interesting ramblings, that you might return to the description of your homeland, good Zhuyun, not to be pronounced zooyoon."

The Yuntaiman laughed and slapped his thigh. "I do ramble! Quite a lot. It is a disease we who travel develop, ah?"

The distant cackling of a flock of running guinea fowl greeted the procession. The birds ran across the road on skinny legs sweeping from underneath dome-like feathery bodies.

"Strange birds," Malker Argen said. "Do they taste similar to other types of fowl?"

"I wouldn't know," Zaiyera replied. "We do not eat everything we live with, especially friends who eat the ticks and other insects that would leave us battling horrible diseases."

Malker pursed his lips. "I … see."

" … Great green hills and mountains that turn white with snow in the winter," Zhuyun went on. "There are trees with trunks that grow like the shape of a slithering snake, and ones that grow on the side of the mountains that see more rain and mist in a year than sun."

"Your home sounds dark and damp, Yuntaiman," Jaide said.

"Misty and damp, yes," Zhuyun agreed. "But only a region of it. My actual home is the flatter lands to the south. Surely it hasn't escaped your notice that I'm not a tall man by your standards, ah? Southern Yintish people, we do not grow tall. But in the north, they grow as tall as you, and in the mountains, taller still. A Yintish woman from the mountains would look straight into your eyes."

The landscape became completely green, as if the caravan had passed over a border separating the town from the desert. Thatch-roofed huts made of mud and sand squatted amidst the flourishing vegetation. The inhabitants emerged from their homes or stopped their tasks long enough to take note of the long procession of northerner wagons that spoke of the arrival of foreign goods.

Zaiyera glanced at the locals, then back at the procession. The once jovial caravanners looked haggard and beaten. While some wagons made the journey relatively unscathed, many arrived with their wooden enclosures and cloth tops shredded or bearing large holes—holes the size of speeding screamers. The traders of Burkiba would not like the prices coming their way.

Mr. Vose trotted his camel up to the group, who made way for him to reach Zaiyera. He looked tired. His beard had filled in over the past day and a half, more gray than blond. Looking at the man now, slumping in the saddle, the whites of his eyes red from a mixture of lack of sleep and sand blown in his face, she thought perhaps the gray might be a result of this journey.

"Dare I hope that my tired eyes don't lie to me?" Greg Vose said. "Is it a trick of this cruel land, or are we truly arrived?"

"Neither your eyes nor the land lie to you, Mr. Vose," Zaiyera replied. "We have arrived in Burkiba."

"Praise Jokolta," the man sighed. "Another day may well have killed me."

Zaiyera didn't reply. As hard as she and the others of her team worked to protect the caravan, nature was an adversary impossible to defeat. She hoped the souls of the slain had received the warm embrace of Shakimah—or Jokolta, she guessed the northerners' divinity to be—and were enjoying the paradise of *Sojalleh*, or whatever name their God had placed upon the world of bliss.

Greg stared at her. "I ain't claiming to read minds, miss milady, but every one of us knew the dangers of this harsh place you call home. You needn't carry the burden of their deaths on your shoulders. We hired a small group of you, and you've gotten most of us here alive." He offered a half smile. "Maybe a touch heat-exhausted mixed with normal exhausted, but alive."

"The families of the dead might not think so highly of us," Zaiyera replied. "Our best efforts failed them."

"We traders choose our work with full knowledge of the hazards," Greg countered. "Our families know the risk. We Dor'haigheners are a hearty folk and we take care of each other. Death ain't but another of the hardships we face in life, and the end of the hardships we face when it's over. Don't you worry none about those we lost. Maybe say a prayer to whoever your God is, but don't feel guilty."

Zaiyera nodded. "I shall try."

The man had barely moved his camel away when Malker and his superior took his place. Zaiyera pressed her lips together.

"This is a surprising city," Malker said. "I hadn't expected to find any green vegetation in Samhar, yet it's everywhere." He jerked his chin in the direction of the distant plateaus. "Even there."

"You must have only traveled through the mid and northern regions of central Samhar," Zaiyera said. "The far south, east, and west are quite different."

"They'll all look the same if we don't succeed in our mission," Malker replied. "Desolate and lifeless." A look from Dyren Faust, and Malker inclined his head. "My apologies."

"Malker can be quite focused," Dyren said. "It is our duty to ensure the safety of people everywhere from the deadly nature of the addicted. It's the main part of the oath we swear upon attaining The Mark."

"I'm sure your cause is a noble one," Zaiyera replied, not knowing what else to say.

"Noble or otherwise," Dyren pressed, "many will die, should we fail. This land is foreign to us, and our quarry is powerful, and native to it. We're at a considerable disadvantage."

"Perhaps you could send for aid," Zaiyera offered. "There are runners at every city and town in Samhar. Hire one to send a message posthaste of your need of greater forces."

"How many will die in the time it takes the message to reach our king and queen?" Dyren asked. "And how many more by the time a decision is made, and reinforcements reach us?"

Zaiyera stared at the thick patch of mane between Sadiq's shoulders for a while. "I know what you want of me, but I fear that whatever you saw of my battle with the two streamdancers was through the filter of your semiconsciousness."

"You undersell your skills," Malker said. "I've never seen a lancer who could actually cut through the flow of another lancer."

Zaiyera felt a spike of cold shoot through her stomach. "I assure you, Malker Argen, I am not what you think."

Both men gave her a perplexed look. Dyren looked at Malker, who spoke up. "Only a lancer could have done what you did. You destroyed their flows as though slicing through a wedge of butter."

"Do you recall seeing a dance-resin form from my movements?"

Malker was silent for several moments, then shook his head. "I don't believe so. But I can't fathom how you would counter the flow in such a way without lancing, yourself. How *did* you achieve such a feat?"

"Ah!" Zhuyun said. Zaiyera had forgotten the man was there. "Perhaps she is a talented conjurer. They never reveal their secret, *ixu*?" He pointed ahead. "And it looks like we've reached our destination. And more importantly to my exhausted bones, rest!"

The Yuntaiman's words were true, for the center of town lay ahead. Word of their arrival had preceded them. Men and women pulled two-wheeled carts laden with a variety of goods toward the city trade square.

"Perhaps we can speak of this at a less busy time," Dyren said.

"If time permits," Zaiyera replied, pretending not to notice the even look Dyren cast Zhuyun, and the barely subtle scowl of Malker.

The shydon hunters fell back to talk amongst themselves, and Zhuyun, Jaide, and Barum moved in until all four of them rode tightly together. Zaiyera gave Zhuyun a thankful nod. The Yuntaiman winked.

"Those two are persistent," Barum said. "Though I don't understand why you're so wary of them, it's not the best manners for them to be so pushy. I can't imagine what in the name of Jokolta they think a non-lancer could do against an addicted."

Having years of practice, Zaiyera kept her flinch at that last word internal.

5

In all the times Zaiyera had been to Burkiba, never had it been this subdued. The caravan trundled into town to little more fanfare than quiet waves in greeting. Trade was normally an exuberant occasion. Samharans generally looked forward to the arrival of foreign traders, and the haggling that followed.

When the wagons stopped and the traders dismounted or exited their beaten-down wagons, negotiations began in quiet tones. The locals, in their multicolored robes and turbans and keffiyehs took in the sight with what looked like not only sympathy, but lack of surprise. That was worrisome.

Zaiyera and her three companions dismounted. Sadiq followed her to a grassy patch of land where he stopped to graze. "Enjoy your hard-earned meal, my friend," she said, giving him a pat on the side.

"I'll see you later today before sleep." Sadiq responded with a friendly groan, and lumbered away, followed by the other three camels once their riders had relieved them of their gear.

"I cannot for the life of me understand how you trust they don't just wander off or get themselves stolen," Barum said. "Not to mention how you control the beast with no reins." He looked questioningly at Jaide.

The Viriksani shrugged. "I ride with reins the same as you, northerner. The people of Kushtanja are different, yes? They have a closer relationship with nature than the rest of us Samharans."

"Don't see how that's possible," Barum said. "Every Samhari I've met seems to be pretty close to their animals. Like they're family."

"Do you not care for the animals that share your lands, Barum Hurst?" Jaide asked.

"Eh. We like 'em good enough, but they ain't friends 'n family like what you folk seem to think. We do find most animals are useful in some way."

"Then more servant than friend," Jaide replied.

"They're animals," Barum said.

"Aren't we all, Barum Hurst," Jaide said. "Aren't we all."

Zaiyera stole a glance at the Viriksani. He always had a smile at the ready beneath those oceanic blue eyes. The men in Viriksan were known as being handsome, sometimes bordering on pretty. Jaide Amadi was beautiful, even for a Viriksani male. Then, there were his eyes. Dark blue eyes among the brown-skinned people of Samhar was an extremely rare occurrence.

"Something has happened, recently," Zhuyun observed. He nodded toward traders and the surrounding spectators. "Unless these people of Burkiba"—he took his time to pronounce the word—"are normally this sober, something unfortunate has befallen this place."

Zaiyera had a feeling she knew what the cause of the dour mood was, as would the shydon hunters. It made her want to leave as soon as possible.

"Sounds like an opportunity to learn what news we might," Jaide said.

"Info gathering?" Barum asked.

"Being nosy," Jaide replied. He looked to Zaiyera. "If I may begin my nosiness with you, might I ask of your plans? Assuming you're not trying to drive the price up for guarding Mr. Vose back to the border, I'm assuming you aren't planning to take the work."

They squeezed through the gathering crowed. Sandstone buildings surrounded them, some with stone stairs ascending to a second floor, while others were a single floor with a flat roof. Many of those had large sturdy ladders leaning against them, providing access to a flat roof with chairs and tables. The air carried the light, crisp smell of plant life, as well as grilling meat, and the aroma of baked goods wafted from open doors and windows.

Barum looked at the clusters of people loitering about in the sparse shade. "Do Samhari folks even feel the sun? I'd die, standing out there unmoving with it beating down on me like that."

"You're probably right," Zaiyera said. "But I imagine you do the same in the frozen lands of your home, Barum Hurst of Dor'haighen."

"Ugh. There you go with the formal stuff," Barum said. "Surely I didn't say nothing to irritate you."

Zaiyera responded with something of a grin. "Not at all, Barum Hurst of Dor'haighen."

Beside her, Jaide guffawed.

Barum frowned then shook his head. "You like messing with my head, don't you, miss milady?"

Zhuyun chuckled at that.

"What are our plans, now?" Jaide asked. "We've delivered the caravan to their destination and are now effectively jobless, yes?"

"Mr. Vose has need of caravan guards for their return journey," Zaiyera said. "All you need do is speak with him and you'll find yourself employed once more."

"We?" Jaide asked. "But not you?"

"Not me," Zaiyera confirmed. "My path takes me back to Kushtanja. Perhaps even farther south." *As far away from those shydon and their quarry as I can get.*

"Hmm." Zhuyun scratched his chin. "I admit I am not of this land and that this is my first visit. But that sounds like a long and perilous journey to make alone."

"The Yuntaiman is right," Jaide said. He winked. "You should hire a team of guards to escort you."

"Eh," Barum said. "She couldn't afford us."

Despite her mood, Zaiyera smiled. "You've a living to earn. And it's true, I couldn't afford you."

Barum rolled his eyes. "Pfft. You think I ain't seen what you can do with that scimitar? More likely you'd be paying to protect *us*?"

"Speak for yourself, northerner," Jaide said. He patted the shamshir at his hip. "I do just fine."

"I'd hope so," Barum replied. "You're too pretty a man to be walking about not knowing your way around a sword. Ain't no sense in a man with them delicate features and eyes sparkling about. Ain't a rugged bone in your body. Not even so much as stubble on your lip."

Jaide laughed. "What can I say? Some of us are blessed with beauty and wicked charm, and some of us … wicked ruggedness." He sniffed. "And a rugged odor to match."

"Man smell," Barum shot back.

"Man stink," Zaiyera added, rubbing her nose. "And we all reek." She started down a trail that led to a section of town referred to as the Shared Homes, where locals rented rooms in their home to travelers. "I'm in need of a bath."

"Will you be about town later?" Jaide called after her. "We made a good team. A shame to dismantle so abruptly and with no fanfare."

"The Round Huts," Zaiyera answered. "You will find me there until nightfall."

"Very well," Jaide answered. "We will see you then."

Zhuyun trotted up beside her. "Might I join you?"

Zaiyera arched an eyebrow at him.

"Oh. Heh heh." He offered a respectful bow, his legs still moving as he walked beside her. "Apologies. Perhaps I should speak more clearly. Might I join you, for a moment before you reach your place of bathing?"

"What do you wish of me, sir?" Zaiyera asked.

"You will leave before first night." It wasn't a question.

Zaiyera glanced at him. "You have visions of the future, Zhuyun?"

"I pay attention and see things," the Yuntaiman corrected. "One doesn't travel the world alone, oblivious to his surroundings, and survive long, *ixu*?" He looked over his shoulder at Jaide and Barum. "You seem one who allows for few friends. Those two are good men, and good friends, should you let them be such for you."

"Is there something you're trying to tell me?" Zaiyera asked.

Zhuyun went silent and she thought he might not answer. She let the silence stretch with no intention of breaking it.

"There are times," he finally said, "for solitude, and times for allies. I believe you will need allies for your road ahead, Zaiyera Tuneesh of Kushtanja."

Zaiyera felt her palms tingle. "What ... makes you think so? Pardon my words, for they aren't meant to be rude, but we've just met. I am grateful for your aid against the screamers, but we hardly know each other."

Zhuyun slipped his hand up the side of his keffiyeh and scratched. "I know these things protect us from the sun. Surely my hair would be hard and brittle, and snap off my head much like dried straw, ah? Still, they make my head itch.

"Forgive my intrusiveness, if that is what it is," Zhuyun went on. "But traveling the world for more than half one's life grants some degree of insight."

"I suppose that insight extends to my life journeys?" Zaiyera asked.

"I wouldn't think of telling you about your life," Zhuyun said. "But I would be remiss not to at least offer an observation."

The trail led to a small village of houses amongst the trees. Ankle-length grass grew everywhere, kept in check by grazing goats, and the occasional donkey. A series of grunts and squeals sounded from a patch of rocks near a tree. A sharp, tiny scream answered.

"What in the name of he Sisters was that?" Zhuyun asked.

"That was a family of hyrax," Zaiyera said, chuckling. "They're small and round but can give you quite a startle if you're not used to them being around."

"They sound near to being murdered," Zhuyun said.

Just then, two rotund rodent-looking animals nosed their way out of the grassy wall along with three smaller ones. They spared Zaiyera and Zhuyun little more than a glance before scurrying across the trail into the patch of grass on the other side.

"Ah! Fat and adorable," Zhuyun said, then looked at her again. "It isn't solitude you prefer, more than a different kind of company." He pointed in the direction the round little animals had gone. "Their company. And the trees and rocks, the sun, moon, the stars."

Zaiyera grinned at him. "They talk less." Her grin disappeared when she realized how rude that must have sounded. "Not … not that I mean you talk too much, good Zhuyun of Yuntai. I meant in general …"

Zhuyun smiled and held up a hand. "Apologize not, lovely lady. I've spent enough time among the monks and mystics of my own homeland to understand your meaning. Nevertheless, I will not fill the rest of your time here with my burbling. But I hope you'll consider the help of would-be friends. The two men you saved have the look of those who are not enemies, but not necessarily friends. I don't know your personal story, nor would I think to pry. But they look like trouble. If you find yourself unable to be free of them, you'll welcome the help of friends."

With that, the Yuntaiman waved and turned away.

* * *

Zhuyun's words stayed with Zaiyera long after his departure. How many years had it been since she'd had a friend?

She passed the square-roofed huts with their green yards and scurrying rodents, navigating playing children and the occasional goat that wandered across the trail to get to a 'better' patch of grass than the one it had already grazed.

How long? A rhetorical question, even if only in her own mind. More than half her life she'd avoided friendship. It was safer that way, for her and anyone else. And if she was honest with herself as she tried to be, it was because she didn't deserve to have friends.

She finally reached the section of town where the huts were made of the same sandstone, but were round instead of square, with pointed thatched roofs. Each hut had a small yard enclosed by a waist-high stone wall.

Zaiyera couldn't imagine living her life surrounded by walls. Her people, the Kushtanji, were nomadic. There was little of central and southern Samhar that Zaiyera hadn't seen in just her first thirteen years of life. In the years hence, she'd seen even more of the lands stretching to the north, from coast to coast. It was a hard life with no deficiency of peril. But it was the life she had. The life she'd earned for herself, whether it was a pleasure or a penance.

She finally reached a circular hut with a pointy thatched roof, a little walled yard attached to the side with chairs and a couple tables. Even from a dozen feet away, she could smell the sweet odor of Ngoji root. She closed her eyes and inhaled deeply, smiling inwardly when a young woman's voice broke her reverie.

"I think this is why you come to my home every time, Kushtanji."

Zaiyera grinned at the other woman's accented but steadily improving grasp of Kushtanji *Soloush*. She opened her eyes to see Oloma standing just outside her door, feet in a wide stance, hands on her hips in mock disapproval. She thought of the Burkiba woman as young, but by the looks of her, she could well be an older girl or Zaiyera's mother. With their smooth, coal-colored skin, bright white eyes and shining teeth, the beautiful Burkibi were the most difficult to age in all of Samhar.

Oloma was even shorter than Zaiyera, barely above five feet tall. She wore a purple, ankle-length skirt with rust colors fading in the material. It swayed lazily in a passing breeze and looked far more comfortable than Zaiyera's riding clothes. The woman's sturdy tunic of the same color, with its loose sleeves, hung slightly big on her, but Burkibi wore their clothes that way.

Zaiyera inclined her head respectfully. "I don't know what you mean, *niyima*. Your home is clean and beautiful. Why would I not return to share it when I arrive?"

Oloma's mock scowl morphed into a toothy smile, and she stepped forward and wrapped Zaiyera in a crushing embrace. The woman may be a head shorter than Zaiyera, but she was strong. Zaiyera thought that hug would crack her ribs.

"I don't believe you," Oloma shot back in her aggressive humor. "I'm the only one who scents my house with mint and ngoji, and you like it. Come in and be home." She turned back toward the door, and Zaiyera dusted off her pack and followed.

"Another caravan travel you bring?" Oloma asked.

Zaiyera shrugged out of her shoulder pack. "I suppose you could say I brought them. Though I'd say they brought themselves and I helped them get here."

"What is that word?" Oloma asked. "Browt. What is that?"

Despite being fluent in the universal tradetongue, Oloma had insisted on mastering Zaiyera's mother tongue. Zaiyera had insisted that she may be the only Kushtanji Oloma would ever meet, and thus it was a poor use of time, but Oloma had insisted. "We are all Samharan," the woman had said. "We should be able to speak to each other in every version of our beloved *Soloush*." And she lived by that philosophy. Oloma already spoke seven Samharan dialects including the tradetongue, and a smattering of *Dreuga*, since Dor'haigheners came so often to trade.

"Br*ought*," Zaiyera replied, "is the past tense of bring."

"Oh," Oloma said. "Br ... ought. You ... brought ... another caravan."

Zaiyera smiled. "Yes."

Oloma nodded. "You know where your room is. When word arrived you caravan travel coming, I drew fresh water from the well. Is still cool."

"Thank you, *niyima*. I would love a cup if only you will have some with me."

They enjoyed the water in silence, Zaiyera holding her ceramic mug in both hands and staring into the water's depths. When she finally looked up, it was into Oloma's studying gaze. "Always you troubled since I first meet you. But you more troubled today."

Zaiyera sighed. That was the one thing about staying here. She might hide her inner turmoil or foul mood from anyone else in the form of being contemplative, but not Oloma. The woman could see right through her. And there was no point in lying unless she wanted a genuine tongue-lashing about lying to friends and holding toxic feelings inside.

"Nothing more than the normal concerns of life," Zaiyera said.

Oloma seemed to think on that. "Any of these 'concerns' have to do with the tainted one?"

Zaiyera's heart dropped into the pit of her stomach at hearing someone she had come closer to thinking of as a friend than anyone, refer to an addicted dancer such. True that anyone who'd syphoned the lifestream from another was guilty of a most heinous act, but could not a person be capable of redemption? Then again, considering the nature of the crime, did an addicted streamdancer deserve such a chance?

"Word of the darkdancer found its way to me via two shydon hunters," Zaiyera admitted. "I aided them when they were in trouble. Now they wish to hire me." She didn't know why she was telling Oloma all this, but it felt good to confide in someone.

Oloma sucked air through her teeth. "You have a dilemma. Easier to have left them to their fate and be done with it. But not easier for you, Kushtanji. You would have stacked that moral burden on your shoulders along with the other you carry."

"Other?" Zaiyera asked.

Oloma gave her a level gaze over her mug that suggested she'd go along with the charade as long as Zaiyera wished. "You save them, yes. And now that you can continue to live with yourself, you have problem of denying two shydon on the hunt."

Zaiyera took another sip. She wanted to drink it all down in one gulp, but she forced herself to drink slowly, savoring the refreshing water as long as possible. "Yes, that is my problem, *niyima*."

Oloma took a long draw from her own mug then sat it down with a sense of finality. "You will be leaving quickly. To get away from these men before they can pry further. Tomorrow?"

"Morning," Zaiyera confirmed.

Oloma sighed but nodded. "Of course. Likely I would do same. You would leave tonight if you needed not to rest, I think."

Zaiyera arched an eyebrow at that. What did this woman think of her, that she imagined Zaiyera would be in more of a hurry to get away from these men? What did she suspect, if anything? Or was Zaiyera just being paranoid?

"The one they hunt is a man from the south. Zalrabi. Word of the destruction he's wrought came four days before your arrival, and more news early this morning. He drinks lifestream without restraint and has passed from the dark into the shadow." Oloma gazed out the window. "He has moved beyond darkdancer. He is now *kivuli dayasa*."

Zaiyera's mouth went dry despite the water. "One who dances in shadow. You're sure?"

Oloma nodded. "He is lost to himself and the world." She turned her steely gaze on Zaiyera again. "Only Shakimah can cure his insanity, now."

Zaiyera didn't disagree. One who'd passed so strongly from light to dark, then into shadow was beyond saving. This man had fully succumbed to the addiction. That addiction burned away any morality he'd had left.

Oloma still held her with that uncomfortable stare. It was an effort not to squirm under it. "You know what it means? To cross into shadow?"

"I … believe I do," Zaiyera answered carefully.

"That he kills anyone who would stop him from drinking the stream? Man, woman, child? He has killed all, Zaiyera Tuneesh. To him, there is only the stream. There is nothing else."

Zaiyera opened her mouth, then closed it. What could she say? This was all true, of course, but why did Oloma tell her what she already knew, and with a tone that seemed almost … reminding?

The Burkibi woman finally broke eye contact, and Zaiyera relaxed.

"But that is for others to deal with, I think. I am but a little Burkibi woman who gardens and sometimes rents a room in my dusty home to a person I can tolerate."

Zaiyera smiled at that. Oloma kept her home as free of dust as any person she'd ever met.

"The shydon will find *kivuli dayasa* and kill him, or he will kill them." She shrugged. "Then he will kill and drink from the stream until not a hundred or a thousand dancers combined could stop him. Then we all get to bask in the love and light of Shakimah. And so it is."

Zaiyera listened to it all, not knowing how to feel. Or rather, not wanting to know how to feel. She pushed it all away. "And so it is."

"I have work to do." Oloma stood, Zaiyera standing with her. Perhaps I can finish my chores quickly that I may find more gossip about the world. I'm not a world traveler like you, Kushtanji. Just a dusty little woman who travels through her ears."

"I've hardly traveled the world, *niyima*," Zaiyera said. "And you're hardly dusty."

Oloma waved her away. "You are home, today, and every day you wish to share, here."

"Thank you, *niyima*, my friend."

The other woman waved her words away as she walked out the door.

After dropping her shoulder pack in her room, Zaiyera unstrapped Shatr from her waist and stepped out onto the little walled yard. She sat in one of the chairs and unwrapped her keffiyeh, letting her skinny braids spill out over her shoulders. She sighed in contentment, letting her head fall back to enjoy the mild warmth of the early evening sun on her dark brown face.

I can't remember how many caravans I've safely seen to their destinations, she thought. *I've helped many people survive to see their families again. Saved lives when I could. Does this make you smile on me, just a little, Shakimah? Do I carry even a spark of your grace in my soul? My lifestream?*

When she finally opened her eyes, she looked on the other side of the trail to see Zhuyun sitting cross-legged against a tree. He stared off into the distance, though whether it was somewhere in front of him or much farther away, she couldn't tell.

The Yuntaiman must have felt her gaze on him. He looked in her direction and his eyes lit up. "Awake finally!" He hopped to his feet. "You have a nice nap?"

"I only closed my eyes for a moment," she said.

"If a moment means my shadow leaning a bit more to the east, then yes."

Zaiyera frowned. Then yawned. *Maybe I did fall asleep.* She stood and stretched with a contented groan. "You're just sitting under a tree? Daydreaming?"

Zhuyun shrugged. "Only until you wake from your slumber."

She realized he was still standing on the other side of the road and laughed. "Come and join me. Unless you prefer conversation at a distance?"

Zhuyun offered a slight bow and joined her, easily vaulting over the little stone wall. "Sadly, I cannot enjoy your divine company for long. I came to share news."

"Of *kivuli dayasa*?" Zaiyera asked. The Yuntaiman blinked in incomprehension. "The shadowlancer," she translated.

"Ah. Yes." His expression darkened. It was the first time Zaiyera had seen him such. She found it unnerving. "He's razed an entire city whose name I cannot pronounce, to the ground. More than half the population is dead, and anyone who's ever, as you call it, danced the stream, had their lifestream drained."

One after another the words hit Zaiyera like a punch to the stomach. How many dead? Hundreds? More?

"He moves south," Zhuyun continued.

Kushtanja was south. "How do you know?" Zaiyera asked.

Zhuyun's hesitation set Zaiyera's heart pounding.

"The … bodies, my friend Zaiyera. "It seems he has encountered travelers."

Zaiyera's lips parted. "He's slaughtering everyone in his path."

"If there is any good in this grim news," Zhuyun said, "it is that no, he isn't indiscriminately slaughtering. He only attacks those who have touched the stream."

"To feed his addiction," Zaiyera said.

"But why leave others to spread word of his movements?" Zhuyun wondered. "Surely he knows he is hunted or will be."

Zaiyera tried to swallow the lump in her throat. "He has syphoned enough of the stream from others that his power is probably immense," Zaiyera said. "He might even welcome the challenge."

6

Zaiyera awoke well before the rest of the world. She opened her eyes and stared at the ceiling for many long moments. She and the other guards had delivered the caravan safely to Burkiba and there were enough guards left from her team and likely a few others loitering in the city to provide safety for Mr. Vose's return trip.

If she left immediately, Zaiyera could be gone before the shydon hunters came looking for her. But what of Barum, Jaide, and Zhuyun? The Yuntaiman had spoken of them as potential friends. She recognized the wisdom in his words, but she didn't have friends. Or rather, she didn't allow for friends.

Zaiyera crawled out of bed and let out a quiet groan as she stretched her arms and back and legs. She slipped out of her night-clothes and into a fresh set of traveling robes. She noticed her previous day's robes missing when she went to pack, then moved to the doorway to see them sitting neatly folded and clean on the floor. *Shakimah bless you, Oloma.*

Finished, she shouldered the pack and with Shatr in hand, quietly slipped out the door to her room. The sound of rhythmic breathing mingled with the aroma of recently cooked food. When she reached the front door, Zaiyera saw that the delicious food smell came from a little pack sitting on the floor right beside the door. She gently untied it to see two rows of skinny rolls of flatbread, baked yams and other roots, shoko paste, and colama nut butter. She'd also packed several pieces of fruit.

Zaiyera retied the pack and stood. She hugged it to herself, uttering another silent blessing upon the kind woman, then slipped out into the blue world of predawn.

Only the elderly milled about at this hour, tending gardens or simply walking and chatting in the peaceful and less harsh warmth. Saddle in hand, Zaiyera moved off the main walking trail and maneuvered out into the brush. Having been to Burkiba so many times, she easily navigated the green rocky terrain until she arrived at the place where she'd parted with Sadiq the previous day.

The camel grazed several dozen feet away, accompanied by a handful of other camels who'd been tethered to a stake in the ground with long ropes.

Zaiyera patiently watched as her dear friend enjoyed his breakfast alongside his tethered companions. Sometime later, the camel finally lifted his head and looked in her direction. She grinned, watching his jaw move sideways and his big camel lips flapping as he chewed his meal.

Sadiq grunted as he lumbered toward her. Zaiyera watched his approach while a wrinkled grin crept across her face. She reached up and gave him an affectionate rub on the side of his face, then a pat on the neck. "Time to leave, my friend. Will you join me, and bear me as a burden again?"

The camel chewed for several moments, swallowed, then grunted and butted his head into her side. Sadiq lowered himself to the ground, fore and hind legs tucked under himself. Zaiyera secured the saddle over his single hump and climbed up.

She smiled at the occasional waving resident as she and Sadiq navigated the snaking trails of Burkiba. Once she finally crossed out of the city border, she turned west, then south toward Kushtanja.

It had been years since she'd been to her homeland. When she'd left her Kha—still practically a child—they'd been in eastern central

Kushtanja and moving south. She wondered if they'd continued south or gone someplace else. Then she wondered why she wondered. Though she missed her people, her family, she would never see them again. How could she face them?

The little town receded in the distance behind her, and with Sadiq's every step, Zaiyera's anxiety ebbed. She took a deep breath and almost choked on it when she saw four camelback figures in the distance ahead.

"No." She shook her head. "Why? Why can't they leave me alone?"

She let Sadiq continue his leisurely pace, delaying the inevitable meeting as long as possible. In the predawn light they became distinguishable only when she was but a couple dozen feet away. Dyren Faust and Malker Argen sat to one side, watching her approach. Barum and Zhuyun sat a few feet from the two shydons, speaking quietly amongst themselves.

She relaxed a bit at the sight of the latter two. Friendly companions would be a good offset to the grim hunters.

Dyren and Malker inclined their heads. She returned the gesture.

"Ah. And so she arrives!" Zhuyun smiled and also inclined his head. The Yuntaiman had once again wrapped his long braid about the top of his head and had it tucked inside his brown keffiyeh.

"'Bout bloody time," Barum said. The Dor'haighener smirked at her. "Thought you were the early rising type."

"Do not let our northern friend fool you," Zhuyun said. "It took an effort to pierce his snoring enough to shake him awake, and even more effort to ignore his complaints."

"It appears we've all had the same idea," Dyren said. The commanding shydon hunter sat erect astride his camel. His stony face looked satisfied. "And apparently we're all headed in the same direction."

Zaiyera didn't miss the look Malker cut Zhuyun and Barum. The hunters must have thought to head her off, here, and the other two men were an unexpected addition. She looked at her companions and gave them a half smile in thanks.

Barum offered an exaggerated wink, which made her smile broaden just a bit, and Zhuyun simply responded with a firm-chinned downward smile and a nod. The man couldn't be more than five or ten years her senior, but the expression gave him the look of a village elder.

Zaiyera urged Sadiq onward, the other four falling in around her. She closed her eyes for a moment to enjoy the refreshing wind breathing over the distant plateaus, the soothing chirp of the crickets as they sang their last songs before the sun fully arose. Morning filled one with life, that they might endure the harshness of another day.

"If yesterday's news holds true," Malker said, "our quarry is possibly about two days ahead of us."

Zaiyera released the breath she'd been holding in an annoyed puff. She didn't respond. What would she say? She hadn't agreed to accompany these men and she hadn't expressed any interest in hunting down an addicted dancer. Once again she questioned the wisdom in not having pretended she hadn't seen these men shackled in that little enclosure. She silently chastised herself for the thought as soon as it came. *What would you have done? Left them to die? Are you no better than the man they hunt?*

Tension hung in the air between these men. She felt it as surely as she felt the clothes on her skin. What was going on with them?

From the corner of her eye, she noticed Malker and Dyren share a look. On her other side, Zhuyun and Barum shared a similar, hesitant look. It was Zhuyun who finally cut the silence.

"There is ... more you should know, my friend Zaiyera."

She looked at him. "More?"

He nodded. "If my memory still serves me, you said that your people hail from the land of Kush ... Kush ..."

"Kushtanja," Zaiyera finished for him, feeling little pinpricks attacking her stomach. "What are you trying to tell me, Zhuyun?"

"The man our stern companions hunt," Zhuyun continued— Malker frowned at that assessment—"was last seen moving in that direction. A survivor we spoke to said that she'd heard him proclaiming something about the corruption of the Sheiks and

Sheikhas, and that they would sell all of Samhar and its people to the north."

"That sounds like the ravings of a man gone mad by the addiction," Zaiyera said, inwardly flinching at her own words. "Was this person really a survivor? Hasn't the addicted dancer left entire cities in ruin and killed everyone he encounters?"

"The woman we spoke with," Malker said, "was not a lancer and had never touched the stream. From what she and other survivors say, the shadowlancer would not have attacked a non-lancer unless threatened."

"Does this … shadowlancer, have a name, Malker Argen?" Zaiyera asked.

"Does it matter?" Malker replied. "He is a murderer who must be put down. Evil need not have a name."

"Everyone has a story, *shydon hunter*," Zaiyera said. "Even the darkest of us have a story. Otherwise, might we just be walking breathing titles someone else has given us?"

"We don't know his name for certain," Dyren Faust said, "but he is one of a handful of emissaries on his way to the capital of Dor'haighen. All of this has happened rather quickly, and we've not had the time to discover his identity."

Zaiyera frowned. "Did you not engage him once already?"

"That confrontation was … swift," Dyren replied.

"Ah!" Zhuyun said. "You mean he put the beating on you too fast for you to get a good look at him."

Dyren's expression hardened. "I don't appreciate your choice of description, Zhuyun of Yuntai. We lost three comrades. But you or correct."

Zhuyun cupped his right fist in his left palm and bowed his head in solemnity. "My apologies to you and my prayers for your fallen."

"Seems to me one question just led us all the way across the Great Sea from our original conversation," Barum commented. He tugged at his robes and fanned his face. Surely he couldn't be hot already.

"You're right." Malker looked at Barum. "If I hear you correct, your accent places you from Denberest."

"Good ear," Barum said.

"The shadowlancer"—Dyren leveled his gaze at Zaiyera—"was said to have been ranting about the corruption of the lords of this land. The Sheikhs and Sheikhas. We believe it may be related to the ill-fated mission of the emissaries of which he was one. Things happened quickly. People died, he survived, and came out of the entire mess a tainted lancer."

The sun finally peeked over the eastern plateaus and started to warm the left side of Zaiyera's face. She untied a piece of her keffiyeh and let a flap of the cloth hang down the left side of her head. The others watched her and did the same. Or tried to. While Zhuyun more or less got it right, Barum's large hands threatened to unravel the entire piece, and Malker and Dyren fared little better.

After silently enjoying their struggles, Zaiyera called for a halt long enough to help.

"By the time word came to Nanshaigha," Malker continued sometime later, "Four days had passed. We hadn't the time to investigate first. King Eredin Nansheig dispatched a team to discover what befell the emissaries and tasked us with hunting down the shadowlancer."

"Despite the tragedy he's already inflicted," Dyren said, "we've been lucky. For reasons we haven't yet determined, he didn't begin killing and syphoning other lancers until we were dispatched from Nanshaigha. One would think he'd have immediately begun building his power." The younger-looking shydon stared at the back of his camel's head. "There is still so much we don't know."

He didn't immediately begin syphoning dancers because he spent those days struggling with what he'd become, Zaiyera thought. She, too, stared off into a distant place far beyond the increasingly sandy brown landscape stretching before them.

The man they hunted had likely defeated a streamdancer and for whatever reason, syphoned his lifestream. Then he'd probably gone into hiding, curled up someplace alone, trembling as he fought off the raging fires burning inside his skin and the freezing cold icing his bones. How long had he endured the sensation of spikes grinding in his stomach, the thirst that no water could quench, the emptiness that left him feeling brittle and hollow, before he'd finally succumbed?

Zaiyera felt a tiny spike pinch her own stomach. The feeling of hollowness crept into her, and she pushed those thoughts away. After several moments and a few deep breaths, the feelings subsided.

When she looked up, it was to see Zhuyun watching her. She looked away.

"… severely underestimated him," Dyren was saying. "That mistake cost many lives."

"Ah, but could you have known?" Zhuyun asked. "From all that I've heard this last day, I don't think these shadowlancer folk are common. You had a plan, but a plan's lifespan ends once it is implemented, ixu?"

"I appreciate your kindness," Dyren replied. "But had I planned more appropriately, three of our companions and many more lives across Samhar might have been spared."

"You said he defeated you so swiftly you hadn't been able to identify him?" Zaiyera asked. "I mean not to squeeze the wound," she said when both men bristled, "but I ask for a reason."

"Yes," Dyren said stiffly.

"Then it's likely you would have just lost more of your comrades, had you brought a full team."

Dyren arched an eyebrow at that. "How so?"

"If he was able to defeat five of you that quickly, he would have beaten eight or even ten of you. And if you'd pushed him close to his limits, he might have syphoned all of you after it was done. You may have had a larger team, Dyren Faust, but you would not be here, now."

Dyren said nothing for a while, and Zaiyera thought perhaps she'd struck a nerve.

"How do you know so much about this?" Dyren asked.

Zaiyera felt a stab of ice shoot through her heart. She'd said too much. How could she be so stupid? She glanced at Dyren, but the shydon hunter faced forward, his expression unreadable. On his other side, Malker stared at her with an open curiosity that clashed with the wizened look of his gray and black hair, and the creases on his face and at the corners of his eyes.

"Do they not teach you in Dor'haighen of the terrible things people do," Zaiyera replied, "that those things not be repeated? How can you know to prevent something if you know not how it happens?"

Dyren thought on that, then nodded, while Malker tilted his head in a shrug that said it made sense to him. Zaiyera let out a relieved sigh.

"And once again," Barum Hurst said, "it seems like my job in all this is to keep the discussion on track. The deranged lancer heads south, raving about corrupt leaders as he marches toward Kushtanja. From what me and Jaide found out last night over a mug of the most bitter tea I've ever had in my life, this guy just might be planning to visit every major city in this dusty place and kill their leaders. Nobody knows why, yet, but that's what we've got."

The mention of the other caravan guard drew Zaiyera's attention from the matters at hand. How could she have forgotten about the good-natured Viriksani?

"Ah, she finally remembers the pretty man," Zhuyun said.

Zaiyera rolled her eyes but asked anyway. "Has he gone back home?"

"Not unless home is south, ahead of us," Barum replied. "After all the grim news of our man headed in that direction, Jaide rode out early and fast to spread the warning."

"Let's hope he doesn't stumble into the maniac on his way," Malker said. "That would be a quick end to your friend."

"Jaide isn't a dancer, as far as I know," Zaiyera said. "He may well not attract attention to himself if he doesn't challenge the man."

"Too many dead men envisioned themselves heroes," Dyren said.

"Not the smart ones," Zhuyun replied.

Zaiyera pointed ahead. "There. The first dune between Burkiba and Shanhazai. We should take our rest there."

"We don't have time for that," Malker said. "Who knows how much of a lead the shadowlancer has on us, and we're to lean against a mountain of sand and break bread?" He half turned in his seat and swept his hand out behind them. "We should have been moving faster to begin with."

"Our pace is the fastest we can go without injuring our camel companions, Malker Argen," Zaiyera replied. "The sand is thick and the soil is soft in this region. Perhaps dismount and walk for a while, that you might experience the extra labor."

Again, she indicated the dune, growing larger as they approached. "Samharans have traveled this route for thousands of years. In the endless desert you see around us are markers we use to gauge our distance from one point to the next. And some of us, having lived our entire lives here, simply know the land, as we are a part of it. I'm sure the same is true of Dor'haighen and its people."

Malker opened his mouth, but Dyren held up a hand. "Please excuse our impatience, Zaiyera Tuneesh. We're simply anxious to reach the shadowlancer before he can deal any more calamity."

"Heat and exhaustion will have long claimed our lives if we charge headlong across Samhar," Zaiyera said. "Unless this man can fly, which would mean your cause is hopeless, he'll have moved at a similar pace to ours and stopped here."

She promised them a brief rest, but one long enough that human and camel alike could resume strong and energized. She shared her fruit, but kept the other food wrapped, as it would dry moisture and add to their thirst. The sun passed overhead and had just begun to tilt west when they resumed.

"We should reach Shanhazai before night," Zaiyera said. "It's a large enough city that we might catch up to him before he's gone."

"Hopefully he hasn't destroyed the place," Barum said.

No one responded to that, for surely they all thought the same. Shanhazai would likely be left in ruin, its leaders dead, their dancers syphoned.

Thinking of that gave Zaiyera a moment of hesitation. What was she doing? She hadn't agreed to help these men. They weren't paying her, and she had no desire to cross a kivuli dayasa, a shadowlancer. She should point them in the right direction and continue on her way.

Perhaps she could do the same as Jaide, simply warn the cities further south."

That path would almost certainly end with Dyren and Malker dead, Zhuyun and Barum as well if they were foolish enough to try to fight. Could she live with that?

Curse them for this, she thought. *This is their fight, not mine. Curse them, curse my conscience, curse all of this. Goddess Shakimah. Is this part of my penance?*

On the other side of Zhuyun, Barum grumbled about how even the wind from their speedy pace felt like it came from a kiln. Zhuyun and the two shydon spoke little, but their discomfort was no less evident. The Yuntaiman had pulled the lower cloths of his keffiyeh over his face so that only his eyes were visible through a narrow slit.

She paid close attention to Sadiq as well. Her loyal companion galloped uncomplaining across the open desert, passing by many a shady tree. The smell of the perspiring camel filled her nostrils, a reminder of the strength of their friendship over the years.

Zhuyun pointed at the sky ahead where large black birds circled. "That bodes ill. How far are we from this place I cannot pronounce?"

"Another few hours yet," Zaiyera replied. "That is too close."

They kept going. After some time, even the ever-uncomfortable Barum had settled into the rhythm of his camel's lope. They crossed flatlands that turned to mild rolling hills and winding trails when they finally reached the area of the circling birds.

"Tell me this is some horrible mirage," Malker said.

Zaiyera swallowed the bile in her throat.

They slowed the camels to a walk as they passed through an area strewn with corpses. Buzzards half as tall as Zaiyera fussed and picked over the dead.

"What beast leaves people to die in the open land to be picked at by scavengers?" Malker spat. "This is why we hunt him," he said to Zaiyera. He spread his hand to encompass the sight. "This is why, despite your greatest wish to be rid of us and go about your lovely way, we persist in practically pleading for your aid."

"That's enough," Dyren said. He looked to Zaiyera. "Malker

became a shadow hunter for the same reason I and every one of us does. To prevent horrors like this. If we push at you, it's because we're trying to stop this. To save lives."

Zaiyera took in the carnage with growing anger. These people were nomads much like her own people, though their lighter skin marked them as from northern Samhar. Kivuli dayasa had no reason to kill these travelers.

"Some bear weapons," Zhuyun said, his tone respectfully solemn. "Could be there were a number of *tokailan* among them, ixu?" At Malker and Dyren's questioning looks, he clarified. "*Tokailan*. What you call lancers." He indicated a dead woman with a pair of long daggers at her side. "Maybe these people tried to fight."

"*Jakta skree*," Barum cursed. "How could anyone lay so many people to the ground like this?"

"Let's get moving and ask him ourselves," Malker growled, "right before we kill him."

Though it pained her to leave these people to the scavengers, Zaiyera didn't disagree. They might still aid the living.

They moved on, the camels needing no encouragement to put so much death behind them.

"We're an hour or two from Shanhazai," Zaiyera said.

"Those people haven't been dead for long," Malker said. "If we ride hard, we might catch him. He's not expecting …"

Malker trailed off at the sight of a lone figure walking toward the city of Shanhazai, which just barely came into view. "There's the bastard right there."

Zaiyera sensed the flow building inside the younger shydon hunter, followed by Dyren, who touched the stream much quicker and deeper. She felt the senior shydon hunter pull back until his depth matched Malker's.

"Manipulate the flow in sync," Dyren said. "Combine our power, share the price."

Malker narrowed his eyes at the solitary figure ahead. "Lance the stream as one."

The lone figure stopped walking and turned toward them.

"He felt us," Dyren said in a surprised tone. "He felt us as soon as we touched the stream."

"That's impossible," Malker said. "We're too far away."

"It must be another addition to his power," Dyren guessed. "Having syphoned so many, he may well be so powerful that he can feel someone lancing from even this far away."

Zaiyera felt a chill in the pit of her stomach. If that were true, this man could access a lot of power.

The camels groaned and tried to pull up, but the riders urged them on. Zaiyera leaned forward and patted Sadiq on his side. "Will you still carry me, friend?"

Sadiq grunted. He felt the wrongness of the man the same as the other animals, but he ran on.

My loyal friend. I will do all in my power to keep you safe. Zaiyera drew Shatr.

Beside her, Zhuyun unstrapped his staff and tucked it under his arm. Barum drew his longsword.

Zaiyera wished they had stayed behind. Their weapons would do no good, here.

The brown-clad man had stopped walking and waited as they rode down on him. He extended his arms, but otherwise did not move. As they drew closer, Zaiyera saw that he was smiling. She clenched her teeth. There was no concern on his face. *Perhaps Shatr will change your mind, lightless.*

The two shydon hunters lanced the stream and collected the flow in unison. Zaiyera clenched her legs against Sadiq's sides, prepared to leap free.

Their enemy laughed. The ground shook.

7

The stream. It was art, life, creation. The stream was an expression of Creator Goddess Shakimah Herself. It was the goddess's blessing.

It was Zaiyera's curse.

She narrowed her attention on the monster smiling back at them. The ground trembled, the camels groaned in fear.

Zaiyera ignored it all. She pushed away the sensation of the blissful power of the flow that the two men beside her built, molded, and shared between each other. She blocked out what that must feel like, what she *knew* it felt like. She blocked out the enormous power building in front of them. It was an impossible amount of power for a single person to access without paying a deadly amount of lifeprice, yet this man, this kivuli dayasa, continued to pierce deeper into the stream.

The ground stopped shaking. Zaiyera glanced at the two shydon hunters, but if they'd stopped the tremors, they showed no sign of having done so. Both remained focused on the man ahead.

They were close enough now that she heard the brown-clad man's laughter. It wasn't the maniacal laughter of a madman, but that of amusement. Had he been testing them?

The shadowlancer suddenly turned his focus on Zaiyera. With a flick of his wrist, he grasped what looked like a transparent whip. It slithered into being as though being drawn out of an invisible pouch.

He flicked his wrist at Zaiyera. The translucent whip arced through the air, its deadly tip curling down toward her.

Shatr flashed across the air in a horizontal cut. The whip dissipated before the surprised eyes of the shadowlancer just as the five riders reached him.

Dyren Faust and Malker Argen unleashed their built-up power in the form of a shockwave. The shadowlancer merely grinned and swept his hand aside. The air in front of him warped as though his hand had slashed through a body of water.

Zaiyera swallowed. That burst of power washed over her like a blanket of bliss, waiting to envelope her. She tightened her grip on Shatr to keep her hands from trembling.

The hunters pulled their camels up and dismounted. Relieved of their burdens, the animals fled.

Barum and Zhuyun also hopped down from their mounts. Zaiyera gave Sadiq a little pat on the neck and swept off his back. "Be safe, my friend," she said to him. The camel grunted once and trotted in the direction the others had gone.

"Not dead after all," the shadowlancer said. "I remember defeating five shydon hunters before the arrival of that band of raiders. A shame I hadn't shed my inhibitions yet. I might have done away with all of you and would not be wasting my time now."

"You mean sucking more lifestream from your victims." Malker spat. "Say what it is you do, leech."

"What I am is beyond your comprehension," the shadowlancer snapped. "You and your organization who hunt those who have fallen into darkness. Your mighty sacred order who crusade to exterminate what you don't understand." The muscles in his jaw knotted, the veins at his temple bulging at his barely repressed rage. "Spare me the lecture, child. Your pedestrian knowledge of the stream is wasted on your immaturity."

"Grand words for one who has murdered countless innocent

people," Dyren Faust said. Where Malker's voice was thick with passion, the senior shydon's was cold, icy. He drew his longsword and held it before him, his stance defensive.

The shadowlancer watched as Dyren squared with him while Malker circled around to his right. Zaiyera remained where she was, partly because Barum had moved behind the man while Zhuyun took the left side. No need to draw attention to herself yet.

Unfortunately he turned his attention on her, practically ignoring everyone else. "Now, you," he said, pointing at Zaiyera, "are interesting."

Zaiyera said nothing. She tried not to be cowed by those cold dark eyes shadowed by thick black eyebrows. His face was hard, as though forged on an anvil made of a thousand taken lives.

The shadowlancer tilted his head. "Are you unable to speak?"

"What would I say to you?" Zaiyera said. She held Shatr at her side, tip pointed toward the ground.

The shadowlancer narrowed his almost black eyes at her. "So you judge me as well, I see." He'd switched from tradetongue to *Soloush*. "You judge what you don't understand on the words of two foreign shydon hunters. You are Samharan. You should know better."

"I am Samharan, yes," Zaiyera said. "Being Samharan doesn't mean syphoning someone and murdering countless people to feed your addiction."

"You think I decided this path of my own will?" the man yelled.

His sudden passion caught Zaiyera off guard. What was going on here?"

Before anyone could react, the shadowlancer curled his fingers and stabbed them into the air, which again warped in front of him. He raked his fingers sideways and drew forth a transparent whip that he waved at the two shydons in front and beside him. He hadn't even bothered to look in their direction.

"You have no idea what their king and our 'illustrious' rulers would do with our land," the shadowlancer shouted, "our resources. I've seen it first-hand. I know what they're about and I won't let them do it. They have no right!"

While the shadowlancer ranted, flicking his whip at them with barely a thought, Dyren and Malker went on the defensive. They drew their swords with one hand and lanced the stream to form a transparent blue disk. The whip crashed into them with such force, both shields shattered and they were thrown backward.

"You wouldn't stand beside them if you were a dancer," kivuli dayasa said.

"They only hunt the likes of you," Zaiyera replied.

He laughed at her. "You know that's a lie." He waved a hand at Malker and Dyren, who were still picking themselves off the ground. "Their kind, the Dor'haighen. They merely tolerate those who dance the stream. It's fine as long as their dancers are useful. Their warrior class is filled with them. But a civilian who dances the stream rightfully fears their freedom in the north. You must be their tool."

"Says the murderer," Zaiyera replied.

"Idiot!" He slashed his hands through the air and sent a blade-like arc racing toward her.

Zaiyera charged, at the same time sweeping Shatr upward. The magnificent blue-steel scimitar sliced clean through the stream-born blade. Zaiyera kept running as the two parts dissipated on either side of her.

From the corner of her eye, Zaiyera saw Zhuyun and Barum charging in as well, the former angling closer to the Dor'haighener for some reason. Unless they secretly had the ability to dance, this would be their end.

The shadowlancer spared them an amused grin. He thrust his finger into the air and drew forth a large pulsating blue disk. Dozens of circles opened in the disk.

Barum cursed.

Blue shards shot out of the disk and raced toward the big Dor'haighener.

Staff spinning, Zhuyun kicked sand and dirt into the air as he skidded to a stop. The Yuntaiman moved so fast he seemed to sweep his staff in every direction at once. Even as he worked, Zhuyun leapt into a sideways flip and landed in front of Barum. His staff didn't fend off the assault but *collected* it.

Zhuyun kept the staff moving, collecting every bit of the stream the shadowlancer hurled at him. Finally, his staff practically buzzing with built-up power, Zhuyun leapt forward. He curled his body backward in the air passing over several more shards. With a growl that rumbled from deep in his belly, the Yuntaiman slammed the end of his staff to the ground.

The impact released the collected power and sent it rippling through the ground back at the shadowlancer.

The shadowlancer's eyes widened in surprise, but he quickly recovered. His hands flashed up before him in a quick pattern that produced another disk. The returned power burst through the shield and lifted him off his feet.

Dyren and Malker produced transparent whips from the air and each lashed at the airborne enemy.

The shadowlancer snarled. Once again his hands flashed out into intricate patterns, one in the direction of each shydon. Before he touched the ground, he thrust both hands back at the hunters, blasting their whips apart. The force of the counter struck the two warriors full on. They dropped their weapons as their bodies shook with violent spasms as though electrocuted.

As soon as his feet touched the ground, the shadowlancer slapped the palm of his hand toward Zaiyera. The air between them rippled as though he'd slapped a body of water.

Crackling energy sped toward Zaiyera. She swept Shatr upward and cut through it. The shadowlancer was working even as she defeated his attack. He thrust his hands toward the ground and it rippled underneath her. The tremor tossed her up at the same time he drew a whip from the air and flicked it at her.

The stream-born whip stung like a physical one, drawing blisters on her hip where it struck. She cried out, but the sound came out like a chirp, for she'd been midair from the first attack.

Zaiyera gritted her teeth as she hit the ground in a backward roll. Another ripple crashed into her from behind, halting her momentum and tossing her in the opposite direction. She skipped across the ground like a pebble until finally crashing into the still shaking Dyren Faust. They rolled in a tangle of limbs, robes, and dirt.

Zaiyera ignored the screaming pain in her hip and spat a mouthful of grit and a little blood. She looked to the side to see Malker struggling to lift himself up to his forearms. In the haze of her rattled mind, she heard the muffled sound of the shadowlancer's voice.

"I'm done wasting time on you," the shadowlancer hissed.

Zaiyera's body vibrated as she felt the drawing of a large amount of the stream. It was glorious. She knew the power was being drawn to kill her, knew something terrible was coming, but it was difficult to focus with all that power swirling around her.

She sighed with pleasure, but as soon as the sound left her, Zaiyera felt a fresh wave of revulsion. She turned over and growled as she climbed to her hands and knees.

Somehow, Zaiyera had managed to keep hold of Shatr. She gave her head a shake and climbed to a kneeling position. While she struggled through her daze, a huge shadow passed overhead.

And stopped.

Zaiyera lifted her gaze upward first, then she craned her neck to look up at the sky. A sky made of … sand. She closed her eyes and whispered, "I am released."

The sky of sand fell.

* * *

The crushing weight of the world never came. Or perhaps it did fall on them, but she'd felt nothing, simply been snatched from life into oblivion the instant of impact.

The stream. She felt the stream. Did her soul swim the stream now, in the bliss of *Sojalleh*? Dare she even hope that Goddess Shakimah would welcome her there?

No. She didn't swim the stream. She felt the power, but it was outside herself, nearby. The sensation warmed her like a campfire just close enough that she could feel its heat. Zaiyera opened her eyes to darkness broken by the faint golden glow of Dyren and Malker's dance-resins.

"We must make a move, Senior Hunter," Malker said, "or we'll dry up long before we reach the end of this."

Zaiyera coughed, then swallowed. "End of what?"

"He dropped an entire sand dune on us," Malker said. "We're in the middle of it but there's no telling how big it is."

"Remain focused," Dyren said. "Keep your movements matched to mine. We share the lifeprice. We can survive."

Zaiyera climbed to her feet. She looked about the tiny hole in the middle of what most likely was a massive dune. How far were they from freedom? Fifty feet? A hundred? Could these men hold that long before the lifeprice claimed them both?

"I'm about to give you a condensed lesson in compounding," Dyren continued.

"I'm listening, Senior Hunter," Malker replied.

"Release your anxiety and focus. This will not be easy. If we stay in unison, the lifeprice will be minimized. We may only pay half a day each of life. Maybe a day."

In the golden glow of their dance-resins, Malker nodded. "Yes, Senior."

The two men danced the stream, or rather, "lanced the stream", as non-Samharans referred to it. They moved their arms in precise gestures, up and around, sweeping down, left, then right, up, repeat. The movements were smaller and less flourishing. It was the way northerners danced. Their unsullied resins trailed golden beauty after each movement.

"You know the pattern," Dyren said. "Make it part of you. Internalize it so that you don't have to think about it; that you don't have to watch me to remain in sync with my movements."

Zaiyera kept quiet. There was nothing she could do to help except let them concentrate on saving the three of them from a crushing death.

"All right," Dyren said. "As you continue the pattern, remove one hand as though you were holding a weight with both hands and have to take one away. Good. Keep in sync. We've already drawn from the stream and paid the price. No more is paid so long as we simply maintain the flow. Now, lance the stream with your other hand. Allow the power to build. Gather it. Hold it."

Dyren and Malker let their free hands hang at their sides, palms facing upward, fingers curled. Their hands began to tremble as the power built, and the soft golden glow of their lance-resins brightened.

Zaiyera moved to the other side of the hole from the lancers, though it was only five or six feet. She placed a hand on the wall and leaned against it, eyes squeezed shut. She wanted to touch it, to taste it. Just a bit. She only needed but a tiny sample of what it was like. Touching the passive stream was good, but to touch the true stream, the actual power. There was nothing like it. No feeling in the world, no sensation could compare to it.

Her body gave an involuntary shudder, and Zaiyera turned and leaned her back against the wall. Eyes still closed, she hugged herself tightly to keep from shaking. Hot and cold, all at once. And the longing, the *need* to have it. It was right there. Just out of reach and all she needed to do was reach out and grab it.

"Are you all right, Zaiyera?" Malker asked.

The sound of the man's voice created a tiny crack in Zaiyera's torment, and she grabbed hold of it like a lifeline. "Yes." She gasped. "I'm fine."

"Are you claustrophobic? Ill luck that we get buried under a mountain of sand."

"H … hardly a mountain, Malker Argen."

"Doesn't matter does it?" he replied.

"Not if your focus fails," Dyren quipped.

"Apologies, Senior."

"Focus into the stream and feel how much I hold," Dyren said. "Can you match it? Will the price be too high, even if we share it?"

Malker closed his eyes. A moment later he gasped. "That's far too much for me to wield. The price could shave decades of my life away or render me feeble. Either way, I would die out there in the heat if we escape."

"Hold as much as you can on your own," Dyren said. "I will match you."

The junior shydon hunter did as instructed while Zaiyera focused on her breathing.

"We are aligned," Dyren Faust said. "Follow me."

The hunters moved both hands in opposite patterns in unison, as though mirror images of each other. Zaiyera had broken into a cold sweat by then, but she was nonetheless impressed by the display.

"One blast," Dyren said. "On my call, thrust the flow against the far wall."

Zaiyera started to feel lightheaded and breath came with an effort. She hoped they'd finished soon or they would smother in short order.

"Ready," Dyren said. "One. Two. THREE."

They thrust their free hands toward the far wall. Zaiyera shielded her eyes against the explosion. When she looked back, she saw that they had blasted a huge section away, but they were still buried.

"Maintain the flow you've already drawn!" Dyren said to Malker.

While his subordinate complied, the senior shydon hunter continued to hold his defensive lance against the sandy tomb as well. He lanced again and sent another shockwave into the wall.

Zaiyera watched Dyren work. He kept his hands moving, not expending the lanced flow, but using it to keep the sand dune at bay while repeatedly swiping at the wall. With each swipe, more of the lanced power would be expended until it was depleted, and he'd need to touch the stream again, requiring more lifeprice.

Malker dropped to one knee, but kept his hands moving, helping to maintain the barrier between them and certain death.

Zaiyera slid down to the ground, each breath a wheezing gasp. She tried to draw shallow breaths to afford Dyren as much of the remaining air as possible.

Dyren slashed at the wall of sand repeatedly, knocking thick sheets away as he walked through the corridor he'd created. Zaiyera helped Malker to his feet, and they shuffled after Dyren. The senior shydon faltered but kept his footing and pushed on. He was weakening. Too little air.

Another swipe. Sand tumbled away, and crumbled until a tiny sliver of light shined in. It went dark immediately as more sand slid down the slope and covered the hole.

"We've made it," Malker said.

He was right. Zaiyera felt a gust of fresh air sweep in through that slit before it covered over again.

With one last thrust, Dyren sent a final shockwave of the remaining stream into the fragile slope. It burst open, letting in an ocean of sweet fresh air. Everyone inhaled deeply, filling their lungs. To their credit, Malker and Dyren maintained their protective lance until they were safely outside the dune, then released the flow.

Both men dropped and rolled onto their backs, arms and legs spread, chests heaving.

Zaiyera also fell over, wheezing as she drew in sweet life-giving air. That was close. She wasn't sure if she felt relieved or disappointed to have survived, but she had, so that was that. She was glad Dyren and Malker were all right. She might wish to have nothing to do with them, but they were here to save lives.

Save lives. And what if she turned away from them? What if her aid could help these men save lives? If she abandoned them, would they survive in an unfamiliar land with climate that was hostile to them? Unlikely. Their deaths, along with any others at *kivuli dayasa's* hands, would be on her soul.

With a resigned sigh, Zaiyera climbed to her feet and looked up at the displaced sand dune behind them. Malker's exaggeration didn't seem far off the mark after all. Standing this close and looking up, the dune did indeed look like a mountain whose peak she couldn't see.

A familiar, distant voice made Zaiyera's heart leap with relief.

"Ah! So hope and a little luck still exist in the world!"

Zaiyera turned to see Zhuyun trotting toward her, shielding his eyes against the descending sun to the west. How long had they been buried?

Overhead, a murder of crows cawed as they passed, angling south and west. Zaiyera watched the black cloud of birds as they receded into the distance. The day was late, and it was almost time for them to roost for the night. A patch of trees must be nearby, possibly with vegetation and water.

"Across my homeland and the Great Sea, to lands around the world I've traveled." Zhuyun stooped to help Malker and then Dyren stand. "And never have I seen anything so amazing." He gestured at the dune. This great thing dropped on your heads, and you burst out the side of it! I am truly amazed."

"I'm glad … to provide … your amazement, Yuntaiman," Dyren huffed. "You've a great deal of faith in our abilities that you waited for us to dig out of this." He waved a hand over his shoulder.

"Well," Zhuyun said. "I hadn't many options. Figured I would wait and see if you were alive, since I would likely not be if you failed to emerge, ixu?"

Zaiyera looked past him in the direction he'd come running.

Zhuyun followed her gaze. "You must be looking for our stocky Dor'haighener friend, ah?" He pointed north. "Seems not being *tokailan* has its benefits. After our powerful enemy dropped half the world on you, and blasted me and Barum to this side of oblivion, he left. Must have figured us for dead."

"You are indeed lucky," Dyren said. "He doesn't bother syphoning non-lancers."

"Lucky for us and your homeland, perhaps," Zhuyun replied. "Our friend Barum realized from our confrontation that his sword and his skill was of no use in this fool's errand. He turned north to your capital called Nan … Nansheeg …"

"Nanshaigha," Malker said. "He went there to warn King Eredin, I presume?"

"Yes," Zhuyun said. "I doubt help could arrive in time to assist us by the time we catch up with our quarry, but your homeland will be prepared."

"I think," Zaiyera said, "we should rethink our strategy."

"Our?" Malker said.

Zaiyera moved a stray braid away from her eye, inconspicuously sliding her fingers over each of the red four-point marks on her face. "Unless you no longer desire my help?"

"Your help would be most welcome," Dyren said. "We're just surprised by your change of heart."

"Revenge can be a great motivator," Malker said.

Zaiyera's expression darkened. "So can the desire to prevent more deaths, Malker Argen of Dor'haighen."

Malker raised his hands in a warding gesture. "Apologies. I meant no insult …"

"He's nearly killed you twice, now," Zaiyera said. "He quite easily defeated the five of us, and if he'd chosen to be more thorough, we'd be dead."

"We'll need to change tactics," Dyren said. "We could use up every second of our lives against him and still he'd likely defeat us."

"Not likely at all," Zaiyera replied. "A certainty. Our enemy is stronger than our bodies, but not our minds."

"Wisdom," Zhuyun agreed. "There is Yintish saying. The sharpest weapon is between your ears."

"We have a similar expression in Samhar," Zaiyera said. "There is no weapon sharper or more versatile than your mind." She shrugged. "Of course, the mind is only a weapon when need be."

"Making it all the more versatile," Zhuyun replied.

Zaiyera nodded. "As to our problem. We have no choice but to pursue him, but if we're not smarter, he'll crush us."

Dyren looked to the sky in the direction of the setting sun. Already, the evening breeze grew cooler. "We should find a suitable place to camp for the night."

"There is vegetation that way," Zaiyera pointed in the direction the crows had gone," but I don't know how far it is. We're also close enough to reach Shanhazai. I recommend we press forward, either to search for vegetation and a possible watering hole, or on to Shanhazai."

"The shadowlancer probably reached the place already," Dyren said. "He may be there now."

"Possibly," Zaiyera agreed. She gestured at the encompassing desert awash in the golden glow of the evening sun. "There are things out here that might avoid a caravan but consider the four of us an opportunity. I recommend we move on to Shanhazai. He may have already moved on, but if he's still in the city when we arrive, it's big enough that he won't know we're there."

"And if he is still there?" Malker asked. "What then?"

No one answered.

8

Jaide Amadi shook his head then slapped his clean-shaven face. Beneath him his camel panted, the poor animal lathered from the hard ride from Burkiba. He'd only stopped to allow the animal enough rest that it didn't die of exhaustion.

"I'll see to it you're well rested and fed soon, my friend," he said to the animal. He gave it a pat on the neck. Viriksani may not be as closely tied to animals as the Kushtanji, but they still appreciated them.

Jaide had taken a roundabout path to Shanhazai, hoping against hope that he'd beat kivuli dayasa there. Through some miracle Jaide had indeed reached the city before him and managed—with some difficulty—to obtain a brief audience with Sheikh Ahreid.

The man had been skeptical of the degree of the threat, given the many years that had passed since Samhar had seen an actual dark-dancer, let alone a fully fallen kivuli dayasa. In the end Jaide had convinced Ahreid to at least send word to his garrison of *dakhiva*, as well as any dancers in Shanhazai who could or were willing to fight.

Of course, the sheikh had *agreed* to do so. Whether he actually did send word wasn't Jaide's concern. He'd done his part.

Jaide thought of Zaiyera and the others as he crossed into the Kush-tanja. It was possible they'd already encountered kivuli dayasa, and

87

that was why Jaide had gotten to Shanhazai first. The Viriksani had no desire to pass within a dozen miles of the fallen streamdancer, but he didn't like the other possibility either. Anyone who could soundly defeat five shydon hunters *before* laying waste to an entire city could probably kill them all with ease. But then, Zaiyera was a force of her own with that beautiful scimitar.

Jaide patted the shamshir sheathed at his hip. The weapon had been with him through many a conflict and had served him well. It was a weapon of both functional and sentimental value, but even the well-crafted weapon paled terribly in comparison to the marvelous blue-steel scimitar.

The sun sat low enough in the western sky that it dipped out of sight when Jaide passed close enough to the frequently appearing dunes. He unwrapped his keffiyeh and let his long black hair fall free. "Much better," he sighed.

Short stubby euphorbia plants that inhabited the harsher parts of the desert grew scarce, while their larger, bush and tree-like cousins became more common.

A pack of black-spotted dark brown chukita cats appeared a few dozen feet away. The small wild cats raced alongside Jaide's camel, yipping and yowling. Jaide let out another sigh of relief. Chukita cats in such numbers typically lived near human settlements and civilizations. Kruwa Outpost was close.

Jaide, his camel, and their chukita escort reached the outpost just before dark. He slowed the camel to a walk just as the town came into view, tied his hair up again, and rewrapped his keffiyeh.

A dark-skinned man with a map of age creases upon his smiling face greeted Jaide as he entered Kruwa. He did well to hide his amazement at the Viriksani's eyes by speaking at once. "You look tired, my friend." He looked at Jaide's panting camel. "But she looks even more tired, hmm. Maybe a little longer and you'd have killed her, I think."

Jaide didn't miss the disapproval in the man's tone. "Be assured, *dyenbe*," he said with as formal a bow as he could manage in the saddle, "I wouldn't have pushed her so, if it wasn't urgent."

The old man blinked at the sound of Jaide's voice, with a higher pitch than what was typical for a man. Jaide was used to it by now. "Any news?" he asked as the man squinted at him.

"Em, nothing important, young traveler," the man said, still trying and failing to study Jaide's features. "Just the typical gossip that flies through." He waved a dismissive hand. "Not much happens out here, so people passing through think to amaze us with grand tales of adventure and danger. Whole cities falling to a single man. Beh!"

Jaide tilted his head. "Please, sir. I would ask you to share such a story with me."

He dismounted and handed the reins over. Kruwa wasn't unlike any other Samharan outpost. Small homes spaced just enough apart not to crowd each other, yet close enough for protection against the elements as well as any predators that might wander in. The circular mudbrick homes with their thatched roofs sat in socialized clusters, their inhabitants busy cooking, building, crafting, and cleaning.

As with most outposts in Samhar, there were no enclosing gates or walls, so the surrounding landscape could be seen from any direction.

The old man led Jaide along the outskirts of the home cluster toward the area sectioned for animals—the only place with a fence. Two women strode past them, each leading a dolm by a rope with one hand and the other holding a woven basket upright atop their heads. The short, thick-legged animals scraped the ground as they walked, their giant paws like flippers ending with black claws. Though they managed all right above ground, dolms were better suited to digging and tunneling.

As with the old man whom Jaide followed, the women conversed in southern *Soloush*, which sounded like a sharper and more clipped version of the language to his northern Viriksani ears. The women smiled at them while not missing a beat in their conversation.

Jaide and the old man bowed their heads. Jaide heard a snatch of the conversation. A town north of Burkiba and an outpost south of the city had been destroyed by a single man that could wield the power of an *orashaklmah* sandstorm. Jaide let out a sharp breath.

The old man glanced at him. "The gossip of people with not enough to keep them busy. Don't believe it."

"You think it lies, *dyenbe*?" Jaide asked, only half listening.

"As I said," the old man replied. "Gossip. And you can stop it with the formal talk. I appreciate the respect, but every youngster calling me *dyenbe* all day sounds like I'm being ushered respectfully to the grave, hmm. You can call me by my name, which is Kjale." He glanced at Jaide. "Your accent places you to the north if my ears hear true. Lirshan? Trystia?"

"Close," Jaide said. "Viriksan."

"Huh," the old man said. "Never met anyone from there. All the men as woman-pretty as you?"

"You were going to share news with me, *dyen* … Kjale?" Jaide asked.

The old man snarled. "A waste of time, but if you must hear it."

They reached the enclosure and he opened the gate and released the camel. The animal meandered its way across the open area to a patch of vegetation and started to nibble.

"If you heard the women we passed," Kjale said, "you have the majority of it. Likely some rogue or lone raider quick with the blade has murdered a good handful of people and stolen things. Probably struck at night and has avoided capture. All this talk of wielding enough power to rival Shakimah Herself and bringing it down on these cities is ridiculous."

Jaide fought to keep the dread from playing on his face. "So, you don't think this man dances?"

"Beh." Kjale spat on the ground and kicked dirt over it. "If a man was so foolish as to dance so much of the stream, he would use up his life. He would use up two lives! And a darkdancer?" He rolled his eyes. "Not one has lived since long before you or I were born, boy. And I'm your age twice over."

Jaide's typical light mood felt far away. Residents of larger cities and villages were more likely to believe the danger than an outpost of little more than thirty to fifty people out in the middle of nowhere. He remembered his audience with the overtly skeptical Sheikh Ahreid, then thought perhaps not. Jaide wondered if the sheikh had heeded his warning and done at least something to prepare. Or was his great city of tall buildings, libraries, and public speaking squares, rock gardens, and craftsmen and women known throughout Samhar for their ornately designed pottery, little more than a smoldering memory.

Kjale eyed him. "You believe every bit of it don't you? That's why you came in riding that camel near to death."

"Yes, *dyenbe*," Jaide admitted. "I've already warned the sheikh of Shanhazai. I can only hope he's martialed his forces and that they're enough. If they fall, and there are any dancers among the population …" he let the rest hang in the air.

Kjale's expression changed from dismissive to grim. "You want to provision and be gone on a fresh camel, hmm. Even with the dangers of being alone out there at night."

"I must," Jaide said.

The old man whistled through his teeth. "These old ears have heard a lot over the years. Many rumors of world-ending events, epidemics, insect invasions, sandstorms that would level every city in Samhar. People have a flair for the dramatic, young man. You're so sure of this?"

They reached a structure that consisted of little more than six mudbrick pillars and a woven cover tied on top. People under the shade of the tent conversed mostly in some form of accented *Soloush*. A trio of Dor'haigheners bartered in tradetongue over a small cache of shimmering zimastones native to their land in exchange for three camels, provisions, and a hut for the night. They smiled in satisfaction, oblivious to the lackluster deal they'd gotten.

"We're safe out here in nowhere," Kjale said in an assured tone tinged with hopefulness. "Can't imagine anyone wanting to come bother folk all the way out here."

Jaide wanted to smile and tell old Kjale that indeed, no one would put themselves out to travel so far into nowhere to bother the dusty old place. Instead, he asked a simple question. "Are there any dancers in this humble outpost?"

* * *

Not for the first, or second, or even fifteenth time, Barum frowned openmouthed at the cloudless Samhari sky with its relentless, evil sun. As much as he wanted to remove some of these blasted robes, he dare not. Early on in their travels with the caravan, Jaide Amadi had warned him against it, and Zaiyera had repeated those warnings.

He thought of the beautiful—if aloof—Zaiyera and those two shadow hunters, squashed by a huge sand dune by the shadowlancer. She'd been a formidable woman; better with the blade than any of the caravan guards. Such a sad waste. And the Yuntaiman was probably feeding the buzzards by now as well.

Barum wondered about the odd foreigner from across the Great Sea. He'd insisted on waiting to ensure Zaiyera and the shadow hunters were dead for sure. "Hmph. How could they not be?" he muttered to himself. He gave his camel a little kick. The animal groaned and swung its head around to nip at his leg. Barum pulled on the reins, just barely stopping the damned temperamental beast from taking a plug out of him. It had tried to bite him twice already. Barum couldn't begin to understand how Samhari managed any kind of working relationship with the stinking, knobby-kneed animals.

Dusk had arrived when he saw the first colama tree. Barum thrust his fist in the air with a bark of triumph. His camel groaned and threw its head, nearly unseating the big Dor'haighener.

"Jakta skree!" he cursed. "Hold steady, you musty animal."

He pulled on the reins. The camel grunted. Barum grunted back at it. You never saw a rasadon lizard jumping out of its skin at every sound. Good, sturdy animals, those lizards. Not like these spitting, spindly-legged beasts.

More colama trees started to appear. Barum thought he just might survive after all. When that crazy traveler had told him which way to go, Barum had been skeptical. Neither of them was familiar with this land. But the Yuntaiman had insisted that to survive as a world traveler, one needed the skill of being good with their sense of direction. Zhuyun had told Barum every recognizable landmark he would encounter on the way back, and by *Jakta Skree's* black toenails if he hadn't been right about every single one.

He took a swig from his waterskin. The colama and other type of trees appeared in more abundance now, reaching ten to twenty feet in the air with dull green leaves and curling limbs. He heard the yipping and yowling of small animals, but never caught sight of them beyond a distant silhouette. When he caught sight of the plateaus ahead to his right, Barum smiled.

The charming little town of Burkiba came into view as soon as he passed the last of the Great Dunes. He'd actually survived the horrid desert.

Barum's smile faded when he thought about the others' sacrifice. Zaiyera and those shadow hunters were dead, no matter what the crazy Yuntaiman wanted to hope.

He had to get back home fast. The sacrifice of his companions demanded it. Barum hoped that smooth-faced Viriksani had gotten past the tainted maniac without being caught.

Burkiba was just as quiet and sleepy as he'd left it. Barum wished he could stay a day or twenty. Hot as Samhar was, it was cooler—well, less scorching—than everywhere else he'd been in the south. The people were friendly and accommodating, too. And of course, there was the beer.

He rode straight into town as far as was considered polite, then dismounted and led his camel the rest of the way in. He waved to the same boy who'd tethered his camel what seemed much longer ago than it was.

"Oy, boy!" he said in *Dreuga*. The dark-skinned lad laughed. It reminded Barum of Nyko, his own nephew, likely the same age as this boy; barely seen fourteen winters if he'd seen any.

"Oy, boy!" the lad repeated in likely the only two words he knew in Barum's home tongue.

He reached out and grabbed the young man's hand in a firm grip. "Halei, if I'm remembering?" Barum said, switching to the tradetongue.

Halei nodded. "My name is still the same, north man."

"I'm movin' fast today," Barum told the boy. "I need you to move my gear to a fresh mount and have it ready in a few hours. I'll be heading out tonight."

"Dangerous," Halei said. "You want to get eaten, north man, you go out there at night." He pointed a slender finger in the direction of the outside world. "Best you wait till morning."

"I wish I could," Barum said. "No time. You just get me a fresh one of those stinking things to ride. Preferably one with two humps."

"You in a hurry or not?" Halei asked, laughing. "Two humps is luxury. One hump is speed."

"Guh," Barum grumbled. "Fine. Speed."

He made straight for the Trade House, as they called it here. It was the same mudbrick, thatch-roofed structure as every other, only larger than most, and with a fenced area attached to hold animals.

The place buzzed with buyers, sellers, and traders. A man offered several goats in exchange for some weird-looking hairy animal with thick legs and flippers. Others traded silks, cloth, footwear, even food stuffs.

To Barum's surprise, a Dor'haighener milled among the hagglers. She stood head and shoulders above just about everyone, with fiery red curls bouncing beside her pale, freckled face. A Dor'abereenian.

She lifted a sack the size of both Barum's hands, and carefully emptied it onto the counter. Large green zimastones sparkled in front of the Burkibi trader. Nearby eyes lit with appreciation, as the beautiful stones could only be found in Dor'haighen, and even then were plentiful in only a few places even then.

The trader had kept a neutral face through the haggling, but once the redheaded woman dumped those stones on the counter, his brown eyes grew so wide, they reflected the stones.

Barum chuckled to himself. The two finished their transaction and the towering redhead turned away from the counter, and immediately spotted Barum.

"Ay then!" she called, in her shrill, accented *Dreuga*. "Be sure that yer the first Dor'haighener my eyes've seen since I got here yesterday." She came toward Barum with a long stride and grabbed him in a crushing hug.

"Oomph," Barum grunted, feeling the air squeezed from his lungs. His ribs protested that they'd soon crack. Despite his bones being slowly ground to salt, he rather enjoyed the tight embrace.

"Ay, but quit yer complainin'," the powerful woman said, laughing. She'd fully lifted Barum—not a small man by any account—clean off his feet by then. She sat him back down and stepped back.

Though the woman didn't tower over Barum like the locals, she still stood a head taller, and he had to look up at her. She possessed a feminine kind of power signature to most Dor'Abereenian women; tall, curving dimensions, pale skin that she undoubtedly had to cover completely in this harsh sun, and freckles that gathered together above a brilliant smile.

"You won't hear me complaining about a hug from any woman. Least of all from a tigress of Dor'Abereen."

"You've got the tongue of one 'uh' them dainty folk from the capital," the woman said. "A Nanshaighaner, fer sure." She gave him a once-over. "I suppose yer not too dainty. Got at least a little muscle on ya."

Barum let out a great belly laugh, 'accidentally' flexing his arms as he did. "The name's Barum Hurst, miss milady. And I'm not from the dainty capital of Nanshaigha, but Denberest. Tell me what brings you all this way south. You came on your own?"

"Yer well met, Barum Hurst from Dainty Land Denberest. My name's Sherin Macostia. I came alone only if it means not countin' the guides that got me here." She secured her keffiyeh back on her head and around her face—only her green eye showing through a tiny slit— and grabbed him by the elbow.

Barum 'allowed' himself to be led away from the Trade House and to the local social house.

Men and women leaned against the walls or stood all about the floor, conversing over mugs of drink or in between crunching into crisp fruit or handfuls of colama nuts.

They made straight for the counter where Sherin finally released

Barum. He thought he could still feel the woman's fingers clenched into his arm from that iron grip.

The lady behind the little counter took one look at them and went to one of several large round lids in the floor. She grabbed the rope and with an effort, pulled the heavy lid up until it stood open on the hinges. She dipped a metal ladle into the buried cask and poured two clay-fired mugs full of pale reddish liquid. The unmistakable color of euphorbia beer.

She replaced the heavy lid with a thud and returned with the two mugs and a smirk. "Never have to guess what north people want to drink," she said in accented tradetongue. She sat the mugs on the counter as Barum fished out several coins from his pouch.

The two Dor'haigheners clinked their mugs together and downed them in one draw. They sat their empty mugs down and stared at one another.

"You gonna tell me," Barum said, "that you came down all this way, risking being burnt to a crisp, to sell a couple zimastones?"

"You ever buy euphoria beer back home, Nanshaighaner?" Sherin replied.

Barum chuckled at her use of the beer's nickname, which did provide happiness aplenty back home. "Can't deny I have, miss milady."

Sherin responded with a good-natured backhand to his chest. "That big pouch 'uh' stones just bought a couple months' supply of the stuff. I sell back home and the drink finds its way all over Dor'haighen." She gave him a once-over. "You can find a way to thank me later."

Barum could think of a few ways he'd like to do that. "Surely you're not telling me you supply all of the north with this wonderful drink."

"It wouldn't be true," Sherin replied, "but you're free to think it. Puff up my ego a little bit, maybe. You know my business here, Barum Hurst. What's yours?" Her red eyebrows rose when his features tightened. "Looks like nothin' good, I'm guessin'."

"Sadly not," Barum said. "Lost some friends on the road south and had to turn back home."

"Sadly indeed," Sherin said. "The heat get 'em?" When Barum shook his head, she frowned. "How far south?"

"Close to that city with the long name hard to pronounce."

She gave him another backhand to the chest. "All the names in the south are hard to pronounce."

Barum conceded the point with a nod. "Shen … Shan …"

"Shanhazai?" Sherin offered.

Barum waved at the bartender, who waved back in acknowledgement while working on another drink. "That's the one."

Sherin's freckled face darkened. "Aye. He's moving fast."

"So, you've heard the news?"

Her curly red locks bounced as she nodded. "Seen it myself, I have. Well, the aftermath. More terrible than anything I've put my eyes on, Barum Hurst. Terrible enough to make me of a mind that nobody has business lancing the stream. She gazed out one of the windows. "*Jakta skree*, but I've never seen anything like it."

The bartender arrived with the mugs, but this time Sherin insisted on paying.

The cheerful mood of the tavern felt like a shocking contrast against the news. Word seemed to be traveling swiftly of the calamities caused by the shadowlancer. Barum had heard plenty of it himself. The little city of Burkiba had been subdued when he'd passed through here with Zaiyera and the others, but for whatever reason the shadowlancer had passed this place by.

He looked at the laughing, smiling patrons, some bareheaded, some donning elaborately woven keffiyehs matching their robes. Maybe they celebrated their luck, or maybe they took time to be happy while they could.

"What're you thinkin' about, Denberesterner?" Sherin asked.

Her voice snapped Barum back into the moment. "Eh. Nothin' worth conversing about. And another sad thing. I don't have much more time to converse about anything, Miss milady Sherin Macostia. I have to get word about all this to the capital." He glanced about and lowered his voice. "He took down five shadow hunters. Nearly killed me, too."

Silence stretched between them for several moments. She nodded as though coming to a decision. "Can you remember something and forget that you heard it, Barum Hurst?"

He downed the rest of his second beer and nodded. "I can do that."

Sherin looked at the floor, then out the window, and finally back at Barum. She held his gaze with those fiery green eyes. "Take it for what you will. But Eredin unleashed this plague on these poor folk." She discretely swept a hand to encompass the room. "That plague is gonna come back to his house many times stronger."

Sherin Macostia finished her euphorbia beer and set it on the counter. "You take your news back to your king nice and fast. But don't be surprised if you find stuff you don't like when you get back home."

"He's your king, too," Barum replied.

"Aye," Sherin agreed. "Just as a child's parents might abuse her, they're still her parents, worthy of the title or not."

Barum didn't like the suddenly sober direction this conversation was taking. "You really think he's going to return to Dor'haighen."

"What I hear," Sherin replied, "from the survivors of several destroyed towns and cities the monster has passed through, is that he rants about the royalty of the south, and *our* king as well. He hates them all but hates Eredin more. Has the sound of something personal, if you ask me."

The Dor'abereenian woman gave Barum's shoulder a squeeze. "You ever find yerself in the east, you stop yerself in my hometown. My name is known because of my trade. We'll have a"—she gave him another once-over—"happier time."

They stood and Barum gave a shallow bow. "Then I'll finish my business quick and get myself east."

She took his head in her hands and kissed him. Even that was powerful. Sherin Macostia broke away and gave Barum a playful shove. "Go do what you have to do, dainty man." She spun on her heel and strode into the milling patrons.

Barum stepped outside and made for the Trade House. Sherin Macostia had so distracted him that he'd forgotten his business. He had nothing to trade, but he did have coin. He paid for the service of a guide, provisions, and the remaining balance on the credit he'd received for his camel.

The sun had already set when Barum Hurst and his hired guide rode out of Burkiba. Sherin Macostia's words haunted him all the way out of town and into the night. What could King Eredin have done to cause a man to take such a dark turn? The feeling deep in his gut told him he wouldn't like the answer he found.

9

Malhadiev rode right into the little village. Nearby, cackling guinea hens scattered at his approach. Crows, lizards, any form of life capable of movement gave way before him. Even the plants and trees seemed to lean away.

Good. One should know their place when in the presence of absolute power, absolute change.

His light brown robes rustled about him as he swung down from the camel. The camel shuffled nervously beside him. It wanted nothing more than to bolt, if only he would release its reins. He could feel the terror in the animal; see it in the beast's large dark eyes.

He turned away ·from the cowardly animal toward the village. Buntara Village, he thought it was called, south of Shanhazai, between Kushtanja and on the way to Zalrabi.

Mudbrick homes with roofs made from mud and animal dung stood quietly in welcome. Trade tents with tops made of animal hide sagged in the middle as though unkempt. Rodents scurried from bushes into rock clusters and burrows.

Malhadiev smirked. His eyes darted left to right as he looked the place over. "I'm to believe the once inhabited village of Buntara is now abandoned?" He strode casually along the main artery, occasionally

101

taking a side path around the back of a house. He led his nervous camel toward the back of the village and the iron smelting pit.

He squatted in front of the pit and held his hand in front of it. No warmth. He grinned again, half turning his head to cut his gaze back toward the main village.

Malhadiev stood and made as if to continue on his way, then turned back. He strode right into the center of the village, near a trade tent. "A fine, crisp morning and I find myself in a village with no welcome. I know you're here. All of you. I can smell you. I feel your fear. I can taste it floating in the air."

He remained still, his eyes scanning the area. They were watching him. Waiting to see what he'd do. "No matter what you've been told, I do not go from city to city, village to outpost, leaving waste and ruin in my wake. Great injustices have been and are being committed against us, the people of Samhar. Our so-called nobles, the ones who have appointed themselves and their descendants, the rulers of this land have betrayed us, and have been betraying us since long before I or any of you were born."

Silence.

"I've no quarrel with anyone here. I simply wish to have a meal and replenish my supplies. Perhaps rest and rejuvenate, that I may continue to take my fight to the corrupt powers of Samhar."

He felt the twist in his stomach. Then came the coldness that crept into his bones while his skin felt like it was on fire. The sensation swirled inside him, reversing so that he was cold on the outside and burning inside. He felt hungry, yet he had no desire for the meal he spoke of.

There were dancers nearby. Every civilization, no matter how small, had at least one. The stream permeated everything and everyone. It was everywhere, including the air they breathed. How could at least one person not touch it?

He would find those who danced the stream. They might resist, but that was okay. The lion must eat and the deer must feed the lion. But the lion couldn't expect the deer to come to it and offer its neck.

Malhadiev swallowed the burning bile in his throat and touched the stream. He felt the sensation of it creep into him, like dipping a finger into a river. He drew his finger out of the river, but instead of droplets of water falling free, a black wave trailed.

He rotated his arm, swishing his finger into the stream, splashing the flow from it, taking it in. He exalted in the sudden rush of lightness in his body. He felt light enough that he might take flight, yet strong enough that he could lift the entire world in his hands. Lift it in his hands and drop it upon every ruler in Samhar.

He drew in more and more of the stream, allowed the flow to enter him, build inside him. Pure bliss replaced burning icy torment. He drew in more, filling himself with a torrent of power until he felt the strain. The ground shook as he guided the flow and sent it into the ground. The tremors grew violent. The towering poles of the trade tent swayed until the ground cracked beneath them and they fell over.

Tiny wrinkles appeared on Malhadiev's hands, and he knew they creased his face as well. He practically felt his black hair turning gray beneath his keffiyeh.

A nearby house collapsed into a cloud of dust and a pile of rubble.

There. Finally.

He felt someone touch the stream nearby, like an interruption in the flow of the river when another placed their hand inside it. He felt the dancer moving, drawing in a pittance of the stream, moving it around themselves offensively. What did they think to do with that? It was like throwing a pebble at an elephant.

Malhadiev turned in the direction he felt the power building, and saw a single man moving toward him, his arms moving in great flourishing gestures, his steps swooping, his body turning. It was a beautiful dance, one that Malhadiev himself had once enjoyed. But it was a waste of energy and movement. He was so far beyond the need to dance the stream that this man seemed a child to him.

His pure golden resin trailing his movements, the streamdancer slapped his hands together, rotated them, and opened them wide. A transparent whip extended between the space in his hands. The dancer kept moving as he flicked the whip at Malhadiev.

Malhadiev swatted the whip aside as if waving a fly away from his face. He grinned in satisfaction at the astonishment on the stream-dancer's face. "You'll have to dance a little deeper into the stream if you wish to best me."

He felt a second dancer pierce the flow. To the side, behind one of the houses.

The second streamdancer glided over the top of a hut and slapped her hands together. A wave of fire roared at Malhadiev. He looked up into the flames, through them, at the wavering form of the woman whose short soft hair, like the wool of a sheep, began to sprinkle with gray.

Malhadiev swept his hand into the flames and drew them away with his right hand. As he turned his body, he swept his left hand toward the still airborne dancer. He grabbed the flow supporting her and yanked it away.

Her shout of surprise choked off in her sudden plummet of more than twenty feet to the ground. The sound of bone snapping preceded her screams of pain when she hit.

Malhadiev continued his turn. He swept the fire in an arc and flung it at the first streamdancer, a whip of fire instead of air.

The dancer had been in the midst of forming another attack. A transparent blue disk formed in front of him. The whip of fire shattered it as though it were a pile of leaves, and swept over the surprised man. He hollered in agony as the flaming whip burned his skin.

Malhadiev swept one hand around and slapped it against the whip of fire. The sudden influx of air into the fire turned the whip into a wave that washed over the unfortunate streamdancer. His howls turned to screams as the flames fully engulfed him.

The shadowlancer pulled his two hands apart while swiping his left hand in a circle. With a gesture like slapping his hand at the air, he hit the flames with a gust, then drew all of it away. With no oxygen to feed it, the flames burning the agonized man winked out.

The poor man stood trembling for only a heartbeat before he fell over. Before his body hit the ground, however, the shadowlancer continued the sweep of his hands. He wrapped the flow around himself, turning it, reforming it. He lashed it out in the form of another transparent whip. It wrapped around the horribly burned man and Malhadiev yanked his arm back. The transparent whip pulled the man off his feet and sent him speeding toward the shadowlancer. Malhadiev used his other hand to guide the remaining flow and wrapped it around the streamdancer. He swung his prey around himself several times, then stopped him in the air right before his eyes.

The shadowlancer barely had to move his hands while he continually moved the flow, holding the streamdancer aloft. He reached up with his free hand and touched the man's chest. The robes had either been burned to nothing or melted into the horribly charred skin, which peeled and flaked away under the constant gusting wind of the flow Malhadiev maintained.

He felt the streamdancer's chest, the charred skin, the heartbeat. "Ah. There." The lifestream. It flowed weakly through the man, indicating his life was nearly over, but it was still there.

Malhadiev closed his eyes and felt the power in the dying streamdancer's body. He touched that lifestream, letting it run along finger, two fingers, a third. The man made a choking sound and squirmed.

Eyes still closed, Malhadiev nodded. "Your body hurts and your life is at its end. I will release you. Know that you will aid me in destroying the very structure which presses its foot down on our necks, gambles with our lives and livelihoods.

He pulled at the man's lifestream, guiding it away from his dying body. Pure golden light seeped out of the man's eyes, mouth, ears, and every pore on his body.

"Ghrgh. GAGH!" The streamdancer's back arched as the last of his lifestream fled his body. The tiny bit of flesh not charred from the flames faded until all that was left was lifeless, ashen brown skin. The man hung limp in the air, and Malhadiev gently lowered him to the ground.

The golden cloud swirled around the shadowlancer. He inhaled deeply, and the cloud funneled into his body. His hair, having grayed from plunging so deeply into the stream, regained its black shimmer. The faded light in his eyes brightened again. The wrinkles in his skin smoothed and tightened.

He stood for a time, holding his breath. Holding in the bliss. Then he exhaled a lightless black puff and smiled.

Malhadiev left the empty husk that was the male streamdancer and walked to the broken woman. Despite her obvious anguish, she tried to drag herself away from him with her arms.

He crouched over her and shook his head with regret. "The pain must be unbearable." He looked at her ruined legs. "I will relieve …"

She spat in his face. "Soul thief. Addict. Soulless dung. Shakimah curse you." She gritted her teeth as she adjusted herself to sit upright. "What you steal from me, Goddess Shakimah will have back from you, and you will be nothing. A nightmare dead at dawn."

Malhadiev wiped his face and glared down at her. "Seems to me our goddess doesn't care much about what happens to Her children. Look what has happened." He spread his hands out. "Look what men do. If our goddess truly cared about us, why would She leave us to this fate?"

"You are truly lost, soulless," the woman said. She adjusted again, and nearly cried out at the pain. "Shakimah gave us choice without interference. It is the grand gift. To make of our lives what we will without Her will imposed."

"To what point?" Malhadiev asked. "What good is it to leave men to their lives if they create nothing but ruin?"

The woman stared at him with incredulity. "A question to ask yourself. Or to ask the goddess at your end, before she takes back what you've stolen, and there is nothing left of you but an empty husk of evil that She blasts to nothing with but a breath."

Malhadiev listened to it all, his face tightening with each word. But he owed her that much. She was about to contribute to his cause, willingly or not. The least he could do was hear her final words. Could he blame her? What words might he speak if another was to bring about his demise?

The woman finally stopped talking. "Ugh," she groaned, her voice little more than a squeak of repressed agony.

Malhadiev appreciated the effort. Even at the end, she showed strength. He placed his hand over her and she didn't try to stop him. "My cause becomes yours. Your lifestream strengthens mine."

She stared into his dark eyes. Her words would haunt him for many a day after. "May you ever feel Shakimah's gaze upon you."

* * *

Beside him, Jaide's camel snorted in fear. He placed a hand on its side and willed the animal to remain quiet. He was taking a risk that bordered on stupid, but he had to see for himself what they were up against.

The brown-robed kivuli dayasa had beaten the two streamdancers so easily. Jaide now understood how he'd managed to reap such destruction.

The Viriksani warrior's hand tightened on the hilt of his shamshir, but what could he do? This man had just dispatched two streamdancers with little more than a thought.

Jaide released the hilt. He had no illusions that his weapon, formidable though it was, had the same capabilities as Zaiyera's magnificent scimitar. He'd known that blade was dancecraft the first time the Kushtanji woman had used it to cut apart a dancer's flow.

He remained crouched behind the wall of the farthest-most house, watching helplessly as the monster syphoned the lifestream from the injured woman. He finished, rose, and walked away, leaving the streamdancer's graying body as empty as a hollowed-out tree.

The man retrieved the reins of his nervous camel. It seemed the poor animal was too afraid of the man to flee.

Jaide decided to wait until kivuli dayasa had left the village. Perhaps he could talk to the locals after they came out of hiding. Find out if there was any news—"

The man swept his hand in an upward arc—his black lance resin trailing the movement—and set fire to a small building to his right. He swept his hand upward again, lifted an entire house, and dropped it on another. He produced a tremor that leveled an entire section of houses and buildings. As the flames spread, the screams started.

Jaide realized he was gripping the hilt of his shamshir again. Maybe if he crept up quickly and quietly. He might be able to run the forsaken man in the back before he knew Jaide was there. No. He needed to help any survivors he could find.

He ran around the house and skidded to a stop in front of a giant ripple of earth and fire rolling through the village. Jaide's mouth fell open. It looked like a wave at the beach of the Great Sea, only made of earth and fire.

Jaide turned and ran to his camel. *After* his camel. The already fleeing animal was surely smarter than he. Jaide clenched his teeth and sprinted for his life. The disoriented camel hadn't broken into a run yet. It groaned and loped, head swinging left to right.

He finally caught up to the animal and grabbed the reins. The camel danced around, groaning in protest, but Jaide finally climbed into the saddle, turned north, and gave the mount its head.

Jaide spared one last look over his shoulder. Houses, tents, buildings. Everything in the path of that ripple of fire and sand rose, then went down in a crash of flames, splintering and burning wood and thatch. Jaide heard those screams in his head well into the night and the next day.

10

Not you four, or four hundred can kill him.

Sheikh Ahreid's words echoed in Zaiyera's mind long after they'd left the grievously wounded noble behind. They'd reached Shanhazai after kivuli dayasa had battered the city and moved on.

Broken stone buildings, blasted mudbrick homes, beautiful smooth reddish-brown structures made of sand, mud, and clay, exploded like a child's sandcastle. And the dead and wounded.

Zaiyera shook her head as if trying to rid her mind of the images. So many dead, broken, bleeding. So much blood in the sand.

All inflicted by a single man. And the dancers; syphoned dry and discarded like a drained waterskin or mug of euphorbia beer.

Zhuyun moved his camel closer to hers. Zaiyera's three foreign companions had given her space after they'd departed Shanhazai. For the past few hours the Yuntaiman had engaged the other two often enough, but Zaiyera saw the way the man kept an eye on her. Despite her dour mood, he reminded her of a fatherly rooster, if such a thing could exist. The thought made her smile inwardly.

"Senior," Malker addressed his superior.

"At ease, Malker," Dyren replied.

Malker nodded. "Dyren. If I may speak freely, we're riding to our

109

deaths. The man has practically leveled every city he's passed through, and there's no telling how many lancers he's drained since then. He may well be invincible by now."

"No one is invincible," Dyren said. "There is always a weakness, a flaw, or fault in the armor. We must find his."

The foreigners sighed in relief when the shadow of a cluster of clouds passed between them and the scorching sun. Although they passed the odd community of euphorbia plants—short, green, and hardy—out in the endless desert, little else in the form of vegetation dotted the landscape. But there were lizards, patches of sand that swirled in the occasional breeze, and of course, the Great Sand Dunes.

"Agreed," Malker said. "We must find his weakness before he utterly crushes us."

Zaiyera wondered if Malker heard the irony in that last statement.

Dyren looked at her, then at Zhuyun. "I confess, you two are somewhat of an anomaly to me."

Zaiyera spared him a quick glance, while Zhuyun leaned forward to look around her at the senior shydon hunter. "How so?" the Yuntaiman asked.

"You used the *flow* technique against the shadowlancer, yet you emit no lance resin. You," he looked at Zaiyera, "somehow, are able to sheer through the power, yet you also emit no lance resin. As a shadow hunter, we study every form of lance technique, *offensive, defensive,* and *flow*. All require touching the stream in some way, which requires one to be a lancer. A lancer leaves a lance resin when they touch the stream and manipulate the flow they draw from it. In my thirty years as a sword-lancer and twenty-seven years as a shadow hunter, never have I encountered or heard of anyone possessing the ability to hide their resin."

"Ah!" Zhuyun smirked. "Is that all? I can help with that. We in Yuntai often live quite long lives. Such cannot be the case if one were to go around touching the stream, ixu?"

"Are there no lancers in your homeland?" Malker asked.

"Oh, there are," Zhuyun answered. "But we do things differently. As for what you saw me do against our adversary back there"—he jabbed a thumb over his shoulder—"that was a similar technique to what you call *flow*.

"I gathered the force he sent at me into a single focal point, that being my trusty staff, here." He patted the long flexible weapon strapped to his camel.

"I don't see how that's possible," Malker said. "The amount of power he threw at us should shatter that thing to splinters."

Zaiyera silently agreed with the shydon's assessment. Unless it was a dancecraft artifact, like Shatr. She kept that to herself. She didn't know about the people of Yuntai, but the north tended to frown upon any item enhanced by the stream.

"It's a difficult thing to explain, ixu?" Zhuyun continued. "What I describe to you is accomplished through a lifetime of study and practice. Much like your study of the stream. And if you think what I've done was even a little remarkable, you should see what the masters can do!" He thrust a finger in the air this time. "They don't need staffs like mine, or anything else as a focal point. Had we one of the masters accompanying us on this little venture, it would already have reached its conclusion."

Dyren Faust rubbed his chin. "A technique similar to *flow* lancing, but without actually lancing. That sounds useful."

Zhuyun bowed his head. "Perhaps if you find yourself with an extra ten or twenty years free, you might study the technique in Yuntai, ah?"

The senior shydon's face soured at that.

"What of you, Zaiyera Tuneesh?" Malker asked. "Unless you've studied these skills in the land of Yuntai, how is it you're able to cut through the flow as you do? Is there a similar thing here in Samhar?"

That was the last question Zaiyera wanted, yet one she knew was coming. "I'm aware of no such skill in Samhar that Zhuyun has described," she answered.

When the silence stretched, Malker leaned forward to look at her around Dyren—who also looked expectantly at her.

Zaiyera glanced at them several times, then finally sighed. "Forgive me for not being more forthcoming. I am Kushtanji. We tend to be a contemplative folk."

"Sounds … quiet," Malker remarked.

"You aren't wrong," Zaiyera said. "We are a nomadic people. Our travels take us mostly east to west, just south of central Samhar. When last I saw my Kha, we were moving southwest from Xair. I left not long after our departure. They would have reached Zalrabi, where they would trade with locals who lived on the outskirts."

"What did you trade?" Zhuyun asked.

Zaiyera turned her head toward him just briefly enough to offer an appreciative smile. "The keffiyeh and robes all of you wear are not uncommon in Samhar, obviously. But every society has its own style and signature." She indicated her own headwear and robes. "The purple colors mixed with red are the colors of the Kushtanji nomads." She pointed to the four-point dots on her cheeks and forehead.

"North, south, east, west," she indicated the dot in the middle of each four-point mark, "and center. We are a people of and from everywhere and nowhere. We start here, move someplace else, then another. Our home is the land beneath our feet, and the endless sky above, where our spirits ascend while we sleep."

Malker frowned in puzzlement at that. "Why would your spirit leave your body to travel to the dark sky at night?"

"Not always at night, Malker Argen," Zaiyera replied. "But we ascend to be with The Dancers. Sun Dancer and Moon Dancer, daughters of Goddess of Creation, Shakimah.

"When we dance with Sun Dancer, her joy and playful nature reminds us to be young and happy, no matter how many years we've seen in this life. When we dance with Moon Dancer, we know things quiet and mysterious. When Moon Dancer holds sway at night, it is a time of love and contemplation. It can also be a time of playfulness. Moon Dancer is said to be shy, and soars through the dark night sky above. We chase her among the stars."

"That's quite interesting, Zaiyera," Dyren said. "I've only traveled to Samhar once before, and it was a brief visit across the border. It seems a shame that our two peoples live so close yet can know so little about each other."

"It's understandable," Zaiyera replied. "Your land is deathly cold to us, while Sun Dancer seems cruelly hot to you."

"Our summers are warm," Malker offered.

"To *you*," Zaiyera replied.

Malker chuckled. "I suppose that's fair."

Dyren had been quiet through it all, devouring every word. Finally, he spoke. "You sound like a fascinating people, Zaiyera of Kushtanja. I would wager that the story behind that magnificent scimitar is equally fascinating."

Exasperation flashed across Zaiyera's face, but she quelled it quickly. Still, the shydon hunter saw it.

"My apologies if it seems I press you, but you've seen what we're up against. Any advantage is a better chance at survival."

"If there was anything about my blade that could be replicated to aid you," Zaiyera said, "be assured I would share it. But however much I might wish, that is not the case. I've never seen its like. Perhaps there are others with the same qualities as Shatr, but I've not encountered one."

That last bit wasn't exactly a lie. If there was another way to help them, she would do so. But the creation of the blue-steel scimitar was something unique unto herself, like every other lancecraft artifact to its possessor.

"Shatr," Dyren repeated thoughtfully. "I don't know this word, but it sounds powerful. What does it mean?"

"Shatr," Zaiyera answered, "means 'sunder' in *Soloush*, my mother tongue."

"Sunder." Dyren nodded in appreciation. "From what I've seen of the remarkable blade, it is aptly named."

"It has served me well, for sure, Dyren Faust," Zaiyera said. "I hope you won't be offended, but I wish to move our conversation in a different direction. I understand your curiosity, however, we are still new to each other."

Dyren held up a hand. "Of course. Excuse our insistence. We

shadow hunters can be rather forward, which makes others … uncomfortable. We are an organization dedicated to the defense of the world against those who would spread death, misery, and ruin upon it."

"I understand," Zaiyera replied. She started to say that perhaps another time they could talk about it but stifled the reflex. She didn't want to talk further about it. Ever. Especially with these two.

"I wonder how our other friends are faring," Zhuyun said. "I sent our muscular Dor'haighener back to Burkiba with the best directions I could remember from our journey. He should hopefully have arrived by now, or nearly so. Jaide," he nodded his chin ahead, "hopefully reached civilization farther south by now. Perhaps he's headed back our way?"

"If he's not dead," Malker added. "Wasn't he supposed to warn Sheikh Ahreid about the threat? You saw what we arrived to. Most of the man's forces were decimated. And the lancers," he shook his head. "Ten drained lancers before I stopped counting."

Zaiyera thought about the time she'd spent in Jaide Amadi's company. They'd done a few caravan jobs together here and there. The man was swift on a camel when he needed to be, and he also had incredible stamina. Zaiyera could easily see him traversing great distances, stopping only long enough to acquire a fresh camel before heading straight out again. She'd even heard him brag about how Viriksani were trained at an early age to ride in a semi-lucid state, just aware enough of their surroundings that they could nap, but snap awake in an instant. Whether that was little more than exaggeration or the truth was another matter.

Thinking of the jovial warrior brought a mental smile to Zaiyera. They weren't exactly close, but there was a camaraderie between her and the Viriksani that she couldn't put words to. Like they understood each other in a way that Zaiyera couldn't place, but Jaide fully understood. A secret that only one of them was in on.

"Ah. I put my gambling hand on him being alive," she heard Zhuyun say.

"Is that so?" Malker asked.

Zhuyun pointed ahead. "I don't expect you to see as far as my sharp Yintish eyes, but you will see."

The others strained to see what Zhuyun saw. After a few moments, a solitary figure appeared on the horizon. Someone on camelback, their image swaying in the heatwaves rising from the ground. The figure rode across the imaginary oasis that teased the parched and heat-exhausted no matter which direction they turned.

"*Jakta skree*," Malker whispered, then bowed his head in apology when Dyren arched an eyebrow at him.

Zaiyera still hadn't gotten used to the dynamic between them. Dyren was clearly the older and more experienced of the two, yet Malker looked his senior by possibly two decades, due to his aggressive dancing of the stream.

Zhuyun stretched his hand into the air with a big wave, and the figure—now distinguishable as Jaide Amadi—waved back.

11

"I don't envy the decision you must make," Jaide said to the shydon hunters.

"I've made few decisions that are enviable," Dyren Faust replied. "Nevertheless, I would have whatever news you offer, that I can make it."

Jaide took a deep breath and seemed to blow out most of his good spirits when he exhaled.

As if to punctuate the incoming dark news, a few clouds drifted lazily across the sky, casting shadow over the group.

"I'm good at avoiding being seen when I've a mind for it," Jaide said. "But I had no small bit of luck getting around that monster. And a monster he is." Jaide's sea colored gaze swept over all of them. "There is a darkness you can't see that swirls around him. I could feel it even as far away from him as I was."

"So, you did see him," Dyren said.

The Viriksani nodded. "Oh, yes, I saw him. I watched helplessly as he leveled Buntara village."

"He did what?" Zaiyera breathed. "Leveled? All of it?"

Again, Jaide nodded. "He killed and syphoned two streamdancers as though they were little more threat than children. Then he set about destroying the place as he walked through." Jaide ran a hand over his smooth face. "He razed the village to the ground with a huge ripple of land and fire. Buntara collapsed and burned. People, homes, everything."

Zaiyera dismounted and walked off a short distance. She bent over, one hand on her knee, the other over her heart. Buntara was filled with kind and hospitable people. Her oldest memory of the village was when her people had been driven northwest by the largest sandstorm central Samhar had seen in over a decade. Buntara had welcomed them with food, shelter, and kindness.

A spear of guilt punched into her chest. She should have ridden faster. She should have ridden as hard as Jaide, caught up to the forsaken bastard, and driven Shatr through his heart.

Zaiyera sank to her knees, bowed her head, and closed her eyes. There, she remained in prayer to Sun Dancer, that She keep warm the souls of the dead. She prayed to Moon Dancer that the pale light of Her smile would show the unfortunate souls the majesty of creation as She led them to *Sojalleh*. She prayed to Shakimah, but for what, Zaiyera didn't know. There was no need to pray for the souls of the dead to be welcomed by the goddess, for they would be. Finally, Zaiyera prayed that Shakimah grant her the wisdom and strength to endure, and to stop the monstrous kivuli dayasa.

A hand gently touched her shoulder.

Zaiyera opened her eyes to see Zhuyun looking down at her. The Yuntaiman's kind brown eyes were soft and hesitant. Forgive my rudeness, Zaiyera my friend. But we must go. As you have warned, when night approaches, things come out to eat, ixu?"

She took a deep breath and stood. "Yes."

"So we go," Zhuyun said. "But the question is, where?"

Zaiyera gazed out at the sublime dunes, hearing their deep humming song as the steadily cooling air passed over them. She looked at the scattered clumps of hardy bushes, the open swirling sands of the beautiful desert dotted with ogko trees, their green-leaved branches reaching as if to embrace the sun. She inhaled the dry smell of a world of sand, the camels nearby, man perspiration.

"I don't know," she finally answered.

They heard the last of Jaide's descriptions of the destruction of Buntara as they returned to the party. Zaiyera was glad she'd moved away. She'd heard enough horror for one day.

"Are you all right?" Malker asked.

"I'm fine," she said, surprised to see concern on the man's face. "Thank you." She glanced at Dyren to see his sympathetic nod.

"We've a boon to ask of you, my lady miss," the senior shydon said. "We ask your assistance in leading us back to Dor'haighen and accompanying us to the capital. With yours and Jaide's testimony added to ours, we may convince King Eredin to allow us to return with a full force of shadow hunters."

Travel to the heart of the shadow hunter organization, then return surrounded by them. Zaiyera swallowed. "How ... many number in a full force?" she dared ask.

Dyren's face hardened with determination. "That depends on how many are away from the capital on missions. But likely over a hundred."

Moon and stars! "It would be weeks before we return. Maybe months. By then, he may have leveled every city and village in Samhar."

"I doubt he can cover all of Samhar in a year," Dyren replied. "I don't make light of your people's plight, but we need a larger force. By your own countryman's testimony and what we've already experienced, just the five of us confronting him again would result in certain death."

"To flee now means certain death to everyone in his path," Zaiyera countered.

Dyren looked out at the endless ocean of sand and wiped sweat from his face.

Zaiyera realized that sitting out in the middle of the heat, even past midday, was likely dangerous for these foreigners. "Let us talk while we ride. There is an oasis two hours away, west of here."

"This will sound callous," Dyren said as they rode. "But the truth is, if we ride him down now, the only difference will be our deaths numbered among the civilians he slaughters after he's finished with us."

The senior shydon hunter's face screwed with distaste at the admission. "Lives will be lost. But we can save more by getting help."

"If I may speak on this?" Malker Argen asked. He'd been quiet for so long, Zaiyera had forgotten he was there.

"Every perspective is welcome," Dyren replied.

"He will soon enter what we call a cocoon period," Malker continued.

Dyren frowned in thought. "I've heard of this, but I've not researched deeply into it."

"It isn't a widely known fact," Malker said, "because it's been so long since a shadowlancer has walked the world. We've only had darklancers appear here and there. They usually struggle against what they've become until finally succumbing. Even then, they syphon victims infrequently, as the practice is disturbing, from what I've read."

"I never knew you studied this side of it so deeply," Dyren said.

Malker's jaw tightened. "A darklancer killed my younger sister, sir. She had been a developing lancer before I'd begun my training. I made it my purpose to learn everything about them. Some call it obsession. But I dug into every book in the library of Nanshaigha that I could find on the subject."

Interesting. "You were speaking about a cocoon period?" Zaiyera asked.

"Yes," Malker replied. "Despite cheating the lifeprice by syphoning other lancers, the body must adjust to the massive amounts of the lifestream that it is now a conduit to, as well as the larger reserve housed in the body. A few drained lifestreams are relatively negligible, and the body can adjust. But as many as he's syphoned ..." Malker snarled. "The bastard will have to curl up and let his body adjust, or it'll eat him away from the inside."

"Any chance he doesn't know this and will meet such a fate?" Zhuyun asked.

Malker shook his head. "The books say it's a reflexive function, much like how a caterpillar is compelled to cocoon so that it can emerge as a butterfly."

Zaiyera felt a chill at that last part.

"And as a caterpillar emerges from the cocoon to be a beautiful butterfly ..." Jaide said, the tone of his voice echoing Zaiyera's fears. "He will emerge with a body stronger and able to hold and wield more of the stream than any army of streamdancers should be capable of."

"How long is this cocoon period?" Dyren asked.

"That isn't clear," Malker answered. "The speculation ranges from several days to several weeks. Other books vary on this. All of them agree, however, that this can happen more than once. My guess is it happens after so many leaps in power."

"That gives us some time," Dyren said. "Not enough, but better than nothing."

"There is one question that hasn't been asked," Zhuyun said. "What is he after? No man seeks power just for the sake of it, ah? He intends to wield it in some way; effect some sort of change. I remember his words when we first battled him." He looked to Zaiyera and Jaide. "His thoughts are fixed on the rulers of this land."

"That's true," Jaide said. "I also heard him ranting about how the rulers of Samhar used their people as the ground upon which they walk. He went on about how they care nothing for us, and that he will use their lifestreams to add to his power and kill them all." He shook his head. "It made little sense."

"Because we only have part of the story," Zhuyun said.

"He's a madman addicted to the power he's stolen from others," Malker replied, an edge to his voice.

"I am not a man of vast wisdom," Zhuyun replied, "but in my travels I've found that things are rarely that simple."

They rode on in silence for a while, each person no doubt digesting the information Malker had shared and the perspective Zhuyun presented.

Zaiyera found herself wondering about *kivuli dayasa*. What had driven him to this? What had some ruler done to him or his family that he would become the very thing he claimed the rulers of Samhar were, and that he'd rid the land of?

If Malker spoke correctly, their best hope was for the man to enter the cocoon stage soon. Yet when he emerged from it, how much worse of a monster would he be?

12

"This land of Samhar has no small number of surprises," Malker said. He removed his brown keffiyeh and ran a hand through his short salt-and-pepper colored hair. He squinted up at the early evening sky as he moved to a nearby palm tree and sat down against its base. "I confess, I never thought to find water anywhere in this endless world of sand, much less a beautiful oasis such as this."

Zaiyera grinned at the shydon. It was the same with any foreigner on their first visit to Samhar and a subsequent stop at an oasis. "This one is small, Malker Ar … Malker," she said. "There are other oases many times the size of this one, with huge, deep waters, towering palm trees and plants that grow so tightly together at the water's edge, you could not see the ground."

Malker looked around at the oasis where they currently took their rest. The palm tree he leaned against stood over fifteen feet tall, its fan-like leaves swaying in the breeze. Several feet away, the camels drank from the blue-green pond and grazed on nearby reeds.

The little oasis was a paradise nestled in the middle of several mounds encircling it like a bowl. As with so much of Samhar, the sand was smooth, with shallow grooves slithering away as far as the eye could see. The distant roar and deep hum of the wind as it passed over the nearby dunes washed through their camp like an endless lullaby.

A trio of chukita cats trotted a few dozen feet away from Dyren, then Zhuyun. They crossed a little closer to Zaiyera and Malker, giving little yips as they passed.

"They're getting bolder," Malker remarked after the felines' fourth pass. "Keep close watch of your food."

"They ask for us to share," Zaiyera said.

"Ask?" Malker chuckled. "Share? Likely they'll raid our packs and be off with our food while we sleep."

"Life in the heart of the desert is harsh," Zaiyera said. "Yet we find common ground." She reached into her pack and produced a handful of dried meat, which she tossed to the trio. The sandy brown cats snapped up the food quickly and trotted away toward the water.

"May as well have left a bowl of milk out," Malker said. He stretched and slumped in the shade of the palm. "Better your pack than mine, I guess." He closed his eyes.

Zaiyera smiled at the trio of yipping cats, their black tipped ears swiveling backwards as they crouched at the pond to drink.

Having similarly relieved himself of his keffiyeh, Dyren Faust strode quickly from his place of shade to hers. He knelt beside her, forearm resting on his knee.

"Am I correct to assume the beauty of this oasis belies potential danger that might find us in our sleep?" he asked.

"That would be a correct assumption," Zaiyera said. "I will keep watch."

Dyren shook his head. "We need you fresh for tomorrow. I will keep first watch." He straightened, and Zaiyera stood with him.

"I know what to look for," she said. "There are things that live out here that can sneak up on you, if you don't know how to look for them."

"Actually ..." Jaide Amadi strode over from visiting with Zhuyun. The Viriksani was little more than a dark silhouette against the descending western sun. "I would be the most logical person to keep watch."

"And why is that?" Dyren asked.

Malker cracked an eye open.

"You know the reputation of us Viriksani, *niyima*?" Jaide asked Zaiyera. The man's usual lighthearted charm had returned in some measure. He grinned at Dyren Faust. "My people can travel on less sleep than any other Samharan. It's why I managed to get so far south and return to you before you found the lion and stuck your heads into its mouth."

"Anyone can live on less sleep when need be, Viriksani," Dyren said. "It's not a special trait exclusive to any one person or people."

Jaide shrugged. "Do as you will." He turned away.

Dyren watched Jaide walk away. When he reached Zhuyun, he said something in too low a voice for them to hear. After a moment, the Yuntaiman threw his head back and laughed.

Jaide secured his gear near the base of a palm, produced a piece of dried meat, and stood facing the pond as he ate.

"Anything specific I should watch for in the night?" Dyren asked. He belted his longsword and strapped on a throwing knife.

"Snakes roam the grounds around the water, as well as large lizards. They're more active at night." Zaiyera untied her bedroll. "Jaide will spot the more subtle threats, should they wander near."

Dyren looked over his shoulder at the Viriksani and frowned. "I'm aware that he's not under my command, but a team can't survive if they don't listen to each other."

"You're right," Zaiyera said. She watched Sadiq wander over. The camel gave an affectionate grunt, then shuffled his stance and lowered himself beside her. Zaiyera rubbed the camel on his side, then on his forehead. She turned on her side and pressed her back against her large friend.

"How can you stand the smell?" Malker asked. He'd opened both eyes and was looking from her to the camel.

"I've smelled man-sweat all my life," Zaiyera replied. "I'm used to it by now."

Malker's mouth worked in search of a response until he finally gave up and closed his eyes again.

Zaiyera reached back and gave Sadiq another pat on the side, then drifted asleep.

13

Dawn brought with it a pack of giant lizards called Slyvra. After a desperate battle that left the party fleeing the crocodile-sized creatures, fate hadn't finished with them just yet.

"Ora … what?" Malker yelled beside Zaiyera as they angled northwest. They crossed a landscape varying from barren, to sparsely vegetated, to inhabited by scattered dunes as far as the eye could see.

"Orashakimah," Zaiyera answered. "A sandstorm you don't want to experience, Malker Argen."

They kept the camels at a comfortable canter so as not to tire them out, but the looming threat of being caught by the distant sandstorm had her casting more than a few wary glances over her shoulder.

Jaide had insisted that the sandstorm wasn't behind them but coming in from the east. That meant they needed to move quickly in hopes of getting north of it before it hit.

Zaiyera spared a glance at the Viriksani warrior, looking over his pretty face. How long would Jaide would keep up the facade? She returned her attention ahead. It wasn't her business, but she thought she understood the reasoning.

They stopped long enough to allow the camels to rest, and for the foreigners to take the rare comfort of shade under trees when they found them.

As soon as the camels were rested, they continued on. The Great Sand Dunes heralded their passage, the deep humming of the wind sliding over their peaks sounded like the buzzing of a cloud of insects passing through a tunnel.

Their flight across central Samhar had been hot, and the non-Samharans needed extra rest and shade early on. But as they progressed further north, the blistering heat, endless swirling sand, and the great dunes gave way to more vegetation, more frequent oases—which the Dor'haigheners eyed warily—and a steadily cooling temperature.

"By the cold breath of Jokolta Himself," Malker said with a sigh of relief. He unwrapped his keffiyeh. "I'd forgotten what it was like to breathe cool air."

"Indeed," Zhuyun said, though he didn't remove his head wrap. "This time of year is summer in my homeland. While the heat here is like the inside of a kiln, in Yuntai it is like breathing water."

"I don't know which would be worse," Malker said.

"Humidity is good for the skin," Zhuyun offered.

"If you don't smother trying to breathe it," Malker countered.

Jaide sniffed the air, then moved away a bit. He looked to the east and gazed into the distance. "Zhuyun. Lend me your Yuntai eyes."

Zhuyun moved beside him and squinted in the direction Jaide pointed. "Looks like a hint of a dust cloud on the horizon," he said. "Small …" he trailed off.

"Small-looking from here," Jaide added.

"How fast do sandstorms move," Dyren asked Zaiyera.

"Very fast," she replied.

Everyone looked at each other.

They spurred the camels into a gallop. The animals' long-legged strides covered ground quickly, but the riders held them in check. If they allowed the animals to tire out too quickly, they were dead.

Half an hour into their flight, the ominous dark wall of the storm rumbled into view. The wind picked up, buffeting their hair and robes.

As the storm drew closer, Zaiyera strained to listen.

"What is it?" Dyren asked, noting her concentration.

Zaiyera continued to listen, then straightened in satisfaction. "Nothing, fortunately." At his questioning look, she elaborated. "It is a simple *orashakimah*; breath of Shakimah, or sandstorm. The storm that hit us when we met in the caravan was a screamer storm."

"I'm content to live the rest of my life and never experience another of those," Malker said.

"Then ride on, Dor'haighener," Jaide said.

Ride, they did.

The sandstorm drew nearer with every minute. Having kept the camels at a conservative canter, they now gave the animals their heads.

Everyone took regular glances to the right. The sandstorm was close enough now that they could see the wall of stirring sand and rock. In that wind, the debris would be like millions of tiny blades grinding the skin off their bones.

Zaiyera kept stock of the dunes, that were growing scarce the further north they moved. She looked back to the storm. It was too close.

"We need to stop!" she yelled over the howling wind. "Now!"

"Have you gone mad?" Malker said.

"We can't outrun it to the next town," Zaiyera replied, slowing Sadiq to a stop and dismounting. "We need to take cover."

"We'll die out here!" Malker said.

Zaiyera didn't bother to reply. She coaxed Sadiq to lay down, then shrugged off her pack. Jaide was also swinging off his mount.

Dyren pointed back toward the sand dunes they'd passed. "Can we not hide on the leeward side of those dunes?"

Zaiyera shook her head. "We'll be buried alive."

"If we stay out here, we'll be *skinned* alive!" Malker replied.

Zhuyun clamped a hand on the top of his flapping keffiyeh and looked east. The sandstorm was nearly on top of them. "I defer to those who live here, ixu?" He dismounted and led his camel near to Sadiq.

"Wet a handkerchief and hold it over your nose and mouth,"

Zaiyera instructed. She hunkered down against Sadiq's side. He curled his head around and nudged her, seeming not at all concerned.

The others gathered their camels as closely as possible. They followed Zaiyera's lead and coaxed their camels to the ground. It didn't take much effort. The animals willingly folded their legs and lay down.

Everyone huddled against their camels opposite the storm, wet their handkerchiefs, and pressed them to their faces. They pulled the extra wrappings of their keffiyehs around to cover their faces.

The breath of Shakimah fell over them.

Damp cloth tied over her nose and mouth, the last thing Zaiyera saw before she covered her face was a world of darkness and swirling, deadly air.

* * *

The party endured the sandstorm in blindness. The howling and whipping wind shouted at them in its passing.

After what felt like a lifetime, it finally ended.

Zaiyera kept her face covered and lifted her head. What must have been a pound of sand slid in rivulets down her head. She lifted the cover from her eyes to see that Shakimah's breath had passed.

The cleaned the sand from their heads and bodies as well, while the camels still lay on the ground, chewing their cuds as though nothing had happened.

Dyren dusted himself off. "Luckily we weren't buried alive."

"Ah, but that would have been the case, were it not for our smart friends, here." Zhuyun grinned and bowed to Zaiyera and Jaide. "I mean, our resilient camel friends, of course." He then bowed to his camel, who returned the gesture with indifference.

Jaide laughed.

Zhuyun opened a hand toward Zaiyera and Jaide. "Many thanks again to you both for ensuring our survival. You make a good team, ah?"

"Of course," Jaide replied.

"Perhaps," Zaiyera allowed, to which Jaide sighed.

The Yuntaiman looked from Jaide to Zaiyera and back. He looked at Jaide again, then nodded his head at Zaiyera with an exaggerated wink.

Zaiyera had begun sipping from her waterskin and nearly choked. Despite herself, she spat up water, sputtering in her attempts not to laugh.

The side of Zhuyun's mouth twitched.

"I doubt I'm … his type, Zhuyun Xaiylin," Zaiyera said.

Jaide cleared his throat. "Yes it's true. I like my … women a little more …"

"Stocky?" Zaiyera offered.

"Yes. Stocky." Jaide grinned at the Yuntaiman, who laughed and turned back to his camel. The Viriksani turned his blue-eyed gaze on Zaiyera. Those eyes asked a question he didn't want to verbalize.

Zaiyera thought about what it was like for her to operate in certain capacities with men. Her expertise, or abilities with the sword were often doubted or considered secondary to her male counterparts until she'd proven otherwise. How much easier would it have been in her line of work, had she been a man?

She looked Jaide in the eye and nodded. Jaide returned the gesture with an expression of appreciation, then went to retrieve his own camel.

Zaiyera took another swig of water, then stoppered it and stood. The sand hissed as it slid off her robes. She brushed away as much dust as she could, then stuffed her waterskin back in her backpack.

Dyren and Malker had moved to talk. The senior shydon indicated his junior's torso, and Malker gave the area of his wound a pat and nodded his head.

Zhuyun sifted through the loose sand until he grabbed hold of something buried. "Ah!" He lifted his staff. "I'd held onto it until I was forced to let go and hold the cover to my face. Good that I found it or I'd be no use to any of you, ixu?"

The others began trying—and failing—to get their camels to rise again. No matter how hard they pulled on the reins, the animals simply lay there chewing their cuds.

Zaiyera got Sadiq to stand with minimal coaxing. With a little more effort, Jaide got his mount on its feet as well. The two Samharans went to help the others who—with the exception of Zhuyun, who seemed to be negotiating with his animal—pulled at the reins and barked at the animals, who simply ignored them. With Zaiyera and Jaide's help, the foreigners eventually got their mounts to stand.

"We are ready to resume when you are, my lady Zaiyera," Dyren Faust said as he shouldered his pack. "The sooner we make the capital, the sooner we can return."

"Hopefully with an army at our back," Malker added.

A few hours into their resumed journey, the great dunes of Samhar disappeared and the ground grew harder as the sand grew more scarce. Having never traveled so far north, Zaiyera found the landscape unfamiliar, the air cool. The speed at which the camels moved made the air cooler still.

She wrapped her robes tighter about herself. Despite her love of her central desert home, she found the crisper air here refreshing.

The Dor'haigheners visibly relaxed. Even the more conservative Dyren Faust sighed with a bit of a grin.

Malker leaned his head back and closed his eyes. "It's still somewhat hot, but bearable, now."

Zhuyun also looked more at ease, though the Yuntaiman had endured the central Samharan heat more stoically than the other foreigners.

"Aaaah," Jaide said with a content smile. "This is more like the weather in Viriksan. Perhaps you will visit my homeland one day."

"A most welcomed prospect," Zhuyun said. "When this is done, should we still draw breath, I would be pleased to visit this homeland of yours."

"Looks like something up ahead," Malker said. "Village, maybe?"

"Oasis trade outpost," Zaiyera said, pointing out the tents that typically lined the borders of outposts.

"Another oasis," Malker said in a flat tone.

"An inhabited one," Jaide replied. "Whatever horrors akin to those we encountered at the last one would have been driven away, if they lived here to begin with. Any outpost on an oasis will have a big enough population to deter predators."

The party dismounted in front of the opening between a crowd of flourishing palm trees. Zhuyun's mouth fell open as he took in the lush foliage growing around the tall green palms.

They passed several traders sitting or standing in their tents, various types of wares, from jewelry to pottery and much more, lying on blankets spread on the floor.

A woman trotted up to them from one of the tents. She wore a tan ankle-length skirt stitched with tiny beads the color of the Great Sea. Her top was a shade darker and similarly ornamented. Her necklace of seashells clanked as she spread her hands and offered a shallow bow, which the other two Samharans returned. "I am Myisha, travelers. For a small cost, I can have your camels accommodated. They will not be able to navigate the terrain beyond this point."

The three non-Samharans looked questioningly to Zaiyera and Jaide.

"Ah," Myisha said, noting the expressions. "Apologies," she said, switching to tradetongue. "We don't often see visitors from the north." She repeated her offer.

"How far are we from the Great Sea of the west, *niyima*?" Zaiyera asked.

Myisha smiled while absently running her fingers along her necklace. "A week and more of swift riding, *niyima*. We are not close, yet not far from the Great Sea, and so we frequently trade with the people who live there."

Zaiyera nodded. "How far are we from the Samhar Dor'haighen border?"

"Farther still," the woman replied. "At least a week of swift riding. Possibly two."

Deflating news. The party looked at each other in disappointment, but in the end they took the woman up on her offer. True to her words, the cost to care for the animals was fair.

"I'll see you soon, my friend." Zaiyera wrapped Sadiq's curved neck in a hug. The camel grunted when she released him and offered an affectionate head-butt.

Myisha tilted her head. "Kushtanji?" When Zaiyera nodded, her smile broadened. "I couldn't quite place your accent other than being from the south of here. I've only known Kushtanji to have such affection for animals."

She called to another woman, who jogged over to take the reins of the Dyren and Malker's camels, while Myisha herself took Zhuyun's and Jaide's. Seeing that Sadiq had no reins, she looked questioningly to Zaiyera.

"May I?" Zaiyera asked, indicating the other woman's hand. Myisha offered it, which Zaiyera lifted to place in front of Sadiq's nose. The camel snuffled over the woman's hand, then grunted.

"Follow her, Sadiq," Zaiyera said. *"Oolip soo."* She pressed Myisha's had to Sadiq's nose, then slid her hand along the side of the camel's face and onto Myisha's hand.

Sadiq gave short groan, then moved to stand closer to Myisha.

"Truly amazing," the woman said. She indicated a path leading straight through the foliage. "Be welcome to our beautiful Malajanna."

They continued through a patch of palms that gave way to full green-leaved trees and bushes. The smell of greenery surrounded them, as did the chirping of insects, singing of birds, and the occasional yip of a chukita cat.

Once they finally passed through the multilayered greenery, Zaiyera shared the others' amazement.

They had apparently been at the top of a hill. Below lay a sprawling city of sandstone and mudbrick homes and buildings surrounding a huge oasis lake. Distant music drifted up the hill to welcome them, as did the laughter of children and adults alike.

"If this is what your trading outposts look like," Dyren said, "I fear your cities will render ours in Dor'haighen quite primitive."

Zaiyera responded to the man's uncharacteristic humor with a half chuckle. "This is my first venture so far north. I've only ever seen outposts built around oasis." She waved a hand over the city below. "My eyes are as new to this sight as your own."

Jaide Amadi whistled through his teeth. "I've seen many a north Samharan oasis city, but nothing to rival this."

To the left, a wide path of stone steps descended in an arch down to the city. The party followed them down, all the while marveling at the massive blue lake, the foliage around it, and the buildings nestled along the shore. Malajanna sat at the bottom of a partially enclosed bowl. A solid stone wall enclosed the city in a horseshoe shape, with the open-end facing north.

The wonders didn't stop once the party reached the bottom of the steps. Buildings were carved into the stone itself. Some had sharp sloping roofs while others had flat roofs with sloping awnings made of animal hide.

From the stone wall buildings, the city extended toward and around both sides of the lake. Women similarly dressed to Myisha strode by, their conversation light and pleasant.

Men dressed in robes of light cloth material pulled two-handled, two-wheeled carts along the hard stone street.

Many an upraised eyebrow followed Malker and Dyren down the various avenues, while Zhuyun received openly curious stares.

"Looks like you're even rarer a sight than we are, Yuntaiman," Malker said.

"I'm feeling particularly exotic, this day," Zhuyun replied. When they passed a trio of staring women, he swept into a low bow of the Yuntai style, clasping hand in fist, and bending at the waist.

The women responded with friendly grins and responding nods that carried an air of regality.

"The people here seem kind, ah?" Zhuyun said. "I wouldn't mind remaining for a time."

Jaide gave him a sidelong smirk. "I'm sure you would, Zhuyun."

"There is so much to see here. Just look!" Zhuyun pointed with an open hand at a magnificent building made of sandstone. Smooth, worked stone steps descended a few feet up to a pair of massive pillars fronting a building so large they couldn't see the other side of it. Where the steps ended, a smooth brick-worked stone floor led to a towering entryway. On either side of the entryway stood wide, shallow bowls filled with burning coals standing on three crisscrossed legs.

"Such amazing architecture and artistry," Zhuyun continued. "Never have I seen such a captivating place."

"Filled with captivating women?" Jaide added.

Zhuyun cleared his throat. "Well, that too. Perhaps we'll find a place of eating and drinking, that we might find lovely women to talk to, ixu?"

"Perhaps," Jaide replied.

Zaiyera looked away to hide her grin. When she looked back to the path ahead, she noted the Viriksani eyeing her from the periphery.

We should re-provision first, then find food and a bath," Dyren said. "I'd like to have a little time to relax before we return to hardship's embrace."

Zaiyera silently agreed. She'd almost forgotten what her skin felt like without several layers of grime coating it.

After asking directions, they found affordable accommodations along the interior of the city.

Malker and Dyren shared a room. Zhuyun offered to do the same with Jaide to save money, but the Viriksani declined with thanks.

Once their rooms were secured, everyone went their separate ways.

Jaide stopped Zaiyera halfway up the stairs. "May I have a word, *niyima*?"

Zaiyera nodded. "Of course."

They entered her room, which was modest and clean with a bed and two windows above an alley on the side of the building. Zaiyera made for the little balcony overlooking the avenues below, now lit by the golden glow of torchlight as evening arrived. She leaned on the rail and stared at the golden flames while Jaide sat his backpack down by the door.

Jaide leaned on the rail beside her, similarly admiring the beautiful gardens and snaking stone streets. "How long have you known?"

"I'd suspected for some time during our job with the caravan," Zaiyera replied. So long ago, that seemed. "But you slipped when you mentioned your Viriksani stamina when riding, and that you require less sleep."

Zaiyera looked into those wary blue eyes. Such a color was almost nonexistent in Samhar. "I know Viriksani stamina is legendary across Samhar. I also know that it's a trait exclusive to its women."

Jaide let his, or rather, *her* head hang. After a self-deprecating sigh, she reached up and unwrapped her keffiyeh. It was a distinctively feminine movement that contrasted starkly with the Jaide Zaiyera had known up to this point.

Long raven hair spilled down over Jaide's shoulders, and she let out another little sigh, this one relief. "My first slip in five years," she said.

Zaiyera's breath caught at the sound of the woman's voice.

Jaide's high-pitched laughter sounded musical. Yes, Kushtanji. This is my true voice. Being able to deepen it," she continued, her voice taking on its more masculine depth, "is a skill I learned as a child."

"Why?" Zaiyera asked.

Jaide leaned sideways on the rail. Her posture grew more feminine as she relaxed. One woman to another. "Can you not guess?"

"I suppose I can," Zaiyera replied. "I recall the day Mr. Vose hired our team."

Jaide made a disgusted sound and leaned her back against the balcony rail, propping her forearms up. "You were introduced as the team leader from the first."

"Yet he often deferred to you when he failed to catch himself," Zaiyera said. "Or to confirm my information when he thought I wasn't around."

Jaide rolled her eyes. "Grimy old man took for granted that my skill with the blade was superior to yours." She grinned. "Well, it is."

They shared a laugh at that.

"Odd," Zaiyera said. "I've met a number of Dor'haighen warriors easily as capable in combat."

"Central and northern Dor'haighen," Jaide agreed. "But not southern. Don't mistake me. Southern Dor'haighen women are hardy, but typically run more of the businesses, commerce, things like that. Few are warriors or travelers like their kin further north." She ran a hand through her hair, fidgeting with the tangles. "It's not just Dor'haighen, though."

Zaiyera found herself nodding before Jaide had finished that last statement. Even in Kushtanja, most women were homemakers, and similarly dealt with trade and commerce. There were other parts of Samhar that were the same. In those societies, she'd found herself having to work twice as hard to convince a man, and even some women, that she was capable of protecting travelers.

She thought back on Mr. Vose. The man hadn't thought her stupid or inferior, per se, but women such as Zaiyera were apparently uncommon.

"You have my appreciation for not revealing my secret to the others," Jaide said.

"It's not my secret to reveal," Zaiyera replied.

Night arrived. Birdsong gave way to the chirping of insects, the low din of passing conversation, the warm glow of torchlight up and down the streets. The smell of baking flatbread with herbs and imported garlic crept along the streets like a culinary seducer.

Zaiyera's stomach groaned at the smell.

Beside her, Jaide held a hand to her belly as well. She turned a sarcastic grin on Zaiyera, the expression much the same as the 'male' Jaide she'd traveled with all this time. But with her hair down, and her posture more feminine, it was like looking at different person.

"I'd better have that bath before my hunger takes control," the Viriksani woman said. "I'd forgotten how hungry I am."

After Jaide left, Zaiyera set about unbraiding her thick black hair, then went to her travel pack and found her only other pair of fresh robes. She packed everything in a sack and took them with her downstairs. At the direction of one of the inn's staff, she found the women's bathhouse.

She walked to the edge of the steaming pool and dipped a toe in. The water was hot, but it felt good. She untied her robes. As soon as she let them fall, a rush of chill bumps covered her unclothed body.

She stepped down into the steaming pool with a gasp, then a contented sigh as she sank into the hot water and leaned against the side.

One of the staff placed two folded towels, a bowl of nogori oil, and a bar of black soap beside her. Zaiyera smiled in thanks.

She sank further down to her chin in the soothing hot bath, then dipped underneath. Her hair spread out above her head, then hung soaked and heavy when she surfaced.

Zaiyera scooped a handful of nogori oil into her hand and ran it through her hair. The oil softened it, and she basked in the energizing tingle while massaging it into her scalp.

The soap did for her skin what the oil did for her hair. By the time she was done, Zaiyera's dark brown skin felt smooth and energized. She sat in the heavenly water for a while with her eyes closed, until she finally had to force herself out.

Dried and dressed, Zaiyera found the social house and spotted Zhuyun and the shydon hunters. They sat at a table off to the side, the former waving her over.

Jaide entered almost right behind her as she started toward the others. They went to the counter to order a couple bowls of boiling hot stew and flatbread, then navigated the mass of people toward their companions.

"Another slip," Zaiyera said to the now male Viriksani. "You take as long as a woman to bathe and freshen up."

"That bath was worth it," Jaide replied barely above a whisper."

"Ah, the stragglers arrive!" Zhuyun said. He raised his mug and patted the empty space next to him. "I was telling our stern friends here that you learn patience in Yuntai, for the women there take just as long to bathe and clothe as you, here in this grand desert world."

"Some things must be universal, eh, Yuntaiman?" Jaide said, reverting to her masculine voice.

Though she'd already heard the woman switch from one timbre to the other, Zaiyera still found the contrast jarring.

The stew was hotter than anything Zaiyera had ever eaten, but she found it delectable. She tore off a piece of flatbread, folded it, and dipped it in the stew. "Mmm." She closed her eyes and savored the bite.

They ate in silence for most of the meal, only remarking here and there about provisions and how much longer they had to travel.

"I'd hoped we were closer to the border," Dyren admitted.

"Perhaps there may be a way to speed our journey," Zhuyun said. He lifted the bowl and slurped the last of its contents.

"Speed our journey?" Malker said. "How in the name of Jokolta would we do that?" He looked to Jaide, then Zaiyera. "Are there faster animals in this land that we don't know about?"

Both Samharans shrugged.

"Could be nothing more than an exaggerated sales pitch," Zhuyun said. "But while I waited for the rest of you slow bathers, I walked these lovely warm streets. Lots of things to do! Gaming houses for dicing and playing the stones, ah? Lots of things to do."

I came across a little shop run by two sisters who must have taken me for a traveling foreigner. Can't imagine why." He winked at them.

"Are you nearing the part that concerns us?" Malker asked.

"I am," Zhuyun replied. "Perhaps I'm not the first visitor here from Yuntai. They drew me into their shop with kind words and shiny items. And if there is one thing we Yuntai love, it's shiny items." Seeing the expressions of strained patience surrounding him, he pushed on.

"Everyone is in such a hurry, *ixu*? They asked me how long I was to stay, and my destination. When I told them I needed to reach your difficult to pronounce homeland"—he waved a hand at the Dor'haigheners—"they showed me a most interesting bowl. They said that it had the ability to speed my journey and reduce my time of travel to less than half."

Malker rolled his eyes. "Please tell me you didn't fall for such foolery, Zhuyun Xaiylin."

Zaiyera quietly digested the information, as did Jaide beside her. Across from them, Dyren looked thoughtful.

Malker noticed the sober expressions around the table. "Don't tell me you're considering this?" He looked at his superior. "You, too, Senior?"

"A fool falls for the foolish," the senior hunter said.

Malker raised his hand and let it drop with satisfaction.

"But," Dyren continued, "a fool also passes a possibility out of hand without at least investigating that possibility."

Zhuyun lifted his hand and let it fall with satisfaction, earning a glare from Malker.

Zaiyera shared a look with Jaide. They both knew what it likely was that Zhuyun had stumbled upon, and the northerners wouldn't like it.

14

"Come! Come in!"

A woman in modest brown robes and a head scarf beckoned to Zhuyun, her dark face glowing in the torchlight. "No such thing as coincidence. I know this. You are here for the basin. I know this too." She took note of the others. "You bring friends! Good, kind foreign man."

Zhuyun bowed and introduced the others.

They entered the little candlelit shop. Shelves upon shelves of decorated pottery and glassworks lined the walls. Three ornately designed walking staffs leaned crisscrossed in the corner to the left of the door.

The sweet smell of incense thickened the air and put the patrons at ease. They trailed in behind Zhuyun onto a multicolored, handwoven throw rug, where a second woman greeted them. Obviously the shop owner's younger sister. Her long thick hair was tied away from her face, ending in a big puff at the back of her head. The corners of her eyes creased when she smiled at them.

The sister who'd first greeted them went to the back of the shop. "Our friend from across the great western sea has returned, Tamiya."

"So I see, Lamaya," the younger sister replied. "But what of your friends? Please peruse our wares. There is something here for all of you."

"Our companion has spoken of a special item you possess, *uluma*," Zaiyera said, addressing her with the term of respect for an elder woman. "Please forgive my forwardness, but it has been a long and perilous journey here, with farther still to go. Time does not hold us in its favor."

Tamiya searched Zaiyera's face and her tone sobered. "Then waste not another moment in decision." Lamaya returned with the bowl and handed it to Zaiyera.

"We call this a swift basin," Lamaya said, handing it over.

Zaiyera turned the bowl in her hand. It was handcrafted, painted with a wavy blue river flowing around the side, and an eye surrounded by haze sitting above it.

"As your foreign companion has surely told you," Lamaya said, "this basin can make your steps swift and enduring. You will cover great distances in half the normal time or less." She lifted the basin to provide them a better view. "Only water will activate it."

"You may drink from the basin as many times as you wish," Tamiya added. "But the gifts it bestows number only six."

At the back of the shop, Malker snorted.

Zaiyera gave him a warning look from over her shoulder. "An item of such value would come at a high cost," she said, turning back.

A heaviness settled in the shop as the two sisters nodded. "The cost was paid. The man who sold it to us was in need, or he would have never parted with such a valuable item. We paid him handsomely for it."

Zaiyera glanced at Dyren Faust. The senior shydon hunter's expression changed from confused, to comprehension, to discomfort. Then stubborn refusal.

"If you'll excuse us, please," he said to the shop owners. He turned a look on Zaiyera that suggested they speak outside, then strode out the door, sweeping a confused Malker in his wake.

Zaiyera turned back to the shop owners before the shydon hunters were out the door. "Please excuse the ill manners, *uluma*," she said, reverting to *Soloush*.

Lamaya held up a hand. "You need not apologize. My sister and I traveled near to the northern border in our youth." She glanced at the door where the two men had exited. "Once you've seen a shydon, you know them even without the uniform."

"Your situation must be dire," Tamiya said, "not only for you to travel with shydon, but to bring them here to buy a dancecraft artifact."

Lamaya looked at her sister, though her expression was far away. "So, it *is* true; the rumors of kivuli dayasa."

Zaiyera was aware that Zhuyun and Jaide were still in the shop; the former unable to follow the conversation. She switched back to tradetongue. "It's true, *uluma*. The rumors of kivuli dayasa, the one who dances in shadow, are not rumors at all." She spread her hands and bowed. "Please excuse me."

She left Jaide and Zhuyun with the sisters and exited into the night to find an agitated Malker and an outraged Dyren Faust.

"You bring us to a vendor who sells blood artifacts." The senior shydon's tone was even and heavy with controlled anger. "Perhaps you've had too little enough interaction with us of the north, Zaiyera Tuneesh. I shall open your eyes.

"We of Dor'haighen frown upon—*heavily* frown upon—the creation, sale, and use of lancecraft artifacts of *any* kind. Their creation is a blasphemous spit into the face of God Jokolta, and the precious life He bestows upon us."

Beside him, Malker Argen blinked at his superior. "If I may, senior …"

Dyren talked right over him. "To exploit someone to lance their entire lifestream into the creation of some bauble, in order to give it a unique function, is the most deplorable act one can commit. Worse than murder."

Malker took a half step away from Dyren and looked in a different direction.

Still as a statue, Zaiyera listened to the rant. Her anger built with every word, but she held it in check, lest she allow it to explode right here in the street.

"We of the shydon, and all of Dor'haighen, value life over—"

"I will stop you there, shydon hunter," Zaiyera interrupted, "before your next words commit irreparable damage."

The senior shydon hunter's mouth was still open. He slowly closed it; icy light blue eyes boring into her.

Zaiyera met his gaze and saw a flicker of surprise at her lack of being intimidated.

"You of Dor'haighen have your customs, traditions, *culture*, which you've so vehemently barked at me. And so now I will share an aspect of *mine*.

"*We* of Samhar *also* value life, Dor'haighener. We revere it. While you *lance* the stream, thrusting yourself into the flow and drawing from it, we of Samhar *dance* the stream. We touch it, dip our hands into the flow, drag our fingers along it and allow it to flow around and through us. The stream is life, and we dance in honor of it."

Passersby in conversation continued down the avenue, their curious gazes lingering on the trio. A few male locals stopped just behind the shydon hunters and stared. When Zaiyera took note of them, one of the three large men looked into her eyes, then at the Dor'haigheners, then back again.

Zaiyera inclined her head and held up a hand. The two men nodded back, and continued on. After several steps, one of the other two glanced over his shoulder.

Malker noted the exchange but remained relaxed, though he did have his thumbs tucked in his belt, near his sword.

Dyren opened his mouth to speak and Zaiyera narrowed her eyes at him and kept going.

"And as to the creation of a dancecraft artifact, shydon," she went on. "Whatever is done in *your* homeland to bring one into being, here, it is the greatest, gift from a loved one ready to move into Shakimah's embrace."

She thought of Shatr. How her aunt, who had created it, would never have done so had she known how it had been imbued. Zaiyera kept talking, guilt and hypocrisy mingled with indignation.

"That basin was created by an elder ready to cross into *Sojalleh*. It was created as a final gift to someone close and it helped the elder cross swiftly from this world to the next. That the man who'd sold it to those sisters had done so, speaks to the level of desperation he must have felt at having to do it.

"So, interpret our culture however you wish, view it as a spit in the face of your God if you will, but I'll not spit in the face of another's no doubt painful sacrifice in giving up so dear an item.

"I'll leave you to contemplate your desire to continue with your mission, shydon. And also to balance your willingness to involve me and other civilians in this dangerous business against your *un*willingness to use an item whose creation you do not understand."

She spun on her heel before the man could respond and entered the shop to a group of sober expressions. Well, except for Jaide, who held a fist over her grin and looked away.

"You heard that, didn't you?" Zaiyera asked.

"Please excuse, my friend Zaiyera," Zhuyun said. "It was difficult not to. But I've gotten an education at least, ixu?"

She heard Jaide's muffled voice from the side. "That was quite a tongue-whipping."

The younger sister—Tamiya?—held the bowl cupped in her hands. She crossed the shop and held it out to Zaiyera. "If this will add to your chances of survival against that terrible monster, please have it."

Zaiyera spread her hands and bowed. "Thank you, *uluma*, and to you, *uluma*." She repeated the gesture to Lamaya. "We will not take this without payment."

"It is our gift to you," Lamaya argued. "Please."

"And you have a store to run," Jaide spoke up. "We all have some modest means about us. Let us combine our efforts and pay you fairly."

Zaiyera, Zhuyun, and Jaide fished into their money pouches. The door slowly opened, and Malker Argen ducked halfway into the shop.

He looked around the room, seeing every gaze directed back at him, and stepped in.

"My … apologies for my skepticism earlier, my lady … *ulooma*."

Across the room, a neutral-faced Jaide bit her lip.

Malker noticed the trio, hands in pouches. He stepped forward and reached into his own. "I would also contribute."

They paid the sisters well for the basin and the women saw them out the door with many thanks.

"One last thing, young woman," Tamiya said to Zaiyera. She took the bowl from her and turned it so that Zaiyera could see an eye surrounded in haze. "As you know, dancecraft can have a second manifestation, like a side effect."

She pointed at the rushing river. "This symbolizes speed, to quicken your journey. This," she touched the eye, "will provide you with a vision, though I don't know what. It could be of anything or anywhere."

"Only the first sip will grant the side effect," Lamaya warned. "Beware obscure visions, girl. They can be a boon or a curse if you interpret them wrong."

Zaiyera inclined her head. "Thank you, *uluma*."

The others waited for her in an uneasy silence. Dyren Faust stared down the street, features tight, icy fire kindling in his eyes.

Nighttime strollers gave the senior shydon hunter a wide berth, except for the occasional sword-clad local, who gave him lingering stares as they passed.

Zhuyun cleared his throat. "I presume there is nothing left to do but take our sleep for the night? We've a long way to go yet, and I fear if I remain in this beautiful paradise too long, I'll not leave."

"Then we meet at the north side of town, yes?" Jaide asked, looking from Malker to Dyren.

"We ride at dawn," Dyren said. He left without another word, his stride quick and precise as he angled down the winding avenue toward the inn.

"That one is all a-cheer," Jaide Amadi said.

"The senior shadow hunter is unaccustomed to being challenged," Malker replied.

Zaiyera noted the undecided look on the man's aged face and had to remind herself that he was likely close to her age, though he looked more than twice that. That became more apparent than ever the more she saw him waver between agreeing with her on using the basin, yet feeling the need to respect his superior. "Where do you stand, Malker Argen?"

He seemed to only consider the question for a moment before responding. "My Dor'haighen sensibilities balk at the idea of using lancecraft for anything. Maybe I trade my morality for the greater good, but if it will help us kill that shadowlancer before he breaks the world, I will continue with you and use that thing," he pointed at the swift basin, "if I must. I pray Jokolta spares me His ire."

Malker started away.

"What if your superior refuses?" Zhuyun asked.

The shydon hunter stopped and looked back. "I have no authority over him."

"But he has authority over you," Zhuyun countered.

Malker nodded that point. "I'll see you at dawn."

Zaiyera stared at the man's back, honestly wondering how she felt about continuing on with those two.

She heard Zhuyun beside her whistle through his teeth. "If but a gaze alone had physical power, you'd have incinerated him, my friend."

Zaiyera snapped out of her musings. "Hmm? What?"

"Zhuyun was just remarking on how you look ready to throttle the departing shydon hunter," Jaide said.

Zaiyera gave her head a shake and ran a hand through her braided hair. "Just thinking."

Jaide pointed at the diminishing figure of Malker. "About throttling him?"

Despite her mood, Zaiyera smiled.

"Since we Yuntai actually require sleep," Zhuyun winked at Jaide, who chuckled, "I shall retire for the night as well."

"A good idea for us all," Jaide replied.

Zaiyera wanted, *needed*, to dance the steam. It had been days. Just the thought of it made her aware of the creeping knots in her stomach, the sensation of being hot and cold at the same time, the thirst that no water could quench. She needed to be close to the stream.

A hand gently touched her shoulder, and she nearly jumped. She turned to see Zhuyun's concerned face. Behind him, a similarly concerned Jaide looked on.

"Are you all right, my friend Zaiyera?" Zhuyun asked. "I'm sure at dawn our party will still number five. Ten, if you count our camels, ixu?"

Zaiyera strained to smile. "Just thinking about what's to come." She felt bad for the lie, but what else could she say?

The walk back to the inn was filled with grand stories from Jaide about historical events of Viriksan, and how they produced some of the most formidable warriors in all of Samhar.

Zhuyun joined in the storytelling, speaking of the disciplined soldiers of Jintai, ruled by the shrewd Empress Aidai. He spoke of the great mountain named Deishaun, and the *tokailan* monks who lived there.

"Have I mentioned that we of Viriksan are also geniuses, Zhuyun?" Jaide said with a snap of her finger. "I've had an idea that is certainly worthy of the title. When this dark business of death and kivuli dayasa is finished, we three will visit each other's homelands, yes?"

"A fantastic idea!" Zhuyun looked at Zaiyera. "What an adventure that would be, ixu?"

Zaiyera smiled politely. "That does sound like a lovely idea, should we survive."

Jaide blew air out of her lips, making a deflating sound. "So cheerful."

15

Malhadiev smirked at the armed force standing between him and his home city of Zalrabi. The expression belied the strange sensations churning in his body. He'd syphoned three more dancers since Buntara. Since then, his body felt … stretched, like an overfilled sack fraying at the seams.

He closed his eyes and drew a long breath. He sensed the static energy in the air. The anxiety, determination, fear. He felt the wariness of nearby animals, trees, every form of life in the area. Even the rocks at his feet feared what he might do.

Malhadiev let the breath go. They needn't fear him if they would all just stand aside. Only Sheikh Jegried need fear for his life. As well he should.

"One chance only," he shouted across the gap between himself and an army of what must have been a hundred *dakhiva*. There were more than just these soldiers, of course. Jegried would have them surrounding him like the coward he was.

The spearmen shifted into throwing position, the swordsmen at their backs.

Malhadiev sighed. How many must die at the whims of their lords? Why wouldn't they at least *listen*?

Even as that last thought played in his mind, the hunger struck. It had been a week since he'd syphoned his last dancer. If these people would stop opposing him, he wouldn't have to draw from the stream. He wouldn't need to kill them and replenish himself. If only they'd step *aside*.

There were dancers here. Zalrabi was Malhadiev's home. He'd been one of the city's streamdancers. How long had it been now? How long since he'd actually *danced* the stream? It seemed like a lifetime ago. With as much power as he had readily available, there was no longer a need to dance the stream. There wasn't a single dancer in the world powerful enough to access enough of the stream to do little more than amuse him.

The commander of the *dakhiva* forces didn't bother ordering him to stand down or surrender. They simply stood in battle formation, waiting.

Word had spread.

Malhadiev's grin evaporated. Who had gotten past him to send word ahead? A surviving soldier? A witness he hadn't noticed? Might it be unwise to leave survivors in his wake until his work was done?

Another pang of withdrawal struck. Its simultaneously icy and fiery hands twisted his stomach, burning his skin and freezing his bones. His body felt as though it expanded and contracted in an attempt to contain the immense power flowing within.

He suddenly wanted to sleep.

Malhadiev shook away the feeling and called out once again. "However many your numbers are, every one of you may be spared, this day. You have only to step aside and allow me to deal with your true enemy. There isn't a weapon or skill among you, not even your courage, or indomitable spirit, or warrior's stoicism, that will prevent the inevitable. Jegried *will* die."

His eyes moved while he spoke, scanning left to right as he assessed the formation. "Don't be the pawns of a man who schemes to the detriment of his own people."

A wall of silence answered him.

Malhadiev sighed. "Very well." He started forward.

Someone barked a command and the spearmen lifted their weapons and took aim.

Malhadiev continued his steady approach.

They waited until he was within a hundred feet. Another order was called, and the swordsmen behind the spear-throwers roared, and flowed forth around them. The spearmen let fly.

Spears arced over the heads of the charging soldiers who bellowed their battle cry, swords held high.

Black as a starless night, Malhadiev's tainted lance-resin glowed around his body. With a simple wave of his hand, the missiles fell aside like a jumble of twigs.

The first soldiers to reach him died on their feet. Malhadiev struck directly into their lifestreams, his tainted resin like a poison injected into the blood.

Their momentum carried them stumbling past the steadily advancing *kivuli dayasa*. He strode into the heart of the force and made the ground rumble beneath their feet. He produced defensive disks to ward against their blades. With a flick of his wrist, he lashed them with a transparent whip entwined around his wrist.

He produced more glowing disks from the stream that sent hundreds of needle-like projectiles tearing through leather armor.

Malhadiev would have poisoned all their lifestreams if he could. It would have been quicker for him and the dying. But to touch the lifestream of even ten people required a good deal of concentration.

In the end it didn't matter. Most died, and those that survived lay broken or torn upon the blood-soaked ground.

The battle lasted as long as it took the shadowdancer to walk through the *dakhiva* force to reach the towering sandstone walls of Zalrabi.

Malhadiev strode up to the great wooden door, more than three times his height. He drew from the stream with his left hand and produced another glowing blue disk that sent projectiles the size of spearheads shooting into the gate. With his right hand, he produced another transparent whip, this one several times larger.

The shadowlancer drew his arm back and swung it forward repeatedly. The spearheads punctured the great wooden doors while the whip splintered every place it struck.

Malhadiev grimaced. Such a waste of wood. How much of it had to be harvested from far away and brought here? Had Jegried overcome his cowardice, he would have saved his people from all this loss of resources and life.

The giant door exploded in a shower of wooden splinters. The shards rained down on Malhadiev as he passed through, while vultures circled over the carnage behind.

"They're dead, Jegried!" kivuli dayasa shouted. Soldiers struck from both sides, but he dispatched them with little effort. "And the rest will die. They die because of you! I am your fate. Come face me and save them!"

No hidden attack point worked. No soldier was able to sneak up on him. How could they? This was Malhadiev's home. He knew every alley, every corner. His advantage was his enemy's disadvantage. The Sheikh of Zalrabi knew nothing of the origin of his adversary.

The streets welcomed him home with palpable silence, save the groaning of injured *dakhiva* and regular soldiers squirming behind him. Through soaring spears and swinging swords, kivuli dayasa advanced toward Sheik Jegried's palace.

He felt the twinge in his stomach again. The hunger no food would sate. He quickened his step. Every dancer in the city known to Jegried would be gathered in the palace as a last defense.

Malhadiev ascended the steps to the palace unchallenged and entered the main antechamber.

A small force of *dakhiva* awaited him, shamshirs at the ready. Behind them stood a dozen unarmed men and women clad in woven blue and green robes, whose beauty was second only to the robes of the man who stood at the top of a set of steps behind them.

Two of those unarmed protectors were women, both with shaved heads and fierce eyes that gave Malhadiev pause. One of them had a tattoo along the side of her head.

Malhadiev looked beyond them all, into Sheikh Jegried's cowardly eyes. "You sent many to their deaths today, Jegried," he said. "Must you condemn all these people to the same fate? Are you such a coward that you would sacrifice them to delay your fate a few moments longer?"

"Submit yourself to our lord," the captain commander ordered, "and you will be spared. You stand before the greatest of the Zalrabian *dakhiva*."

Malhadiev ignored the order and continued to stare into Jegried's eyes.

Sheikh Jegried's chest heaved. He looked back across the room into Malhadiev's gaze. "When first I heard about the ruin you left, far to the north, I'd thought the stories exaggerated. But every account grew worse as you made your way here." He frowned. "Who *are* you?"

Malhadiev narrowed his eyes. "Of course you wouldn't remember me. A man who orders men and women to their deaths while entertaining guests and filling your coffers— "

"What are you talking about?" the sheikh interrupted.

" … wouldn't recognize one of the very delegates you sent to negotiate with the treacherous lord of the north."

Fear and frustration gave way to recognition, and Jegried's eyes widened before he regained control. "You were part of the delegation that was assassinated." The words came out calm and controlled, but Malhadiev didn't miss the quaver in his voice. "That is what all this is about? I assure you, had I known there were survivors, I would have sent aid. How could I have known?"

Malhadiev's mouth stretched into a half smile that didn't meet his eyes. "I suppose I understand why." He shrugged. "I'd been a cramp in your side for years, hadn't I? Always opposing your schemes to cut out other nations within Samhar. I routinely made it difficult for you to justify making quiet deals with the northern king to import zimastone and valuable metals and materials straight to your glorious Zalrabi."

"You only see part of the whole," Jegried argued.

"Oh?" Malhadiev waved a hand to encompass the room with its massive handwoven throw rug, the polished stone floor, the many pieces of art adorning the walls.

"You've murdered countless people out of resentment," Jegried said. "You murder out of jealousy of my family's wealth, passed down through generations."

Malhadiev winced when the hot/cold pain twisted tighter in his stomach. "I resent your greed. I was your trade advisor, remember? Do you think I didn't know about your interests, your ambitions to cut off trade of the most valuable resources from the north, so that the rest of Samhar would be forced to trade and buy from you? And you made all who knew disappear. Well…" He shrugged again. "Except me, that is."

"Remove him," Jegried ordered.

"Please, don't," Malhadiev said, his imploring tone surprising even himself. "I promise you, I will spare their lives." He indicated every *dakhiva* in the room while conveniently omitting the streamdancers surrounding the sheikh. "You *will* die. That is a certainty. They need not share your fate."

The first line struck and died. Then the second. The streamdancers —all but those strange two—buffered the efforts of the remaining troops, but Malhadiev easily neutralized their efforts.

In mere, moments only Malhadiev, the captain commander, the twelve streamdancers, and Sheikh Jegried remained alive.

The captain commander moved in front of his lord, and the stream-dancers in front of him. The odd duo moved beside the sheikh.

Malhadiev watched the dancers' pure golden dance-resins trail their graceful movements. Half of them formed their defense and settled in place, while the other half formed their offense.

He chuckled at their concerned looks. They must have realized their doom when they saw him patiently waiting for them to finish.

"Ready?" he asked. "Are you prepared to meet Goddess Shakimah?"

"You sully her name when you speak it," Jegried spat.

"No man can sully the name of the Goddess," Malhadiev countered. "Were you a man with some sliver of faith, you'd know this—"

The streamdancers struck. Malhadiev drew from the stream and countered so quickly, the astonished expressions on every dancer lasted only a heartbeat before they lay broken, gasping, and squirming on the ground.

The two beside Jegried never moved; never even blinked. It was as though the deaths of the *dakhiva* behind Malhadiev and their fellow streamdancers meant nothing.

Malhadiev studied the pair as they stepped away from Jegried. Both women lifted their knees high, and stepped lightly sideways. They raised their hands above their heads and crossed them, then lowered them in front of their faces, sternum, stomach, waist. They repeated the motion again. This time a transparent dark orange glow trailed one of the women's movements.

A darkdancer, Malhadiev thought. *Intriguing.* He looked at the other woman with the tattooed head. *But what of that one?*

The women continued to move as one, their dance graceful, poetic, perfectly in sync. Then the darkdancer struck.

She punched two fingers into the air, which rippled before her. She drew a long transparent whip from the air and turned a circle.

The tattooed streamdancer spun beside her in the opposite direction. Both women stretched their arms out wide as they turned. The darkdancer dipped the fingers of her other hand into the flow and drew forth another whip from the air just as hers and the tattooed woman's hands passed each other.

The lazy grin on Malhadiev's face evaporated. The darkdancer passed the first transparent whip to the tattooed woman, who slid it along her body like a serpent.

This will be interesting. The inky black aura of Malhadiev's tainted resin lined his body.

Both women struck.

Malhadiev ducked the left whip and chopped his hand across the right. Instead of severing the whip and cutting off that bit of the stream, the whip wrapped around his wrist.

When he moved to sever it with his other hand, the darkdancer on the left dealt him a stinging blow.

"Gah!" Malhadiev stumbled sideways.

The tattooed woman yanked back on her dancewhip. His shock at her strength was complete as his feet left the polished stone floor.

Malhadiev used his free hand to reach into the stream once more.

He thrust his hand down, blasting the drawn power into the ground. At the same time, he tucked his feet under himself and straightened. Instead of falling onto his stomach, the extra space beneath him allowed Malhadiev to land on his feet.

As soon as he touched down, he yanked on the whip with all his strength.

The sudden pull jerked the tattooed woman toward him. Instead of resisting his pull, she leapt down toward him. The darkdancer flicked her whip at him again, but this time Malhadiev raked his hand across the air and shredded it. The whip fell apart and evaporated in the same instant the tattooed woman turned in the air and thrust her foot out.

Malhadiev tried to turn his head away, but the woman's kick snapped into his nose and broke it.

He hit the slope of the tiny crater he'd created a moment before, but barely felt the impact. Tears welled in his eyes as his nose swelled. He gasped when pain suddenly exploded between his shoulder blades. The other streamdancer.

The tattooed woman landed as light as a feather, then sprang out of the crater.

Malhadiev groaned and tried to rise. Pain shot down his back and up his neck. He gasped again, nearly choking on the blood trickling down his throat.

From behind, the darkdancer leapt straight up and turned her body in the air, her arms spread wide. A thin orange line traced her movements and when she landed, she swept her left, then right hand in an arc from right to left. Two glowing orange arc blades sliced through the air toward him.

Malhadiev swept his arm left. The first arc shattered. He swept his arm right, just as the second transparent arc reached him. He saved himself from being sliced in half, but just enough of the blade slipped past and cut through most of his hand.

He let out a choked scream and tried to cradle his hand, half of which dangled by piece of skin.

The tattooed dancer pulled on her whip again and dragged him sideways.

Malhadiev turned a murderous glare on her, yet she returned his look with equal promise. He drew from the stream again. He would heal his hand and break these women until they begged for him to syphon and release them into death.

As soon as he drew from the stream to heal, a golden aura surrounded the tattooed woman's body that extended down the whip. It washed over Malhadiev like a river, flowing around his body as it passed. The sensation of bathing in so much untainted stream was bliss. He had to focus not to simply bask in it.

The wondrous bath of purity quickly turned to horror. The golden aura that extended from the tattooed dancer touched his black resin and intermingled with it. As soon as the two dance-resins touched, they flowed inside each other and then through his body.

His eyes widened. He fought against the whip, but her grip was strong. She'd also stopped him from healing his hand, and that pain was becoming unbearable.

From his other side, the darkdancer produced another lancewhip. She wrapped it around his ankle and she pulled his leg out straight.

Held at an awkward angle, his right arm stretched to its limit, his left leg similarly extended, Malhadiev felt his very lifestream being pulled from his body. She was syphoning him.

No.

Her resin tangled with his, becoming more and more indistinguishable. The darkdancer waved her right hand. It was a subtle gesture, yet Malhadiev's damaged hand moved in that same direction against his will, his black dance-resin trailing the movement.

She turned her hand so that her palm faced him, then turned it to face her. She slowly curled her hand into a fist.

Malhadiev felt himself touch the stream as if someone else were doing it using his body. He drew it into himself to heal his hand, then turned his arm so that his hand hung sideways, that the skin and bone could knit.

He looked from his healing hand to the tattooed streamdancer. She was using flow, but not in a way he'd ever encountered it. Her dance-resin continued to link with his own. It was slowly dominating it.

A stab of panic shot through Malhadiev's chest. *She would make me her slave, her weapon.* He glanced at the other streamdancer that held his ankle, thinking of their perfectly synced dance.

Never. NEVER!

Rage lit his blood afire. He plunged himself into the stream. *How much can you hold, adversaries?* He submerged himself into the stream of power, allowing the flow to wash over him; through him.

His body lit with pleasure and burning pain. He had already drawn enough of the stream to burn a normal streamdancer from the inside out.

"What are you doing?" he heard Sheikh Jegried demand.

Malhadiev spared the coward a glance. His eyes were wide with fear.

The sheikh gestured at Malhadiev as he yelled at the women. "You have him. Kill him!"

"He is a sword of unequalled power," the tattooed woman said. Her high-pitched voice contrasted starkly with her strength. "A sword that will be mine, for I will be the hand that wields him."

During the brief exchange, Malhadiev filled himself nearly to bursting. His body grew weary, aging rapidly with each heartbeat. A few locks of hair fell over his face, not black or gray, but white.

The tattooed streamdancer blinked at him. Then frowned. Her eyes narrowed in realization, and she tried to pull away.

I think not. Malhadiev flooded her with the stream, tainted from passing through him.

Her eyes widened and her mouth fell open in a silent scream.

Malhadiev felt her lifestream diminish and absorb into his own.

The darkdancer cried out and started to move her free hand.

Malhadiev shattered the tattooed woman's whip with but a flex of the massive power still flooding through him. He felt the lifeprice exacting it toll. He had to be quick.

Malhadiev swung his arm and chopped his uninjured hand in front of his body. A black arc swept across the air. It sliced through the transparent whip and both of the darklancer's legs.

The woman screamed as the lower half of her legs fell apart. She toppled to the ground, still screaming.

It happened in little more than the span of two heartbeats, during which Sheikh Jegried ordered the captain commander of the *dakhiva* to cut Malhadiev down.

Malhadiev snarled and swept his hand back toward the captain, then thrust it forward. A black arc blade like the one that had cut down the darkdancer raced toward the captain. Malhadiev flicked his hand in a circle while moving his fingers. A pulsating black disk appeared in front of him. The disk opened at the middle, then burst in a geyser of channeled flow, a dam opening to release a raging river.

The unfortunate captain commander had already been on the move and thus committed to the motion. To his credit, he reacted quickly. He flipped his sword down to block the speeding arc blade. It sheered through the sword as though it were silk and sliced cleanly through his torso. The poor man barely had enough time to choke on his own blood before the second attack, the blast of tainted black flow, crashed into him. When the blast cleared, all that remained of the man painted the far wall.

Feeling his rapidly aging bones creak, Malhadiev moved quickly to the darkdancer, who lay bleeding to death on the floor. He needed to get to her before her lifestream dried up.

He slapped his hand on her chest and drained her lifestream so quickly, her back arched. The influx of power filled him, healed his hand, and satisfied the hunger. His hair darkened again as the lifeprice reversed. The wrinkles in his skin smoothed, his body growing stronger again.

Malhadiev took a deep, shaky breath. It was the first time he'd syphoned a tainted dancer. It hadn't felt as blissful and invigorating as a pure lifestream, but it replenished him.

He looked over his shoulder at the bald tattooed woman. On hands and knees, she wheezed, mouth agape as she tried to refill her body with that which had been taken.

"You are unique," Malhadiev said as he approached. He swept a hand at the side door to the anteroom. A vertical black arc blade split the air and sliced into the wall beside it. Inches from the quietly fleeing Jegried's nose. The sheikh cried out and stumbled backwards.

Malhadiev flexed his healed hand. His palm itched from the newly stitched skin. He squatted beside the gasping woman. "You're unique because you are the first to experience only part of your lifestream syphoned away."

Her back arched upward as she let out a long, agonized wheeze.

"It must be torture." He leaned forward and whispered into her ear. "I am no one's weapon, yet you will be mine." He slapped her on the back, planting her flat on the stone floor.

Malhadiev felt what was left of her pure lifestream. Because he already held some of it inside him already, it was as though two parts of a whole sought to reunite. It made syphoning her that much easier.

His hair fully returned to its black color, and all the remaining strength returned to his body. He moved to the other streamdancers. Most lay unconscious, or barely so. He drained them one by one until all lay empty and dead, and he, renewed.

Still kneeling over the last drained dancer, Malhadiev slowly turned his head and leveled his livid glare through his shimmering black hair at Jegried.

He took his time to rise, then stalked toward the still sitting man. He stopped right in front of Jegried. "Stand."

Malhadiev had expected the man to protest against being given an order, but Jegried climbed to his feet, straightened his back, and squared his shoulders. The two men stared at each other.

"A last bit of courage to face eternity." Malhadiev nodded with a downturned smile. "Perhaps you are deserving of some tiny bit of respect after all. I do have a question." He spread his arm in the direction of the dead woman with the tattoo on the side of her head. "She and the other one obviously aren't from Zalrabi, or Samhar, for that matter." He concentrated on not letting the pain in his body show on his face. So much power straining against him from the inside. "Who are they?"

Jegried said nothing. Just stared at him.

Malhadiev sighed. "Death is something we prepare for the older we get. But the crossing from this life to the next is the mystery we fear, is it not? Allow me to shed some of the mystery, though I can't promise to do the same for your fear.

"Tell me what you know of those women, and your death will be quick. Otherwise …" he shrugged.

Jegried's mouth started to move, then he clenched his jaw shut and raised his chin. "You have me." He spread his arms. "Do what you must."

Malhadiev eyed the sheikh's intricately woven linen robes. Tiny slivers of zimastones were sewn into the white, purple, and blue fabric. The green stones glittered in the light peeking through the windows. His eyes narrowed.

"You've killed everyone and left the city defenseless," Sheikh Jegried continued. "My beloved Zalrabi can easily be invaded, now. What more would my death accomplish for—"

With curled fingers, Malhadiev grabbed Jegried's chest and syphoned a tiny bit of his lifestream, just a flicker.

Jegried collapsed in a wide-eyed gulp. Malhadiev crouched in front of him, and when the sheikh looked into his eyes, all defiance had given way to terror.

Malhadiev hid his pain behind a grin. "It hurts, and can last a very, *very* long time, Sheikh Jegried.

Moments later Malhadiev worked his way out of the anteroom. In the end, it had been over as fast as it began. A non-dancer's lifestream was much smaller, and Jegried had little to offer. Still, Malhadiev reveled in the irony that the very man who had started all of this would aid him with his revenge and setting things right.

The sheikh's revelations just before his death, however, tempered Malhadiev's smugness.

He struggled along the walls under the weight of a new influx of lifestream flowing through him. It felt like a raging river of fire that was his blood, sinew, and muscles. He could barely contain it.

"H …h …hav … have to … rest." He clamped a hand to his chest, doubled over, and emptied his stomach on the smooth stone floor. He braced his forearm against the wall for support and kept going. Having been in the palace many times over the years he'd served the sheikh, Malhadiev knew exactly where Jegried's bedchamber lay.

When he reached the sheikh's private rooms, he smiled in relief that they were empty. Whatever his grievance had been against the now dead Jegried, at least the man had enough decency to send his family away.

Malhadiev ignored the gaudy sleeping chamber, made his way past the handwoven pieces of art, clay-fired and painted pottery, and throw rugs. He climbed into the bed that could easily hold a family of six and lay on his back. He crossed his ankles, interlaced his fingers and rested his hands on his stomach, and closed his eyes. He didn't know how, but Malhadiev knew that when he awoke, he would be near invincible.

In three breaths, those thoughts faded away into the blissful oblivion of hibernation.

16

The ride out of Malajanna had been a quiet one. Zaiyera, Zhuyun, and Jaide rode at the front of the party, while Dyren and Malker brought up the rear.

Zhuyun had once again fallen into jovial accounts of the many adventures of his travels. The Yuntaiman had traveled through much of his homeland but had also gone to faraway places on continents across the Great Sea.

"I once traveled by boat to land at the beach of a civilization of builders," Zhuyun said. "Grand women of stone, as tall as any mountain, stood guard at each side of the entrance to the gulf awaiting our arrival. It is a place of huge structures made of wood and stone. A matriarchal society where the people are clothed and fed, yet possess little wealth in the way you and I know it, *ixu*?"

Jaide frowned at that. "How could such achievements be attainable without some form of trade or currency?"

"Ah, but I said wealth in the way *you and I* know it. These are a different people, who see wealth through different eyes, ixu?"

"As you say," the Vıriksani replied.

Behind them, Dyren Faust rode in a silence that was every bit as loud as their conversation. Malker Argen tried throughout the day to engage the senior shydon hunter, but with infrequent and brief success.

The dunes of Samhar had long disappeared to be replaced by more green vegetation. Thick-barked ogko trees grew in clumps everywhere, as well as niyabi trees with their long leafy branches reaching out to embrace the world itself.

Zaiyera took it all in. The such sights this far north were unfamiliar and beautiful. Vines with strange fruit lay on the hardened ground. She wondered if they were edible but didn't ask. Perhaps it was the tension she could practically feel from Dyren, behind her. Or perhaps it was the hunger.

As soon as thoughts of the latter entered her mind, she pushed them away. It took concentration to keep the urges at bay. She focused on the conversation, or rather, Zhuyun's endless stories. Thank Shakimah these two were with her. Having Jaide and the Yuntaiman around made it easier to forget the urges, if only for a little while.

As Zhuyun went on, Zaiyera found her mind wandering. She thought of home and wondered where her *ka* was now. Were they on the move east, or west? Perhaps they moved south, toward the fertile regions where vegetation grew thick and tall.

For twenty years she'd been separated from her people. The feeling of missing them could be likened to the urges, only less physically and mentally painful.

Before she thought to stop herself, her mind went back through the years to when she had first learned the sword. She'd been fourteen years old at the time; little more than a child.

Despite the disapproval of most of the *ka*, Zaiyera's father—and with some coaxing, her mother—believed she should be trained to survive in the same manner as any boy in the tribe. She'd split her time between gathering roots, herbs, and vegetables with the other girls, and hunting with the boys.

Zaiyera mentally smiled at the memory of creeping along the dunes in search of large rodents and great horned lizards as long as a man was tall. They'd shunned her at first; jogged an extra fast pace to tire her out. They'd succeeded in wearing themselves out instead. Zaiyera's father had known what the boys of the *ka* would try. He'd known they would try to make her feel inferior, weaker, believing it themselves. So he'd pushed her hard since she'd been old enough to endure it.

Then came the time for the blade. Her training had progressed from tasks as simple as finger exercises to working her wrists, footwork, basic stances and motions. It was the time young Zaiyera had waited for, and she'd thrown herself into it with single-minded focus. She'd obsessed over perfecting everything she'd been taught, spending the hours the children were at play practicing her lessons.

At ten years old, no boy in the *ka* could defeat her with the blade. Except for one.

The tiny smile that had crept onto Zaiyera's face disappeared.

Aried Dom.

Once again she remembered his dark brown eyes practically glittering in triumph after their first practice, and her first defeat. She'd bested him at hunting, time and again, but in the practice circle with their carved wooden scimitars and shamshirs, he dominated.

Zaiyera had lost terribly that first time. But she studied him, learned from her mistakes, practiced every free minute she had.

He'd defeated her every time they sparred. But she was getting better. Every time they met in the circle, she'd come a little closer, forcing him to backpedal, putting him on the defense. All of the younger and older children of the *ka* would come to watch the two most skilled children clash in the sparring circle. Even adults started to show up.

And every time, they'd showed up to watch Zaiyera's defeat. After one rather painful loss, Zaiyera had collected her wooden scimitar from where it lay in the dirt, having been knocked from her hand. She'd almost disarmed Aried in that match. She'd seen the panic in his face turn to ferocity. He'd recovered and come at her with the savagery of someone attempting to kill their adversary. It quickly felt like a life and death battle that left Zaiyera "dead". Eyes downcast, she'd limped toward the camp, rubbing her sword hand.

When she looked up, however, she saw that many of the younger girls were watching her with admiration in their eyes. Despite her defeat, they'd still looked up to her.

"One day you will win, Zai Zai," a girl had said to her.

Tears brimmed in Zaiyera's eyes at the memory. She masked wiping her eyes by pretending to check her keffiyeh.

She'd practiced through the two weeks her father had ordered her not to spar so her body could heal. She'd gone over every technique she knew, moving slowly to get them right, then faster and faster. In her little hand, the wooden scimitar had whirled, sliced, and stabbed. Zaiyera had taken her frustration out on Aried Dom in her mind, punishing her imaginary opponent, reveling in the look of desperation in his eyes.

Then it happened. A faint golden glow trailed her movements—

" … any minute now, right, Zaiyera?"

Zaiyera blinked. She looked to her right at a grinning Zhuyun. "Hmm?"

On the Yuntaiman's other side, Jaide chuckled. "Our foreign friend was saying that you would snap out of your open-eyed sleep any minute now. I was about to wager that you'd slide off of your camel before waking up, but he cheated and called your name."

"Mmph."

Jaide and Zhuyun recoiled.

"Grumpy?" Jaide asked in her man voice. The Viriksani smiled, but Zaiyera saw the question in her eyes.

"I'm sorry," she said. "My mind wandered to dark places."

"Ah, but how could it not?" Zhuyun replied. "Dark places we're bound for, no doubt. And speaking of such," he lowered his voice, "should we not be moving at a blistering pace?"

Zaiyera spared a hint of a grin for the ever-discrete Yuntaiman, then turned to Jaide. "You spoke of one last oasis?" When the other woman nodded, she looked back to Zhuyun. "We will try the basin at dawn. Our speed advantage is best reserved for the coolest hours of the day."

The oasis turned out to be a fair-sized lake surrounded by palms and reeds, a pack of chukita cats drinking from the shore off to one side. A pack of wild camels lounged near the water, not far from the drinking felines.

"What in the name of Jokolta is that?" Malker pointed to the other side of the pond. "Over there."

Zaiyera and Jaide sucked in a breath through their teeth and pulled their walking camels to a stop.

A tan-colored animal with a five-foot long, slender body from head to tail lay curled on the ground several feet from the pond. It noted their approach and lifted its scaled head. Sunlight glimmered off the red horns growing from the back of its skull. It flexed its leathery wings, then settled them back in place.

"Urufirun," Zaiyera whispered.

"It looks predatory," Malker said. "Yet camels and small animals rest near it."

"Because it's full," Jaide said. She sniffed the air. "After they've eaten, their bodies perspire due to the effort of digesting their meal." She sniffed again and wrinkled her nose. "It's a rather distinct odor."

"A sharp nose indeed," Zhuyun said. "I smell nothing."

"You will," Jaide replied.

"It looks similar to the frost worvas that roam the skies of Dor'haighen," Malker observed. "Only that one is much, much smaller."

"We should move on," Dyren Faust said. It was the first time he had spoken to anyone but Malker since their departure from Malajanna.

"If you wish," Zaiyera replied. "But they grow lazy after they've eaten. It won't move from that spot for a day or two."

"How do we know how long it's been since it's eaten?" Malker asked.

Jaide tapped her nose. "Judging from the strength of that smell, I'd say it ate sometime earlier today."

"If it makes you feel better," Zaiyera added, "as long as the animals are content to share the oasis with it, we're safe."

The urufirun lowered its head and shifted the end of its barbed tail in front of its face.

"Indifference if ever I've seen it." Zhuyun said.

They set camp, and everyone except Zaiyera tethered their camels near a patch of grass. The animals grazed, occasionally looking across the lake, but largely unconcerned by the presence of the sleeping urufirun.

While the others talked around a campfire, Zaiyera looked around at the darkening, flat landscape. A few hills lay sprinkled about, not far away. She spotted one a hundred or two yards from the campsite. That would be good enough.

She went back to her gear and picked up Shatr.

Malker looked from the sword to her. "Is something wrong?"

Zaiyera held up a hand when he moved to rise. "Nothing is wrong. I'm just going to … practice for a while."

"A great idea, actually." He rose anyway.

Zaiyera sighed.

"We've traveled so far and not once have we practiced together."

Zaiyera stole a quick glance at the privacy of the distant hill, lying there like a shadowy sanctuary. "I'm sure the four of you can challenge each other without me. Your numbers would be even, as well."

"Malker is correct," Dyren said.

Zaiyera looked across the camp at the senior shydon. He sat with his legs crossed, back erect, staring out at the black circle in the darkness that was the lake. "I'm sure he is," she said carefully as she studied his profile. Shadow and the orange glow of the campfire danced across the side of the senior shydon's stony face.

"Then please join us." Dyren grabbed his longsword, unfolded his legs, and stood. "It's a benefit to know how we each move, that we might complement each other's tactics."

Zaiyera stared into his hard eyes. This was a challenge. She didn't know if he was *that* outraged by their argument back in Malajanna, or if there was more to this. Whatever the motivation, Zaiyera knew a challenge when she saw one.

She forced herself not to glance at the distant hill. It would be perfect on the other side. No one there to talk into her ear. No one to challenge her to spar. No one to witness her shame. Zaiyera clenched her jaw in order not to flinch at the twinge of pain from the hunger. She needed to feel the stream. She *needed* to feel its rushing currents flowing around her. She pushed down her growing desperation. "Maybe another time."

"Nonsense," Dyren said. He moved to stand beside Malker. "You and Malker first? Your prowess with that most curious blade will provide a good challenge. Then, perhaps, you and I."

Malker looked from Zaiyera to Dyren. "I would love nothing more than a friendly crossing of blades, my lady miss. But if you wish not to …"

"I'm feeling quite forgotten over here," Jaide said. She walked up to the trio with her customary sarcastic grin. "Let our grumpy companion have her solitude from our incessant banter and draw your blade with me. I'm sure I'll give you enough of a challenge, Dor'haighener."

Dyren ignored her. "Unless you do not intend to see this errand through to its conclusion, my lady Zaiyera, we should become familiar with each other's abilities. We shydon are expertly trained. You may find you'll learn something from the experience."

I'm sure. Zaiyera embraced the withdrawals twisting and burning her insides. She took a deep, steadying breath, and responded with a tip of her head. "Very well."

From the periphery, she saw both Jaide and Zhuyun watching. They both looked … concerned.

"Very well," Dyren said as well.

Zhuyun drew a large circle in the sand with the butt of his staff. "No crossing out of here, unless you plan to flee for the hills, ah?"

"Sounds like you've already considered the option, yes?" Jaide quipped. "I promise I won't beat you too badly."

"Such a kind man, you are," the Yuntaiman said.

The two took opposite ends of the circle. Zhuyun whirled his staff and rammed the butt into the ground. He placed his fist into the palm of his other stiff-fingered hand, bowed, and pushed both hands out.

Jaide placed her hand below her opposite shoulder and bowed.

"Won't my blade sheer through it?" she asked as they slowly circled each other.

The Yuntaiman grinned. "It is made of durable materials. But first you must make me block or parry, to worry about that, ixu?"

Jaide laughed. "Okay."

She dashed in with an overhead slice that Zhuyun simply side-stepped. He swept his staff at the back of her feet, but Jaide had antici-pated the counter. She lifted her left foot while sweeping her shamshir in a backward cut.

His staff already at the perfect angle, Zhuyun slapped Jaide's wrist as she swung her blade toward him.

The maneuver had her twisted at an awkward angle as well as dropping her sword. The Viriksani warrior turned at the waist and hopped into a diagonal spin. As soon as her feet touched the ground, she crouched and swept a foot toward the Yuntaiman's ankles.

Sand and dirt sprayed out of the circle as Zhuyun lifted his left foot over Jaide's sweep and stepped back. Jaide continued her turn and swept her second foot, which Zhuyun also avoided while stepping back.

The counter hadn't been to actually trip him up, however. Jaide regained her weapon on the second sweep. She rose and stabbed forward. Zhuyun simply leaned away.

Jaide launched into a flurry of swipes and cuts, slicing her scimitar in upward and downward arcs, swinging it sideways.

Always, Zhuyun was one step ahead of her. Rarely did he bother to parry her blade aside, and not once did he block.

Jaide broke off the attack. "Thinking to tire me out, Yuntaiman?" she asked. "You'll be waiting a long time."

Despite her good-natured bluster, Zaiyera saw that Jaide had real-ized she was outmatched. The Viriksani woman had performed an uncanny combination of attacks and counters, stringing together a flurry of offensive combinations that would have left an above average swordsman disarmed long ago.

Zhuyun had simply avoided them all.

The Yuntaiman came forward.

Jaide attacked, and he spun around her blade while at the same time, spinning his staff vertically around his body. Back-to-back with her, Zhuyun stopped the shaft of his staff just short of the side of her face. Both combatants stood frozen until Jaide threw her elbow back.

Zhuyun ducked his head away, then turned while bent over. He swept the butt of his staff at her ankle. When Jaide lifted her foot, Zhuyun snapped his staff up. It caught her in the front of her ankle, just below the shin, and Zhuyun lifted. The sly maneuver overbalanced the Viriksani warrior. She hit the ground with a resounding "oomph."

Jaide lay face down on the ground for several heartbeats before her body started to shake with muffled laughter. She rolled onto her back and took Zhuyun's offered hand. He pulled Jaide to her feet, and she clasped a firm hand over Zhuyun's and shook it.

"A good lesson, yes? You and I will spar again, Yuntaiman! I can't remember the last time I've been so firmly planted. I'll learn your tricks yet."

Zhuyun grinned. "You are an expert swordsman. I will be happy to spar again. And help you to kiss the ground again as well, ixu?"

They exchanged salutes and exited the circle in an endless loop of jokes.

The shydons watched the exchange in silence. Once the combatants were seated, Malker stood. Longsword in hand, he moved into the circle and waited silently.

Zaiyera took a deep breath and picked up Shatr.

* * *

Zaiyera and Malker exchanged salutes. They circled each other for several heartbeats, taking each other's measure. Zaiyera had been content to wait as long as need be, but the junior shydon went quick to the offensive.

He closed the distance faster than Zaiyera expected, but her reflexes and a lifetime of training easily saw her avoid the downward strike. They clashed blades several times, Zaiyera mostly parrying to get a feel for how heavy his blows were.

His two-handed longsword had more heft to it than her scimitar, which added to the power of his blows, but compromised speed.

Zaiyera remained on the defense. She slapped Malker's stabbing blade aside with Shatr. He went for a horizontal cut, then snapped back and brought the blade around and down. Zaiyera read the feint as though it happened in slow motion.

With one hand, she swept her scimitar up and stopped it in front of his neck. When she removed the blade, they clashed again, ending in a similar result, this time with the junior shydon doubled over and the cutting edge of Shatr resting at the back of his neck. Three more times they clashed, each time ending with Zaiyera stopping short of a killing blow.

When they finally stopped and exchanged salutes, Malker stared at her with an unreadable expression. "Your skill," he said between breaths. "I've fought beside you but seen nothing of this. Another of your secrets, then?" He stalked over to the campfire and sat. He looked like a gray and black-haired child sulking.

Once again, Zaiyera sighed and turned to leave the circle. She found herself facing Dyren Faust instead.

"I've warned him about his ego, before," Dyren stated. "When he perceives an opponent to be lesser, he fights with more aggression to end the exchange quickly. The tactic has served him well up till this night. You've taught him a lesson."

"I'm no teacher," Zaiyera replied. She wished the man would step aside.

Dyren conceded the point with a nod. "Now that I've seen your skill, perhaps I may offer more of a challenge."

Zaiyera refrained from sighing yet again. He'd seen her defeat his junior shydon. That was hardly much of her skill. The younger man was good, better than most men she'd fought, but he wouldn't defeat a Samharan master. In fact, Zaiyera was certain he wouldn't defeat Jaide either.

Dyren misread her tiny grin. "Feeling confident?"

"Fond memories came in the moment," she replied. "They're gone, now."

"Then let us spar."

"Can we not do this another night, Dyren Faust?"

The senior shydon unsheathed his sword and tossed the scabbard outside the circle. "This is as good a night as any."

Zaiyera thought about just walking away, but that wouldn't solve the problem between them. The man obviously had something to prove. But was it his own superiority, her, or something else? She felt another wave of fire scorching her insides. Some irrational corner of her mind blamed the senior shydon for her torment, though the man knew nothing of the pain burning her from the inside out.

"Come, cross blades with me, Zaiyera Tuneesh," Dyren called.

Zaiyera turned back to the circle. She took a moment to check her anger before entering again.

They saluted.

Dyren lunged with a stab, retracted, then spun forward with a downward sweep of his longsword.

He was much faster than Malker, and far more precise. The stab feint had been easy enough to avoid, as was the sweep. The bottom of his foot, however, was not.

Air blasted from her lungs when Dyren's kick connected with her chest. She rolled backwards and came to a kneeling position. She had just enough time to draw a wheezing breath before diving aside to avoid Dyren's descending chop.

He turned the blade and followed up with a one-handed horizontal slice that flashed right in front of Zaiyera's face.

The senior shydon pursued, matching her step for step. Every block or parry bought her only enough time to block or parry another attack. Behind that wickedly flashing blade, she saw the smug snarl on his face, flickering in the nearby campfire.

"Does your lancecraft weapon not gain you advantage in melee, then?" Dyren asked. "Have you nothing more to offer, warrior? Have you no other weapons to access?"

That was it, then. He thought she was a dancer capable of touching the stream in a subtle way. After the incident at the shop, he must have puzzled out that Shatr was dancecraft. He thought the scimitar gained her an advantage in normal blade-to-blade combat.

Zaiyera continued to give ground in a circle, not allowing him to force her out, yet not gaining advantage. The idea that he thought so little of her abilities, despite her having saved his life, *both* their lives, lit a fire inside that enveloped the flames of the withdrawals.

Dyren feinted a cut left, sliced down, sliced left again. He stepped back, then lunged forward and cut his sword right.

The shydon's blows came fast and heavy. His feints were well-placed and the follow-ups deadly accurate.

Zaiyera stopped moving back. Shatr batted a stab sideways, then chopped down. The tip of the scimitar passed right in front of Dyren's surprised face. Zaiyera took the offense. Dyren parried a swing and tried to counter, but she snapped her scimitar back and around his countering swing so quickly that he overbalanced in the opposite direction.

Dyren cursed as he stumbled forward. Zaiyera had him. She could have easily brought Shatr down to stop at the center of his back and end the contest. Instead, she snapped her foot into his stomach. He let out a heaving gasp an instant before Zaiyera smacked the flat of her scimitar against his back.

The match should have ended there, but Dyren recovered and attacked again. His blows were heavier now.

Zaiyera beat each attack away and looked at his face. Cold determination. This was no longer a sparring match. Or was it ever?

Very well.

Zaiyera exploited every mistake. He delivered an overhand chop that was too slow, and she spun around close to his side. As she did, she reversed Shatr so that the non-cutting edge faced away, and sliced Dyren along the side of his waist as she passed.

His eyes widened at the sensation. He reflexively touched the area and looked at his hand.

Zaiyera stood several paces away, the tip of her scimitar hovering just above the ground.

Dyren launched into a ferocious attack of sweeps and stabs, horizontal cuts, thrust feints. His movements began to glow with a golden aura.

He's going to dance against me? Zaiyera parried a chop at her head, over and down. She stepped in and delivered an elbow to the side of his head.

He stumbled sideways with a grunt, then thrust out his hand. A cloudy whip formed in the air and lashed at her.

Zaiyera snarled. With a flick of her wrist, Shatr cut through the whip. It dissipated in a puff. Zaiyera gave a mental nod. *Passive dance.* Dyren was doing what she did when practicing the blade in solitude. His attacks would serve only to let her know when she was struck and give her the mild sensation of what the effect would be. It was how streamdancers sparred without harming one another or paying the lifeprice.

Dyren growled and came at her again. His attacks were a mix of blade and offensive streamdancing. He delivered a two-handed chop left, then released the sword with his left hand and swept it back. A cloudy blue disk appeared in the air and shot across the space between them, straight for her neck.

Zaiyera leapt forward, snapping Shatr up to cut through the disk.

Dyren's blade was already in a downward arc even as she passed between the two pieces of the severed disk. She turned the scimitar sideways and blocked the descending blade.

Zaiyera fell to one knee and spun. She slid Shatr along the other sword and turned and rose to a crouch. She slid the scimitar free, stepped back, and turned the blade just as it came free of Dyren's sword.

Again, the non-lethal edge sliced across Dyren's side. He ignored what would have been a disemboweling injury and waved the hand closest to Zaiyera in a quick pattern.

A disk appeared in the air and launched dozens of tiny blades at her. Zaiyera swept Shatr in an upward arc as she stepped sideways. The scimitar blasted the first wave of needles apart as she turned. The second wave passed harmlessly by.

Zaiyera never stopped moving. On instinct, she dropped to one knee and sliced the scimitar down and right. Shatr blasted another transparent whip apart as it lashed at her. It also blasted away the triumphant look on Dyren Faust's face when he thought he'd tricked her. That smirk turned to a scowl when Zaiyera closed the distance between them.

Zaiyera defeated his quickly offered defense in three moves and ended the match with her scimitar hovering a hairsbreadth in front of his throat.

17

"I suppose it is time." Zaiyera took one last look around. This was the last of Samhar, where the sand stood thick, and where it still swirled in the wind. The last of the warmth.

She reached into her pack and retrieved the swift basin. Without a word, she left the group and started toward the pond. The sound of trotting came behind her, followed by Zhuyun's voice.

"My friend, Zaiyera," he said, slowing beside her. "Given the last experience we had with an oasis of this kind, perhaps I might join you."

"I appreciate it, Zhuyun, but I assure you, I'm quite safe." She pointed at the sleeping Urufirun. There is one thing that would wake it immediately, and that's a slyvra. They tend not to like each other. If there are slyvra in this pond, they will not chance an attack, even at the water's edge."

"Do you think there are any in there?" Zhuyun asked, staring at the pond.

Zaiyera looked at the body of water, far too small to be a lake, yet larger than a watering hole. "If there are any in there, they would be cramped for space."

Despite Zaiyera's words, Zhuyun held his staff at the ready when she crouched at the shore and dipped the basin into the crystalline water. The basin filled, she stood and they started back. Zhuyun glanced over his shoulder.

"Nervous?" Zaiyera asked.

"Careful," Zhuyun replied. "Em …"

Zaiyera arched an eyebrow.

"I would like to practice with you, when the opportunity arises, my friend Zaiyera."

She blinked several times and looked away.

"No, no, please." He opened his hand. "I have no wish to challenge you for the sake of it. But last night I had the opportunity to view your skills, whereas before"—he grinned with a shrug—"not so much. Given that we were trying not to die."

"What is it about my skill that interests you, Zhuyun?"

The Yuntaiman glanced at the waiting party. "For now, I will just say that your skill is formidable, and I may learn a thing or two from you. I may also have some tools to share that you might like, and that our enemy most certainly will not. Given the attributes of that blade you carry, you would be … more formidable, ixu?"

Back at camp, Jaide waited with her customary slanted grin. Despite being in her male persona, Zaiyera had no trouble visualizing the Viriksani as a woman now. She stifled her chuckle.

Having finished securing their gear to their camels, Malker and Dyren stood to the side talking amongst themselves. Their conversation faded when Zaiyera and Zhuyun approached. Malker offered a stiff nod while Dyren stared at the basin in her hands.

"Speak your misgivings now, shydon hunter," Zaiyera said, "that we may get it over with and move on, either together or our separate ways."

She stopped directly in front of Dyren Faust and noted the veiled surprise in his eyes at her directness.

"You already know my misgivings," he replied.

"I do," Zaiyera said. "Unless you consider me a liar about how dancecraft artifacts are made in Samhar, you know how this was created." She lifted the bowl.

"We all must sip from it," she said to everyone. "Including the camels. Though I personally would prefer to take my drink before them."

"Woah, woah, woah!" Jaide recoiled in mock surprise and grabbed Zhuyun by the shoulder. "Was that … was that a hint of *humor*? I didn't know you had it in you, *niyima!*"

Zaiyera ignored the other woman and looked down at the basin. She thought of the sisters' warning that the basin's side effect would happen upon the first sip; some sort of vision. She took a sip.

The water felt cool and refreshing. She denied her desire to take another draw and passed it to Jaide.

"Best water I've had in days," Jaide remarked. "Makes me want to dive into that pond, mouth first."

Zhuyun sipped next, then handed it to Malker.

The junior shydon hunter held the basin in his hands, looking as though he pointedly didn't glance at his superior. He took a deep breath and sipped from the basin. After a few heartbeats, he looked to Dyren.

The senior shydon took the basin without a word, stared at it for only a moment, and took his sip. He quickly handed it back.

Zaiyera took the basin from Malker and held it under Sadiq's flapping lips. The camel continued to chew even as he lowered his head to the water. He slurped a couple times and Zaiyera pulled it away before he started to drink too deeply.

She went to each of the other four camels and repeated the process until they had all taken their drink, then went to the pond to rinse out the basin. She returned and slipped it into her backpack.

"I don't feel any different," Malker said.

"Perhaps our shop owners exaggerated the properties of the basin," Dyren remarked.

Zaiyera said nothing. She gave Sadiq several pats on his side, and the camel lowered himself to the ground. Once she settled into the saddle, he stood again.

Mounted and ready, the riders turned north.

"Let's see if it works, my friend." Zaiyera leaned forward and gave Sadiq a pat. *"Heyup!"*

Sadiq groaned loudly and lurched into a full run, his body swaying as he extended his neck. The others were right there, their camels also fully stretched out.

"How do we know the basin really worked?" Malker asked.

"You'll have your answer soon, yes?" Jaide said. "Camels can't sustain this speed for long."

As time stretched and the sun moved between the eastern horizon and midday, the camels showed no sign of tiring.

The animals didn't slow even when their shadows stretched from the west, to directly below them, to moving east as the sun began its descent. The riders shared little conversation, mostly focused on the animals. Not a one showed signs of fatigue. No lathering of the mouth, or heavy breathing. Not a single camel stumbled or tried to slow down.

"This is exhilarating," Zhuyun yelled, the loose ends of his keffiyeh flapping behind him. "Never have I ridden at such a speed for so long!"

The wild-eyed excitement in Jaide's eyes mirrored the Yuntaiman's sentiment. Malker also looked to be enjoying the swift ride, and even the stern Dyren Faust looked to be … not unhappy.

The last of everything familiar about Zaiyera's beloved Samhar disappeared by twilight. They entered a land of trees like she had never seen, some with no leaves.

Malker noticed Zaiyera's interest and pointed at a leafless patch. "They are not dead. The north has a variety of trees. Some have leaves that turn from green to red, to yellow, to gold. Then they fall to the ground and the tree goes into a dormant slumber. When spring arrives, they awake, and leaves bloom anew."

Zaiyera nodded absently, still taking in the unfamiliar sight. The largest gathering of trees she'd ever seen appeared on the northern horizon. "How can so many grow in one place like that?"

"This is but a small patch of woods," Malker replied. "There are forests in Dor'haighen that dwarf that one a hundred of times over."

Zaiyera gave him a skeptical look but said nothing.

As they drew near a patch of woods, Jaide pointed out a trail and they angled toward it.

Zaiyera's mouth fell open. The world outside might never have existed as they entered a world of trees that grew so tall and broad, with branches extending so far, that the sky above could barely be seen. Most were bare but sprinkled in between were others bearing the multicolored leaves that Malker had described.

The farther in they went, the darker it grew. Soon the wondrous forest became a shadowy mystery that could hide any manner of creature large and small.

"I know it's dark," Malker said, "But I recommend we camp on the other side of these woods. Near the outside."

"How do you know how far that is?" Zaiyera asked.

"Though we have forests in north Samhar," Jaide said, "there is not enough water for them to grow as big as those in Dor'haighen. I've heard these forests stretch for many miles."

"That is so," Malker replied. "You could spend your entire life roaming them."

"How is that possible?" Zaiyera asked, more to herself than the northerner.

"Ah, but you should see the mountains of Yuntai!" Zhuyun said. "They are home to zhodai lan. The forever green," he clarified at the blank expressions. "The mountains are carpeted with trees whose green leaves never change and never fall. And the mountains! Ah, the mountains. They stand tall enough to touch the clouds."

"You tease us, Yuntaiman," Jaide said. "But you make me wish to see this place one day."

"And so you shall," Zhuyun replied.

Zaiyera refrained from adding, "if we survive."

* * *

Bustling stone streets. Buildings made of white and red brick crowded the many avenues, while farther beyond, larger and more fortified buildings loomed over the streets like grim sentries, the downturned archways of bridges scowling down at the streets that passed beneath.

Strangely clad soldiers with hard faces patrolled the quiet streets.

Behind a series of buildings that looked like barracks, men and women with shaved heads sparred in openhanded combat. They fought against each other in pairs, each ally complementing the other's movements perfectly.

Their movements were acrobatic, their attacks sharp and ferocious with cold precision. One person from each pair had sudden a yellow or orange color trailing their movements. They danced the stream, drawing passively of the flow. They sent foggy yellow disks speeding at opponents that burst apart when they struck their targets. Foggy orange whips lashed at opponents that dealt no injury yet stung enough that the opponent knew they were hit.

A woman with an odd tattoo stretching along the side of her clean-shaven head charged her adversary in a burst of red lance-resin glow around her body. Her movements were so quick and precise that her opponent found himself on the ground in less than two heartbeats.

The tattooed woman straightened over her defeated foe. She swept her hands into an outward arc, red lance-resin trailing each arm, and brought her hands together in front of her waist. Hand atop hand, palms facing up, she lowered her head and lifted her hands in a some form of salute ...

Zaiyera's eyes popped open. She looked at her right hand where she held Shatr in a white-knuckled grip. Once she realized she lay in a bed of leaves at the edge of the woods among her companions, she sat the scimitar down.

What was that? Where was that? Zaiyera remained on her back, eyes moving left and right, scanning the moonlit woods. *Was it the vision the sisters spoke of after drinking from the basin?*

From the corner of her eye, she noticed a figure move into view and stand facing her. She lifted her head and saw that it was Zhuyun. Darkness obscured his features, but she was certain he was looking at her. They stared at each other for several moments before Zaiyera finally climbed out of her bedroll.

Staff in hand, Zhuyun turned and moved down the trail. Zaiyera grabbed Shatr and followed. Her feet crunched softly in the leaves while the Yuntaiman's footfalls were as silent as the night.

She followed him off the trail and into the woods until their sleeping companions were out of sight.

Zhuyun leaned his staff against a nearby tree. "You'll not need it," he said, indicating her scimitar. Zaiyera looked around at the surrounding foliage aglow in the pale light of the fresh new moon.

"I assure you, during my watch, the area is quite safe. We are closer to camp than it appears."

Zaiyera hesitantly leaned Shatr against a tree, still within reach. "Why are we here?"

In answer Zhuyun began to move. "Follow me. Replicate my movements."

The Yuntaiman's legs bent, his steps sweeping and circular, his body low to the ground. He held his hands out before him, one just behind the other. He kept his arms extended, hands out but turned slightly sideways. He stepped in a wide circle, the top half of his body unmoving, his bent legs keeping him at the same height with each step.

Zaiyera started to demand what this was about, but Zhuyun had already begun to move. Though she kept her legs bent as he did, Zaiyera found her steps not nearly as smooth. She tried to mimic his hands and found it difficult to keep her wrists bent so that her fingers faced the sky, her hands turned sideways.

She stepped as he did, her strides jerky and bouncing. Zhuyun remained opposite her as they moved in a circle together, torsos slightly facing each other.

Zhuyun slowly turned away, placed the butt of both hands together and curled his fingers upward. It looked as though he were cupping a flower in his hand. Every action, every flip of his wrist or turn of the hand executed a graceful and delicate pattern.

Despite her best efforts, Zaiyera's movements were awkward and less fluid.

Zhuyun closed the distance between them and continued to move. Now facing each other, he guided her movements, slowly enough that she could follow.

"What you call the stream, we in Yuntai call *irshunaqi*. It is also what flows inside of you." He tapped his chest. "Your *irshunaqi*."

He swept both arms up from right to left, over his head as he stepped sideways to the right. Zaiyera followed.

"In every moment, through our every movement, breath, laugh, cry, shout, we swim the currents of *irshunaqi*, for it is life."

Zaiyera tried to focus on his words while keeping up with his movements. What was he trying to teach her?

"To take from your own *irshunaqi* and send it away is to send a piece of yourself away. Though it is all connected, our bodies house only so much *irshunaqi*; lifestream."

Zaiyera nodded. "The true word for the lifestream in Kushtanji *Soloush* is *haiyasha*.

"A beautiful word," Zhuyun replied. "One day you must teach me more of your mother tongue." He stopped, lifted his hands in an arc, and turned. "When we deplete our bodies, they expire. But the world, this great world that we live on is huge indeed in comparison to us. We are but a grain of sand upon its surface. There are some who learn to draw from our world's *irshunaqi*, while others learn to simply swim in it like a running stream. Others still, learn to dip their hand deeply into the flow, until their fingers grasp the river floor. And there, they drag their fingers through the forever-wet soil, scrawling, tracing beautiful patterns that immediately wash away with the current.

He stepped back and Zaiyera followed. He dipped into a low crouch, torso still upright, and formed his hands—one over the other—as though he were holding a sphere. He remained in his crouched stance, as though he sat astride a camel.

Beside him, Zaiyera copied his stance.

Zhuyun extended his hands over his head, swayed his torso to the right while whipping his arms in the same direction.

He stepped back with his right foot and thrust his left forward. Golden light flared into his hands, sending a transparent ripple into the air. He quickly drew his hand back and held it to his chest. The ripple of air stopped and funneled back into him.

Zaiyera's mouth fell agape. "You're a streamdancer," she whispered.

"No," Zhuyun replied. "But I have an understanding of what you call dancing." He looked up at the moon, peeking down at them from between the reaching tree limbs. "That is enough for today." He looked back to her and grinned. "Not bad for you, tonight. You never know what the body can do, when you get the mind out of the way, ixu?"

Zaiyera looked down at herself and realized she still stood in her squared riding stance. She noticed a faint warmth radiating from her core that felt as though it waited for her to release it. As soon as she became aware of this, it winked out, and the chill of the night returned.

Zhuyun laughed as she straightened. "Whatever you punish yourself for, your heart still glows golden, ah? I hope this small bit that I've shared will help."

Zaiyera froze and stared at the man. "Help with what, Zhuyun Xaiylin?"

His cheeks bunched as he smiled, his almond-shaped eyes creasing at the corners. He bowed his head. "With whatever you need of it."

She remained for some time after Zhuyun left, wondering if he knew what she was. "Whatever you punish yourself for, your heart still glows golden," he'd said. Did that mean he knew? But how could he? Zaiyera had spent most of her life mastering discretion with regards to her secret.

Zaiyera took deep, measured breaths to settle the panic welling in her stomach. No. She could think of no way he would know. Maybe he was referring to the guilt she'd felt about the caravanners who hadn't survived.

She'd barely taken a few steps back toward camp when she froze. Her eyes widened; her breath caught. The hunger. It was gone.

18

Trees.

Zaiyera tried counting them, differentiating them, guessing at what kinds of small animals or insects might live in them. Every attempt at distracting her mind from the previous night lasted only as long as it took to return to the memory of it, and the undeniable conclusion that Zhuyun knew her secret, no matter how much she tried to rationalize against it.

The last of the Samharan desert faded away as the camels raced toward the northern border. Aided by the gift of the swift basin, the camels ran nonstop through morning, day, and into the evening. As with the first time, the riders had also partaken of the basin's gift to augment their stamina and stay awake for so long.

Zaiyera gazed out at plant-covered hills like the plateaus of Burkiba. A world carpeted in beautiful swirling sand became one of multi-colored bushes, clusters of boulders the northerners had called "outcroppings", and beautiful, wondrous patches of woods.

Thinking of the exotic trees towering over her head with their red, gold, orange, and green leaves almost distracted her from the concerns swirling in her troubled mind. Almost.

"We have left the land of sand, then?" Zhuyun asked. "The world grows greener and cooler."

"Not yet, Yuntaiman," Jaide Amadi said. "But we will reach the border today, yes?" She looked ahead with a wide smile. "Those lovely sisters back in that paradise of an oasis told us true. We have covered over two weeks of distance in but a few days!"

Zhuyun spotted a town coming into view on the horizon ahead. His gleeful announcement came just as Zaiyera began to realize that whatever the Yuntaiman had done to ease the hunger had been temporary.

The closer they drew, the more it became apparent that this was indeed a border city. A green flag with the image of a camel in the center flapped in the wind high above.

"I know this flag," Jaide said. "It is Demenin Waypoint."

"I thought you hadn't traveled this far west, Viriksani," Malker replied.

"I spoke true," Jaide replied. "However, it is a boon to those of my profession to know as many flags as possible of the cities we're likely to encounter, yes?" She pointed at the distant flag, flapping in the wind. "For example."

"Yes, yes," Malker said. "Point taken, my good man." He looked at Zaiyera. "You're even less talkative than usual? What do you brood on this day?"

Zaiyera looked at the junior shydon hunter. Malker returned her gaze with a nod and a partial smile. She tried to ignore the hot/cold fire creeping into her blood and skin, and forced herself to smile back. "I am thinking about the future, Malker Argen." She released a handful of Sadiq's mane and pulled her robes tighter about herself. "And it is cold."

Malker laughed at that. "Then, you are in for quite some misery, Samhari. But not without a bit of luck." He pointed at the rapidly approaching city. The tops of three stone buildings peeked at them over a white brick wall that looked tall even from that distance. "Border towns specialize in warm clothing and piping hot food and drink."

And noise, Zaiyera came to learn.

* * *

Roaring laughter, loud talking, drinking games. Zaiyera thought she'd make herself dizzy from looking this way and that. As soon as they led the camels through the southern gate, Demenin Waypoint's joviality washed over them like a crashing wave from the Great Sea.

The smell of animals, gathered humans, baking goods, and roasting meats found her nostrils. Combined with the crisp cold air, Zaiyera found it overwhelming. She covered her nose with the free-hanging part of her keffiyeh, lest she inhale too deeply and freeze her brain.

To the right of their entrance, she noticed a crowd of people cheering. As they passed, Zaiyera saw through a gap in the spectators. Two men with axes stood side by side. They drew back and hurled the axes at a wooden target that looked to be thirty feet from their position.

The axes flew end over end. The sharp-bladed axe heads bit into their targets, the one on the right slightly high and left of the center. The axe on the left went far low of the center.

The axe thrower on the right raised his fists in the air. A good portion of the crowd roared and thrust their fists in the air as well, while others groaned. Money was then exchanged.

"A gambling game for throwing axes at wood?" Zaiyera asked.

"Popular tradition, in the north," Malker said.

"It looks like it could be fun," Zaiyera commented, "but it's a waste of a tree."

"Wood is far more common in the north than what you're used to," Malker replied. "The forests grow far and thick."

They found the stable in the west side of town. Three young grooms trotted out to meet them. The two girls were obviously sisters, as they had the same smile and similar facial features. While their eyes were as blue as Jaide's—lighter blue, actually—the third groom, the boy, had eyes the color of shimmering green zimastones.

The eldest girl greeted them in southern *Dreuga*. Zaiyera caught a word here and there, but her grasp of the northern tongue was less than proficient.

Malker said a few words to her, and the girl switched to tradetongue.

"You wish to house only?" the girl asked, "or house and exercise?"

"Housing will be fine," Dyren replied.

"I will have housing and—"

"Exercise for your friend," the boy spoke up.

Zaiyera's eyebrows raised, and she nodded.

The boy smiled at her. A very wide smile and bowed.

The younger of the two girls elbowed him in the side and looked at Zaiyera. "He thinks you're pretty, miss milady."

The boy's mouth bobbed open and closed several times as he struggled for a response.

"We don't see many people from so far south, miss milady," the eldest girl said.

Zaiyera smiled at the clearly mortified boy. "Em … how did you know I'd wish exercise in addition to housing for my companion?" She gave Sadiq a pat on the neck.

"Because you're Samhari, miss milady," the boy answered. "Your people like camels a lot."

Zaiyera laughed. "We like all animals a lot. My name is Zaiyera."

"Ary," the boy said. "My name is Ary."

"And he will pledge his undying love for you when finally he's old enough," the girl—probably his older sister—teased.

Zaiyera pretended not to notice the wave of red creeping up Ary's neck as he turned to glare at his sister. "May I take your reins, miss milady?"

"Must not pay much attention to Samhari," the girl said. "They don't use reins."

"Some do," Ary growled through his clenched teeth, the crimson wave washing over his face.

Jaide held a fist up to her mouth and cleared her throat. "Quite right you are, my friend Ary." She lifted the reins in her hand and made a regretful face. "Unfortunately, we of northern Samhar do not have the same level of affinity for the animals we share this world with, as our more southern kin."

The boy looked up at Jaide and frowned. "You're kind of pretty, for a man … hey!"

His sister elbowed him again, then whispered loudly in his ear. "That ain't polite, you straw head."

"Stop calling me that."

The older sister sighed. "Only housing for you two sirs?" she asked Dyren and Malker. "We give discounts to shadow hunters."

"That is correct, young lady," Dyren replied.

The girl bowed, then lightly slapped her younger sister on the side of the arm.

"Don't hit me," the girl protested, but she took the reins from Dyren and Malker and led the camels away.

"For you, sir?" she said to Zhuyun.

"I will follow the lead of my friends from Samhar, ah?" Zhuyun replied. "This hardy beast has borne me far and endured my endless chatter, ixu?"

"You sound different," the boy said.

"That is because I hail from a land far across the Great Sea, boy." Zhuyun spread his arms out wide. "A voyage of many days and nights aboard a ship with giant sails and long oars! It is a journey of great adventure, but not for the light of stomach."

The boy's eyes widened. "Did you see a great green diver? Atta says the Great Sea is home to great green divers that leap high out of the water."

Zhuyun's expression sank and he let out an exaggerated sigh. "Sadly, I did not. Ah! But now that you've told me, I can look for them the next time I sail the endless world of water, ixu?"

"If you please," the eldest sister said, tiredly, "the inn is there." She pointed to a building next to the stable. Like every other structure in Demenin Waypoint, it was made of light gray brick, and wood. "You'll be able to pay for your camels' lodging there. We can take your animals from here if it pleases you."

"Of course," Zhuyun said. He handed his reins to the remaining sister, as did Jaide.

"I'll let your soon-to-be-betrothed handle yours," Jaide whispered to Zaiyera as she passed.

Zaiyera coughed to hide her chuckle and turned to Sadiq. She gave him another pat on the neck. *"Ngomaila rafiki."* She reached out her hand to the boy. He hesitantly took her hand, then his fingers snaked between hers so that they were entwined.

She blinked, then lifted Ary's hand in front of her. "I … will need you to hold my hand lightly so that I can introduce you," she said as gently as she could.

"Oh." Ary uncurled his fingers in hers, and she held his hand to Sadiq's nose.

Once she finished the introduction, Zaiyera turned to Zhuyun, who'd waited behind for her.

"What was that you said to your camel friend?" Zhuyun asked. "I've not heard that before, ah?"

"It is a *Soloush* introduction of friends," Zaiyera answered.

They joined the others inside the adjacent inn where they secured lodging. Dyren, Malker, and Jaide sat in a couch near the room's central fireplace. The two shydon were deep in discussion while Jaide simply listened.

Zhuyun carefully removed his keffiyeh. His long single braid spilled out of the wrapping and fell over his shoulder. He swiped it behind his back and sat. "Deep conversation about our road from here, ah?"

"Winter is past its peak," Dyren replied. "Our path is still packed thick with snow and ice, but the season for blizzards and shard rain has passed."

"Both of those words sound unwelcoming," Jaide said. "I've heard of this blizzard you mention but haven't seen one before. And shard rain sounds most unpleasant."

"A blizzard can freeze you to death," Malker said. "Shard rain can kill you outright. The air gets so cold during a rainstorm that the falling droplets elongate as they freeze. "Armor is essential."

"What of our animals?" Jaide asked.

"Those native to Dor'haighen have adapted their own defense.

Rasadon lizards, for instance. Shard rain does nothing to them because their thick leathery hide has outer scales. In the winter, they grow thick fur between the plates of their scales, further protecting them. One of the hardiest animals you'll lay eyes on."

The junior shydon hunter pulled out a map of Dor'haighen and unfolded it. "We're here." He pointed at a spot at the bottom of the map. There is more than one route to the capital, and it all depends on the weather."

We're nearing the end of winter, so we shouldn't encounter any heavy snow. The snowpacks haven't melted yet, nor have the lakes begun to thaw." Malker glanced at his superior and cleared his throat. "Given that we still have several uses left of the swift basin, we should make Nanshaigha within two days."

Zhuyun scratched his head at that. "Our camels are more adapted to what we left behind, ah? I don't see them surviving in this world of snow and ice."

"He's right," Zaiyera said. "They'll not survive long, even if this frozen climate is in the end of winter."

"White camels live in this region near the border," Malker replied. "They are better adapted to the milder climate of Dor'haighen than their desert relatives. We will ride white camels from here and head northeast. Our first stop will be in Denberest. Normally we'd stop sooner, but we have ... an advantage to get us there quicker."

Zaiyera thought of Sadiq. How long would she have to leave her loyal friend here?

"At Denberest," Malker continued, "we will trade our mounts for rasadon lizards. They can move through the best and worst conditions Dor'haighen can throw at them. They'll get us to Nanshaigha well within the second day."

"Sounds like we've got ourselves a plan, yes?" Jaide said.

Malker looked up at her. "You're used to this kind of weather, aren't you, Viriksani?" He nodded at her keffiyeh. "Isn't your head hot, yet? Or is your head shaven?"

"I may hail from one of the most northern regions of Samhar, my good man," Jaide replied. "But I am still Samharan. My blood does not run so thick that I'm made for these frigid climes."

Malker shrugged and was about to say more when Dyren spoke.

"You can … trust the word of those you will buy your furs from."

Zaiyera kept her features neutral but nodded her acknowledgement. Was the senior shydon trying to be amicable after all this time?

"Due to the nature of its location," Dyren continued, "border town merchants specialize in garments to keep foreigners from freezing to death."

Dyren pushed away from the table and stood. "There are two garment shops in Demenin. Mention my name to either of them and they will offer you their wares at a discount." He waved to one of the serving staff. "The tab for this table will be settled by myself—Dyren Faust."

The server blinked in surprise but recovered quickly and bowed his head. "Of course, Senior Shadow Hunter. An honor to have you and your friends."

Dyren turned back to the table. "I must excuse myself. I have a contact here that I must search out."

"Perhaps we should meet back here before settling in for the night, yes?" Jaide suggested. "There may be news of the south."

"Good idea," Malker said.

"This evening, then." Dyren left.

Zaiyera, Malker, and Zhuyun watched him leave while Jaide gave her order to the server.

"That was as close to an apology as I've ever seen from him," Malker said.

Zaiyera shrugged. "We're all born into customs and beliefs that might not be compatible with others."

"Yet the sign of a wise person," Zhuyun said, his voice taking on an uncharacteristically sagacious tone, "is the ability to listen and see without judgement, and recognize when one fails to do so." He nodded his head in the direction of the door Dyren had exited through. "I believe he's coming to realize his earlier failure to do the latter, ah?"

The meal turned out to be the hottest, spiciest, and hardiest Zaiyera had ever experienced. She'd asked for something to warm her up, and the server had brought a large bowl of what he'd called jackroot stew.

"Best food I've had in many days," Malker said. "No offense intended," he said to Zaiyera and Jaide, "but there's nothing like a big pot of piping hot stew to warm the bones."

"It is good food, Malker Argen," Zaiyera agreed. "Rather spicy to my tongue, but not without flavor."

Zhuyun pushed back from the table. "Indeed. My belly is full and my bones are warm. I'd like to see more of this cold place. I doubt we'll have to look far for fun, ixu?"

It turned out that fun wasn't far away. Despite her typical reluctance—or perhaps, because her companions wished to strike a heavy blow against it—they explored the streets and found fun seemingly around every corner. They returned to the south side of town to watch the axe throwers—a different pair, this time—and made their way along the streets on the east end of town. Given that Demenin Waypoint wasn't a big city by Dor'haighen or Samharan standards, most of the homes sat on top of each other two stories high.

"You're going to hurt your neck if you keep arching it back like that," Zhuyun teased.

Zaiyera tore her gaze from their surroundings to see the Yuntaiman smirking at her. Having abandoned his keffiyeh, he now wore his long braid wrapped around his neck.

"So much brick and wood," Zaiyera said. "I've never seen this much in one place."

The corners of Zhuyun's eyes crinkled as his smirk turned to a smile. "Amazing, isn't it? In all my travels across the Great Sea, and even within my own homeland, peoples and places can be so different, yet at the same time, so similar."

"And in that spirit," Jaide declared, "I'd like to hear about these adventures of yours, world traveler. Perhaps you'll infect me with this same itch to see the world over as you have, yes?" She gestured at a building with a sign over the door that read "Roosters' Truce".

"Ah, but can my stories possibly compare to the one behind how that inn received its name?" Zhuyun replied.

Jaide gave him a slap on the back. "Let's find out!"

As intriguing as she found the Yuntaiman, Zaiyera's thoughts went to her loyal friend, Sadiq. "Will you be here a while, my … friends?"

"Oh ho!" Jaide leaned back and swept her hand out at Zaiyera. "Good people we must truly be, Zhuyun Xaiylin! Did you hear that? Friends!" She elbowed the Yuntaiman. "Though it did sound strained, as though she had to chew on a mouthful of sour root. But I'll take it."

Zaiyera leveled on Jaide what was quickly becoming a signature mock glare, just for her. "I won't be long."

She heard Jaide's receding sarcasm as she walked away. "Probably off to some stern meditation session …"

Zaiyera moved quickly. Though it wasn't far past midday, night fast approached. A second walk through town would hopefully solidify the surroundings in her memory before it got dark.

After having to ask directions twice, Zaiyera finally found the stable. She knocked on the large barn door and waited.

She turned her back on the door and wrapped her arms around herself. The sun hadn't completely set, yet the air had already gone cold. The scattered serenade of night insects crept out of grass and random piles of straw and along walls and corners everywhere. As daylight faded, torchlights were lit in sconces on building walls and inside places of public gathering.

Behind her, the muffled sound of an unlocking bolt preceded the creak of the large barn door as it opened.

A little head with sandy blond hair and bright green eyes appeared in the opening.

Zaiyera smiled. "Hello, Ary."

"Oh, I … hello, miss milady." He pushed the door open. "I didn't know you was coming, otherwise I'd have gotten him ready for you."

"I'm just here to visit." Zaiyera smiled at him again, and the boy blushed redder than she'd have thought possible.

A loud groan sounded from farther in the barn. Sadiq's long head appeared out of one of the stalls and turned in their direction.

Ary laughed. "Hasn't made a sound all day."

"He is my very good friend," Zaiyera replied.

"I'll be sure to take good care of him as long as he's here, miss milady."

Zaiyera entered the stall and gave Sadiq a pat on the neck. "*Migisa, rafiki,*" she whispered in *Soloush*. Sadiq grunted and swung his head around into her side. Zaiyera chuckled.

Ary scratched his dusty blond head. "I'll just be about my work, milady. Let me know if you need anything at all."

"Thank you, Ary," Zaiyera said.

As soon as the boy was gone, she wrapped Sadiq's neck into a tight embrace. She pulled back and wiped away a few tears. "I don't know how long I'll be gone, my friend." She sniffed. "And I don't know if I'm treating you fairly."

Sadiq moved to a pile of straw and folded his legs to lay down. Zaiyera waited till the camel was comfortable, then sat and leaned against him.

"Your life is not mine to command, dear friend. Should I turn you loose and hope we meet again? Should I have done so long before we reached this unfamiliar land?"

Sadiq groaned softly.

Zaiyera thought about all the adventures she and Sadiq had experienced together. They'd covered so much of Samhar. She thought of every time they'd stopped to rest. She'd never tethered him or used reins to ride. Even in the presence of other camels roaming wild in the desert, he'd never left her to join them.

In the end, whether it was because she understood that he was content to wait for her, or that she rationalized her own selfish need of him, Zaiyera decided to ensure his comfort until her return.

She settled herself with her back against his side, smelling his strong camel odor, feeling the rise and fall of his side with each breath. Soon her big companion's body heat warmed her, and she forgot about the biting cold that nipped at the air outside.

Zaiyera's eyes drooped. She absently gave Sadiq a pat on the side, her breath going heavier and more rhythmic. Her eyes fluttered one last time before slipping shut.

Again, Aried Dom had defeated her. Again, and again, and again.

Zaiyera sat on her backside, seething at the sound of the older boy's laughter.

Beside her hand lay her new blue-steel scimitar. Just a month earlier, Grandma Ochima had tasked a blacksmith with its forging. The ka had settled just outside Kuzenei for several days to trade. Grandma Ochima had taken what few coins she had and Kushtanji robes she'd handwoven and gone to the blacksmith.

Zaiyera had been practicing with her first steel scimitar all day, as well as the streamdancing she'd begun to learn. Father's pride at her possibly becoming the first bladedancer—one who could dance the stream while fighting with the sword—motivated her and weighed heavily on her shoulders.

Despite other girls in the ka wanting to learn the blade after watching her, Zaiyera still remained the only girl to do so. Perhaps if she could just defeat Aried.

Two days after they'd left the outskirts of Kuzenei, Grandma Ochima had come to her with a long, crushing hug, and a half day of conversation.

"You've grown so much, my Zai Zai," Ochima had said. "Promise me you will continue to be who you are, no matter if it is to train as the boys do, or craft and forage. Your father, my son, sees something special in you, as do I. Let it grow, Zai Zai."

Grandma Ochima blurred behind the tears brimming in young Zaiyera's eyes. "Not yet Uta. Don't ..."

Grandma hugged her. "Would you deny me my reward, my beloved girl? Beloved Shakimah calls to me. I hear Her call louder every day."

Zaiyera had fallen asleep against Grandma Ochima and awoken to the sobbing. She opened her eyes and saw Grandma Ochima lying on a raised platform, her hands resting peacefully on her stomach.

For several heartbeats Zaiyera stared. Uta wasn't gone. Just sleeping.

But Uta's chest didn't rise and fall as it should with each breath. She lay too still. And there was the blue tinge to her skin.

The entire ka gathered around Grandma Ochima and sang beau-

tiful songs of mourning that gradually changed to celebration. Stories were told, tears were shed, and a life now transitioned was honored.

Hours later, the ka *started to drift away for sleep. Zaiyera sat cross-legged, staring out at the starlit sky, wrapped in the dark cloak of night.*

Father came to her carrying something long and wrapped in a purple and red cloth. He sat down beside her and for a long time they said nothing. Finally he set the item next to her and left without a word.

The blue-steel scimitar. Uta's gift, and the one Aried Dom had disarmed her of.

He stood over her, laughing. "You're getting better. It took me longer to sit you down this time. You're good, Zaiyera." He shrugged. "You'll just never be as good as me. And your shiny scimitar won't change that."

He hadn't meant it as an insult to Grandma Ochima. Even Aried wouldn't sink that low. But the words hurt. That hurt mingled with her frustration and rage at her failure—at Aried's superior laughter.

Zaiyera picked up her scimitar and stood. She settled back into her stance. Today she would beat him. Today she would take away his smile.

They clashed again. Aried taunted. Zaiyera surprised him. She took his superiority. She took his smile. She murdered her innocence.

19

Zaiyera bolted upright and opened her eyes. After a few fluttering heartbeats, she forced her breathing to slow. Behind her, Sadiq lay contentedly chewing his cud. He swiveled his head around to look at her, jaws moving side to side.

Feeling the weight of her decade-old yoke settling back on her shoulders, Zaiyera climbed to her feet. "I'll see you before I leave, my friend." She patted him on his hump.

Sadiq grunted.

Further down the barn toward the door, Ary raked out a stall while a white camel supervised in the far corner. He looked up when Zaiyera came by.

"I came to check on you, milady. You looked so peaceful, begging your pardon for saying so. I didn't want to disturb you."

"How long have I slept?" she asked. Given her dream, she wouldn't have minded being woken.

"Not long," Ary replied. "There's still plenty of drinking and talking left to do, if that's your concern." He went back to raking.

Zaiyera's nose gave an involuntary twitch when the smell of camel dung and urine mixed with straw and dirt in an enclosed area finally hit. Ary seemed not to notice.

"I'll come to visit him once more before I leave," she said. "I hope to return before spring is over." She hesitated.

Ary stopped raking and looked over his shoulder at her. When he saw her expression, he smiled. "I've met a few Samhari people, milady. I understand how he's your friend." He jerked his head in the direction of Sadiq's stall. "I'll take extra good care of him; stretch his legs and keep him warm."

At the sight of Zaiyera's relieved smile, the boy quickly turned away. "Ain't no problem, really. We treat the animals well, here."

Zaiyera didn't miss the blush rushing up the boy's neck to redden his face. She'd been used to northerners being red mostly from being burned by the sun. Did they always blush so often? "My deepest thanks, Ary. I'll see you tomorrow."

She quickly navigated the streets of Demenin Waypoint. Even though she'd been here for hours, now, she still marveled at the architecture, so foreign from Samharan cities. Homes and buildings alike were made of wood and brick. Giant piles of straw crouched in corners by two-wheeled, two-handled wagons.

Zaiyera found The Roosters' Truce with little difficulty. As soon as she opened the door, a wall of thunderous joviality crashed into her ears. She sifted through the crowd, squinting until her hearing adjusted. Some sort of music battled the cacophony of yelling and roaring laughter.

She moved along the wall while searching for the others. A duo of men held small round instruments with long handles tucked under their chins. Attached to the handles were long cords that extended down to the circular body. The men slid long slender instruments up and down the cords. They reminded her of a variation of the musical instruments people played in the southernmost regions of Samhar.

In the giant cauldron of loud music and conversation, the aroma of cooking food, pipe smoke, and many bodies clustered together, Zaiyera almost missed Zhuyun's waving hand just ten feet away.

"We were beginning to wonder if you'd opted to go to sleep early," Malker said once she sat down.

Jaide sat with her head leaning on her fist. "We thought to wait for you before we ate, but we figured you were likely having your meal with your camel."

The mention of food made Zaiyera's stomach growl, so she missed the Viriksani's jab. She waved down a server and placed her order.

"According to our friend here"—Zhuyun opened a hand toward Malker across the table—"Dor'haighener spiced chaffa is something not to be missed. We decided to wait for you, that we might enjoy or suffer together."

Malker snorted.

Zaiyera hadn't realized how cold she was until she felt the warm stew going down after the first couple bites. Once she finished, they ordered a mug of spiced chaffa. The steaming pot came with two chaffa leaves at the bottom. The leaves were as large as a person's hand, folded several times.

While the tea steeped, they talked of the journey ahead. Malker again cautioned them that while Dor'haigheners considered this time of year to be mild weather, the others might still freeze to death.

"Ah, but the cold here feels not so bad," Zhuyun replied. "In Yuntai, we get lots of rain, and that means moisture. Nothing colder than damp cold that hangs on you, ixu?"

Zaiyera listened while the others discussed the next step in their travels to the capital. Ever adventurous, Jaide seemed ready to simply gear up and hit the road, stopping as little as possible. The Viriksani warrior seemed to share Zhuyun's hunger to see new places and peoples. The two talked as though they'd been traveling comrades for years. Zaiyera wondered how Zhuyun would react if Jaide revealed her secret.

A faint streak of the hunger hit her just then. The telltale sensation of being hot and cold at the same time sent a nervous chill through her stomach, but she shoved it down. The others continued talking and joking about various things. Between a humorous rant involving Zhuyun's father and an angry heron, the Yuntaiman twitched an eyebrow at Zaiyera.

The expression came and went so quickly that everyone but

Zaiyera had completely missed it. Was the timing coincidental, or did Zhuyun somehow know when the withdrawal struck?

"As much as it galls me to admit it," Jaide said after taking another sip. "This hot spiced chaffa you northerners drink feels good going down, and better in my belly."

"Why does it gall you to admit the truth?" Malker asked.

Jaide lifted her mug at his smug grin. "That, right there. You Dor'haigheners possess a boisterous pride that's groan-worthy, yes?"

"If it makes me feel less likely to freeze solid in this ice world," Zaiyera said with a forced smile, "I'll gladly inflate a northerner ego."

"Ah! Here's to that!" Zhuyun raised his mug.

Everyone lifted their mugs in toast.

They shared an animated conversation and many laughs during the walk back to the inn. Try as she might, Zaiyera only half listened, contributing shallow laughter during moments of humor.

The hunger sent her thoughts back to the many painful childhood sparring matches against Aried Dom, the older youth mercilessly dishing out beating after beating. She remembered the bruises and frustration. She remembered the fear.

Father had supported her, yet emphasized that in life, there would be many things to strike fear in her. Life could be beautiful and rewarding, but also brutal and relentless. So she'd kept going back, receiving her painful defeat time and again.

Zaiyera remembered the first time she'd touched the stream. She remembered her parent's shock when they'd discovered this, and how they'd rushed her to the *ka's* master streamdancer to begin lessons. Zaiyera had learned quickly how to incorporate dancing the stream with dancing the sword. She'd secretly practiced that, determined to master the technique. One day, it would help her defeat Aried. Unfortunately, that day did come.

She blinked away the dark path her memories had taken and looked to the starlit sky. Her breath clouded in her face as the temperature continued to drop.

From the corner of her eye, Zaiyera noticed Zhuyun shooting glances at her. As nervous as the Yuntaiman made her of late, she would need to have a conversation with him before the uncertainty got the better of her.

Zaiyera let out a long cloudy breath through her nostrils. It seemed like everything sought to drive her mad, lately. First, her inability to escape becoming entangled with the two shydon hunters. Then the inability to passively dance the stream as often as she needed to, to stave off the hunger. Now it was her uncertainty about what Zhuyun knew or suspected about her, and how he felt about it.

Her thoughts grew so undisciplined during their walk that she didn't bother trying to participate in conversation any longer. What had Zhuyun been trying to teach her back in the woods? Zaiyera had gone over it time and again in her mind, visualizing the movements and the effects she'd felt.

She thought of their nearly fatal battle with *kivuli dayasa*. Though Shatr had cut through his efforts as effectively as any other dancer she'd fought, the sheer magnitude of power the man had brought against them was too much for any one person to stand against. She needed to find another way to deal with him.

They entered the mostly empty main room of the inn to see Dyren Faust waiting for them. Typical of the senior shydon's personality, he went straight to the point once they were seated.

"My contact has eyes and ears across Dor'haighen," Dyren said. "They've brought him news of the assassination of Sheik Jegried. He received a letter via storm hawk two days ago from Nanshaigha." He looked them over while the information sank in.

Malker leaned forward and rested his forearms on the table. "What of the king, sir."

A shadow passed over Dyren's expression, but it disappeared quickly. "Nansheig is keeping that information close. He hasn't, or at least, *hadn't* informed the captain of the Nanshaigha Shadow Hunters as of the sending of the letter."

A letter that arrived here two days ago. Zaiyera chewed on that bit while Dyren spoke.

"We may well find our division mustered and ready to march by the time we arrive," Malker said.

No one said anything to that, but the way Zhuyun tapped his fingers together suggested he may share Zaiyera's doubts about how informed anyone but the king would be. Even Jaide's responding nod was stiff.

Dyren stared at the table. "Perhaps. It matters little. We'll know the whole of it once we arrive." He looked up at the others. "We leave before dawn."

* * *

It took all Zaiyera's restraint to keep from looking back over her shoulder at Demenin Waypoint, receding in the distance behind them. The previous evening had ended with her spending some time with Sadiq before going to sleep. She'd refrained from seeing him before their departure. Temporary or not, that goodbye would have been too much to bear.

Now astride her white snow camel, Zaiyera looked around at a world covered in white powder. Having escorted many Dor'haigheners across central Samhar from coast to coast, she'd heard many a story about a world opposite her own. While hers was a brown world of sand and dunes sparsely populated by trees and small plant life, Dor'haighen was a land of towering trees and mountains covered in snow.

Zaiyera had never truly believed her charges when they'd told her that even the ponds and lakes froze solid in the winter. Now, encased in layer upon layer of warm furs, her doubts had long frozen brittle and shattered in this brutal cold.

She tugged at the head wrapping covering her head and most of her face; much thicker than her traditional keffiyeh from home. She'd learned quickly to breathe through the thick material, to avoid the freezing air stinging her lungs.

Ahead, the two Dor'haigheners wore little more than hide jackets —which they wore open—and trousers. Both men sat erect astride their white camels, swaying back and forth between the two humps.

"It's an odd ride," Zhuyun said, "sitting snuggled between these two humps. I wonder if I even need this saddle."

"It does feel kind of strange," Jaide agreed. "Feels like I'm wedged between two soft hills."

Malker frowned at her. "You've never ridden a two-humped camel? You live in a world of camels."

"You're not wrong, Dor'haighener," Jaide replied. "But in Viriksan, we require speed more than comfort." She patted one of her camel's humps. "Try to imagine these towering humps flopping around when this thing tries to run."

"I'm sure it manages fine when it needs to," Malker said.

"Yet their single humped more slender relatives manage even better, yes?"

Malker looked to Zaiyera, who shrugged.

The trail leading west finally bent north, taking the party through small snow-carpeted woods and the occasional sprinkling of homes. On their pass through one such community, Zaiyera noticed smoke lazily drifting from a short, rectangular tower attached to the back of a house.

"Malker," she said, pointing to the house. "There is a fire in that home? Perhaps we should see if they need help."

The shydon hunter chuckled. "All is fine, my southern friend. That is a chimney. Do you remember the tavern and inn we stayed in last night? Remember the little square brick thing with the burning wood in it?"

"That's what that is?" Zaiyera replied.

"I supposed you wouldn't have noticed," Malker said, "since we arrived in the day, and no hearths had been lit, yet."

"Fascinating that people actually start fires inside a home or building," Jaide said.

"You don't have hearths in your homes, then?" Malker asked. "What about cooking your food?"

"When we cook with fire," Zaiyera answered, "we do it under the canopy of Shakimah's queendom. The nights are cold, but among

Kushtanji, a big bonfire with food and family provides warmth." She looked to Jaide Amadi. "What of you in the north?"

The Viriksani warrior blinked and looked off in the distance. "Similar. Dinner is the meal shared together by the community, though in pockets of communities. Since our cities house hundreds to thousands of people, it would be one mighty bonfire if we all gathered at once, yes?"

They climbed a hill covered in ankle-deep snow. It crunched under each step as the camels high-stepped up the hill.

Dyren's jaw tightened once they reached the top. Zaiyera followed the senior shydon's gaze to see a ceiling of dark clouds drifting in from north and slightly east. "That looks ominous."

"Your eyes tell you true," Dyren said. "If there were no trees, you'd see what looks like a distant fog, but is actually a snowstorm. We must find shelter and quickly."

"I see nothing for miles," Jaide said. "We might have to take cover in the woods, yes? Or at the base of a hill opposite the storm."

"We'll need to shelter against some large conifer trees if we can't find an alcove or cave," Malker said. "Our snowstorms don't skin you alive, but they will bury and freeze you solid."

"How long till that reaches us?" Zaiyera asked.

"Two hours," Dyren said. "Maybe three."

"How far are we from the next city or town?" Zaiyera asked.

"Close to the same amount of time," Dyren said.

Zaiyera pursed her lips. "How fast can the camels move in this?"

"They can high-step trot as long as it's not as high as their knees," Dyren said. "They can move in snow up to their flanks, but it would be slow going from that point. What are you thinking?"

"I'd wanted to save the use of the basin for more friendly terrain," Zaiyera answered. "But even a fast trot might keep us ahead of that storm."

She braced herself for an argument from the senior shydon, but he nodded.

"A good idea. We might be able to reach Denberest before the storm swallows us."

Zaiyera climbed down from her camel and fished the basin and waterskin from her pack. She offered the water to her camel, but it showed no interest. Zaiyera stepped away and blinked. "She won't drink."

"Oh, I'd almost forgotten." Malker twisted in his seat and rummaged through his travel pack. He produced a brick of some sort and handed it down to Zaiyera. "I'd climb down and help, but it would be an ordeal getting back up. I'm not good with these animals."

Zaiyera reached up to accept the brick. "What is this?"

"Salt block," Malker said. "I knew we'd be using the basin again, and Dor'haighen camels require even less water than their southern cousins. We keep a salt blocks in their pens that they lick and bite. They like it."

"Good thinking, Malker Argen," Zaiyera said. She offered the salt block to her mount, who licked it several times, then took a small bite. The other camels did the same. She waited patiently until the animals tried to dip their heads to lick the snow. The riders held their animals' heads up by the reins while Zaiyera offered her camel the first drink.

Soon the party descended the hill and took to the trail, the camels moving at a gallop across patches with little snow and trotting through the thicker areas.

From time to time they looked to the north. The storm crawled closer. The camels proved to be efficient in picking the best paths with the shallowest areas of snow, or the firmest snowpacks. They managed a gallop as frequently as a trot.

The wind picked up. The chirp of sparrows and native birds grew quiet. Only the caw of the crows and ravens broke the building silence. Soon, even the hardy black birds faded away to be replaced by the cavernous sigh of the encroaching storm.

Despite the growing desperation of the situation, Zaiyera smiled at the sight of white fog blowing across the ground ahead.

"Kind of reminds you of home, yes?" Jaide asked beside her.

"It does," Zaiyera replied. "Except it won't scratch our eyes and fill them with grit."

White flakes meandered their way down from the sky, drifting left to right to collect on the ground. Zaiyera's mouth fell open at the sight. "Moon and stars." She held out a hand. "It's amazing; beautiful."

Malker grinned. "I envy your first experience of it. I admit Samhar had a similar effect on me, though I was more able to appreciate it at night when the sun wasn't trying to kill me."

Jaide pointed at the approaching clouds. "As that seeks to kill us?"

Malker conceded the point with a nod.

Denberest came into view just before the storm caught them. Tiny pinpricks of torchlight shone from the distant town, a beacon of hope for the storm-harried riders.

Zaiyera's sense of wonder at the drifting snowflakes changed to urgency. The snow now fell diagonal in much the same manner as rain. It was better than rain, in that they weren't immediately soaked, but visibility grew steadily worse.

She squinted through the white deluge, looking for anything that gave an indication of their whereabouts. Her efforts were futile. All around she saw nothing but whiteness. Even the towering trees became little more than a silhouette and were only visible when they were close enough.

The storm howled through the woods and fell over them in gusts. Zaiyera immediately knew when her ear, or wrist, or any other patch of skin was exposed, for the cold struck like a knife.

"I see nothing!" she yelled. "Are we lost?"

"Stay close!" Dyren Faust replied. "Stay very close. We can lose each other with but ten feet between us. We're nearly there."

Zaiyera and the other non-Dor'haigheners had no choice but to trust the shydon.

The cold patiently wove through layer after layer of Zaiyera's furs until it finally reached her body. Had she been dressed just a bit lighter, she would likely have succumbed to the cold that already had her teeth starting to chatter. Beside her, Jaide faired only a little better.

They were practically in front of the town of Denberest by the time its lights came into view. Zaiyera couldn't have imagined a more welcome sight.

Malker pounded on the thick wooden door with the side of his fist. A slot at eye level opened to reveal a pair of astonished eyes that looked them over. Dyren moved his camel closer and flashed the shadow hunter insignia on his coat. The eyes widened further and the slot shut.

Bolts and locks clicked, and the door swung open. "Apologies, noble shadow hunters. Please c'min out of this nasty storm."

The old doorkeeper stepped out of the way and opened the door wide enough to admit the riders still astride their camels. He shut the door with a huff and patted the snow off his furs.

"I can only think of one thing might have two shadow hunters on the road in a storm like this," the doorkeeper said. "You must've got word about the king gathering his forces, hmm?"

Dyren and Malker glanced at each other.

The doorkeeper caught the exchange. He slid a few strands of wispy white hair out of his face. "You've heard word, surely? There's some kind of tension between the capital and some eastern city that sits right near the border. Some place called Rexzen. Apparently the king and the emperor of that place had an agreement that didn't go as planned."

"What agreement was this and what happened?" Dyren asked. He climbed down from his camel and stepped up to the old man, who shrank away.

Dyren Faust held up a hand. "Be at ease, good man. We've been away, and I would know any news you have."

The man relaxed a little and wiped his hand over his head. "Well … I can't say as I know everything, but what I've told you is the most of it that I know. Word came through Denberest some days ago, so there's no tellin' what's happening now."

"Thank you for the information, Mr …"

"Laxy," the old man said. "Beggin' your pardon. Shoulda offered that sooner."

"Our thanks, Mr. Laxy," Dyren replied. "We remember."

The old man perked up at that and bowed deeply.

"What's with that last bit?" Jaide asked. She looked over her shoulder at the old man, who'd resumed his post in the enclosed little shelter to the side of the giant door.

"It's short for 'the hunters of shadow remember,'" Malker replied. "It's a maxim of our organization."

The storm spilled into the little town of Denberest, but the walled city proved a safe haven from what would have been a hopeless situation had they arrived but an hour later.

Dyren Faust led them to the stables where they bartered their camels in exchange for a pack of rasadon lizards. "We'll select our mounts in the morning," the senior shydon said. "For now, we'd best replenish our supplies and find an inn. This will be our last night of comfort until we reach the capital."

"How far away are we?" Zaiyera asked.

"In less hostile weather, five days by lizardback," Dyren replied. "If we use your … the basin, about two days."

Zaiyera nodded.

The party went quickly about the business of replenishing their food and gear. At the Dor'haigheners' advisement, Zaiyera, Jaide, and Zhuyun traded up and acquired warmer furs, head, and face wrappings.

Dinner in the inn's common room passed in a quiet and subdued manner as each of them digested the old doorkeeper's words.

Zaiyera replayed in her mind what she saw of the shydon hunters' skills with the blade and the stream. She mentally went over her sparring match with them, as well as Zhuyun and Jaide's match.

She took a sip of hot spiced *chaffa*. The Viriksani would be all but helpless against *kivuli dayasa*, and that worried her. Zaiyera would need to speak with Jaide in private about her concerns.

Zhuyun, on the other hand, had already battled their enemy and proven capable of some form of defense and indirect offense.

Zaiyera replayed their defeat by the man, which worried her further. He'd nearly killed them all, the first time they'd fought him. Now, as she thought about these worrisome developments, *kivuli dayasa* was likely in his hibernation state that Malker had spoken about. He'd awake even more powerful.

They agreed to meet back in the common room at dawn to break their fast. Zhuyun and Jaide must have sensed her mood, for they simply wished her a good sleep and went to their rooms.

In her own room, Zaiyera undressed and slipped under the covers of her bed. For a time, she lay on her side, staring at the wall. Her mind raced through the news of the apparent tension between the king of Dor'haighen and this emperor in the east, in a place called Rexzen.

She thought about her vision from the basin. That colorful place brimming with people on the surface, and with a grim underbelly inhabited by streamdancers used as living weapons. But none of that mattered. Their only concern was *kivuli dayasa*. If they were to survive they must find a different way to deal with him, or they would be obliterated. Zaiyera clamped her eyes shut. As if all those dark thoughts were an invitation, the hunger struck.

20

If Zaiyera had been blessed with any form of luck, it was to not suffer from claustrophobia, as most Kushtanji did. She lay in bed and stretched.

Another bit of luck was that the only other woman in their party happened to be passing as a man, so it would have looked suspicious, had Jaide asked to share Zaiyera's room. This afforded her the opportunity to passively dance the stream in her room to stave off the withdrawals for a while. The hunger remained, however. Barely sated. Dancing the stream outside the confines of a structure left her more satisfied until the hunger struck again. Inside, she could only feel so much of it. Better than nothing, however.

Zaiyera yawned as she sat up and ran a hand over her face. Outside, the weather was still and silent. Everything lay covered in a soft blanket of snow, the only sign of the storm's passing the previous night.

She arrived downstairs to see only Jaide and Zhuyun waiting. Shortly after, however, Dyren and Malker arrived. They reached the stable to the familiar smell of camels, but also something else.

"What is that?" Jaide said. She held a finger under her nose. "Smells musty, gamey, and stifling all at once."

"That would be the mounts who will bear us the rest of our journey," Malker said.

The stablehands led them to the lizard pens where they each selected a mount.

"Good morning," Jaide said to a huge scaly gray and white-patched lizard with thick legs and a long body. "You stink."

The lizard swiveled a blue eye in her direction, and a long forked tongue flicked in and out. It turned its head toward her and flicked its giant tongue at her again.

"What's it doing with that thing?" Jaide asked, stepping back.

The blonde woman chuckled. "Tasting the air. Or rather, tasting you. It's how they catch your scent in the air."

"Charming," Jaide said. She looked at the lizard again. "You still stink."

"Yet another new experience, ah?" Zhuyun said to Zaiyera.

"Another of many we're likely to have in this land," Zaiyera said. She watched as the two Dor'haigheners mounted their lizards. She also watched that big thick tongue flicking in an out.

She'd seen the smaller lizards common in Samhar use their tongues to catch insects. Zaiyera tried to do a mental calculation of the proportionate size of this lizard and herself.

"No need to fear, milady," the stablehand said, laughing. "I know that tongue looks strong enough to grab hold and suck you into that big mouth, but I assure you they're docile. You've nothing to worry about unless you suddenly wake up a rodent, small to medium-sized bird, or a particular kind of leaf."

"Thank you," Zaiyera replied absently. *"Migisa rafiki,"* she said softly in *Soloush*. "Hello, friend. Will you bear me on our journey?" She ran a hand down its neck, careful not to cut it on those rough scales. The lizard tilted its head in her direction and flicked its tongue out.

The ride out of town and into the wild was the oddest experience Zaiyera had had on the back of any animal. The reptile's relaxed walk consisted of curling its body left to right, swinging its front outside leg forward for the next curling step. The effect had the rider partially turning to one side while moving forward. Zaiyera concentrated on keeping her stomach steady, lest she empty it.

"You'll grow accustomed to their unusual gait," Malker said. "It's straighter when they move faster."

"Then … let's move … faster," Jaide warbled.

Zaiyera looked at the other Samharan woman and wondered if her complexion had the same greenish tint to it. She pressed a hand to her churning stomach. Probably.

Once they spurred the lizards into a trot, their gait did indeed smooth out, as did the swirling in Zaiyera's stomach. She glanced down at her lizard. Its neck fully extended as it moved, short thick legs pumping quickly back and forth. "Such a drastic difference in the ride," she said.

"That it is," Dyren agreed. "Only their walk takes some getting used to. Every other speed is a bit bouncy, but the ride is easier."

"Horses are still best, ah?" Zhuyun said. "But this is not bad, given the terrain we cross."

"You have horses in Yuntai?" Zaiyera asked. "We have them in Samhar, but they're rare from the central region northward."

"We do," Zhuyun replied. "All across Yuntai."

"I've never ridden one," Jaide said. "But I hear they are the swiftest animal one can ride."

"Only on solid ground," Malker said. "The rasadons of Dor'haighen do not run as fast as a horse, but they're still swift. And thick snow barely slows them."

"We're sufficiently outside the boundaries of Denberest," Dyren stated. "Now is a good time to use your basin, Zaiyera."

The party stopped, and Zaiyera filled the basin. The riders drank, then lizards, and soon they were moving again.

Zaiyera learned quickly to pay attention to where the sun sat in the sky, for its light reflection on the ice stung the eyes.

The lizards ran tirelessly through the day and into the night, the riders equally alert.

The effects of the basin started to wane close to evening of the following day. The lizards fell back to a leisurely trot, before finally returning to their sideways curling walk.

"We should find shelter for the night," Dyren said. He pointed to a nearby mountain strewn with rocks, boulders, and hardy green-leaved trees. "The wind blows in from the northwest. We should be able to find shelter in a crook of those mountains and build a fire."

The senior shydon led them past several bends in the base of the mountain that Zaiyera would have thought sufficient. The sun had nearly dipped below the western mountains by the time Dyren found a suitable location.

As soon as they moved into the bend, Zaiyera understood his decision. Their camp sat nestled against an almost U-shaped crook in the base of the mountain. Though the west-facing part of the camp opened just enough to be a potential trap, should danger find them, it completely sheltered them from the northwest winds. It was a risk they'd have to take.

Malker and Jaide left to hunt and later returned with several large rabbits. The Viriksani woman foraged some edible green plants and roots as well.

In the warmth of the cook fire, Zaiyera crossed her legs and sat erect. She closed her eyes and went through the confrontation with *kivuli dayasa*. She contemplated the immense power he accessed, and how he wielded it. She remembered how Shatr still managed to cut through the stream, and the tainted dancer's surprise. She couldn't count on that surprise again.

She remembered how aggressively he manipulated the flow against them. Unlike a normal streamdancer, this man could continuously access the power and attack; seamlessly touching the stream and manipulating the flow to his bidding.

Zaiyera sensed someone's approach and opened her eyes to see Malker squat beside her.

"Apologies for disturbing you," the young shydon hunter said. "I'd planned to wait until your meditation was finished … to ask if you'd like to spar."

Zaiyera raised an eyebrow, but seeing the effort it took the proud

Dor'haighener to come to her, she bit back the sarcastic remark. "If you wish."

"This should be interesting," she heard Jaide mutter to Zhuyun. The Yuntaiman's expression stayed neutral. Not neutral, Zaiyera realized. Studious.

They moved to the far side of the campfire and faced each other. Shatr at her side, Zaiyera bowed her head to Malker, who returned the gesture.

Malker drew his sword and started to circle. This time, however, Zaiyera merely drew her scimitar and remained where she was, only turning to keep him in front of her.

The shydon tilted his head, then shrugged. Zaiyera held her blade out at her side, tip just above the ground.

Malker came in with an overhead chop that she quickly side-stepped. Not quick enough.

The attack missed, but Zaiyera was too close. Malker spun, turning his back to her, and hooked his elbow around. Zaiyera turned away. The blow missed her head, but caught her shoulder. The weight and strength from the hit sent her stumbling forward.

I'm slower. She spun to face her opponent, who looked at her with suspicion. He hadn't expected to land that elbow, she realized. A gust of cold air stirred her head scarf. She glanced down at the snowy ground as Malker approached.

This time, Zaiyera moved with him, angling sideways, forcing him to pursue. This time she felt the stiffness of her movements, the drag of her feet through the snow. The cold. It held onto her like a giant hand, stiffening her joints, slowing her movements. She hadn't experienced cold like this, before. Hadn't realized the effects it could have. The nights in Samhar were cold during the non-summer seasons, but not like this.

She felt a wave of gratitude toward Malker. The situation might have been dire, had she learned this for the first time in a life-or-death situation.

Zaiyera took a deep breath and adjusted her stance. No relying on speed.

Malker moved in with a quick stab.

Zaiyera saw the feint for what it was, and simply stepped back. Malker darted forward for another stab, then quickly flipped his sword up and around in a sideways chop.

The sword passed over Zaiyera's head when she ducked. Crouched, Zaiyera stepped past him as she turned and snapped her scimitar upward. Malker brought his sword down to block. The two blades sang as they clashed.

Malker would try to use his strength to force Zaiyera's blade down. He easily outweighed her by fifty pounds or more and was physically stronger, and he knew it. So did Zaiyera.

As soon as their blades touched, she turned in the opposite direction and brought Shatr around and down toward his back.

Malker knelt and thrust his sword backward over his head. *Not bad,* Zaiyera thought. *Seems you're a little faster than I thought.* She made a mental note that the cold also didn't seem to affect his movements as it did hers.

They clashed again and again. Malker continued the pursuit, attacking low, high, then feinting to avoid becoming repetitive.

Zaiyera went with it, studying the way he moved. This one had a mind for offense more than defense, yet his defense seemed relatively solid.

Her joints were starting to warm, as was her confidence in moving in this white powder.

Malker prodded with several feints, which she ignored. As he jabbed with one more feint, Zaiyera sprang into an offensive flurry.

She instantly had him on his heels. The man snarled, blocking and parrying, working for an opportunity to counterattack. She gave him no such opening.

Malker turned in a fluid motion and swept his sword around in a horizontal cut toward her head.

Zaiyera ducked and turned. She slapped the flat of her blade against his midsection as she passed.

Malker growled and slapped his fist to his stomach.

He might be frustrated, but Zaiyera found herself panting after the brief exchange. They had executed but a handful of exchanges, yet she heaved with every breath. Her limbs felt heavier, and even her scimitar felt many times heavier in her grasp.

The young shydon hunter shook snow out of his gray and black hair and came in again. He quickstepped in with a stab, then cut left. When Zaiyera parried the blow, he leapt forward and smashed his shoulder into her.

It was a move she would normally have avoided, but she was winded. The strength of the blow combined with the larger size of the man knocked Zaiyera clean off her feet. What little breath she had left blasted out of her, but she managed not to gasp long enough to hit the ground in a backward roll. She stopped in a crouch and sucked in a wheezing breath.

To the side, Jaide and Zhuyun watched, the former's brows knitted together in puzzlement, the latter still watching with that same unreadable expression.

Zaiyera stood, chest heaving in a show of catching her breath. It was easy enough, given the display was more sincerity than bluff.

Malker looked not at all winded by their exchange. He approached with his sword up before him, his steps measured but confident.

It must be this climate, Zaiyera realized. *The air is so cold. But why can't I breathe?*

Malker stopped a few feet away. "Perhaps we should stop for now," he said. "You haven't yet adjusted to the cold or the altitude yet."

Zaiyera wanted to keep going. She wanted to push through and finish the match. Malker's skill was formidable, but she could beat him, *would* have beaten him already, had she not been so ill-affected by this environment.

"No," she said. "I'm fine."

"You're swaying on your feet, Zaiyera," Malker said.

She tried to blink through the dark spots in her vision, while watching Malker straighten and lower his blade.

Zaiyera glared at him and tightened her grip on Shatr. If the fool wanted to drop his guard, she'd make him pay for it.

They silently faced each other, neither making a move. He couldn't beat her. They both knew it. Under any other circumstances she'd have already finished this. Zaiyera closed her eyes, took a long deep breath, and opened them again.

Where is your ego, Zaiyera?

Hands clenching Shatr in a trembling, white-knuckled grip, she stared at the shydon hunter, who returned her gaze with a perplexed frown.

Zaiyera barely noticed Malker's confusion as she looked right through him into a time many years ago. A time when despite her best efforts, she'd been defeated over and over again.

"Raise your sword," she said to Aried.

"Zaiyera," her opponent said. "Why? You're barely standing. If you keep this up you'll pass out …"

"RAISE YOUR SWORD."

Aried took a step back. He blinked at her.

So many defeats. So many matches ending with her flat on her back, the tip of his sword at her throat. "You're dead," he'd say to her. "Again." Then he'd laugh. A game. Nothing but a game to him. She'd been nothing more than entertainment. No matter how hard she trained, only once had she come close to defeating him. And oh had he punished her then. His strikes had come harder and faster, his offense aggressive to the point of brutal.

And the mocking laughter.

"You're good for a girl," Aried would say. "Maybe use that sword to dig up roots faster, eh? Why not just leave the swords alone? You're never gonna beat me, Zaiyera. Never. You'll always lose."

The cold of the frosty evening fell away, forgotten. She remembered a promise she'd made to herself, long ago. She would never feel helpless again. She would win or she would die, but she would never know the bitter taste of the helplessness Aried had inflicted on her.

Zaiyera leapt across the eight feet between them. Malker growled and brought his sword up to deflect the incoming chop of her scimitar.

The piercing ring of steel striking steel shattered the silence of the camp. Zaiyera barely registered the openmouthed frown on Malker's face. She came at him again. A swipe high, an underhand chop. She struck again, forcing the shydon hunter to use more power to defend.

Just when Malker began to adjust to her offense, Zaiyera switched to the more traditional style of Samharan sword combat.

She didn't have much time. She refrained from taking large breaths, the sting to her head and lungs would be overwhelming. Malker tried to form a counterattack, but when the young shydon parried her overhead chop and cut back, Zaiyera simply spun away.

Malker brought his sword up to block Zaiyera's descending blade. But the blow had no power behind it. It simply slid downward. Having expected a heavier blow, the shydon overbalanced. Zaiyera pursued step-for-step with the stumbling shydon, and in three moves had his sword knocked wide, and the edge of Shatr pressed against his throat.

Malker glared at her over the top of the blue-steel blade. She saw the icy fire blazing in his angry blue eyes. Those eyes divided into four, then back to two, then four again.

Zaiyera blinked. Her vision blurred. She shook her head and let out a sigh that echoed in the darkness that enveloped her.

21

Zaiyera awoke to the warmth of a crackling campfire on her face. A dark sky filled with stars stared down at her. As memory returned, she imagined the stars likely gazed down on her with disapproval.

"And so she wakes," she heard Zhuyun say.

She lifted herself up to her elbows. Zhuyun smiled at her from a few feet away. The clang of steel rang behind her, and she twisted to see Dyren and Jaide sparring. At the edge of camp, one of the huddled rasadon lizards let out an openmouthed hiss as it settled beside another. The giant reptiles lay unmoving, aside from the occasional flick of a forked tongue.

The sound of grinding drew her attention to the far side of the fire. Malker sat cross-legged, sliding a whetstone along the blade of his sword. His eyes flicked up to meet hers once, then he returned to his business.

Zaiyera looked down at her lap for a few heartbeats. She got up and dusted the snow off herself, then moved around the campfire to where the shydon hunter sat. She stopped a few feet away. He ground the whetstone along his sword again.

"May I sit?" she asked.

Malker never looked up. "I do not own this land."

"Does anyone truly own any land?" Zaiyera asked. No response came, so she sat.

For a while she remained silent, staring into the fire while Malker Argen continued to sharpen his blade. Across the camp Jaide and Dyren's sparring match grew more vigorous. Given her homeland's proximity to Dor'haighen, the Viriksani woman looked to have less difficulty with the thin air and climate.

"I ... my apologies, Malker Argen."

The grinding grew louder. "What is there to apologize for, Zaiyera Tuneesh?" Every word sounded strained.

Zaiyera opened her mouth, then closed it. "That ... I turned a friendly sparring match hostile."

"Is a sparring match not a simulation of the exchange of hostilities? Are we not practicing how to kill an adversary?"

"It's also an opportunity to learn in a safe space," Zaiyera replied.

Malker stopped and stared into the fire. "Well, we're safe. You're awake, and my throat isn't slit. Sounds like the match was a success."

The distant ringing steel and the crackling campfire filled the silence while Zaiyera struggled to think of something else to say.

"It's a horrible feeling, vulnerability."

Having moved to stand, Malker stood half crouched and frowned at her. "What?"

"The feeling of vulnerability," Zaiyera said. "Of ... being unable to defeat your opponent."

Malker's face tightened. "Thank you for that." He stood.

"I swore to myself that I'd never feel vulnerable again, no matter the cost. Even if it means my demise."

Confusion mixed with irritation on the young man's age-creased face.

Zaiyera took a deep breath and pushed on. "During our match, I felt that vulnerability creeping up on me, and I succumbed to it."

"I believe you conquered it," Malker replied, his tone laced with acid.

"No. I failed. My ego drove me for the rest of that match, all the way into unconsciousness."

The shydon hunter softened a bit. "That must have been what you were feeling along with that claustrophobia when the shadowlancer dropped that dune on us."

Not at all. "There was a time in my youth when someone made me feel vulnerable; inferior. I projected him onto you."

Malker's responding chuckle held little mirth. "I understand this is your awkward attempt at an apology, my lady miss, but it's doing a fair job of further bruising my ego."

Zaiyera huffed quiet laughter at that.

Malker squatted beside her. "Only a blind and deaf man could miss the fact that you have some past damage that haunts you. Whatever burden you carry that keeps you so silent and your laughter forced, I wish you well in resolving it."

The junior shydon hunter stood. "I can't think of many injuries easily mended alone. But if it can be done, Zaiyera Tuneesh will work her way through it." He bowed at the waist and went to unpack his bedroll.

She felt eyes on her and looked to the side of the fire to see Zhuyun watching. The Yuntaiman met her eyes with the heaviest gaze she'd ever seen from him. He gave a quick nod and looked away.

Zaiyera went to her own pack to untie her bedroll.

Jaide and Dyren finished their match and returned to camp. Jaide spoke in her usual jovial manner while even the ever-serious senior shydon hunter spoke in a lighter tone than usual.

They shared dinner and conversation over a range of topics. Zaiyera forced herself to take part. She genuinely laughed at one of Jaide's quips. Mostly, though, she listened to everyone with half an ear as she contemplated Malker's words and concentrated on keeping the hunger at bay.

She lay awake long after everyone had gone to sleep and Malker took first watch. When sleep finally found her, it came with dreams of repeated defeat, humiliation, a final triumph, and the tragic creation of a powerful weapon.

* * *

The bear found them just as they were mounting the lizards.

Zaiyera had secured her backpack on her shoulders and the rest of her supplies on her mount's rear, when they saw the large white animal in the distance. It meandered left to right across their field of vision.

Zaiyera stood frozen, her hands still raised, halfway finished tying the last pack. "Do you think it'll move on?" she asked Dyren, who'd already mounted his lizard. The reptile shuffled beneath him and let out series of short hisses.

"Unlikely," the senior shydon replied. "We need to be gone now, before it gets too close. Rasadon lizards only have one major predator, and that's it."

A roar came from the edge of the camp to the right, where the protective crook of the camp began. A second bear rounded the corner and galloped toward them.

The lizards hissed in alarm and took off.

"Hey, now!" Zhuyun protested at his fleeing mount.

Jaide had already lifted herself up on one foot and was about to swing her leg over when her lizard bolted. Her foot got caught in the stirrup and the giant reptile dragged her away.

Zaiyera's mount turned and fled so quickly, its thick tail struck her in the back of her shoulder and sent her flying.

Malker and Dyren fought to regain control of their thrashing lizards, but unlike any other animal in the world, lizards could bend and curl their bodies violently. They flipped their bodies sideways, curling left to right like giant fish flopping out of water.

Dyren and Malker struggled with the reins, but the thrashing mounts dislodged the shydon hunters. Relieved of their burdens, the lizards fled, tails snaking behind them as they disappeared into the distance.

"*Jakta skree.*" Malker ripped his sword from its sheath.

Dyren drew his sword as well. "We'd not outrun a bear in the best conditions. We'll have to fight them."

Zaiyera drew Shatr. "Maybe we can scare them off if we work together."

"Cave bears don't discourage easily," Dyren replied. "Especially when there are two of them."

They turned back-to-back, Zhuyun and Zaiyera facing the bear at the side of their camp, Malker and Dyren facing the other. The first bear waded in, and Zaiyera took a swipe at its face.

It snorted and shrugged away to stalk around the side, big dark eyes boring into her. The bear's head was the size of her torso. The indentations its paws left in the snow were easily bigger than her head, and the claws six inches long.

"Keep formation and work our way out," Dyren said. "We can't get trapped between them.

The group moved sideways. The nearest bear pursued but didn't strike.

Zaiyera stole a glance past Dyren at the second bear, who'd nearly reached them.

The closer predator circled around and took another swipe. Zhuyun hopped back, then sprang forward. With a twist of his wrist, he thrust his staff straight into the bear's muzzle and twisted. The bear recoiled with a snort and came in again. Zhuyun's staff flashed forward in a confusing corkscrew. The flurry distracted the animal enough that he landed a few solid blows to the head, which did little more than anger it, but still bought them time.

The second bear trotted along their path of retreat to head them off while the bear to the rear followed.

"If we can't discourage them," Malker said, "we'll have to kill them."

Despite the serious danger they were in, and the undesirable prospect of being eaten alive, Zaiyera thought furiously for an alternative.

"Can we deal enough injury that they'll give up?"

Malker responded with a nervous laugh. "You'd have to deal enough damage to get past the rage. Hurting a cave bear enough will make it *very* angry."

From the corner of her eye, she saw the golden hue of Dyren's dance-resin trailing his movements.

"Reserve yourself," the senior shydon commanded when Malker began to touch the stream. "On my signal, Zhuyun and Zaiyera. Both of you attack the one that follows. Just one quick burst of offense, then run."

"On your signal," Zaiyera replied.

One hand on his sword, the other turning at the wrist, Dyren Faust touched the stream. "I know your feelings for animals, Zaiyera of Kushtanja. Pray this works, or we must kill them both."

Zaiyera did just that, offering a prayer to Shakimah that they wouldn't be forced to kill these animals, who were likely a mated pair.

"NOW!"

As quickly as Zaiyera sprang forward, Shatr leading, Zhuyun shot past her. The Yuntaiman struck with such speed and force, he left the bear momentarily disoriented and stung. The whirling staff struck it several times in the face by the time Zaiyera dealt it a cut across the paw as it tried to swipe.

The bear roared and rose up on its hind legs. Zaiyera turned and ran, Zhuyun beside her. She heard the snorting sound of pursuit, but they kept running as Dyren had instructed.

Zaiyera focused on the ground in front of her, the danger behind, her pumping legs, anything to distract her from that glorious flow of the stream in which the shydon hunter dipped his hands.

Dyren skidded to a stop, at the same time spinning and swiping both hands left to right. A transparent blue arc slammed into the ground, creating a wave of snow and ice that crashed into the bears.

Zaiyera looked over her shoulder and saw nothing but white carpet. It looked as though the animals had never been. She and Zhuyun trotted to a stop. "You buried them alive."

Dyren started running again. "I bought us time but it won't take them long to dig out!"

Zaiyera and Zhuyun looked at each other and took off again.

"We must find Jaide," Zaiyera said.

"Hopefully he still lives," Malker replied. "The way his mount dragged him off by the ankle, all it would take is one swat to the head by that thick tail ..."

"There." Zhuyun pointed ahead and to the left, where a solitary figure hiked toward them. "A lucky one, ah?"

They altered course and ran for Jaide just as a distant roar sounded from behind. The Viriksani must have heard it as well, as she turned and fled ahead of them.

Dyren and Malker guided the party to a patch of woods where they stopped to catch their breath.

"Glad to see you all right ..." Malker trailed off and tilted his head at Jaide. "You've ... lost your headwrap."

A flicker of uncertainty flashed across Jaide's face. It was there and gone in a flash, but Zaiyera caught it.

"Yes, yes," Jaide said, flipping her exposed wet hair behind her back. "Long hair, face devoid of stubble. You won't be the first, tenth, or hundredth person to tell me I'm rather pretty for a man, Dor'haighener."

"Well, I mean"—Malker stumbled over his words while Jaide stared at him.

Zaiyera hid her laughter with a cough.

Zhuyun wrapped his long thick braid around his neck and looked around at the sparsely vegetated woods filled with hibernating trees. "If the bears here are anything like their smaller relatives in my homeland, they can smell food for miles. And since those back there have deemed us food"—he pointed back the way they'd come—"I'd make a fair guess they might still be after us, ixu?"

"Strong possibility you're right, Yuntaiman," Dyren said. "We should keep moving. If they're hungry enough, they'll pursue us until they cross easier quarry, or we tire out."

"Ah! Lucky for us we have an advantage there."

"Unless you packed that basin in your bags," Jaide said, "which is the only passenger on your lizard, now."

Zaiyera pulled the bowl free and sat it on the ground. "Fortunately for us, I keep it in my personal pack." She looked at the others with a half-smile. "Never know when an animal might take off."

"Since we don't run as fast as a camel or those giant reptiles," she said, pouring water into the basin, "I estimate we have just enough to get us to your Nanshaigha. Or close enough, anyway."

Dyren responded with a stiff nod. "Then let us be gone now. The day is early."

They passed the basin around. Once empty, she stuffed it back into her pack. "Let's go."

They hiked through thick patches of snow and ran when the terrain grew less difficult. Not long into their speedy trek, the Dor'haigheners removed their hide jackets and tied them to their backpacks.

"How can you not be on the verge of freezing?" Zaiyera asked, looking in disbelief at the two men. They wore only thick woolens, now.

"The same way we wondered how you didn't die of heat exhaustion in your sweltering homeland, Samharan," Dyren replied.

Zaiyera grinned at the senior shydon's attempt to break the ice between them.

Their fortune at eluding the cave bears came at the price of hilly terrain and knee-deep, soft snow. Despite the aid of the swift basin, the trek grew more laborious.

"As cold … as you find it … here," Malker huffed from in front, "You're fortunate it's not winter. The temperature … drops so low … your hair and even eyelashes … freeze and break off. And further north … the air can freeze a pot … of boiling water … the instant you toss it … into the air."

"That sounds … like a tale growing more grand with each telling … Dor'haighener," Zaiyera replied. "You try … to impress your foreign guests?"

He smirked at that. "This is … spring, Samharan. Take off … your furs and … feel it fully."

When the effects of the swift basin waned, they stopped long enough to eat and drink from it again.

To her astonishment, Zaiyera found that the muscles in her legs didn't complain as the terrain started to incline, though it did leave her more easily winded. She hoped they wouldn't crash into a week-long slumber once they reached their destination. That random thought had her wondering if their unnatural endurance would come with a cost to be paid in full once they stopped. The animals hadn't exhibited any such effects, but then, neither they, nor the riders had drunk from the basin more than once at a time. This was their second round without stopping.

They passed through thinly wooded areas filled with naked-limbed trees where small and larger birds roosted, the former chirping at them as they flitted through the woods. The shydon hunters stopped at the top of a snow-packed hill and waited for the others.

"That," Dyren, nodded at a range of mountains looming over a forest below, "marks the beginning of the end of our journey. Those mountains separate the Denberest territories from the capital Nanshaigha."

"Please, Dor'haighener," Jaide said, leaning against a tree. "Please tell us we'll have the joy of climbing all that." She waved her hand at the mountains in mock excitement.

"We will," Dyren replied, "but there's a trail in that direction." He pointed left, where the mountains sloped downward. "Also, mind. As thin as you've felt the air become, it will be thinner still, up there. Take care you don't push too hard too fast and black out."

Zhuyun looked up at the sky. "At the pace we've kept, we should reach the base of that mountain at dusk."

"Then let's get moving," Jaide said, "before this super water wears out."

They turned sideways, half stepping half sliding down the soft snow of the hill.

"Would that we had shields to ride down this hill on," Malker said. He stumbled and fell waist deep in a thick patch of powder. "We could have ridden all the way down to the woods."

"Why *don't* you use shields?" Zaiyera asked. "I've seen pieces of art from foreign traders depicting northern warriors with them."

"Of the four classes of warriors," Dyren replied, "shadow hunters alone do not carry shields."

"Most don't even carry weapons," Malker added.

"Truly?" Jaide said. "Interesting. I would have thought any warrior would wish to have a blade to fall back on if a fight got too close."

"Not those who devote their life to mastering the art of lancing the stream," Dyren replied.

"Yet you two carry swords," Zhuyun said.

"We do," Dyren replied.

"Sworddancers," Jaide waggled a finger at them. "I've heard of your type. You dance the stream while wielding the sword. A rare skill, yes?"

"While we're called sword*lancers* in the north," Malker said, "it is a discipline most don't aspire to."

"Why's that?" Jaide asked.

Malker picked his way around a protruding boulder and grabbed hold of a sturdy bush just beside it. He eased himself down past the boulder. "For one thing, it's a lonely …"

Zaiyera raised her eyebrows when he trailed off and looked to the sky. "Malker. What do you see?"

From high in the gray sky, a distant shriek answered.

22

"Moon and stars," Zaiyera breathed. "What now?"

The party had stopped at the thunderous sound, all eyes focused on the overcast sky. The shriek split the silence again, closer.

"I don't know what that is," Jaide said, "but I'm happy not finding out."

"Frost worva," Dyren said. "Hurry!"

They scrambled down, no longer concerned with being half buried on their slide to the bottom. They reached the base of the hill just ahead of a mini avalanche.

Zaiyera scrambled out of a pile of snow and grabbed Zhuyun under his shoulder to help him out. The sputtering Yuntaiman held up a hand once he'd gotten to a kneeling position.

They heard another screech and looked to the sky. Something with a long body and huge wings glided into view.

Zaiyera clenched her teeth. "That thing looks big even from this far away."

"Keep moving," Dyren yelled.

The slog through the shin-deep snow took a lifetime. Zaiyera looked to the sky after another screech. The thing Dyren had called a frost worva banked toward their left on its descent. She looked ahead to the tree line, mockingly close yet so far away.

"We're not gonna beat that thing to the woods," Jaide said. She, too, turned her blue-eyed gaze to the sky, worry creasing her brow.

The trees were close, but the white-gray monster was closer. Long before they could have reached the sanctuary of the trees, the monster landed behind them in a ground-shaking explosion of snow and ice.

They turned and shielded their eyes against the blast, then drew their weapons. Jaide looked at her shamshir and chuckled nervously. "A toothpick would do my chances just as well against that horror."

Twenty feet long from fanged mouth to the tip of its horned tail, the frost worva threw its head forward and screeched at them.

Malker's golden resin flared as he scratched curled fingers through the air, left, then right. He turned his body and brought both hands around in a downward swing.

At the same time the junior shydon ripped into the stream, Dyren Faust slapped his hand into the air, much like one would slap their hand into the surface of a pond. His lance-resin flared to life around his hand like a splash of water.

Dyren made a grasping gesture and drew his hand back. He guided the flow from the stream and wrapped it around his turning hand. With small, conservative gestures, he molded the flow, spinning it in his hands, and thrust his right hand toward the worva's cavernous maw.

A transparent blue shard-disk sped across the space between him and the giant scaly beast. It stopped just in front of its mouth and discharged a barrage of tiny blades down its throat.

Malker's blue arc sliced through the air right behind the disk. It struck the worva across the face just as it coughed on Dyren's assault. It recoiled when the blades bit into the inside of its neck, then fell sideways when the arc blade struck the side of its head.

"Conserve yourself," Dyren said to Malker. "We combine our efforts to delay it. Too much effort to kill."

The shydon hunters moved their hands in unison, their lance-resins intermingling as they touched the stream together.

"Keep moving," Dyren said to the others.

The worva scrambled back to its feet, shook its horned head, and screeched again. It tucked its leathery wings back and stomped in pursuit.

Dyren and Malker continued to move their hands, the latter following his superior's gestures as closely as possible. Once they'd drawn what they needed from the stream, they manipulated the flow using the technique named after it.

They swung their hands up and over their heads repeatedly as though swinging a long implement. A giant transparent whip—larger than if they'd individually created one—swirled in the air between them. Together, they swung their hands down.

They worva flinched when the whip struck it across the head. Dyren and Malker flicked their arms upward, lashing it up across the face again. Several more times they struck the winged reptile. They started moving backwards as they struck, the whip growing slightly more transparent, smaller with each lash.

Zaiyera and the others raked through the snow ahead of the shydon hunters, creating a trail for them to back into the woods.

The worva's red eyes blazed with fury as it stalked toward them. Every lash of the ethereal whip succeeded in knocking its head aside, but it continued to advance. Those murderous red eyes, so stark a contrast to its white-gray body, bore into them with an angry awareness that sent a shiver down Zaiyera's spine.

"The neck!" Dyren yelled.

The shydon hunters swung their arms around and back, then lashed forward. The whip wrapped around the worva's neck. Dyren thrust his hand into the air and pulled a smaller whip from the stream. At the same time he lashed one of its wings, causing it to curl away. He and Malker yanked their shared whip down.

The smaller whip stung the worva's wing enough to draw its atten-tion. The distraction occupied it enough for the shydon hunters to catch it off guard. They pulled the beast into an awkward stumble forward where it fell onto its shoulder.

Dyren and Malker released the flow and ran for the woods. The others having scraped a trail to the woods, the shydon hunters were able to make a more swifter retreat.

Another earsplitting screech preceded the crack of breaking tree trunks.

Zaiyera looked over her shoulder. The worva plowed through the woods, snapping branches and knocking over smaller trees while snaking its way around larger ones. It extended its long neck forward and snapped.

"Haiya!" Jaide squeaked in a distinctively non-masculine voice. "It's right on my back!"

"Sounds like it bit you someplace intimate," Malker remarked. "Run faster."

The worva followed on their heels. The sound of an impact and the groan of cracking woods preceded a frustrated screech. Zaiyera looked back. The worva whipped its head left and right as it pushed and thrashed against the trees. It rammed itself repeatedly against the large trunks. Snow rained down from the shaking branches, and the tree trunks cracked and splintered.

They kept running. When the worva broke through, it fell forward. Luck was with Zaiyera as the worva's mouth was closed. It still managed to her in the back and sent her sprawling. She barely registered the muffled 'crack' she heard when the beast crashed into her.

Malker stopped and grabbed her under the elbow. He hoisted her back to her feet and they continued their flight. They passed between the largest trees and clusters that might slow the worva down.

Zaiyera looked ahead with relief as Zhuyun slipped between another pair of giant heavily barked stoic greens. Her relief evaporated when she heard his shout.

"No, no! Not this way!"

By the time she realized what he was saying, they'd followed him between the trees and come to a wall of tree trunks so tightly packed that even they couldn't pass, it was too late.

Jaide crashed into Zhuyun in a tumble of limbs and furs. "Up we go, Yuntaiman," she growled, helping him to his feet.

"Dead end," Zhuyun said.

They pressed themselves against the wall of trees just as the worva's scaly horned head pushed through. It opened is fanged maw wide and lunged for them, snapping just short of Zaiyera's and Dyren's faces.

It drew back and rammed its shoulders into the obstructing trees again and again, snapping no more than a foot short of its prey.

"Lovely breath," Jaide gasped, turning her head away.

The worva thrashed and snapped against the unyielding trees. It screeched in their faces, straining mere inches from its quarry.

It snapped at Zaiyera again and opened its maw wide. She received a clear view of rows of knife-like teeth with bits of rotted flesh between them. The worva stretched its tongue toward her in desperation, the long fleshy thing trembling in front of her.

Whether it was survival instinct or the refusal to be basted by that slavering tongue, Zaiyera snarled and snapped Shatr from its sheathe in an upward arc from left to right. A foot length of tongue flopped to the ground in a splatter of blood.

The worva let out a high-pitched scream almost like a yelp. It threw its head back, spitting blood everywhere, some of it spattering over the five companions.

They watched the horned head drop to the ground repeatedly as it retreated back through the trees, tromping back the way it came.

Backs flat against the trees, no one dared move until they heard the telltale swoosh of giant wings when the beast took flight.

"Let's get moving," Dyren said.

They followed Dyren Faust through the woods, the senior shydon picking the thickest patches of trees to move through. Zaiyera tried to look through the treetops, but despite their barren branches, they were still too thickly intwined to see much of the sky. "You think it's still out there?"

"It's definitely out there," Dyren replied. "They're stupid in some ways and smart in others. It'll try to wait us out."

Zaiyera looked about the eerily quiet woods. No chirping birds or even buzzing insects. The area felt like it was holding its breath.

They reached the edge of the tree line with little more than an hour before the sun dipped behind the mountains. Dyren held up a hand to stop the others and crept out a few steps to peek at the sky. He quickly ducked back in. "It's circling."

"How long do you think it'll wait?" Jaide asked.

"Depends on how hungry it is," Malker answered. "Considering that and how it's likely enraged at losing part of its tongue, we may have to wait till sundown."

The party settled in to wait out the circling frost worva, who occasionally split the silence with an enraged screech.

"What a horrible sound," Jaide said. "Someone really ought to have a talk with that thing, yes?"

"Ah, good idea," Zhuyun replied. "You first?"

Zaiyera shrugged out of her backpack. She raked a thin layer of snow away from the base of a tree and settled down against it. When she sat her backpack down, she heard a clinking sound and froze. She looked down at the pack. *Moon and stars.*

A sinking feeling weighed down her stomach. Zaiyera gingerly untied the pack, opened the top flap, and reached in. She lifted out a thick cloth to the sound of more clinking and let out a resigned sigh.

"What is it?" Jaide said, half turning. She noted Zaiyera's expression, then looked at the cloth in her hand. "Oh, no."

The others gathered around as Zaiyera crossed her legs and opened the cloth in her lap. The swift basin lay in pieces inside the cloth, shattered, like their chances of returning to Samhar from the capital in less than half the normal time.

Malker closed his eyes. *"Jakta Skree."* The curse came out of his mouth in a white puff.

"Should have known that beautiful basin wouldn't survive once we left Samhar," Jaide said. "Without Domahir to protect it."

"Who is this Domher you speak of?" Zhuyun asked. "One of your gods?"

"Domahir," Jaide replied, "is the spirit of good luck who rides the winds of Samhar." She rubbed the bright blue stone on the chain around her neck. "Shiny things keep him, and most importantly, his luck, nearby."

"We'll need to have a talk with your *Domahir* about crossing country lines some day," Malker said. "Looks like we'd better enjoy whatever brief time we have in Nanshaigha. It'll be a swift ride back with little rest along the way."

Zhuyun squatted beside Zaiyera and picked up a piece of the ruined basin. "I don't suppose," he said, turning the piece over in his hand, "that reassembling the basin will restore its helpful properties."

"No," was all Zaiyera could bring herself to say. Her thoughts traveled across the hundreds and hundreds of miles back to Samhar. Had *kivuli dayasa* already gone into hibernation? Had he awakened? How many more had he killed? How many more villages and cities had he razed to the ground or scoured of life? How many more, by the time they returned to confront him?

Dyren went back to the edge of the woods and peered at the darkening sky. "If it's still here, it hovers in the clouds, just out of sight."

"But it can still see us, though we can't see it," Zaiyera replied, remembering how they'd heard the beast long before seeing it.

"Only in the thinnest clouds," Dyren replied, still scanning the sky. "Its vision at night is no better than ours. Our only advantage is that it doesn't know which direction we travel. Once we reach the mountain, it won't be able to safely get to us. As soon as the sun dips, we go."

They secured their gear and waited until the sun dipped below the mountains. Dyren kept the party close together and led them. As silently as possible, they crunched through the snow, constantly looking to the sky.

Zaiyera glanced about the expanse they traversed, feeling terribly vulnerable. Her labored breath sounded like a shout through the quiet darkness out in the open like this.

When their destination finally came into view they angled left, toward the trail Dyren had spoken of.

The hairs on the back of Zaiyera's neck stood on end. She looked over her shoulder and her heart almost stopped. The frost worva quietly glided out of the darkness, claws extended and ready to snatch them up.

"DROP!" Zaiyera hoped they reacted in time; she didn't wait to see. She collapsed onto her stomach in the snow. Less than a heartbeat later she felt the swoosh of the beast's passage and heard the frustrated screech that followed.

She hurried back to her feet and sprinted for the trail with the others. Zaiyera noticed the golden glow of Dyren's lance-resin as he moved his hands. She wondered if this was the Dor'haighener form of dancing the stream, with movements more conservative than that of Samharans.

The frost worva let out a long piercing screech as it banked to the right.

"Whatever I do," Dyren said, "keep moving."

"No fatal heroics, shydon hunter," Jaide replied. "We need your austerity to kill the humor on our journey, yes?"

Dyren didn't respond. He continued to move his hands, his golden lance-resin glowing like a beacon in the night.

The worva glided toward them again. Blood streamed down its mouth like crimson saliva.

When the transparent whip drew out of the air over his head, Dyren leapt sideways and lashed one of the horns extending backward from the base of the worva's skull. The whip wrapped around the horn.

Dyren Faust bared his teeth and growled. With the momentum of his falling weight, the senior shydon hunter yanked the whip down with all his strength.

The worva might be twenty feet long, might outweigh them several times over, but its neck was too long, its head not large enough to withstand the pull at its horn as it flew by.

The worva's scaly white-gray neck curled around when its head jerked sideways. At the same time, the weight of the falling beast launched Dyren Faust into the air.

It hit the ground in an eruption of snow and soil. The flying debris blasted into Dyren as he fell.

Malker slapped his hand in the stream and swept it at the ground. A blue arc hit the snow in front of him and sent it piling under the senior shydon hunter.

Dyren fell fifteen feet and landed flat on his back in the mound of snow. He disappeared with a loud puff.

Zaiyera looked at the dazed worva while the others ran to dig out the shydon. It had skidded a good way back, and now scrabbled to right itself. It gave its head a shake.

"Got ya!" Zhuyun grabbed hold of Dyren's coat and together they pulled him out.

Moments later they were again running for the trail, practically hopping through the shin-high snow.

A screech from behind spurred them on. Zaiyera looked back and saw the relentless beast stand. It extended its great leathery wings and crouched. With a great flap, it leapt into the air.

They reached the mountain trail and kept running. Zaiyera's foot nearly swept out behind her when she stepped on a patch of ice. Only the nearby Malker kept her from a painful face-plant.

They followed Dyren up the tricky path, navigating around patches of ice and grabbing hold of foliage within reach to aid their climb.

The frost worva rose up behind them with a flap of its wings. The wind buffeted the five companions, but Dyren urged them to keep going.

Zaiyera tried not to think about that thing grabbing her in one of those huge claws and carrying her away. She chose to interpret the screech as one of anger, that the worva couldn't reach them.

She could no longer ignore the temptation to look when she felt a heavy thud from below, followed by the sound of falling rock. The worva clawed desperately at the ground below, sliding down as much as moving up. It barked out a series of short screeches, fumbling its way up the slippery narrow trail.

They reached a flat point in the trail and stopped briefly to look down at the struggling reptile, now mostly a shadowy silhouette in the failing light.

"Keep going," Dyren said. "We don't want it to take off again and try to land here."

They crossed a path of flat terrain and continued their ascent. More sounds of slipping and scrabbling came from downhill. With a final screech of frustration, the worva leapt away from the mountainside.

They climbed in silence as they listened to the diminishing sound of its flapping wings.

"Endless … excitement," Jaide huffed. The ever-increasing altitude finally having an effect on the Viriksani.

Even Zhuyun labored more than usual, though with him it was barely noticeable. "I wouldn't mind if you … tell us your beloved capital … is on the other side of this mountain, ah?"

"It is," Dyren said. "Talk as little as possible until you've adjusted to the air up here. We'll stop for you to catch your breath if we can. Altitude sickness isn't a fun experience."

They did have to stop, several times. Zaiyera and Jaide weren't able to maintain the brisk hike for long before having to stop. As soon as night fully arrived, the temperature plummeted and continued to drop with every foot they climbed.

Zaiyera covered her face up to her nose so that only her eyes were visible.

Dyren and Malker donned jackets and fur hats with flaps that covered their red ears.

"We're nearly to the top," the senior shydon called back.

By the time they crested the last hill, darkness had enveloped everything. Occasionally the full moon peeked at them through gaps in passing clouds. Zaiyera held her fur scarf over her mouth and looked up to her right. The enormous shadow that was the rest of the mountain towered over them, and she was glad they didn't have to climb that way.

Dyren and Malker walked to the end of the trail and looked over the side.

"We've reached Nanshaigha." Dyren pointed down. "Capital of Dor'haighen, and the seat of her power."

Zaiyera looked down into a valley of darkness lit by countless pinpricks of torchlight. She took in the sight with openmouthed amazement. The lights spread all across the huge valley, from one end to the other and a great distance back. If those lights told truly of Nanshaigha's size, the great city could hold two Shanhazais and a large village.

The sound of a bowstring drawing taut, and an unfamiliar voice pierced her reverie.

"Dach'desisa."

23

A brief exchange in the tongue of Dor'haighen, and a flash of the shydon hunter insignia had the party descending the hill with an armed escort. Five hidden scouts had revealed themselves and bowed in deference to Dyren first, then Malker.

Zaiyera wondered where shydon hunters ranked in Dor'haighen society.

"Am I correct in assuming," Jaide jabbed a thumb over her shoulder, "that that was some variation of 'stay where you are or die?'"

"Close enough assumption that you'd have survived the encounter," Malker said. "*Dach'desisa is Dreuga* for "stay where you are or we will shoot you."" He shrugged. "More or less, anyway."

Jaide arched an eyebrow. "More or less?"

"There are words in *Dreuga* that don't translate to tradetongue or other languages, Viriksani."

"Ah," was all Jaide said in response.

At the front of the procession, Dyren Faust conversed with one of the scouts, though they spoke too quietly for Zaiyera to hear. The other scouts spoke *Dreuga* around them. None seemed particularly friendly, but they didn't seem hostile either.

Zaiyera moved closer to Zhuyun, who smiled at her approach.

"Ah! Looking for conversation you can understand, my Samharan friend?"

"You must be thrilled, Zhuyun," she said. "Another foreign city to visit in your travels."

"Indeed," Zhuyun agreed. "Though regretfully, I'll not have much time to enjoy it. Our errand wouldn't permit my normal indulgence, ixu?"

The chirp of crickets as well as the unfamiliar rattling of unfamiliar insects heralded their approach to the walls of Nanshaigha.

Zaiyera looked at the traveler from faraway Yuntai. "Why *are* you involving yourself in this, Zhuyun?"

"Why?" he repeated.

"You have no stake in this. Samhar is not your home, though of course I welcome you as though it were. Dor'haighen is equally foreign to you."

"You already know this, Zaiyera my friend," Zhuyun replied. "I am a traveler of the world. I collect sights, sounds, experience, and knowledge. I weave all of these things into the tapestry that is my life."

"You could easily do that without the danger of being obliterated by a tainted streamdancer," Zaiyera persisted.

Zhuyun conceded the point with a nod. "If you welcome me into your home out of the rain, and your roof starts to leak, should I just leave to find a different house? Or move to a different room while the rest of your home floods, leaving you to your efforts?"

"Hardly the same," Zaiyera said.

"Yet *somewhat* the same," Zhuyun countered.

Zaiyera looked ahead to the towering walls of Nanshaigha. "Somewhat."

"What of you, Zaiyera Tuneesh of Kushtanja?" Zhuyun asked. "If you come to visit my homeland and trouble arises, would you flee or step aside?"

"Mmph. You've cornered me with your logic, Zhuyun," Zaiyera replied.

"That means she wouldn't help," Jaide Amadi said from behind.

Zaiyera's mouth fell open. "I said no such thing!"

Zhuyun laughed.

When they finally reached the enclosed city, one of the scouts called to the guardhouses atop the wall on either side of the giant iron gate. The guards called down in response. Moments later, gears ground from the other side of the wall as chains were drawn taut, and the huge doors split inward to admit the procession.

The scouts escorting the party saluted Dyren and Malker again before trotting back into the night.

"Before we retire," Dyren said, "we must meet with the captain of the Fist of Light."

Nanshaigha's status as the capital of Dor'haighen was made immediately apparent once they stepped through the gates.

Torchlight cast its golden light on Zaiyera's face from both sides of the street, illuminating wooden signs hanging from chains attached to metal poles. The signs creaked as they swung back and forth, advertising everything from tailor shops, to taverns, weaponsmiths, eateries, food shops.

The surrounding stone made Zaiyera a little claustrophobic, but provided relief from the freezing winds of the wilderness.

She inhaled the smell of roasting herbs, cooking meats, baking breads and pastries as they passed what must have been a section of the city for dining.

Their boots crunched along the streets scraped of snow, while small clumps of it crouched against the sides of buildings. She looked down at the walkway. Tiny white granules lay scattered everywhere. "What is that?" she asked, pointing.

"Salt," Zhuyun answered. "We use this in my homeland as well. It melts the snow and keeps it from becoming ice, which keeps us from slipping and opening our skulls on this unforgiving street, ixu?"

The five companions navigated the streets largely alone, as not many citizens moved about this time of night. The occasional street urchin skulked about the edges of the streetlight, but shrank away at the sight of the two shydon hunters and their well-armed companions.

Zaiyera grew hopelessly lost after just a few minutes of navigating the gray stone avenues of the endless city. Streets extended as far as she could see and wound in different directions. Stone and wood-built neighborhoods sat on hills or downhill along various paths. Towers gazed over the city like the watchful eyes of parents, supervising their smaller children.

They passed under a stone walkway bridging clusters of buildings. Zaiyera looked to one side of the walkway as they passed under. Candlelight flickered from inside the windows of homes and businesses open in the late hours of night.

They followed the shydon hunters up a flight of stone steps alongside a building connected to another stone bridge. They moved through an alley that eventually opened on one side, while the other remained a solid wall. The open side of the walkway revealed a view of yet another section of the city.

Zaiyera slowed, almost stopping to take in the endless forest of rooftops spanning into what seemed like infinity.

Smoke drifted lazily from brick chimneys, either at eye level or below their position. She glanced further down the walkway to where Dyren and Malker had noted her absence and turned back. The walkway they traversed was one long rooftop extending to the end of the block and around the corner.

"Moon and stars," Jaide said beside her, echoing Zaiyera's sentiment.

"I can't imagine so many people living in one place," Zaiyera said.

"I've been told of cities as grand as this in Samhar," Jaide Amadi said. "Though I have never been to one. I find Viriksan more than large enough to suit me. This is too many people in one place, yes?"

Malker moved beside them and pointed southwest. Rows and clusters of rooftops climbed uphill toward the silhouette of an imposing structure towering above all else. "That," the junior shydon said, "is Citadel Nanshaigha. The seat of power of all Dor'haighen."

They continued across the rooftop walkways, passing over thick stone bridges overlooking walkways below. They came to another set of stone steps, these descending to an iron door.

Dyren knocked on the door in a series of patterns, then uttered a barely audible phrase in *Dreuga*. The response came in the sound of several locks being disarmed, then Dyren opened the door and stepped in.

The others started to follow, but Malker held up a hand. "Civilians must wait until your presence is made known." As a show of politeness, Malker Argen waited out in the cold with them. Quite some time passed, and Zaiyera and Jaide began shifting about, trying to ignore the cold.

Jaide leaned over and whispered in Zaiyera's ear, her voice reverting to its feminine pitch. "I wouldn't mind them opening that door any time, now."

Snow flurries had just started to fall when the heavy door creaked open again.

Malker stepped aside to allow them entrance, then shut the heavy door behind them with a resounding thud.

The room appeared to be some sort of chamber. Candlelight guided their shadows in an endless dance along the brown brick walls. A chest-high fountain filled with clear water stood against the wall to the right. Malker bent over it and splashed his face.

A man stood talking with Dyren at the far side of the chamber. He wore dark green trousers and a matching leather jerkin emblazoned with a hand grasping a bolt of light. Everything about the man spoke of precision. His long black hair hung neatly tied behind his back, his black boots so polished they reflected the dancing candlelight. Even his goatee was immaculately manicured, sloping from the top of his lip, down the sides of his mouth, to end at a point under his chin.

He stood at rest, feet slightly past shoulder width apart, hands clasped behind his back. He had a hard look, though not unattractive. His muscular arms and legs, as well as his broad chest were unusual compared to what Zaiyera had seen as typical of a shydon hunter. They were usually lean, as Malker and Dyren were. Most didn't wield anything more than a dagger or maybe a short sword, given that their discipline lay with dancing the stream.

Malker waved a hand at one of the two wooden benches lining the wall on the other side of the room. "Make yourselves comfortable."

The visitors sat, while Malker stood in front of them. The younger shydon hunter watched Dyren and the other man as they talked.

"This is a rather grim chamber," Zaiyera observed. She tried to ignore the stone walls looming over them.

"It's a holding chamber," Malker replied, "where business may be discussed or visitors may wait without entering the main building."

Zhuyun rubbed his chin as he looked about the warm yet cold chamber. "I'm assuming not many civilians have seen the inside of the main building, ah?"

"You could assume none," Malker replied.

"Who's the polished boots over there?" Jaide jerked her head in the direction of the talking men.

"That is Valyer Captain Commander Stavra Riaidas," Malker answered. "Leader of our prestigious ranks."

"A title far too self-indulgent, Shadow Hunter Malker Argen," the shydon named Stavra said as he and Dyren moved to join them.

Zaiyera and the others stood.

"Valyer," Dyren Faust said. "I introduce you to Zhuyun Xaiylin of Yuntai."

Zhuyun clasped fist in hand and bowed.

"Jaide Amadi of Viriksan, Samhar," Dyren continued.

Jaide pressed her palms together in front of her chest and bowed her head.

"And Zaiyera Tuneesh of Kushtanja, Samhar."

Zaiyera used the same silent greeting as Jaide.

"You stand in the presence of Valyer Captain Commander Stavra Riaidas, of the Shadow Hunters of Dor'haighen. The Fist of Light."

Stavra inclined his head. "You must trim that introduction back, old friend," he said to Dyren. "Eredin might hear you, and the herald's job will be threatened."

Dyren responded with a tiny grin.

"So long in your travels, and still your smiles remain conservative," Stavra said. He looked to Malker. "And you, my boy. Looks like Senior Shadow Hunter Dyren has had a positive impact on you. After all, you've gone on an entire mission and not only survived, but managed not to age yourself past my grandparents."

Malker slapped his fist to his chest, and partially snapped his fingers open, leaving them curled over his heart. "I've learned much, Valyer Captain Commander."

Stavra shook his head. "Including Dyren's conservatism. I suppose it's necessary in the presence of civilians." He gave the younger man a curt nod. "Very good, Junior Shadow Hunter."

Zaiyera watched all of this with no small amount of confusion mixed with humor. This man was obviously the highest-ranking man in the room, yet seemed not to like being addressed as such. When he snapped into formality, an air of power practically focused on him. Zaiyera suspected Stavra's humility belied a great deal of skill and a lot of power. She stole a glance at Dyren Faust, who did a good job of keeping too much admiration from showing in his face.

"And you three." Stavra turned to them. "A Yintish visitor and a Samhari man and woman who look to have endured a lot to get here. He stopped at the Yuntaiman and rubbed his chin. "Zhuyun Xaiylin."

"Indeed that is my name," Zhuyun said. "You pronounce it well for a first time, ah?"

Stavra narrowed his eyes in thought. "I've some small experience with your people, but I can't place your regional accent. Southern Yuntai?"

"Hah!" Zhuyun's features lit up. "A worldly man indeed. You've spent some time in my homeland, then?"

"Not long enough," the captain commander said. "And it was many years ago, early in my calling as a hunter of the shadow. It was a memorable experience, mostly due to painfully learning that I didn't know what true spice was."

"Oh, your poor easterner tastebuds." Zhuyun shook his head in mock regret. "You found yourself eating in Uren Province. Are you able to taste food again?"

Stavra laughed. "I've been tasting again for years, Zhuyun Xaiylin. But I confess I couldn't taste anything until after my second week back home."

The captain commander looked to Jaide, then Zaiyera. "Our two southerners. As rare as visitors from Yuntai are, Samhari this far north are even fewer. Ironic, since you live so much closer."

"I'm sure Dor'haighen is a most hospitable place," Zaiyera said, "but your climate is not."

Stavros nodded at that. "I suppose it's not, for a southerner. Though if you find this weather cold, best you remain in the southern regions of the north during the winter. And what is this about you're *sure* Dor'haighen is hospitable? Have you not experienced the extremes of northern joviality?"

"Unfortunately not," Zaiyera replied. "The urgency that brought us here leaves little time to experience your intriguing and … frigid, homeland."

The valyer captain's features darkened. "Your words ring true, sadly." He looked at Dyren. "I received your storm hawk barely a day ago."

Zaiyera didn't like the look on Stavra's face, and judging by Dyren's frown, the senior shydon picked up on it as well.

"Ill news," Dyren said dryly.

"Eredin isn't likely to supply the forces you want for your return to Samhar," Stavra said, all semblance of his amiable tone gone. "And I'm not sure he'll allow *you* to return either."

Dyren's gaze lowered, his eyes moving back and forth as if searching the floor for answers. "Sir. Did you … relay my message to King Eredin?"

"I personally delivered it and tried to have a conversation with his majesty at length about the implications of the tainted one."

Zaiyera flinched inwardly.

"*Tried*, sir?" Malker asked.

Stavra's nod fell like a headsman's axe.

"He refuses to send forces, then," Dyren said.

"Eredin didn't refuse out of hand," Stavra said. "But he refused to talk further about it until hearing your account firsthand. He said he had … other matters of great importance to attend."

"Other …" Dyren trailed off. "Sir, with respect, what could be more urgent?"

Zaiyera glanced about the chamber while listening to the shydon. As the news grew grimmer, the shadows seemed to darken. Their candlelit dancing mocked her as if employed by *kivuli dayasa* himself. The stuffy air in the chamber seemed to grow even more so.

"… might not be as irrational as he sounds, however," Stavra was saying. "Apparently some agreement or mutual endeavor with the eastern city of Rexzen went awry, and relations have soured in a big way."

"Rexzen?" Dyren repeated.

Zaiyera noted the obvious disgust in the man's voice, having practically spat the word.

"Why would King Eredin have anything at all to do with such a place."

"Sometimes it's necessary to deal with those you would like nothing to do with," Stavra replied.

"They bind lancers to their will and use them as weapons, sir," Dyren said, his words dripping with venom. "They would enslave *us* just the same, if given the opportunity."

Zaiyera felt the pit of her stomach go cold. She again recalled the vision the swift basin had given her. The lively and colorful city with a stern underbelly bordering on unfriendly. Most terrifying of all, though, was the vision of warriors sparring in pairs, one clearly held in check by an invisible binding.

"You've no need to tell me any of this," Stavra replied. "You, I, and every other shadow hunter to the last man and woman feel the same. Given the chance, I would march us on that city and eliminate every seeker and *shlieth* everywhere. But I am not king of Dor'haighen; only his vassal."

Dyren looked to chew on that information for a time. He finally nodded. "It seems our errand just became more urgent and uncertain all at once."

"Then, waste no more time here," Stavra said. "I doubt I'll see the rest of you again," he said to the others. "May your travels be safe."

* * *

"Mind if I ask why you turned to stone back there when they mentioned Rexzen?" Jaide asked Zaiyera in a quiet voice. She walked at the back of the group, and the Viriksani had fallen back to join her.

Zaiyera watched Dyren and Malker. The two men were engrossed in conversation of their own, the latter somewhat animated. "The swift basin. Do you remember the artwork on it?"

Jaide thought about it. "I remember blue wavy water flowing around it, with something else above the water. An eye?"

Zaiyera nodded. "An eye. Since I drank from it first, I received the side effect; a vision."

Jaide looked at her. "Okay?"

"I saw a place brimming with color and life, with people crowding clean streets—"

"Sounds lovely to me," Jaide interrupted.

" … with a presence underneath the surface that felt extremely dark. I think it had to do with a faction of their warriors. I witnessed a sparring match between two pairs of warriors. Each pair were bound together by an invisible part of themselves, entwined together. One seemed under the control of the other."

Jaide's cheeks puffed as she let out a long slow breath. "Yup. That sounds like Rexzen."

"You know of the place?" Zaiyera asked.

"I do." Jaide's normal joviality disappeared. "I've been there only once. It's not quite as bad as your vision seems to paint it, yes? The people weren't what I'd call jolly, but they were polite and friendly. There is a mixed history in Rexzen that makes the place somewhat different. I've heard stories of the bound warriors you speak of, but I've never seen them."

Zaiyera absorbed all of this as they navigated the various avenues. Being from the capital, Dyren and Malker knew where to take the visitors for food and lodging, so their route was fairly direct. "Why was my vision of the place so intimidating?" she wondered.

"Perhaps it has something to do with the strained relations between them and the King of Cold who rules this frozen land," Jaide said, a hint of her humor creeping through. She shrugged. "I wish I could say more that might add some clarity. Perhaps I felt safe because I'm not a streamdancer."

"They don't like streamdancers there?" It was only half a question.

"Ooooh, not at all," Jaide said, chuckling.

They started walking uphill, and Zaiyera found herself huffing again.

Light flurries of snow drifted from the dark sky. In the surrounding lights of the candles in sconces on either side of the street, the falling flakes were beautiful.

Jaide started to slip. When Zaiyera grabbed one of her flailing hands, she slipped as well.

Zhuyun reached back and grabbed Zaiyera's free hand and steadied her, which helped her to steady Jaide.

Jaide managed to stop her shuffling feet from flying out from under her and steadied herself. "Moon and stars. How does anyone *walk* on these frozen stones of death?"

"You get used to it," Zhuyun said. "A lifetime of walking on frozen ground and your body's muscles remember and hold you stable, ixu?"

"Watch for patches of black ice under bridges," Malker called from further ahead. "One step on that and you'll have a view of your feet on your way to your back."

"Thanks, Dor'haighener," Jaide called back.

Malker gave her a friendly salute. "Of course, my good man."

Once he was sure Zaiyera and Jaide were stable, Zhuyun carefully released her hand. "I shall leave you to your conversation."

"Feel free to listen if you wish, Zhuyun," Zaiyera said. She surprised herself with the invitation. Though she and Jaide were from faraway places in Samhar, they were both Samharan. The Viriksani was a pillar of familiarity in this cold and foreign place. But the Yuntaiman, she found, made her feel … safe. Not in the sense of a protector, but in his knowledge and simple presence. The Yuntaiman traveler had seen much, learned much. Perhaps he'd have insight on the discussion.

"As you wish, friends. Though I enjoy conversation with myself quite a lot, I can drag myself from it for your company."

Zhuyun listened without interruption while Jaide caught him up on the conversation.

" … and so we were just coming to the part about the ruler of Rexzen's disdain for dancers," Jaide finished.

Zhuyun frowned. "I cannot imagine why anyone would dislike dancing so much that they would condemn them to forceful servitude."

"*Stream*dancers," Zaiyera clarified. "In Samhar, the way we touch the stream is a form of dance. Those who dance the stream are called streamdancers, or dancers, in short."

Jaide frowned. "After all this time together, how have we not spoken of this?"

"What do you call streamdancers in your land, Zhuyun Xaiylin?" Zaiyera asked.

"*Tokailan*," Zhuyun replied. "But I would rather hear the rest of what you say, first, ixu?" He indicated for Jaide to continue.

"Streamdancers," Jaide said, "are considered dangerous in Rexzen. Only one form of dancing is openly practiced. And even then, only by an organization of warriors called Seekers. I don't know exactly what they do to streamdancers, or how they do it, but you need only to mention the word seeker to a streamdancer to induce fear. No one who dances the stream willingly goes near Rexzen."

Zhuyun stroked the long braid wrapped around his neck. "One need not, as you say, dance the stream, while in the city, no? I've not heard of a person, or not, who could detect another without them touching the stream first."

"True," Zaiyera said. "But I imagine simply being close to such hostility to who or what you are would be uncomfortable."

They came to a five-story tall building with a carved bear over the door. Arching over the carving were the words "The Cave Bear's Den."

"That's a name that brings back unwelcome memories," Zaiyera said.

"I wonder," Jaide said, "if bears build inns and social houses and name them 'The Human's House?'"

"That is truly an odd question," Malker replied. "Maybe even for you."

Unlike the inns and social houses from the last two Dor'haighen cities they'd passed through, The Cave Bear's Den had a more cozy common room. Wooden rocking and reclining chairs occupied the large open space, many of which crowded around a crackling hearth.

Zaiyera caught a whiff of something sweet and pungent. She wondered if the smell came from the smoke puffing from the mouths of men in the chairs farther from the hearth. Their pipes bobbed in their mouths as if involved in the scattered conversations.

A young man greeted them in *Dreuga*, then repeated in tradetongue, "please rest wherever you like." He opened a hand toward the sitting area.

They found a group of chairs the like Zaiyera had never seen. She ran a hand over the smooth padding of one chair-backs. The material felt smooth yet durable, and stitched over some kind of soft, puffy filling. She sat down on the chair and felt herself sink. The chair felt like a large pillow.

"Try to at least hide your amazement a little, Kushtanji," Jaide said in her disguised male timbre. "You'll make our Dor'haighen hosts think we're not used to luxury."

"I'm a nomad, Jaide," Zaiyera replied. "I'm actually *not* familiar with this kind of thing."

"My poor uncivilized friend," Jaide said with a smirk. "She reached over and patted Zaiyera on the leg. "We'll get you used to the finer things in life yet."

Zaiyera arched an eyebrow.

"You've an interesting way of flirting, my good man," Malker snickered. "Has your face gone so long without a handprint on it that you wish another?"

The serving man who'd greeted them arrived with five mugs of steaming *chaffa*. He waited while the companions arranged into a circle, then sat the mugs on little round tables between the chairs. After taking their food order, Zaiyera noted the young man's gaze lingered first on her, then Jaide and Zhuyun before he left.

"What's our next move?" Jaide asked. "I imagine we'll be out of here as soon as possible, yes?"

"You heard what the valyer captain commander said," Malker replied. "We might be on our own. *You* might be on your own."

"More fun for us," the Viriksani replied dryly.

"We don't know anything, yet," Dyren Faust said, taking a sip of *chaffa*.

Caught up in her thoughts about that very topic, Zaiyera hadn't realized she'd been holding her own mug halfway to her mouth. She took a sip of the hot, spiced drink. It slightly burned her tongue but felt good going down.

"Consider other possibilities if you must," Dyren said, "but we won't know how to act until we've had our audience with King Eredin."

"We, as in you and Malker?" Jaide asked.

"We as in all of us," Dyren answered. "Expect an audience tomorrow with the king and queen on the morrow." He sighed. "I would rest easier if we had more information."

The server returned with two steaming bowls of stew, then left and returned twice more until everyone was served. He then turned to Zaiyera and Jaide. "Begging your pardon, sir, and my lady miss. I think I might have a message for you."

Zaiyera's eyebrows raised. "For me? Us?"

The young man produced an envelope with a wax seal. In the middle of the red seal was a logo featuring a feather dipped in an ink bottle.

"I think you're mistaken," Zaiyera said. "I'm visiting here and know no one."

"All the same, my lady," the young man said with a bow. "The man who left this letter described the three of you such that there can be no doubt. A beautiful woman with skin darker and smoother than a mug of *chaffa* mixed with coco beans." He pointed to his forehead, chin, and both cheeks. "With red markings on her face." He turned to Jaide. "A Samharan man with eyes the color of the Great Sea, and a face absent of even the slightest bit of stubble. He said a little on the pretty side, begging your pardon."

The corner of Zaiyera's mouth twitched.

"And you, sir," the young man said to Zhuyun. "If it was ever possible I could mistake them, I could not mistake you. A man from west, across the Great Sea. Long black hair, likely in a single braid. Dark brown eyes shaped like the almonds imported from the far south, and similar of height to his Samharan companions.

The server looked at Dyren and Malker. "The man said two shadow hunters might or might not be in company of these three companions, which is why I addressed them first. I beg pardon." He bowed.

"No offense given, young man," Dyren said. "Our thanks."

The server bowed again and left.

Zaiyera turned the letter over in her hands.

"That wax symbol is a standard logo for all Dor'haighen notaries."

Zaiyera broke the seal and opened the letter. Her eyes widened, and she looked up. "It's from Barum."

24

Malhadiev opened his eyes. For a while he lay staring at the top of the bed's canopy, absorbed in Sheik Jegried's soft pillows. At least five feet of empty bed lay on either side of him. Malhadiev remembered his own bed. Having been a man of some small status, he'd been able to afford a bed that could fit himself and his wife without them having to sleep shoulder to shoulder.

He continued to stare straight up at the canopy without seeing it. Jegried's death left him and Kima only half avenged. His heart lurched, and he forced thoughts of his brother away. *No. I won't think about him. I can't.*

Malhadiev sat up and ran a hand over his smooth face. A face unblemished by so much as a scar, let alone any creasing the lifeprice might have exacted. *Should* have exacted.

He stretched his arms with a groan, then swung his legs over the side of the bed and stood. He stretched again, then looked about the lavish surroundings. Silky purple curtains hung closed over the windows, yet the sun shone through them enough to dimly illuminate the room.

A huge portrait depicting the marvelous city of Zalrabi hung from the wall opposite the windows. Malhadiev looked over the giant image.

It seemed odd, viewing the place with this overhead perspective. One of Zalrabi's two canals flowed right behind the palace where he now stood, the other connecting the far end of it with the river to the east.

The artist captured the towering palm trees, the various shapes and sizes of the buildings and homes populating the city, and even people walking along the tan-colored streets.

Malhadiev's face darkened when he finished his scan of the portrait. The work was so large it covered a good portion of the wall, yet Zalrabi's poorer district had been omitted. No. Not omitted. At the very edge of the painting to the south, a couple of less fancy homes could be seen. Well, part of them. It was as if the artist meant to note the less desirable side of Zalrabi without actually including it.

He thought back to the expedition he'd been a part of. As an emissary of Zalrabi, he'd thought the task given to him by Jegried was to negotiate better trade terms to bring more wealth to the city. He'd hoped the poorer districts might be gentrified.

He thought about the first time he'd been to Nanshaigha. He remembered seeing the same poverty in certain secluded areas of the capital.

"How naive," he muttered.

The sound of his own voice startled Malhadiev. He blinked a few times, then hummed. It felt like his voice made the air itself vibrate. "What is this?" He'd said it in a low voice, but the words came out in a powerful rumble.

He stood frozen while trying process this new development. "Mmmmwwwoooaaaaaaaah."

The room vibrated as though a tiny tremor shook it. Malhadiev's eyes widened. Still looking around, he closed his eyes and opened himself. He felt it—the stream. It moved around him, through him, through and around everything that was.

Everyone knew this, of course. Dancers more intimately so. But this was different. A streamdancer dipped their hand, foot, or even their body, into the stream. Once they drew the power out, it became the flow. They guided it, molded it, wrapped it about their perpetually moving bodies. Some drew tiny lines from the stream like a finger digging a tiny canal from running water; guiding that little bit from the whole that they needed.

Malhadiev was no longer a streamdancer. He'd ascended that existence long ago. But this, as far above normal folk as a streamdancers were, Malhadiev was many, *many* times above an army of powerful dancers. He didn't dance the stream. He *was* the stream. He lay in the enormous, infinite river of power, allowing it to carry him in its never-ending current.

He opened his eyes and looked at his hands again. Black as liquid night, his dance-resin glowed. He clenched his hands shut and let his head fall back, reveling in the immense power coursing through him.

He noticed a mirror leaning in the far corner of the room and went to stand before it. The man looking back at him shrank away in a mimic of Malhadiev's shocked reaction. Heart racing, Malhadiev moved closer to inspect himself.

Unsurprisingly, his pitch-black dance-resin glowed around his body. But unlike a visible transparent aura like before, it danced about him like black fire. And his eyes!

Kivuli dayasa leaned forward until his face was inches from the mirror. What should have been the whites of his eyes were now black, along with his pupils. Instead of light brown eyes surrounded by white, the face looking back at him housed unsettling pure black orbs.

Malhadiev straightened and forced himself to stare at his reflection. He faced the horror of the hard face and black eyes that blended with the matching black fire dancing about his body. He'd crossed a line. That thought made him chuckle aloud. *A* line? He'd crossed many. Too many to count. But this was different. If there had been a shred of possibility for him to alter the course he'd set upon seemingly a lifetime ago, it was gone.

He felt power of such magnitude that he had no doubt he could level the entire Zalrabi civilization, should he choose. But that inferno of power bubbling inside had come at great cost. He thought he could feel the Goddess Shakimah turn Her gaze from him.

The realization came not with a voice in his head, or a hunch, but a feeling of some tiny spark dying inside of him and fading away. *Am I damned, then?* He turned away from the mirror and walked to the window.

With a casual swipe of his hand, the glass shattered and the wall crumbled away like a curtain pulled to the side. He looked out at the sprawling city below. His home. Or was it, still? He could remain in Jegried's palace and take it as his own. Who would stop him? A hundred shydon hunters would be nothing to him, let alone any normal streamdancers that might try to oppose him.

He dashed that idea to the winds of his mind as soon as it formed. What would he do with a city? He had no desire to rule anything or anyone.

Malhadiev looked to the north. Then east. Rexzen. If what Jegried had told him was true, those linked streamdancers had come from there. He remembered the sensation of having his lifestream attacked. It had felt akin to someone trying to harness the blood inside his body and bend it to their will.

Despite the immense power flowing through him, Malhadiev shuddered at the memory. If there were streamdancers in Rexzen capable of binding another dancer's lifestream to their own, that made the northeastern city a priority.

Malhadiev looked to the northwest, where the capital of Dor'haighen sat hundreds of miles away. He hadn't killed everyone in his path, so Malhadiev was reasonably certain that King Eredin knew about him. He had probably assembled every soldier and shydon hunter in his kingdom to march against Malhadiev.

Kivuli dayasa smiled at the thought. No. Eredin wouldn't do that. He wouldn't know to do it. The Dor'haighener king would have only the faintest idea of what Malhadiev had become. He looked back northeast. Rexzen would fall first. However much power Malhadiev wielded, he wasn't delusional. If not one streamdancer could bind him, then the combined efforts of many could do it.

Eredin and Nanshaigha were of no concern for the time being. There weren't enough dancers in his kingdom and likely all of Dor'haighen and Samhar combined to bring Malhadiev down. That could wait.

He curled his fingers, grabbing fistfuls of the stream. He whipped his arms around in a backward, circular motion. Two enormous transparent whips, each nearly as large around as the tower he stood in, drew from the air and curled backwards. They sliced through Jegried's bedroom like knives through parchment and curled around the tower of the palace.

The sound of crumbling sandstone rumbled from the structure below. Malhadiev snarled and yanked his arms forward. The enormous whips cut through the tower section of the palace and sent it collapsing straight to the ground.

Malhadiev floated above the crashing rubble below. Dust drifted up from the destruction but not high enough to reach the hovering shadowlancer. The only limits to his power, now, rest within that of his own mind. He could do anything, and that anything would start with the obliteration of Rexzen.

2 5

L oud conversation, roaring laughter, and the sound of things breaking seeped out of the bursting seams that was The Flying Mug, the building straining to contain the exuberance within its walls.

Zaiyera opened the door and squinted when the noise spilled out onto the street. She took a careful step inside and looked around the establishment. The place was loud. Very loud.

Jaide stepped in beside her, followed by Zhuyun. "Wow," the Viriksani said when a mug arced through the air to be expertly caught by a pair of raised hands, not a drop spilt.

They kept to the walls, as that seemed to be the easiest route around the forest of patrons.

"Amazing that I'm no longer cold," Jaide said. "Must be this massive glob of bodies, yes?"

Zaiyera expertly navigated around several insistent offers to dance, hardly slowing her pace. Barum had said the easiest place to find him would be at the bar. She looked at the long counter stretching at least thirty feet from end to end.

A gray-haired bartender's head and shoulders were barely in view through the crowd of drinkers. He poured a foaming mug of beer and slid it down the counter. Patrons along the bar lifted their mugs and the

271

drink slid past. By the time the targeted patron snatched her drink up, the barkeep had poured another and launched it out of the bar. There was a resounding "oooh" followed by sad grimaces when the missed beer shattered on the floor, splashing drink on nearby feet and ankles.

A nearby woman with thick black hair flowing down her broad shoulders yelled above the cacophony in *Dreuga*. She held her mug up in toast.

The room raised their mugs in a collective "AYE!" and continued drinking and shouting at each other.

Zaiyera was about to cross around a big barrel-chested man leaning against the wall. He staggered away from the wall to block her path and spoke to her. Zaiyera made a gesture indicating she didn't speak his language and tried to keep moving. "Hold on, my lady beautiful," he slurred, this time in tradetongue. She pretended not to listen, but he didn't move. "Hard of the hearing?" he asked, louder. "I said, beggin' your pardon, but I'd like to exchange a dance with you for a mug of frost beer." He offered her a grin as greasy as his watering eyes that took her in, head to toe.

"Not this night," Zaiyera replied. "Please step aside."

"Aw, but what fun is a place like this without a little dancing? I insist, my lady beautiful. The hospitality of Dor'haighen is something to experience." He looked past Zaiyera at her companions. "Your friends won't have to wait too long, be assured."

Zaiyera stole a quick glance over her shoulder. Jaide's hands rested crisscrossed with her thumbs in her belt where Zaiyera knew she had a pair of daggers. Zhuyun looked relaxed, but Zaiyera knew that was a well-hidden lie.

She didn't need a scene. Especially not a stabbing. Zaiyera moved closer and leaned toward the large man. Her shoulder barely reached above his midsection. "Perhaps another time."

Just as the man started to put his arm around her, Zaiyera ran a palm up his midsection and thrust the butt of her hand into his solar plexus.

She let her hand slide down the gagging man's stomach while helping him turn to face the wall as he began to convulse.

Zhuyun pursed his lips and gave the vomiting man a pat on the back. "I should apologize on behalf of men everywhere," he said with a laugh. "Tiring, it must be, to deal with such a thing, *ixu*?"

"Indeed," Zaiyera replied. She stole another glance at the smug Jaide Amadi and sighed.

The gray-haired barkeep flung mugs about the bar with the grace of a dancer who didn't touch the stream. Zaiyera slipped between the lingering gazes of two patrons and finally reached the bar.

When the barkeep finally noticed her, he waved them to the left, and made his way from behind the counter.

Barum sat nursing a beer at the end of the bar. When the barkeep arrived, he perked up and turned to see Zaiyera and the others.

"*Jakta scree*, but I half believed I'd never see any of you again!" He wrapped Zaiyera in a tight hug and lifted her off the ground. Zhuyun cried out in surprise and laughed when the big Dor'haighener lifted him off the ground as well.

"I will settle for a handshake, my burly friend," Jaide said.

"Bah gimme your blasted hand, then." Barum snatched Jaide's proffered hand and pulled her in to a partial sideways hug.

Zaiyera snickered.

Barum released Jaide and looked them all over. "I'm not going to lie and say you don't look road weary. Surely you didn't just arrive?"

"We have," Zaiyera said. "Not long ago. How did you know where to find us?"

Barum nodded toward a vacant table at the back of the establishment. The barkeep, now armed with four foaming mugs, hollered something in *Drouga* over his shoulder at his subordinates as he followed behind the group.

"Ole Jassy, here is a longtime friend," Barum explained. He dropped an affectionate hand on the older man's shoulder. "He keeps this spot free for me."

"Every time you pay for it," Jassy added, placing the frost beer on the table. He wiped his hands on his apron. "Anything else for ya?"

"This should do for now, Jass. I need to be sober."

Jassy snorted at that and waded back through the mass of bodies to his counter.

Zaiyera watched the man go. He looked like a grizzled old war veteran skulking back to the trenches.

"I see you're without your shadow hunter friends," Barum said. "Are they here, or have they fallen, then?"

"They're in the city," Zaiyera said. "They had business to see to with their organization."

"I'm sure they did," Barum said knowingly.

"Which brings us back to the lovely lady's initial question," Jaide said. "You were about to share how you found us, yes?"

"I *didn't* find you," Barum replied. "Not really. I left a letter at the common room of every inn in Nanshaigha. Cost me no small bit of coin, but luckily there aren't *that* many inns; else you'd have found me begging on the street."

"Your news must be urgent to put you to such trouble to find us," Zaiyera said.

Barum nodded. "That it is. I have to confess, our Yuntaiman friend here is of a stronger faith than me. When that tainted bastard dropped an entire sand dune on you, I'd had no doubts you were dead." He lifted his mug to Zhuyun, then to Zaiyera. "Here's to friends of faith and your survival, miss my lady."

Zaiyera smiled widely at the rugged formality Barum had bestowed on her, what seemed like ages ago.

They tapped their mugs together in toast and drank. The beer was cold and bitter, with a hint of sweetness. Zaiyera set her mug down on the table and looked for something to wipe the foam off her upper lip.

Barum wiped his mouth with his coat sleeve and Zhuyun followed suit. Jaide slipped a little brown kerchief out of her jacket pocket, talking great care to grip it in her palm like a man would, and roughly wiped her mouth.

Zaiyera had no handkerchief, so she hesitantly used her hand.

Barum slapped the table in laughter. "I can practically hear your mind screaming for a cloth, miss my lady. Accept my apologies. Rowdier places such as this don't tend to supply such refinements."

"I'm fine, Barum," Zaiyera said, taking a more careful draw while wiping her hand on her knee.

"Now, about that news." Barum's expression sobered. "I've got me a few contacts spread across Nanshaigha." He glanced around, then leaned in closer. "Word has it there's more to this situation than simply a man syphoning a bunch of lancers to become powerful."

Zhuyun shrugged. "His rantings during our first confrontation indicate as much, *ixu*?"

"Well, here's the whole of it," Barum replied. "Or at least as much as I've been able to find out. Our shadowlancer's name is Malhadiev. He was a trade emissary from a Samhari city named ..." He looked up as he recalled the memory, "Zal ...raybi? Aye. Zalraybi. That's the name of it." He looked from Jaide to Zaiyera. "Either of you familiar?"

"That's Zal*rabi*, my linguistically challenged friend," Jaide replied. "And I'm only vaguely familiar. It's far south of my homeland. Past central Samhar."

"I've been there twice," Zaiyera said. "My people trade with every city in the regions they roam. Zalrabi sits in that area."

"Well, that's where he's from," Barum said. "My contacts say that he was part of a trade delegation tasked with negotiating a new trade deal with the monarchs of our great capital, here.

"Turned out that this Malhadiev fellow argued with the sheikh of Zalrabi on more than a few occasions on what to trade, the prices, and how best it would benefit the poorer areas while still increasing overall wealth."

"Doesn't sound like the same man who almost obliterated us all," Jaide observed.

"I'm gettin' to that." Barum downed the rest of his beer. "Malhadiev had been a cramp in Sheikh Jegried's side for years. Rich as he was already, the sheikh apparently has an insatiable taste for wealth. When word came to Jegried from King Eredin that he wished to discuss new trade terms, he used it as an opportunity to be rid of his troublesome trade treasurer.

"He appointed Malhadiev as trade emissary to Nanshaigha and allowed him to choose the team to accompany him. Malhadiev saw such a great opportunity in this that he didn't even think to second guess how strange it was that his ruler actually *selected* his biggest financial detractor to oversee trade with the biggest source of wealth to the city."

Barum gave a slow, sad shake of his head. "Malhadiev selected his younger brother and six others to represent Zalrabi. Sheikh Jegried readily approved the man's selections except for one, which he'd replaced with a personal choice.

"Since the woman was a skilled negotiator who appeared to have no stake in the situation, she'd seemed harmless, and Malhadiev didn't argue against the choice. Jegried sent him off with four guards." He paused. "Two of them were armed. Apparently, some kind of "accident" befell our little traveling trade group. Malhadiev walks away from the ordeal as the only survivor. The official word is that they were attacked by raiders."

"A single person survives a raider attack," Jaide said, "and it's a trade treasurer?" She leaned back and rolled her eyes.

Barum shrugged. "That's the *official* word."

"Yet the official word says nothing about how this treasurer survives the ordeal and walks away a darkdancer," Zaiyera said.

Barum snapped his fingers. "No mention at all of anything to do with that. When your shadow hunter friends were deployed with their team, they were told only that a darklancer had been discovered in north central Samhar.

"Two pieces of luck got word to Eredin, who sent word back to Jegried before dispatching Dyren, Malker, and their team. Malhadiev's brother. He'd thought his brother had been killed, since he'd fallen off a bridge into a running river below where the skirmish took place. The attack had been in the middle of the night, I should add."

"So, Malhadiev and his brother couldn't find each other," Zaiyera said.

"Yup," Barum replied. "And about that luck? Yeah. Two pieces of luck, good and bad. The attack had happened less than an hour's ride from the nearest village. Since the attack had failed, the camels they'd ridden hadn't scattered. Malhadiev's brother managed to ride one to the nearby village. How he survived, I can't begin to tell you.

"The man had good luck to actually reach the village, which is where his luck ended, and Eredin's began. Apparently the woman Sheikh Jegried had appointed to accompany the delegation was the person supposed to do the actual negotiating—"

"After Malhadiev and his team had been disposed of?" Zaiyera asked, catching on.

"You've got it," Barum replied. "She was supposed to meet Eredin's escort and accompany them to the capital."

"But instead, they found Malhadiev's barely alive brother," Zhuyun surmised.

"And they brought him back to Nanshaigha," Barum said. "Eredin had the man nursed back to health so that he could question him. The brother had been no wiser to the plot against them than Malhadiev, so he'd fully cooperated."

Zaiyera frowned at the table. "But, how would your king have known to send shydon hunters in pursuit of Malhadiev. The brother couldn't have known he'd syphoned those streamdancers."

"I'd wager it a guess, ah?" Zhuyun said. "If the brother had known two of the attackers had been *tokailan*," he cleared his throat at Barum's blank expression, "lancers, as you call them, your king might have sent his team of shadow hunters just in case."

Again, Barum nodded, then looked to Zaiyera. "This brings us right up to the time when you found Dyren and Malker."

Zaiyera still had questions. Malhadiev had to have been a dancer in order to syphon his attackers. Only a streamdancer could syphon another streamdancer. And how large must the stakes have been for Jegried to plot the murder of not only his trade treasurer, but the other innocent members of the party?

The most important question, however, rested on King Eredin. Had he been complicit in Sheikh Jegried's plot? If so, Zaiyera could guess at how much success Dyren would have in beseeching the monarch for aid that would likely see as much as three-quarters of the capital's shydon hunters deployed from Nanshaigha. And with the apparent tensions with Rexzen—

"What are you thinking?"

Zhuyun's voice jarred Zaiyera back into the moment. "I'm thinking about being gone from this place by dawn. If I wasn't so tired, I'd say as quickly as we could secure mounts."

Jaide took a deep breath and let it out through her teeth. "There is a saying in Viriksan that I think all of Samhar probably shares, yes? 'Politics will strip your bones dry—'"

"Faster than a grinder," Zaiyera finished.

"Mmm." Zhuyun replied with a sagely nod. "It seems this is a thing the world around. From across Yuntai to my travels to lands all around the Great Sea, people beware the scheming of their rulers, ixu?"

"I see where your thinking is going, miss my lady," Barum said. "Before I got back here, I'd have argued tooth to nail that it wasn't true. King Eredin has been a good ruler and the wealth of Nanshaigha and its territories are proof."

"And now?" Zaiyera asked.

"I don't know." Barum sighed. "I've met folks from right here in my beloved homeland who trust our King no more than you. I don't know."

"Apologies if I sound rude, Barum, my friend." Jaide swiped a hand across the air in front of her. "But I care not about anything but being free of this."

That drew an openmouthed frown from the big Dor'haighener. "Then, why did you travel all this way through cold and snow that I know your thin Samhari blood struggles to handle?"

"That was before learning this is wrapped up in monarchs and bloody trade deals," Jaide said. She looked to Zaiyera "Why would we risk our lives in this dirty business? Let's say through some grand miracle, we bring down this *kivuli dayasa*. Their king"—she waved a hand to encompass the tavern—"and the southern sheikh will prosper all the easier for our efforts. They might even try to have *us* eliminated."

"Sheikh Jegried is dead," Zaiyera said.

A heavy silence settled over the table for a long while.

"How can you know that?" Barum asked, but Jaide was already nodding in agreement.

"She's right," Jaide Amadi said. "On the way back, I saw *kivuli dayasa*. He tore through a small town on his way south after destroying Shanhazai. His direction pointed south and west. Just like when he fought us, he kept ranting about making rulers pay for their greed. If your story is true, Barum Hurst, Zalrabi is likely where he was headed, yes?"

Zaiyera's mind kept returning to the eastern city of Rexzen. Given what she'd heard the shydon say about the place, and what Jaide had shared with her, the city played some kind of role in this. The timing was too suspect.

"Thinking again, ah?" Zhuyun said. "What do you say to all of this?"

Zaiyera looked up to see three expectant faces staring back at her. "If we don't fight *kivuli dayasa*, he will kill many more people, including the king of this land, from what I gather of this news. He may do it anyway, after stepping over our dead bodies. I can't fathom how powerful he must be by now."

"You set me all afire to go meet our enemy," Jaide drawled. "Let's just assume for a moment that Dyren and Malker come back with us to challenge that monster. We'd have two shydon hunters accompanying the four of us. And none of us are streamdancers. That leaves me with only one question. How quickly the slaughter would take?" She shook her head. "I'm not sorry to say this holds no appeal for me."

"We can leave this business to the Dor'haighen king," Zaiyera said. "And Malhadiev will probably level this entire city and everyone in it. He'll syphon every dancer *and* every shydon hunter."

Jaide plunked her mug down and looked away.

Zaiyera didn't blame the Viriksani woman. All anyone at this table wanted was to scratch out their own small place in the world and be comfortable. Maybe experience some adventure. Now they sat around a table discussing a problem they hadn't created, but that would almost certainly affect every person north and south of the Samhar/Dor'haighen border.

Everyone sat in silence, beers forgotten, each digesting the news and its implications.

From their previous conversation, Zaiyera knew Zhuyun would fight beside her still. Jaide's very frustration about the situation made Zaiyera fairly confident she would fight, too.

She looked across the table at Barum, the only one to remember his beer. He lifted it, realized that it was empty and sat it back down with a grumble.

Zaiyera had a better idea of what they were up against than anyone sitting at this table. By all rights, she *shouldn't* allow any of them to come. Even if Eredin agreed to send every streamdancer in Nanshaigha against *kivuli dayasa*, the casualties would be immense, if they didn't all die. What could three—albeit formidable—warriors do against him?

Perhaps this was Zaiyera's penance. Perhaps this was the task that would cleanse her soul, that Shakimah might smile on her again. Zaiyera's thoughts traveled out The Flying Mug, through the many dark avenues, up and down the hilly streets, and into her room. Strapped to the underside of her bed lay quite possibly the only hope at defeating Malhadiev. Her hope, and her shadow.

"Oh, one last thing," Barum Hurst said, interrupting her thoughts. All eyes turned to him. "That brother of the shadowlancer? Yeah. He happens to still be a 'guest' of King Eredin."

26

Dyren Faust had been correct, and Zaiyera had returned to her room to find an invitation waiting for her. Now, she prepared to meet a King and Queen. When the knock on her door came in the morning, she opened it to see a nervous-looking girl wearing a white apron and a scarf tied to her head. She'd spread her apron out as she curtsied, then told Zaiyera that a carriage waited to take her to the castle of Citadel Nanshaigha.

The girl's nervousness had barely followed her out the door by the time a team of handmaids had arrived with a metal tub and buckets of steaming hot water.

The handmaids had insisted on bathing her despite her protests, which lasted through her undressing and stepping into the tub. They'd even insisted on dressing her when it was done.

Despite her misgivings about being bathed by a bunch of strangers —she was perfectly capable of doing it herself—the memory of that heavenly bath with the smooth black soap and unfamiliar but lovely scented oils left her closing her eyes with a contented sigh.

Apparently, the black soap of central and southern Samhar numbered among the many goods Dor'haighen traded for with the south. After days of either no baths at all, or using the rough soap of the north, the soft and soothing black soap combined with the scented oils left her skin shimmering and revitalized.

She looked in the mirror at the silver dress she wore. It had a pale blue swirl flowing down the side. Simple yet elegant.

She turned around and looked over her shoulder at the dress with an approving nod. Originally the dress had hugged tightly to her waist, pushing her bust upward, and fit her hips and backside like a second skin. That was a fight the handmaids didn't win.

Zaiyera had assured them that ten kings could descend on her little room in this inn, and all would be told no. The head handmaid had conceded with a frustrated sigh and sent for pin and needle. In short order, the woman had taken the dress out a bit at the waist and hips and loosened the bust.

Careful not to dirty the exquisite dress, Zaiyera knelt and looked under the bed. Shatr lay strapped on top of one of the cross boards of the bed frame.

Satisfied, she stood and took the silver hair clamp they'd left on the bed. She pulled her thin braids back away from her face and applied the clamp.

As soon as she stepped out of the room, the handmaids whisked her down the hall, across the common room, and to the waiting carriage where Zhuyun sat waiting. Jaide came only a few steps behind, a red-faced manservant trailing behind.

The man glared at the Viriksani woman's back as she climbed into the carriage. The driver smiled with an affectionate bow and closed the door.

Zaiyera couldn't contain her smirk as she took in the other woman, resplendent in her gold doublet with silver embroidered patterns and dark green breeches.

"That fellow didn't look happy with you, ah?" Zhuyun observed from Zaiyera's other side.

The carriage rocked as the horse team started forward. Such an odd feeling.

"Pfft. I don't care what he thinks," Jaide replied. "I've dressed myself all my life and I don't need a man to do it for me now."

A tiny frown creased Zhuyun's brow. "You'd have preferred a handmaid, then? That might not be appropriate in this fine place, ixu?"

Zaiyera kept her features neutral.

Despite the slip, Jaide kept her cool and shrugged. "What I meant was that I don't need anyone dressing me, Yuntaiman."

The carriage rocked and swayed along the street. After a while, Zaiyera noticed the crunch of the large wooden wheels on the salty streets became more of a grinding noise. She peeked out the window and saw that the road they traveled was now a well-kept dirt and gravel trail. Likely easier for the horses to walk the sloping streets without slipping.

The trio talked of the foreign sights that filled their journey through Dor'haighen, and the immensity of Nanshaigha. According to Zhuyun, there were great civilizations in Yuntai equal to the size of the Dor'haighen capital. Jaide spoke of the ancient civilizations to the southeast near Viriksani, still inhabited today, huge and sprawling. Hearing the woman talk, Zaiyera thought she might wish to visit these places with their efficient irrigation systems, towering palm trees, and immaculately designed sandstone and clay structures.

Conversation eventually came around to their impending visit with the King and Queen of Dor'haighen. Though it was a point everyone silently agreed on, they nevertheless relaxed when Zaiyera mentioned keeping every detail they knew about the situation with Rexzen, as well as Malhadiev and his brother, to themselves.

A slot at the front of the carriage opened, and the driver's face appeared. "Begging your pardons, but if this is your first time to the castle, you might open the shades at either side.

Zaiyera moved to the other side of the carriage and looked out the window just as they passed through a huge arched opening the driver called a portcullis.

The clip clop of the horse team's hooves echoed in the enclosure beyond the portcullis. Dozens of little holes lined the walls like eyes watching their progress. "What are those?" Zaiyera asked the driver. "Those little holes?"

"Arrow slits, my lady miss," the driver replied. "And if you were able to look overhead, you'd see more of them, though those aren't exactly for arrows."

"What are they for?" Jaide asked.

"Let's just say you'd prefer the arrows."

They passed out of the enclosure and into a large open courtyard the driver called the inner ward. Citizens dressed in all manner of finery milled about the fragrant gardens and snaking walkways, admiring red and blue, green and yellow and pink flowers. They sipped drinks in between conversation, most smiles looking prim and superficial. Despite what Zaiyera considered extremely cold weather, most people were dressed lightly. "They look … to be enjoying themselves," she said.

There was a snort from the driver's window. "They look like nobles posturing with each other, mingled with aspiring nobles to elevate their own status. You might find it an attractive atmosphere, my lady. Certainly nothing wrong with a man or woman looking to improve their position in life."

"I wish them luck," Zaiyera said. She grinned when she heard the snicker of agreement.

"We are now in First Castle," the driver said.

"*First* castle?" Jaide asked.

"Ruled by Prince Varadonis Nansheig. And a good ruling hand he has."

Zaiyera noted the way the driver's tone perked up at the mention of this Prince Varadonis. Since she'd been in Dor'haighen, she'd never heard anyone speak of the king and queen with such fondness as the driver had with the prince. No one spoke ill of the king and queen— who would dare?—but there seemed to be a more positive air about their son, if the driver's sentiment was any indication.

"First Castle," the driver continued, "wasn't actually built at the same time as Nanshaigha Castle. It had originally been the main structure where I'm taking you now. This bridge and the royal barracks being the last line of defense. Something of a citadel, if you will."

"So, the monarchs of your great city had a small castle constructed for their son, when he came of age?" Zaiyera asked, keeping the disapproval from her voice.

"Ha. By Jokolta, no. The entire royal family used to live in Nanshaigha Castle."

The carriage passed across the inner ward through a second portcullis leading to the huge stone bridge.

Zaiyera leaned out the carriage window to get a better look. At least three carriages as large as the one they rode in could travel side by side on the bridge. Like the rest of the structure, the stone was made of the same light gray color.

The massive structure that was Nanshaigha Castle looked down on them even from across the bridge. The roofs of the various towers were painted red, some with little structures on top that looked almost like houses. Zaiyera wondered how many flights of stairs one must climb to get that far up. Perhaps those little houses were to sleep in, as who would want to climb back down again after that?

"The capital," the driver continued, "has a good relationship with most of Dor'haighen except one … faction, if you will. There's a whole population up in the far north. Even past Argastonia, the farthest town up. It gets cold up there like nothing you'd believe."

"I find it hard to imagine anything cold enough to make a Dor'haighener say that," Zaiyera said with an involuntary shiver. "How is that possible?"

The driver laughed. "Very possible and very cold, my lady miss. Anyway, the people who live that far north have been unfriendly with the ruling family since long before I was born, and things came to a head again. Over a decade ago."

The chatter of passersby speaking in *Dreuga* filtered into the carriage. Zaiyera found it a heavy-sounding language, with dips in the tone instead of the more rhythmic, flowing *Soloush*.

"A band of over four hundred North Argastonians came sprinting down the mountain. And when I say sprinting, I do mean *sprinting*. Their people are a different breed, my foreign friends. They are big and tough, with blood as thick as molasses."

"But only four hundred against an entire regiment of trained warriors from this fine city?" Zhuyun replied. "Seems suicidal, *ixu*?"

"Normally it would have been," the driver agreed. "But the self-proclaimed king of those people never declared war. Never even sent demands. Just sent four hundred marauding warriors through the mountains and down to the capital.

"Of the ten scouts out there, only three were lucky enough to have made it back to bring warning. Because of the surprise, shadow hunters had to be included in the ranks, which is normally not a practice unless the situation becomes desperate. The battle was brutal as only one could be involving North Argastonians, which brings us to our prince.

"Varadonis went out at the head of an elite team of shardlords."

"Shardlords," Jaide said. "They sound formidable."

"A title well earned, my good man," the driver said. "Shardlords are the highest-ranking soldiers in Nanshaigha, very intimidating, and are activated only under the direst of circumstances.

"Over six hundred soldiers had been deployed and cut down when Prince Varadonis rode out at the head of a team of twenty shardlords. They cut through the enemy ranks and turned the tide in what should have been an impossibly short amount of time. It was the most impressive thing I've ever witnessed to this day."

"You saw it, then?" Zaiyera asked.

The driver's stony face appeared in the slit. "Aye. I was there. On the battlefield surrounded and praying to Jokolta that I take at least one more enemy before I met a swift death.

"Varadonis led us to win the day and earned the nickname, the Iron Prince. His parents hadn't known he'd gone out and weren't exactly happy. But Queen Orianna had been first to recognize the love her son had earned, and even greater respect and loyalty, not only from the populace—who already adored him—but from every soldier in the capital.

"After that battle, Varadonis developed a quick bond with his shardlord team, and had insisted on taking residence in the royal barracks. King Eredin had protested, but Queen Orianna had eventually assented."

He chuckled again. "Eredin wouldn't stand for his son living in soldier type conditions, no matter how luxurious they were, being the royal branch. What we've just left behind took five years to build, and became First Castle. Varadonis resides in the mini keep, as it's known."

Zhuyun whistled through his teeth. "Quite a story that is."

"And unfortunately," the driver replied, "the last one for now. We've reached our destination."

The carriage rolled to a stop and the carriage rocked as the driver climbed down. A moment later, the door opened.

Zaiyera climbed out first, followed by Jaide and Zhuyun. The latter whistled through his teeth again. "Amazing."

Jaide stared openmouthed at the huge, sprawling inner ward and the towering structure at the other side. "All the stones in the world must have been used to make these two castles and the bridge connecting them, yes?"

"Seems like it," Zaiyera said.

A stately woman with a huge book cradled in one arm waited for them at the base of the front steps. Without a word, she inclined her head in greeting, turned on her heel, and started up the steps. The three companions glanced at each other and followed.

"Good day and welcome," the woman said in tradetongue, once they caught up. "I am Mari Dorae, Stewardess of Nanshaigha."

"Good day and thank you, Mari Dorae, Stewardess of Nanshaigha," Zaiyera replied. "I am Zaiyera Tuneesh of Kushtanja, Samhar."

The corner of Mari's mouth stretched into a faintly amused expression. "This is your first time to the capital?"

Zaiyera nodded.

The stewardess nodded as if she'd suspected as much. "And what of you?" she said to the others.

"I am Jaide Amadi, of Viriksan," Jaide said. "I have ventured north on a few occasions, but never so far as this fine kingdom."

Zhuyun gave his customary greeting. "I am Zhuyun Xaiylin of Yuntai. Of the many lands I've visited in my travels across the Great Sea, Nanshaigha distinguishes itself with its grandeur."

The stewardess cut him a quick glance. "I see you've attended court before, world traveler."

Mari Dorae led them through halls filled with long red drapes hanging from windows as tall as a house. It seemed every hallway they turned had a set of curving stairs leading somewhere.

The air smelled of wine, food, and perfume. The din of conversation and laughter added to the mixed cauldron threatening to overflow Zaiyera's sensibilities. She leaned over to whisper into Jaide's ear. "How many families must live in this giant home? It seems half of Nanshaigha could live in here."

Jaide held a hand to her mouth to muffle her laughter. "Oh my uncultured, nomadic friend," she whispered back. "Based on the royalty I've been subjected to in our own great homeland, I doubt that more than the royal family themselves, the second highest ranking nobility, and their immediate staff live in this grand castle."

"Their rooms must be truly impressive," Zaiyera replied, though in her mind she wondered what so few families needed with so much space.

Mari led them down another series of hallways where fewer people milled about. Their steps were muffled by a long red carpet that flowed away into the distance. They reached two sets of stairs facing each other that curled up to meet at a balcony overlooking the grand hallway.

Zaiyera frowned. How many people must travel this area, that two sets of stairs wide enough for the carriage they rode in on were needed? And why the big curve? Surely the architect knew that it took more steps on these roundabout staircases than if they just went straight up.

"I've spoken with Senior Shadow Hunter Dyren Faust," Mari informed them as they ascended the stairs. "Given the nature of your visit, I thought it best to come for you myself.

"I gathered from my conversation with Senior Shadow Hunter that your news comes not on the wings of a dove, but those of a raven."

At the puzzled looks she received, Mari clarified. "It is an expression regarding ill news."

They turned down another endless wide hallway, the red carpet extending into infinity. Zaiyera took a relieved breath. Fewer people here meant less of that strange perfume that threatened to plug her sinuses.

"Please listen carefully," Mari Dorae said. "King Eredin and Queen Orianna are practical, and will hear your stories. They may share with you the information they've received or they may not. Whichever is the case, you are not to make any inquiry of them unless given leave." She looked at them for comprehension, then clarified. "Unless asked to do so. Whatever their decision on the matter you bring before them, it will be final."

A servant trotted up, gave a shallow curtsy, and spoke to Mari in *Dreuga*. Mari opened her giant tome and made a few notations, then sent the girl on her way.

They followed her down through hallways even more extravagant than before. Zaiyera made an effort to ignore the paintings, voluminous curtains, and other decorations that adorned the halls in order to focus on Mari's instructions.

They finally arrived at the end of yet another hallway and stopped at a set of tall double doors with an armed guard, sword and dagger at each side.

"Wait here, please," Mari said.

"Sounds like this will be interesting, ah?" Zhuyun remarked in a quiet voice.

"Maybe so, "Jaide replied. "But I find that I don't much care so long as I'm gone from this cold land with its cold monarchs. At least the royalty in Samhar house multiple families in their big extravagant homes, yes?"

Zaiyera found that she agreed with Jaide. Though Samhar had its benevolent and not so benevolent monarchs, they were still familiar.

The doors opened again and Mari stepped out and beckoned them forward. "Wait at the back of the room with me while you're announced, then follow me forward."

Once they entered the auditorium, a man dressed in black and gray robes emblazoned with the house livery loudly proclaimed their arrival, then informed the party in whose presence they were in, as if they hadn't already known.

Through the herald's speech, Zaiyera looked across the mostly empty throne room at the king and queen, seated next to each other in matching thrones as white as the snow covering the land outside.

King Eredin stared at them through the speech, and when the herald finished, he spoke a single word. "Come."

They followed Mari Dorae across the red-carpeted floor. Though she kept her head straight, Zaiyera looked around the giant throne room. Facing the two thrones on their raised dais were two long booths, one on each side. In each booth men and women analyzed the party as they passed. Zaiyera found those stares frosty.

To her surprise, she saw Dyren Faust standing beside the booth on the right, and Malker the left. They faced forward and didn't look at her at all.

They stopped behind Mari at the base of the steps leading to the dais. The stewardess dipped into a low and graceful curtsy. Zaiyera imitated her, while Zhuyun and Jaide bowed low.

"My Lord King," Mari Dorae proclaimed once she'd straightened. "My Lady Queen."

Both monarchs gave a slow and silent nod in response.

Zaiyera focused on the steps at eye level. She could feel the weight of the queen's gaze on her, but she denied her desire to make eye contact. She kept her head straight, chin not too high, but her gaze not lowered, either. She would give these royal figures their due respect without being submissive.

Mari had finished talking some while ago, yet nothing more had been said. Zaiyera stole a glance up to the right, at Eredin. The king of Dor'haighen caught her gaze and held it fast in an icy embrace.

27

Eredin Nansheig looked to be of average height and build. Not that he was a small or frail man, but he wasn't physically imposing. His gray and white hair hung over his shoulders. Each strand seemed to have been combed and perfectly placed. His clean-shaven face bore an angry scar in the shape of a V on his cheek, just below his cheekbone.

Not wanting to hold his gaze too long and risk offense, she bowed her head as respectfully as she could, and straightened, then returned his gaze again.

The king responded with a soft exhalation that could have been a quiet chuckle, then looked past her on the right. "Senior Shadow Hunter. You may assume position with your most recent companions, should you choose. Or you may remain where you are. It matters not to me." He looked to the other side. "The same applies to you, Junior Shadow Hunter."

The two shydons came forward to stand at their respective sides of the party, much to Zaiyera's appreciation.

Queen Orianna spoke in a voice that rang as powerful as her husband's. "You may speak."

As Dyren stepped forward and knelt, Zaiyera stole a quick glance at the queen. Her hair hung perhaps half a foot longer than Eredin's, and was also perfectly combed, and the color of steel. If her hair was the color of steel, her eyes were made of it. The queen snapped up Zaiyera's gaze, and she felt as if the other woman read her inside and out in that one brief moment.

Zaiyera held her ground as respectfully as possible. Though she'd been through too much in her life to be cowed by the stern gaze of a king and queen, she could imagine how common folk might curl in on themselves under the weight of those stares.

Dyren straightened and stepped back. "My Lord. My Lady. I've been informed that you have some details regarding the shadowlancer?"

"We have," Eredin replied. "Apparently he eluded your attempts to immobilize him, if I'm correct."

"He … decimated my contingent, my lord. Only Malker Argen and I survived to continue pursuit."

And so Dyren told the tale of their first confrontation with the shadowlancer and their subsequent defeat and near death. He told them of how Zaiyera had found and rescued them, and their travels together.

Eredin and Orianna listened without interruption, though several members of the panel seated at the booths behind them asked the occasional question.

Once Dyren reached the point of their second defeat, he shifted the focus to Jaide. "During our efforts to free ourselves from beneath the sand dune, and our continued pursuit south, our companion, Jaide Amadi rode on."

The king and queen turned their gazes to the Viriksani, who bowed low and cleared her throat. "I rode hard, that I might be able to ride wide of his position and overtake him without being seen. *Kivuli dayasa* had been riding at an easy pace …"

Zaiyera watched the expressions of Eredin and Orianna as Jaide related her story and the murders and destruction she'd witnessed. Their expressions gave away nothing.

"And what of you, world traveler from Yuntai?" Queen Orianna said after Jaide finished her tale. "How does an unlikely visitor to the deserts of the south find himself embroiled in such a conflict?"

Zhuyun gave another Yintish salute, then told the tale of his journey across the Great Sea, arriving at the western coast just north of the border, and paying for passage with Mr. Vose's caravan.

Zaiyera smiled inwardly. Of all the stories they'd told thus far, the Yuntaiman's was by far the most grand.

"You weave quite a tale, Zhuyun Xaiylin," Queen Orianna said. "Your skill begs an offer as Master Storyteller in our court."

Zhuyun smiled. "I am honored, My Lady. But I must at some point return home."

The queen tipped her head. She turned her iron gaze on Zaiyera, but it was Eredin who spoke. "And you, young woman of the Kush-tanji. I find myself most interested in this ability of yours to cut through the efforts of a lancer without, yourself, touching the stream."

Zaiyera remained silent for several heartbeats as she gathered her thoughts. If she was to avoid being enveloped in northern politics, she needed to tell them as little as possible. She wished she hadn't been compelled to come to this audience in the first place.

"Raiders are not uncommon along the paths between cities," Zaiyera began. "I've been a caravan guard for years because of this. Streamdancers often number among those who prey on caravans. My blade … is able to cut through the flow. Because of this, I can survive against those who dance the stream."

"The young lady is possessed of no small amount of … modesty, wouldn't you say, Eredin?" Queen Orianna's smile didn't look hostile, but there wasn't anything comforting in it either.

The more she interacted with these people, the more Zaiyera wanted her sword at her side and her feet on the road as soon as possible.

"Indeed," King Eredin replied, equally scrutinizing her. "From the way we've heard it so far, Zaiyera Tuneesh of Kushtanja, *survive* isn't quite the word that comes to mind. Does this sword of yours touch the stream, in some way?"

"It does not, King Eredin." Zaiyera thought to leave it at that, but it would only invite more probing questions. "The blade is but one of an infinite number of objects around the world possessed of unusual properties, I'm sure. But truly, it was Shyd … Shadow Hunter Dyren Faust and Malker Argen who are the reason we stand before you now. Their combined efforts saved us from being crushed beneath the sand dune."

Eredin leaned forward in his throne. "Yet it was your ability to prevent everyone in your party from being obliterated by an obviously far more powerful enemy. Am I incorrect?"

"That … to some degree, yes, King Eredin."

"I would be interested to know how you do this," the king said. "Perhaps it would provide an advantage of some sort. Can the sword's crafting be duplicated?"

"I've never seen its like," Zaiyera replied carefully. "It was a gift to me from my grandmother."

"I see." He sat back again. "I would be interested to see if our best blacksmiths might find out. If you would be willing to offer your sword you would be compensated. Once our blacksmith is finished studying the blade, it would be returned to you, unspoiled, of course."

Zaiyera's heart shuddered in her chest. "I fear there may be no time for this, King Eredin," she said. "He roams my homeland still. My heart aches at the death and devastation he brings."

The king rubbed his chin. "Mmm."

Zaiyera forced her expression to remain neutral. Did this man not care anything about her people? They had given their accounts of murder and destruction; a dangerous addicted dancer growing more so by the day. And he seemed more interested in her scimitar than the countless lives ending.

To her surprise, Dyren Faust spoke up. "My Lord, if I may?"

The king responded with a subtle nod.

"Zaiyera is correct in that we have little time to spare. The shadowlancer has left death and ruin everywhere he goes, and it's a matter of time before he's leveled every major city in Samhar and turns his sights north."

The king's gaze snapped to attention. "And what makes you think this addict would be interested in Dor'haighen, Shadow Hunter?"

If Zaiyera hadn't been looking at Dyren's profile, she might have missed the twitch in his left eye. It was subtle enough that she might have missed it, had she blinked.

"A logical conclusion, my lord," Dyren replied. "Once he's finished south, nothing would stop him from moving toward us."

"Perhaps he simply wants to conquer the south and rule it as his own," Eredin countered.

Zaiyera clenched her teeth.

"Not an impossibility, my lord," Dyren said. "But a man bent on conquest of this sort wouldn't be likely to stop there. And even if he were, my lord, would you wish to treat and trade with such a monster? What might happen, should any disagreement happen? His power is already enormous. The longer we leave him be, the more powerful he will become. Perhaps we might gather allies in the south, from surviving cities. If we don't bring him down soon, I'm not certain all the shadow hunters and civilian lancers in all of Dor'haighen would be able to stop him."

"That is a serious statement," Queen Orianna replied.

Dyren bowed at the waist. "I would not make it, were I not certain, my lady. It is why today, I request a large contingent of shadow hunters and soldiers to march south."

"A large contingent?" Eredin replied. "How large, exactly?"

"As many as can be spared, my lord."

King Eredin arched an eyebrow. "That is a rather substantial request."

"My lord," Dyren replied. "I've felt his power and seen what he can do. He touches the stream and manipulates the flow with barely a thought. He wields massive amounts of the flow without fear of the lifeprice. Twenty shadow hunters would age and expire against him while he remains strong."

From the corner of her eye, Zaiyera saw a man from the left booth behind them stand and bow. "My Lord, My Lady, this matter must be taken into advisement. I propose we enter closed council to discuss."

A man from the right booth stood. "Are we not in discussion now?

How long must we talk of this when Dor'haighener lives could be at stake?"

"Decisions of this magnitude are not made on anecdote alone," the first man said.

"A full team of shadow hunters dispatched and only two return alive with tales of one man wielding monstrous amounts of the stream, and you consider this anecdote?" the second man said.

"In times of danger," the first man calmly replied, "especially when one is directly involved, memory can be creative."

A woman in the booth to the right stood. "Do you suggest the testimony of two shadow hunters, one a *senior* shadow hunter, and three civilians to be embellishment? And their stories align. Perhaps they gathered beforehand and rehearsed?"

"You merely plead my case for me," the man in the left booth replied.

"What reason would they have—"

The king raised his hand and all three parties quieted and sat.

"This matter must indeed be put to discussion," Eredin said. He looked each of them over as he said this.

To the left, Malker's mouth fell open before he caught himself and closed it. Jaide gave a barely audible sigh. Even Dyren blinked at the news, a tiny frown creasing his brow. "My lord," Dyren said. "I assure you our accounts of the events are—"

"Accurate to the best of your memory, yes," Eredin interrupted. "However, I'll not empty Nanshaigha of our best soldiers to send against one man, no matter how powerful. We have barbarous enemies to the far north, who would like nothing more than to see all of Nanshaigha's most powerful shadow hunters march out of its walls."

Zaiyera knew what the outcome would be before the king spoke it. The fate of her people, their southern neighbors, weren't once mentioned as a concern in the discussion other than by Dyren to help as allies. The only concern, here, was the impact to Dor'haighen and its people.

Jaide was right. It was time to go.

28

"That couldn't have gone better," Jaide remarked, her tone as dry as the frigid air.

Dyren showed open disappointment, an unusual display of emotion from the senior shydon hunter. "None of us can know the weight of responsibility ruling a kingdom places upon its monarchs' shoulders. The matter must be taken before the imperial bench before the king can make a decision."

"Is *that* what that flock of chirping sparrows were?" Jaide asked.

"Careful," Dyren warned. "They hold sway in every major decision impacting the capital and Dor'haighen as a whole. Do not underestimate the imperial bench."

Jaide looked toward Zaiyera and rolled her eyes.

Zaiyera, however, found her gaze lingering on Malker Argen. The junior shydon had been largely silent through the audience. The muscles in his jaw were tense, his expression stony.

Zhuyun stroked his long braid in thought. "How long might this deliberation take, ah? I've seen a situation such as this take days to settle. Sometimes longer."

"You aren't wrong, Zhuyun Xaiylin," Dyren replied. "I've no way of knowing."

"I doubt it matters," Jaide said. "The king's mind is already made up, yes?"

"I heard no such thing," Dyren replied.

Jaide looked at him as though he were naive. "You cannot question your king and queen, so I will spare you that burden. He did not mention his dealings with the Sheikh of Zalrabi, the attempted assassination of Malhadiev that he surely knew about, nor did he mention word coming from the south from the widowed shaykhah about her husband's death and *kivuli dayasa's* subsequent change in direction to Rexzen."

Dyren's stare hardened through her speech. "The king does not discuss matters of state with his subjects, in case you didn't know this, Viriksani."

"Even when that subject is a high-ranking member of his most elite warrior class, *Dor'haighener*?" Jaide shot back.

"You walk a dangerous line," Dyren said his voice going quiet.

Despite the shydon hunter's admonitory tone, Jaide laughed. "That's amusing, because I thought we've been walking a dangerous line this whole time, yes?"

Zaiyera stepped between them and leaned close to Jaide. "Enough, my friend. Please."

Jaide took a deep breath and nodded. She turned away, Zhuyun following her down the gravel path snaking across the low-cut grass of the inner ward.

Zaiyera turned to Dyren. "He's not wrong," she said quietly. "Neither your king, queen, nor the members of your imperial bench mentioned the fate of my people, many of which have already been murdered."

Dyren stared hard at her. "No. He did not mention the ill fate of your people. But before we return to that, I'd like to know who *mentioned* word arriving from Sheikh Jegried's widow, the conflict with Rexzen, and the shadowlancer's new destination."

Moon and stars, Jaide. Curse your fast tongue. "It matters not—"

"It matters *indeed*, Zaiyera. If someone in the royal household has a tongue so loose that three foreigners newly arrived have found out such sensitive information, I would know about it."

"I assure you there are no loose tongues spreading word across your noble city, Dyren Faust."

"Nevertheless—"

"This path will lead you nowhere," Zaiyera snapped. "Your rulers played a part in creating the monster that ravages my homeland, yet have taken no consideration for my peoples' safety, so someone must." She pointed a short distance away to where Jaide leaned against a wall, gazing out at the scenery beyond. "He is a proud Samharan, as am I. Your king and queen show no concern in even warning Samhar, let alone any interest in joining with us. You discuss the fate of my homeland as though we have no stake in the outcome. We resent this, Dyren Faust."

"You've an interesting way of speaking to an ally," Dyren said.

Zaiyera almost laughed. "Is that what I am to you, or just a possible advantage that failed to sway your royal leaders?"

The senior shydon hunter maintained his composure, but anger flared in his blue eyes.

Zaiyera met that anger with her own. "You don't like my words. That is unfortunate for you. I do not like what I heard in that audience." She pointed to the doors behind him. "Your people have made up their minds. We've made up ours."

Dyren frowned. "You intend to leave on your own. You will return to confront the shadowlancer yourselves." When Zaiyera didn't reply, he shook his head. "You will die. Both of you. And if you allow your loyal friend to accompany you, he will die beside you."

"I cannot control the actions of anyone but myself," Zaiyera replied. "If it is *kivuli dayasa* who writes my life's conclusion, so be it."

They stared each other in the eye as the silence between them lengthened.

"There's a chance he *will* send us with a force, Zaiyera," Dyren finally said.

"As large as the one we know is required to stand a chance?"

Zaiyera asked. She glanced at Malker, who stared at the ground, his jaws still tight, then looked back to Dyren. When the senior shydon didn't answer, she turned away. "I look forward to your king's decision."

* * *

Zaiyera joined Jaide and Zhuyun at the side of the bridge. She rested her arms on the chest-high stone wall and gazed out at the enormous body of water.

"I'm told this grand thing is called Endless Lake," Zhuyun said. "Seems fitting. Almost looks like a tiny ocean, ixu?"

The lake was indeed huge. The pristine surface reflected the surrounding trees and mountains as though they were twins growing upside down. A perfect replica of this world beneath the depths.

"I don't suppose," Jaide said, "it would be believable if I said that I usually never let words fall out of my mouth without forethought."

Zaiyera patted the other woman on the back. "We aren't perfect, are we? It happens."

"That could have been a dangerous slip in different company," Jaide replied.

"But it wasn't, so things are fine." She looked out at the water again. "Take it as a lesson that came with little cost."

"I'd like to think I need not tell you this," Zhuyun said after a while. "But whenever you plan to disappear, likely best at night, mind you, please notify me, that I won't have to track you down."

Both Zaiyera and Jaide looked at him. He returned their stares for a heartbeat, then the corners of his eyes crinkled when he smiled. "Yes, yes. This is your fight. I am a foreigner from a land so far away. I didn't travel across the Great Sea to potentially die in a conflict that has nothing to do with me." He swiped his hand sideways. "Now that I've listed all of your arguments, let us just assume I've *already* told you that you have become great friends to me, and I would see this through to the end; beside you both."

"What makes you think we're planning to sneak out?"

Zhuyun responded with a lazy smile and a slow blink.

"All right," Zaiyera said. "Stupid question. But for my own conscience my friend, I feel the need to warn you that we stand even less of a chance of surviving without Dyren and Malker."

Zhuyun nodded to that point. "However. There is one piece to this puzzle you haven't considered."

Zaiyera slid her thin braids away from her face and stared at the Yuntaiman, her dark brown lips pursed. "Oh?"

"Every situation has a starting point," Zhuyun said. "Something that happens to spark the fire."

"The attempted assassination of Malhadiev and his brother," Jaide said.

"Only, his brother survived also," Zaiyera said, catching on. "He's here."

"Which presents us with another problem," Jaide said. "I doubt Eredin is keeping him in a luxurious suite where he can have visitors at his whim."

"But I doubt he's being held prisoner in the traditional sense either," Zaiyera countered. "He didn't commit any crimes."

"If you were part of a conspiracy to have a ranking official and his family member assassinated," Zhuyun asked, "and they both survived, given the circumstances, would it behoove you to have that family member able to come and go as he pleases? Particularly, *go?*"

Zaiyera thought on that. "If Barum's information is correct, and the brother is here, he'd be the most powerful shield King Eredin has against Malhadiev."

"He would," Zhuyun agreed. "My guess, and it is only a guess, understand, is this Dor'haighen king keeps his shadow hunters and the rest of his military force close, while assessing relations with Rexzen. If or when the shadowlancer arrives at his walls, Eredin will have the man's brother as a bargaining chip against attack, ixu?"

"Meanwhile, who knows how many more people in Samhar die while the man makes his way here," Zaiyera replied. It was a truth that came with a bitter taste to it, but there was merit in Zhuyun's thinking.

"All right," Jaide said. "We know that the brother is somewhere

here. Assuming we actually want to find him, my question is why? What do we have to accomplish that's worth the risk of making the royal pants in there"—she waved a dismissive hand at the castle keep —"angry at us? I don't much like the notion of imprisonment in a foreign land. Especially one this cold, yes?"

While leaning on the wall, Zaiyera noticed small structures built into the side of the fortress. She leaned forward to get a better look. There were at least half a dozen of them built right into the castle. Further down on the small island upon which Nanshaigha Castle sat, larger structures hugged the building. No, not hugged. They were built as part of the castle as well.

She leaned as far as she could, straining to see further down. Small structures were even built onto the side of the bridge connecting Nanshaigha Castle and First Castle. There were more structures attached to the towering walls of First Caste as well.

"What has you so enraptured that you're about to fall over the side of this wall, Zaiyera The Reckless?" she heard Jaide ask.

Without a word, Zaiyera pointed.

The other two leaned forward and looked.

Zhuyun whistled through his teeth. "Quite efficient use of space, ah?"

"Not bad," Jaide admitted with a grudging edge to her voice.

"Didn't Barum tell us Malhadiev's brother was being kept as a guest, and that his view of the water was amazing?"

Zhuyun nodded slowly. "I remember a bit of sarcasm in his tone at that."

"I wonder," Zaiyera said. "Could this brother be housed in one of those structures?"

Jaide narrowed her eyes at Zaiyera. "What are you planning?"

* * *

Zaiyera hid her surprise at the ease in which she'd been admitted into the holding quarter of the castle. Apparently, security was tighter for the prisons and harsher dungeons. The section housing those who hadn't necessarily committed a crime but were important people seemed to be less strict about visitors.

She thought on everything she'd learned so far while she followed the guard down the hall. According to Barum, this brother of Malhadiev's wasn't a prisoner in the traditional sense, but he wasn't allowed to leave, either. In the end, it was still politics. Malhadiev's brother was a safety bargain chip against attack. He could roam certain sections of the castle, and even come up to the inner ward for fresh air and to stretch his legs. But never into the main city, and always accompanied by guards.

A prisoner in all but name.

After traveling down several flights of stairs, they came to a long hallway lit by candles in wall sconces. Zaiyera swallowed and focused on her thoughts. She constantly reminded herself that the walls weren't closing in on her.

As they moved along the hallway, passing the occasional door, Zaiyera took note of where they'd been when they started down the stairs, and the direction they were moving. Judging from where she'd been escorted into a building in the inner ward, opposite the keep, they were actually *inside* the giant bridge.

The guard stopped at a thick door made of solid wood with iron hinges. He gave a loud rap on the door. "Got a visitor for you!"

The voice on the other side of the door sounded surprised. "Visitor? Maybe someone to finally escort me to the headsman's block?"

"That again," the guard grumbled, his annoyed tone indicating this wasn't the first time the subject came up. "Keeps talking about the stupid headsman's block despite how many times I've told him the king has no intentions of executing him."

"Yet," added the voice from inside the cell.

Zaiyera stifled a snicker.

"Don't know why you'd want to visit this man," the guard said. "He's got nothing but sarcasm and irritating conversation in him."

He's a prisoner, she thought. *No matter what you say to the contrary.*

The guard gave her a once-over. "Well you're from the south as well, from the look of you. I guess it makes sense."

"Thank you," Zaiyera responded. "Might I speak with him inside the cell?" When the guard raised his eyebrows at her, she said, "please be assured, I can take care of myself. Thank you."

The man shrugged and looked back to the door. "She's coming in."

"She?"

He unlocked the door and pulled it open. After Zaiyera entered, he closed and bolted it shut again. "Just let me know when you're ready to come out."

Though she wasn't a prisoner, Zaiyera felt a shudder at the thought of never being able to leave this place. To her surprise, the 'cell' wasn't the dank and dreary accommodations she'd been expecting. To be sure, it was not a luxurious suite, but there were no piles of rotted straw in the corners, no rodents scurrying about the place. There was a decent-sized window looking out at the lake. A basic but comfortable-looking bed sat to the side of the room beside a large throw rug. Sunlight shone through the room's only window, partially illuminating the plain gray walls.

Against one such wall stood two shelves filled with books. There was also a small square table with two chairs at each end.

She looked upon the man standing against the far wall next to the window. He was a bit lighter in complexion than she, though his features were obviously Samharan. The whites around his light brown eyes shone brightly from the shadow in which he was standing. The beginnings of an unkept beard coated his chin and jawline, and his hair, though somewhat short, also showed signs of neglect.

He bowed in the Samharan fashion, looking as though he knew less of what to expect than she did. "Had I known I would have a visitor, I would have made an effort to at least *look* like I cared about my appearance, *niyima.*"

Zaiyera smiled at hearing *Soloush*. Though his was an accent from southern Samhar, it was still Samhar.

"I'm sure your guard would prefer our conversation spoken in tradetongue, would he not?"

The man looked at her and accurately read the question in her expression. "They speak no more *Soloush* than we speak their harsh-sounding *Dreuga*. Be at ease. Why have you come here? Is there news of …"

"Of what?" Zaiyera asked when he hesitated.

"Anything," came the reply. "Is there any news of our homeland? Any news of the outside world at all?"

"You've been in the north for some time now," Zaiyera said. "You speak in curves like them."

He shrugged.

"You must have some idea of why I'm here," Zaiyera said. "How many from Samhar come to visit you?"

"Perhaps to glean information out of me," he said, casting her a suspicious look.

"Yes. That is exactly why I'm here."

That set him back on his heels. "You're a horrible spy."

"Hardly a spy."

"Oh?" He tilted his head.

Zaiyera studied the man's features, so similar to the man who'd almost killed her not long ago. "Let's save time, since I don't know how long I'm allowed to stay. I'm sure you're guessing I'm here because of your brother. You're correct. But I haven't been sent by anyone other than myself, in my desire to know what to do in this situation I've been swept into."

"You've encountered Malhadiev," he said. Zaiyera watched a range of emotions cross his face before he finally leaned against the wall and slid down to sit against it. He rested his arms on his knees and ran a hand through his disheveled black hair. "I can't say I'm not surprised you're alive and standing here talking to me."

"Barely." She moved closer, but not too close. "My name is Zaiyera Tuneesh."

He bowed his head in greeting. "Kima Imrian."

They were silent for a while, Zaiyera wrapped in her thoughts, Kima no doubt deep in his own. She didn't know where this man stood, but his reaction seemed pained on the subject of his brother.

He looked up and studied her face. "You're not sure where I stand, are you? You're not sure if I share the same sentiments toward the north as my brother."

"You're imprisoned here while your brother is being hunted down. It's a rational sentiment to have, is it not?"

Kima sighed. "Yes, it is. I'll admit my brother and I share a similar thought toward the north, but mine is less extreme." He stared at her for several tense moments. "Whether you take my word or not, I'm not going to grow hostile and attack you." He offered a rather sad grin and indicated the space next to him. "If you'd like to sit."

Zaiyera hesitated a moment, then moved closer. She looked out the window, making a note of the water, the distant mountains. Finally she sat next to him. "You said you were surprised I'm alive. You know what your brother has become?"

Even Kima's nod was sad. "Unfortunately, yes. I heard of his actions shortly after I awoke."

"Can you tell me of this?"

Kima looked at her, then nodded. "I'd assumed you hunted Malhadiev. Do you know nothing of him?"

"I've heard news of his actions in Samhar, north to south," Zaiyera replied. "But I'd like a better understand of what caused all this."

Kima chuckled, but there was no humor in it. "I can only imagine the rumors of what a monster my brother is. They doubtlessly paint him as a directionless monster, killing for the sake of killing. They would convince everyone he needs to die before he destroys the world."

"I would hardly say 'convince'," Zaiyera said. "After but one encounter with him, I'd say he has become somewhat … different, from the man you know." She raised her knees up and wrapped her arms around them. "I wish I was here to say otherwise, Kima Imrian.

But your brother must be stopped before he razes every city to the ground from Samhar to Dor'haighen

"Your concern for this land is heartwarming," Kima replied. "But I assure you the north cares little about us."

"And I assure you, that Malhadiev cared little about Shanhazai and its people."

Kima stiffened. "Shanhazai?"

Zaiyera nodded. "Destroyed, and those who hadn't escaped are dead. The city's dancers were even less fortunate, as I'm sure you can guess. I saw the aftermath with my own eyes. And word came from the south that he's already attacked Zalrabi."

Kima's face darkened. "I have little remorse for Jegried."

"What about Zalrabi's people?" Zaiyera pressed. "Those who have nothing to do with your quarrel with Sheikh Jegried? If they were anywhere near the conflict, he probably killed them."

"How can you be sure of that?" Kima asked, a note of accusation in his tone. "You said you heard word of the conflict? You weren't there."

"I bore witness to the desolation of Shanhazai. There have been other places, too. I saw the terror in the faces of those who escaped." She studied his face, saw the lines of despair forming. "I'm sorry for bringing such news, but it's the truth, *osa*."

His responding grin was a mix of sad and hopeless. "It's been long since I've heard that word, *niyima*," he said, referring to her use of the traditional *Soloush* term referring to a male. "I miss home."

Zaiyera sighed. "I wish I could tell you otherwise …"

He held up a hand. "No. I don't want to believe it, but I'd rather not sit here in ignorance, lying to myself. He's getting worse. I allowed myself to be naïve enough to hope he would fight the urges and overcome the addiction. Impossible."

"Nothing is impossible," Zaiyera said.

"How would you know?" Kima snapped.

"How would you?" Zaiyera countered.

"Spare me the false hope," Kima said. "It's well known the addiction can't be overcome. I've had to endure little more than silence on the fate of my brother. And every tiny morsel of information I've been fed has spoken of his steady descent into madness. I took it as Eredin's cruel lies because of what happened, but now I know otherwise." His voice cracked. "And here I sit, torn between the desire to hear news that he's destroyed a Dor'haighen civilization, or that he has finally fallen, and is no longer a terror to the world."

Zaiyera frowned at him. "You wish him to wage a personal war with the north?"

Kima looked at her from the corner of his eye. "You truly know nothing at all. What do you plan to do with this information, should I divulge it to you?"

"I...don't know." Zaiyera leaned her head back against the cold stone wall. "When I battled him, Malhadiev seemed to have a strong hatred for the north. He mentioned this land more than once with a fair bit of contempt. I suppose I'm involved in this, or rather, I was. I'm not in the habit of being used, and I know little of the events leading up to now."

"Again I ask, what would you do with this knowledge?"

Zaiyera took a deep breath. "From what I've learned, you and Malhadiev have been wronged. Horribly wronged. But should the unwitting people of Dor'haighen pay the price as so many of our people in Samhar have already paid?"

That reached him. "Our people."

"I already told you, he destroyed much of Shanhazai. Did you think he picked through the population, sparing every Samharan who cowered in fear or ran away? No. And he's syphoned so many stream-dancers, there can be no doubt that the addiction has taken him." It hurt to say those last words, despite their truth.

"Enough, please." Kima held up a hand. "You might be right, but I hate this." He stared across the room, looking into a place much farther away than the "room" in which they sat.

"I was part of a delegation representing one of the five major cities of Samhar in the negotiation of furthering trade with Dor'haighen. Malhadiev's surprise had been equal to mine when he'd been informed that he would be part of the delegation. Since he'd constantly been an objective voice in Jegried's trade schemes, surely the man would have wanted to keep Malhadiev out of such an important part of his plans."

Kima wrinkled his lips in anger. "Malhadiev saw it as an opportunity and jumped at it. Just as Jegried knew he would. The members of the delegation were selected, myself among them due to my skills at negotiating. We set out just two days after Jegried's announcement.

"Several days into our travels, we stopped for the night at an oasis. I'm a light sleeper. When I heard the slightest movement, I figured an animal had come upon our camp. It *was* an animal. One of Jegried's animals.

"He and Eredin had come to an agreement long before our delegation was dispatched to this cursed ice ball. Jegried had an assassin planted in our midst to kill us while we were en route. Surviving that, it didn't take much for me to figure out that once we were out of the way, Jegried's man would continue on to meet with a group of escorts to bring him here. I arrived at a village on camelback, barely alive. Eredin's men had been waiting, just not for me."

"How could that have worked?" Zaiyera asked. "Once the other cities found out what happened—"

"How would they have known anything but what was told to them?" Kima interrupted. "The scavengers would have long ago devoured all but our bones by the time an investigation was launched. Any manner of tragedy could have been concocted."

Zaiyera took a deep breath to keep her anger in check. "What happened during the assassination attempt?"

Kima almost growled the words. "I awoke and alerted the others. But the man was good. He'd already killed four of the seven of us by the time I'd woken. He was quick and efficient. By the time Malhadiev and I got to our feet, he'd leaped clear across the campfire and stabbed another representative from Zalrabi in the neck."

The man shuddered, and Zaiyera could only imagine what that night must have been like; what horrible images it left burned into Kima's mind.

"He never slowed. After he killed the man, I dove into a roll as my brother danced the stream against him. He kicked me in the stomach.

When I doubled over, he sprang upward and drove his knee into my nose, then spun me around.

"When Malhadiev saw the blood on my face, he hesitated. Shakimah be praised, it was at that moment I tried to break free. The dagger aimed at the middle of my back went below my shoulder instead. Painful to put it lightly, but not fatal." He leaned forward and lifted his tunic. Zaiyera took in a sharp breath at the sight of the angry, bubbled scar.

"He struck me in the back of the head with the butt of his dagger, and I dropped to my knees and fell over. As I blacked out I heard my brother screaming, and the ground rumbled."

He went silent for a while. Zaiyera used that time to digest all of this.

"It must have been by the power of Goddess Shakimah that I somehow crawled out of the river and wrapped my shoulder tightly to slow the bleeding. I got to my camel and rode north while falling in and out of consciousness." He gave a helpless chuckle. "I don't remember doing it, but at some point I managed to find and apply Ogko tree bark sap to block the wound and rewrap it. The last clear memory I have is waking up in the infirmary here, in Nanshaigha Castle. The surgeon told me that the king had made it clear no effort or expense was to be spared to ensure my survival. He also told me that the Ogko sap was the only reason I hadn't bled out and died. Still, she hadn't expected me to live."

He chewed his lip. "All those dead men. For wealth."

"How do you know all this?" Zaiyera asked.

Kima responded with another chuckle, this one bitter. "Interesting how in some lands, the higher on the social level one is, the more arrogant they can be. These idiots believe we are like them. That not a single person in all Samhar would understand their language."

"I don't."

"It doesn't matter," Kima said. "I don't know every language in the world, but I've traveled to Dor'haighen enough times to learn it. They assume I would never have learned their tongue."

"So they spoke freely around you," Zaiyera surmised. She glanced back at the door. "A mistake best learned from, is it not?"

"One of the skills you learn when in my position, is how to read a face. I've said some things around these people that would have elicited a reaction from a statue. There are some in Nanshaigha who speak *Soloush*, but none of them work anywhere near here. Trust me when I tell you that I've had plenty of time to figure out who speaks our tongue and who doesn't.

"When I first arrived, I listened when they thought I was unconscious. The king always had an advisor with him when he came to loom over me. They'd discuss their options should I die. They spoke in curves, never outright saying what they meant."

Zaiyera nodded at that, recalling her own experiences.

"Despite what this northern royalty think, I'm not stupid. Jegried is as conniving as he is ambitious." He turned his angry gaze on Zaiyera. "His name was mentioned in every conversation Eredin and his advisor had while standing over my bed.

"The idiots spoke about the assassin's orders, and how Malhadiev had gone crazy. The king was putting together a contingent of shydon hunters to track and kill Malhadiev before he grew too powerful and came here."

"And King Eredin keeps you in case his plan failed and your brother comes for him," Zaiyera said.

"His shield," Kima spat, "or whatever he plans to use me for. If the idiot had had me healed and released, I might have stopped Malhadiev from becoming what he is. But, if what they say is true ...""

Zaiyera reached for his shoulder, hesitated, then gave it a squeeze. "It's true, Kima. I've a friend who saw with his own eyes as Malhadiev syphoned dancers, and I heard his hatred for Dor'haighen with my own ears."

"He's going to come here and kill Eredin."

Zaiyera shook her head. "If Shanhazai is any indication, he's going to come here and kill everyone."

"And here I sit," Kima said. "Useless."

Zaiyera made up her mind. "I must leave soon to return to Samhar.

The nights are so very cold here." She stared into his eyes. "I'll come to visit you once more before I leave. In two days."

Kima studied her expression as she willed him to understand what she meant. A quick look into her eyes and he nodded. "I'll see you then."

29

"*Z*aiyera, the risk taker." Jaide lifted her mug in toast.

Zhuyun and Barum did likewise while Zaiyera rolled her eyes and lifted her mug as well.

Little more than the crackle of flames in the hearth broke the relative silence in the inn's common room at this hour, just before dawn. Having finished setting up and cleaning for the day's business, the serving staff milled about, attending to the odd chore during casual talk. The smell of cooking food thickened the air like soup.

Zaiyera held her warm mug cupped in her hands, silently enduring the burn of withdrawals.

"It seems you have a surprise or two about you, yes?" the Viriksani said. "I wouldn't have taken you for the type to take such a risk."

Zaiyera took a sip of her hot spiced *chaffa*. "Not so big a risk."

Jaide snorted. "Oh? You asked to see a prisoner of the kingdom without leave to do so by the king or queen. What do you think might have happened if Eredin had found out?"

"Kima isn't officially a prisoner," Zaiyera said. "There's no reason to deny him a visitor."

"Maybe not," Jaide replied, "but you run the risk of the guard informing the Cold King up there in his ice castle that his unofficial prisoner had a visitor. How far of a reach do you think it would be to figure out it was one of us?"

"A risk it may be," Zhuyun said. "But the king failed to mention Malha—" he glanced around. The place was still nearly empty, but he lowered his voice anyway. "Our 'friend' had a brother to begin with. He had plenty of opportunity to mention that little detail but didn't."

"Which means he wants the presence of this brother," Jaide looked at Zaiyera, "Kima, you said his name was? Seems to me the Cold King wants to keep him a secret."

"If that were the case, I'd think Eredin wouldn't allow visitors," Zaiyera said.

"Unless he doesn't want the situation to be suspicious," Jaide countered, "and simply told his guards to admit anyone, but report back to him if someone did come."

"All possible," Zhuyun said. "But consider the circumstances. Who would come looking for this man? Even his brother thinks he's dead, and Jegried certainly wouldn't have launched an inquiry, ixu?"

Jaide pointed at the Yuntaiman in concession. She looked back at Zaiyera and raised her eyebrows. "I think I know you well enough, now, that I should feel nervous at that look."

"Hm?" Zaiyera looked up from her drink.

"You've been staring into your mug as though it holds the answers to life's most profound musings," Jaide replied.

Zaiyera took another sip and continued to stare. "I'm going back to visit him in two days." When she looked up again, she saw the other two staring back at her.

Zhuyun responded with a slow, deliberate nod. "I see."

Jaide blinked. "I'm guessing … you intend to leave after this visit, yes?"

Zaiyera nodded.

"Well, then." Jaide leaned back in her chair. Should we secure some of those nightmarish lizards?"

"That would be good," Zaiyera said.

"I'm sure I don't want to know how you intend to … visit him again?" Jaide asked.

"Probably not." Zaiyera finished her *chaffa* and sat the mug down with a heavy thud.

"I'm going to find Barum," Jaide said. She pushed her chair back and stood. He'll want to be part of this."

Zhuyun took a final draw from his mug as the Viriksani swept out the door. "Come. I'd like to talk."

"There's hardly anyone here," Zaiyera said, looking about the mostly empty common room.

"I like to walk while I talk," came the reply.

Zaiyera looked longingly at the warm crackling flames as she pushed her chair back.

The crisp morning air clouded in front of their faces with each breath and with each word. A frozen breeze snaked its way down the distant snowy hills and sighed along the hard stone streets. Zaiyera wrapped her furs closer and secured her scarf over her mouth. After but a few steps, she wrapped her head. The air felt like frozen fingers sliding along the spaces between her plaited hair.

"We're headed back toward the castle," Zaiyera said once the massive structure came into view.

"Indeed," Zhuyun said. "I find the grounds between the gates separating Nanshaigha and its royal home to be relaxing."

Zaiyera swallowed her annoyance. The perceptive Zhuyun surely knew she'd want to be making plans for getting Kima out. This must be important. When the hunger burned and twisted her insides again, she recognized that as another source of her impatience.

They went through the open gates and walked uphill, passing between mounds green with winter grass, and the many trees and multicolored bushes filling the grounds.

He led her off the path and through the trees, along the side of the garden with a view overlooking Endless Lake. She looked around, noting their hidden location. "Is this where you hit me over the head and take my coin purse, Zhuyun?"

He laughed. "You've caught me, my perceptive friend. Come. Stand beside me; just there." He pointed at the ground several feet away.

Zaiyera moved to the designated spot and waited. She blinked at him, beneath her frown.

"Now," Zhuyun said, the word little more than a sigh escaping his lips. "Move with me."

He raised his hands, palms sweeping upward until they faced out, then pointed them down and lowered them. At the same time, he bent his legs. He swept his arms outward and took a step to the side.

Zaiyera remembered the time in the woods and followed the Yuntaiman's lead. The pattern was the same at first, and so she easily moved in sync with him. Then Zhuyun entered a new combination of movements. Despite the unfamiliar patterns, Zaiyera managed to keep up, though she suspected it was because he slowed down for her.

"The body has its own energy within; its own flow." Zhuyun closed his eyes as he moved. "In Yuntai, we call this energy *qikai*." He cracked his eyes open in a sideways glance at her and said it again, slower. "That's *chee kai*."

"*Qikai*," Zaiyera repeated.

Zhuyun nodded. "*Qikai* flows through the body of every living thing. Us, the animals and trees, insects, birds, the mountains, the creatures swimming in the depths of the Great Sea and even in this beautiful lake before us."

Zaiyera continued to follow his movements, matching the sweeping and arcing of his arms, dipping low into a crouching stance as she moved sideways to rise tall again.

"Feel your *qikai*," Zhuyun whispered. "Feel it flowing through your body. It can warm you, invigorate you, give you strength beyond what you think is possible."

Zaiyera closed her eyes. Despite not being able to see him, she somehow felt Zhuyun's movements and followed them. The energy he spoke of flowed through her body like blood through her veins. It felt similar to touching the stream, though smaller than a fraction in capacity.

Her body warmed, the hunger slowly dissolved, and the stiffness brought on by the cold fell away. Her body moved with the fluidity of water itself. She suddenly became aware of the smell of the trees, the bushes, the lake, and the scent of a patrolling guard at the far end of the garden.

She sensed Zhuyun's presence beside her. He shone in the pitch darkness of her closed eyes like a golden flame. What was this?

Time fell away, long forgotten as Zaiyera released herself into the flow of her *qikai*. It felt as though she lay in a running stream, opening her arms as she floated on her back, carried away by the current.

Zaiyera hadn't realized Zhuyun had stopped speaking until she finally stilled and opened her eyes. The sun had risen above the eastern horizon and lit the bluish dawn with its golden rays.

Zhuyun stood a few paces away, smiling at her. Zaiyera blinked in puzzlement, then noticed the yellow glow of her tainted dance-resin coating her shoulder. She looked at her hands and the rest of her body, then turned her wide-eyed expression on him. Her dance-resin faded away, but her shock and horror remained.

Zhuyun held up a hand. "Please, be calm. How do you feel?"

Despite the Yuntaiman's words, Zaiyera's breath came in rapid puffs. Her heart pounded in her chest. She glanced about in search of, what, an escape route?

"Zaiyera." Zhuyun's deep voice vibrated in the air and settled over her like a warm cloak. "Be at ease, my good friend. You have found your *qikai* and blended it with the stream. That is a very difficult thing to do."

She stared at him, her lips still parted in a combination of panic and horror. He'd seen her tainted dance-resin. He'd seen it!

He took a careful step forward. When she didn't react, he reached out and took her hands in his. Heat radiated from his palms into hers and spread up her arms, into her chest, and traveled through her body.

"How do you feel?"

Zaiyera stared at him. "I ... don't you know?" She looked down at their joined hands.

Zhuyun gave a slow nod. "Yes. You are calmed. How do you *feel*?"

She knew what he was asking. She'd known the first time he asked. She just couldn't bring herself to acknowledge it.

"I am your friend, Zaiyera. Friends help each other. I will help you in any way I may, if you allow me to do so, ixu?"

Zaiyera responded with a trembling nod.

"How do you feel?" he asked a third time.

"Steady. Balanced." She took a steadying breath and still found it shaky. "I can't put it into exact words, but the"—She took another deep breath and forced herself to say it. "The hunger is gone."

The corners of Zhuyun's eyes crinkled above his half smile. "If you continue this, the effects will grow more lasting. I wish I could tell you whether it can be permanent, but it will help."

"Why?" It was the only thing Zaiyera could think to ask.

"Have I not just said?"

"But, you know. You've known for some time now, haven't you? You know I'm a … you know what I am. So why help me? I don't deserve it."

"Don't you?" Zhuyun asked. "I don't understand why not. You are a kind and caring soul, my friend Zaiyera. You help others at the risk of your own life."

"I'm paid to do that."

"You know what I mean," Zhuyun said. "You could have refused to aid Dyren and Malker, but you didn't. You knew the risk of being discovered and could have left them to die. No one would have been the wiser. Instead, you saved their lives and endure every hardship beside them to aid in a mission that has nothing to do with you."

Zaiyera opened her mouth, then closed it. Despite Zhuyun's kind words, it felt like a pall of shame settled over her shoulders and she turned away to gaze out at the lake. The sun sent a stream of golden light burning across the water from shore to shore. Bird chatter raced through the brisk fresh air. She closed her eyes and felt the cold crisp air on her face, inhaled the fragrant winter foliage surrounding them.

A strong hand fell on her shoulder and squeezed. "I don't know what circumstances led to your state, but only a person with an indomitable will and a powerful sense of honor and morality could manage the withdrawals. I've encountered more than one *ying'tokailan* in my travels. Good people many of them were. Not a one ever managed the burden for long."

"I've no right *not* to manage the … hunger," Zaiyera said. This conversation felt like a stab to the heart, her words bleeding out of a wound that never healed; that she didn't deserve to heal.

Her legs threatened to give out as the grief and guilt rolled over her.

Zhuyun placed a comforting arm around her. "I meant not to cause you pain. Perhaps this old fool talks too much, ah?"

Zaiyera shook her head. "No. You've given me a gift I don't deserve, but I thank you for it."

"I don't know what in your past keeps you from forgiving yourself," Zhuyun said, "but you must do this. Self-hatred will eat you from the inside out, *ixu*?"

Zaiyera had no reply to that. Aried Dom had more of a right to live than she did to forgive herself, yet he was long dead while she lived. Thinking of Aried, dead before his fifteenth birthday, sent a fresh wave of shame washing over her.

"The dead cannot be returned to life," Zhuyun said in a quiet and compassionate voice. "But they can be honored or redeemed by the actions of the living."

Zaiyera's expression hardened. "Then I should have died years ago. I'm no better than the man I've pledged to hunt down."

A frown creased Zhuyun's brow. "I doubt that, my friend."

"I don't."

"I think—"

"There isn't anything to think or discuss, about what I am, Zhuyun Xaiylin." The words came out more harshly than she'd intended. "I am the same kind of monster we're trying to stop. No words or kindness changes that, so discussing it is useless."

Zhuyun bowed his head and said nothing.

Zaiyera glanced at him, then took a long deep breath and let it out in a frosty cloud in front of her face. "I was eleven years old."

Zhuyun raised his eyebrows but remained silent.

For a while, she said nothing more. The nineteen-year-old memory still twisted her insides into a knot. Speaking the words aloud made it burn.

"My … my mother raised me in the way of a woman. I learned how to forage, how to recognize where roots and edible plants lived. I learned how to read the land to find food and water. My father, taught me how to defend myself. I learned how to hunt, how to track, how to fight. I learned the sword.

"Among my people it's unusual for a girl to be raised in such a way. Men and women each have their roles to play in maintaining the *ka*. My father believed his only daughter should be prepared for anything this harsh life might throw at her. He wanted me to be able to fight, to have any option in life to choose from."

The sun rose higher above the eastern horizon, slowly but surely bringing warmth and light to Dor'haighen. Soon the rest of the population would be awake, and the seclusion of the garden would fade.

"The boys of the *ka* thought it odd that a girl ran with them to learn to track and hunt. I was the smallest, and they treated me as if I was the weakest. Whenever I joined the hunt, they would run faster, climb faster, do everything they could to leave me behind. When they couldn't, some came to respect me while others refused."

Zaiyera smiled ruefully at the memory. "I couldn't understand why they treated me that way, until Baba one day told me that the boys saw me as a girl invading their space. They didn't like me challenging their place in Kushtanji society. To me, I was simply learning survival.

"By my ninth birthday Baba began to teach me the sword. A year later I had beaten every boy my age or older. Except for one boy. Aried Dom."

Zaiyera let out an involuntary shudder at speaking the name.

"He was fifteen years old and the best with the sword of any child in the *ka*. The first time we sparred, he beat me till I was bruised all over. It went this way every day for the first half year. Despite his constant taunts and insults, his superior skill aided my growth. I got better, but only at receiving fewer bruises after every defeat.

"On my twelfth birthday, my grandmother used all the money she had to commission a blacksmith to forge a scimitar for me." Zaiyera took another deep breath to stall the tears welling in her eyes."

Zhuyun placed a gentle hand on her back. "If you are uncomfortable sharing this memory—"

"No, no. You have shared something special with me. I owe you this much, at least."

"You owe me nothing," Zhuyun replied.

"Then indulge my sense of personal obligation, my friend Zhuyun." She stared out at Endless Lake, growing more golden by the minute. "I was young and didn't fully understand what it meant that she spent everything she had on this scimitar for me. When it was finished, she showed it to me, then took it back and declared that it was time for her to go out into the desert to finish it.

"That was when I knew she was at the end of her life. Uta had been a powerful streamdancer and had even begun to teach me how to dance the stream. As her final gift to me, she intended to reforge the blade into a dancecraft artifact. That is the way of Samhar. To create a dance-craft artifact for a beloved when at the end of your life is the greatest show of love you can express when your time has come."

Zaiyera wiped away the tears spilling down her eyes. "She had imbued the scimitar with the ability to absorb whatever properties I wished, but only once. It was a powerful gift, but a power I wouldn't learn to unlock for another year, after I'd learned more about the stream.

"When we began practicing with real blades it had been difficult adjusting to the weight of a steel scimitar while being mercilessly punished by that boy.

"One day after Aried Dom had defeated me yet again, he taunted me. He said I didn't deserve my scimitar, and that such a weapon and sacrifice was wasted on me." Zaiyera's smiled mirthlessly into a faraway place.

"Something inside me went cold when he said that. I took up the blade and challenged him again. The fight started as any other; Aried taunting me as he blocked and parried my advances. But I began to gain the advantage. I saw the way he moved like I hadn't before. In my cold focus, he seemed to move slow.

"My anger narrowed my focus and drove my skill to a new level while I drove my opponent to his limits. When Aried realized this, he began to touch the stream. I finally had him on the brink of defeat and he was about to cheat me out of it. I fought as though my life depended on it, and eventually bested him and stabbed him through the shoulder. I was so angry …" Zaiyera closed her eyes. "I was so angry I didn't realize what I was doing until it was too late.

"I'd touched the stream, too, the moment I'd stabbed him. To this day I don't know how, but I syphoned his lifestream. Not only that, my touching the stream at the same time as syphoning him, had activated my scimitar's power. When Aried had touched the stream to dance against me, my reflexive response was to cut through his dance. When I stabbed him through the shoulder and began syphoning his lifestream, I'd activated the blade with my power and intent."

Zaiyera shook her head. "It happened so quickly. He died staring at me in horror. I panicked and ran. I went home and packed a little food and a waterskin and left the *ka* for the nearest city, several hours away."

"The open desert sounds like a dangerous place for a child," Zhuyun said. It was the first time he'd said anything since Zaiyera had started talking.

"It is," she said. "Which is how I first saw what would be one of the two constant reminders of what I'd become. A pack of raiders tried to kidnap me. I danced the stream as Uta had taught me. For a mercy, I wasn't strong enough or experienced enough to kill them. That might have broken my young mind. Still, I left them all badly injured, but alive."

Zaiyera twisted the end of her coat between her fists. "I had no right to use grandma's gift after what I'd done. My punishment was to see my golden dance-resin tainted orange. The tainted resin of a darkdancer."

"Did your family ever find you?" Zhuyun asked.

"No."

"Have you ever gone back to find them?"

"No," Zaiyera repeated. "I fled my *ka* like a murderous coward and never looked back. I had shamed myself and my family. Better that Baba never have to look upon the disgrace I had become."

They sat in silence for a long time before Zhuyun finally spoke. "Would you allow this humble fool a word?"

"You're hardly a fool, Zhuyun Xaiylin." Zaiyera still stared out at the lake. She couldn't bear to look at him.

"I do not make light of the life that was lost," Zhuyun began in a careful tone. "But I know a mistake when I hear one. My friend Zaiyera, you were a child who made a horrible mistake, but a mistake it was. We all serve penance in one way or another for our misdeeds in life. We serve them, and we move on and do better, ixu?"

Zhuyun stared at her until she finally looked at him. The compassion reflected in his brown eyes nearly undid her.

"You've been serving this penance for nineteen years," Zhuyun said. "More than half your life. How long will you punish yourself so?"

"Until it is my time to leave this world and return to *Sojalleh*, if the Goddess Shakimah will have me."

"Your tone suggests you don't hold much hope for this."

"How could I deserve such a reward?"

That warm crinkle-eyed smile returned. "Your work has saved a good many lives in the short time I've known you, ah? I'm sure you've saved many more before then. And you've done what I've seen no other person in your circumstances able to do. You've refused to touch the stream."

He gave her shoulder a friendly pat, then stood. "You are a good woman with a painful past. I see the way you look at your scimitar. You think of it as a constant reminder of your past. Just as you do your lance-resin. Perhaps both could serve not as a reminder of a terrible past, but hope for a future."

Zaiyera frowned. "Hope?"

"There are many who carry the taint of actions they wished they hadn't committed. How many of them fight against the hunger, refusing it as long as possible before they finally succumb? Who could be more of a beacon of hope than one who shares their burden, ixu?"

He left her to ponder his words. What was Zhuyun suggesting? What could a darkdancer be, other than rightfully reviled by every society in the world?

She sat for a long time, contemplating his words. The distant chatter of conversation drifted up the hill as the city awoke.

Zaiyera stood and walked through the gardens toward Nanshaigha proper. She filed the conversation away and set her mind to exploring the streets. She'd be leaving soon, and the monarchs of Nanshaigha wouldn't be happy.

30

Zaiyera awoke at dawn the next day, and immediately recalled the path she and the guard had taken to get to Kima's cell. She didn't plan on her second visit being that way, but best to be prepared. Bundled in her furs, she left the inn and made straight for First Castle.

People moved about the streets in various amounts of clothing that told of how far north or south in the country they lived. She received more lingering gazes than in the two previous cities she'd passed through, as southerners were even more of a rarity this far north and west.

By the time she reached First Castle, the city was fully awake. People on foot and in carriages passed about the populated streets, and Zaiyera took careful note of the lesser used avenues.

Unlike the first time she'd passed through First Castle, Zaiyera had time to explore the inner ward. She paid special attention to the direction the front doors to the keep were facing, as well as every window.

Archers patrolled the parapets, keeping watch of the populace below and beyond the walls. Zaiyera had made sure to come when there were more people about, so as not to look suspicious while she studied the layout.

When she reached the huge bridge, she moved to the left side and leaned on the chest-high wall. She raised up onto her toes and peered out at the distant mountains enclosing Endless Lake. She stretched with a contented groan, and continued her casual stroll, occasionally glancing at the mountains. When she came to a spot where the mountain range was at a familiar angle, she leaned on the wall and again raised on her toes to peer over the side.

She huffed in satisfaction when she saw the red roof of a small building growing right out the side of the stone bridge.

"If you come out here just before dawn, the morning haze is glorious."

So intent on her task, Zaiyera's heart skipped when she heard the voice. She turned to see a man with blond hair and green eyes smiling nervously at her.

He held up his hands in a placating gesture. "Apologies, my lady miss. I didn't mean to frighten you. I was just admiring a beautiful sight."

"It is beautiful," Zaiyera said, looking back out at Endless Lake and beyond. "Everything is beautiful in the tranquility of dawn."

"Indeed," the man said, and Zaiyera refrained from rolling her eyes. "May I?"

She glanced at him and nodded.

"You've the look of a southerner," the man said. "Such a beautiful specimen, you are."

"Do all northerners use such odd complimentary terms?"

"I suppose every land has something strange about it to its visitors." He offered a shallow bow. "I am Jered Malgo, of Nanshaigha."

"A pleasure," Zaiyera said.

"And you are?"

"A woman in a strange land who would love to be more acquainted with it."

"Well," Jered Malgo offered a slanted smile and bowed. "I'm at your service, my lady miss. I have lived in Nanshaigha my entire life. What would you know?"

She leaned sideways against the wall and smiled into his crystal blue eyes. "I find this castle magnificent, but I confess," she pointed down at the many structures at the base of First Castle. "There are balconies and doorways, I see. Where would those people go?"

She listened with half an ear as Jered Malgo told her of the construction of First and Nanshaigha Castles, remarking on more than one occasion that he was the descendent of one of the head architects who'd designed them.

"Interesting," Zaiyera said with more enthusiasm than she felt. It wasn't *exactly* a lie. "I can't imagine how they built these places right into the side of the bridge."

Jered perked up. "That is actually one of the many prides of my family and Nanshaigha. There is no other place in all the world with such a design!" He pointed over the side. "They're difficult to see from here, but the stone masons used larger bricks as steps to link those small platforms that look like balconies."

Zaiyera's eyes widened. "Moon and stars! Why would anyone want to walk along that?"

"To finish the construction," Jered replied. "The builders and painters needed a way to get from one structure to the next without having to go through the inside of the bridge, which was loaded with supplies at the time."

Jered led Zaiyera along the bridge, pointing out the many architectural accomplishments of his forefathers. She felt a small bit of guilt, using the man like this. *A greater good,* she reminded herself. *He will indirectly help me to help many.*

"I'm boring you, aren't I?"

Zaiyera blinked away her musings and looked at him. Jered's lips were compressed, and his brow knitted to a peak. The guilt returned. "You aren't boring, Jered Malgo. I just have much on my mind."

His face brightened. "Then perhaps a drink to ease it?" He spread a hand back toward Nanshaigha proper. "I know the best places for a steaming bowl of stew and a cold mug of frost beer, or spiced *chaffa.*"

She placed a hand on his arm, felt him flex, and tried again not to roll her eyes. She could practically hear Jaide Amadi's smug laughter in her mind. "Another time, I'm afraid. I have somewhere I must be."

"Might I escort you to your destination?"

"Is Nanshaigha so dangerous?"

"I … no."

Zaiyera smiled. "Then I believe I should be fine. I have a number things to do that I'm confident will thoroughly bore you. Perhaps we might meet again in a few days."

Jared Malgo bowed again. "I shall look forward to it, my lady miss."

Zaiyera left him with thanks for providing such fascinating information. She thought about what she intended to do and hoped it wouldn't come back to haunt him.

She lingered until dusk before making her way back to the city proper. She'd navigated these streets at night once already and felt confident she could do so again while in a hurry. She took the rehearsed route without issue on her way to meet with Zhuyun, Jaide, and Barum. They didn't like the idea of escaping with Kima in tow, but Zaiyera had made up her mind. She'd be leaving with the man tonight.

Zaiyera ended the day with a hot meal and carefully laid out plans. She'd spent hours studying the structures alongside the bridge, spied the protruding walkway stones Jered had spoken of, as well as the planks linking them. She would make the climb at nightfall.

* * *

All too soon the tranquil oblivion of sleep faded, and Zaiyera's eyes popped open. She lay in the darkness, collecting her thoughts. Gathering her nerve. She closed her eyes again and envisioned the path to the cell. She tried to recreate in her mind the climb from the roof of the cell to the top of the bridge wall. She visualized the flaws in the integrity of the window, the width of the walkways, the protruding stones the builders had used.

Zaiyera slipped out of bed, lit a candle, and quietly dressed. She strapped Shatr to her waist, concealed underneath her coat, and slipped out of the room. She made her way down the hallway leading to a door to stairs at the rear of the building.

The streets were mostly quiet at this time of night, though Zaiyera passed the occasional nighttime stroller. She still couldn't believe anyone would voluntarily be out in this freezing cold.

Zaiyera took her planned departure route in reverse, once again ensuring she would remember when it was time to leave in a hurry. Soon she reached the open gates to the hilly garden leading uphill to First Castle.

Conscious of archers patrolling the parapets, she kept her pace casual and walked close to a clump of people in front of her. She nearly swore when she saw a pair of guards standing at the portcullis to First Castle. She quickly unstrapped her scimitar and re-secured it to her hip in plain view. Fortunately the people here moved about with swords strapped to their backs or hips anyway.

They passed through the inner ward and continued onto the bridge. Several well-dressed people strode toward them, making casual conversation in *Dreuga*. Zaiyera smiled at them.

She broke away from the group at the end of the bridge just before the portcullis to Nanshaigha Castle. The night was dry and cold, and the wind gave it an extra bite. Zaiyera didn't relish the thought of what it would feel like on the side of this huge stone bridge. Standing flush against the wall and out of view of the patrolling archers, she leaned on the wall, pretending to gaze out at the partially moonlit lake while studying the structures below.

As she'd noted before, the first little building had a flat roof and was less than a dozen foot drop. It connected to a circular building via a stone walkway that she hoped wasn't covered in ice.

Another pack of nighttime revelers strolled through the portcullis just as she was about to climb over. Zaiyera waited as they stopped walking at some crucial point in the conversation. She tapped her knuckles on the wall during the ensuing laughter. *Hurry up!*

Finally they moved on. As soon as they were halfway down the bridge, and the archers on First Castle turned, she slipped over the wall and dropped to the flat roof.

Her feet slipped out from under her as soon as she landed on an invisible layer of ice. Years of training and footwork saved her. She twisted even as her feet slipped upward and landed on tips of her fingers and her toes in a crouch.

She carefully shimmied sideways until she reached the wall for support. Confident no one had seen, she tested her gloved hands on the stones, gripping the protruding pillars next to her. There was a bit of frost, but luckily no ice. She simply dusted it off.

Over the side of the roof looked like a two-hundred-foot drop to the rocks and water below. She leaned back and took a deep breath, then sat down and hung her legs over the side. She turned onto her stomach and placed her hands on the roof. Muscles developed from a lifetime of training bunched in her arms as she lifted herself to an upright position.

She used her toes to slide downward as she carefully lowered herself until she was hanging down the side of the building, her feet only several feet above the path. She let go and dropped softly and soundlessly.

Zaiyera took another deep breath and turned to face the stone walkway. It was wide enough for two people to walk abreast, but the layer of ice and the cold wind moaning in her ears made her hesitate.

No going back now. She placed her foot on the bridge and put some of her weight on it. She slipped and almost fell. After staring at the frozen walkway for a moment, Zaiyera knelt and crawled on hands and knees. Though her heart hammered in her chest, she made her way across with minimal slipping, and came to the next building.

Back pressed against the cold stone wall, Zaiyera moved around the circular building using the narrow built-in walkway. Pieces here and there had broken away over the centuries, so it was slow-going as she tested each step before placing her weight down.

She made gradual progress from one building to the next in a similar manner, carefully crossing the linking pathways on hands and knees. When she finally came to the small building next to Kima's "room", she looked down and saw two twin structures far down on the pillars of the bridge. She shook her head, thankful he hadn't been put down there.

When she came around the side, she let out a misty sigh through her nostrils. Time had worn away some of the stone, and the walkway had cracked and fallen away at certain points. She eyed the icy platform and saw her death waiting in front of her.

Another freezing gust of wind caressed her face. She took a deep breath and reminded herself what was at stake. Her homeland. Her people. Her family and every person between Malhadiev and Nanshaigha. She would free Kima and get his help to stop his brother, or she would die in the effort. Better that than returning home to absolute devastation.

Zaiyera said a silent prayer to Shakimah, took a few quick breaths, and bolted for the walkway. She led with one foot as she slid toward the cracked gap, then crouched and jumped. Several pieces of stone crumbled and fell away. As soon as her feet touched down on the far side of the walkway, they slipped out from under her.

Feet over head, Zaiyera landed on her back. The wind blasted from her lungs as she slid the rest of the way to crash into the wall. She lay there for many heartbeats, panting as she pushed her panic down. Several moments later, she finally heard the broken stones plunge into the lake below. *Moon and stars*.

Zaiyera huddled in on herself while she martialed her courage again. Then she heard someone softly calling her name. She climbed back to her feet and moved around the walkway to peer into a pair of shutters slightly cracked open. Kima's alarmed eyes widened from the other side of the window when he saw her.

Kima looked over his shoulder at the door behind him, then turned back. "Moon and stars, woman!" he hissed through the cracked window. "What madness has taken you?"

Despite her terrified heart hammering in her chest, Zaiyera felt some small comfort in hearing *Soloush* spoken again. "I told you I was coming back."

"Of course, but ... this?"

Zaiyera shivered. "It's cold out here, Kima. We need to get moving. Now."

"You don't expect me to go out there and die."

"I expect you to think about the stakes," Zaiyera hissed, "find your courage, and do what must be done. And I expect you to do it quickly!" She opened the shutters a bit more. "Don't open the window all the way. If there's a gust of wind, it'll howl right through and make too much noise."

"I can barely fit through that," Kima said.

"Do your best," Zaiyera replied.

With one last glance at the cell door, Kima muttered a curse and climbed up. He slipped one leg out the window, then the other.

"We have to hurry," she said once he was beside her. "We only need to cross two walkways and there's a flat roof where we can climb back to the bridge." Zaiyera handed him the spare fur cloak and gloves she'd packed. Kima complained about the minimal protection from the cold, but quieted when she offered to take it back. As they moved around the small building, Zaiyera kept careful watch on him. Kima wasn't shivering yet, but he had his arms crossed in front of his torso.

She led him across the first walkway, showing him how to crawl over the icy stone on hands and knees. Kima improvised, using his forearms and the balls of his feet to spare his already cold hands and knees. Zaiyera tried not to look down at the terrifying height as they continued around the next structure.

Beside her, Kima gasped, and she grabbed his wrist. "Look at where you're going, not down." They made it around to the next walkway and did the same as before. *Now the hard part.* "Time to climb." Zaiyera pointed to the roof of the structure they stood next to.

When Kima didn't respond, she looked at him. He stood hunched over, breath billowing from his mouth like a chimney, his arms wrapped around his torso with his hands tucked into his underarms. Zaiyera wished she'd found him thicker gloves. "How are your hands?"

"Right now, tucked, they're fine." He looked up. "I don't like this."

"I haven't liked it from the start," Zaiyera said. "Let's go."

Despite it not being a long climb, it was slow-going. Each stone was either covered in light frost, or a thin layer of ice or both. When Zaiyera encountered an ice layer, she slipped her hip dagger out and cracked it with the butt of the hilt and swiped it away.

Once Zaiyera reached the roof, she slipped over the side and rolled away from the edge. She looked over the side to see Kima already climbing. Moments later, he reached the edge of the roof and she reached down and grabbed him under the arm to help him up. She waited while he huddled against the wall and slapped his hands against his legs to get the warmth back. Kima cupped his hands and blew into them, then flexed his fingers. "Ready."

When they turned to look at the protruding stones on the wall, Zaiyera slapped her hands on her thighs as she considered their options. They could either climb from here, which was a farther climb to the top, or traverse yet another cracked and broken walkway to the last small structure on the bridge wall. The climb from that structure, sitting higher up the bridge wall, would be shorter.

Kima followed her gaze. "There's wood on that building. "I'll take more wood and less stone."

Zaiyera nodded in agreement. They climbed down the other side of the building and stood at the broken path. Zaiyera ran and like before, slid part of the way, then jumped the remaining distance. Pieces of the walkway fell into the freezing water below.

On the other side, Zaiyera silently watched Kima working through his fear. She waved at him. When he looked up, she stared unblinkingly into his eyes, willing his courage to the surface. He gave a stiff nod, then took a step back and crouched. He trotted forward and slid unsteadily over the icy walkway, then jumped.

Kima landed in a hard fall, and a chunk of stone broke apart. Pieces of the ancient bridge crumbled apart behind him as Kima scrambled toward Zaiyera's outreached hand. He threw himself forward and slid the rest of the way on his stomach.

His slide was awkward, though, and the lower half of Kima's body slid over the side. His eyes widened above his silent scream as half his body slid over the side just as Zaiyera grabbed his hand.

Kima's breath came out in panicked gasps. One hand holding the ledge and one in Zaiyera's grasp, he looked over his shoulder.

"Don't look down!" she hissed at him. "Look at me!"

Half dangling over his death, Kima looked up in to her eyes. Zaiyera nodded to him. "Pull."

They growled in unison, each pulling with all their strength. Inch by terrifying inch, Zaiyera pulled him over the edge and helped him to his feet. They huddled next to the building, steadying their nerves while Kima tried to warm his hands again. Ever aware that time wasn't on their side, Zaiyera looked toward their destination and gave Kima a slap on the shoulder and pointed. "Come."

The next climb was higher, but the handholds were larger and more plentiful. They stopped for a brief rest on the slightly sloped roof, then moved to the wall. Only ten feet up to their destination; ten feet of smooth cold stone.

Zaiyera went first, once again brushing away frost or breaking away ice on each stone as she made her way. Below her, Kima waited.

She finally made it to the top and carefully peeked over the side. She ducked back down when she saw a handful of people coming, and waited till the talking receded. She looked over the side again, and when the way was clear, climbed up and swung her legs over.

Once her feet were on solid ground, she breathed a sigh of relief that she nearly choked on when she heard a familiar voice.

"Oh. Hello again."

Zaiyera turned on her heel to face a smiling Jered Venadonis. He swept her a low bow.

"Fate must smile upon me that just as I walk through that grim entryway to the ward, I come upon you once again, basking in the beauty of Endless Lake."

By the blazing sun! "Hello, Jered Venadonis." Zaiyera leaned her back against the wall to block his view. She said a silent prayer to Shakimah in the hope that Kima hadn't started up yet.

"Still so formal," Jered said. "I admit I'm surprised to see you out in what must be freezing cold to you."

"Hardly voluntary," Zaiyera said. She had to get rid of this man before Kima froze to death or slipped off. "I'm afraid I am forced to meet with someone and this was the designated spot."

"An odd place to meet when there are warmer places indoors."

"Scenery," Zaiyera said. "There is nothing like it in Samhar."

"Meeting with a Samhari countrywoman, then?" Jered asked,

clearly fishing. He looked out at the lake and mountains beyond. "Cold or not, I understand. It's a beautiful sight."

"He finds Dor'haighen, quite interesting, if different."

Jered's expression fell. "Oh. I see."

Zaiyera forced herself to laugh. "Your disappointment is noted, Jered Venadonis, but unnecessary. He is an acquaintance and nothing more." She heard a soft whistle from below.

"Did you hear that?" Jered said, moving toward the wall.

Zaiyera intercepted him, pressing her body against his. "The cold is relentless to penetrate my furs. After my meeting is done, might I see you again? Perhaps over a mug of your delicious *chaffa*? Someplace …comfortable?"

Jered looked down into her brown eyes and a smile twitched at the corner of his mouth. "That would be lovely."

Zaiyera fought down the urge to push him back, as Jared had misinterpreted her action. If she'd been more acquainted with the man, she might not have found his physical reaction to their closeness so off-putting. "Please, give me this time with my countryman that we might sooner meet."

"There is a little tavern just inside the gates to Nanshaigha—"

"The Stout Tap," Zaiyera interrupted, hearing another soft whistle.

"I shall see you there?" Jered asked.

Zaiyera smiled in response, and he gave another bow and left.

As soon as Jered was out of sight, Zaiyera spun and looked over the side. Kima stood huddled against the wall with hands tucked under his arms. She whistled down at him and he glared up at her, then started up.

Zaiyera made a show of leaning on the wall to gaze out at the moonlit lake, while keeping an eye on Kima. Hopefully no one would appear on the bridge. She looked down. Kima was halfway up and moving slowly. She knew his hands must be growing numb, but she wished he could climb faster.

"You're almost there!" she whispered down at him. Kima growled as he grabbed the next stone. Zaiyera glanced up and down the bridge, and up at the patrolling archers on Nanshaigha Castle. "Come on, Kima! You can make it!"

Kima faltered and lowered his head. Zaiyera saw his shoulders rising and falling with each breath. *No, no no! Not this close!* "Pull, Kima!" she hissed. Focus!"

"Hands … freezing," Kima gasped.

Zaiyera glanced around again to make sure no one was looking, then climbed onto the thick wall and lay flat on her stomach. She held onto the side with her left hand and reached down with her right.

"You can't lift me," Kima whispered.

"Let me worry about that. Be silent and reach!"

Kima groaned and pulled himself up. He reached for her with curled fingers that looked more like a gnarled claw than a hand.

"Reach!" she hissed

"I can't straighten my fingers."

"Just reach."

Kima stretched as far as he could while Zaiyera did the same. She grabbed his hand and pulled him up to the next step. Once he was closer, they adjusted their grip and held onto each other's wrists. The feeling in his hands must be nearly gone, for she barely felt his grasp.

Zaiyera clenched her teeth and pulled. With her help, Kima made it to the top, and she hopped down and pulled him the rest of the way over.

"Thought you'd … abandoned … me." Kima gasped. He tucked his hands under his arms.

Zaiyera grabbed him by the shoulder and turned him toward the way out. "After all I went through to get you? Don't be simple.

"I know you're nearly frozen," Zaiyera said as they passed back through the inner ward of the Iron Prince's castle, "but straighten yourself and look comfortable, or you'll draw attention."

They crossed the ward and made it to the snaking trail leading downward to Nanshaigha Proper. Zaiyera scanned for patrolling guards but saw none. In the darkness they could be hidden anywhere.

"What now?" Kima asked.

"We walk back into the city, through the streets and out the gates."

Kima looked at her as if she was insane. "We can't—"

Zaiyera kept her focus forward. "Yes, we can." *If it's all we have left, I'll go with hope.*

"No, you can't," a voice said from several paces to the side. Her hope quivered.

31

Zaiyera thought quickly. If she could catch the speaker by surprise, she might be able to knock him unconscious and drag him in the bushes.

"If I didn't know you better, I'd probably be within striking distance of you, Zaiyera," the voice said. This time it sounded familiar.

"Malker?" Zaiyera ventured.

The shydon hunter stepped into view from around a tree. "At your service."

Zaiyera remembered their situation and continued walking. Kima and Malker fell in step on either side of her. "At my service?"

"Did you think we'd let you do this on your own?" Malker asked.

"What choice did I have?" Zaiyera said. "Your king isn't interested in seeing reason."

Malker's face hardened. "No, he isn't. And that leads me to suspicions I'm not particularly happy about."

They followed Zaiyera's lead and passed through the lesser traveled alleyways. Zaiyera tried not to hurry, but she could practically feel their time running out.

"How long ago did you plan this?" Malker asked. "You seem to know exactly which route to take."

"Does it matter? What's important is that we get out of the city as soon as possible."

"And you plan to do this how?" Malker asked. "They'll not simply open the gates for you."

"Should we be trusting this *shydon?*" Kima asked in *Soloush*. He said the last word as though it were a curse.

"I believe we can trust him," Zaiyera replied.

"Believe?"

"Mind including me in the conversation?" Malker said. "Otherwise, it makes me think you're talking about me."

"We are," Zaiyera replied.

Her honesty caused the junior shydon to hesitate over his response.

"We climb." Zaiyera pointed ahead. "Some of these rooftops sit close enough to the city walls that we can jump across."

"And drop over thirty feet to your deaths," Malker added dryly.

"The snow is thickest on the east-facing wall not much farther ahead," Zaiyera replied.

Malker blinked at her. "You really have planned this out."

They turned down a quiet street and saw three figures leaning against the wall. When they spotted her, they straightened.

"Of course," Malker said.

"Where is your superior?" Zaiyera asked.

"Shadowing us," Malker answered. "Best if at least one of us remain unseen …"

They looked over their shoulders at the sound of barking far behind, then picked up the pace.

"Now it begins," Malker said.

"Hunting us with dogs," Zaiyera said just as they reached Zhuyun, Jaide, and Barum.

"We'd stand a better chance if they were dogs," Malker said. "Those are trained tundra wolves. Nasty beasts."

"Sounds exciting," Jaide said.

Zaiyera looked at the large Dor'haighener up ahead. "What are you doing, Barum? You're not supposed to be here."

"Yet I am, miss my lady," Barum replied. "You're not the only one that cares about people enough to do something."

The barking was getting closer.

"Discretion is useless, now," Kima said, reverting to the tradetongue. "We must run."

Behind them, the barking turned to howling, then more frantic barking.

"They've caught a good whiff of our scent," Malker said. "They'll turn the beasts loose, now. We'll not outrun them."

They turned a corner and came face to face with two members of the city guard. Without missing a step, Malker and Zhuyun crashed into them. Malker punched one man in the stomach and followed up with a blow to the head to knock the guard unconscious.

Zhuyun tossed his staff at the other guard who reflexively caught it. Zhuyun leapt forward and snapped his foot up and under the guard's chin. As the man's head fell back, Zhuyun grabbed his staff and rode the man to the ground. They hit with a loud "umph", as the wind blasted from the guard's lungs.

"My apologies, ah?" Zhuyun struck the guard over the head and left him unconscious on the ground.

An arrow whizzed by Jaide's face, and she pulled up short. "By the blazing sun!" she swore. "They try to kill us?"

More arrows zipped around them. They kept close to the sides of the buildings as they ran.

Overhead there was a cry of surprise that cut off abruptly. A heartbeat later, there was the sound of a body thumping down on a roof. After that, Zaiyera noticed the number of arrows chasing them grew fewer until none rained down on them any longer.

Malker took the lead. "We're close to the gates. This way." He led them down an alley, then turned down a side street Zaiyera wasn't familiar with.

"How are we to get out through the gates?" Zaiyera asked. "You said yourself that they won't let us through. I doubt the sound of our barking pursuers will be any more persuasive."

"Well make a way out," Malker said.

Further down the street a group of guards rounded the corner and drew swords as soon as they spotted the fleeing party.

Malker's hands started to glow, his golden dance-resin trailing his tiny movements.

"Malker Argen," Zaiyera hissed. "There are other ways. You needn't pay the—"

"There's no time for other ways," Malker said. He finished the pattern he weaved in the air and turned his hands so that his palms were facing to the right. He placed them together and swept them sideways.

An invisible force struck the guards and sent them crashing into the wall.

They came to the end of the walkway, but Malker never hesitated. He hopped off the edge of the street down to a lower street. Jaide dropped down next, just as a snarl drew Zaiyera and Zhuyun's attention.

An animal resembling a wolf skidded around the corner and sprinted for them. It stood easily taller than a man's waist. In the moonlight, Zaiyera saw a muzzle long enough to bite half her arm off. Its fur bristled on its back like the coarse fur of a warthog.

"I've no desire to meet that thing up close," Zhuyun said just as he turned and hopped down. Zaiyera didn't disagree.

They ran full-out down the alley now, with the sound of booted feet on the street to the left.

"They're trying to flank us," Malker said.

The hairs on the back of Zaiyera's neck prickled. On instinct she leapt and turned midair. At the same time, she drew Shatr from its sheath in an upward cut. The blue-steel blade sliced right through the disk speeding toward their backs. She had just enough time to see the disbelieving shock on the attacking shadow hunter's face before her feet touched the ground. She landed in a backwards roll and came back to her feet without missing a beat.

A transparent whip of air flashed across them from a side street. It missed but struck the corner of a building. Dust and rock assaulted them, but they pushed on.

They'd barely cleared the cloud of dust and rocky debris when five shadow hunters appeared further down the street, all completing a series of movements. The air in front of them rippled as three horizontal lines split the air, rotated, and formed into disks. The transparent blue disks pulsated blue light as dozens of holes opened in each one and tiny blades shot towards the fleeing group. Malker touched the stream. He drew forth a transparent green shield that absorbed the shards while Zaiyera sliced Shatr downward, then sideways.

The blue disks shattered in the astonished faces of the shadow hunters ahead, an instant before an invisible force struck them from atop a side building. A figure dropped from the roof and waved them on.

"He thinks we're jogging, yes?" Jaide quipped.

Behind them, the barking and snarling drew closer. Much closer. Zaiyera spared a glance over her shoulder and wished she hadn't. Those long muzzles had lots of teeth. Even the paws on the tundra wolves were armed with sharp claws that clicked on the ground with each step.

"Front gates ahead," Zhuyun said.

"I remember those gates when first we passed through them," Zaiyera said. "They're thick and iron-bolted."

Malker touched the stream and created a blast of wind that Dyren compounded. Their combined efforts produced a force strong enough to bend the iron bars and buckle the gates open. The guards on each gate tower trained arrows on them and let fly while their partners sounded horns.

Dyren drew from the stream and created a burst of air that turned aside the arrows. They reached the buckled gates and squeezed through. The trail ahead lay clear and snaked its way back toward the mountains.

"How long will they chase us?"

"Until we elude them," Malker said.

"Has anyone ever done so?" Jaide asked.

"No."

Zaiyera felt terribly exposed as they sprinted across the open grounds. They heard barking from behind again but pushed on.

The same men who'd intercepted them before appeared up the trail as they started to ascend the hills. They spoke to Dyren in alarmed tones, and the senior shydon hunter responded. Whatever words were exchanged wasn't enough to placate the men. They drew swords and nocked arrows.

Dyren frowned with regret and produced an invisible force like the one back at the gates. He thrust his hands forward and the force dug up a wave of snow that fell over the sentries.

"It won't take them long to dig out," Dyren said as they hurried past.

"We need to slow those wolves down," Malker said. He stopped and moved back a few feet to face the slope. The tundra wolves had just reached the base of the hill and were loping up toward them.

The junior shydon touched the stream. Zaiyera watched him, noting that every Dor'haighener streamdancer she'd ever seen used smaller, more conservative motions when they danced the stream, whereas in Samhar, they used dramatic, flourishing movements.

Malker sent an avalanche crashing down on the four wolves. It swept over the snarling animals and sent them tumbling away in a tangle of long, muscled limbs and paws.

The younger shydon noticed Zaiyera looking on him with concern and turned back toward the hill. "Worry not. That looked more costly than it was. I assure you I paid no more than a few minutes of the lifeprice."

Barum led them up the trail, helping them to navigate around patches of ice. As it turned out, the thickly muscled Dor'haighener was an expert at traversing snowy terrain.

"I thought … you were from … southern … Dor'haighen," Zaiyera huffed.

"Aye," Barum replied. "But just like you spend a lot of your time in north Samhar, guiding expeditions, I do a lot of traveling in the harsher north, where the zimastones are more plentiful. Bigger struggle yields bigger reward."

"This … is true, yes?" Jaide said. "Life itself … wishes for us to fail or die … before we succeed.”

Not so, Zaiyera thought. *People make their lives difficult. The world is as it is. We create most of our hardships.*

“Can … we please … stop,” Kima said. “I’ve been … here long enough … to endure the altitude, but I’ve not … been given the chance … to exercise.”

“All right,” Dyren said. “We’ll take a brief rest, but touch nothing. The wolves will pick up your scent on anything you touch.”

Zaiyera responded by simply pointing at the trail they’d left behind.

Dyren nodded and moved his hands in a pattern, then reached a hand to the sky and swept it out to the right.

Zaiyera watched as the shydon hunter moved through the last of his pattern. Snow began to fall and the wind picked up. Soon they stood in the midst of a mild snowstorm.

“It will travel down the path behind and sweep up our tracks and our scent before enveloping our pursuers. A little while longer and we must get moving.”

Once the Samharans caught their breath, the party continued on. Some bit of luck found them when the snow lightened on the trail, and they were able to move more quickly.

Zaiyera looked up at the dark sky just as a layer of clouds passed across the bottom half of the nearly full moon. If not for the circumstances, Zaiyera would have marveled at the beauty of the surroundings, illuminated by the moon’s pale light.

“We’re almost to the top,” Barum said from the front of the group. “Once we start down, it’ll be easier going for us and harder for the tundra wolves to catch up. They don’t do so well downhill.”

“Let’s hope there are no lancers among them,” Malker said. “Otherwise we could find ourselves buried under an avalanche.”

Zaiyera concentrated on slogging through the shin-deep snow, putting one foot in front of the other. Barum had set a pace the Samharans could manage, as the big man moved along with far less effort.

All too soon the barking started up again. Everyone turned to look back down the trail.

“Do my ears deceive me,” Jaide said, “or the barking sounds rather angry, yes?"

"Yes." Zaiyera did her best to control her breathing. The days she'd spent in the higher altitude had forced her body to adjust at least some bit. It was still a labor, but if this had been back when they'd first come, she might have fallen behind.

The trees started to thin out, revealing the open trail ahead. They hiked on, and Zaiyera thanked Shakimah that the snow wasn't any deeper than it was. If it had been closer to winter than spring, they'd have been in trouble.

"Double-time," Barum yelled over his shoulder. "Only a couple hundred feet until we start downhill."

They moved single file across the field, with Barum more or less plowing a trail for the rest of them.

Zaiyera looked around the open field. The ground, the trees and bushes, all covered in snow. It was tranquil and refreshing, but for some reason it also felt ominous.

"You feel it too, ah?"

Zaiyera looked over at Zhuyun, who gazed up at the clear moonlit sky, and at the surrounding shadows of towering stoicgreens.

The barking sounded closer, prodding everyone to move even faster.

"We're not going to outrun them," Malker said.

"If we can't run, then it's time to fight." Zhuyun stopped and spun, his staff whirling over his head and around to slam under his arm. His stance was wide and solid. Zaiyera had never seen the mild-mannered storyteller so grim.

Dyren stopped and turned as well. "He's right."

Zaiyera turned and drew Shatr in one motion. Malker and Kima were a few feet away, the former moving away to spread the space between them all, the latter looking helpless. Zaiyera slipped her thigh dagger free and tossed it to him. "Don't lose it."

Kima nodded in thanks. To her relief, he flipped it in his hand and tested the weight like someone who knew how to use a weapon.

The tundra wolves slowed as soon as they came out of the woods. Even from several dozen feet away, Zaiyera saw the muscles in their legs bunch together as the wolves slowly advanced, their large heads in line with their necks and shoulders. Their muzzles drew back to reveal canine teeth half as long as her index finger. Zaiyera took a deep breath and lightened her white-knuckled grip on her scimitar.

The four tundra wolves spread out to form a semicircle around them. Zaiyera felt torn as she stole glances at Dyren and Malker, who were readying themselves to dance. The animals were deadly, but they would stand little chance against the two shydon hunters wielding the flow.

Someone barked an order in *Dreuga*, and the wolves held their positions. The sound of boots crunching through the snow preceded the arrival of six armored soldiers. They looked the situation over, then one of them addressed Dyren.

Dyren nodded and replied in tradetongue. "Soldier."

The man lifted his helm from his hand and tucked it in the crook of his arm. He looked from Dyren to Malker and sighed. "Senior Shadow Hunter," he said, reverting to tradetongue. "Why are we out here, sir?" He indicated the group. "You entered as respected hunters, sir. You brought them," he indicated Zaiyera and the others, "under the hospitality of King Eredin, and now leave as fugitives. You've removed his majesty's guest and fled."

"Hardly a guest," Kima spat.

"We are well aware of the circumstances of our arrival and departure, soldier," Dyren said.

Zaiyera kept an eye on the tundra wolves, who fanned out just a little more.

"Why, sir?" The soldier asked. "Why have you done this and forced us to track you down?"

"There is more at play than you understand," Dyren replied.

"Then, please come back and explain it to his majesty."

The tundra wolves started growling again. The one nearest Jaide snapped its jaws and sent drool flying. The soldier to the right of the speaker barked an order and the wolves quieted.

"What is your name, soldier?" Dyren asked.

"Devon Corgin, sir." He saluted.

"You seem a good man and a good soldier, Devon Corgin," Dyren replied. "I understand you must follow orders. That is honorable and it is our duty. But sometimes even the highest of us err."

Around Devon, the other soldiers were growing restless. They looked to him, then back at Zaiyera and the others.

"Sir." Devon looked regretful. "I've admired you through my entire training and career with the Nanshaigha guard. You are held in high esteem amongst us all. Please, don't make me do this."

"No one is making you do anything, Devon," Dyren said. "You can turn away." He glanced at the others. "All of you. Right now. You can turn away and tell your superiors we eluded you."

"I can't do that, sir." Devon looked regretful. "And my honor will not allow me to return without you."

Zaiyera watched the conflict play across Devon's face. *He's not going to let us go.* The thought had barely finished in her mind when the soldier's jaw set, his eyes hardened.

"I am sorry, Senior Shadow Hunter Dyren Faust." Devon's tone turned formal, now. All attempt at being personable gone. "We must return you and your accomplices and the guest to Nanshaigha Castle to receive the king's justice." He placed his helm back on his head. "I will do what I must."

Zaiyera looked at Dyren. The man looked truly pained. "As will I, soldier."

"Try not to kill them," Malker said to the others. "They're following orders."

Jaide glanced at the snarling wolves and snorted. "And while I'm at it, I'll try not to be ripped apart."

The soldiers unsheathed their swords and moved forward, the tundra wolves in step with them. The man Zaiyera figured to be the lead handler barked a command and the wolves bounded forward.

Malker touched the stream and launched himself into movement. Almost instantly, a gust of wind struck two of the animals and sent them tumbling away. He'd barely released the flow when one of the soldiers came in, sword swinging. He blocked the sword and muscled the soldier backwards.

Zhuyun leapt into the fray, battling staff against sword. In less than a few heartbeats he'd lain one man low and smacked a lunging tundra wolf on the side of its head. The animal let out a pained yelp and staggered to the side. That instant was enough for the Yuntaiman to whip his staff around and down. The staff struck the wolf in the side of its foreleg at the same time the other end blocked a sword from a second soldier aimed at his head.

While the wolf barked and hobbled sideways, Zhuyun popped the high end of his staff sideways. The movement was so quick, the soldier didn't register it. The end of the shaft smacked him in the side of his helm so hard he fell away, unconscious before he hit the ground.

Zaiyera had her adversary on his heels. She used the slicing movements signature to her homeland, parrying and countering, sweeping high and cutting low. She could see in the man's eyes that he knew he was outmatched. "I'll not kill you," she said to her adversary just before kicking him in the groin. When he doubled over, she struck him in the side of the head with the butt of her scimitar.

"Zaiyera!" Malker called. "Take my place!"

She leapt into the fray, Shatr a blur of movement that quickly had her new opponent on his heels. Before he could formulate a proper defense, she had him disarmed and on his rump, looking up the length of the magnificent blue-steel blade.

The two wolves Malker had sent tumbling downhill came loping back into view. Malker threw himself into touching the stream again but hesitated when the large animals skidded to a stop and backed away. They growled and snapped their jaws not at the embattled fugitives, but past them.

Zaiyera watched in confusion as the wolves continued their steady retreat. Kima cried out and she stole a quick glance at him, then in the direction he was looking.

Zhuyun looked to the sky. His laugh held no humor. "Our unwelcome friend returns!"

Zaiyera shook her head and backed away from the soldier she'd defeated. All eyes looked to the sky to see a giant winged figure illuminated against the moon.

32

"**M**oon and stars," Zaiyera breathed.

"What in the blazing eyes of Sundancer is that?" Kima asked.

The soldier Zaiyera had defeated scrambled to his feet and snatched up his sword. Like the others, his attention went skyward, all thought of fighting lost. Both groups moved away from each other, focusing on the incoming beast.

"It's headed straight for us," Malker said.

"Great observation," Jaide replied.

"Run!" Dyren waved irritably at the soldiers. "Get yourselves out of here!"

Zaiyera and the others ran toward the thickest concentration of trees they could find while the soldiers scrambled to leash their snarling tundra wolves. With an effort, they pulled the animals back into the trees.

The frost worva let out a deafening screech. Everyone crouched and clamped their hands over their ears. It landed in a splash of snow and whirled to roar in the direction the soldiers had gone. It whipped its armored tail into nearby trees as big around as two men standing abreast. The trees snapped like twigs.

Zaiyera kept her eyes on the monster as she and the rest of the group continued to back away into the woods.

The frost worva swung its horrible gaze in their direction, and everyone froze. Zaiyera feared the beast might hear her heart hammering in her chest.

From behind the tree line on the other side of the winged beast, the tundra wolves barked. The worva whipped its head around in that direction.

"Poor stupid animals," Zhuyun whispered. "The domesticated blood is too thick in them to know better."

The worva screeched again and started toward the trees. It swung its head into a nearby stoicgreen. The steady cracking and groaning of the falling tree sounded as though a building had been toppled. The giant beast tucked its wings against its side and rammed its way through another cluster.

Zaiyera heard curses and steel being drawn. Beside her, Kima looked her in the eyes and she saw his intention as clearly as if he'd spoken it aloud. She slowly shook her head at him. "We can't leave them to that thing."

"We save them so they can take us back to that cursed place?" Kima replied, incredulous. "We can be long gone—"

"You can be long gone if you start now," Zaiyera cut in. "We each make our own choices."

Kima licked his lips, glancing from her to the worva still crashing through the trees. "You choose death."

"Better death than living with myself for running away." *No more dishonor.*

Kima ground his teeth. "You wouldn't say that if it was you rotting away in the cell disguised as a guest's quarters."

Zaiyera turned at the sound of snarling and barking. The wolves had come out of the woods and surrounded the worva. They snapped at its heels and retreated before it could catch them. The beast roared and swept its tail around. The giant scaled tail sent snow spraying everywhere. One wolf hadn't been quick enough to avoid the tail. It yelped once as it was thrown high into the air. It crashed into a tree and tumbled downward toward the ground where it landed in an unmoving heap.

The sight of the doomed animal's final moments lit Zaiyera's blood afire. She snatched Shatr from its sheath and stalked toward the conflict.

"Are you insane?" Kima hissed from behind, but she barely heard him.

The wolves snapped at a monster that was ten times their size, fearlessly defending their human handlers who crouched just beyond the tree line. She wanted to flee. It would have been so easy. But it wasn't those animals' faults for how they were trained.

She sprinted toward the fighting, Shatr at her side. The worva swept its tail on the ground again, and a wave of snow flew at her.

Zaiyera leapt straight through the white rain and brought her scimitar around and down, scoring a hit on the beast's tail.

It recoiled more out of surprise than any injury she might have dealt. Whether sensing she was an ally, or more concerned with the bigger threat, the tundra wolves paid her no heed. They leapt in again, snapping and biting, retreating and attacking.

Zaiyera darted between them, hopping over the worva's low sweeping tail, dropping to the ground when it swept at her head. The worva turned in the direction of a wolf that bit its clawed foot. As soon as it did, Zaiyera leapt in and stabbed it in the side of the leg. Shatr bit through the scaled hide and sank halfway in.

The worva screeched and swept its wing backward at her. Zaiyera snatched her blade free and ducked. She realized her mistake immediately, in the form of huge jaws closing in on her. She dove aside just as the jaws snapped at the spot she'd been in just an instant earlier.

A transparent whip struck the monster square in the face. The force of the blow snapped the worva's head sideways, causing it to stumble aside.

Malker ran toward the beast as he produced a large blue disk. The disk pulsated and sent a stream of shards into the worva's face.

As the shydon hunter ran by, Zaiyera saw the tiniest hint of 'crow's feet' wrinkle at the corner of his eyes that hadn't been there before.

She sprang forward at the worva again, but Zhuyun reached it first. Just as Malker sent forth another stream of shards, the Yuntaiman leapt into their path. The young shydon hunter cried out in alarm, but just as he had done when they'd battled the shadowlancer, Zhuyun snatched the shards out of the air. The Yuntaiman whirled his staff, reforming the physical manifestations of the stream.

He whirled the staff in a vertical blur from the left to right side of his body, all the while charging at the beast. The worva shook off Malker's first attack and turned toward the shydon hunter. It stretched its neck out toward Malker, mouth agape.

Zhuyun made it pay for that mistake. He leapt high and brought the blue glowing end of his staff down on its outstretched neck.

The impact sent bits of scales and blue sparks exploding into the air. The monster's neck dipped and it fell to the ground with a high-pitched screech.

One of the tundra wolves seized the opportunity and bit down on the tip of a leathery wing while another clamped onto one of the finger-like appendages connecting the membrane.

The monster didn't know which threat to deal with. Zhuyun pounded at its neck while the tundra wolves bit at its right wing and ankles. Dyren sprinted through the trees and leapt out at it. His sword sliced and stabbed, cutting part of the membrane of the left wing to shreds. He stabbed up and under the scales of one leg and into the flesh beneath.

"Nanshaigha!" The four soldiers finally found their courage. They sprinted out of the woods, hollering the battle cry that was their homeland. They struck fast and hard, and the sudden heavy blows stunned the worva.

Devon quickly reined them in, however, smartly realizing the formidable beast was far from finished. They coordinated their efforts. Every time the beast swung its head around to bite at the pesky tundra wolves or Zhuyun, the soldiers would lunge in and stab at it.

Still in close, Dyren moved as it moved, keeping to the vulnerable area where neither tail nor jaws could reach him. He continued to punish its flank, and soon a trail of blood flowed down the beast's scaly leg.

Zaiyera caught her breath and went in again. With a powerful downward stroke, Shatr severed one of the finger appendages on the wing. The monster arched its neck and let out an agonized wail.

Though she couldn't see them on the other side of the worva, Zaiyera heard Jaide and Barum Hurst's roar as they too engaged the beast.

Before it could begin to respond to the newest threat, one of the tundra wolves leapt at the exposed neck, the only area not covered in scales. Long canine teeth sank into the leathery flesh. The worva screeched and bucked. It swung its neck left to right, but the tundra wolf's powerful jaws kept hold.

One of the soldiers thought to move behind it and chopped his sword down on the thick tail.

Malker shouted in warning, but it was too late. They worva snapped its tail up and into the man's chest. It lifted the soldier into the air as though he weighed nothing.

Despite the tundra wolf attached to its neck and another clamped down on its wing, the frost worva turned toward the dazed soldier. Dyren Faust dealt it blow after blow from his advantageous position, and try as it might, the beast just couldn't get to him.

With soldiers stabbing and cutting at it from one side, a wolf at its neck and wing, and the rest of the party punishing it from all sides, the struggling soldier made an irresistible target.

The frost worva opened its perpetually grinning maw, revealing awful, jagged teeth, and lunged for the soldier. Zaiyera winced as Malker dove toward the man, sure that the beast would bite them both in half. But Malker had been the faster. He tackled the other man aside, barely throwing them both out of the path of the snapping jaws.

Another soldier stabbed at its flank, and the worva screeched and swung around again. The sudden movement finally dislodging the wolf clamped onto its neck. The tundra wolf tumbled away, but not without tearing free a hunk of bloody flesh.

A stream of blood flowed freely from the gaping wound. The

worva's pained screech choked off into a gurgle and it went into a frenzy. It stumbled sideways and bumped Dyren with its thigh, sending the shydon hunter tumbling away.

A tundra wolf hopped away, narrowly avoiding being stomped into the ground by the enraged beast. Zaiyera backpedaled as it swung its wing at her. She brought Shatr around in a downward chop as the wing passed over. The blue-steel blade sheared through bone and thick leathery membrane.

Zaiyera dove headlong away from bloody, snapping teeth. Despite a host of grievous wounds, the thing just wouldn't die.

It swept its tail at Zaiyera. When she leapt away, it swept its tail back at her again. Zaiyera saw the giant tail coming and reflexively turned away from it. The world spun end over end when a glancing blow sent her flying and tumbling in the air. She hit the ground hard in a cloud of snow and dirt.

Zaiyera groaned and tried to quickly rise, but her head spun. She collapsed to the ground and lay on her back, breathing slowly and hoping the thing wasn't still coming for her.

A man's agonized scream pierced the fog in Zaiyera's head. She rolled on her side and looked in the direction of the sound, then wished she hadn't. The giant worva had a soldier clamped between its bloody jaws. Everyone fought to free him, stabbing and slicing, frantically working their weapons to hurt it and draw its attention.

Barum let out a mighty bellow and brought his large sword down on its foot. The blade broke through the tiny scales and bit into the flesh beneath.

Unfortunately for the poor soldier, the worva clamped its jaws shut and bit him in half, then swung its head around.

Jaide circled out of its line of sight and waded in as it passed. The worva moved much slower now. "How's this blasted thing still alive?" the Viriksani shouted. She sliced it across the membrane of the opposite wing Zaiyera had injured, ducking when it curled its tail around to strike at her, then stabbed it in the thigh.

Zaiyera struggled to her hands and knees, rubbing her head. She heard another tundra wolf yelp and another soldier bellowing in anger.

From the corner of her eye, she saw Dyren and Malker dancing the stream. They drew forth and guided the flow in the northerner fashion, with small, conservative movements.

The beast tried to lift its ruined wings to take flight, but it buckled and collapsed instead. It was finally succumbing to its injuries.

Zaiyera rose and found her feet steady. She searched for Shatr and found the scimitar lying several feet away. She grabbed it up and jogged toward the struggling worva. The stubborn monster continued to bite and claw at the surrounding enemies.

While its neck was curled away from her, Zaiyera drove her scimitar into it. She yanked the blade free as the worva rocked sideways and swung its head toward her. Zaiyera ducked while delivering an overhead chop. Shatr sliced through the vulnerable flesh under its neck, cutting through the same spot where the tundra wolf had torn a chunk free.

Zaiyera bolted from under the long and heavy neck. The worva dropped onto its belly. It let out a sound that was half wail half screech as it flailed in its attempts to rise.

Finally the frost worva shuddered, and its head fell into the snow with a loud thud, blood flowing between its teeth and staining the snow beneath its parted maw.

From somewhere on the other side of the dead beast, Zaiyera heard a command shouted in *Dreuga*. The tundra wolf closest to her loped away with a noticeable limp, the other two joining it.

Spread out around the felled monster, the soldiers of Nanshaigha and the seven fugitives looked at each other, some doubled over, some on hands and knees, everyone exhausted.

Zaiyera's gaze fell on half of the dead soldier, and she looked away.

A hand appeared in front of her. She looked up to see Zhuyun, bruised and bloody, offer a reassuring nod. She grabbed the proffered hand.

"On your feet, little desert flower," Zhuyun groaned as he pulled her upright. "Time to see what happens next."

"A frost worva *that* determined wouldn't have given up," Devon said. The leader of the soldiers looked as though he'd been bludgeoned by an army of clubs. One of his eyes was swollen shut and he had a cut along the side of his jaw. "I can't believe you aided us when you could have easily escaped."

Dyren stared at the man, then held out an open hand in Zaiyera's direction. "If you offer thanks, offer it to her. She struck the first blow."

The soldier turned toward Zaiyera and began to labor in her direction. She went to the man to save him the struggle and he offered his hand. She took it.

"Thank you, southerner."

"You're welcome," Zaiyera said. "What now?"

He offered a weak nod and looked over at Dyren. "Straight to the point, eh?" He turned back. "Casting aside the notion that we couldn't arrest a band of children in our current state, I'd be severely lacking in gratitude and common sense were I to insist upon your arrest."

Those who were in better shape, helped the injured, and seeing that their handlers were no longer aggressive to their quarry, the tundra wolves sat on their haunches.

"We'll have to dig a temporary grave for Rickard," Devon said, swallowing the lump in his throat at the grisly remains of their comrade. "We can't carry him in our condition, and have nothing to carry him with nonetheless."

Zaiyera waited, but the man said nothing more as they started to dig. She walked up to Devon and pointed at the lifeless body of the fallen tundra wolf. The handler crouched over the dead animal, head bowed in grief. The other three wolves had followed him over and sat a few feet away. They lifted their heads to the sky and let out a collective howl.

"What of your other fallen comrade?"

Devon looked where she pointed. "Oh, the wolf. She won't be wasted. The pelt is thick and warm, so we'll skin her." He took a step back at the anger and horror on her face and glanced at Dyren.

"Samhari think differently about animals than we," Dyren said.

"Skinned and discarded as a reward for loyalty and bravery."

Zaiyera stood. "An animal's first instinct in the presence of a greater predator is to flee. That wolf fought because of you." She stared at him and was about to say more, but just turned away.

Zaiyera found a decent sized branch and carved it as best she could, then started digging. Jaide joined her, followed by Zhuyun.

From the corner of her eye, she saw the other soldiers standing by, looking from each other to the diggers and Malker and Dyren, who'd started to help as well. Two went off into the woods while the others finally went to help dig. By the time both groups were finished, the graves were as deep as they could be under the circumstances.

They carefully lowered both halves of the dead soldier into the first grave and covered it with the large stones the two soldiers had collected. They repeated the process for the fallen tundra wolf as well.

The wolf handler came to Zaiyera and offered his hand. She took it and he gave her a firm shake. "Maybe it's because I have a close relationship with them," the man said. "But I never much liked the way we treat 'em after death, no matter how much they call it practical use of the animal. Thank you."

"I hate to put a rush on this," Barum said. Aside from a tear in his furs, and a handful of cuts, he seemed mostly unharmed. "But we've got to get moving. You might be willing to let us go," he said to Devon. "But once you report back, I don't see King Eredin giving up."

"Time isn't on our side, regardless," Dyren said. "Our business is urgent."

"Very well, sir," Devon said. "Be safe in your journey."

"Impossible," Dyren said with a grin. "But our thanks."

"Peace to you," Zaiyera said.

They parted ways, Devon promising to relate the tale of what happened this day, and how Zaiyera and the others had saved them from what would surely have been their deaths.

Malker whistled through his teeth. "An adult frost worva. Can't say I ever thought I'd fight one of those things and live to tell the tale."

"Surely you could defeat such a beast, or at least, discourage it using your other abilities," Zhuyun said.

Malker nodded. "Yes, but it wouldn't be much different. The

amount of power it would take to singlehandedly bring down an enraged frost worva would see me to the grave before my grandparents."

The presence of more gray in his hair and the newly acquired 'crow's feet' creases at the corners of his eyes punctuated the junior shydon's point.

By the time they reached flat land again and had the mountain range at their backs, the first hints of dawn glowed blue on the eastern horizon. They worked their way south and east, choosing to skirt the border to Samhar, as the terrain would be more easily managed.

Watching the huffing Kima from the corner of her eye, Zaiyera tried to imagine what it must be like to officially be declared a guest, but held captive in that cold place of stone. No freedom to come and go from the capital—or even the castle, for that matter—as he pleased. How many hours of the day did Kima spend sitting in that cell, wondering if he'd ever get to go home?

A murder of crows glided overhead, cawing back and forth at each other.

"Let me guess," Malker said to Zaiyera when he noticed her grinning up at the black birds. "You like crows, too."

"Why wouldn't I like them?" she asked, still watching as they glided toward a patch of dormant trees.

Malker shrugged. "What is there to love about a scavenger that picks over the dead?"

"Not wholly scavengers," Zaiyera said. "Though I don't see anything wrong with that, either."

"In Yuntai," Zhuyun said, "crows are thought of as the bringers of misfortune and at the very least, ill tidings."

Jaide arched an eyebrow at him. "That's a rather harsh burden to place on the unwitting birds, yes? In Samhar, the crow and the raven are revered because of their intelligence."

Zhuyun bowed his head. "I've seen many a superstition in my travels. I wonder what the animals and birds of every land think of humans."

"Trouble," Malker said. "That's why the smart ones flee our coming."

The conversation reminded Zaiyera of Sadiq. She missed her camel companion and hoped he was warm and well.

"Once we reach Denberest," Barum said, "I'd recommend horses over camels or rasadons. Since we're going further south from there to skirt the border, horses're faster."

"Agreed," Dyren Faust replied. "You are a Denberesterner, aren't you? Will you remain in your home city or continue with us?"

"Aye." Barum nodded. "Denberesterner born and bred. And no, I got no intentions of staying behind. Ain't nothing there for me that won't be there when I get back, which is little to begin with. I'm seein' this through to the end."

"Good to know there is at least one other person as suicidal as me, yes?" Jaide slapped the much bigger Barum on the back. "I do not know what it is I can do against a *kivuli dayasa* with godlike power, but my pride and arrogance strangles any good sense."

Jaide waved a hand at Zaiyera. "I'm still not convinced she'll not bolt on us as soon as she's reunited with her camel friend."

Zaiyera snorted. "Keep talking, Viriksani. I may just bolt as soon as we meet *kivuli dayasa*. Surely you'll be fine without me."

"My dear Zaiyera," Jaide said. "I do believe that was the most personality you've let slip, yet. Careful. You may enjoy some of this journey more than your normal grimness, yes? Or rather, you'll neglect us again once you're able to talk with your camel friend once more."

"A high likelihood," Zaiyera quipped, to the collective chuckling of all but Kima.

"We'll reach Demenin Waypoint and get you to your friend before you know it," Zhuyun said. "I'm sure with every bite of his delicious cud, he thinks of his wayward friend, ixu?"

Zaiyera laughed, then coughed on the cold air.

They walked on in silence for a time until Zaiyera finally broke it. "Do you not have animal companions or human loved ones that miss you, Zhuyun Xaiylin?"

"No animal companions," Zhuyun replied. "I do have some family and friends that may miss my stories more than myself, ah?" He had a self-deprecating chuckle at that. "I likely don't remain home long enough for anyone to remember who I am."

"I'm sure they do," Zaiyera said. She gave his shoulder a friendly squeeze.

Zaiyera noticed Kima silently watching the exchange. He'd hardly spoken since their escape. She wondered what he was thinking.

Their relief at the approach of dawn was colored by the specter of approaching clouds from the northwest.

"Now that looks bad," Malker said. "That's going to completely cover the sky."

"Snowstorm?" Zaiyera asked.

"A late winter storm," Malker answered. "One of the last of the snowstorms we get before the final thaws of spring. "We should find shelter."

Shelter proved hard to come by while visibility was clear. An hour later when the storm overtook them, visibility diminished to no more than a twenty to thirty feet in any direction.

"Moon and stars!" Jaide shouted over the howling storm. "Does this angry land punish us one last time before we escape it?"

Zaiyera shrank into her furs until as little of her face was exposed as possible.

Beside her, Zhuyun let out a loud openmouthed laugh, joined by Barum Hurst.

"Cave up ahead." Malker yelled over the wailing winds.

The group looked to where he pointed and saw a cave that looked like it could easily house them all, even from this distance.

Without a word, Kima marched forward and caught up with Barum, who caught him by the shoulder. "Stick with the group, good man. There's things that patrol the storms that you don't want to meet up with alone."

Kima looked up at him and nodded.

They pushed on, the strengthening storm mocking their efforts. The land grew rockier, with scattered boulders and even a few outcroppings dotting the white landscape. They trudged by towering stoicgreens coated white, climbed over and moved around boulder clusters in a straight line for the cave.

When they were but a dozen feet from their intended sanctuary, Zaiyera could practically feel the warm relief the cave would provide. Then she heard the roar.

33

"**M**oon and blazing stars," Kima cursed.

Zaiyera felt the relief drain out of her. *What more can go wrong?*

Jaide laughed and clapped his hands together. "Of course there would be a large animal living in a cave, yes? How ironic if this is how we meet our end; freezing to death or killed by a large animal before freezing to death."

"You have an interesting coping method, Viriksani," Dyren said, his voice as dry as the cracked ground in a dead oasis.

They trudged on cautiously for the cave. Another deep roar came from inside. Zaiyera felt it vibrate in her chest. "Anything that can make a sound I feel in my bones from this far away, I don't want to disturb."

"There are many things I'd like not to do," Dyren said, "but we need that cave." He glanced at her. "Unless you know how to talk to it and get it to share?"

Zaiyera wasn't sure if the shydon hunter was being sarcastic. "One doesn't try to befriend an angry or wary animal, predator or not."

A large set of eyes twice as high as the tallest of the party appeared from inside the cave. The sight of those eyes had everyone hesitating.

With another angry roar, the giant four-legged animal emerged from the cave. It had long shaggy white fur, and a large wide head the size of a man's torso. It stretched out its neck as it made is moaning roar again.

"Cave bear," Malker said. "*Another* cave bear."

"We've disturbed its home," Zaiyera said.

"Maybe we can scare it off," Malker said. He threw his hand in the air and shouted at the animal.

The bear roared at him, then swiped at Dyren when he came too close. It snarled back at Malker when he tried to approach.

Zaiyera watched the exchange with a deepening feeling that something wasn't right.

Beside her, Zhuyun had his staff in his hands, but looked hesitant. "It's not moving away from its cave," he said.

The shydon hunters drew their swords and swatted at the giant bear, and it swiped back at them. No matter what they tried, it didn't pursue, but remained blocking the opening.

"It's protecting its home," Zaiyera observed "but it still doesn't attack."

Zaiyera waved frantically at Dyren and Malker when she saw them sheathe their swords and begin to touch the stream. "No! Stop!"

"What?" Malker yelled back. "It won't go, Zaiyera. We need sanctuary! If we kill it, we'll have meat for our travels and furs as well."

"You can't kill her!" she shouted.

"What do you mean, *her*?" Dyren asked.

"Get back!" Malker said. He and Malker began to weave a pattern in the air. "It's the beast or us. We're not going to die out here!" The shydon hunters attacked in coordination.

Shatr was instantly in Zaiyera's hands. She sliced through their flow so quickly, the two men barely registered what had happened.

The cave bear lunged at Dyren, and he skittered backward, shouting curses.

Malker glared at Zaiyera. "You're reverence for life is misplaced! You would sacrifice our lives for an animal?"

"A family!" Zaiyera shot back. "She protects her little ones!"

"How can you know that?"

"Look." She pointed at the bear, who stood upright to tower over the intruders. It roared at them again, but never moved from its spot in front of the cave. "If she were just protecting her home, she would chase us off. Even if we did go in, she'd trap us in there and kill us. She's protecting her little ones."

"Her little ones are better equipped for this environment than we are," Malker countered.

Zaiyera's skin prickled and she whipped Shatr up and down with a flick of her wrist. Once again the scimitar sliced through the flow drawn by Dyren Faust.

"Take care your actions, Zaiyera," Dyren warned.

"I'll not stand aside and watch you slaughter a family and steal their home," Zaiyera said. She took up her scimitar in a two-handed grip and faced the shydon hunters. Farther to the side, Kima stood back watching.

To her other side, Zhuyun leaned on his staff. She knew the Yuntaiman could spring into action faster than she could react, but she was confident he wouldn't move against her.

"Look at her," Zaiyera pleaded. "She's not trying to attack us. She's protecting her home and what's inside."

Dyren's hands glowed with a golden aura. She saw the anger and indecision on his face. Malker's glower shifted from Zaiyera to his superior while he waited for Dyren to make a decision.

Dyren looked from the cave bear to the warm cave several times, then cast Zaiyera a dark look and backed away. "We move on!" he barked.

The group slowly backed off from the large and angry bear, who was still barking and growling at them. Zaiyera kept her attention split between the cave bear, the two shydon hunters, and Kima. Although the latter was from her homeland, she wouldn't take for granted that desperation wouldn't prod him to betray her.

They circled around the bear and when they'd moved a safe distance away, it dropped back to four legs and watched them. Occasionally snorting at the air.

Zaiyera glanced at Zhuyun, who gave a subtle nod of approval. She hadn't realized how much the traveler's opinion mattered until she felt the wash of relief flood through her.

It was a quiet and tense trek through the harsh and cold winds as the group hunted for a safe and warm place to wait out the storm. Though no one spoke, Zaiyera felt the anger. Malker and Dyren remained focused in their search for shelter, but she could feel the angry looks they *didn't* cast her. Kima remained silent as always, watching everyone.

"Ah!" Zhuyun yelled. "Unless these snow-blown eyes deceive me, I see a cluster of boulders up ahead!"

They picked up their pace until finally reaching the boulder cluster, then tentatively approached.

"Hopefully nothing lives in there," Malker muttered, peering inside. "I'd hate to evict a family of coneys.

Zaiyera narrowed her eyes at him.

When it looked safe to enter, they crept into the small space. Kima gave a leaning bolder a test shove, then after a wary scan of the other giant rocks, he stepped in. Zhuyun was next into the shelter, followed by Jaide and Malker. Zaiyera and Dyren faced each other after Barum, the last of the group, entered. The wind howled again, and a strong gust blew at them from the northwest. Loose straps on their gear whipped in the wind, and stray strands of hair slapped at her face.

Zaiyera didn't know what to say, so she stood there, waiting for the senior shydon hunter to speak. The silence stretched, and from the corner of her eye, she saw Zhuyun peek out of the rocky shelter.

"I will keep first watch," Dyren said.

For several moments more, Zaiyera didn't respond. Those icy blue eyes were angry, but there was something else there as well. Was it disappointment? Indignation?

She respectfully inclined her head and crept into the outcropping. The narrow enclosure opened into a cramped campsite. Snow still drifted in from the entrance and the gaps in the boulders around and overhead. Still, the wind was far less harsh.

With a quick and aggressive gesture, Malker produced a fire in the middle of the camp. Flames flared to life, and the others recoiled, then settled back. He lanced using the technique flow, to keep the fire going long enough to warm the place.

Zaiyera inclined her head in thanks and pulled her gloves off. She understood their frustration with her, and she wished she could have found a way to resolve that conflict without bruising their pride.

Malker carefully moved the air around the fire to warm the camp. The effect was immediate, and soon the camp was filled with warmth. Without a word, Malker got up and left the camp.

Kima watched him go. His gaze flicked from the departing shydon hunter to Zaiyera, then to the other three.

Zhuyun gave Zaiyera an encouraging nod. "Time settles the burn."

"And time it will take, my friend," Zaiyera said. "For I've burned them well today."

"It was the right thing to do," Jaide said.

Zaiyera folded her hands in her lap and stared at her palms. "It was. But not without cost."

Zhuyun looked at her, his expression saying he understood her meaning. "There is always a right and wrong way to do something. I can't say I know another way it could have been resolved."

"It's done," Zaiyera said. She settled down and withdrew into her thoughts.

Time passed with Zhuyun, Jaide, and Barum exchanging tales of their many adventures. Often, Zhuyun found a way to make Zaiyera laugh, and even prodded her into sharing a story or two. She intrigued the foreigners with the many facets of Samharan culture and customs. Kima watched in silence, occasionally joining in the laughter with a chuckle of his own.

At the sound of shuffling coming from the opening further down, they went silent. Malker appeared and sat down in the circle. He rifled through his pack without looking at any of them and fished out a sack of provisions. After taking his portion, he tossed the sack to Zaiyera.

"I'm not hungry, but thank you ..."

"The cold is harsh and food in your stomach helps. Hungry or not, eat."

Zaiyera allowed him the retort and opened the sack. She took a portion of some kind of dried meat, then passed it around. They ate in tense silence until the snack was done.

"Has our watchman partaken of the meal yet?" Zhuyun asked.

Malker shook his head.

"Ah! Then I shall—"

Zaiyera placed a hand on his arm, still looking at Malker. "Please. If I may?"

The junior shydon shrugged and tossed the sack back to her.

She crept out of the shelter to a storm less powerful. Right in front of the opening, Dyren Faust stood with his hand resting on the hilt of his sword. When he noted Zaiyera's approach, he looked over his shoulder, then look back. "Zaiyera," he said.

She remained where she was for a moment, staring at his back. Then she came out to stand beside him and watched those icy blue eyes scan the environment.

"We've had our meal," she said. "I've come to bring yours."

"Thank you." He accepted the sack but did not open it.

"My ... apologies, Dyren Faust. For undermining your authority, and in the presence of your protégé and others. It wasn't my intention."

Dyren was silent for a long time and Zaiyera, figuring he wouldn't speak, turned to leave.

"You were right," he finally said. She stopped and turned back. He stared out at the surroundings, obscured by the blowing snow.

Zaiyera didn't know what to do, so she said nothing.

"When Malker came out, I went out to scout the area. Or so I told him. In truth, I needed to know, if not for my own piece of mind, then to prove you wrong." He stood still as a statue, his breath clouding with each word.

"They were outside," he continued. "The cubs rolled and played once the storm died down. The mother was already facing my direction." He turned a grudging grin on her. "They can smell for miles. She knew I was approaching and was waiting for me. She watched me while I watched them."

Zaiyera looked at him, still not knowing what to say. "I'm … glad they are all safe," she ventured.

Dyren made a sound that was half sigh half laugh and looked back out at the snowy expanse. "You may have been wrong to undermine my command, but you've balanced the infraction by sparing me the guilt of having slaughtered a mother and condemned her cubs to die."

"There was no easy way to handle the situation."

Dyren chuckled again. "I appreciate the attempt, but you're terrible at misplaced sympathy, Zaiyera. You were right and you know it. But I do appreciate and accept your apology while offering my own."

"Apology accepted," Zaiyera said. "Thank you, Dyren Faust."

"Please stop distracting me. I have a watch to keep."

She flinched in indignation, then saw his grin. She smiled back and inclined her head.

Zaiyera returned to camp intending to apologize to Malker as well, no matter who was present. When she returned, however, she found the northerner and Zhuyun chuckling over some conversation. They went silent at her approach, and when she opened her mouth, Malker nodded. They shared a look of understanding as effective as any words might have been, and she nodded back.

Off to the side, Kima continued to watch, and Zaiyera wondered what was going on in the man's head.

* * *

Zaiyera took careful note of the position of the camp once more, then turned again toward the copse of snow-coated stoicgreens. The storm had picked up again, so she drew her dagger and marked the tree facing directly toward the camp, now completely obscured.

The others had thought her insane to venture away from camp in the cold—well, cold for a southerner   but she'd insisted her furs kept her warm enough. Knowing what she was about, Zhuyun had taken her side, insisting that it was quite a burden to be the only woman in a group of smelly men, and that she needed a break.

Zaiyera chuckled at the thought as she passed through the woods. When she finally found a suitable place, she stood still for a moment and closed her eyes. Many moments passed as random thoughts came and went. Her mind took her from the past to the future, concerns that occupied her, regrets that plagued her.

She waited patiently through all of them, letting her mind have its say. Finally, her thoughts slowed and her mind grew quiet. Normally she would achieve this balance through passive dancing of the stream. This was different.

Zaiyera folded her hands at her waist, one atop the other, palms facing upward. She slipped her foot out sideways as she raised her hands above her head and settled into a wide stance. She shifted her weight onto her left leg, moving her right back in, while bringing her hands up again, then pushing them down.

Legs bent, she started to move in a circle. Her torso partially turned toward the circle she continued to walk, and she moved her hands in various patterns she'd learned as a child. She felt the flow right beside her, ever flowing, ever powerful, ever within her reach if she only extended her hand to touch it.

Zaiyera moved beyond the sensation. With an effort, she ignored the recurring guilt that sprang up whenever her tainted yellow dance-resin appeared. The transparent yellow glow trailed every sweep of an arm, flip of the hand, every sway and turn.

She closed her eyes and reached deep within herself. Her body remembered the movements and so continued of its own accord. Zaiyera went into her mind, her soul. She swam ever deeper inside herself. The sounds of the storm faded. The sweet and earthy smell of the stoicgreen trees drifted away.

Zaiyera sank ever further into herself until even the stream fell away. There was no sound, no smell, no sense of touch. Zaiyera's body continued to move in the void.

The cold of the storm faded to be replaced by the warmth of the stream. No, not the stream. *Her* stream.

Zaiyera felt warmth flow from her hands, through her arms and torso, down her legs to her feet. Her beating heart blazed with heat as though touched by Sun Dancer Herself.

Qikai, Zhuyun had called it. Her personal stream of power. Zaiyera swam in its depths and allowed the current to sweep her away. She dipped low to the ground and swept her hand in a scooping gesture, rising again. Her feet came together as she spun a circle, her hands cupped together in a bowl above her head.

Zaiyera rotated her hands and bent her arms in an intricate weave as her body turned. With a feisty flick of her hips, she felt the power of her personal stream flare inside.

For an eternity she danced the stream, *her* stream, until finally she came to stop. Zaiyera's hands rose and fell. She took a deep breath and realized she was smiling.

34

Power was an interesting thing. It created all sorts of possibilities.

Malhadiev casually strode along a path between two sand dunes. He'd decided against riding camelback, and instead decided to walk to his next destination. He'd been walking for days since leaving Zalrabi. What was the rush?

Incredible, infinite power coursed through his body like a river. Day and night Malhadiev walked across the endless desert with its flowing mounds and towering dunes, unconcerned for any predators he might come across. Of course, no predators challenged him.

Not the animal kind, anyway. They seemed to intuit the presence of a creature greater than them, and even the largest fled his coming.

Human predators, however, had no such ability. He'd left two groups of bandits dead in his wake, any streamdancers among them syphoned, adding to his life, his power.

Though there were still limits to how much of the stream he could touch—it was infinite, after all—there wasn't a streamdancer in all the world who could challenge him. Not a dozen, or a hundred, or a thousand.

Malhadiev continued out of the enclosing dunes and was afforded an open view of the landscape once again. A dust cloud in the distance informed him of yet another band of raiders heading straight for him. *Kivuli dayasa* slowly shook his head. This had ceased being amusing days ago. These last few days, he didn't even bother to break his stride as he dispatched his attackers.

The bandits would be on him in minutes, which meant they had minutes left to live. He wondered what it must be like to ride unknowingly to one's death. Was it the same as hunting an animal and failing to kill it, only to have it turn and kill the hunter instead? Perhaps like a soldier going into battle?

No, not the latter. A soldier knew that there was a possibility they wouldn't return from battle every time they engaged. Bandits, however, preyed on those weaker than themselves. No doubt when their scout returned with news of a lone traveler foolishly walking out in the open, they saw him as easy prey. There wouldn't be much of value to take off a lone traveler's corpse, but he might fetch a fair price in the labor markets of the more remote places in the world.

A narrow-eyed smile slithered across Malhadiev's face at that thought. There was little he enjoyed more than watching the life flicker out of a would-be slave trader. He usually took his time with them, letting them know that their efforts were futile. He enjoyed watching the predatory expressions change to surprise, then alarm, then finally to desperation.

It had eventually grown boring, however. Now, he simply dispatched them and moved on.

The raiders finally caught up and encircled him with their camels, not bothering to brandish their weapons.

"You must be sick or a fool, traveler," a man who must be the leader addressed him. He had a long scar running down the middle of his face to the left side of his nose, all the way down his lips to his chin. His body was thick with muscle, apparent in one large arm as he pointed at Malhadiev.

"Maybe you are homeless and looking for a master?"

Malhadiev never stopped walking. "Hardly that, thief. Best be on your way."

The statement was met with a ripple of laughter, as always. The circle didn't move as he drew closer to the two blocking his way. Their laughter faded at the unconcerned and rather confident expression on the shadowlancer's face. They glanced at each other then looked past Malhadiev; at their leader, no doubt.

"You must be a streamdancer to be so confident," the leader said from behind. "You think we're not prepared for that, fool?"

"I think you're anxiously speeding toward the end of your lives," Malhadiev said. The pair blocking his way shifted nervously in their saddles. They were only a dozen paces away, now.

Malhadiev stopped in front of them and touched the stream simply by thinking about it. "I've killed more people than any of you could ever imagine in all your nightmares combined. Many did not deserve to perish, but they stood in my way while I was in the grips of blood-lust. I can't say why I'm feeling a moment of generosity, but I am."

He half turned to look back at the bandit leader, then his comrades. "None of you deserve it, but I will extend, one last time, my offer to leave you alive. I've a long walk with a lot of death waiting at the end of it." He touched the stream a bit deeper.

The camels beneath the bandits shuffled nervously. The bandit leader drew his curved sword, the rest following his lead.

Malhadiev shrugged. "So be it." Black dance-resin trailing his movements, he drew forth a transparent whip from the flow and struck in a circular motion. The whip swept through the bandit behind and to the left of Malhadiev, and continued through every bandit around and behind him to the left.

For several heartbeats, the struck bandits sat trembling astride their mounts. Then, one by one, the top half of their torsos toppled over. The severed torsos hit the ground with loud thuds, blood pooling in the sand and spilling down their now frantic mounts. The animals groaned in terror and lurched away. The bottom half of their dead riders slid free as the animals receded into the distance.

Right arm still extended behind him, Malhadiev watched them gallop away. He watched until the last of the animals was finally out of sight, then turned to look up the length of his arm and the transparent whip. At the end of the whip, the bandit leader sat stiff in the saddle,

Malhadiev's stream whip wrapped around his neck. The man's eyes bulged so large in his head they looked like they'd fall out.

"Well, now." Malhadiev tilted his head at the muscular raider. "Looks like I've been forced to kill all your comrades, haven't I? That is regrettable, but you needn't continue on alone. Let's walk together."

With barely a flick of his wrist, Malhadiev snatched the man from his saddle. The camel bolted before the bandit hit the ground.

"Come," Malhadiev said with ominous cheer. "Walk with me."

He saw the fear in the bandit leader's eyes as he quickly surveyed the carnage Malhadiev had wrought.

Malhadiev turned away and started walking. He smiled when he felt the expected trickle of lifestream flow through the whip and into his body. "Careful," he said without turning. "We are linked through my little tool, here. If you try to use the flow against me, you'll simply send me your power, little by little," he shrugged, "or in one big torrent. That depends on you."

"Why did you spare me?" the bandit growled. "To take me to the nearest city for trial? They'll execute me, so you might as well do it now. Or better yet …"

Malhadiev could practically see the man licking his lips in his mind's eye.

"… we could work together, no? Think about it. We're both powerful streamdancers, no? Just the two of us, we could gain great wealth."

Malhadiev snorted. "Before I respond to that, thief, answer this one question. If our positions were reversed, how likely would you be to accept such an offer?"

"But I know the best places to wait for travelers and caravans," the bandit leader protested, a hint of desperation creeping into his tone. "I know the best places to ambush outside the watch of any major cities. There are outposts ripe for the taking …"

Malhadiev listened with half an ear to the man's small-minded ideas. He didn't think the fool believed his own words any more than Malhadiev did, but he was in a bad situation with nothing but his own severely lacking wit to get him out of it.

The bandit finally went quiet. Malhadiev arched an eyebrow and looked over his shoulder. "Tired of talking? Or are you planning our world conquest in silence?"

"I thought you weren't listening to me."

Malhadiev shrugged. "More or less, I was."

"You're not interested." It was more a statement than a question.

"It wouldn't make sense," Malhadiev replied. "I've no need of you in any capacity. Besides, how long do you think you'll live to put these plans into motion?"

The bandit leader's throat worked as he swallowed. "If you're going to kill me, why didn't you do it back there?"

"That wouldn't have been much fun," Malhadiev said. "Now, I have someone to accompany me on this long walk of mine."

The bandit stopped walking. "I'm not a toy. Kill me now or set me free."

Malhadiev kept walking. He fed the whip a bit more from the stream until it was twice its former length. He left the bandit standing there, now more than fifty feet away. A hundred feet.

A grin spread across the shadowlancer's face as he fed tiny pinpricks of razor-like shards of energy through the whip. A quick, tiny burst. A moment later he heard the bandit's surprised cry of pain.

He didn't bother to look back to see if the bandit was walking again. Malhadiev gave him another shock, then another. The footfalls grew rapid as the bandit started to jog. He gave the bandit one last shock that sent him into a full run.

Malhadiev heard his reluctant companion's heavy breathing as he caught up and fell in step beside him. Malhadiev didn't bother to look at him. "Careful, now. I'd remain a couple steps back, if I were you."

"I'm no sla—argh!" He dropped to his knees. Malhadiev gave him another shock, and he scrambled back up.

"You exchanged your freedom for mine, when you tried to take it," Malhadiev said.

The bandit leader narrowed his eyes. "You plan to sell me to slavers."

Malhadiev almost laughed. Bandit raiders made a business of

selling prisoners to the same slavers this man pretended to be afraid of. Being more of an asset running free to find more human captives, the slavers would more likely try to take Malhadiev and turn his captive loose. "Hardly."

They walked through the day and into the night. Malhadiev ate when he grew hungry and drank when thirsty. For the bandit leader, he spared just enough to keep the man going and sent frequent tiny shocks through the whip when he started to slow.

Through most of the day, the man had glared hatefully at Malhadiev, who merely smiled back in response. By nightfall, the worn-out bandit leader had grown tired and weak. Now, in the mostly full moon-lit night, the man barely walked without dragging his feet, which he mostly stared at more than anything else.

Malhadiev knew the bandit—also a streamdancer—could feel him syphoning away tiny bits of his lifestream. At first Malhadiev had only done it the few times the man had gotten angry and tried to use the flow against him. But he'd quickly learned the futility of that. So when he'd stopped, Malhadiev had simply taken to syphoning tiny bits of his lifestream.

Ever since his hibernation-like sleep, and his body's subsequent change, Malhadiev had little need of rest. He'd planned to walk through the night and the next day, but his captive had simply collapsed.

Malhadiev sighed and sat a few feet away from the exhausted man. He cut off the constant trickle of the man's lifestream to himself and closed his eyes. He thought of Sheikh Jegried, and his partially avenged brother. He thought about the other Samharan rulers who were complicit in the web of trade deals that benefitted themselves at the cost of their people.

Only a small handful of societies experienced the shared wealth of their resources and trade. Malhadiev held no illusions of the benevolence of the rulers of these places. It was only a matter of time before they, too, became greedy. No matter. Greed was a disease, and Malhadiev himself was the cure.

"How long ... will you torture me?"

Malhadiev looked over at the bandit, lying on his side, propped up on his elbow.

Malhadiev frowned at him. "Torture?"

The bandit spat. "Stop toying with me. You plan to kill me. Just get on with it."

"Ah." Malhadiev reached into his pack and pulled out a waterskin. After a mouthful, he replaced it in his pack, pointedly ignoring the longing in the other man's eyes as they followed the waterskin back into the pack.

"I suppose slaves do feel tortured by their captors, no?"

"You said you weren't going to sell me to slavers."

"I spoke true. You see," Malhadiev shifted so that he sat cross-legged facing the man. "The problem with this world is that we do the things we do without knowing how it feels. Figures in power make decisions that affect their subjects, yet do not know the feeling of being subjected to another's rule. They do not know the feeling of breaking their back to survive while others live in excess wealth and comfort."

The bandit growled and slapped his hand on the ground. "What in the blazing sun of Samhar are you talking about, madman?"

"Only," Malhadiev replied calmly, "that one should experience how their decisions and actions affect another." He gave the bandit a lazy wave of his hand. "You've no doubt sold people into captivity. Should you not know what it's like? I'm providing you with education through experience."

"What does that matter if you're going to kill me anyway?"

Malhadiev shrugged. "Maybe you can return to the next life with this knowledge."

The man stared at him with open disgust. "You teach me a moral lesson and you've admitted you've killed many."

Malhadiev's expression darkened. "I have. And I've felt every death. I've died with each of them. Every one. Their souls ascend to dance with Shakimah in eternity, while my soul, blacker than this night, continues on. It is the price I pay to be the hand that slaps down the tyranny of men."

To Malhadiev's surprise, the bandit leader laughed. "The tyrant who fights tyranny? You are truly insane."

"I see the world for what it is."

"So do I, no?" the other man said. "I know what I am. At least I don't try to pretend otherwise, no?"

Malhadiev stared at him for a time. "What is your name?"

"What does it matter? My name will be lost to the wind soon enough, no?"

"It will," Malhadiev promised. "But I want to know it anyway."

The man stared at him for a long time.

Malhadiev looked around at their surroundings while he waited for the answer. The pale light of the moon lit the otherwise dark expanse of desert. In another two nights it would be gone, leaving the stars to sparkle in the black canopy. Somewhere in the distance he heard the yip of a chukita cat. Cold air slid over the dunes and swirled around them.

"Ijra," the man finally said.

Malhadiev nodded. "Well, Ijra. I don't pretend to be anything other than the monster I am. But I am the monster the world has created and so, I am the monster the world deserves. I am the mirror of the hearts of men."

He was staring at the ground in front of him, now. "I'll bring chaos. I'll bring smoke and fire, pain and death. I will leave despair and broken souls in my wake."

Ijra listened with narrowed eyes. "You want to burn the world, no?"

"Did you know?" Malhadiev asked, "that in some places where there is lots of vegetation, that fires spark and burn millions of acres of land, leaving them charred and black. But out of that burning and destruction and death, the soil becomes rich and fertile. Life springs forth anew."

Ijra stared at him for a long time, then snorted and rolled over, putting his back to the madman.

Malhadiev's level gaze lingered on the man's back for a time before he finally stood. "We move on."

Ijra didn't move. "Then go."

"I shall." Malhadiev started walking. "And you with me."

"Shakimah blight your eyes," the other man said. Kill me now or leave me be. I have robbed and beaten. I have sold others into captivity, yes. But I am no abomination."

Malhadiev looked down at his right hand. He'd long since used its namesake to tie off the flow around his wrist. Whenever it started to weaken, it simply drew a bit more lifestream from Ijra. He snarled, clenched his fist, and sent a stream of acidic barbs slicing down the bandit leader's throat and through every inch of his body.

Ijra convulsed, his mouth agape in silent agony. When the fit finally stopped, the bandit leader lay heaving and sprawled on the ground. He rolled over and wretched up what little food remained in his stomach before struggling to his feet. "Shakimah—"

"Blight my eyes," Malhadiev finished for him. "Yes, you've already cursed me once. If the Goddess would be inclined to do so at your request, I'm sure she heard you the first time. Come."

Malhadiev started away, but when he saw the other man standing on wobbly knees, barely able to hold himself up, he sighed and reached into his shoulder pack. He fished out a couple pieces of dried meat and tossed it to the man, who nearly bit his own fingers gobbling it up. Malhadiev tossed him one of his waterskins, which the man downed in one long gulp.

They walked through the night and the next day, and the night after. Malhadiev allowed Ijra just enough nourishment and rest to keep him alive through it all. On the fourth day of their journey together, the man had visibly lost weight and had black rings around his eyes. He strode behind the shadowlancer like a ghost barely attached to this world.

When they came within sight of the mud and thatch roofs of village houses, he heard Ijra sigh in relief. An odd reaction.

"Feeling some glimmer of hope?" he asked the bandit. When he looked back at the man, Ijra looked away.

They continued toward the village until it came fully into view. At the leisurely pace Malhadiev kept them at, they were about an hour away.

Ijra's steps grew stronger, if only a bit. He seemed to drag his feet less. Even his back straightened a bit.

Malhadiev pondered the little transformation. Perhaps the man hoped they might be spotted and someone would come to his aid. Or perhaps he simply hoped Malhadiev would take them into the village for a good night's sleep. Maybe relent, just a little, and allow him a full meal.

The more he thought about that, the more Malhadiev thought that might be a cruel carrot to dangle in front of the man.

Through the whip attached to both of them, he syphoned Ijra of his lifestream. The bandit made a strangled sound and tried to grab at the insubstantial whip wrapped around his neck. He fell to his knees, wheezing as he tried futilely to draw breath.

Malhadiev watched him until he fell forward, sand clinging to his face where tears had spilled, in view of the close yet so far away village. He let the whip dissipate into the air and turned north.

Carrion crows found Ijra's corpse before Malhadiev had gone a few hundred paces. That had become a common occurrence since he'd left Zalrabi.

The birds were smart. They knew that Malhadiev was a food source. He grinned. Soon they would feast.

35

All but Zhuyun cast puzzled glances at Zaiyera the following day. The last storm of the season had finally breathed its last puff, and a ceiling of gray clouds were replaced by the sun in a bright blue sky.

Wildlife came out of hiding. The distant call of animals large and small, as well as bird chatter, layered the peaceful surroundings, softened further by the sound-absorbing snow carpeting the world in every direction.

Zaiyera ignored the bemused expressions of her comrades. Though she didn't smile, per se, she found herself in a bright mood. How could she not? After exercising the gift Zhuyun had given her days ago, she felt no sign of the hunger. Of course, the withdrawals would return, but this was the first time since that fateful day she'd become a darkdancer that she hadn't felt even a hint of the hunger.

A flicker of guilt sparked deep inside. She still wasn't sure she deserved any relief at all. Regardless, for the time it lasted, she felt free. It was as though she'd stepped outside into the sun for the first time in her life, instead of looking at it from the inside.

"We'll easily make Denberest before midday," Barum said. "From there it's a matter of if you want to continue or spend the night. The town is still a bit north of the border for horses to be common enough to get, but it's a possibility."

"An expensive possibility, no doubt," Jaide added.

"Aye," Barum replied.

"We'll continue on as soon as we've acquired mounts," Dyren Faust said. "I've little experience in Denberest. Can we bargain, Barum?"

"Aye," Barum said again. "Denberesterners will bargain with you to a point. Just remember the town ain't that big and makes a good deal of its income as a place between major destinations. They'll not bend too far."

"Noted," Dyren replied.

Two hours later Denberest came into view. As soon as they reached the town, they split up. Barum and the shydon hunters went off to bargain for mounts, while Zaiyera, Jaide, Zhuyun, and Kima replenished their provisions. It turned out that Denberest had no horses at that time, so Barum and the shydon hunters acquired snow camels instead. The price had been reasonable, yet more expensive since they had no mounts to trade in the deal.

Their tasks done, the party met just outside town and continued on.

Zaiyera took a deep breath and let it out in a contented hum. The air was getting warmer as they drew closer to the border. She'd enjoyed the way the snow muffled sound and quieted the environment. The endless expanse of white-carpeted flatlands, rolling hills and mountains had been breathtaking. She'd marveled at the towering stoic greens, their needle-like leaves ever green, yet ever coated in white.

Now that she wasn't stiff with cold and trying to prevent her face from freezing, Zaiyera found herself reflecting on the northern landscape with fondness.

Jaide's sarcasm penetrated her thoughts. "Moon and stars, woman. What are you grinning at?"

Zaiyera blinked. When she opened her mouth to respond, Jaide waved her hands at Zaiyera, palms facing her. "No, no. Never mind. Any ray of light that penetrates your magnificent grimness is welcomed, yes?"

Behind her, Zhuyun and Barum chuckled.

Zaiyera glared at the Viriksani woman, but with no anger. "Not all of us have so few thoughts that we remain in a state of euphoria, Jaide Amadi."

"Oh ho *ho*," Jaide said. "Wit and beauty in a woman. A dangerous combination, yes?"

Zaiyera gave her a direct look. "You tell me."

Jaide cleared her throat behind her fist. "How far till we reach the border, Dor'haighener?"

"Dusk," Barum called over his shoulder.

Barum's words held true. By the time their shadows began their retreat to the east, signs of Samhar started to appear. The snow had all but disappeared, only patches of ice in low areas signifying they were still in the north.

"We're about an hour north of the border, now," Barum said. "I'm figuring we should turn west now. These camels may be cousins of your desert kind, but they're adapted to colder weather and light snow. If the ground gets too hot it'll fry their feet."

"Is there no other town near or south of the border where we might acquire horses?" Dyren asked.

Barum shook his head. "Not between here and Demenin Waypoint on either side."

"Then we turn fully east from here," Dyren stated.

They rode into the night until fatigue set in. Barum declared that they were about a half-day's ride from Demenin Waypoint so long as they didn't encounter any extenuating circumstances. They awoke at dawn and continued on. For a mercy, no extenuating circumstances found them, and they made an uneventful journey straight to the border town.

Zaiyera wanted nothing more than to gallop in a straight line for the stables as soon as they crossed through the gates of Demenin Waypoint. She kept the urge in check, however, if not for any other reason than to spare herself from Jaide never letting her forget it.

Their path to the Inn and stable that housed Sadiq was painfully slow. Zaiyera tried to occupy herself with people-watching and taking note of the various smells and sounds of the place. Zhuyun guided his snow camel over to Zaiyera's side and spoke to her in a low voice. "After we've secured lodging, I would like to venture out of town a little. It would be my pleasure if you'd join me, ixu?"

Zaiyera thought that a little odd, but perhaps there was something more the Yuntaiman wished to teach her regarding management of the hunger.

Barum did the bargaining for desert camels in exchange for their snow cousins, with very little to pay on top. Zaiyera made out ahead in the deal, since she'd already paid a deposit to house Sadiq. Snow camels were of great value in Demenin Waypoint, so she'd had to pay almost nothing for the exchange.

After the stable business was finished, Malker walked up to her. The junior shydon hadn't said much of anything to her since the incident with the cave bear, so it came as a surprise when he approached Zaiyera.

"You're probably hiding your agony to visit with your camel friend," the young shydon hunter said. When he smiled the creases at the corners of his eyes deepened, and his hair—more gray than when she'd first met him—spoke of someone easily twice his age. "We will secure the rooms and meet for a meal in an hour." He jerked his head in the direction of the barn. "Go be with your friend."

Zaiyera inclined her head with a smile. "Thank you."

She made a show of taking her time to enter the barn, but once the door was closed, she practically ran down the middle. She'd made it halfway to his stall before Sadiq's head emerged further down. It swiveled in her direction and he let out a long groan.

Zaiyera laughed like a girl when she reached the stall. She climbed over the door and wrapped her arms around Sadiq in a tight hung. The camel let out an affectionate grunt, and she laughed again.

"I've missed you, my friend," she said, her head resting against his neck. She leaned back and gave him a pat. "I hope you've been good."

"He's been great, miss milady." It as Ary's voice.

Zaiyera turned to look at the boy. He still shifted his feet awkwardly when he looked at her, his bright blue eyes blinking with a hidden crush, his sandy blond hair still tousled about his head. "Hello, Ary. And good. It wouldn't do to associate myself with a troublemaker."

"Oh no, miss milady," Ary replied. "He's been a good camel. Always steps away when I clean his space. Never tries to bite or spit … much." He scratched the corner of his head. "He does like to rub his head all over me for some reason, though. Leaves me covered in a right bit of foamy slobber. A little disgusting, pardon my saying so."

Zaiyera chuckled. "Sadiq has a bit of a sarcastic side." She gave her companion another pat on the neck. Sadiq swung his head around to rub it on her, but Zaiyera placed a hand on the bridge of his nose and stopped him short. "That's how you keep him from slobbering all over you."

"I guess now's a better time to learn than never," the boy said. He shuffled his feet, then pointed off toward the direction of the other stalls. If you'll excuse me, miss milady. I still got more stuff to do."

"Of course." Zaiyera leaned over the stall door and gave the boy a kiss on the cheek. "My deepest gratitude for taking care of my friend."

A blush appeared on the boy's neck and swept up to cover his face. Even his ears looked like they'd caught fire. "I, er … it's my pleasure, miss milady. I should go."

Zaiyera looked after the boy with a crinkled grin, then turned back to Sadiq just in time to see a pair of incoming giant lips smack into her midsection. With slow, powerful, lazy ease, the camel dragged his foamy lips across her body, then nudged her shoulder from the other side.

She looked down at herself in disgust, then up at her now chewing companion. "Ugh. Sadiq!"

The camel grunted and blinked his long eyelashes at her.

* * *

"What are the chances your king sent soldiers in this direction to find us?" Jaide leaned over her elbows on the table and looked from one face to the other.

Around their circular table, a low din of conversation filled the air, atypical to the normal rowdiness of a Dor'haighen town. Servers swept in and out of clumps of patrons, serving food and taking orders. Candles burning in wall sconces, combined with the fire crackling in the hearth, cast a golden light on the place.

"Maybe," Jaide continued, "he thinks we make a straight line for Rexzen, yes?"

"Assuming he knows that we know about Rexzen," Malker replied.

"That we encountered no pursuit after our fight with the worva says that word came after the snowstorm hit," Dyren said. "To send a team out into that would have been folly. By the time he was able to send another team to track us, all trace of our passage would have been long gone. Our tracks, our scent, everything, gone. He'd be left to guess our first stop."

"That wouldn't be too hard a guess," Barum said. "Denberest's the likeliest stop between the capital and here."

"Best to assume he guessed correctly," Dyren said. "We shouldn't linger here and lose our lead."

Jaide ran a hand over her face. "Moon and stars, but this road has driven us hard, yes?"

"With a lot more driving to go yet, my good man," Zhuyun replied. "Best to get a good night's rest, ixu?"

"True words," Barum said, sliding back his chair. "And if I'm gonna get a good night's rest myself, I need to get to work now."

"Work?" Zaiyera asked.

Barum winked at her. "News ain't gonna gather itself." He stood. "We leavin' on the morrow?"

Dyren looked around the table at the weary group. "We're all tired, but we must push on as hard as we can to Rexzen."

Tired nods responded all around, except for Kima, who sat in his usual brooding and unresponsive silence.

Zhuyun spared a quick glance at the Zalrabian man. The Yuntaiman's expression was unreadable, and the look came and went so fast it might not have been.

"Just after dawn, then," Dyren said. "The extra couple hours will do us all some good."

They'd mostly eaten in silence after the discussion. Zaiyera had gone up to her room to drop off her gear when there was a knock on the door. She ran her hand across Shatr's hilt. "Come in."

The door opened and Jaide stepped through. She closed it behind her and took off her warm head wrappings. Her long black hair fell in volumes down her shoulders. "Oh, that feels good," she said, switching to *Soloush*. "It gets extra oily under all that wrapping every day."

Zaiyera arched an eyebrow. "Longing for woman talk?"

Jaide laughed. "Hardly." She looked at Zaiyera, who was still standing, and then at Shatr, still strapped to her waist. "Do you have a little time?"

"A little," Zaiyera replied.

"Then, I'll get straight to it. What are your feelings on riding this thing to its conclusion?" Jaide waved a hand behind her. "Those shydon hunters wouldn't be a match for *kivuli dayasa* if there were two hundred more at their back. You know this. *They* know this."

"Which is why we have Kima," Zaiyera said.

Jaide snorted. "That one? If I hadn't heard him speak the two words he uttered at the beginning of our flight from Nanshaigha, I'd have thought him a mute."

"Consider his circumstances," Zaiyera countered.

"Lone man traveling beside a group of people out to kill his brother," Jaide said. "Who happens to be a monster, yes? I suppose I can understand that. And speaking of that monster," Jaide's green-eyed gaze again fell on Zaiyera's scimitar. "Our shydon companions rest their hope and our lives on the edge of your blade."

"It looks that way."

"A dangerous gamble."

"What alternatives do we have?" Zaiyera asked. "There isn't a streamdancer or a hundred streamdancers who could overpower

Malhadiev. When you can't overpower your adversary, you find another way." She patted the hilt. "Shatr can cut through any amount of the flow. Whether a trickle or a raging ocean."

Zaiyera had never tested Shatr against the amount of power Malhadiev would wield against them. It had done its job against him the first time they'd fought, even if the man had ultimately beaten her. She had to believe the scimitar could defeat any amount of the flow, as long as Zaiyera herself possessed the skill and strength to wield it true.

Jaide tossed her hair over her shoulder, a distinctly feminine motion that contrasted heavily with her masculine alternate persona. "A trickle or a raging ocean. How many raging oceans of the flow has your magnificent blade encountered, Zaiyera?"

Zaiyera thought back to the scimitar's creation, and the power her grandmother had used in completing its forging. It would be enough. Shatr had never failed her and it wouldn't when the time came to face *kivuli dayasa*. "None."

Jaide closed her eyes and smiled. "None." She turned to the door.

"You have no obligation to this," Zaiyera said.

"I appreciate you not pointing out that I'm all but useless in this fight," Jaide said to the door. "But just as you've found a way to manage the withdrawals, I'll find a way to help you destroy this monster."

Icy blades of fear shot through Zaiyera's stomach. "What …"

"Don't try to deny it, Kushtanji." Jaide turned back. "Our shydon friends only *hunt* dancers who've fallen. They spend only enough time with a darkdancer to kill them. I know the subtle signs all too well. The distant expression. Clenched jaw, the look of concentration for no reason at all."

Zaiyera listened to her with a growing sense of dread.

Jaide let out a long exhale. "I know the signs because I used to see them in my brother. He resisted the hunger for months before he started to give in. The horror of that first syphoning broke something inside him."

Moisture crept into the other woman's eyes. It was such an alien sight on the normally jovial Jaide's face that it almost made Zaiyera forget that she was in a dangerous situation, here.

The moment passed, and Jaide's face hardened as though she was angry she'd let her emotions slip. "He spent the rest of his days trying to fix what was broken in him and failed. I kept his secret, and it fell to me to help him die when the hunger threatened to turn him into a monster like the one we hunt.

"So, yes, I'm aware that I'm likely to die fighting *kivuli dayasa*. But I feel a responsibility to my brother and my homeland to try."

She'd been looking at Zaiyera without seeing her. Now her fierce green eyes refocused. "Put your worry to rest, Zaiyera Tuneem of Kushtanja." A fractured version of her normal flippant smile returned. "Despite your normal brooding personality, I like you. It feels like we're something like friends."

Zaiyera found she didn't disagree. "You honor me with your friend-ship, Jaide Amadi."

"Honor you." Jaide chuckled and turned back to the door. "And just when I thought you were starting to loosen up."

Zaiyera stood rooted to the floor in the middle of the room as she watched Jaide Amadi slowly open the door and peek out, then leave. She stood there for a long while.

* * *

So wrapped up in her thoughts, Zaiyera almost walked right by Zhuyun on her way to the common room.

"This land of snow must have made me pale as a ghost, ah?" Zhuyun said as she passed by. "Otherwise, how could so perceptive a lady walk right by without seeing me?"

Zaiyera snapped out of her trance and turned back. "Oh. I ... had some things on my mind."

"You?" Zhuyun said. "Zaiyera Tuneesh had something on her mind?" He widened his eyes at her in mock amazement.

Zaiyera could only offer a self-deprecating chuckle at that.

She said little on their walk through the streets of the border town, preferring to listen to Zhuyun's endless supply of stories. She smiled whenever he shared such stories, for they always came punctuated with wide, flourishing gestures.

"Is there a corner of the world you haven't visited, my friend?" she asked him.

"Of course," Zhuyun replied. "I hadn't been to Samhar or Dor'haighen before this grand adventure brought us together. There are many places I have not seen. Perhaps I might survive to see more yet, *ixu*?"

When Zaiyera noticed they were nearing the city walls, she glanced up at the sky. "Are we leaving?"

"Only for a short distance," Zhuyun said. "I thought we might have some room."

"For?"

Still looking ahead, Zhuyun responded with a devious grin. "Exercise."

Zaiyera felt a thrill shoot through her stomach. "You do realize there are usually training circles and halls for just this sort of thing?"

"Yet an actual fight in one is unlikely," Zhuyun replied. "I judge your skills beyond one in need of a training hall."

They exited the city and moved not more than fifty feet away from the city walls.

"Why are we doing this now?" Zaiyera asked. "We've traveled together for so many days I've lost count, yet you've not once expressed interest in sparring with me."

"Time," Zhuyun said. "I needed time. You see, everyone takes part in this journey because they feel they can be or wish to be of some use. Despite his carefree demeanor, your countryman, Jaide Amadi, carries weight from his past that forces him on despite the likelihood he can do little more than die against so powerful a foe. Our friend Barum's motivations are as simple as they seem. He's an adventurer, comrade in arms, and a loyal friend. It's who he is."

Zaiyera slid a stray braid from the side of her face back into her head wrapping. "This is a long path to the answer, Zhuyun Xaiylin."

The Yuntaiman laughed. "Ah, forgive my traveling storyteller nature. The answer is that I needed time, my Samharan friend, to see what use I might be to you."

"To me?" Zaiyera frowned.

"That's what I said, ah?" Zhuyun flipped his staff to tuck under his shoulder with a casual spin. "You're the best hope of all of us surviving this." He pointed at Shatr. "That magnificent blade of yours can cut through anything the shadowlancer can throw at you."

"As far as I know," Zaiyera replied carefully. "I've never fought anyone as powerful as he probably is now."

"So, you're unsure you can cut through larger amounts of the flow." Zhuyun nodded. "Instances like this, you do your best to avoid the answer if you can. The best way to do that, is cut off the flow before he can draw it from the stream, *ixu*?"

Zaiyera's puzzled frown deepened.

"Cut through the flow before he can fully draw it from the stream," Zhuyun clarified.

"How would I do that?" Zaiyera asked. "How do you cut through the flow when it hasn't taken shape?"

"Ah, but you know the moment he touches the stream," Zhuyun said. "Stop him then. Cut off the flow as soon as he draws it."

"What you describe requires reflex more than speed," Zaiyera said.

Zhuyun smiled at her. "Your speed, precision, and power with the blade are formidable. You also possess the intuition of the stream that only a *tokailan* can. I suspect not one of our party could defeat you." He held up a finger. "However, I am faster than you by enough of a margin that you would not match me in a month or a year."

The Yuntaiman had spoken a simple truth, without ego. "I've seen you fight," she agreed. "I don't doubt that."

Zhuyun bowed his head, fist clenched in hand. "So how, then, would you defeat an enemy like me?" The setting eastern sun cast shadow over the left side of his face, hardening his features.

* * *

T he night had long since arrived by the time the two finished their sparring match and started back into town. Despite the numerous bruises to her body and her ego after repeated defeats by the Yuntaiman, Zaiyera felt a sense of exhilaration. The man possessed unbelievable speed and a precision in battle that saw his whirling staff slipping through her defenses time and again. But the lessons! Moon and stars, the lessons she learned from each defeat brought her closer to solving the conundrum of how to defeat Malhadiev. She didn't know why she felt this, but she was sure of it.

"What would you have done if it were not me you fought, but Jaide, who is likely your closest match?"

The question seemed abrupt, but Zaiyera didn't have to think much about it. "He," she said, careful not to let the woman's true identity slip, "fights in the same manner as all Samharan's, though each region has different variations. We use slicing and stabbing attacks, mostly. And we prefer to parry than block, though we will if necessary. Ours would be a dance of the sword until someone draws first blood. In a real fight, I would need to continuously deal injury until he slowed and made a mistake.

"Ah," Zhuyun said with almost childlike excitement as they entered through the gates and past the guards. "Exactly! He is your closest match, so yours would be quite a battle. Who could keep their movements crisp and sharp the longest? Who would outsmart the other? Who would be the first to falter? *That* would be a sight, *ixu*?"

"Perhaps we might perform for you someday," Zaiyera replied dryly.

Zhuyun chuckled. "I ramble. More to the point, what of me? How would you fight one whom you could not match in speed? One whose tactics are something you've not seen?"

They parted ways with the question left unanswered. Zaiyera went to sleep with that question on her mind. The more she thought about it, the more she realized how lucky she was to be alive. It wasn't often one survived defeat in a real fight. She replayed her match with Zhuyun, visualizing that spinning, stabbing staff. She considered his dizzying speed. Beating the Yuntaiman would require more than strategy, for she'd never have enough time to form one.

Zhuyun hadn't asked the question of her lightly. More than just her life was at stake. Somehow she knew that if she managed to piece together the puzzle of how to defeat Zhuyun, she would figure out how to defeat Malhadiev.

Zaiyera closed her eyes. Nightmares of desolation greeted her.

36

Zaiyera's first journey outside her beloved Samhar came full circle the instant Sadiq's foot touched down on the first bit of sandy soil.

The air was still cooler than further south, but the time Zaiyera had spent traveling through cold snowstorms and thin air in the high elevations made breathing easier, and the chill air seem warm.

She took off her head wrapping and stuffed it in her pack. She might don her keffiyeh later at some point, but it felt good to feel the brisk breeze caressing the areas of bare scalp between the plaits of her braided hair.

Zaiyera leaned her head back and closed her eyes with a contended sigh. "Indeed, Kushtanji," she heard Jaide say.

"Nice to be where the sun's light brings warmth, yes?"

"Yes," Zaiyera replied.

"I'll take it," Barum Hurst said. "It ain't that hellish heat you're content to swelter in further south, but it's warmer than farther north." He snorted at that. "You'd probably have died traveling to the capital just a few months earlier. You think what we left behind was cold?"

Malker chuckled. "This, coming from a Denberesterner. You might as well be Samhari, living practically on top of the border."

"And this," Dyren Faust said, "coming from a Nanshaighaner. Your coldest winters in the capital are a balmy day in my home of Argastonia."

Malker Argen waved a hand at that. "Pure stubbornness. Only stubbornness would keep anyone in that frozen wasteland after enduring one winter. If ever there's a place nature itself doesn't want a man to live, it's that perpetually frozen bed of ice."

"Or this perpetually baking land of sand," Zhuyun added. "Or my perpetually soggy homeland of Yuntai, where it rains for months in the autumn and winter. In my travels, I find the wisest people I've met live on big islands in the Great Sea, where the temperature is a steady warm but not hot."

"Until a storm rolls in and crashes over it." To everyone's surprise, it was Kima who'd spoken. "You must have visited one of these islands during their summer, Yuntaiman."

"Ah, this is true!" Zhuyun said. "But I have not visited every island, only two. Namaiyla and Sepai. Sister islands in sight of each other. The sand is white, the ocean warm, and the fruit juicy. One of these fruits is as big and hairy as a man's head and as hard as a boulder, but with cold sweet water and soft white meat on the inside!"

"You've traveled many places," Zaiyera said to Kima, trying to keep the man engaged. "Have you been to these places?"

"Not those two islands," the man admitted. "But there are many, large and small. Zalrabi frequently traded with the people of Kukishi. It's a huge island, maybe half the size of Samhar, with giant mountains covered in green trees and plants. Animals live in those mountains like none I've seen before. Large cats with thick green pelts like moss, and teeth like swords."

"Sounds dangerous," Jaide remarked.

"Maybe to us," Kima agreed. "But the people who live in those mountains don't seem to have problems with them."

"You sound like a man after my own heart," Zhuyun said. "You've traveled to many paces?"

Kima kept his focus forward as he spoke. "Some. But not as many as you, traveler." I've only been to the places Jegried sought trade relations with."

Mention of the dead Sheikh cast an uneasy pall over the conversation.

"This Kukishi Island sounds like a fascinating place to visit," Zhuyun said. "I could find myself willing to remain indefinitely in such paradise, *ixu?*"

"There's a lot of rocky knolls and rough patches up that way." Barum pointed further ahead where the land grew less flat and rougher. "Once we've crossed through that patch of terrain, it smooths out and we can ride faster."

"Faster by camelback," Malker grumbled.

"Better than walkin'," Barum said. "Sometimes even border cities don't have horses. This is one of those times."

"How far are we from Rexzen?" Dyren Faust asked.

"From where we are right now," Barum answered, "about two weeks."

Dyren and Malker grunted.

Kima settled into a brooding mood at the mention of Rexzen and didn't speak again.

Zaiyera reflected on her sparring match with Zhuyun, and their subsequent conversation. Everything he had said was matter of fact. He *was* stronger and faster than she, and though Zaiyera was more skilled with the blade than anyone she'd fought in her adult life, Zhuyun was likely more so with that whirling staff of his. How indeed could she overcome an enemy that was simply better, or in the case of *kivuli dayasa*, infinitely more powerful?

They rode through mildly warm days and found shelter from the elements to camp through crispy cold nights. Midway through the second week, they set camp for the night in the shelter of a cluster of niyabi trees.

A short distance from the campfire, Zhuyun and Barum watched the shydon hunters spar, while Kima sat off to himself as usual. The clang of metal rang out from the night as Dyren and Malker pressed each other. As the contest grew more intense, the shydon hunters started to passively touch the stream.

Jaide sat on the ground beside Zaiyera and crossed her legs. "A rare thing, yes?"

"Bladedancers?" Zaiyera replied. "Yes. I've never met one." It wasn't exactly a lie. As a child, she'd had the aptitude of a bladedancer, though she'd never finished her training in accessing the stream. Aried Dom would have become a bladedancer; the first in Kushtanji history. Something else Zaiyera had taken from her people.

"Moon and stars, Zaiyera," Jaide said in a quiet voice. "Does everything send you into brooding?"

Zaiyera snapped out of her steadily darkening thoughts. "Hm?"

Jaide stared at her for a moment, then sighed. "Maybe *try* not to torture yourself with your every thought?" She cast her most charismatic manly grin. "Such a beautiful woman should be more concerned with fighting off her many suitors, than bathing in such grimness."

Zaiyera blinked at her. "You have … quite a way of speaking, Viriksani."

Jaide responded with a slanted grin. "You know, *niyima*, when I met you on our first caravan job, you were like a song whose words I didn't understand, but whose tone was obvious."

Zaiyera didn't respond. What could she say against that?

The sweet smell of burning niyabi branches hung thick in the air, providing a calming atmosphere. The campfire cast a golden glow over the Viriksani woman's face. In that light, sitting this close, there could be no doubt that she was a woman. It was odd watching her now, staring at the ground in front of her, talking without her usual levity.

"From the moment my brother went dark," Jaide said, "he struggled with the guilt and the hunger. He tried to keep his spirits up for me, always ready with a smile and a playful quip. But I saw the physical and mental pain in him."

Squeaking and chirping insects filled the night with their song, a background chorus to the cracking campfire and murmur of conversation on the other side of the flames.

Barum leaned back with a hearty laugh and slapped Zhuyun on the back. Kima watched them both with conservative mirth.

Their match ended, Dyren and Malker stood off to the side, the senior shydon hunter speaking while his subordinate listened.

"He turned to meditation," Jaide continued, "and found every opportunity to help anyone else, no matter the cost to himself. He'd always been a kind person, but in his last months of life, he'd become the most benevolent person I've ever known."

With the back of her hand, Jaide wiped away moisture brimming in her eyes. "Every day I tried to help, and encouraged him that through his meditations and being busy helping others, he could beat the hunger. He might never touch the stream again, but there was so much good he could do.

"He did do a lot of good, but he wouldn't be able to carry on forever. He knew that, no matter how confident I sounded while silently praying to Shakimah for it to be true."

Jaide leaned back on her hands and let her head fall back. "In the end, the hunger grew inside him. All I could do was watch as it continued to eat him alive from the inside. I saw the way he watched streamdancers in practice, the longing and pain etched in his face.

"We took one last journey together to the coast, to see the Great Sea. It was there that he pleaded I end his life, that he be buried in sight of the sparkling blue waves."

"Your brother sounds like a brave man," Zaiyera said. "I feel the pain from your words. I can't imagine what you felt, walking that path with him."

Jaide sniffed. "Jiet." Jaide said. "His name was Jiet. There are people like him everywhere. All over the world, I'd wager."

She turned her fierce blue eyes on Zaiyera. "You try to do what's right while enduring the endless guilt and pain, just as Jiet did. But you've done what he could not. I don't know how you've managed the withdrawals for so long. It's supposed to be impossible."

Zaiyera started to reply but held her tongue. What would she say?

"I guess only Shakimah knows why anything happens, yes?" Jaide said. "Maybe I'm wasting my time talking to a woman who's already condemned herself to death. Or maybe you learning to manage the taint, the guilt, and the hunger, can be a gift you give to others."

A tiny bit of horror crept up Zaiyera's chest at the mere thought of it. Helping others who'd killed and syphoned? Aiding murderers like herself?

The shadows dancing on Jaide's suddenly hardened face made her look ominous. "Take care what judgements you make, Zaiyera Tuneesh of Kushtanja. Life is messy. Things happen for many reasons. My brother was no murderer or evil person, nor is every single person who goes dark."

She held up a hand when Zaiyera opened her mouth. "Don't try to deny what's in your mind, it's written on your face at my suggestion. Go and do what you think best. But at least consider my words."

The Viriksani warrior stood and turned away in one graceful movement, leaving Zaiyera wrapped in the cloak of her own dark musings.

* * *

They set out just before dawn. Zaiyera allowed herself to feel every one of the bruises Zhuyun had dealt her last night. The Yuntaiman had come to her with his polite invitation and bow, fist in palm. He'd politely battered her in a number of places in short order, to the surprised amazement of everyone but Kima, who knew nothing of the everyone's individual prowess.

Zaiyera allowed herself some comfort in that she'd almost fought him to a draw the second round. She turned the match over and over in her mind, remembering every mistake that had led to a painful hit. Each one of those hits represented her death.

She glanced at him riding alone at the side of the group. It seemed such a contrast, seeing the serenity on his smooth face and knowing how deadly he was. No matter what Zaiyera had tried, no matter how drastically she'd changed her tactics, nothing worked. She'd even fought left-handed, something her father had been adamant she learn to do. The Yuntaiman had smiled at that, and punished her left and right. If there was an opening, no matter how small, Zhuyun found it.

Zaiyera flexed her arm, certain the bruise on the side of her bicep must be purple by now. She needed to figure out how to defeat him if for no other reason than to avoid earning any more bruises.

Beneath her, Sadiq let out a long groan, then regurgitated and started chewing his cud. Zaiyera gave him a pat on the neck.

At the rear of the party, Dyren and Malker rode mostly in silence. The closer they drew to the east, and thus Rexzen, the grimmer those two became. Zaiyera didn't blame them. She remembered being on the receiving end of Malhadiev's full attention when he'd dropped an entire sand dune on them. The possibility of arriving in Rexzen to confront *kivuli dayasa* and a host of bound streamdancers was troubling, to say the least.

Kima rode his camel up beside her. Zaiyera thought he would say something, but for a time, he rode in silence. She'd just begun to slip back into her thoughts, mentally running through her sparring matches with Zhuyun, when he finally spoke. "What was he like?" Kima asked in their native *Soloush*. "What was Malhadiev like?"

Zaiyera didn't know how to answer that. Should she tell him the truth? That his brother was a monster. An insane man driven mad by the sum of his rage and power? "He was … powerful." It seemed a foolish thing to say, but it was the only neutral answer she could think of."

"Powerful," Kima echoed in a dry tone.

"I don't know what to tell you," Zaiyera admitted. "My experience with Malhadiev wasn't a positive one. I barely survived the encounter."

"Kind of ironic," Kima said. "The first time assassins were sent to kill him, he barely survived. The second time—"

"I'm no assassin," Zaiyera said.

"Oh?" Kima shot back. "What were you there to do? Break bread? Talk?" He jabbed a thumb over his shoulder. "What do you think they were sent to do?"

"Stop him from killing another city full of people, perhaps?"

Zaiyera felt her temper rising. She took a deep breath. "I know he's your brother. I can't begin to understand what you must be feeling. But Malhadiev has brought death and ruin to Shanhazai and Zalrabi. He leveled a trade village and a small town."

Kima looked as though he barely kept himself from shouting. "You think I don't know that?"

"I know you know that," Zaiyera said. "I wish *I* knew how to resolve this differently."

"Isn't that why you've brought me?" Kima asked.

"In part," Zaiyera said.

That got his interest. "In part?"

"My hope is that when he sees you alive, he we might be able to incapacitate him, and maybe—"

Kima cut her short. "Incapacitate the most powerful and dangerous *kivuli dayasa* possibly in recorded history? What would you do, hit him over the head and tie him up?"

Zaiyera stared at him and tried to understand the purpose of this conversation. "If you've any ideas, I'm open to them."

Kima gritted his teeth and stared off into the distance. "Everyone lies. When Jegried's father, Sheikh Malhata bestowed upon Malhadiev the title of trade treasurer and ambassador, the intention was to send him to different lands to negotiate deals to the mutual benefit of Zalrabi and its trade partners. For a while, it went that way. But Malhata was already old when he'd appointed Malhadiev to the title.

"Within four years, Malhata died and his ambitious son became Sheikh."

"He wasn't happy with the trade deals your brother had previously negotiated," Zaiyera ventured.

Kima made a disgusted sound. "Malhata was a good man and treated his people well. He even recognized the differences in his people. Some aspired for great things in life, others wished only to lead a simple and comfortable life, while many had desires that sat in between. He devoted his life to ensuring even the lowest level of Zalrabian society lived with dignity and kindness.

"Jegried, though." Kima's eyes narrowed. "That man had blood as cold as a Dor'haighen winter. Despite how well Zalrabi thrived, and how healthy its coffers grew, he pushed for trade deals that better benefitted Zalrabi."

"And Malhadiev pushed back," Zaiyera said, remembering Barum's account.

"They were in constant disagreement. Every discussion ended in a compromise where neither Malhadiev nor Jegried was completely happy and were often angry."

A crisp breeze swept across Zaiyera's face, the first hint of dusk's approach. The wind picked up with a soft moan that flowed through the scattered copses of niyabi trees and scattered hillocks. The fresh damp smell of rain hung thick in the air.

"I never sat in their meetings," Kima continued, "since I wasn't in any position of importance, other than having trade experience and accompanying my brother when he was dispatched. But I had seen the eyes of Sheikh Jegried before. I didn't trust him."

"But your brother did?" Zaiyera asked.

Kima snorted. "Of course not. But he hadn't thought Jegried would resort to murder. He wouldn't listen to me when I told him of the possibility. He knew of Jegried's avarice, but he hadn't thought Malhata's son would step out of the realm of morality. He was wrong." Kima indicated himself and Zaiyera. "And here we are."

"Here we are," Zaiyera agreed.

Barum twisted around in the saddle to look behind them. "Storm's rollin' in!"

Zaiyera looked back to see a carpet of dark clouds rolling in from the northwest.

"I thought we were done with hellish Dor'haighen's snowstorms," Kima complained.

"We are," Zaiyera said. "That's rain. Do you not smell it?"

"I spent many a day in the north sick," Kima replied. "I hardly smell anything anymore."

"Double-time!" Barum shouted back to the others. "We're close enough to the border that we might find a clump of stoicgreens!"

They urged the camels into a fast canter that the animals could sustain for miles. For a while they stayed ahead of the storm, but the camels couldn't maintain their pace forever, and no patches of stoicgreens appeared.

The rain caught up to them an hour later. They stopped to rest at a patch of niyabis. The tall thick trees with their tiny green leaves provided no shelter from the howling wind and sideways rain.

The camels sat huddled together with their backs against the downpour, while their riders sat against the base of the trees. The niyabis' thick trunks provided some relief from the wind and rain, and they could move about the trunk as the wind—and subsequently the rain— changed directions.

It was a small comfort, however. In short order everyone was soaked and miserable. Zaiyera sat with her knees up against her chest, huddled against the base of her tree and wrapped in her coat.

Zhuyun sat against the tree nearest her. She and the Yuntaiman exchanged a look and she stood. Zhuyun stood as well and picked up his staff.

Zaiyera watched him settle into his stance, with his staff tucked vertically under his right arm, feet slightly wider than shoulder-length apart. He stood so still against the pounding rain he might have been made of stone.

Zhuyun spun the staff and slammed the butt into the ground. Fist in palm, he bowed as if to the storm itself, then kicked the staff into a spin. He turned as he spun the staff over his head and stropped in a forward-leaning stance, front leg bent as he struck out in a horizontal arc.

He leapt back from that stance so quickly it looked like a trick of the eye. Zhuyun's staff became barely a blur in his hands. He hopped over an imaginary foot sweep, while at the same time whipping his staff in a diagonal downward counter. He snapped the staff back in the other direction. If there had been a true enemy there, they would have been struck in the back of the head and in the face before the Yuntaiman landed.

"Damned crazy man!" Barum yelled over the storm. At the tree next to him, Jaide laughed, though the Viriksani didn't look half as amused as she sounded.

Zaiyera watched the dizzying display until she caught Zhuyun's eye. A brief glance and nothing more. *Moon and stars, but I'm crazy, too.* In spite of her own doubts of her sanity, Zaiyera felt a rush of adrenaline as she snatched up Shatr and drew it from its sheath.

She sprinted across the distance between them and launched herself at the Yuntaiman without preamble.

Zhuyun's spinning staff turned her blade aside as though he'd known what she would do. Zaiyera went with the momentum and whipped her foot toward the back of his knees. Zhuyun accepted the counter, but his stance was solid, and Zaiyera found herself falling instead.

She fell forward, away from him, and rolled back to her feet. On instinct she leapt away and turned midair. Up Shatr came to block the incoming staff. Zaiyera landed and the staff came in at a horizontal arc for her midsection.

Zaiyera swept her scimitar into the block once, twice, thrice, a fourth time. A fifth. Zhuyun slapped his staff against her block repeatedly, forcing her to give ground, pounding her defense until her hands grew numb.

That hellish staff came for her again and again with such speed and ferocious power that it was all she could do just to stop it. Was Zhuyun caught in the moment, intoxicated by the rush of unleashing such power in the invigorating storm?

No. He was determined to bring her to the answer she sought. An answer she wouldn't find by simply sitting and thinking about it day after day.

Zaiyera's thin black braids whipped about her head in the screaming storm. Rain blasted them like an endless shower of arrows. The speeding droplets bounced off the combatants, soaking their clothes through.

The infinite power of nature itself humbled her as a mountain would an ant, yet it galvanized her into action. A flicker of light lit the distant sky, and several moments later, a soft rumble bellowed through the roaring torrent.

Zaiyera opened herself to the storm, to a power so great it could snap her from existence with but a flicker of effort.

Her limbs moved with an ease she hadn't felt since the first day she'd crossed into the cold north. Her actions grew swifter, her body moving far too fast for her mind to keep up.

Zaiyera ducked the swinging staff and swept Shatr toward Zhuyun's midsection. He spun the staff back in the other direction impossibly fast and blocked the counter. Zaiyera spun in the opposite direction. She brought the scimitar around for her opponent's head.

Zhuyun met the attack with a sudden last minute block that would have sent her scimitar flying from her hands. But she figured he would block that way. Whether a genuine block or this crafty one, their weapons would meet. Zaiyera stopped the blade short as Zhuyun pulled back on his flexible staff.

The shaft of the staff bent, the tip arching toward Zaiyera's sword. She stopped, leaned away, then ducked and swayed under it. When she straightened, Zaiyera whipped Shatr under and down toward Zhuyun's right leg. First blood would be hers.

Zhuyun's leg wasn't there. Twisted toward his left, the Yuntaiman would have appeared vulnerable. He was anything but. Zhuyun swept his right foot into an upward kick, using the momentum to angle his body down and horizontal while standing on his left foot. At the same time, he whipped his staff down.

Zaiyera saw it as it was happening; saw the incredible improvisation the Yuntaiman had pulled out of his endless bag of tricks. She hopped away and felt the staff hit her back, but it was a soft blow, as she was already falling.

As soon as her stomach touched the ground, Zaiyera pushed herself back up, tucked her feet and planted them on the ground.

Zhuyun was straightening again. He blindly whipped his staff around in the other direction, sweeping it in an upward arc.

Zaiyera jumped straight up as the butt of the staff came around and under to connect with her ribs. She tucked her feet up as the staff passed under her, then kicked out to the side.

When her foot connected with the back of Zhuyun's shoulder, she stifled the elation that threatened to spring into her heart and distract her. Zhuyun accepted the blow and launched himself into a forward roll.

Zaiyera touched down and pursued. As soon as Zhuyun's feet touched the ground, he sprang toward her, turned in midair, and thrust his staff out.

Zaiyera skidded to a stop and whipped Shatr around in a downward chop.

Airborne with his staff still extended, the muscles in Zhuyun's arm clenched as he popped the staff to the side and knocked the scimitar away. Zaiyera allowed the force of the parry to knock the scimitar wide. She held it with her right hand and swept her left around the side of the staff.

Zaiyera clamped her hand around the staff with all her strength and turned at the waist. She tucked the staff under her arm and used the strength in her hips to twist and wrench it from Zhuyun's grasp.

She continued the motion and swung the other end toward his head. Zhuyun ducked the staff and slapped the butt of his palm under Zaiyera's elbow.

The impact hurt, and forced Zaiyera's elbow into an awkward angle, sending the staff flying from her grasp.

Zhuyun snatched his weapon out of the air and spun it around. The staff stopped an inch from the side of her face.

Zaiyera froze, chest heaving from the exertion, and fully aware that the side of her skull would have been broken. A tiny smile crept onto her face that turned into a girlish giggle.

Frozen in place as well, Zhuyun looked down at his left side, where the tip of Zaiyera's blue-steel scimitar hovered a finger's width from his ribcage. She'd reversed her grip at the last instant and drove it backward while he'd been in the midst of his counter.

Zhuyun's proud laugh challenged the roar of the rain and the distant rumbling clouds. The combatants straightened and faced each other. Zhuyun clenched his fist in his palm and bowed. Zaiyera bowed in turn.

When Zhuyun straightened, there was such pride and joy in his dark brown eyes, it made Zaiyera's heart leap.

A crinkled downward smile lit Zhuyun's face. "Now, you see."

37

"I understand, now," Jaide said.

Zaiyera looked at the Viriksani woman. She still wondered how Jaide was able to change the timbre of her voice to be just deep enough to sound masculine.

"I understand the mistake we've made," Jaide continued.

Malker frowned at her. "We're in a straight line for Rexzen and are only two days away. What mistake?"

"We should have dipped farther south, away from the border," Jaide replied. "It is clear that your Dor'haighen hates us, yes?"

"What nonsense are you rambling, Viriksani?" Barum asked.

"Three straight days of rain before the hell clouds decided they've punished us enough and move on." Jaide swept her hand toward the sky. Cold rain for three days, after slogging through a world of snow. How does your frozen land not hate you?"

That brought on a round of laughter.

"Just because your blood is too thin for the cold, doesn't mean our beloved north hates us, southerner," Malker said.

"Nonsense," Jaide countered. "Our Samhar loves us like a mother does her child."

"The warm love of a volcano spewing magma on everything below it," Barum replied dryly. Another round of laughter.

"It is true," Jaide said. "Samhar is a kiln that bakes the skin into a nice leathery armor. And the wrinkles. The wrinkles on our faces are maps of the cracked and barren patches that have not seen rain in a season. This is how we navigate the land, yes?"

"There isn't a wrinkle on your girly face, Jaide," Barum said. "Are all the men from Viriksan as gracefully designed as you?"

Everyone laughed, even Jaide. The comment didn't seem to shake her at all. She must have heard it before.

"Variety is life, Denberesterner," Jaide said. "If all men were walking walls of burly muscle and filthy beards, women would grow bored, yes?"

"Says the man who can't grow a beard," Barum countered.

The sparring of those two and the resulting laughter would have lifted Zaiyera's spirits, if she hadn't already been in a good mood since two nights ago.

Zaiyera replayed her match with Zhuyun that rainy night. She'd fought him to a draw. A draw! And it hadn't been because she'd gotten faster or because he'd made a mistake. She'd begun to feel what he was doing, and by watching him, had started to predict what he was going to do. It didn't always work, as Zhuyun was formidable and simply too quick for that, but for the span of several heartbeats, she'd matched him because she'd managed to see his intent.

Even though it hurt to do so, Zaiyera forced herself to think back to the many beatings Aried Dom had dealt her as a child. He'd been older, bigger, and stronger. And also faster. Her rage at his taunts toward her scimitar had given Zaiyera the unthinking focus to finally beat him.

Now an adult, she endured the knife twisting in her heart. She suffered the needles in her stomach as she forced herself to recall the details of that final match years ago, clear of the haze of her childhood anger.

Aried had led with a backstep followed by a quick forward thrust.

The boy had been good with feints, moving one way, then snapping in another direction, altering an attack, changing an attack into a parry.

Zaiyera had read his every move before he made it and had countered it the instant—or in some cases, before—he could fully execute a maneuver.

She fled those memories in favor of more recent ones. She thought back to their first encounter with Malhadiev. He could hardly be called a streamdancer, for he no longer danced the stream when he touched it. A simple gesture from the tainted man was enough to bring a torrent of the flow to his command.

Shatr had been equal to the task of battling that much power, but Zaiyera could only be in one place at a time; could only withstand so much force against her. Similarly, she could only move so fast against Zhuyun. She was only so dexterous, so strong, while the Yuntaiman was physically stronger, faster, and more agile. Just as Aried had been.

Malker Argen pulled his camel up beside her. "I would say that you've the look of someone with things on her mind, but that's always the case with you."

"That isn't a lie," Zaiyera said.

"You're thinking about our impending confrontation with the shadowlancer."

"His name is Malhadiev," Zaiyera replied. "Yes. How could I not?"

Malker's blue-eyed gaze leveled on her. "You accord him more dignity than he has to the people he's murdered."

Zaiyera kept her voice low. Kima was far enough back not to hear over Barum and Jaide's banter, but still. "He is a monster, but he wasn't always one, from all I've learned of the man. It seems to me that seeing people as little more than implements toward a desired end has created the monster we hunt."

"No," Malker said. "He turned away from what is good and what is right. He chose to syphon lancers, avoid the lifeprice, and murder innocent people. He is a monster because he chose to become one."

Zaiyera looked into Malker's eyes, willing him to understand what she was trying to say. "I do not agree or sympathize with what Malhadiev has become, and what he does. But I understand what led to his fall and dehumanizing him only opens us to the possibility of someone else replacing him one day."

Malker stared at her through it all, then looked behind him at Kima. The man had gone back into himself, staring at the ground in front of his camel. What thoughts must occupy his mind, traveling with a band of warriors intent on killing his brother?

"How much hope do you have that he'll be able to reach the shadowlancer … Malhadiev?" Malker asked. "Do you truly see even the most remote possibility of a peaceful outcome because his brother is alive?"

Zaiyera looked out at the distant mountains to the north, carpeted with stoicgreens powdered with snow. Those mountains stopped at the border. To the south lay nothing but a thin layer of sand covering the hard earth, clusters of large stones and the occasional outcropping, and scattered patches of niyabi trees. The majestic sand dunes lay farther south. Her heart longed to see them again, smell the dusty odor of the endless carpet of sand and hills, inhale the damp fresh air after a good rain.

"Anything is possible," Zaiyera finally replied. "I wish I knew what was going to happen, but no one can. I do know that leaving Kima in that cell to use as a bargaining chip against his brother was wrong." 'Cowardly' was the word she was thinking, but kept that to herself.

Malker considered that. "What I think is that we're affording the two of them one last reunion before at least one of them dies."

He was probably right. Even if Kima somehow managed to reach his brother—assuming he didn't betray them all and join Malhadiev—what could she expect to happen? Enduring the hunger on a daily basis as Zaiyera had done all these years was a constant challenge.

Malhadiev was fully in the thrall of the power he'd stolen. The man was at least as powerful as a full army of streamdancers. He must feel like a god. Even if things did come to a peaceful conclusion, Malhadiev couldn't be allowed to live. Not with that much power, and likely the insanity that went with it.

When she looked back at Malker again, she noticed that his hair was almost completely gray, now. The creases at the corners of his eyes were a little deeper than they had been before setting out from Dor'haighen.

"You must be careful, Malker Argen," Zaiyera said as she looked him over. "You have a good heart to do what you must, but the lifeprice draws heavily from you."

Malker's lips pressed together in a faint smile. Combined with his aged appearance, the expression gave him a wizened look that belied his true age. "Sometimes there is no other way. As you said, I do what I must."

"There is always a way," Zaiyera said. "Not everyone dances the stream."

Barum's voice drew their attention to the head of the group. "Soup up ahead!"

At the sound of Malker's sigh, Zaiyera turned a questioning look on him. "Soup?"

"A term south Dor'haigheners use," the junior shydon replied. "They get more fog down here."

Zaiyera looked past the lead riders to the wall of fog waiting for them. It stretched as far as she could see in either direction.

Barum and Jaide came to a halt and waited for the others to reach them.

"We need to talk about this," Barum said, once they were gathered.

"Is it a fair guess that entering that fog will come with some form of danger?" Dyren Faust asked.

"More like a certainty." It wasn't Barum, but Jaide who answered the question. "The border region between central and east is home to an animal called tugyre. They tend to hunt in packs, are fast and strong, and live primarily here and in the hilly regions farther north of the border."

"And you're just telling us about them now?" Malker asked.

"That was before we came to that," Jaide said, gesturing at the waiting fog. "This is the start of the land I'm familiar with. This fog is not always here, and tugyre do not typically hunt out in the open."

"We can try going around it," Malker suggested.

Jaide shook her head as she pointed north. "We cannot see the end of this fog, but up there is a range of mountains tall enough to touch the clouds." She pointed south. "And that way, well, you can see. This is a lowland area. The fog can go for many miles south, and it could sit here for days, maybe weeks, yes?"

"How far do you think we are from Rexzen?" Dyren asked.

Barum and Jaide looked at each other, and Jaide answered, "If my memory serves me, we could reach Rexzen by morning or midday tomorrow at the latest."

Everyone chewed on the information in silence.

"Have you encountered these animals before?" Dyren asked Jaide. "Can you tell us anything about them that will help, if they attack us?"

"Not personally," Jaide answered, "but I've heard stories, yes? They're large and fast pack hunters. If we stay together we stand a good chance of survival. Get separated and you're done."

Dyren sighed. "We move forward."

"I recommend we dismount once we reach the fog," Zaiyera said once they were moving again. "If those things come on us, your camels will be spooked and want to bolt."

"Then better to control them astride," Malker replied.

"You're not on horseback," Zaiyera said. "You'll find yourself dismounted from a terrified camel quickly. Best if your feet are on the ground and you hold onto the reins if you can."

"I suppose you'll not have that problem." Dyren nodded at Sadiq, walking along with no reins and only Zaiyera's legs and body cues to guide him.

"He is my friend," Zaiyera said. "He will stand by my side or flee as he chooses. I'll not force him to remain."

As she'd recommended, the riders dismounted and led the camels by the reins into the fog.

At first, everyone walked as close together as they could, each keeping an eye on the ten feet of visibility around them before Zaiyera had an idea.

"Wait. Stop." She looked to Kima, then the others. "Everyone hand your reins to Kima." She turned to the wary Zalrabian. "Keep the camels together. We will surround you." Kima looked past her at the ominous fog and gave a nod. He reached out for everyone to hand him their reins.

"Good idea," Dyren said. "One person at the front and rear, one person at each side between the middle and front and rear. If the lead or rear guard needs help, you'll be able to aid them."

As much as Zaiyera wished they could have ridden full out through this thick haze and be clear of it, it wasn't possible. Visibility was too poor, and with the wind blowing in their ears from the speed, they wouldn't hear a quiet predator until it was right on them.

Time disappeared along with everything else in the world, as the fog hid the sun. The occasional ghostly figure of a niyabi tree appeared out of the haze like a specter whenever they drew within a dozen feet of one. The first couple times it happened, Zaiyera nearly jumped out of her skin. Not being able to see anything until it was that close had her on edge. When she looked at Barum, she saw the same uneasiness reflected in his face.

On her other side, Zhuyun walked at ease, but his step was light, and his eyes shifted to and fro.

"Does this haze swallow sound as well?" Malker whispered from the other side of the camels. "I hear nothing but my own breathing and our footsteps."

"Nothing with its sanity intact would be in this," Barum whispered back.

"There are plenty of animals that roam foggy lowlands," Jaide said.

"He's right," Zaiyera whispered. She looked around and saw nothing, but the hairs on the back of her head stood on end. Shati was in her hand before she'd even thought to draw it. "Something's out there, and it's keeping just out of sight."

As soon as those last words left her lips, Zaiyera smelled them. The gamey odor of a large furry and sweating animal.

She heard collective swearing and drawing of swords. To her right, Zhuyun had his staff gripped with both hands. He crept along on the balls of his feet; a cat ready to spring.

Something shot in and out of Zaiyera's peripheral vision so quickly she wasn't sure if it was real or her imagination. It happened a second time, a large shape crossing her periphery without a sound.

"Our hunters reveal themselves," Zhuyun said.

"Hold onto the camels," Zaiyera said over her shoulder to Kima. "We'll protect you." She hoped Sadiq wouldn't panic and bolt. Out there alone in that fog, he would be pulled down and killed.

At the front, Dyren swore loudly and there was the sound of scuffling, followed by an inhuman howl. "*Jakta skree!* They're big and *fast*. Be ready!"

Rrrrruuuuuuuh gukukuh kuh kuh kuh kuh.

"Moon and stars," Zaiyera breathed.

"*Jakta skree,*" Malker cursed from the rear of the group. "I just saw one. It walked right past me on two legs, in and out of the haze! It was taller than I am!"

Rrrrruuuuuuuh gukukuh kuh kuh kuh kuh.

The call came from the right, then the left, then from the front, the back. Zaiyera felt a chill go down her spine. "We're surrounded."

"We should have ridden fast through this," Kima growled.

It was his fear talking. Zaiyera prayed to Shakimah the man didn't mount a camel and take off.

Zaiyera caught sight of a large shape walking upright. Its back was curved, and its legs were long and slim, with the knee joints backwards, typical of a four-legged animal. Its forelimbs hung long, with large hand-like claws flexing at its sides. The fur on its back stood on end like spikes. It turned its wolfish head in her direction just as it disappeared back into the fog.

By now the camels were shuffling and groaning nervously. Zaiyera didn't blame them. What she just saw sent shivers down her spine.

"Keep moving!" Dyren called from the front. "There's no telling how many there are."

Another of those awful calls split the ominous silence, to be answered further ahead.

"Sounds like they're organizing," Zhuyun said. "They study us from a far and pick their targets."

"That means they see better in this soup than we do," Barum said.

"They are animals, remember," Zhuyun said. "On two legs or four, they're attacks are limited. Bites, slashing claws. Maybe tackle you. These are the weapons of our foe."

A four-legged creature stalked through the fog toward Zaiyera, its muscly shoulder blades protruding with each step. It stopped when Zaiyera lifted Shatr. The tugyre looked from the scimitar to her face with unnerving comprehension.

Zaiyera craned her head back as she watched it rise to its full height on its hind legs. It had a muzzle like a wolf's, only wider. It stared down at her with round yellow eyes. Those eyes narrowed, and its lips drew back into a toothy snarl.

She didn't dare take her eyes off the thing, but from the corner of her eye, Zaiyera saw another one standing in front of Zhuyun. She suspected the others were having the same face off.

"What in the name of Jokolta are these things about, then?" Malker said from the back. "They're just …"

A tugyre leapt completely over the head of the one facing Zaiyera. The world disappeared behind gaping jaws.

38

Zaiyera dove to her left, barely avoiding those snapping teeth. She rolled back to her feet, spun, and thrust Shatr straight in front of her. As soon as the blade bit into the mouth and through the skull of the tugyre, she retracted.

It was a quick in-out stab that saved her arm. Whether it was a jerk from the nervous system or one last bite before death, the tugyre snapped its jaw shut just as the tip of her sword came free.

Judging from the sounds around her, something similar must have happened to everyone else. Which, considering the initial standoff, meant they might be fighting at least twelve of the things. Her eyes flicked down at the dead monster in front of her. Well, eleven.

The tugyre that had been standing in front of her bound over its dead comrade toward Zaiyera. She spun to the side and chopped down. The beast snapped at the space she'd just occupied but shrugged back before the scimitar found its neck.

With but a flick of long, muscled legs, the tugyre hopped diagonally at her. The much heavier body hit Zaiyera with enough force to lift her off the ground and send her tumbling into the fog.

* * *

Zhuyun kept his movements snappy and efficient. These weren't cave bears or frost worvas. Those long muscular yet slender limbs were built for speed, jumping, and dexterity. Swinging attacks would bring more power with momentum but required too much distance to travel. No matter how fast he was, he couldn't match the kind of fast twitch bursts of action these horrors were capable of.

He'd knocked the tugyre that leapt over the head of the first one down with a quick pop to the throat. He smacked it on the back of the head when it crashed to the ground. Now, the beast that had been facing him lowered itself to all-fours again and stalked forward.

Zhuyun saw Zaiyera kill one of the things, and nearly behead another. He slowly gave ground as the snarling beast moved toward him. It would lunge and bite or lunge with a swipe of those long-fingered foreclaws. Or it might simply try to tackle him.

He heard a high-pitched grunt. Zhuyun's gaze flicked past the tugyre just in time to see Zaiyera's feet sweep up into the air as she flew backwards and disappeared into the fog.

Zhuyun's blood went cold at the sight. He tried to work around toward her, but the monster hopped sideways and blocked his way. He tried circling the other direction and again, it hopped in front of him.

Smart, he thought. "Stay in pairs!" he shouted. "They try to separate us!"

The only response came in the form of grunts, curses, and ripping flesh. Zhuyun hoped it was the tugyres on the receiving end of the latter. The tugyre in front of him snarled. It lunged forward but stopped and crouched while leaning sideways. Zhuyun's stabbing staff shot safely over its left shoulder.

It lunged again and snapped up at his arms. Zhuyun had been holding the end of the staff when he'd leaned forward into the thrust. When those jaws came for his extended arms, he lifted onto his left foot and twisted his body upward and to the right. He arched his back —which was almost parallel to the ground—so that his stomach was facing diagonally upwards. At the same time, he spun the staff around from right to left.

The tugyre missed Zhuyun's rib section by mere inches while his staff arced around and smacked its right hip. Despite his awkward angle, Zhuyun swung with enough force to bend the shaft of his staff. He heard the telltale 'snick' of snapping bone, and the tugyre let out a high-pitched yelp that didn't match its large and menacing appearance.

As its hindquarters dipped from the injury, Zhuyun planted his right foot back to the ground. He turned to the right while sweeping the staff around. At the last moment, he pulled back. The shaft bowed just before the end struck a whip-like blow to its side.

This time there was a loud 'crack'. The tugyre dropped as Zhuyun spun in the opposite direction, his staff speeding around for the killing blow. He nearly lost his grip when the weapon suddenly came to a halt.

Long clawed fingers wrapped around the shaft of his staff and held it tight. The newly arrived tugyre opened its maw in a growling snarl and yanked Zhuyun in.

* * *

*K*eep moving. One thought. The only thought Jaide had time for before hell erupted in claws and teeth. She ignored the burn in her shoulder from where a tugyre had almost gotten a hold of her. That would have been … bad.

A tugyre lunged in to bite at her, and Jaide swung her shamshir into the side of its mouth before sidestepping. It wasn't the most graceful counter, but she'd almost died learning that a sidestep before countering wouldn't work. The tugyre were smart and far too fast.

Jaide kept turning. Her shamshir sliced across the face of the tugyre and spattered her with blood. When its head dipped away, she completed her turn and chopped down. The blade buried into furry hide, through hardened flesh and between ribs. Jaide gritted her teeth and pushed down.

The tugyre yelped and howled as the blade sliced through it. *Spare me*, Jaide thought as she slid the blade free and backed away, just as the juggernaut that was Barum tackled her to the side.

They hit the ground in a tumble. Jaide glanced over Barum's shoulder and saw a monster flying past the spot where she'd been standing. It collided with the dying monster she'd just injured. It rose with a shake of its head and turned toward Barum's exposed back.

"Oomph." Jaide shoved at the big northerner. "Your back, man. Your back!"

Barum rolled off Jaide and swung his broadsword. The tugyre flinched away, but not fast enough. The sword split its mouth while Jaide rolled forward and stabbed it in the throat.

Jaide pulled her shamshir free, stabbed the struggling monster to her left that should have been dead by now, then pulled free again. She swept the blade out, catching the persistent tugyre across the face as it tried to bite at her.

"You all right?" she said to Barum. The big man bled from several slashes across his back and side.

"Been better, been worse," came the answer.

At the front, Malker dispatched one monster just as another came up from the side. It rose to its full height and swiped at him. The junior shydon met the attack with his blade and severed the limb. The tugyre let out a pained cough and staggered in the direction of the injury. Malker centered his stance and swept his sword back across its midsection.

The disemboweled monster shuddered, then collapsed to the ground as its lifeblood and organs spilled out onto the ground.

More large forms glided from out of the fog, one, two, three. Each form landed on the back of a camel and simultaneously bit down and broke its neck.

The horrible groan the dying animals made broke Jaide's heart, but she had not time to mourn the poor camels' fates. Three more tugyre's approached.

Two went for Barum while the third came for Jaide. She leaned away from a swiping claw and countered with a series of slices. She cut down and right, ducked another scratching claw, and cut right again. Jaide cut left and scored a hit across its face, but it cost her.

The tugyre caught her leg and swept it out from under her. She landed flat on her back and the wind blasted from her lungs. Jaide gritted her teeth and stabbed out across her body.

Her instincts saved her life. The tugyre had snapped at her head, and so her shamshir struck into its mouth and out the side of its jaw. The beast threw its head from side to side so violently it tore the weapon from her grasp.

The tugyre continued to swing its head about, with Jaide's shamshir still lodged in the side of its jaw. It bucked and pawed at the sharp end of the blade protruding from its jaw, which cut its paw. It finally reached up and grabbed hold of the hilt and wrenched it free.

Jaide had already brandished her dagger by then. She forced herself not to react as she watched the monster throw her weapon aside. She leapt and wrapped an arm around its neck just as it tossed the weapon sword aside. With her other hand, Jaide punched the dagger into its throat repeatedly.

The tugyre stumbled under the onslaught but managed to grab her arm. Jaide screamed. When the beast grabbed her, its claws cut her side as those long fingers wrapped around her arm. The monster hurled her away. She hit the ground and tumbled into the corpse of one of the camels. The large body jerked once, then slid away, one of the monsters dragging it into the fog.

Jaide felt a brief pang of sorrow for the fallen animal but reminded herself she would share its fate if she didn't get back to her feet and find her shamshir. It lay on the ground, barely in sight at the edge of visibility in the fog.

The injured tugyre struggled toward her, teeth bared, eyes narrowed with murderous intent. Jaide ignored the pain and warmth spreading in her side and settled into a defensive stance. The dagger in her hand felt like a toothpick.

From somewhere out in the fog, she heard a scream. It sounded agonized. The tugyre made is slow way forward. Jaide held the dagger in a white-knuckled grip. Another scream penetrated the blanket of fog. No, it wasn't agony. It was rage.

* * *

Zaiyera heard the terrified and dying screams of the camels. She heard the crunch of bones and breaking necks, the gurgles and sliding bodies. Her left shoulder ached, and she felt the warmth of her blood trickling down her right leg and soaking through her pants.

One of the three tugyres that surrounded her, the one to her left, moved with a noticeable limp. Zaiyera had dealt that one a good cut across the foreleg. The other two had minor cuts but nothing that hampered their mobility. Once they'd gotten her alone, the three animals tried to overwhelm her. She'd barely managed to stay ahead of those snapping teeth and slashing claws, but her situation was still desperate.

She kept the three monsters in her vision but didn't focus on any of them. She let herself see them from her periphery, catching any subtle movement that might indicate an attack or opening.

The two on either side of her moved sideways towards her back. Zaiyera paced them, though she had to figure something out. They were drawing her further away from her companions.

When she heard another camel cry out before it died, a surge of fear and adrenaline shot through Zaiyera's body. *SADIQ!*

The thought that that scream could have come from her dear friend, that Sadiq might have fallen to be devoured by these things, lit something primal inside of her.

Zaiyera launched herself screaming at the tugyre in front of her. The two at her back sprang forward. She skidded to a stop and dropped onto her back as the front tugyre leapt at her.

As the dark striped monster passed overhead, Zaiyera cut its underbelly. Blood rained down on her and she rolled to the side. The tugyre on the right less than a dozen paces away. Zaiyera rose to her knee and swept Shatr sideways.

The intelligent beast hopped away at the last second while the third tugyre came snarling in from the side. It slashed out at Zaiyera's face, but she rolled backwards. She felt the whoosh of air as those horrible claws missed by inches.

Images of Sadiq, dead and being devoured flashed through her mind. Her loyal companion, killed and eaten by these *things*. Zaiyera didn't care if it was by natural law that these predators hunted their prey, she was the reason Sadiq was here and in danger. She would not die here. And if she failed to defend her friend, they would pay a dear price for whatever meal they claimed.

The tugyre she'd cut lay thrashing on the ground, its entrails spilling on the bloody ground beneath it. The two remaining beasts flanked and crept in.

Zaiyera darted to the left. She cut downward at the beast, forcing it to move back. As it did, she completed the chop by stepping around and bringing the scimitar in an upward arc.

As she'd predicted, the large cat-like monster behind her was nearly on her back. It was in motion, lunging in to tackle. Committed to the action, the tugyre couldn't reverse course. It glided right into Zaiyera's upward cutting scimitar. It sliced up its face from bottom to top.

As though she were a turning wheel, Zaiyera followed the motion through again. The tugyre she'd forced to recoil charged back in, its head turned sideways to clamp those large teeth into her torso.

As though in the steps of a dance, Zaiyera continued her turn as she cut the tugyre up its face. The monster's head arched back from the painful injury as Zaiyera completed her pivot and chopped down again.

Shatr sliced into the top of the tugyre's muzzle.

In the span of three moves and three heartbeats, two more tugyres lay dying at her feet.

Zaiyera sprinted in the direction of the fighting. She kept her body low, Shatr in her right hand at her side. To the right, Malker felled a tugyre and was now rushing to the aid of Barum, who faced two. To the back of the group, Dyren Faust beheaded one beast, reversed, rolled sideways to avoid another monster falling on him from the air, and sent a dagger spinning into its neck. It hit the ground in a hard tumble. The senior shydon stabbed it through the ribs before it could rise.

Her footsteps quick and quiet, Zaiyera closed in on the injured tugyre towering over Jaide. She faced off with the monster holding nothing more than a dagger.

She spotted Jaide's shamshir and altered course to grab it. She scooped it up in passing, reversed her grip on Shatr, and slammed it in its sheath an instant before she leapt the last few feet onto the standing tugyre's back. With Jaide's shamshir in a reverse double grip, she drove the blade between the monster's shoulder blades.

Her momentum sent the beast falling forward. With the blade protruding through its chest, the tugyre fell face first on the ground. The impact pushed Jaide's shamshir partially out, and Zaiyera drew it free. She tossed it to Jaide as she sprinted off toward another tugyre closing in on one of two surviving camels, one of them bound by no reins. Sadiq!

Kima's eyes were wide with fear. He wildly swiped the dagger left to right in front of him, but the tugyre paid little heed. It rose to its full height and roared at him.

Rrrrrruuuuuuuh gukukuh kuh kuh kuh kuh!

Kima hollered and let go of the reins. As soon as he let go, the camel bolted. The tugyre ignored him and started toward Sadiq. It held its arms out at its side, fingers curled as it leaned forward and roared again.

Sadiq let out a terrified groan and shuffled away. The monster closed the distance and Sadiq turned sideways and kicked his hind leg at it. The kick didn't have near enough range to hit the stalking tugyre, but it provided that instant of distraction Zaiyera needed to reach it.

She saw the monster's ears swivel back in her direction when she was less than five feet away. Zaiyera dropped to the ground and slid on her side. An instant after she threw herself to the ground, the tugyre rounded on her and snapped. She heard biting snarl overhead as she slid under the tugyre's body.

Zaiyera swung her scimitar with her right hand. The blue-steel blade sheered through the monster's right leg. It gave an agonized roar and fell sideways. Zaiyera regained her feet while the injured tugyre flailed, blood splattering from its severed stump.

She ran Shatr through its upper rib cage and into its heart.

* * *

Little more than reflex kept Zhuyun alive. After that tugyre had appeared out of the fog and grabbed his swinging staff, only his quick reflexes and dexterity had saved him from being gutted.

He'd managed to tuck the shaft under his arm as he spun, and twist with his torso. The maneuver had not only saved his life and wrenched the weapon free, but smacked the fallen tugyre he'd previously felled.

He held his staff in a two-handed grip, right hand at the end, left hand farther out. The tugyre he'd dropped with that smack to the side of its skull rose and shook its head. It narrowed its eyes at him, its lips peeling back to reveal fangs in front of a row of yellow teeth.

Zhuyun reversed his momentum and swept the staff down and up between the legs of the monster that had grabbed his staff. He stepped around as he did this, tangling its legs and forcing it between himself and the rising—and angry—tugyre at his right.

He rotated the staff and yanked down, then up. The tugyre stumbled, and as soon as the other one was within reach, Zhuyun hopped forward with a jab of his staff. The tugyre barked and swatted at it, but Zhuyun had already retracted. With a twist of his right hand at the end of the staff, he thrust forward again.

The other end of the staff came forward in a circular thrust. The motion confused the snarling monster, and so it had trouble tracking the incoming object. Zhuyun scored a hit to the side of its eye, and when it flinched, he scored another hit under the jaw.

Zhuyun slid the staff in his hands to ram the butt of the other end into the mouth of the tugyre that was lunging in at his back, jaws agape. The staff punched into its throat, causing it to gag. The

Yuntaiman pulled the staff free and sent it stabbing into the face of the tugyre in front.

When it flinched back, he stepped in and snapped the staff up and down. It whacked the beast in top of the head again, then flicked it up. The shaft bowed like a whip, and the butt of the weapon struck the tugyre under the jaw. If it had been a human, or a smaller animal, the blow would have broken its jaw. But the tugyre was larger and much tougher.

The hit did cause it to stumble away long enough for Zhuyun to sweep his staff back around to smack the beast behind him in the fore-leg, reverse and smack the beast in front of him in the side, then reverse again, and whip the monster behind him in its lower foreleg.

With muscles honed from a lifetime of training, Zhuyun sprang backwards as the tugyre glided toward him. Still midair, Zhuyun tensed his core and whipped the staff toward the monster's shoulder.

As before, he pulled back at the last second, creating the devas-tating whip effect. The impact tore through the animal's hide and broke bone.

Zhuyun landed and fell into a backwards roll. He planted his feet and rose into a low stance, then jabbed his staff backwards with all his strength.

The tugyre creeping on him from behind took the butt of his staff in the mouth. It coughed and spat blood and teeth, just enough distraction for Zhuyun to spin and smack it in the side of the head. Much as he'd done when sparring with Zaiyera, he whacked the beast in the side of the head repeatedly with all his strength.

The monster couldn't recover. Between trying not to choke on the blood pouring from its ruined mouth, the repeated heavy blows to the side of the head left the tugyre in a stumbling daze.

Zhuyun knew the other monster would be coming. He smacked the tugyre in the head a sixth time, rotated his rear hand and sent the staff into an arc over the monster's head. The staff bowed and struck the beast on the other side of the head, then Zhuyun reversed the motion and whacked it on the injured side once more.

That last attack finished, he backpedaled so that he was facing the space between the two beasts. He swept the staff into an upward arc. When the tugyre now to his right stopped short, Zhuyun feinted left, right left, left again. With his rear hand rotating the staff, it created a dizzying spin on the other end.

Just as before, the tugyre couldn't easily track the movement. Its frustration flared, and the monster roared and charged forward. As Zhuyun had hoped.

Zhuyun skittered backwards and sidestepped. He brought the staff up quickly and smacked it down hard on the tugyre's head. He kept smacking it on the head, kept backpedaling as it charged. He circled around, conscious that he didn't want to move too far from the others and get caught alone in the fog.

The tugyre pursued, but it visibly slowed. It lunged in, then scrambled sideways and swatted at the troublesome staff. Zhuyun kept moving, kept his buzzing staff between him and claws that could shred him with one swipe.

It lowered itself to the ground and crept sideways, much like a hunting cat. It circled to his left, which forced him to position his back to the injured beast he'd battered a moment ago. "Clever," Zhuyun whispered.

He hopped in for a quick jab at its face, then hopped back. The injured tugyre crept around behind him. Now stuck between them, Zhuyun set his staff whirling. He lunged at the beast in front of him, then spun the staff back to swipe at the beast behind him. Neither attack connected, but that wasn't the point.

The monster in front of him backed away barely quick enough to avoid getting hit, while the injured one behind him escaped only because it stumbled.

Zhuyun held his staff in a two-handed grip and waited as the tugyres closed in. Once they were within reach on either side, he launched into action. He drove his staff into the front beast's face, then stabbed backwards at the one to the rear. He dove into a sideways roll and swept the staff at the front monster's legs.

When it hopped back, Zhuyun spun back to his feet and launched himself forward. He swung the staff around and pulled back, creating the whip-like impact. The blow hit the tugyre in the side of the head, near the eye, with concussive force.

It slumped to the ground and didn't rise again, blood trickling out of its nose.

Zhuyun turned away from the dying creature, his focus solely on the other. Behind it, he saw the tugyre with the broken mouth. He'd forgotten about it since it hadn't joined the fight. Even now it looked hesitant, only moving in closer when the tugyre with the broken foreleg stubbornly hobbled closer.

This is not normal for any predator, he thought.

Blood dribbled out of its ruined mouth. It made a gurgling sound, spat blood, and rose onto its hind legs. Zhuyun lifted his gaze as the creature loomed over him.

"Thank you." The Yuntaiman set his staff to whirling. When the tugyre swiped at him, Zhuyun met the sweeping limb with the speeding shaft of his staff. Despite its injuries, the striped monster was still quick and dangerous. It dealt the Yintish warrior a nasty slash on his arm that might have shredded his skin off, had he been slower. But Zhuyun personified speed.

He ignored his burning wound as he beat the monster back, pounding limbs and jabbing its torso. His tactics did little more than frustrate the tugyre, but that was his intention.

When the beast grew angry, it tried to power through his offense and tackle him. Zhuyun made it pay. He struck its arms repeatedly every time it slashed at him, until finally there was the telltale 'crack' of a bone. The tugyre howled and retreated a couple steps, one arm dangling. Zhuyun swept, stabbed, and swept again, his staff in constant motion until finally the stubborn and battered monster crumpled to the ground and moved no longer.

39

They found the camel that had run off only twenty feet away. As soon as the large still form appeared through the fog, Zaiyera redirected around the corpse, keeping it out of sight of Sadiq. He might not have been able to see the poor animal, but he could smell the death and blood. Sadiq shuffled about and gave a plaintive groan.

While Barum and Zhuyun crept toward the dead camel to retrieve whatever gear they could find, Zaiyera rubbed and patted Sadiq's neck, and spoke softly to him. She managed to calm him down enough that they could keep moving.

Twice their progress took them across a trail of blood leading off to one side or another. The non-Samharans sighed with regret, while Zaiyera, Jaide, and Kima murmured prayers to Shakimah that the animals made a speedy transition to Her peace.

With Sadiq now their only surviving camel, his job changed from riding mount to pack animal. Zaiyera stayed close to the camel. She still couldn't believe how fortune blessed Sadiq to have been the sole survivor of all seven camels, but she silently thanked the Goddess again and again.

She ran her hand lightly over the cloth wrapped around her left upper arm, and also her torso. The latter was starting to soak through with blood. Zhuyun had assured her that despite her death having been a hairsbreadth away from those swiping claws, her cuts weren't deep enough to worry.

The Yuntaiman hadn't escaped injury either. Zaiyera had helped him wrap a bleeding wound of two cuts across his right forearm. It must have stung, for despite his stoicism, Zhuyun's right eye had twitched when she rinsed the cuts and bandaged them.

No one had come out of that desperate fight unscathed. Malker and Dyren sported several cuts and bruises. The junior shydon hunter wore a cloth bandage across his face, tied off at the back of his head. He'd been lucky. If Malker had been but an eye-blink slower in leaning away from those slashing claws, he'd have lost an eye, or perhaps his entire face.

Barum's left shoulder sported a bandage where a tugyre had bitten him. The man's responding roar of pain and rage would have given a cave bear pause. The injury was bad, but the tugyre had paid for it with its head.

With no indication of how close they were to the end of the fog, and Rexzen beyond, the bloodied, battered crew rationed out the food and water. Barum had suggested they take meat from the dead camel they'd found. It was a good idea, but no one wanted to stick around in case the tugyre came back for it, which Jaide assured them was a certainty. Zaiyera had been secretly relieved at the collective decision to move on. The thought of consuming one of their former animal companions had made bile rise in her throat.

The dampness and terrible visibility hung heavily on the beleaguered group. Between the snowstorms of the north, the cold torrent of rain days earlier, and this thick, damp fog, it felt like the land they traversed fought them every step.

Patches of vegetation started to appear again as the cracked dry earth grew moist. When Sadiq made no move toward the weeds and shrubs, Zaiyera gathered a handful and offered it to him. The camel ignored the proffered snack and kept walking.

She stuffed that and a few handfuls more into her pack on his back for later. Sadiq likely felt as they did, wanting little more than to be out of this place.

They camped in a circle around Sadiq that night. Zaiyera took first watch, and when Dyren relieved her, she went straight to her friend, who was finally chewing some of the shrub she'd offered him. Once he'd finished with the shrubs, Sadiq settled to the ground, and Zaiyera sat with her back against him. The rise and fall of his side lulled her into slumber.

When Zaiyera opened her eyes again, it was still dark. Malker stood watch, and Zhuyun stared into the fog on the other side of the group, standing with his staff resting over his shoulder.

"In Yuntai," he said when she came up beside him, "it is to Jie Mei that we pray."

He repeated himself when Zaiyera tried and failed to pronounce the unfamiliar words. As foreign as *Dreuga* might sound, Yintish felt even more so.

"Jie Mei," Zhuyun said. "The Sisters. All life on this world has a beginning and end. Fu Mei brings cleansing destruction, that her sister Fu Huo may plant the fresh seeds of resurrection. Life."

Zhuyun continued to look out at as though he could see the world beyond the ten to twenty feet of fog. "I've never seen predators that don't give up after being wounded. Perhaps they were spawned of evil or simply just hunting, but our camels paid the price to Fu Mei, that we didn't have to battle them all to the death, *ixu*? They paid the price, that we can continue."

Zaiyera might not have heard of the Yintish deities, but it was much the same in Samhar. Sun and Moon Dancer, daughters of the Goddess Shakimah. Light and dark, warmth and cold, death and birth. "Our camel companions paid the high price of their lives that we could carry on," she said. The words sent a spike of pain and guilt through her heart and she hated speaking them.

The rest of the camp stirred. The telltale deep voice of Barum groaning as he stretched, penetrated the quiet. Soft conversation filtered through the gloom as the others gathered what gear they had into their backpacks and prepared to set out.

"I may not be familiar with your Goddess and Her daughters," Zhuyun whispered. "But if they're anything like Jie Mei, they smile upon you."

The Yuntaiman's shoulders bounced with soft laughter. "Your doubts of my statement practically waft off you, my friend Zaiyera. Yours is a heart as big as the Great Sea. Whatever your past, I can see no kind and just God or Goddess *not* smiling upon you."

Zhuyun gave her shoulder a squeeze and turned away. "Time to go. Say a prayer of thanks to the souls of the camels, and your Goddess, Zaiyera my friend."

* * *

The sober mood of the previous night draped over the group like an extra layer of the fog. They cast their gazes in every direction for potential threats, but none came. In spite of that, conversation remained muted.

Dawn came with the bonus of finally reaching the end of the fog. When the misty surroundings started to lighten, and visibility lengthened, everyone walked with a little more energy in their step. Even Sadiq's step quickened.

They finally slipped free of the fog like prey escaping grasping claws. Sighs of relief and prayers to respective deities ensued, but no one stopped until they were a few hundred feet away.

"I hope to never cross through that again," Malker said. He came to stand beside Zaiyera, everyone taking a short break to look down at the world of fog that stretched for many miles in the distance. "I can't believe we passed through all of that."

"Yet the real challenge lies ahead," Zaiyera replied.

"*Jakta skree*, but I hope he's at least encountered some of the trials we have," Malker said. They glanced at Kima, standing a dozen paces away. Zhuyun engaged in his customary animated conversation while Kima mostly listened. If the Zalrabian man heard Malker's words, he gave no indication.

Now on foot, travel across the last stretch of land was slow going, with terrain ranging from hilly and rocky to flat and parched.

Vegetation started to appear in abundance, and the once frigid damp air grew warmer with every step.

Kima worked his way around the group until he walked beside Zaiyera. "How do you plan to kill my brother?"

Zaiyera thought on the question but found the answer difficult. How could she answer a question like that?

"This … isn't a question I can answer," she said finally. "This mission is not mine to command."

"Yet you alone are the best chance anyone here has to survive."

Zaiyera forced herself to look into the man's eyes. Pain, anger, and resentment stared back at her. "That is what others say, but no one knows anything for certain."

Kima made an irritated sound. "You are the only person among us with a weapon that can cut through the flow. I saw it with my own eyes against that cave bear. I've heard the shydon hunters talking. They hope you'll be able to cancel my brother's power until they can kill him."

Zaiyera tried to see things from Kima's perspective. This was his brother, after all. But the man's constant prodding and disdain wore on her patience. "Do you have any suggestions?"

The question hung between them as she continued to hold his gaze.

"Do you possess any information, abilities, insight, *anything*, that can lend us an advantage to overcome Malhadiev without killing him? Is there anything we could do, should we even be able to capture him alive, to contain his immense power until he could be rehabilitated?"

"There is no rehabilitation for the tainted," Kima growled. "They can't be cured of the addiction. That's common knowledge."

Maybe not cured, she thought. "If there were a way to capture your brother alive and bring him out of the depths of his addiction, I would try," Zaiyera said. "So, please share with me any knowledge you have that could help us achieve that end."

Kima looked ahead and wiped the moisture from his eyes. "Even if I did know something that could save him, why would you do it?"

Zaiyera pressed her lips together as she considered the man. "You've a talent for asking difficult questions."

"If you weren't walking beside the brother of a *kivuli dayasa*, would that question be so difficult?"

Zaiyera didn't hesitate in her answer. "No."

"Yet you hesitate now."

"I …" Zaiyera sighed. "This is not a mission of revenge, though there are an endless number of people who would be entitled to such an undertaking. "We've endured the hardships that lay behind us because to not do so would mean death for many more people."

She tried to soften her tone as she spoke, but she found it hard, given all that Kima's brother had done. "Malhadiev has destroyed entire cities, Kima Imrian. He's left destruction and death in his wake. Were all the people he's killed co-conspirators in the schemes between Jegried and Eredin? And however greedy or despicable those two might be, or in Sheikh Jegried's case, might have *been*, they didn't kill whole villages and cities of people."

Kima's shoulders seemed to bow under the weight of every word she spoke, but he needed to hear them.

They walked on in silence for a time. Kima ran a hand over his short curly black hair. "He was kind, once. He always thought of others, fought every inch he could to ensure that the less wealthy of Zalrabi were not forgotten. How could he have fallen so far?"

His voice quavered. Zaiyera wondered if he'd asked himself these questions during his time in Nanshaigha. Probably not. It would be much easier to see King Eredin and Sheikh Jegried as the sole malefactors of his predicament, and the catalysts of his brother's descent to darkness.

But since his freedom, he'd had time to think. Zaiyera saw resentment in him for what she and the others planned to do, but Kima couldn't deny the necessity of it.

Having lost heart for conversation—to which Zaiyera was relieved —Kima fell back to the side of the group and wrapped himself in his thoughts once more. Zaiyera noticed that Malker walked little more than a stride or two away. Dyren had the man in eyesight as well. It seemed overcautious, considering he wouldn't be able to overwhelm everyone. And even if he could, how long would he last out here alone?

"Oh, by the warm kisses of Sun Dancer Herself, yes!"

Zaiyera looked up at the sound of Jaide's voice. In her relief, the woman had let a bit of femininity slip into the word "yes".

Zhuyun arched his eyebrow at her, though his expression remained otherwise unreadable. The others missed the moment, however, as they were too relieved at the first signs of civilization arriving on the horizon. Stone towers of white and red shone across the distance as a beacon of relief.

Small patches of farmland came into view on either side of the trail. The cackle of guinea fowl tumbled through the air, mingling with the heavy odor of water buffalo grazing the fields and pulling plows to the urging of the farmers who guided them.

"Now, that is something," Jaide said. "Not many animals are meaner than water buffalo, yes?"

"They must be well trained," Malker said.

Zaiyera chuckled at that. "You'll not find an animal more difficult to even attempt to train than a buffalo, Malker Argen. You must make friends with them first."

"Friends with a buffalo." Malker shook his head.

"Considering our good friend Sadiq accompanies us by choice," Zhuyun said, "while carrying our gear, no less, makes me slower to dismiss this, *ixu*?"

The sweet smell of ngoji roots and the bitter citrus odor of fen berries welcomed them as they passed between the irrigated farms.

Men and women dressed in bland, stout, robe-like garments looked up to regard the newcomers, then returned to their work.

Mounted soldiers patrolled the farmland, along with the occasional duo of finely dressed men and women. They looked to be no more than out for leisurely walks outside the city, but they had the hard look of warriors.

Malker visibly tensed at the sight of the latter. "Relax your body and your judgement," Dyren Faust ordered him in a quiet voice. He kept his eyes forward. "Whatever our beliefs, this is not the place to show our disapproval."

Ogko and Niyabi trees populated the surrounding landscape through the farmland and out past either side of the city ahead as far as they could see.

Zaiyera glanced up at a nearby tree. A man with light brown skin, short hair, and light brown almond-shaped eyes lounged in one of the branches. He glanced down at her with little regard, though Zaiyera noted the arrow-tipped spear resting across his lap. He looked Samharan, yet reminded her of Zhuyun as well.

As if to punctuate that observation, the man looked past her and gave a nod of respect. Zaiyera followed his gaze to see Zhuyun return the gesture.

"Desert family," Zhuyun said at her questioning look. A note of wonder crept into his voice. "Four hundred years ago, the ancestor of Noble Queen Aidai, Noble Queen Mai Hua, sent adventurers across the Great Sea. Two of those ships landed on the eastern shores of Samhar." He jerked his head back toward the sentry they'd passed.

"This must be the place the expedition landed, ah? The adventurers were escorted to meet with the royal family of this place. After a month of North Samharan hospitality, the members of the expedition returned home.

"Noble queen Mai Hua had been pleased with the trade and kindness the people of Samhar had shown her adventurers. She sent two more ships laden with gifts and items for trade. After years of building relations between the two lands, Samhar made a big gesture. One that would make Yuntai as family. They sent what your people call a link family bearing a peace-child."

Zaiyera perked up in recognition. "A link family was sent that far?"

Zhuyun nodded. "Indeed. And Queen Mai Hua returned the gesture. The families of both lands were treated as one of their own, and their children solidified ties between the two lands.

"The result of hundreds of years of intermingling has yielded entire segments of the population in certain parts of Yuntai that we call, 'the brown family'."

"You seem to know a lot about a lot, Yuntaiman," Dyren Faust said.

"A poor world traveler I would be, if I didn't make a study of the world, *ixu*?

That warm bit of history was at odds with the sense of foreboding Zaiyera felt, the closer they drew to the city walls.

The walls were made of light gray stone with red trim painted along the top. Ox carts, horse-drawn wagons and man and woman-powered rickshaws flowed in and out of the front gates and passed back and forth across their line of sight.

The party of seven merged with the flow of two and four-legged bodies. Zaiyera remained close to Sadiq and kept a hand on his neck. As with any other city or village outside Kushtanja, the camel was likely the only animal not leashed or with reins. Sadiq regurgitated and chewed his cud.

They wandered the streets for some time, trying to work their way to a quiet street where they could at least make a plan to find food and lodging. Though the party's bruises and bloody bandages drew the eye of many a passersby, the shydon hunter insignias on Dyren and Malker's jackets quickly turned those eyes away. Some eyes, however, lingered on the insignias before rising to look at the faces of the men who bore them. Zaiyera noted every one of those exchanges, the latter of which she took as a chilling warning.

Most of the people they passed looked to have the same blended ancestry as the guard in the tree. There were others, too. Dor'haigheners milled about, towering at least a head over everyone else. That there were more than a few about the streets gave an indication of Rexzen's proximity to the border. There were also Samharans from further south, as well as an occasional group of Yintish people.

"Ah! This is a sight I hadn't expected," Zhuyun said. His eyes lit up when he spotted a trio of Yintish women walking by. They shared a collective bow in greeting and conversed in their native tongue for several moments before the trio moved on.

"There is a stable along the southern wall of the city where you can house Sadiq," Zhuyun told Zaiyera. "As for ourselves, there are a number of inns in Rexzen, but my countrywomen recommend the one closest to the center of the city. It is called the Silk River Inn."

"Silk River?" Zaiyera asked.

"A name from the ancient days of trade," Zhuyun answered. "The silk traders flowed in caravans right through the center of Rexzen like a river of wagons bearing loads of silk."

"Then let us be quick to the stables and even quicker to this Silk River Inn of yours," Dyren said.

"Aye," Barum said. "I don't know what I want more, a bath to wash off this crusted blood and death clinging to my skin, or enough food for three men."

Jaide sniffed at Barum's arm and smirked. "In your current state you will make any meal spoil instantly. Take the bath first, yes?"

Housing Sadiq turned out to be more expensive than she'd thought and had nearly drained the last of Zaiyera's money. She wondered if the stablehands had a hayloft she might sleep in for the night. If not, she may well be sharing Sadiq's stall.

She said nothing about her situation, of course, but Jaide Amadi had noticed her consternation in short order. "We will talk later, yes?"

"About what?" Zaiyera asked, but the Viriksani ignored the question.

If someone were to blindfold Zaiyera and drop her in the middle of Rexzen, she would have thought herself in a foreign land, perhaps somewhere across The Great Sea. The building architecture had sharp edges, with roofs of semicircular tiles that curved upward at the corners. Encircling some of the buildings were covered patios and walkways lined with smooth, painted stone columns.

While those things made Rexzen seem foreign, the artwork was distinctly Samharan. The columns were the same light sandy brown as the earth they were built from. The plants that inhabited the finely kept gardens were the most colorful plants and shrubs in all of Samhar.

Some buildings were painted white, with the patio columns a shimmering red. According to Zhuyun, these were colors and designs distinct to Yuntai.

"It's beautiful," Zaiyera said as he showed them the various types of Yintish architecture. "That statue." Zaiyera pointed to a life-sized statue of a golden-skinned androgynous figure with shining bracelets and eyes of silver stone that sparkled when the sunlight hit them. "That is Domahir, spirit of good luck."

"A taste for wealth, ah?" Zhuyun said, noting the gaudy bracelets and jewelry on the statue. He squinted. "Though I cannot say whether it is male or female."

"It is both and neither," Zaiyera said. "Domahir is attracted to shiny things. Not necessarily wealth, as not everyone has it, but anything shiny."

By the time they reached Silk River Inn dusk had arrived. The inn's architecture was the same blending of the two cultures, though this one was dominant in Samharan style with Yintish accents.

Zaiyera remained at the back of the line as each of the companions went to the desk to pay for a room. Barum had offered to share a room with Jaide to cut the cost, but she'd deflected, reasoning that the gesture would be better served to Kima, who had no money.

Kima had protested, saying he would take lodging in a hayloft in exchange for a night's work, but in the end, Barum's persistence had won out.

Dyren and Malker took a room together, which left Jaide and Zaiyera.

"You two can share a room with any of us," Malker said. "It hardly seems fair that you should bear the full price of a room because there are no women to share with. And you," he said to Jaide, "needn't be the odd man out."

"If there is a shydon in this world that has a heart, it beats in the chest of Malker Argen, yes?" Jaide clapped him on the shoulder. "Many thanks, but I confess I have a selfish streak. I like the luxury of a room to myself."

"I will manage as well," Zaiyera said. "Thank you, Malker."

The junior shydon hunter shrugged. "As you wish." He left to catch up with the others, sifting between the wooden chairs and milling patrons and servers to find an empty table.

"You will share a room with me," Jaide said to Zaiyera.

"I would stay close to Sadiq," Zaiyera replied, "since he is our only camel, now. I will get lodging in the hayloft."

"Oh, for the allure of a stable filled with dung and animals." Jaide waved a hand at her. "Do not let anyone see when you enter my room."

The Viriksani woman paid for her lodging and waved off Zaiyera's many thank-yous. "We are Samharan. You would do the same for me, yes?"

"Yes," Zaiyera said, surprising herself with how readily she answered.

They turned toward the common dining room and started toward the direction the others had gone. It was then that a pair of women entered the establishment. Zaiyera froze before she could stop herself. Both women had shaved heads, one with a tattoo on the side.

4 0

Zaiyera kept her features neutral and moved on. She could feel both sets of light brown eyes on her back as she and Jaide made their way through the dining room.

"You recognized those women," Jaide whispered when they were out of earshot.

"We'll talk about it later in private," Zaiyera replied.

It wasn't until they sat at the table and Zaiyera had her first euphorbia beer that she realized how hungry she was. No one said a word when the meal came. After days out in the wild and having to survive on the rations left after the tugyre attack, a full hot meal felt as much like an experience as sustenance.

"I'm guessing," Malker said after finishing his last bite, "by the conditions here that our ... friend, has not yet arrived."

"On camelback he should've been here by now," Zaiyera said. "Or at least be near."

"What is the closest major city to Rexzen?" Dyren asked.

"Trystia," Kima answered, surprising everyone. his next words sounded as though they were dragged painfully out of him. "Malha," he glanced around. "He will stop there first."

There were shared glances all around.

"There is a lot of distance between Zalrabi and Trystia," Zaiyera said. "We might beat him there."

"This is possible, yes?" Jaide agreed. "Rexzen is one day from Viriksan, which is two days from Trystia. If what you say is true about this hibernation period, the distance, terrain, and weather would likely have him and us arrive there close to the same time. Possibly."

"Possibly," Dyren echoed. "We won't know if we can beat him there unless we have any news of his last movements," Dyren said.

"Good luck with that, Dor'haighener," Jaide said. "This is the last place anyone with certain … capabilities would come within miles of. No one in their right mind would even talk of this, yes?"

"We'll have to be creative in our approach, then," Dyren said. "Even if it takes a couple days here, we need to know what's happening before we ride headlong on a diverted path. For all we know he may well have bypassed this Trystia and is even now making straight for here."

"As much as I'd like to clean up and get fresh bandages," Barum said, "we've still got a good bit of daylight left. Best we split up and get moving. I don't know where anything in this crowded city is. If I'm going to find a tavern or social house or whatever they call it here, by tonight, I need to get looking."

"I shall leave the interrogating of drunken revelers to you, Denberesterner," Jaide said. "I will return to the fields while it's still light."

The more Zaiyera thought about what she'd seen of Rexzen so far, the surer she became that this was the city from her vision after using the swift basin. She needed to be sure, though. It would determine just how swiftly she wanted to be gone from this place. "I'm going to have a look around as well."

Malker regarded her with curiosity. "What do you know?"

"Nothing," she answered honestly. "I'd like to change that."

"A word of caution," Dyren Faust said. He glanced about the common room and lowered his voice. "Rexzen is a city with many sights and safe streets. But be careful who you talk to and about what. You already know that lancers are not looked upon with favor, here. Those who lance the stream are considered walking weapons, swords without sheaths. Be *very* careful how you approach your questions."

That brought grim nods all around.

"What of you two?" Zhuyun asked.

Dyren stared at the table for a few moments. "We will spend the rest of the day preparing."

They waited, but the senior shydon hunter said no more.

Once outside the Silk River Inn, Zaiyera flexed the muscles in her legs and arms, and gave her back a little twist from left to right. Every cut and bruise protested.

Barum Hurst may have been right that they should get the urgent business done before relaxing, but it didn't stop her from wishing she could have had a bath first.

Dyren and Malker exited behind her, talking amongst themselves.

"You realize you won't get far with your insignias showing?" Zaiyera asked.

Dyren nodded. "We won't be able to do much to help in information gathering. We must leave that and replenishing the supplies to the rest of you. I suspect we may not garner the best prices either."

"Why not take your insignias off?" Zaiyera asked.

"As shadow hunters of Nanshaigha, the code forbids it."

Zaiyera stopped herself from offering a diplomatic response in the spirt of how stupid that rule was, considering what was at stake, but she bit it back. It wasn't for her to say what did or didn't make sense.

The rest of the group exited the inn. Barum and Jaide headed toward the heart of the city, while Zhuyun and Kima lingered with Zaiyera.

"Mind company?" Zhuyun asked.

It turned out that the city of Rexzen was easily as large as that of Nanshaigha, but also more colorful. Zaiyera could only try to imagine how the towering buildings were constructed.

The mixed heritage of Rexzen was evident on every street. Zaiyera recognized the Samharan influences while Zhuyun pointed out the various accents of Yintish culture.

"These streets go on forever," Kima said. "We've had representatives from Rexzen in Zalrabi, so I've heard their stories. I still hadn't imagined it this big."

Zaiyera pulled aside an older boy carrying a sack on his back and asked him in *Soloush* where they could find a doctor. The boy tilted his head and asked a question she more or less understood. Kima stepped in and spoke to the boy. Moments later they were on their way again.

"Do they not speak the tongue of Samhar, here?" Zhuyun asked.

"A northern version of it," Zaiyera answered. "It's called *Solsha*. We share a lot of the same words, but it's different enough that we don't perfectly understand one another."

"And few people here speak tradetongue," Kima added.

They found the physician's building by the time dusk started to settle in. Zaiyera hoped she might be able to buy a few bandages for cheap, as she didn't have much money left. She also hoped to come across news here.

The clinking of hanging beads heralded their entry. The office was large inside, easily as big as a family home. Bottles of various colored herbs and liquids lined the shelves, including unidentifiable plants and roots pickling in jars.

Muffled conversation drifted from behind the closed door of one of several rooms down a hallway. A woman wearing a sandy brown head wrap and matching, simple cut dress welcomed them from the desk to the side of the room.

She was nearly Barum's height, closer to six feet than five, and clearly of full Samharan ancestry. Her warm smile lit her light brown eyes. When she got a good look at them, her smile faded. "Did you escape death itself to get here?" she asked in *Solsha.*

Zaiyera asked in *Soloush* if she spoke tradetongue for the benefit of herself and Zhuyun.

"Of course," the woman said in a fast-speaking accent. She looked Zaiyera over. "Southern Samharan. Kushtanji?"

"You've been to the region?" Zaiyera asked.

"Only twice, but your people are memorable for their kindness, and also your markings." She pointed at her own face in the places Zaiyera had the red four-point tattoos.

She looked the other two over, offering a bow to Zhuyun before turning to Kima. "I do not recognize where you are from."

"South Samhar as well, *niyima*," Kima replied with a bow.

When it became clear he would say no more, she turned back to Zhuyun. "A Yuntaiman friend from far across the Great Sea. Welcome, *ai'mosheng*."

Zhuyun bowed. "I've traveled many lands, *ai'lushr*, but none so fascinating as this great city. Rexzen is spoken of with fondness, in Yuntai."

The woman's light brown eyes seemed to sparkle when she smiled. "I hope to one day visit the land that has so influenced my home. If you have time, I wish to hear about it."

Zhuyun bowed again. "I would love nothing more, *ai'lushr*. But sadly, that must wait for another time."

"Of course," the woman said. "Please forgive my negligence. You require treatment?"

"We wish to buy bandages and healing creams, *niyima*," Zaiyera said.

Those light brown eyes returned to her. "Of course you do," she said, looking them all over once more.

After some polite haggling, Zaiyera and Zhuyun pooled their money together and paid for the supplies.

Down the hall, a male physician—dressed similarly, only in sandy brown breeches and tunic—exited a door and another several paces further away. The man looked exhausted.

The woman looked over her shoulder, then turned back, remorse coloring her features. "I pray to Shakimah this will end soon." She jerked her chin at them. "Another of the lucky ones to survive?"

"I'm afraid we don't know what you're talking about," Zaiyera replied. "We've arrived here from a long and terribly freezing trip through Dor'haighen."

"Better that frozen land than what awaits you in your home regions," the woman replied, looking from Zaiyera to Kima. "The safest place for you is right here in Rexzen. Shakimah bless her name, Queen Adaora takes steps to keep us safe. But our office is starting to fill, and other offices across Rexzen are also feeling the strain."

"What happens?" Zhuyun asked.

"Bad things. Best that you stay here."

That evasion alone revealed that Malhadiev must be on the move again.

"We plan to return home," Zaiyera pressed. "If there is an animal about, or raiders, we can defend against such dangers."

"Would that it was only that," she replied. "The people who come to my office were brought here by litter, often on their backs. Burned, broken, barely clinging to life."

"The raiders have become that aggressive?" Zaiyera asked.

"Not raiders," the woman replied, taking the bait. "I am a physician. We do not speak in gossip and hearsay, but I'd like for you not to return broken, as others have. She lowered her voice. "We are not to speak of him, or his name, or what he is."

Beside Zaiyera, Kima tensed.

"A man. A single man who has left cities, towns, villages, even *trade outposts* in ruin. The number of dead and injured has the look of war." She held up a finger and looked at each of them. "One man. A terrible force."

"Where is he now?" Zaiyera asked. "We would know, so that we could avoid him on our way home."

"You might find your nomadic people," she said to Zaiyera. "But you," she turned to Kima, "wherever you're from. Ruin and death may be what you'll find." She looked to Zhuyun. "Please stay here where you are safe and among many of your people."

A door down the hall opened to admit a young girl who looked no older than ten years old. She had a bandage wrapped around her head, and her arm in a cloth sling. The attending physician escorted the girl and her father out the door.

Zaiyera noted Kima watching the girl as they passed. Eyes downcast, the little girl practically stared at her feet. Zaiyera watched them until they disappeared out the door. The sight stabbed at her heart.

They left the physician's offices in a somber mood, saying little on their way back to the inn. Zhuyun seemed to be deep in thought, as was Zaiyera. Kima looked as if he was being ripped apart from the inside.

* * *

The bath that evening was composed of two parts, and both felt like they had been sent from Shakimah Herself. Despite the sting of Zaiyera's wounds, the steaming hot water boiled out all the impurities, aches, and stiffness. All the crusted and caked-on blood on her skin and in her hair broke apart and left her body.

After soaking away all the blood and grime, she transferred to a second steaming bath with rejuvenating oils.

Zaiyera sighed in remembrance of how soft and supple the bath oils had made her skin feel. The black soap had been lovely, and the oils had been like the breath of the Goddess.

The outdoor patio attached to the common room of the inn had no roof, so afforded an unobstructed view of the stars. Zaiyera lingered long after night arrived and the masses had mostly retired for the night.

Poles with burning candles lined the quiet nighttime streets, their swaying light casting graceful shadows that danced down the stone avenues and against the sides of buildings.

Zaiyera didn't know why she'd felt such apprehension about Rexzen. Whatever its conflict was with Nanshaigha, it had nothing to do with her. She closed her eyes with another contented sigh.

Visions flashed across her mind in a flood that almost knocked her over. Fierce warriors in strange foreign armor with helms cast from a mold in the image of a face with a ferocious expression. The warriors wielded swords but no shields. Archers, spearmen, all imposing and ready.

At the front of the endless rows of fearsome warriors stood a row of women divided in pairs. They stood side by side, bound together by an invisible force more powerful than any chain. Their heads were shaved clean of hair, yet one of each of the pairs of women had a tattoo on one side. And their eyes…

Somehow, Zaiyera knew that this one row of women were more mighty a force than the army at their backs.

"It is time to close for the night, *niyima*," the innkeeper said from behind.

Zaiyera's eyes popped open and she jumped.

"Apologies, *niyima*," the old man said when she shot out of her seat. "I did not mean to startle you." He spoke in tradetongue, as most merchants and business owners did.

"It is nothing, *dyenbe*, she said. "A question, if I may?"

Halfway through the door, the innkeeper turned back, his smile creating creases in his weathered and sun-toughened skin. His dark complexion and almond-shaped eyes spoke of mixed ancestry.

"I saw soldiers earlier today," she lied. "Their armor looked foreign to me, and their helms were molded in the image of faces.

The innkeeper responded with a grave nod. "They are the elite Kreshada Warriors, *niyima*. The shieldless warriors, as some call them. If you do no wrong, you need not fear them. But I advise you to keep your distance anyway."

"I see. One last question, if I may?"

"Please speak it," the innkeeper said.

Zaiyera had a feeling she needed to ask this question carefully. "I saw … two women today who looked like none I've ever seen. Their heads were shaved, and they—"

"They are not anything to be concerned about, *niyima*. Now, it is time for me to finish my duties. These old bones are tired and the work never ends, does it?"

"Of course, *dyenbe*," Zaiyera replied. "I am sorry to bother you."

"Not at all."

Zaiyera went to leave the patio and explore. Hopefully she might come across a social house or somewhere she could find out more about the two women.

"Please do not linger long at night," the old innkeeper called after her. "The city guard frowns upon loitering late into the night when businesses are closed and there is little more than trouble to find."

"My thanks," Zaiyera replied. "I just wish for a little fresh night air and I will return. I've spent a long time in the cold north and miss the less freezing nights of home."

The innkeeper waved and disappeared back inside.

Zaiyera kept to the less traveled streets. It had been easier to figure out in what direction everything lay from the Silk River Inn's central location.

She made her way east. Jaide had told her that was the direction of not only the home of Queen Adaora, but the barracks were near there as well. She hoped the training grounds weren't too far inside.

Zaiyera made indirect progress toward her destination, frequently ducking around a corner when a duo of patrolling city guard walked by.

When she came to the most imposing building in the city, she knew she'd found the barracks. It looked to be three stories high and as large as a village. Zaiyera's mouth fell open at the sight, but as impressive as the structure was, there must have been more than one in Rexzen, if her vision proved true.

Metal clanging on metal drew her attention. Zaiyera looked in the direction of the sound, which brought her to a ten-foot wall. It went for about fifty feet to the right, then bent left down the neighboring street.

Zaiyera backed into the safety of the shadows once more and crept along the street until the wall stopped and turned. After checking both ways, she darted across the street and followed the wall, hoping to find some gap to peek between, or some way to scale it.

She found nothing. Zaiyera crossed the street and waited in the shadow of the tall stone wall. Sure no one was coming, she felt along the stone. It was solid, but rough. It might have just enough grip.

After two failed attempts to run up the wall, she heard quick footsteps and darted back across the street to hide in the shadows behind a building. She crouched in the darkness. The footsteps grew louder, but once they reached the corner, they stopped. For a long time, there was only silence. After a while, Zaiyera lowered herself to the ground and peeked around the corner.

Three uniformed men armed with scimitars looked up and down the street. They didn't appear alarmed, so Zaiyera wasn't sure if they'd heard her, or were simply on a routine patrol. She assumed it was routine and waited them out.

Zaiyera saw them turn down the street in her direction. She backed away from the corner and crept around the other side of the building.

Once the sound of footsteps receded around the corner, she waited a little longer, then gave the wall another try. This time she nearly touched the top. She backed across the street, listened for footsteps, and waited till she heard the clang of swords again. When another clash began, she ran for the wall again.

Zaiyera jumped for the wall and pumped her legs as quickly as she could, hoping the clanging swords would continue long enough to mask the sound of her scraping feet. When she knew her upward momentum reached its end, she gave a little jump. The jump pushed her away, but not too far that the top of the wall was out of reach.

Teeth gritted, Zaiyera stretched to her body's limit and managed to grab hold of the top of the wall by her fingertips. She grabbed hold with her other hand before she lost her grip.

Zaiyera realized how vulnerable she was, hanging on the side of that wall. She took a quick look left and right, then slowly lifted herself up. Pulling her bodyweight wasn't in itself difficult, but doing it slowly, however, was. There wasn't a choice in the matter. The last thing she wanted to do was carelessly hoist herself up and in view of anyone who might be training in sight of the wall.

The soft sound of footsteps came from around the corner where the three guards had gone.

She pulled the rest of the way up and saw that a bit of luck was with her after all. The wall was as wide as she was tall. Zaiyera could easily lie atop it and not be spotted.

As soon as her shoulders were in line with the edge, Zaiyera swung her left foot up onto the edge and pulled herself the rest of the way up. She lay flat on her back staring up at the stars without seeing them, not daring to breathe. In that moment it occurred to her that if the city hadn't bothered to position archers to keep watch in the event someone committed an act as foolish as she just had, it might be a testament to the prowess of the warriors below.

The footsteps grew louder until they were right beneath her, but they kept going. She leaned over to peer down at the same three members of the city guard just before they rounded the corner.

Moon and stars, what am I doing?

Still lying on her back, Zaiyera didn't dare to move. She slowly turned her head toward the inside of the wall. An open yard of grass and dirt stretched out below. Weapon racks populated one wall, housing items Zaiyera had never seen before, but could barely make out from this distance and in the dim light.

Men and women trained in sparring circles using wooden versions of the foreign weapons in those racks.

The circles were numerous, and dozens of soldiers challenged each other with wooden spears and swords in the design of scimitars and shamshirs. Some of the practice blades were shaped like nothing Zaiyera had ever seen in Samhar or Dor'haighen.

She spotted one circle nearest the middle of the training yard. Four white robe-clad figures faced each other on either side.

Zaiyera took in a sharp breath. All four were women, heads shaved. One of the women on the right side of circle had a tattoo on the left side of her head, and Zaiyera was certain that one of the women on the left side did as well. What was the significance?

The women on the far end of the circle each raised a single hand opposite the woman standing beside her, fingers straight, palms facing left as though in prayer. The women on the side closest to Zaiyera raised their hands in the same manner. All four women made the gesture in unison. A salute.

One step brought them into the circle, where commenced the most graceful, beautiful, and deadly dance Zaiyera had ever witnessed. Four bodies flipped and spun, glided and flipped through the air. They stabbed at each other with stiff fingers, chopped at each other with rigid hands flat like daggers.

One of the tattooed women leapt toward her opponent in a backwards spin and snapped her foot out. Her opponent ducked under her spinning kick. The airborne woman dropped low as soon as she landed and repeated the same back-spinning kick, only this time at her adversary's feet.

The other warrior leapt into a backflip to avoid the foot sweep, landed, and shot forward. She threw herself at her opponent with a dizzying barrage of knife-handed chops and stabbing fingers. She leapt forward and thrust her knee toward her opponent's chin.

The other two women were no less awe-inspiring. They engaged in the same hand-to-hand combat as the other two women, but then something changed.

A transparent aura began to trail the speedy movements of one of the non-tattooed women. She'd begun to passively touch the stream. That in itself wasn't what nearly made Zaiyera dive off the wall and run as far and fast as her legs could take her. It was the color of her dance-resin.

One woman lashed out with a transparent rolling wave that would have been a ripple in the ground had she been actually touching the stream. A transparent orange aura trailed her every move. Orange!

Zaiyera swallowed. That woman was a darkdancer who had syphoned the lifestream of at least four people. What was happening, here?

The women she fought leapt over the ripple and dodged left against the follow-up disk. She, too, passively touched the stream and created a disk to shoot speeding shards of light at her opponent.

She leapt into a backwards spin and threw her arms out as she turned. Zaiyera's eyes widened.

The other non-tattooed woman's dance-resin shone red! There were only two tainted streamdancers more powerful than one who bore the red taint. The crimson resin of the most powerful of darkdancers, and the black of a *kivuli dayasa*. The woman was only two steps from total darkness.

Zaiyera watched the women passively dance the stream against one another, sending mock versions of incredibly powerful attacks while performing feats of acrobatics that would leave the most conditioned of warriors panting in exhaustion.

She tried to make sense of it all. Tainted dancers were feared and reviled across all of Samhar, the north, and—she assumed—any lands across the Great Sea and the world over. Could there be a different way of thinking among peoples from other lands? Given the shared relationship between Rexzen and Yuntai, was this an indication of Yuntai having a different view of those who bore the taint?

A part of Zaiyera longed for that to be true. What would it be like to not have to hide what she was? Just the thought of being able to touch the stream, fully touch the stream, might be enough to send her on a ship for the land to the west.

The combatants suddenly intermixed, switching opponents at will. Zaiyera watched in amazement as the tattooed women held their own against the darkdancers, even scoring a hit as frequently as they received one.

The red darkdancer waved her arms in an intricate pattern so quickly they blurred in the air. Her tattooed partner made a gesture as if grabbing hold of the red-colored flow, and wove her arms around like two snakes entangled. A golden dance-resin suddenly trailed her movements.

Using the technique of the power's namesake, the tattooed warrior danced the flow, wrapping the power around her. Her partner began to match her movements until both women moved together as though mirror images of each other.

The other two warriors entered into their own dance, moving in perfect unison, gesture for gesture as though they were one person.

Moon and stars! Zaiyera lay transfixed, gawking at the four women, all streamdancers, two tainted, two pure.

The women on the left built on the passive flow and threw one single punch in the air.

A transparent force that looked like a giant red fist slammed into the transparent orange shield the other two women produced in the last instant.

Now on the offense, the streamdancers on the left punched the air in a series of combinations, while the other two produced shield after shield to block from every direction.

Zaiyera watched all of this with both admiration and a growing sense of dread. Despite her distance, she could feel the passive flow as it swirled around the combatants. She'd studied and trained as a streamdancer, fought enough of them to recognize each of the three techniques: offensive, defensive, and flow.

The tattooed warriors were in a constant state of flow that somehow tied them to their ally like a tether. *Tether.* Zaiyera's dread turned to horror.

I've seen enough.

She looked back to the street to ensure no one was around, then carefully scooted sideways to the edge and dropped back to the street. Quick and silent as a specter, she half skulked half ran back to the Silk River Inn. She made it across the street, rounded a corner, and realized, too late, that she wasn't alone.

41

As soon as the figure stepped onto the street, Zaiyera darted in a different direction. She zigzagged her way back towards the inn, hoping she wasn't being flanked.

She heard a whisper that sounded like her name, but she couldn't be sure. She kept moving, keeping low and to the shadows, peeking around corners to make sure she didn't run into anyone else.

"My friend Zaiyera."

Zaiyera skidded to a stop. *"Zhuyun?"* she whispered back.

The same figure as before stepped onto the street a dozen paces away. Now that she wasn't actively trying to evade him, Zaiyera recognized Zhuyun by his stature.

"What are you doing here?" she said in a low voice once they were close to each other.

"I was on my way back to the inn from an evening walk when I spotted you," he answered. "It seems the city of Rexzen has something else in common with my homeland in that it doesn't have much of a nightlife, ixu?"

"And you decided to follow me," Zaiyera said, her tone dry.

Quickly and quietly, they started moving again.

"I wasn't sure if you knew the rules here, ah?" Zhuyun finally answered. "I was going to catch up to tell you when I realized you were moving as though you wanted not to be seen."

"And so you followed me," Zaiyera repeated, even dryer than before.

"Would you not have a friend near, if trouble were to find you?"

"I suppose you saw me climb the wall?"

Zhuyun blew out a quiet breath. "I'm sure you must have known I followed you, for you have sought to give me heart failure as punishment, ixu"

Zaiyera would have laughed if her mind wasn't reeling at what she'd just seen. "We need to get out of Rexzen as soon as possible. If I didn't think everyone would resist, I'd call for us to go now."

They stopped in the darkness of a corner across the street from Silk River Inn. The oldest inn in Rexzen sat in the middle of three different streets like an island of history.

"After weeks of travel and the injuries we've suffered," Zhuyun said, "you must have seen something truly terrible to make you wish to leave so soon."

Zaiyera looked squarely at the Yuntaiman. He returned her gaze with curiosity and no small amount of wariness in his brown eyes. "They have some sort of elite warrior class here—women with shaved heads, and they fight in pairs. They are also streamdancers."

Zhuyun nodded, waiting for the rest.

"I witnessed two pairs of these women sparring," Zaiyera continued. "Of each pair, one woman had a tattoo on the side of her head. They were untainted dancers. The other women had no tattoos, but they were darkdancers."

Zhuyun frowned at that. "You're sure?"

Zaiyera nodded. "One of the darkdancers is so powerful, she's not far from becoming a *kivuli dayasa*."

Zhuyun sucked in a breath through his teeth. "This cannot be true."

"I know what I saw, and that's not all of it," Zaiyera continued. "Once you've touched the stream enough times, you can feel when someone else is touches it. The tattooed women were somehow maintaining the flow dance; indefinitely. I don't know how they do this, but it maintained a link between them and their partners. A link, leashing them together."

Zhuyun stared at her. "You are sure of this?"

Zaiyera nodded. "The memory is forever burned in my mind."

"That is grim news indeed," the Yuntaiman said. "Grim especially for King Eredin, should relations between Nanshaigha and Rexzen continue to deteriorate."

"Hardly the worst part of it," Zaiyera said. "Imagine if Malhadiev learned this technique."

Zhuyun took a deep breath and looked at the inn as the implications of Zaiyera's discovery settled over him. "Or worse. What if one of these tattooed warriors you speak of manage to bind him?"

That line of reasoning chilled the pit of Zaiyera's stomach.

"I believe you're right," Zhuyun said. "We must be gone from Rexzen, and quickly."

"We don't even know where Malhadiev is," Zaiyera said.

"Thanks to our Viriksani friend, we do indeed," Zhuyun replied. "He's confirmed that Malhadiev moves toward Trystia."

"Then, let's go," Zaiyera said.

They went first to collect Jaide, then Barum and Kima before heading to the shydon hunters' room. The accommodations were more spacious, given the two men had pooled their money for two beds, but it was cramped with seven people in it.

"This must be urgent for us all to be crowded in here," Dyren said while Malker cracked open the shutters.

Zaiyera went straight into it, telling them about the deadly stream-dancer warriors, though she omitted the part about two of them being darkdancers, or the power binding them.

Dyren and Malker listened through it all. When Zaiyera finished, all eyes turned to the senior shydon.

"I admit," Dyren said, "that I've never heard of such warriors, but that hardly calls for us to flee Rexzen before we're properly rested. From what Jaide discovered from the farmers, corroborated by news Barum gleaned, the shadowlancer is still a good distance from Trystia."

"We shouldn't linger," Zaiyera said. "This city is beautiful with a rich history and culture, but there is an underlying danger that makes me uneasy.

"And there's more," she continued. "When I drank from the swift basin for the first time, I experienced the after affect in the form of a vision. It was of a city grand and beautiful, with colorful buildings and beautiful people. And also with a formidable warrior class. The vision left me with a sense of dread."

"You're just telling us about this now?" Malker asked, skeptical.

"Why would I have mentioned it before now?" Zaiyera countered. "Especially given your disdain for dancecraft. But the vision didn't stop there. I saw two women who fought as one. They were fearsome and highly skilled, with heads shaven clean."

She could see that she wasn't getting through to them. The group was exhausted, stinging from their brutal fight against the pack of tugyre, and desperate for a full night's sleep and a day of rest. Zaiyera couldn't blame them. She felt no different. Her bath had only dulled her many aches and pains.

Zaiyera decided to tell them the rest. "There's one other thing. Two of the four women I saw were darkdancers."

Dyren's back stiffened, and Malker hissed through his teeth.

Zaiyera wished she didn't have to reveal the nature of those two women, but she couldn't think of any other way to motivate them. "I saw their dance-resins myself."

"This is a crime," Malker said. "To harbor darklancers is a severely punishable offense. But to train them as warriors is a serious matter. I wonder if Queen Adaora knows she has darklancers among her forces."

"Whether she knows or not," Dyren said, all business, now. "We are duty bound to inform her. And if she knows, we are *then* duty bound to inform the king and queen of Dor'haighen."

Jaide's eyes flicked from the two shydon hunters to Zaiyera and back. "While you two are ruffling each other's feathers for a confronta-tion that might get us all in trouble, I suggest we not forget why we've come this far, yes?"

"What do you suggest, Jaide Amadi?" Malker asked. "That we leave this situation as it is. We are shadow hunters. It's our duty—"

"She's right," Dyren said.

That caught Zaiyera by surprise. She had expected a harder fight than this.

"Although," the senior shydon continued, "when this business with the shadowlancer is finished, we *will* speak with the queen of Rexzen."

Barum snorted. "You mean supposing we survive? Might that he'll just drop a whole city on us next time and be done with it." He glanced at Kima and gave the other man a sympathetic nod. "Pardon me for sayin'."

Kima had been staring at the space in front of him during the whole conversation. He glanced up at Barum and returned the nod before going back to gazing into a place far from where they sat.

As tense as it was for Zaiyera to be in the company of two shydon hunters, one of considerable rank, she could only imagine what it must be like to be in Kima's position. Held captive then released and made a fugitive, for the sole purpose of trying to help everyone around him kill his brother. What inner conflicts must be ripping him apart?

She looked at Zhuyun, hoping for support. He sat back in his chair studying everyone. Whatever the Yuntaiman was thinking, he kept it close.

"Small suggestion," Barum said. "As much as it disturbs me hanging around a city that actually uses darklancers in its military, we might have to swallow our opinions for a day." He groaned as he leaned to the side and stretched his arm. "I don't know about anybody else, but I could use a trip to the healers. If we need to leave quick, then we need fast healing, which will require rest when it's done."

Not you too. Zaiyera gave Barum a hard look, to which he raised his hands in a warding gesture. "Now, don't go givin' me the angry eyes, miss my lady. I'm just saying that if you want me at my best, I'm gonna need some medical attention to get me there. If I raise my arm too fast, I'll tear open the scab that's just barely closed." He looked about the group. "Maybe everyone else is in better shape than me?"

A chorus of noncommittal grunts and muttering answered.

Zaiyera wanted to disagree, wanted to drive home her point that they needed to get moving. Deep down, though, she knew Barum was right. Just that thought alone made Zaiyera aware of every pain in her body. She'd ignored her injuries when she'd climbed that wall, but now that she'd been sitting for longer than a few minutes, the aches returned.

Still, the dread she'd felt from just the vision of Rexzen through the swift basin had her ready to flee at this very moment, injuries or not.

Dyren's suggestion yielded murmurs of agreement from everyone but Zaiyera. In the end, she had no argument against the logic, and so she acquiesced.

"Can I ask a question?" Zaiyera asked in *Soloush* once she and Jaide were alone in their room.

Jaide unwrapped her head and let her long black hair spill out. "Oh, that feels good. I don't know how you can stand keeping your hair wrapped up for so long."

"The braids help," Zaiyera replied. "And some cut their hair short."

"You should move to Viriksan, where it is cooler," Jaide said as she continued to undress. "What is your question?"

"Why the disguise?" Zaiyera asked, waving a hand over the other woman.

"Ha. You are a patient one, yes?" Jaide stripped out of her trousers and tunic, then slipped into one of the room's two beds, closest to the window. "I'd expected you to ask me the day after you discovered my little secret."

Zaiyera leaned Shatr beside the head of her bed, slipped into her nightclothes, then climbed into her own bed. It felt good not lying on cold hard ground. "I almost didn't ask now, but curiosity prevailed."

Jaide shifted on her side and propped her head up on her hand. "Advantage. My parents were traders. As a girl, I watched my father negotiate better deals than my mother. She made most of the wares my parents sold and knew the value of them better than anyone. But when the time came to sell or trade, my father almost always got the better deal.

"The same with certain kinds of interactions," Jaide continued.

"There are things men will tell each other more readily than women." She indicated Zaiyera with her free hand. "Ever tried to get information and find yourself deflecting advances while you do it?"

Zaiyera blew out an annoyed breath. "Need I answer?"

Jaide shrugged. "They're not all like that, but I find it easier in general, and I'm able to do it as long as I look like a very young, pretty man." She touched her chin, a distinctly feminine gesture. "It *can* get awkward if I'm talking to someone and he's particularly attractive."

Zaiyera chuckled. "I'd imagine so."

Jaide shared in her mirth before sobering again. "I know I can't do this forever, but for now, it's a boon. Dor'haighen men give a casual dismissal of women to the south that doesn't carry over to Dor'haighen women, yes?"

"You've seen Dor'haighen women," Zaiyera said, laughing. "Would you?"

"No, I wouldn't," Jaide said. "Big, strong women, yes?"

"Yes," Zaiyera said. "And Samhar men? Have a sword at your hip or your back and you can see them wondering if you can use it and how well."

"Or they think it's cute that you try," Jaide added. "Or maybe you're holding it for your husband. This is more common in central and northern Samhar. I did not encounter it as much the few times I traveled farther south."

"You make me want to don man clothes and deepen my voice," Zaiyera said. "If I could do it without sounding like a little boy."

"I've had many years of training my voice," Jaide said. "Singers are revered in my home, and my mother was friends with many of them. She wanted me to be a singer and forced me to train." She painted a caricature of a sad expression on her face. "Sadly, I had not the voice nor the will for it. But the training has served me well, yes? Though, I barely manage to sound like a young man. What of your secret, Zaiyera? Do you hope to finish this and be away from our shydon friends before they find out? Assuming we survive, that is."

Zaiyera's smile faded. "That's my hope. If I'm still alive after this is done, I'll be happy to be as far away from those two as possible.

They're not bad men, but I have no illusions about what would happen if they found out." It felt odd talking about her condition with someone else. A big part of her wanted to avoid the topic.

"I would think so, yes?" Jaide replied. "I can only try to imagine the feeling of traveling so close with them. It must be difficult."

Zaiyera stared at the other woman without seeing her. "My whole life since I became what I am has been an enduring secret. I keep people at a distance for my own selfish preservation, but for theirs as well. Who would want to be associated with a tainted one?"

"You are like no sick streamdancer I've ever met," Jaide replied. "Even Jiet struggled with the addiction."

Zaiyera smiled regretfully at the mention of Jaide's brother, and also in appreciation of the Viriksani woman's gentle description of her condition. "You can call me a darkdancer or tainted one. It's what I am, and I deserve the title. As for the addiction, it is not something you stop struggling with. You just learn how to manage it as best you can. I've been lucky."

Jaide sighed. "Would that Jiet had possessed such knowledge as you. He might have been better equipped to survive as you have. And however much you feel you should punish yourself for your past, I'll not join you, yes? It helps nothing. And anyone who's spent longer than one conversation with you can see your heart." She sat up and blew out the candle between their beds.

Zaiyera lay awake as she mulled over Jaide's words. Finally, she closed her eyes and reached out her hand. Her fingers brushed Shatr's smooth scabbard.

42

They didn't depart Rexzen until dawn two days later, after the ever-perceptive Zhuyun brought a matter to their attention.

"We've forgotten something important," the Yuntaiman said. "We seek healing lancers, yet this city distrusts lancers, ah?"

Zaiyera wanted to smack her forehead. How could *she* have forgotten such a thing?

Dyren caught Zhuyun's meaning as well and shook his head in resignation. "We must truly be road weary to have forgotten such a detail. If there are any healing lancers here, they'd likely be difficult to find." He looked about the group. "Are you fit to travel, or have you need of another day of rest?"

"I need a *week* of rest," Darum said. "But a day's too much, considering what's at stake."

In the end, the party left Silk River Inn and departed on camelback before the sun fully cleared the eastern horizon.

Small dunes appeared a few hours into their journey. Hot breezes whispered through the air as though from the lips of a burning kiln.

Occasional packs of chukita cats shadowed their progress, indicating that they were near an oasis or some form of human civilization.

Usually it was the latter. At each village they passed, Zaiyera and Jaide inquired of a healer streamdancer, but with no luck.

"It must be the proximity to Rexzen," Jaide surmised after returning from the third village.

"My guess as well," Zaiyera agreed. "Villages are small and vulnerable so far from a major city. There would be at least one streamdancer. Usually two."

"Why wouldn't they help us?" Barum said. "Rexzen or not, are the people in these parts not sympathetic to weary and battered travelers?"

"Fear is a powerful thing, Barum Hurst," Zaiyera replied. "Rexzen's reach is wide. Would *you* admit to a stranger that you're a streamdancer if you lived in the shadow of a place that might well claim your freedom for it?"

They came to the fourth village at dusk. Though it was more a cluster of small thatch-roofed homes than an actual village, the party were able to trade for or buy food and replenish their waterskins at the local well. It was also far enough south that, with some coaxing, Zaiyera managed to get them all a session with the local healing streamdancer.

"We should sacrifice a shiny bauble to Domahir, yes?" Jaide said upon hearing the news. "Luck is truly with us today."

Zaiyera insisted on waiting while everyone received their healing. She tried to argue with herself that her injuries weren't so bad that she couldn't just carry on. In truth, they weren't. But her body needed to be as strong as possible for what was coming.

The thought of receiving that healing, and what came with it, gave her pause.

Barum emerged from the woman's little hut and lifted his right arm to stretch his side. "By Jokolta, but this feels better. Still hurts like fire, but it's better. Makes me feel hungry, too."

"Your first healing this way?" Jaide asked.

"Aye."

"The body heals the body, ah?" Zhuyun said. "One of my many aunts taught us this. Just as when you bandage a cut to hold the skin together that it may knit, this lance healer uses your body's personal stream to quicken the healing process. For a cost, that is."

"That cost being the use of your personal stream," Jaide surmised.

"This, yes," Zhuyun replied. "Which is why we are all now so hungry."

"Your turn," Malker said to Zaiyera. When she hesitated, he narrowed his eyes at her. "You're not about to tell us you have no injuries, woman. None of us walked away from that fight with the tugyre without wounds."

The healer's reddish-brown hut sat in the middle of a gathering of other similar homes, the main difference being the smell of burning incense several feet from the doorway.

Zaiyera looked behind her. A cluster of homes sat between her and the others. She could walk around the side of the house and wait a while, then return claiming she'd received the healing. Zaiyera focused on the wounds she'd be dealt in the fight with the tugyre. She felt sore in a dozen places, and the scratches still stung badly. Her mobility, while decent, was hampered by the natural inclination to avoid certain movements.

The moments passed while she stood there in indecision. If she received that healing, it would trigger the hunger. *Perhaps if I just stretch and apply some of the salve the Rexzen healer sold us…"*

"How long does this lovely girl stand outside my home, hmm?"

Zaiyera had barely finished her thought when the voice drifted outside the beaded entryway.

A woman with skin like polished onyx—and just as smooth—emerged from the hut. She slid a few locks of gray and white hair from her face and smiled at Zaiyera. Her eyes were a startling contrast to her dark skin, for they were as white as her hair. Zaiyera felt the flow swirling about the woman like a running river. She swallowed.

"Please, girl. Come. I'd like to get you mended so that I might release the flow back into the stream."

Zaiyera bowed in respect. "Apologies for making you wait, *uluma*." She followed behind the healer through the beads and into the hut. The woman might be well be twice Zaiyera's age, but her stately posture and the inner power she exuded spoke of years well lived.

The healer led her to the far side of the hut where a bed sat near the wall. She stopped beside it and turned back. "Lie here, girl." She indicated the bed with an open hand.

Zaiyera approached the bed as though it were a poisonous snake. It still wasn't too late. She could tell the healer she changed her mind and felt fine.

"Hmm."

Zaiyera looked up to see a smile on the healer's face. "Hesitant, are we? Is this your first time?"

"Why do you think that, *uluma*?" Zaiyera asked.

The healer's chuckle came out in a single breath. "Your heart is hammering in your chest, girl. And I can smell a wave of anxiety rolling off of you. If you don't calm down, I fear I might drown in it."

"I'm just … I think I may not require your services after all," Zaiyera finally said. "I apologize for wasting your time, *uluma*—"

"You have a number of cuts that have been cleaned well. A standard salve was used. You have bruises as well, and at least one deep cut that is slow to heal." Still looking straight ahead—past Zaiyera, she noted—the woman indicated the bed again.

"I would argue that you do need my services. And before you argue that you cannot pay me, your foreign friend from across the Great Sea has already paid for your session. If he had not, the Viriksani … man …" she cleared her throat, "would have paid instead."

The way the healer spoke of Jaide Amadi made the corner of Zaiyera's mouth twitch in spite of her nervousness. She took a deep breath and went to lie down. The healer continued looking straight ahead but turned when Zaiyera was on her back.

"You are right, *uluma*," Zaiyera admitted. "I have not received healing from someone holding the flow as you do. I feel somewhat guilty in you using some of your life that I might simply mend faster."

"You are a streamdancer?" the woman asked.

"I'm not."

The healer tilted her head. "Yet you know that I hold the stream about me, using flow."

"I've … been educated in the ways of streamdancing," Zaiyera replied.

The slanted grin returned. "Of course. But your education must not have reached the arts of healing yet. If we paid the same lifeprice as others who dance the stream, we would live little more than a decade. Perhaps less, in some of the more conflict-riddled places of the world. To put it simply, I dip my hand into the flow and keep it about me as I need it. The price is paid, but it is small. There's more to it than that, but let it put your conscience at ease."

She lay a hand on Zaiyera's head. "Hmm. More than physical wounds in need of healing." She lifted her hand and let it hover over Zaiyera's head, then passed it over her body from head to toe.

Zaiyera lay on her back as the elder woman slowly passed her hand up and down over her body. After the second pass, she placed her hand on one of the scratches.

Warmth flowed from the healer's soft hands into the wound and spread to every part of her leg. Zaiyera felt a tiny bit of the stream seep into her body and mix with her personal flow. The smaller scratches and bruises closed instantly, while the deeper cuts knitted together only a little slower.

Zaiyera closed her eyes and sank into the bliss. She floated on the stream, then submerged into it. The warm infinite power of the stream passed all around her, through her. It touched every part of her body inside and out, though only a tiny fraction. It mostly concentrated inside her injuries.

It coaxed her, whispered to her, called for her to fully embrace it. It was an ocean infinitely larger than even the Great Sea. Infinitely larger than the world itself. She could experience more if she but reached out for it. There was a limit to how much a single dancer could embrace, but she could augment that capacity…

Zaiyera squeezed her eyes shut and let out a sharp breath. The rapture winked out in an instant. After several controlled breaths,

Zaiyera opened her eyes to see the healer's empty yet seeing gaze upon her.

"I think perhaps you are safe to continue on your way," the elderly woman said.

A stab of anxiety shot through Zaiyera's stomach, but the woman smiled at her and lay a hand on her forehead. Warmth still radiated from her, but this time absent the flow. "Be at peace, girl. Life has many lessons yet to teach you." She stepped away. "My home is always open, should you return."

Zaiyera blinked at the woman in confusion but stood. "I … thank you, *uluma*."

The healer gave a subtle bow of her head. "May Shakimah grace your travels."

* * *

The hunger came as soon as they were mounted and on their way. Its coming was no surprise, but the intensity of it nearly knocked Zaiyera from Sadiq's back.

Zhuyun and Jaide had positioned themselves on either side of her, while the Dor'haigheners rode behind them. The ever-silent Kima rode behind Jaide.

"The healing has taken a toll?" Zhuyun asked in a low voice beside her.

Staring at the base of Sadiq's neck, Zaiyera responded with a barely perceptible nod.

"We've made good time," Jaide announced. "If we camp by nightfall, we will reach Trystia by tomorrow evening."

"And hopefully before he has arrived," Dyren responded from behind.

Zaiyera stole a glance at Kima. If the Zalrabian man felt anything from Dyren's words, he gave no outward indication. She was starting to wonder if he would be a problem when the time came to face his brother.

As the day wore on, everyone rode mostly in silence, to Zaiyera's relief. It took most of her concentration just to manage the twisting, burning pain that seared the inside of her skin. She might as well have not received the healing, for any relief she might have gotten came at the cost of torturous withdrawals. And the deeper injuries—though mended—still hurt.

"How familiar are you with this region?" Jaide asked after they set camp near a patch of niyabi trees. The golden glow of the flames danced across her face, revealing a hint of her feminine features if one knew to look close enough.

"Confident enough to get us there," Zaiyera replied.

Jaide nodded. "Good. My knowledge of the east central region is rudimentary at best."

"You're correct in that we'll reach it by nightfall tomorrow," Zaiyera said in a tight voice.

Jaide studied her face, the Viriksani's eyes glinting in the fire's light like green gems. "Are you well?"

Head lowered, Zaiyera flicked her gaze across the camp. Dyren and Malker sat together in conversation while Zhuyun and Barum shared more audible conversation with more than a few laughs. Kima sat on the far side from them to himself, staring into the flames. "I'm ... hurting, Jaide."

The other woman sighed. "Is there anything I can do to help?"

Zaiyera looked at the moonlit surroundings. For a small mercy, the sand dunes had begun to appear again, though they were too far in the distance. There were some large mounds, however. And they were far enough to hide her from view.

"I need perhaps half an hour," Zaiyera replied. "I need to dance. Otherwise the ... it will drive me insane."

Jaide nodded. "Do what you must, yes? Zhuyun and I will keep everyone otherwise engaged if need be."

Zaiyera looked up at her, and the Viriksani rolled her eyes. "Seriously, woman. You think the Yuntaiman and I didn't figure out that we each knew about," she lowered her voice to a whisper, "your situation? You give us so little credit, *niyima*."

"How long?" Zaiyera asked, her voice heavy with resignation.

"Weeks, now," Jaide replied. "And pick your chin up off the ground, Kushtanji. No one else suspects you, or we'd have told you by now. Go do your dance. And be careful out there alone."

Zaiyera made the usual excuse that she needed time alone to think and meditate, which wasn't untrue. Zhuyun responded with a knowing nod, while the others shrugged, having gotten used to her oddness by now.

Gusts of wind blew across the dark rolling mounds of the desert. The sound of insects and the occasional call of a nocturnal lizard layered the night.

Zaiyera turned back to look at the campfire, now a small beacon of light in the distance. Once she was certain no one followed, she went around the hill.

As soon as Zaiyera was out of sight of the camp, calmness settled over her. The pain of the hunger dulled under the inner peace she felt at being alone. She took a long deep breath, and blew it out, slow and steady between her parted lips.

She began to dance. She moved beside the stream, feeling its power. If she had been an untainted streamdancer, she would not have pierced the stream as a true dancer did. She would have dipped her hand into the stream, swept it out to become the flow, and moved it around and through her body. She would have immersed herself in it and swam in its blissful currents, created an outward expression of her will with it.

Instead, she danced beside the stream, feeling it rush around her, beside her. Instead of dipping her hand into it, she waved her hand over it, feeling the emanating power, but not touching it. Her yellow dance-resin began to trail her movements.

With the grace and precision of a lifetime of dancing the blade and to a lesser degree, the stream, Zaiyera moved with the wide, flourish-ing, sweeping motions of a Samharan streamdancer, her robes rippling as she swung her arms, swept her legs, swayed her body.

Then she closed her eyes. She held her hands out in front of her, one hand extended farther out than the other. She bent her legs and began to move in a wide circle.

At first she simply walked, her arms extended, torso turned slightly toward the inside of the circle she walked. Her body didn't rise and fall with each step but remained slightly lowered as she used the strength in her legs to keep her height steady.

Zaiyera felt the stream slip away to be replaced by her *haiyasha;* her own personal stream. Immersed in the new dance Zhuyun had taught her, Zaiyera felt her inner power flow through her body. It flowed through her blood, her skin, seeped in and out of her pores.

She continued the new dance, eyes closed, hearing, smelling, *feeling* everything around her as she never had before. Time ceased and the hunger faded away as she became one with the desert. As with the other times Zhuyun had guided her in the Yintish dance, Zaiyera felt a sense of wholeness she hadn't felt since the day she'd given up the dance. It still wasn't complete, though. There still remained that bit of emptiness, like a void longing to be filled but never would.

Zaiyera opened her eyes to see a brighter night. Though the moon's pale light illuminated the majestic desert, Zaiyera felt as though she might see just as well if it hadn't been there.

This is new. Intrigued, she looked around. She could see farther into the distance, she felt as though her hearing where more acute, and even the smell of the campfire, from so far away, reached her nose.

As time passed, the new effect faded, and with it a sense of loss. Zaiyera stood where she was and focused on her breathing. The first dance had dulled the ravenous hunger to something manageable, but the second dance had banished it completely. It might not be permanent, but it was the most relief she'd ever had. This night, the dance hadn't diminished the withdrawals like the previous ones. Zaiyera suspected it was the healing she'd received.

That realization cast an ominous pall over an otherwise glorious dance on a beautiful night. What if Zhuyun hadn't taught her this dance to augment her ability to manage the withdrawals. Would her previous methods have been enough?

Zaiyera forced herself to shake off those dark questions with darker implications. For whatever reason, Goddess Shakimah blessed her to have met the Yuntaiman who'd subsequently given her such a tremendous gift. Perhaps the Goddess in Her wisdom had something in mind for her. Zaiyera wouldn't know until she did.

She walked back to camp with a clearer head, slightly less pained body, and spirits lifted. The others noticed immediately. While Zhuyun and Jaide made a show of it by teasing, the Dor'haigheners looked at her with confusion.

"I wish alone-time worked as well for me as it does for you, Zaiyera," Malker said. "I don't know if I've ever seen you so content."

"As much as I'm loath to pull your sudden good spirits down," Dyren said, "we must talk about tomorrow."

"Trystia," Zaiyera said, her mood indeed dampened.

"Trystia," Dyren echoed. "If we reach it before the shad … Malhadiev, we'll need to be ready. We don't know how close he'll be, so we can't afford to spend any time planning."

"What if he's already there?" Barum asked. "What would our strategy be, then?"

"I've a feeling if he beats us to Trystia, we'd need only follow the destruction right to him," Malker said.

On the other side of the fire, Kima ground his teeth as he glowered at the junior shydon hunter.

Malker met the man's glare with his own steady gaze. "I mean you no disrespect, Kima Imrian, but we must speak frankly. We can't afford to slink around the topic because you don't like what we're here to do."

"That's enough, Malker," Dyren said. He looked over at Kima. "My subordinate could have worded things more discretely, but he's not wrong. We must discuss this. Your input would be welcome."

Kima laughed. "My input. You mean you'd like me to help you plan how to kill Malhadiev. You wish me to plot my brother's death with you."

"If you've any knowledge that would make such an outcome unnecessary," Dyren said, "we'd be quick to hear it."

Kima made an angry sound.

Malker's gaze remained lowered through the exchange. He looked back to Kima again, his expression softened. "Apologies for my harshness. I understand what you must be feeling—"

"You understand nothing, northerner—"

"I *understand* … what you're going through, sir. The darkness of the taint has passed through my family as well. I carry that pain with me every day. I wear it as a second skin beneath my uniform, feel its weight beneath my insignia." He placed a hand over the left side of his chest, where the Order of Shadow Hunters insignia sat beneath his robes.

The camp went silent for a while, everyone wrapped in their individual thoughts.

"He was always very focused," Kima said after some time. He looked up to meet everyone's gaze in turn. "Even when we were boys. He had a narrow kind of focus that left him blind to anything on the sides. If he had a goal, he would see it through no matter what. Nothing would move him from it, unless it was a diversion to ultimately aid his goal."

Kima scowled at the campfire. "If he decides to focus on any of you, he will not stop until you are dead. If he wields the kind of power you say he does, expect that force to be directed at you with relentless focus until you are no more. He sees your Dor'haighen king as a tyrant, and I don't disagree with him. But if you stand between him and your king, he will destroy you."

"This focus he has," Zaiyera said carefully. "Is this something we can work with to stop him?"

"I don't know," Kima replied. "My hope is that when we confront Malhadiev, he will relent when he sees me alive. I will speak to him, try to persuade him to another path." He looked at everyone with an expression bordering on pleading. "I don't know what that path will be, but I ask for a chance. I know him. I can reach him. It's all I ask."

Despite the doubtful expressions around the fire, Dyren kept his expression neutral. He sat in silence and thought on Kima's words before he finally spoke. "You will have your opportunity, Kima Imrian. I won't lie to you, however. I don't like your chances. Malhadiev is your brother, but he is a very different man from the last time you saw him. I say this with experience on two different occasions that nearly resulted in our deaths"—he indicated himself and Malker—"but *did* result in the deaths of the rest of my team.

"The man you knew is not the man we pursue." He held up a hand when Kima went to speak. "However, I give you my word. You will have your chance to speak with him. If there is any possibility this can end without more violence and death, I would welcome it."

"If I'm able to reach him," Kima said, his tone growing angry. "It *will* result in death. Your king will never allow him to live."

"I cannot speak for the king of Dor'haighen," Dyren admitted. "All I can offer is my promise to see to it that he is given fair trial for his crimes."

"A waste of time and you know it," Kima scoffed. "What good would a trial do? Assuming your king doesn't lie about what Malhadiev has become, Eredin will have him executed the moment Malhadiev sets foot inside Nanshaigha."

"Again," Dyren repeated, "I cannot speak for King Eredin. I don't deny the real possibility of your words, but I also can't deny that whatever may or may not happen, we cannot allow Malhadiev to continue his course. He's destroyed cities and ended many lives."

"So you say," Kima growled.

"And, so say I," Jaide added.

Kima looked startled at the sound of her voice, as though he'd forgotten anyone but he and Dyren were there.

"I saw with my own eyes what he's done and is capable of."

"We've no need to steer the conversation off track," Dyren said. "In freeing you, we have made ourselves fugitives in the hope that you can help us stop Malhadiev. You wish a chance to speak with him that you might convince him to stand down. You've my word that you'll have that opportunity."

Kima and the senior shydon hunter stared at one another for several tense heartbeats before the Zalrabian man looked away. "I suppose this is all I can expect. If I can get him to relent, might that he can go into exile. Board a ship and leave across the Great Sea."

He got up without another word and went to untie his bedroll. They watched in silence as Kima rolled onto his side, his back to the crackling fire and everyone else.

With nothing left to be said, everyone cleaned up the camp, careful with bits of food so as to not attract any hungry animals nearby.

Crouched over his bedroll, Dyren looked up at Zaiyera's approach.

"A word, please," she said in a low voice.

"I know what you're about to say," Dyren replied.

"You give him false hope."

"I gave him no such thing," Dyren said. "I told him we would figure it out as we go. You heard the conversation, did you not?"

"I heard you imply that there may be hope that his brother would survive," Zaiyera hissed. "You let him believe it was even a possibility, knowing that you've no intention of letting that man live."

"What would you have had me say?" Dyren whispered back. "What words would you have had me speak to the man? Despite every account and every bit of news confirming the monster his brother has become, he still holds out hope that Malhadiev can be redeemed."

Dyren looked past Zaiyera to the lump on the other side of the fire that was Kima. "You know as well as I that there is no hope for him. He's fallen too far."

"Would you have considered there to be hope if he hadn't fallen so far?" Zaiyera asked before she thought better of it."

Dyren frowned at that. "What does that have to do with any of this?"

"You said he's fallen too far to be redeemed," Zaiyera said. "Does that mean he would have been spared, had he not taken all those lives? Maybe if he'd only syphoned one or two instead of countless."

"Only syphon ..." Dyren shook his head. "What are you asking? If we would spare his life if he were merely a darklancer? How much experience have you had with a tainted lancer, Zaiyera Tuneesh?"

Far more than you, Zaiyera thought.

"Once they've tasted the lifestream of another, touched that extra power and sidestepped the lifeprice, there's no turning back. The addiction is too strong. The difference between a darklancer and a shadowlancer is time. Nothing more or less."

"Would that you were this candid with him." Zaiyera jabbed a thumb over her shoulder. "I feel uncomfortable leading a man by his hopes only to dash them later."

Dyren looked down as he nodded. "Fear not, Zaiyera. I suspect Malhadiev himself will convince Kima that he's too far gone."

"And, what if Kima decides he wants to save his brother no matter what he's become?" Zaiyera asked.

Dyren's face hardened, his icy blue eyes as chilly as the desert night. "You already know the answer to that."

43

Sheikha Jawahir clasped her hands behind her back to keep herself from pacing. Word had come two days ago that the *kivuli dayasa* was walking, *walking*, in a straight line for Trystia. The wife of Sheikh Jegried had also sent word of her flight preceding her husband's death.

Jawahir exhaled a regretful sigh. She hadn't liked Jegried as much as his father. She hadn't liked him at all, actually. His trade terms were mostly one-sided and he exhibited a coldness toward the lower class of society she didn't appreciate. But Zalrabi had been a trade partner and ally.

Now, it was rubble. Jegried's palace, that is. Malhadiev had slaughtered every man and woman who'd stood between himself and Jegried, then leveled the sheikh's palace. Yet he'd left most of the city intact.

That was odd, considering how much of other cities the madman had destroyed. As news poured in over the months about *kivuli dayasa's* actions, Jawahir had been trying to make sense of it all. There must be a way to puzzle out some a pattern to the man's actions. The only consistent news she'd gleaned from survivors was that Malhadiev had a potent disdain for Samharan rulers and the king of Dor'haighen.

The musty smell of camels filled her nostrils as the *dakhiva* of Trystia assembled into ranks. Scimitars and shamshirs glinted in the sun. The robes and torso armor of the fearless *dakhiva* shone as green as the blue-green waves of the Great Sea. The proud warriors of Trystia stood tall with spears gripped in tight fists, and swords at their hips.

The mounted units sat erect and focused out at the ocean of sand beyond.

Imrik stepped to the base of the platform and gave a stiff warrior's bow, right hand to left breast. "My Sheikha Jawahir, praise your name. Preparations are nearly complete. The *dakhiva* are in position, secondary troops are nearly assembled as well. We have spear-throwers and archers positioned at the city walls and on rooftops."

"And the streamdancers?" Jawahir asked, still surveying the forces.

"They have accepted your orders with hesitancy, my Sheikha."

Jawahir pressed her full dark lips together. The warrior stream-dancers wished to split into two ranks; one to protect their sheikha, and one at the head of the troops. Jawahir understood the thinking, and in any other situation, it would have been a sound strategy.

But not here. Not with such a monster coming. Jawahir took every account that came to Trystia seriously. News of the wanton devastation had been bad enough, but the stories of the defeated streamdancers were especially troubling. *Kivuli dayasa* had syphoned every single dancer he'd encountered. Every one.

"I want their reassurance again, *Hara Dakhiva*," Jawahir said formally. "I need them to bolster the main troops and your *dakhiva* in hopes of tiring out *kivuli dayasa,* that he might be struck by blade or projectile. If our forces strike him down, it will be a great victory and an end to the nightmare. If we fail ... the warriors are to mount our fastest camels and be away from here as quickly as possible to spread news to every city between here and the northern border."

Jawahir resisted the urge to sigh. She hoped the streamdancers would be successful in gathering the dancers of every other city in a final stand against the man. The hope was as slim as it was naive.

She looked down into *Hara Dakhiva* Imrik's concerned eyes and softened her expression. "I understand their hesitancy and your own, my loyal soldier. But we cannot risk making this man more powerful.

By all rights I should send you all away and confront him myself. It isn't any of you that he wants."

"With respect, my sheikha," Imrik said. "I would sooner drive my own blade through my heart and out my back, than turn it to you and flee. Every citizen, soldier, streamdancer, and *dakhiva* feels the same." He gave another respectful bow. "You can command us to our deaths, this day, or you can give the one command we will never obey." Imrik unsheathed his dagger and placed it at his own throat. "Do you wish to command my execution for insubordination, my sheikha?"

Sheikha Jawahir kept her expression firm to keep the tears at bay. "Remove that blade from your neck, *Hara Dakhiva*," she commanded. "How will you guard me if you're dead?"

Imrik responded with a questioning frown. "My sheikha?"

Jawahir shifted her weight so that her scimitar became visible from her left hip.

Imrik's eyes widened. "My—"

Jawahir held up a hand. "You know as well as I that there will be no stopping him, but there is always luck. I wouldn't escape him anyway. So if today is my final day, I will end it beside all of you."

Imrik left to coordinate with the forces and reiterate her orders to the streamdancers. Sheikha Jawahir remained on her platform, a figure of bravery that bolstered her people. Today the weight of leadership felt especially heavy.

As dusk arrived, even her own shadow looked as though it fled *kivuli dayasa's* coming. Chukita cats darted through the unusually barren streets, yipping at each other. Vultures stood on rooftops, looming over the assembled forces like authorities of death itself. Perhaps they were. The large birds had shared this world with humans long enough to equate large, assembled bodies like this with an impending feast.

Part of her wanted to take up a spear and skewer one of the birds, yet what fault of it was theirs? No force of women or men had ever marched at the orders of the great scavengers.

Imrik returned, dusk casting grim shadows over his face. "The forces are positioned, as are those hidden throughout the city streets.

Catapults are armed and ready, and civilians have been advised to flee as soon as we have *kivuli dayasa's* full attention."

Jawahir gave him a curt nod. Hopefully, after she and her forces were gone, *kivuli dayasa* would show her people the same mercy he had to those of Zalrabi. She didn't take for granted that he would, and so she wanted her people out of Trystia once it was certain Jawahir had his focus. Still, she held out hope. "Very well."

"May I approach, My Sheikha?" At her responding nod, Imrik hesitated, then stepped up onto the platform and knelt before her. "Sheikha Jawahir ... My Sheikha. I must plead one last time that you flee Trystia. Before we fall, we will leave him depleted so that he must rest. You can reach Xair, Viriksan, or even Lirshan. The people of Trystia *must* have their sheikha to lead them."

Jawahir reached down and lifted his chin so that he looked into her eyes. "The people will face the choice of their new ruler whether I flee today or fight beside you. It is me that *kivuli dayasa* comes for. Not them. Rise, Imrik."

The *hara dakhiva* stood. Tears welled in his fierce light brown eyes.

Jawahir smiled at him. "If this is to be the end, let it be the greatest end in all of Samhar. Let it be heard and spoken about across this land and every other. Today we fight to the last and meet Goddess Shakimah with pride and honor.

Imrik pounded his chest. "It has been an honor to serve you, My Sheikha. Today, it will be my honor to die for you."

"Beside me," Jawahir corrected. "Now, we—"

A horn sounded from the city walls. On top of the platform Jawahir and Imrik looked beyond the giant mass of troops to see a lone figure walking toward them.

44

For most of the day, no one spoke much. Everyone fell deeper into their thoughts as the minutes and hours passed, and they drew closer to Trystia.

Barum Hurst shared the occasional comment with Jaide or Malker, while Zhuyun often rode up beside her with a bit of conversation or a question. Dyren said mostly nothing. The senior shydon hunter rode in what looked to be a constant state of thoughtfulness, likely going over his past confrontations with Malhadiev, and how he would combat that much power.

Zaiyera found herself doing the same. She turned that battle over and over in her mind. She thought of every gesture, or sometimes lack thereof. She remembered what it was like to see the flow mold to his will, and how much bigger it had been than the combined efforts of Dyren and Malker.

She had to assume that power was far greater, now. Even supposing Shatr would hold against such immense amounts of the stream, Zaiyera could not. It would be like holding a flat piece of iron against a falling wall. The iron may not break, but the weight of the wall would crush the one holding the iron.

Despite how it tickled the hunger inside her, Zaiyera thought a lot about the stream, and how a dancer accessed it. Whether dipping a finger or a hand or submerging one's entire being into the infinite power of the flow, it was still accessed the same. The stream rushed around and through the object that entered it, and that object would draw a bit of it out and manipulate it. Such uses were mostly dependent on the knowledge and to some degree, creativity, of the dancer.

They stopped at midday to rest under the shade of a cluster of niyabi trees when the raiders found them.

"Jakta skree." Barum unsheathed his longsword at the sight of the not-so-distant dust cloud. "This, we don't need."

"Did we ever?" Jaide quipped, drawing her shamshir.

"By Jokolta Himself," Malker Argen growled. "I'm in no mood." He snatched his sword from its sheath.

"Zhuyun Xaiylin," Dyren said. "What do your sharp eyes see? How many?"

The Yuntaiman peered into the distance for several moments before answering, "Ten. But the dust cloud obscures them. Maybe twelve."

"Hardly seems fair," Jaide said, flicking her wrist and spinning her shamshir.

"How typical is a band of raiders to have a lancer among them?" Dyren asked Zaiyera and Jaide.

"Difficult to say," Zaiyera replied. "The larger the number, the more likely it is. But we might be lucky. We're still far enough northeast."

"What does that matter?" Malker asked.

"Proximity to Rexzen," Zaiyera answered.

The riders were close enough that everyone could see them now. Eight men and four women bore down on them. Their dark faces were painted white, while their lips were painted black. Their eyes and mouths were opened wide as though madness had overtaken them. They held swords with wavy blades high over their heads while hooting and shouting.

One of their number, however, remained silent and had no weapon raised.

"They have a lancer," Malker said, also spotting the man. He had the calmest expression of the band. As though he were concentrating. "We need to remove him as soon as possible."

"I will deal with him," Zaiyera said, moving to the front of the group. She drew Shatr forth from its sheath and held it at her side.

"This dagger would do me more good to pick my teeth as fend off one of those swords," Kima said from the back of the group.

"You'll get a weapon available to you in short order, good man," Barum Hurst said. He hefted his big broadsword and lay the flat of it over his shoulder. "If you can fight, grab one from a dead bandit. If you've no experience, ain't no shame in keepin' safe. We all have our specialties."

Zhuyun stepped up beside Zaiyera. "How far away can you cut through the flow?"

Zaiyera shook her head. "I don't really know. I don't have to be right in front of them, though."

He turned his mischievous expression on Zaiyera. "You can handle at least two of them, ah?"

Zaiyera answered his question with a narrow-eyed grin.

Zhuyun returned the grin, then sprinted off toward the raiders.

"Jakta skree!" she heard Barum exclaim from somewhere behind her, just before she took off after the Yuntaiman.

Adrenaline pumped through Zaiyera's veins. She couldn't stop herself from laughing as she ran behind the faster Zhuyun. This may well be their last battle together before they face *kivuli dayasa*.

The raiders gave a hoot of laughter at the sight of the pair sprinting toward them. The streamdancer at the front of the group and to the right began to move his hands. He was just finishing his pattern when Zaiyera thrust Shatr toward the middle of his hands, twisted her wrist, and flicked the blade upward.

A transparent whip burst apart in his hand the instant it took form. The man looked at his hands in shock, then at Zaiyera, who had angled toward him.

Zhuyun slid his staff forward to hold it at one end, then slammed the butt of the other end into the ground. At the same time, he jumped and vaulted himself up. The staff bowed and propelled the Yuntaiman into the air.

As soon as he was airborne, Zhuyun pulled his staff forward from his right side and gripped it in the middle. In that same instant, he reached the first of the riders. Holding the staff horizontal in front of him, the left side of the staff struck a bandit square in the chest.

The force of the blow unseated the woman with a loud exhale of breath. The force would have sent the midair Zhuyun spinning off balance, but he'd timed it well. An instant after the left side of his staff struck, the raider on his right side had arrived. To his credit, the man tried to duck, but Zhuyun's maneuver had come too quickly. The end of the staff connected with the bridge of the bandit's nose. He fell from his saddle with a face covered in blood.

Zaiyera leapt toward the streamdancer and chopped her scimitar at his side. The man leaned away, narrowly avoiding the blade. She landed in a roll and came to her feet while he circled around, arms moving as he touched the stream again.

As before, just as he finished the pattern, Zaiyera thrust her scimitar toward the middle of each hand and chopped down. The transparent crescent-shaped blade broke in half as soon as it appeared. The man's shout of frustration turned into a cry of surprise and pain.

His camel had barely completed its turn when Jaide caught up to him and drove her shamshir into his side. The streamdancer slumped and bounced in the saddle before finally sliding free. He hit the ground in a heap and lay squirming, his blood soaking into the sand around him.

Two bandits turned toward Zaiyera when the ground behind them rippled.

A pair of spear-like appendages burst out of the ground, followed by many, many more.

"SPINEBACK!" Zaiyera shouted.

As the words left her mouth, a huge creature with a flat body emerged in an eruption of sand and rock. Its flat back was covered in sections of plate armor, the sides ending in hooked spikes.

The unfortunate raiders only had enough time to register Zaiyera's words before two pincers grabbed them up and snapped them in half. A second set of inner pincers swept them into the monster's waiting maw even as it scuttled toward Zaiyera.

Already in a full out sprint, Zaiyera wove between the terrified bandits, all thoughts of battle lost. The giant centipede-like creature pursued the bandits and defenders scattering before it.

Wide-eyed, Kima wheeled his camel around. Zhuyun had already been running for him, and quickly snatched the reins from Kima's hands even as he was—needlessly—urging his camel away.

Sadiq groaned in terror and loped after the other two camels. The bandits still on camelback blew past Zaiyera, right behind the others. Zaiyera found herself at the back of the fleeing pack. The monstrous spineback centipede scuttled after her, its multi-sectioned body swaying as it moved, much like snake. She could hear those countless legs thumping the ground in rapid succession.

Shatr already sheathed, Zaiyera gritted her teeth and sprinted for her life. She heard, and felt, the thumpthumpthumpthumpthump of pursuit drawing closer. She wouldn't outrun it. Her friends were turning about in an attempt to fight it off and give her a chance, but they wouldn't get into position quick enough.

Jaide shouted from the side. "Keep running and come to your left!"

Zaiyera did as she said. From the corner of her eye, she saw Jaide produce a dagger. The Viriksani warrior leaned low in the saddle and urged her complaining camel as close as she dared. The spineback was apparently fully focused on Zaiyera, the easiest target to catch.

Jaide came a little closer. "When I hit it, move for me!"

Zaiyera was panting, now. The thumping and scuttling legs and snapping pincers were right on her back.

As soon as she was in line with its head, Jaide lifted her dagger and waited. When the swaying armor plated body curled away from her, the vulnerable flesh was exposed. She only had that quick moment, but it was enough. Jaide Amadi let fly her dagger. Her timing was perfect and her aim was true.

The dagger punched into soft flesh. The spineback centipede let out a cry that sounded like glass grinding on rock. It flinched and curled in toward the wound, also in Jaide's direction.

Zaiyera dug for her last reserves of energy and surged forward and to the left. Jaide rode up beside her and reached down. Zaiyera grabbed Jaide's forearm and jumped while the other woman pulled. With Jaide's help Zaiyera threw herself across the camel's back, just at the base of its shoulders.

Jaide urged her mount on and away from the angered spineback. "Kima!" she shouted. "This way!"

Kima looked over his shoulder with a questioning expression.

"He follows you!" Jaide pointed at Sadiq, keeping pace just behind him.

Kima looked back and spotted the camel. He leaned his mount left, and Sadiq followed.

Dyren and Malker touched the stream and drew a conservative amount of the flow. They each produced a transparent whip and lashed several of the many legs.

The spineback skidded into a sideways tumble, its long body thrashing like a worm as sand splashed all around it.

"Sadiq!" Zaiyera shouted. *"Kaya yip! Kaya yip!"* Sadiq grunted in response and angled toward them.

Jaide guided her camel closer until it was alongside the other.

With Jaide's help, Zaiyera turned on her side. The camel's bumpy gait threatened to bounce her down on the animal's neck, but she pushed with her right hand while Jaide held onto her.

Zaiyera bent her left lower leg, and lifted her right, while Jaide moved her camel right beside Sadiq.

"All right, girl," Jaide yelled, her voice fully feminine, now. "One. Two. Three!"

Jaide growled loudly as she helped Zaiyera propel herself up and onto Sadiq's back. She slipped into the saddle and grabbed hold of a tuft of mane.

"Ip yip!"

Sadiq surged forward with a burst of speed.

Zaiyera looked over her shoulder to see that Barum on one side and the shydon hunters on the other were harrying the giant centipede, giving her the time she'd needed to get mounted.

Defenders and raiders alike let their camels have their heads, and the animals ran with all speed.

Behind them, the spineback centipede scuttled in pursuit. Zaiyera looked back. It wasn't catching up, but they weren't pulling away from it either.

She heard one of the bandits shout an order, and the band broke off and pulled away in another direction. Zaiyera silently cursed them, as she knew the centipede would continue to pursue her party. It would take more energy to alter its course.

As expected, the spineback ignored the fleeing raiders and continued after Zaiyera and the others.

"It's gaining," Malker warned. He looked at the three Samharans. "Will it tire? Will it give up if we can hold on?"

"Our mounts will tire before it does," Zaiyera shouted back.

"One shot," Dyren said to Malker. "We combine for one shot only. Minimal power."

Malker gave a curt nod.

Together, the two shydon hunters moved their free hands, sweeping their arms, in sync as they drew from the stream and guided the flow. They ended the pattern in a left-to-right sweep of their hands, as though drawing a diagonal crescent shape in the air.

The offensive lance produced a transparent crescent blade that wavered into the air behind them and sped toward the centipede. It struck the monster across the face and sent it into a nosedive in the ground.

The squirming plate-armored body swayed as it pitched forward, numerous legs waving in the air like hundreds of long fingers.

Dyren and Malker turned forward again, and the companions raced onward. Behind them, the screeching spineback squirmed on the ground left to right until it finally righted itself. It continued its pursuit, but the camels had put enough distance between them that after a few anxious moments, the monster finally gave up.

Zaiyera looked back to see it slow down and burrow into the ground.

They pulled their camels up into a more manageable gallop. They rode on in silence for a while, everyone casting wary glances behind them to ensure the monster was gone.

Finally, they slowed the camels down to a walk. Foamy saliva fell from the exhausted animals' floppy lips. They grunted in agitation.

"I hope nothing else tries to devour us while we're defending ourselves," Malker said.

"I just hope nothing else tries to devour us, regardless of the circumstances," Barum replied. "That might have been the worse experience of my life."

"Has your memory of the frost worva faded already?" the junior shydon countered.

Barum grunted. "Good point."

The golden glow of sunset washed over the land when the first shadowy signs of Trystia appeared on the horizon.

Zaiyera felt a weight settle into her stomach when their destination finally came in sight.

"Jakta skree," Barum breathed. "Tell me that isn't what I think it is."

Zaiyera felt a lump growing in her throat. They pulled to a stop and gazed out across a sea of dead soldiers extending beyond the towering sandstone walls.

45

Kima slid off his camel. He looked around in open-mouthed horror at the endless wave of bodies lining the ground all the way up to the walls of Trystia. "What happened here? What could have done this?"

Zaiyera and the others shared a look.

Kima turned his back to them. "He didn't do this." When no one responded, he said more firmly, "He did *not* do this. You can't believe he is capable of this. One man."

"We've … experienced his power firsthand," Dyren said, his usual firm tone touched with a bit of care. "His power has since grown, and with it, unfortunately, his madness."

Kima rounded on the senior shydon. "Stop *saying* that! You bring me to the aftermath of a war and expect me to believe Malhadiev singlehandedly killed all of them?" He waved a hand to encompass the mass of death. Those aren't all regular soldiers, shydon hunter. They are *DAKHIVA*! The elite warrior class of Samhar."

"And no match for a single shadowlancer with his power," Dyren said, his voice soft.

The senior shydon hunter was making an effort to put this as gently as he could, but there was no way to do it.

Zaiyera slid off Sadiq's back and walked up to Kima.

Tears welled in his reddening eyes, threatening to spill down his cheeks. "He didn't do all of this. Even if he came to fight, he must have soldiers at his back."

"If what you say is true," she said, quietly, "then your brother and whatever soldiers he amassed still slaughtered this entire force to a man." She spread her hand out at the carnage. "Without losing a single soldier of his own. These uniforms are all Trystian, and as you just said, a good number, *dakhiva*."

The ground rumbled. At first, everyone looked around in alarm, thinking the spineback had followed them after all. Then an explosion boomed from behind the city walls, nearly a quarter mile away.

"There's no more time," Dyren said. "Whatever the situation, here, we will learn the truth of it now."

Zaiyera and Kima mounted their camels again and the group rode straight down a path between the bodies that left little doubt that this was Malhadiev's doing. It was too neat.

As soon as they reached the walls, Zaiyera dismounted. She wrapped her arms around Sadiq's curved neck. "Stay away and be safe, my dear friend. You've survived so much to bear me so far. I'll not have you perish here."

"What are you doing?" Dyren demanded. "He'll be further into the city."

Zaiyera released her humpbacked companion and turned to regard the shydon. "Ride your camel into this if you wish. But you'll find them less cooperative when more of those explosions happen."

Dyren appeared to think on that for a moment. He responded with a curt nod the looked to Malker. "We dismount."

They secured their mounts to a hitch just inside the city walls—Sadiq loitering nearby—and continued on foot.

Bodies, mostly armored, lay strewn about the ground in pools of dried blood. Limbs lay flopped this way and that, bodies twisted in awkward angles.

Many lay on their backs and sides, staring lifelessly at the sky or the feet of the party as they passed. The coppery smell of blood filled her nose, mingled with the stomach-churning smell burning flesh and death. So much death. Hundreds of bodies.

Zaiyera swallowed the bile creeping up her throat. It didn't seem possible that a single man, no matter how powerful, could have slaughtered so many.

"Tears of the ancients," Zhuyun breathed. "In all my travels across many lands and the Great Sea, I've never seen anything so terrible."

They passed between collapsed buildings, blasted walls, and huge holes in the ground where it looked like it had simply exploded.

An armored body shifted under another lifeless corpse. Zaiyera ran to help. With Kima's help, she pulled the woman free. Her *dakhiva* armor was stained and soaked with blood.

"M ... mon ...ster," she said. "Im ... possible to ... to," she convulsed once, and a final breath fled her body.

Zaiyera closed the *dakhiva's* eyes and lay her down. She remained kneeling over the woman while Jaide approached. The Viriksani and Kima knelt with Zaiyera around the expired *dakhiva* and lowered their heads in prayer that Shakimah speed her journey from this life to the bliss of *Sojalleh*.

Zhuyun and the Dor'haigheners waited respectfully until the Samharan's were finished, then hurried on.

Another boom sounded in the distance. Farther toward the center of the city, an explosion lit the rapidly darkening sky. While the sun was almost down, fires from the rubble-strewn streets lit their way.

Shouting erupted from the same direction as the explosion. Everyone looked at each other and broke into a run. They climbed over crumbled walls, piles of rubble that had once been buildings and homes. Several times they came to a section of the street piled so high with rubble that they had to divert their path to get around it.

The once reddish-brown streets and buildings were now broken apart, covered in upturned soil, splashed with blood and covered with broken bodies. Injured survivors were few, but they were there.

"Sheikha Jawahir must have gotten word ahead of his arrival," Jaide said. "There are almost no civilians here."

Another explosion lit the darkened sky. Malker looked toward the light, then shouted, "incoming!"

Everyone curled against a nearby wall and covered their heads. Rocky debris—and softer things best not thought about—rained down on them. When it was over, they stood and moved on.

Zaiyera focused on her breathing; focused on the path ahead and the confrontation that awaited. But the massive amounts of the stream being used filled the air and sparked the hunger. Every time Malhadiev or whoever else accessed such huge amounts of the stream and wielded it, it felt like being hit by a wave. It was bliss, power, creation. She wanted it. *Needed* it.

She stole a glance at the others to ensure they weren't looking, then gave herself a slap across the face. *Focus!*

They continued their hike through the maze of broken streets, gradually working their way toward the center of Trystia. The city was huge, and though Zaiyera had never been here before, she'd grown up hearing the stories of Trystia's many red clay and sandstone towers, its large buildings and clean, bustling neighborhoods and marketplaces.

As a child, she'd imagined what it would be like to visit the famous city. She'd visualized herself running through the covered marketplaces, looking at all the intricately handwoven rugs, jewels, and precious metals from all across Samhar and other parts of the world.

She'd practically smelled the food, tasted the crisp cool fenberry juice, smelled the sweet burning incenses.

Now, awnings lay shredded on the street. Pottery coated the ground in pieces. Rugs and clothing, food and jewels, trampled and crushed.

"This can't be," Kima whispered. "Malhadiev would never have become such a monster. This is something else."

"Your answer is around the corner, yes?" Jaide called from the front of the group. "It looks like they're fighting in the city square."

"They?" Zaiyera called back.

In the flickering light of the burning buildings, she saw Jaide nod.

They moved to the edge of the partially crumbled wall and peered around the corner. A solitary figure wearing tan and dark brown robes stood in the middle of what was left of a burning pavilion.

Zaiyera caught movement on the roofs of several buildings. Archers. Fifteen bloody and battered streamdancers surrounded Malhadiev. Force of will alone must have kept them on their feet.

In the dancing light of the flames surrounded by the night, Malhadiev looked like the specter of death itself. He stood relaxed, even leaning his weight on one foot. Massive amounts of the stream swirled around him. Zaiyera gasped. The man was standing in the middle of a raging river of power. It would have taken every dancer in Trystia to handle that much of the flow. Maybe more.

"We can't win," Malker said from behind her. Zaiyera looked back. The junior shydon's mouth hung slack below eyes wide with fear. "No man should be able to wield that much power." He looked to Dyren. "We step out there, we're going to die, sir."

"That's possible," Dyren said. "Probably more than possible. But we're not going to let him reap any more destruction and death unchallenged." He gripped Malker by the shoulder. "Still your nerves, shadow hunter. This is our job. Remember your oath."

Malker took a steadying breath and gave a firm nod. "To bring light where there is shadow."

Dyren released his shoulder and gave it a pat. "To live in the light is to cast it upon shadow." He turned to address everyone, his face hardened with determination. "We split up and take up positions around him, concealed in the dark."

"Wherever there isn't anything burning," Jaide muttered.

Zaiyera turned to Kima. "Walk out with me. Try to talk to him."

"You want me to try to talk to him with you at my side." He looked at Shati in her hand. "With that blade in your grasp?"

"You see him with your own eyes," Zaiyera said. "Do you deny the destruction he's wrought? Would you feel comfortable walking out there alone to speak with him?"

A scream echoed from the pavilion, drowning out the crackling flames. They peeked around the wall and saw a laughing Malhadiev fling one of the streamdancers across the pavilion with a transparent whip wrapped around her ankle.

She hit the ground in a sideways tumble and kept going until a hunk of broken building stopped her. The woman rocked back onto her other side and lay still.

"We don't have time to debate this," Dyren hissed through gritted teeth. He looked to Barum. "Take up a position behind him and wait. If you find a spear, or anything that can be thrown, use it. Your sword is a last result."

Dyren looked to Jaide and Malker. You two will wait here. You're fast," he said to Jaide. "Malker can augment your abilities. Just as with Barum, try anything you can do from a distance first. You don't want to get in close unless you need to."

"Do *what*, from a distance?" Jaide asked. "Throw rocks?"

Dyren looked to Zhuyun. "Can that staff of yours harness the flow from friend and foe alike?"

"It is not the staff that does it, Dyren Faust," Zhuyun said. "But I catch your meaning. I can do what you ask."

The senior shydon nodded. "Good. I will have you beside me on the far side."

He turned his hard blue-eyed gaze back on Zaiyera and Kima. The flickering glow of the fires made the V-shaped scar on his left cheek look menacing. "You two are the hope that this can end peacefully. We pray that you can reach him, Kima, that there can be no more violence. But Zaiyera will be there to protect you."

Kima stared at the man. "He's my brother, shydon. I will reach him."

Zaiyera knew Dyren Faust didn't believe it for a second, but to the man's credit, he didn't let it show in his expression.

"Then, the blessings of your Goddess be with you," Dyren said.

Everyone started off toward their positions. Zhuyun hurried up to Zaiyera. "Remember what you've learned, my friend Zaiyera."

Zaiyera looked into his fierce eyes, wondering how she hadn't noticed before now that they were a deep hazel color. "You be careful as well, my friend."

Zhuyun held her gaze for a heartbeat longer, then gave a firm nod and left.

Zaiyera sat against the wall and leaned her head against it. "What do you plan to do?" she asked Kima. "What do you hope to accomplish?"

"I can reach him," Kima said. "I can."

Whether it was the many miles they'd traveled to this point, or the residual injuries that still throbbed in spite of the stream-healing, Zaiyera felt weariness drape over her shoulders like a heavy blanket. She'd never wanted anything to be over as much as she did this ordeal.

She peeked around the corner. The fallen streamdancer still lay where she was, either dead or unconscious. One less ally. The other dancers were talking to Malhadiev, though she couldn't make out their words. Malhadiev had so much power swirling about him, controlling it with such indifference, Zaiyera couldn't fathom what that must mean.

When she leaned back around the wall, Kima was staring at her. "I know you feel you can, Kima. I hope you do. I truly hope you do, because none of us want a fight out of this. But ..." She shook her head. *But what?* "Just ... be prepared for whichever outcome."

The ground shook beneath them so violently, it bounced Zaiyera and Kima away from the wall. They looked at each other, wide-eyed, and Zaiyera crawled over to peek around the wall.

Malhadiev was laughing again. He wielded two of the largest transparent whips Zaiyera had ever seen. They were as thick as the pillars of a building. Though she couldn't see his black dance-resin in the night, even with the scattered flames, she knew he danced the stream. No, not danced. He barely moved.

Kivuli dayasu slapped the giant whips on the ground repeatedly, cracking stone and blasting apart fountains and benches. The warrior streamdancers dove this way and that to get away from the violent onslaught. Every time one of them tried to touch the stream, they had to dive aside or be crushed.

Zaiyera turned back to Kima. "There's no more time. Let's go."

They stood, stared into each other's eyes, and took a deep breath. "I'll take the lead," Zaiyera said.

"No." Kima shook his head. "It should be me."

"If you go out there in front of me," Zaiyera replied, "it will look like you're my captive."

Kima looked like he wanted to argue the point, but he nodded his agreement.

Zaiyera stepped around the wall and walked out into the open square. She glanced back to see Kima following behind her. She kept Shatr in its sheath. Without the scimitar in her hand, she felt vulnerable; exposed.

A grin spread across Malhadiev's shadowy face as he drew back one of his gigantic whips to strike.

46

For whatever reason, Malhadiev hesitated. "You must be an incredibly powerful streamdancer to arrive here by yourself," he drawled. "Or you are otherwise a fool." He'd let the massive whips evaporate in the air and was standing with his arms crossed, a slanted grin on his face. "Has Jawahir sent you as well, while she cowers in her residence?"

"Hardly," Zaiyera answered. She surprised herself at how firm her voice sounded. It came out in stark contrast to the urge to bolt and be as far away from this place as possible.

Malhadiev's brow creased in puzzlement at the sight of her. "You look oddly familiar, woman. Perhaps it's the shadowy light cast by the flames."

The remaining streamdancers were mostly on the ground, having frozen midway through climbing back to their feet. They remained where they were, and Zaiyera could see the uncertainty on some of their faces. Should they move and try to attack while Malhadiev was distracted, or stay still and hope he forgot about them?

"We've met before, Malhadiev," Zaiyera said.

He tilted his head as he scrutinized her, though Zaiyera practically felt his lingering gaze slide up and down her frame a little longer than

503

necessary. "Well, now. This cannot be. The young lady with the shydon hunter friends? If I recall, I dropped a dune on you. How is it you survived?" He seemed not at all concerned. They might as well have been discussing the day over a cup of tea.

"I'm resourceful," Zaiyera replied.

"Nonsense," came the retort. "You must be a streamdancer to have survived that, yet I …" He leaned to the side to look around her. "You've brought another friend. Do you care nothing for the lives of others?"

"Does that mean you'll strike me down, Malhadiev?" Kima stepped around Zaiyera.

Malhadiev fell back a step. "Kima? How … I saw you die." The arrogant nonchalance faded to be replaced by something between disbelief and elation.

"Don't get too far from me," Zaiyera whispered. Either Kima didn't hear, or he ignored her.

"Hello, my brother," Kima Imrian said. "It's been some time. A year?"

Malhadiev stared at his younger brother as though he were a ghost. "Yes," he said absently. "About a year." He looked at Zaiyera, then back. "Have I fallen into madness that I hear and see the dead with my waking senses?"

"Not dead, Malhadiev," Kima said. "I survived. I've come a long way to find you again." He glanced at the surrounding streamdancers who remained on the ground, hesitant to so much as blink. "We've a lot to talk about."

Kima stopped about a dozen feet past Zaiyera. Malhadiev still had the flow swirling about him, but to a lesser degree, now. It was still a massive amount of power, and it called to her in a seductive whisper.

"Kima …" Malhadiev stared at him. "How is it possible? I saw you die. I saw—"

"You saw me attacked and fall while you yourself were still under attack," Kima said. "By the time I came to, everyone was gone or dead."

"Where did you go?" Malhadiev asked. His face hardened when he looked back at Zaiyera.

She met that heavy gaze firmly, though her hand tightened on Shatr's hilt.

"How did she find you?" Malhadiev said, still staring at her.

"We can talk about it," Kima said. "But we must do that away from here." He looked around at the destruction and carnage. "By the grace of Shakimah, Malhadiev. What have you done?"

"More than you can imagine, Kima. And we will talk here. I'm not finished with Trystia yet. It still has a ruler in need of removal."

"Why?" Kima asked. "She's a good and kind ruler."

"She dealt with Jegried," Malhadiev spat. "That's enough. You know what that greedy bastard was about."

"And you know it's not so simple as to simply not trade with another powerful city because you don't like its ruler, Malhadiev," Kima countered. "We both worked long enough—"

"What is this?" Malhadiev cut him short. "You've survived and been lost to me for a year, only to return and preach to me against removing the corruption that has infested our beloved Samhar? Where have you been all this time? Why did you not find me sooner? I'm sure word must have found you of my … deeds."

"If I could have reached you sooner," Kima said, "I would have."

This would turn sour, and quickly. Zaiyera watched the exchange, appreciating that Kima tried to dance around the topic of his incarceration.

"*What* prevented you from reaching me sooner, Kima?" Malhadiev asked, a tinge of suspicion in his voice as he stole another glance at Zaiyera.

"I was severely injured and left for dead," Kima said. "I made it to a nearby town where a healer tended me."

"For a year?" Malhadiev asked. He jerked his chin at Zaiyera. "And, what of the grand coincidence of a woman I thought I'd killed, stumbling across my brother, whom I thought dead?"

Malhadiev looked back to Kima, his expression conflicted. It was the most human he'd looked since Zaiyera had met him. "My heart leaps that you are alive, Kima, but I've done things to blacken it."

"Your heart is not black, Malhadiev," Kima replied. "You're a good man."

"I *was* a good man," Malhadiev shouted. He waved at the ruins of the city square and beyond. "Look around you. Do you see the actions of a good man? I've killed, Kima. Oh, I've killed more people than I can count. And I know she's told you what I've become. I don't deny it. I have syphoned many streamdancers. So many. I am … truly, kivuli dayasa. I dance in shadow. No. I no longer dance. I *am* shadow."

Kima's shoulders slumped. "You must stop this, Malhadiev. You can't go on killing and siphoning other dancers. Goddess Shakimah frowns upon such—"

Malhadiev's laughter cut him short. "Cities, villages, trade posts. I've leveled them all, killed many, and syphoned many. My power is beyond anything a man should be capable of wielding. Do you think Shakimah has not turned her eyes from me long ago?"

Kima opened his mouth, then closed it again.

Malhadiev softened. "My heart may be black as pitch, now, but you are my brother. Walk beside me again. I've already cleansed Samhar of the corruption of Sheikh Ahreid and Jegried." He pointed out into the night, at a distant structure barely visible. "Once I've disposed of Sheikha Jawahir, I will move on Rexzen. From there, the greedy king Eredin."

Kima looked crestfallen. "Brother. How many will you kill? Perhaps Eredin should be made to atone for his sins, but is this the way? The people of Dor'haighen are not cruel. They are a goodly people."

"How would you know that?" Malhadiev said. "Our last trade delegation to the north would have been the first time you'd been there. How could you know what Dor'haighen's people are like?"

"I … that is why I took so long to reach you, brother. I was nursed back to health in Dor'haighen. I've tried to speak to the king that he might treat with you; make things right."

"Nursed back to health in Dor'haighen." Malhadiev narrowed his eyes.

Still off to the side, Zaiyera settled her nerves and with a subtle flex clicked the hilt of Shatr loose from the scabbard. She kept still and searched the darkness with her eyes. Her companions would be in position by now, listening, though only Jaide would understand what was being said.

"Were you truly nursed back to health, brother, or were you imprisoned there?" When Kima looked surprised, Malhadiev laughed. "It's not difficult to figure out. Somehow you ended up in the north. Maybe the assassins took you when they thought you were dead. By the time you were taken before him, the cowardly king of the north had probably already received word of my actions.

"What better way to assure I don't murder him and destroy his beloved kingdom than to shield himself behind my brother? But the question remains, how are you here? I find the possibility of your escaping his clutches remote ..."

Malhadiev slowly turned his gaze back on Zaiyera. She felt a chill run down her spine under that cold dark gaze. "Am I to believe you found him and helped him escape?" he surmised. "You travel such great distance to bring him to me. Why? After you tried to kill me those months ago. Are you a traitor, working with Eredin?"

"Do you truly think the northerner king would allow Kima to leave his kingdom, knowing you will come for him?" Zaiyera replied.

Malhadiev appeared to think on that. "Your words ring true, but it doesn't matter. When I'm done here, I go to Rexzen. When I'm finished there, I will have my *audience* with King Eredin."

"You don't want to go anywhere near Rexzen," Zaiyera found herself saying. Part of her wanted to say nothing, but the thought of even the possibility of this man being controlled by one of those tattooed women was terrifying. Especially given the apparent strained relations between Rexzen and Nanshaigha. "If there is any place in all the world you should avoid, Malhadiev, it is that place."

Kivuli dayasa chuckled. "I know their little secret, woman. I know that they use streamdancers as weapons. They'll not find me so easy to bind." That horrible grin returned. "Now, I would tell you to be gone from this place, that I and my brother can catch up on old times, but of course, you think to stop me."

"I don't wish for this to be a fight," Zaiyera replied.

Malhadiev spread his hands. "How can it not? You know as well as I that neither the king nor any other ruler in Samhar would suffer me to live."

Kima shook his head. "You don't know that—"

"Shut up!" With but a wave of his hand, Malhadiev sent Kima tumbling away."

Zaiyera watched the poor man skipping across the ground until he hit a nearby fountain base, much the same as the other unconscious streamdancer. She saw the others, now. They'd been listening to the exchange and were bracing themselves.

Malhadiev's chest rose and fell as he sighed, staring after his brother who lay groaning on the broken stone ground. He looked back to Zaiyera. "I love my brother, but I hate his misplaced optimism. You and I both know how this must end."

Zaiyera remained still. "It will be as it must."

Malhadiev inclined his head. "Indeed."

He was touching the stream again, drawing massive amounts of the flow. It was enough to age ten dancers. Twenty. Fifty. *Moon and stars, he is a monster.* Malhadiev filled himself with enough of the flow to have aged and died a hundred times over, yet only a tiny streak of gray faded the corners of his hair.

He lashed out with a transparent arced blade and sent it speeding for her torso.

Zaiyera unsheathed Shatr, at the same time slicing cleanly through the arc blade that would have cut her in half. She ran for him, hoping to get in close and end this quickly.

Malhadiev laughed and sent another blade at her, then another. Zaiyera leapt over one, then slid on her back underneath the second one. She sliced upward through a third, then then brought the scimitar down and to her left, cutting through a vertical arc blade.

"Impressive," Malhadiev remarked. He produced two blue glowing shard disks in the air. They were flecked with the telltale black stain of the taint. Dozens of small holes opened in the disks and razor-sharp shards zipped through the air.

Shatr became a blur as Zaiyera blasted the first and then second assault apart. She cut a third disk apart only a heartbeat after it appeared. He was testing her. She was faster, and it surprised him. But she couldn't keep it up.

Malhadiev slapped his hand down, and the air in front of his waist rippled. He swiped that hand into a circle, then followed with his left. The rippling air crackled with power that built in intensity as it condensed close to his body. He threw his arms out at his sides. What looked like black flames danced around the shadowlancer as though held at bay by a dome. The dome retracted, then exploded.

The remaining streamdancers defensively danced the stream, quickly producing shields. Two of their number weren't strong enough, and the blast shattered their shields and disintegrated the poor men.

Zaiyera had barely gotten her blade up in time to cut through the rippling wave of lethal power. She steadied her stance against the offensive flow, but it still pushed her back.

Once the assault faded, Zaiyera looked past Malhadiev to see Dyren Faust picking himself up off the ground. He braced a hand on one of his knees and gave his head a shake. Malhadiev seemed not to have noticed him yet.

He looked around the city square at the survivors. "Not bad."

"Especially for those whose power comes from no stolen lifestreams," Zaiyera retorted.

Malhadiev snarled and created his giant whips again. He moved his arms about, and the whips swayed to his motions like serpents slithering in the air.

Three of the surviving streamdancers produced shard disks that sent the sharp projectiles racing toward the shadowlancer. Malhadiev laughed at their efforts. With a flick of his wrists, both whips blasted the shards to nothing. He struck out at four dancers to his left while swinging his right toward the three on his other side.

Zaiyera sprinted for him again. She chopped Shatr down at the whip in his left hand. Following the motion through, she swept the blade around and up. Shatr sliced cleanly through both of the huge whips and they fell apart.

The four dancers to Malhadiev's left produced whips of their own and lashed at him. The shadowlancer blasted their attacks apart with little more than a wave of his hand.

The three to his right launched shards and lashed out with whips while the others recovered. Working left to right, Malhadiev canceled their efforts out with minimal effort. He thrust his hand out toward Zaiyera and a disk twice her size, the biggest she'd ever seen, materialized in the air. Holes large enough for full-sized spears opened in the disk.

Zaiyera slashed down, then left. As the disk fell apart, two more took its place. At the same time, two more faced the dancers on either side of Malhadiev.

As Zaiyera cut the disks apart, the shadowlancer formed two more of his huge whips. The streamdancers had just finished creating shields against the spear-sized shards when he struck.

The spears pounded into the shields and broke them an instant before the giant transparent whip crashed down on them. Only one streamdancer managed to escape the follow-up attack, but the impact had lifted her off the ground.

Malhadiev slapped down, the air again rippling like water. He raked his hand toward the still airborne streamdancer. A crescent blade formed from the flow and sped towards her.

Barely an instant before it had come forth from the stream, however, Zaiyera cut it apart. She'd tried to get close, but between defending herself and the streamdancers, she'd been forced to hold her ground.

Malhadiev turned his murderous gaze on Zaiyera even as the woman hit the ground in the distance, her screaming grunt sounding above the crackling flames. "You're starting to irritate ..."

A barrage of glowing blue shards zipped through the air past Zaiyera. Malhadiev rotated his hand in the air. A transparent blue shield lined with tiny black flames appeared between himself and the shards, which shattered against it.

The shadowlancer growled and spun on his heel, bringing the shield around to stop the speeding arc blade coming for his head.

Zaiyera slashed Shatr diagonally down in the direction of the shield. Not needing actual physical contact, the scimitar cut through the flow that came from the stream itself to form the insubstantial shield.

Malhadiev cried out as he dove aside. The arc blade missed him by a hand's width. He rolled back to a kneeling position, drew his hands back, and slapped the air in front of him again. A mountainous surge of the flow emerged from the stream. The resulting shockwave amplified Malhadiev's enraged scream and shook the pavilion.

Zaiyera turned sideways and braced herself. She held Shatr downward with the spine pressed against her left arm and leaned against the force of the blast. From her peripheral vision, she saw Jaide hide behind Malker, who produced a large shield. On the other side of the square, Dyren Faust had created a shield to protect himself and Zhuyun.

Whether their comrades were dead or unconscious, only three streamdancers remained standing. They'd come together and combined their efforts to produce a huge shield. Luckily for the unconscious dancer and Kima not far beside her, the shield was large enough to encompass them.

The shockwave parted on either side of Shatr, but the sheer force of it sent Zaiyera skidding backwards, then sent her flipping head over heels backwards. She managed to get her feet under her and land in a backwards roll. She still hit the ground hard, and skipped and bounced as much as rolled. The tumble tore Shatr from her grasp. It went spinning across the ground to rest a dozen feet away. It may as well have been a mile away, as Malhadiev saw it as well.

"What will you do without your troublesome blade?" he shouted from across the square. "We'll find out, shall we?"

Dyren struck. With a motion like submerging his hand into water, he dipped his entire hand into the stream, guided the flow to his will, and created a whip. It wasn't half as large as the ones Malhadiev had wielded, but there were blades at the end of it.

The senior shydon hunter flung the whip at Malhadiev. The shadowlancer produced a shield to his arm and batted the attack aside.

Zaiyera hopped to her feet and sprinted for her scimitar.

Malker Argen sent two spinning disks cutting through the air at Malhadiev. The shadowlancer slashed his hand across the air and what looked like a translucent liquid splashed over the disks and dissolved them.

Dyren struck with his whip again while Zhuyun raced past him for the shadowlancer.

Zaiyera ran at him from the front, while Jaide sprinted past Malker from the right.

Malhadiev sent a spinning disk similar to Malker's but twice as large slicing through the air at Jaide. He whipped his shield arm around to deflect Dyren's whip. Following through, Malhadiev swung his free hand around and sent an arc blade slicing through the air at Zhuyun.

Jaide dropped to the gravel-strewn ground and slid underneath the spinning blade. She planted one of her feet, came upright again, and kept running.

Zhuyun snapped an end of his staff up into the middle of the clear arc blade. Instead of being severed, and Zhuyun cut in half, the staff snatched up the blade-manifested flow. Zhuyun set his staff into a vertical spin, crossing it from the left side of his body to the right.

The Yuntaiman kept the staff spinning, and thus the power of the flow remained attached to his staff without destroying it.

Moving energy, Zaiyera thought in astonishment, *not absorbed, but in a constant state of redirection!*

Zhuyun's staff blurred the air around it as it spun. Dyren lashed out with his whip again and Malker sent another disk tearing through the air.

The shydon hunters were working their way into the square now, assaulting Malhadiev from both sides. While it would have been better for them to combine their efforts, Zaiyera understood why they didn't. Better to keep Malhadiev fighting from as many directions as possible.

Kivuli dayasa created an arc blade that blasted Malker's disk out of the air as it sped toward the junior shydon. He turned back and threw his shield arm up to intercept Dyren's whip.

Somehow, within the space of heartbeat, Zaiyera flicked Shatr up and toward Malhadiev's arm. The shield fell apart in the blink of an eye before Dyren's bladed whip struck.

The blades sliced Malhadiev across the shoulder. Dyren flicked his wrist in the opposite direction, and the whip wrapped around Malhadiev's waist.

Jaide was several paces closer to Malhadiev than Zaiyera, while Zhuyun moved slower as he had to keep the flow—and his staff—moving.

Malker dipped his fingers into the flow, drew forth a more slender whip, and lashed it at Malhadiev. The blow struck the shadowlancer's hip, drawing blood.

Massive amounts of the flow drew into Malhadiev's body. His roar shook the city square.

Such power. Such incredible power. Zaiyera's legs pumped, drawing her every closer to *kivuli dayasa*. If she could run him through with Shatr, she might be able tear that power away from him before he died and it was lost. He didn't deserve it. He used it to kill. Zaiyera could help people; help the world. With the ability to draw that much of the stream to her, Zaiyera could bring every tyrant around the world to their knees. Wars would never happen again. None would commit crimes against another for fear of reprisal.

She could make this world better instead of breaking it as Malhadiev, *kivuli dayasa*, surely would.

Malker lashed with his whip and wrapped it around Malhadiev's arm.

Now held from both directions, the shadowlancer struggled to keep from being pulled down.

Mere steps away from him, Jaide drew her shamshir over her head and brought it down in a diagonal chop. Or she would have.

Malhadiev used his free hand to slap the air in front of her, sending a tiny ripple between them. The ripple hit Jaide like an electric jolt. Her shamshir fell from her twitching hand and she collapsed, writhing on the ground.

Malhadiev repeated the attack on Zaiyera. She skidded to a stop and cut right through it, then kept running. That small moment was all he needed. *Kivuli dayasa* dipped his free hand into the flow, bending forward as though submerging himself down to his elbow. He wrenched his arm upward.

The shadowlancer drew a massive whip from the stream. Dyren cried out and dove aside. The whip broke the ground apart less than a foot from where he'd been standing. The exploding ground catapulted Dyren high into the air and he lost his grip on the flow. The whip he'd been holding evaporated.

Malker yanked hard at his whip. The sudden pull caused Malhadiev to stumble sideways, but then he swung his massive whip over his head at the junior shydon. Malker panicked and lost the flow as he leapt out of the way.

Zaiyera cut Malhadiev's whip apart before it was halfway to her ally.

Zhuyun leapt into the air. He spun the staff around as his body turned and slammed the staff to the ground at the same time he landed. The flow unleashed from the staff drilled through the stone tiles toward the shadowlancer.

Malhadiev thrust his palm downward in front of him. It stopped Zhuyun's attack, but the impact knocked him off balance toward a partially collapsed building.

A thick section of cracked wall shifted and slid forward and fell. Malhadiev looked up in time to see hundreds of pounds of stone just before it fell on top of him.

Barum stood where the wall had been. The thickly muscled Denberesterner huffed as he glared down at the pile of rubble. "Ain't as fast as the rest of you. But I reckon that'll do him just fine."

Zaiyera felt a tickle on the back of her neck, as though a flicker of power sparked to life. She gasped. "Barum! Get way from there!"

The mound of rubble exploded in a geyser of hard stone, directed at the spot where Barum stood. The big man dove back into the building, but the blast of stone hit the ceiling beneath it. A large section of the floor underneath Barum collapsed.

47

It happened so fast, no one had time to react. One moment, Malhadiev was buried under a ton of rock, then next, Barum was gone.

Zaiyera screamed in rage as she ran toward the shadowlancer.

Malhadiev climbed out of the rock and hurled an arc blade at her. Zaiyera planted her feet, skidding forward. She chopped through the translucent blade then continued running. She finally reached Malhadiev and swiped at his head.

The shadowlancer ducked under her sword and slashed the air between them. Zaiyera cut across the attack. Whatever he tried to throw against her fell apart.

Malhadiev backpedaled but Zaiyera was on him. She cut at his head, shoulder to hip, torso. She stabbed at his midsection, cut left, then cut down at his leg. Malhadiev produced shield after shield to keep her terrible blade at bay. Every time a shield met Shatr, the scimitar blasted it apart.

Tiny wisps of gray formed at Malhadiev's temples. He snarled, his concentration now on not being cut apart.

Fully on the offensive, Zaiyera kept her adversary on his heels, shattering every defense he created, keeping him from forming any kind of counter. The world fell away. Only the two of them existed.

Somehow, despite her barrage, Zaiyera couldn't get through. And Malhadiev not only continuously drew from the stream, but his power continued to build even as they fought.

Such raw power. It was sweet. If she could just break through, if Shatr could find its target, Zaiyera could put an end to this conflict—to all conflicts. The stream. The beautiful, blissful stream. She could taste it.

Malhadiev crossed his arms and threw two shields up. The shields layered, one in front of the other, and provided him just enough protection as he barreled into her. The desperate move cost him. Zaiyera scored a glancing cut across the front of his shoulder that soaked his torn robes.

He barreled into Zaiyera and sent her tumbling backwards. She rolled back to her feet with Shatr held defensively across her torso. She needn't have bothered.

Zhuyun threw himself at Malhadiev with a viciousness Zaiyera had never seen in the man. Gone were the crinkles at the corners of his eyes when he smiled, the sparkle in his hazel eyes, and the calm demeanor. The Yintish warrior pounded at Malhadiev's defenses with speed equaled by power. His staff was practically invisible, so fast did it blur.

It wasn't enough. If Zhuyun's staff had the same properties as Shatr, the fight would have been over. But no matter Zhuyun's amazing skill, the staff was still a mundane weapon, and no match for Malhadiev's power.

Just as the triumphant grin started to spread across Malhadiev's face, Zhuyun's staff struck one of his shields and snatched the flow away.

The shadowlancer's surprise was no more so than Zaiyera's, but it still wasn't enough. Zhuyun could have broken through the final shield if he'd been able to build the power in his staff. But that would have required him to keep it moving without contacting another object. The immediate impact of the stolen power at the edge of his staff managed to destroy Malhadiev's shield, but he created another just as quickly.

In that same instant, Malhadiev increased the size of his shield and swiped his hand through the air at Zhuyun. When the Yuntaiman leapt over the resulting arc blade, Malhadiev turned sideways and created a second shield barely in time to stop the slicing blade of Jaide's shamshir as it cut straight for his back.

The Viriksani warrior was no less impressive than Zhuyun. She danced the blade with speed, grace, and power that could likely rival Zaiyera's skill. But as with Zhuyun, Jaide's superior skill meant nothing. And worse, her two allies were blocking Zaiyera from being able to destroy Malhadiev's shields and help her friends.

The shadowlancer gathered more of the stream and shoved outward. Just enough of the flow rippled into the two warriors that they stumbled back. It bought Malhadiev enough time to slap both hands into the air with enough force to send a shockwave out in every direction.

The blast threw Zhuyun and Jaide away as though they were children's toys. Zaiyera chopped Shatr through the wave.

Malhadiev slapped the air again, palm facing toward her. On pure instinct, Zaiyera stabbed Shatr into the incoming wall of the flow. It crumbled. Malhadiev cursed and raked his hands through the air, left and right, up and down.

Zaiyera cut through the first three violent splashes, but they knocked her back. The fourth assault sent her spinning sideways. She managed to keep her feet, but the onslaught kept coming. He was constantly drawing from the stream now, gathering it into a flow and continuously battering her defenses.

Slash after slash, punch after splash after explosive burst, Zaiyera cut through the bombardment, all the while feeling that tremendous power. She thirsted for it. Perhaps if she touched the flow, just enough to defeat him …

Malhadiev produced seven large disks, each over ten feet tall.

Moon and stars. Zaiyera broke off and ran. The first of the disks released a shower of shards that would have ripped her to shreds. She continued to sprint in an arc just ahead of the discharging disks and cut Shatr horizontally through the air.

The scimitar cut four of them apart, but the other three managed to fire again. Several shards caught her leg and hip. Zaiyera gritted her teeth against the searing pain lighting up her side.

Through some miracle she kept on her feet. Zaiyera skidded to a stop and cut Shatr through the air. The scimitar defeated the last three disks before they could discharge another lethal blast.

Her instincts screamed at her. Zaiyera dropped to the ground an instant before a speeding disk sliced the air above her head. She pushed back to her feet as the disk turned. With a downward chop of Shatr, it burst into nothingness.

Malhadiev produced a shield just as a giant transparent blue club pounded into him. The blow fell heavy enough to force the shadowlancer to a kneeling position.

Dyren Faust hammered the shadowlancer's shield with his club. Again and again Dyren struck, his transparent blue club pounding the other man's shield while his golden lance-resin left arcs of blue and gold light in the night air.

Malhadiev had been caught off guard, and the power behind the senior shydon's offense kept him at bay. He dropped to one knee, flinching under each blow.

Zaiyera slashed Shatr horizontally. Malhadiev's shield fell apart and Dyren swung the club into him with full force. The heavy blow threw the shadowlancer into a wall of nearby rubble.

Malker produced two disks overhead that rained shards on the shadowlancer.

Malhadiev created another shield. Zaiyera chopped downward. The shield shattered, but Malhadiev produced a second one that sheltered him from the lethal rain. He slashed the air in Zaiyera's direction.

Zaiyera brought Shatr up in a defensive position. The shockwave parted around the blade but sent her tumbling backwards. Malhadiev slapped the air again, sending another shockwave rippling in every direction. He slapped the stream again, then again. Zaiyera sliced upward through the first assault and chopped down through the second.

The shadowlancer yanked a transparent whip from the stream and swung toward Zaiyera's head. She swiped Shatr in an upward arc over her head, then flipped the blade forward and stabbed through the disk Malhadiev had produced right after.

Dyren swung his club for the shadowlancer's head but Malhadiev slashed the air across it. The club warped before exploding in a rain of golden embers. The senior shydon had barely a heartbeat of surprise before he dropped to the ground to avoid Malhadiev's speeding arc blade.

Malker produced another overhead disk that rained shards down on the shadowlancer, then sent an arc blade of his own speeding toward Malhadiev.

The shadowlancer shielded himself from the assault and occupied the junior shydon with a shard disk of his own. At the same time, he fended off Dyren's attacks by constantly reproducing his shields as Zaiyera destroyed them.

Malhadiev turned left to right, blocking attacks from both sides, and creating spinning disks and arc blades whenever he had a flicker of time between the assaults. He hurled an arc blade at Dyren, who dove aside before being cut in half. As the shydon hunter dodged the deadly blade, Malhadiev spun back toward Malker with the same attack.

Zaiyera gritted her teeth against the burning in her leg and hip and cut the blade apart before it was halfway between the two combatants. The junior shydon wasted no time in lashing with his whip. He struck the shadowlancer across the chest, then flicked it back to wrap around his ankle.

Malhadiev set six glowing disks between himself and Malker just as the shydon yanked his feet from under him.

Zaiyera cut apart two of the disks, then three more as she pulled her blade back. One and a half of the disks managed to discharge their shards. They ripped through the air as Malker dove for the ground. He wasn't fast enough. Part of the volley caught his left leg and arm. Malker screamed as the shards tore through the left side of his body.

Zaiyera had cut the remaining disks apart while Malhadiev landing hard on his back—managed to send an arc blade zipping through the air at her. He sat up and slashed his hands through the air repeatedly.

More power from the stream came forth and the shadowlancer quickly molded the flow into more arc blades. As quick as his hands could move, he sent arc blades continuously speeding toward Zaiyera.

She cut left, ducked, hopped, sliced right, and chopped down. Sweat poured down the side of her face as she worked. Shatr flicked and spun as she wielded the powerful blade with precision earned from a lifetime of training.

Dyren ran for Malhadiev, two small blue disks glowing in front of each of his hands. He leapt into the air and held both hands in front of him. The disks flared and hundreds of shards shot from them.

Malhadiev broke off his attack on Zaiyera, shielded himself from the onslaught, and thrust his hand out in front of the descending shydon hunter. A similarly sized disk as the two Dyren wielded appeared in front of Malhadiev's hand.

Instead of shards, however, it looked as if the shadowlancer had sent the flow itself gushing from the stream.

Dyren crossed his arms in front of him and got his shield formed barely in time. The blast was like rushing water spewing through a broken dam. The blast stopped Dyren from landing and sent him hurtling backwards.

His shield held against most of the assault, but not all of it. Wisps of smoke trailed his singed body as he flew backward. Dyren held his focus long enough to lance the stream again.

As he fell, the senior shydon hunter punched his fist into the stream. The effect was similar to what Malhadiev had just done. The senior shydon sent the flow splashing over his enemy. Caught off guard, the shadowlancer only managed to avoid some of the burning power. It scorched his robes and skin and caused him to lose his focus.

Zhuyun had finally regained his feet by then. He sprinted for the shadowlancer from the side while Zaiyera closed in from the front.

Malhadiev sent shards and arc blades at the Yuntaiman. Zhuyun dove left, leapt right, slid underneath shards, then used his staff to catapult himself into the air.

The shadowlancer grinned at the vulnerable airborne warrior, and lazily produced a tall disk that sent shards speeding for Zhuyun.

Zaiyera's first instinct was to cut the attack apart, but Zhuyun didn't look concerned. In fact, it looked as though he'd counted on it.

The Yintish warrior spun his staff and caught the shards up in both ends of it. The staff now looked like a spinning wheel of blue fire.

Malhadiev's eyes widened. He drew his hand back to produce another whip, but Zaiyera cut it apart. Malhadiev looked at his hand in alarm just as Zhuyun landed.

Back arched, Zhuyun slammed one end of his staff at Malhadiev. The shadowlancer barely got a shield up in time, but the force of the blow shattered it. Zhuyun took a big step forward and swung his staff up, around, and down.

Shaken by the first blow, Malhadiev had no defense for the second. He tried to jump back but succeeded only in falling away. The staff hit the ground right beside him. The stone ground exploded and launched Malhadiev into the air.

He hit the ground in a tumble of robes and limbs, but somehow remained conscious. The shadowlancer got his feet under him, curled his fingers, and spun back around. Eyes wide with murderous intent, he repeatedly struck the air in front the Yuntaiman as though smacking his hand on water. Each time his hand struck and plunged into the stream, the power burst and showered over his enemy.

Zhuyun whirled his staff, catching up the shockwaves, ripples, and splashes of the flow with his spinning staff. He turned his body, whipped the staff around and returned the offensive flow it to its sender.

The shadowlancer let out a frustrated growl as the Yintish warrior canceled out his efforts. He hurled glowing sphere after glowing sphere; left, right, left, right.

Zhuyun rolled and hopped, dodging left and right. The traveler who was more than a traveler, more than a storyteller, could not be caught. Every sphere he didn't dodge, he caught up in his staff and sent it speeding back.

Zaiyera cut apart as many of the spheres as she could, though the crazed Malhadiev kept them coming. He turned part of his attention on her, and Zaiyera quickly found herself dodging, cutting them apart, diving aside.

From the corner of her eye, she saw Malker Argen half running half limping across the square behind Malhadiev. He moved along a partially destroyed building and knelt over the struggling Dyren.

Zhuyun whirled his staff, catching up several speeding disks and pounded his staff to the ground repeatedly. The ground crackled with energy as the offensive manifestations of the flow shattered stone and rock as it sped toward Malhadiev.

The shadowlancer looked to be completely in the throes of madness now. "You've hurt me. Curse your name, foreigner, but you are worthy." He punched his fist into the stream. The flow that sprang from the stream came in a series of blue/black explosions. *Boom boom BOOM BOOM.*

The explosions and the sound of Shatr cutting apart the attacks filled Zaiyera's ears. *Boom boom boom.* Shatr cut them apart. *Whoom whoom whoom.*

Zaiyera kept moving, kept the scimitar moving. If she didn't, she and Zhuyun were dead. She saw Jaide crouched near the rubble where Malker had passed, trying to figure out how to help turn the tide. In truth, Zaiyera didn't know how much longer she could fight this monster. He'd danced enough of the stream to pay the lifeprice of a hundred men or more.

Malhadiev flung several disks into the air. He launched arc blades and explosive spheres. He raked his fingers through the air and sent a burning wave of the flow crashing over them.

Zaiyera stabbed through one disk and cut sideways, shattering the others. Now beside her, Zhuyun caught up the explosive spheres in his staff and kept it whirling as the burning wave of the flow rose between them and their adversary.

Zaiyera took the wave apart with a zigzag cut of her scimitar. As the wave fell, Zhuyun slammed his staff into the ground. The captured power drilled through the ground toward Malhadiev, and Zhuyun turned his body and slammed the other end down.

Malhadiev slapped his hands together and parted them. A huge shield twice as large as his body glowed into being. The double impact of the speeding power pounded into the shield, but it held.

Then Zaiyera destroyed it. She cut the shield apart, but it was for naught, as Zhuyun had released everything he'd had in his staff.

Malhadiev screamed in frustration, then looked past them. Zaiyera followed his gaze to see Dyren and Malker—who seemed to move better than he should have—running to the fight. Off to the side, Jaide ran behind them.

The shadowlancer rose to his full height and produced two massive explosive spheres in his hands and let fly.

The two shydon moved as one. They dove into a roll to the left, came up to a kneeling position, and hurled two arc blades each. They created one large shield to protect against the explosive sphere, then produced two large shard disks, similar to the ones Malhadiev had created.

As the shards sped toward the shadowlancer, Dyren produced two long translucent objects that looked like poles, while Malker pulled two whips from the stream. The shydon hunters pounded at the shadowlancer's defenses. Dyren swung his pole weapons while Malker lashed with his whips.

Behind them, Jaide crept forward with their advance, shamshir in hand.

Malhadiev blocked and countered with more speed and strength than should have been possible. The three men were a war unto themselves, hurling massive amounts of the stream, pulling from it and molding the flow into weapon after weapon, shield after shield.

Somewhere in middle of defending against the onslaught, the shadowlancer produced his own whips and lashed back at his enemies. Where Malker's whips lashed and ripped, Malhadiev's whips shattered and exploded with their enormous weight.

Through it all, the shadowlancer had enough focus to create enough of an attack on Zaiyera to keep her from canceling out his efforts so that the shydon hunters could strike him down.

She fought off shards and spheres, growling in frustration. Zhuyun occasionally managed to catch up some power in his staff and hurl it back at the shadowlancer, but Malhadiev always had a shield ready.

Their combined efforts were moving Malhadiev back step by step toward a stone wall to the side of the ruined building. When he was within ten feet of the wall, a section behind him burst, and two heavily muscled arms wrapped around him.

Bruised and bloody, Barum Hurst lifted the much smaller Malhadiev over his head, and threw him to the ground with an enraged roar.

The sound of breaking bone cracked through the air. Malhadiev screamed in agony but didn't move.

Barum stood heaving over the broken man for several heartbeats, then he toppled over.

"Tears of the ancients," Zhuyun whispered.

They ran toward their fallen comrade but hadn't made it within a dozen feet when the ground between them and Barum and Malhadiev exploded. Zhuyun had been closer and took the brunt of the force. The Yuntaiman was lifted off his feet and landed in a heap several feet away.

The shadowlancer struggled back to his feet and looked down at Barum.

"Impossible," Malker said. "Barum broke his back."

"He did," Malhadiev said, his voice entirely too calm. "But when you have power as I do, you can heal yourself." He opened a hand, and a long shard appeared.

Zaiyera sprang forward and cut the shard in half as Malhadiev stabbed down at the dazed man.

Malhadiev turned on her, his eyes practically glowing with fury. "I've had enough of—"

Jaide's shamshir swept for his neck.

It would have taken Malhadiev's head, but he saw the attack just in time and formed a shield. Jaide continued to pound at him, slicing in every direction with such speed, Malhadiev stumbled away.

Unlike their normal physical counterparts, shields molded from the flow guarded against physical weapons in the manner of two magnets with opposite polarities.

Each strike of Jaide's shamshir turned the weapon aside as though it slipped off the surface of the shield. She kept on him, though, fighting for an opening. Just an inch to slip through.

Jaide's sudden bombardment of the shadowlancer kept him on his heels so that he couldn't offer any offense.

Zaiyera cut through one of Malhadiev's shields while Jaide was already midway into her downward cut. The Viriksani scored a slice into Malhadiev's exposed shoulder. The blade bit through flesh and cleaved through bone. Jaide bared her teeth and pulled back, sliding the sword down and out.

Malhadiev cried out as blood spat from the wound. He slapped the air immediately in front of Jaide. She had just enough time to partially turn away. The shockwave smacked into her body and sent her spinning head over heels away.

Jaide grunted when she hit the ground. Eyes clenched shut, she groaned, her right hand clamped over her limp arm.

Malhadiev's counter had been too fast for the running Zaiyera to anticipate and stop. Worse was that she came just close enough to see Malhadiev snatch the torn sleeve away and the gash in his arm knitting closed.

The stream flowed into him and through the wound.

The shadowlancer threw up two shard disks, which Zaiyera promptly cut apart. The move was only to buy him time, however.

In the time it took Zaiyera to cut apart the shard disks, Malhadiev climbed back to his feet and touched the stream. Zaiyera moved quickly, and in the span of a heartbeat, she was on him. She worked Shatr in an endless flurry of combinations, linking each series of attacks into the next. She came at him low, high, in between. She feinted a stab at his head, pulled up short, and sliced the tip of the scimitar down.

Malhadiev had great power at his disposal, but she kept him too off balance to use it.

The night lit with flashes of blue as every glowing shield the shadowlancer created exploded under the power of Shatr. If Malhadiev had been a normal streamdancer, Zaiyera would have put an end to him right then—long before then. But, Malhadiev was *kivuli dayasa*. Though Zaiyera's efforts were effective at keeping him on the defensive, Malhadiev could still combine his efforts like no streamdancer alive.

He kept producing the shields to guard himself, then drew from the stream with his left hand. Once free, he molded the power from the flow into a small disk in front of his hand. He pushed the disk toward Zaiyera.

Zaiyera saw it coming but couldn't get out of the way fast enough. She sidestepped and chopped Shatr down. The scimitar destroyed most of the shards, but some slipped through. They tore into the skin in her uninjured leg and swept it out from under her.

She landed flat on her back, the wind blasted from her lungs. Pain exploded in fiery pinpricks all through the side of her lower leg. Now with both legs injured and in burning pain, it was all Zaiyera could do not to scream.

Malhadiev swung his giant translucent whip down on her. Zaiyera kept her eyes open. If this was to be her end, she would face it without fear and without flinching.

The end of Zhuyun's staff intercepted the whip. The weapon drew most of the whip's power away and dragged it aside enough that Zaiyera could roll away.

While Zaiyera struggled to stand, Zhuyun battled the shadowlancer with renewed ferocity, kicking and sweeping, his staff whirling.

Cold dark focus colored the Yintish warrior's features. He looked like an entirely different man. His staff never stopped moving, never slowed enough that the flow he'd captured from Malhadiev's whip could be lost.

Zhuyun whirled the staff to collide with Malhadiev's shield. He turned his body in a reverse spin, crashing the butt of his staff against it again. The staff looked like little more than a warping of the air, so fast did it move.

He pounded Malhadiev's defenses, but the shadowlancer's power was still great. Malhadiev managed to dip a finger into the stream and trace a circle in the air between them. He thrust his palm into the circle.

A small explosion of blue fire erupted right in front of Zhuyun. The singed Yuntaiman growled in agony, but the shadowlancer wasn't done. He produced a small disk in front of his other hand and held it in front of Zhuyun.

Zaiyera stumbled sideways but held her balance just enough to swipe Shatr across the air in front of her. She destroyed the disk before it could launch its deadly blast of shards.

Malhadiev shouted in frustration. He rounded on Zaiyera as Zhuyun dropped to his knees, his skin and clothes smoking.

Zaiyera closed off her mind to the pain, forced her wobbly legs to still, and settled into a guarded stance, her scimitar held before her.

The city square lay in complete ruin. Half a building collapsed, the walls broken apart, decorative stone ground crumbled. The surrounding benches and the two fountains that adorned the center of the square lay in pieces indistinguishable from the rest of the rubble.

Cracking flames serenaded the battle. The coppery smell of blood tinged the air and mingled with the scent of burning wood.

"This would have finished long ago if not for you and that *irritating* weapon," Malhadiev said. His calm, even tone carried the weight of his hatred for her. "I'm going to obliterate you and destroy that sw—"

Zaiyera lunged forward with a stab for his heart.

Malhadiev choked off his last words with grunt of surprise. Fell back and threw a shield up. He kept backpedaling, producing shield after shield to keep the unstoppable Shatr at bay.

"What *is* that thing?" he growled. "There is no dancecraft with such power."

"It is Shatr," Zaiyera answered coldly. She stabbed straight through a shield and flicked the blade sideways, dealing him a cut across the chest. "You will know it intimately when it meets your heart."

Malhadiev slashed the air between them and skipped backwards.

Zaiyera cut apart the fiery slash and stepped forward.

The shadowlancer had gotten enough distance between them now.

He wore a triumphant grin. "You can defeat my power, but not forever. How long can you keep going? Malhadiev's body tensed as he submerged into the flow.

Zaiyera gasped. No one could fully immerse themselves into the flow without burning themselves away. The sheer magnitude of what he was doing could topple cities. How did his body not explode? She cut into the flow even as he drew it out of the stream. She cut vein after vein, a knife cutting through endless strands of yarn.

Her efforts were futile. She may as well try to stop an ocean wave with a bucket.

Malhadiev let his head fall back. His sigh filled the air with such weight it threatened to buckle Zaiyera's knees. She became aware again of the pain in her leg and the residual injury from the battle with the pack of tugyre. Her body ached in a dozen places and more, but it felt like nothing in the face of the monster growing before her.

The shadowlancer turned eyes as black as night on Zaiyera. Though the flames had mostly dimmed, and the light faded, she could still see his poisonous dance-resin. The night was dark, but Malhadiev's resin was blacker still.

The pain in her body melted away in the face of all that power. It was glorious and terrible all at once. She wanted to reach out and grab it, consume it, bathe in it. To swim fully in the stream must be pure bliss. What must it feel like? Even a flicker of that much power could heal all her wounds a thousand times over.

Zaiyera snapped out of her trance as Malhadiev took a deep breath and gathered the flow. As though gathering it in his arms, Malhadiev swept his hands inward in an arc, spread his hands out again, and clapped them together.

Zaiyera started to cut through the massive shockwave, but it was so powerful, she stopped the blade halfway and grabbed the spine of the blade with her other hand. Shatr protected her from the brunt of the force. It took everything she had to keep the scimitar from being wrenched from her grasp. When the assault finally ended, she stumbled forward, heaving.

Malhadiev laughed. His deep, rumbling voice swept over the

ruined square like a fog of evil. "Your blade can cut through the flow, but your body cannot." He moved his hand, but Zaiyera slashed left and down.

The shadowlancer narrowed his eyes. He moved again, massive amounts of the flow swirling around him to his command. Long before he could finish molding the power, Zaiyera read him and sliced it apart.

Malhadiev clenched his teeth and moved faster. He tried to create arc blades, shard disks, explosive spheres. Zaiyera cut off his every move the instant he started it; severing the flow before it fully formed.

"How is this possible?" *Kivuli dayasa* threw himself into the flow, flinging everything he had at her.

Zaiyera's thoughts faded away. The burning buildings, her injured friends, the dead, the ruin, all disappeared. There was only her, Shatr, and her adversary. She didn't try to match his efforts, didn't try to slip past his defenses. Zaiyera simply reacted to his movements, studied his body, and through that, his intentions. Her matches with Zhuyun had only been the start that led to her understanding of how to truly use Shatr.

The scimitar was attuned to her, and though anyone could wield it, only she could activate its abilities. To cut through the flow took knowledge of it. Zaiyera had once danced the stream; drawn the flow from it and molded it. She'd felt the nature of the power.

Malhadiev's arms swung back and forth, he flicked his wrists, circled his hands. Massive amounts of the flow came to his bidding. If the power had been allowed to manifest, it would have mowed down everything in its path for miles.

Zaiyera cut it apart instantly. She fell into the dance. Her body moved continuously, slicing through Malhadiev's every attempt to create an offense. The scimitar sang in her hand, and Zaiyera opened herself to it. She would get close enough to clamp her hand around his mouth, and she would drain that undeserved power from him. She would do right by the world; make amends for the wrong she'd committed. She would use that stolen power to make things right.

A cold stab of alarm struck in the pit of her stomach. *No. That's what he sought to do, and what has he become?* Zaiyera pushed the hunger, the temptation, away. She fought the shadowlancer, fought the hunger, walked the narrow path between two raging infernos, either of which would be an end to her.

Zaiyera walked him down, cutting apart his every effort to destroy her. As she drew closer, it looked as though Malhadiev would turn to run. She surged forward, drawing Shatr back, the tip of the blade poised to strike.

Malhadiev created a shield out of instinct, but it didn't matter. The mighty blue-steel scimitar sliced through it and entered the left side of the his chest.

She barely heard Malhadiev's cry, barely saw him fall back as she pushed down. All she needed to do was focus on his lifestream. She could feel it even as the thought came. It was enormous, like a raging river a thousand times the size of any normal lifestream. It was right there, waiting. She could do so much with it. How long would she live?

Zaiyera screamed. She snatched the scimitar free, drawing another anguished cry from Malhadiev, and drew the blade back for the killing blow. She saw a figure behind the shadowlancer and hesitated. *Kima.*

Fingers curled over the heavily bleeding wound, Malhadiev stared at her, then struggled to half turn and follow her gaze. "Brother."

Kima stood several paces away, looking from Malhadiev to Zaiyera. He started forward again, his steps stiff. Kima kept a wary eye on Zaiyera, a look of astonishment and fear on his face.

"Brother," Malhadiev said again as Kima knelt beside him.

The gaping wound in Malhadiev's chest started to knit. Her eyes flicked left to right as she looked from the shadowlancer to his brother. She needed to end this! She needed to finish it before either Malhadiev healed, or she lost her will and did the unthinkable.

"What happened to you, Malhadiev?" Kima let his head hang. Tears spilled from his eyes. "How could you have so lost your way?"

Malhadiev groaned and propped himself up on his elbow. "You can help me, Kima. The darkness of the taint has swallowed me, but you're my light. You can help me find my way back. Please, brother." He swallowed. "Please help me find my way back. Only you can."

Kima's shoulders trembled as he started to sob. "I know, brother. I'll do my best." He thrust the knife he'd hidden in the side of his boot toward Malhadiev's heart.

The shadowlancer caught his wrist. Both men's hands trembled as each struggled to overpower the other.

Malhadiev's black eyes narrowed. "I suppose it couldn't have happened any other—gruugh."

Kima fell onto his backside, heaving in wide-eyed horror.

Malhadiev turned on his side and coughed up a mouthful of blood. He pulled the knife free and coughed more blood but remained propped on his elbow. He was healing himself.

Zaiyera stepped over Malhadiev and drove Shatr home into his heart. She kept the blue-steel blade there until the life drained from his eyes and he slumped over. She slowly stepped back.

Kima's whimper rose into a wail of anguish. He crawled back to his brother's lifeless body and cradled Malhadiev's head in his lap.

Zaiyera heard the rustle of gravel and turned to see her companions —those that were conscious—shuffling toward her.

Instead of relief that it was done, and that they'd survived, Jaide and Zhuyun had expressions of ... pity? Zaiyera frowned at them.

When she saw the shocked and stony expression of Dyren Faust, a tiny part of her knew. Zaiyera had been so focused on surviving, she'd lost control. She looked down at herself now. Like a torch lighting the night, the clear yellow glow of her tainted dance-resin shined about her body.

48

How long they stared at each other, Zaiyera didn't know. The senior shydon hunter's expression ranged from disbelief, to shock and outrage, then confusion. The conflicting emotions battling inside him played a perfect scene across his face.

Zaiyera sheathed her scimitar and waited. Her tainted dance-resin had faded away.

After several long and heavy heartbeats, Dyren found his voice. "I … did not see what I thought I saw, correct? That was my pained and exhausted eyes deceiving me, right?"

Zaiyera just stared at him. What could she say?

"Right?" Dyren shouted. "Speak!"

Zaiyera took a deep breath to steady her nerves. "Your eyes tell you true, Dyren Faust."

"No." He shook his head. The little bit of remaining light from the dying fires lit the side of his face. In that flickering light, she saw that his black hair now had a sprinkling of gray.

"It can't be possible," Dyren said, his voice so quiet Zaiyera could barely hear him. "We traveled together for months. Months! How is it possible you've held this secret from us? How can you be a … a *darklancer?*"

Zaiyera didn't flinch despite how he spat the last word. She spread her hands. "You see the truth of me. What now?"

In that moment, Dyren looked as if every natural year and those of the lifeprice weighed heavily on him. "I don't know."

"What do you mean, you don't know?" It was Jaide who spoke. "This woman traveled beside you, risked her life with you, and *saved* your life—all of our lives. What do you mean you don't know?"

Dyren glowered at her. "This is not your concern. Unless you knew about this." He waved a hand at Zaiyera. "That in itself is a crime."

"Jaide …" Zaiyera said, but the Viriksani held up a hand without looking in her direction. "I knew, Dyren Faust. I've known for some time."

Dyren clenched his teeth, the muscles in his jaws flexing.

"And I as well," Zhuyun said from the side. "I've known of our friend's affliction for some time as well."

Zaiyera thought her heart would break with gratitude.

"Then you are all complicit," Dyren growled.

Malker and a limping Barum Hurst shuffled into the confrontation. The junior shydon hunter's brows knitted together as he looked from face to face.

"Our companion is a darklancer," Dyren said, answering his subordinate's unspoken question. He pointed an accusing finger at Zaiyera.

Malker's eyes widened. "That cannot be possible." He turned his confused expression on Zaiyera. "Surely this is some sort of confusion. We've battled hard and are hurt."

"There is no mistake," Zaiyera said.

"*Jakta skree,*" she heard Barum whisper.

Malker looked down, his eyes moving left to right as if searching for a way to explain this to himself.

"You must be brought before King Eredin," Dyren Faust said.

Malker snapped out of his stupor. "Sir—"

"The law!" Dyren barked. "You are a shadow hunter. Remember the creed. Remember the law. She"—he stabbed a finger at her again—"is the shadow we hunt."

"Yet we've hunted a greater shadow at her side the whole time,"

Malker argued, his voice quiet and careful. "She's fought with us. She's *slept* beside us, sir. How many times could she have syphoned us in our sleep."

Dyren nodded as a thought occurred to him. "That explains the constant need to be alone during our travels. Were you out hunting in the night, syphoning the lifestream of nearby animals to sate the addiction?"

Zaiyera's insides went cold at the accusation. "If you wish to make another enemy this day, Shydon Hunter, you are succeeding."

"Will you attack us, then?" Dyren demanded. "Will you draw your horrible blade and try to strike us down."

Zaiyera narrowed her eyes. "Say what you will about me, shydon, but if you speak another word against this blade—"

"You'll do what?" Dyren interrupted. "Would you fight me? Strike me down? Syphon my lifestream?"

Zaiyera sighed, and her anger fled with the breath. "I'm tired. You've insulted me, attacked my character, and spat on the only item in my life whose worth is beyond what you can comprehend. What do you want of me?"

"You will return with us to Nanshaigha."

"To the justice of a ruler who is not my own?" Zaiyera hadn't realized her fists were clenched until she felt her nails digging into her palms. "Why would I do that? I did not become what I am while in Dor'haighen, and I am not an enemy of your land. I am not subject to your king's justice, no matter what your creed says."

The sound of boots and creaking armor broke the confrontation.

A contingent of *dukhlva* stomped into the ruined city square and divided into precise ranks. They had their weapons drawn, facing the dead shadowlancer and his brother, who sat curled over his face.

Kima had his hand to Malhadiev's mortal wound, and his lips moved as though in prayer. When he heard the approach of the soldiers, he looked up and sniffed.

The warriors parted to admit a woman who could be none other than Sheikha Jawahir. Her smooth dark brown skin bore several fresh scars, yet they seemed to add to her beauty and regality.

Her deep purple headwrap sparkled in the dimming light of the shrinking flames. The intricately woven patterns on her stained and torn purple robes must have taken weeks to create. Despite the obvious wealth such a garb exhibited, they were modest for one of Jawahir's station.

Looking at the bruised and scraped sheikha, Zaiyera felt a surge of respect for the woman who must have fought beside her soldiers, at least until they were forced to withdraw.

She stopped at the front of her ranks and calmly surveyed the scene.

Zaiyera watched her assess the situation, noting how she, Zhuyun, and Jaide stood on one side facing the two shydon hunters. Barum looked to be the only neutral party, standing a bit apart, while Kima was obviously of some relation to the dead *kivuli dayasa*.

"Imrik," she said in *Soloush*, not taking her eyes off the standoff.

A *dakhiva* took one long stride to her side and offered a stiff, formal bow. "My Sheikha?"

"Send a contingent of what remains of our force out to the fleeing civilians. Tell my people it is safe to return home. Any who are closer to Xair should stay the night."

"It will be done." Imrik spun on his heel and strode away, barking orders to several of his soldiers.

"Life is rarely simple," the sheikha said, switching to tradetongue for the benefit of the foreigners. "I should think I'd be grateful, not only for what's left of my soldiers to have survived this night, but with the one who came to kill me and destroy my beloved Trystia, dead." She turned compassionate eyes on Kima, who sat rocking back and forth. He stared into the distance with his brother's head resting in his lap, one hand holding the wound where Zaiyera had driven Shatr home.

"Yet I come here," Jawahir continued, "to find what must surely be a family member grieving, and a conflict between those who, I'm guessing, have saved us all."

An uncomfortable silence stretched while she watched Kima for a few moments more. She looked around the ruined square. Her features growing more sorrowful. "Such death. I'm happy most of my people escaped, but even one death is too many."

"I'm sorry for the loss of your people and the destruction of your great city, Sheikha." Zaiyera bowed with respect. Zhuyun, Jaide, and Barum followed suit. After a heartbeat, the shydon hunters offered a stiff bow as well.

Sheikha Jawahir's eyes snapped back to Zaiyera. "Thank you for your words. I care less for the destruction, it can be rebuilt. Lives cannot."

"Words from royalty who pretend to care," Kima hissed through clenched teeth.

"Temper your words or they will write your fate," Imrik said in a tone so cold it left no doubt that he would follow through on the threat.

"Do not threaten him, Imrik," Jawahir said. "He grieves, and there is no doubt a source to his anger. I would hear about it." She looked to the rest of the ragged party. "All of it. I would hear the story that led to the tragedy that found us standing here this terrible night.

"But that is for tomorrow. For now, I offer you the hospitality of what is left of our beloved Trystia. In the morning we will speak again."

The *dakhiva* parted ranks to admit the sheikha, leaving the party in the care of Imrik.

Zaiyera could feel the angry stare of Dyren Faust. She looked over her shoulder, and into a baleful glare that promised this wasn't over.

* * *

When Zaiyera opened her eyes, it was not to the eastern sun shining through the window of her room.

She climbed out of bed and yawned. She stretched, then flinched at the sharp pain in her legs and ribs. The remaining healers had cleaned and dressed her wounds but they still stung terribly.

Zaiyera leaned out the window to find the sun well overhead. *I slept till midday?*

As best she could, with her injuries, Zaiyera hurriedly dressed and went to the dining hall. The walkways of the clay and sandstone palace were smooth, cool, and quite beautiful. She might have taken better care to appreciate the multicolored woven throw rugs, decorative clay pottery, and walls painted with warm colors, had her stomach not been growling so loudly.

The smell of food guided her through the hallways until she finally found the dining hall.

Zhuyun, Jaide, and Barum looked up from their meals at her approach.

"Well," Jaide said, "the dead finally awake, yes?"

"Don't let our friend, here, fool you, ah?" Zhuyun responded, pointing a spoon at the Viriksani. "We've been awake only a short time."

As soon as Zaiyera sat, one of the kitchen workers appeared with a plate full of roots, vegetables, and eggs.

"Where are the others?" Zaiyera asked around a mouthful of food. As hungry as she thought she was, that first bite lit a ravenous fire in her belly. She made an effort to slow down and not gulp everything down.

"Our two shydon *friends* are likely doing their best work to turn Sheikha Jawahir against us," Jaide grumbled. "They were nowhere in sight when we got here."

"I don't care how duty bound they are," Barum said, his deep voice booming through the dining hall. "Whatever your … condition, beggin' my pardon, we'd have been dead if you weren't here."

Zaiyera looked at the big battered man with gratitude. Despite having not seen much of battle the previous night, Barum had done well to help when he could. Zaiyera still marveled at how he had survived being buried under heavy stone, and then dealt a terrible blow from Malhadiev.

"Well," Jaide said, a slanted grin across her face. "I made a pretty good go of it. Perhaps if the lady, here, hadn't gotten in the way, I might have saved your hides instead, yes?"

The Viriksani's levity drew a round of quiet chuckling.

"You will be fine," Zaiyera said to them all. "Whatever happens, it is I who is the problem. Whatever justice I must face with the lady of Trystia, it will be as it will."

"It will be as it *will*," Jaide echoed with a flair of drama. "Such rich words. No, Kushtanji. You will not face justice alone."

"Aye," Barum said. "I do admit I wasn't none the wiser about your … situation, but you best believe I still count you as a friend. And ain't no friends abandoning each other when things get tough."

"We will stand with you," Zhuyun added. "No matter what Sheikha Jawahir decrees, we will face it together."

"I could be put to death," Zaiyera said to them.

"Oh, well in that case," Jaide said, pretending to stand from the table.

Another round of chuckling.

"As the Yuntaiman says," Jaide said after Barum grabbed her shoulder and sat her down. "We stand together." She held up a mug of chilled fenberry juice in toast. "Shakimah save me, but you've all become my family, yes?"

"Yes," the others echoed.

"Yes," Zaiyera said, moisture building in her eyes.

The sound of someone clearing their throat drew everyone's attention to the doorway. They turned to see a woman dressed in simple white robes with a strip of brown, purple, and gold designs woven into the left side of it. Her headwrap was a beautiful mix of gold and purple.

"Please excuse my interruption," the woman said. She placed her right hand over the left side of her heart with a slight bow. "Sheikha Jawahir is ready to speak with you."

Zaiyera half expected it to be a grand audience with her at the center and on trial. She'd expected to see Dyren Faust and Malker Argen standing in a position of authority near Jawahir.

Instead, she and her friends were led to a far more intimate setting. They entered a circular room filled with a warmth that had nothing to do with the temperature. Paintings depicting past Sheikhas as well as warriors of renown adorned the red-brown walls.

Seven large pillows were placed in a circle on a large throw rug. On one of those pillows sat Sheikha Jawahir. Across from her sat Dyren Faust and Malker Argen.

Jawahir smiled and gestured to the other pillows. The air of regality radiating from the woman felt palpable.

"I'm sure you've reasoned by now that your shadow hunter companions," she said, using the Dor'haighen term, "feel strongly about this situation." She looked straight into Zaiyera's eyes. "Do you have anything you wish to say to me, Zaiyera Tuneesh of Kushtanja?"

Zaiyera sat quietly for several moments, thinking of her life leading to the moment she met Dyren and Malker She thought of everything that had happened after that; the things she'd learned, the friendships that had been forged. For the first time since she'd become a dark-dancer, Zaiyera had friends again. More than friends. Family.

"I've not witnessed a moment yet," Zaiyera finally said, "when Dyren Faust or Malker Argen have spoken or behaved without truthfulness or honor. I trust that every word they spoke about me and their duty regarding me is true."

Jawahir considered her words. "You would leave your fate to these two men without defending yourself?"

Zaiyera looked at the floor in front of her crossed legs. "My past is as tainted as my soul, Sheikha Jawahir. What I did those many years ago has haunted me every day of my life. Perhaps this long road should end with justice finding me after I've made some form of amends."

Through every word, Jawahir looked into her eyes with a brown-eyed gaze that seemed to strip Zaiyera bare. She forced herself not to shrink under that gaze.

"I've held more trials and councils than I care to think about," Jawahir said, once Zaiyera had finished. "They've ranged from disputes over gardening sections of the city, to infidelity, and anything else you can imagine as a symptom of many people living so closely together.

"I've looked into the eyes of men and women of conscience and cruelty. You, young lady of Kushtanja, are not at the end of a long road, because first," she laughed softly, "you haven't been alive enough years for anything to be considered long for you. Second, from your words alone, I hear that you've served your penance quite thoroughly. Why would I enact it upon you again?"

The sheikha looked to each of the visitors in turn. "Every one of you have done not only Trystia, but the world, a great service. All death is regrettable, but this could have ended no other way than for *kivuli dayasa* to die. You are ... *all* of you," she looked pointedly at Zaiyera, friends of Trystia, and welcome here, always."

"If I may speak, Sheikha?"

Jawahir turned her heavy gaze on the senior shydon. "You may, Senior Shadow Hunter."

"The taint cannot be denied," Dyren said. "Once a lancer has tasted the lifestream of another and escaped the lifeprice, there is no turning back. It's only a matter of time—"

Jawahir held up a delicate-looking hand. "Do not presume to educate me on the facts concerning those who dance the stream, or lance the stream, as the north would have it."

Dyren opened his mouth, then shut it again. Beside him, Malker Argen remained silent and thoughtful. The one time he met Zaiyera's gaze, she thought she saw regret.

"With the utmost respect, Sheikha Jawahir," Dyren said. "By the law of Dor'haighen and the creed of we who hunt the shadow, we must bring her to the king's justice."

"I know well what you must do, shadow hunter," Jawahir replied. "And had this young woman committed a crime in your land, she would be subject to the justice of the ruler of your land. But she *saved* Dor'haighen, in addition to Samhar. I'm sure you remember. You fought beside her. We live because of all your efforts, but especially hers.

"So, you are free to leave Trystia whenever you please. When you return home, you may tell your king whatever you wish. Tell him that Zaiyera has died if it makes it easier, for that isn't my concern. But I will not allow one who has long since paid for the unfortunate events of her past, pay again. Nor will I turn a blind eye to the fact that she saved my life and the lives of many Trystians."

"This may not end with our return to the capital," Dyren Faust said. "King Eredin may insist upon bringing her to back for other crimes."

"Oh, yes," Jawahir said, waving a hand. "Breaking out his 'guest'." Sitting on her giant pillow, back erect, the Sheikha of Trystia was the embodiment of elegance. "I would think King Eredin's mind would be occupied more on the mystery surrounding the creation of the monster who has visited not a single Dor'haighen civilization, but upon many of Samhar.

"Surely he would be curious as to what happened to set a once levelheaded member of a trade delegation down such a destructive path. I cannot speak for your king, but it would weigh heavily on my mind, were I in his place."

Dyren knew when he was defeated. "Of course, Sheikha Jawahir. We will waste no more of your time."

"Not a waste at all. These are matters of state between neighboring nations. I'm sure there is nothing here of conflict, especially since Samhar has borne the full brunt of this tragedy. Many, many lives are being mourned, and many homes must be rebuilt. Perhaps share that with your king, that he might divert his thoughts from my guest, to more important issues."

The senior shydon hunter bowed over his crossed legs and replied in a tight voice, "of course, Sheikha."

* * *

Zaiyera stood on a balcony beside the ruler of Trystia, watching Dyren Faust and Malker Argen mount their gear-ladened camels. The guide who would accompany them to Xair, mounted his camel and started forward, Dyren following behind.

Malker followed his superior. After the animal took a few steps, the junior shydon hunter twisted around in the saddle and looked up to where the two women stood. He raised his hand. Zaiyera half lifted her hand, then raised it all the way and waved back.

The Dor'haighen warrior turned forward and soon receded into the distance beyond the towering niyabi, ogko, and palm trees.

"That one has an impetuosity about him," Jawahir said, "but a good heart. He will do well, if he doesn't dance too much of the stream that the lifeprice claims him."

"Yes, Sheikha," Zaiyera agreed. "Dyren is not a bad man either."

"No, he isn't," Jawahir agreed. "But he will break if he doesn't learn to bend." She looked at Zaiyera directly. "What will you do now?"

Zaiyera hadn't thought much about it. If she were honest with herself, she hadn't thought she'd survive the confrontation with Malhadiev."

"Ah. No plan beyond the immediate," Jawahir observed. "Normally I would provide an admonishment about such negative traits of youth, but I imagine you didn't believe you would be alive right now. Perhaps I can offer some direction?"

Zaiyera regarded the other woman. For the first time since she'd met her, she noticed that Jawahir was at least a decade her senior, despite her youthful—if stately—vigor. "Of course, Sheikha."

"Can you tell me how you function despite your condition?"

Zaiyera forced her anxiety down, despite being aware of Jawahir's personal guard standing not two strides away. The sheikha may be confident in Zaiyera's integrity, but Imrik was having none of it. It had been a discussion Jawahir wouldn't win. Zaiyera didn't blame the *dakhiva* one bit.

She took a deep breath and told the ruler of Trystia about the techniques she'd used her entire life, and the new one she'd learned from Zhuyun.

"Fascinating," Jawahir said. "To live as you have for this long, and not only function, but thrive, is something I've never heard of." She looked back out at the ruins of her once beautiful city, and the beauty that was the land of Samhar beyond. "Wouldn't it be fortunate if such skills could be taught to others who might have made such a dire mistake as you have?"

Zaiyera's mouth fell open.

"Careful, child," Jawahir said. "You'll swallow a bird."

"I ... but why, Sheikha? To syphon another—"

"Little in life is straightforward, child," Jawahir said. "There are some who do what they do out of cruelty or selfishness, others out of desperation, greed, self-defense. I'm not asking you to redeem the wicked. I wonder if you might provide a ray of hope for those who have met with regrettable circumstances that led to terrible mistakes.

"Whatever self-hatred you carry, you must work through it. I cannot help you with that, but you have a gift to give to others. If you feel you must pay a penance, do it in this manner. Be the light, Zaiyera. Offer hope to the child who syphoned another without realizing what she was doing. Help the man who panicked in a moment of self-defense and syphoned the lifestream of one who would have murdered him."

Zaiyera listened numbly to it all. She nearly hopped when she felt the other woman's gentle hand rest on her shoulder.

"Think about it," Jawahir said. "You've no need to rush away."

Zaiyera didn't try to fight back the tears welling in her eyes. "Thank you for all that you've done for me, Sheikha Jawahir," Zaiyera said. She placed her right hand over the left side of her heart and bowed in deference.

Jawahir responded with a courtly nod. "I've done little for you, child, but I offer what help I can, whether it's a home in Trystia, or some direction in your life." She placed a hand on each of Zaiyera's shoulders and gave them an affectionate squeeze. "You and your friends are honorary citizens of Trystia. If there is something you need of me, you have but to ask."

Zaiyera's mouth dropped open again before she caught herself and closed it. Even away from her nomadic people, Zaiyera had never remained in a city for longer than a month. "I'm honored … My Sheikha."

Jawahir released her. "Go and be with your friends."

Zaiyera turned to go. Once she passed the stony personal guard, she stopped and looked back. "May I ask a question?"

"Of course," the other woman replied.

"I've not seen Kima Imrian, Malhadiev's brother."

A hint of regret colored Jawahir's features. "He left before dawn.

When one of my staff went to extend my hospitalities, he had already left." She frowned, thoughtful. "Something broke inside of that man."

"The pain of loss," Zaiyera said.

Jawahir shook her head. "Yes, but … it's more than that. The death of someone close carries a terrible pain, but I suspect your companion, Kima Imrian, is broken in a way we may not understand."

"Hopefully he will heal in time," Zaiyera replied.

"Hopefully indeed," Jawahir agreed.

Zaiyera left the balcony and made straight for the guest wing where her friends would be waiting. Something about what Jawahir had said carried a note of foreboding.

"Ah!" Zhuyun exclaimed upon seeing her. The three friends stood. "Finished with your royal audience?"

"I am," Zaiyera replied. Though her heart felt lighter for the first time since she could remember, thoughts of Kima weighed on her. She started toward the stables, and her dear friend Sadiq.

The others fell in step around her. One look at Zaiyera's face, and Jaide threw up her hands. "Our mission is finished, we are alive, and a Sheikha has named us friends and honorary citizens of Trystia. You will not be submitted to the northern king's justice, and you can stay here as long as you like. How is it that in spite of all that, you still find a way to look so dour, Kushtanji?"

"Must be force of habit," Barum said. "Can't imagine anyone pretty as you, miss my lady, being so unhappy all the time. Pardon my saying. He followed that last bit with an awkward walking bow.

Zhuyun searched her face. "It is Kima, is it not?"

They turned down an avenue where the covered stables came into view. Zaiyera nodded, the smell of congregating camels reaching her nostrils. "She told me that by the time someone went to his room this morning, he'd already gone. She believes something is deeply broken in him."

A cluster of camels stood grazing the sparse plants sprinkled across the open ring. One camel lifted its head and turned to look in Zaiyera's direction.

Barum's rumbling laugh vibrated in Zaiyera's ears. "I s'pose you'll perk up after a hug from your best friend over there. Stinkin' beast."

"Careful, Dor'haighener," Jaide said. "You might have to fight her for that."

Sadiq trotted over to the group and stopped in front of Zaiyera, who wrapped her arms around his curved neck. The others stood silently, but Zaiyera didn't care if they watched or not. After all they'd been through together, it was a miracle from Shakimah that her camel friend had survived.

When she finally let go and gave Sadiq a pat on the neck, Zhuyun cleared his throat.

"Our friend, Kima, was a troubled man when we found him, ah? Troubled more, at his brother's death."

Jaide nodded at that. "Let us hope he works through his grief and finds his way, yes?"

Zaiyera leaned against Sadiq's side and looked at the southwest city wall. Her mind's eye looked well beyond it, across the many miles south, to Zalrabi. "Yes."

* * *

Kima stared straight ahead to the south. Home. He didn't know what was left of his beloved Zalrabi, but it made little difference. It would rebuild.

It was just him now. Malhadiev was gone, killed by Zaiyera and her terrible dancecraft scimitar. Rationally he knew there had been no other way to stop Malhadiev. His brother had been too far gone to be saved; he'd seen it in his eyes.

But Kima couldn't shake the image of that terrible blue-steel scimitar plunging into his brother's chest. Even with his waking eyes, he saw it. Malhadiev choking on his own blood. He'd watched the life fade from his brother's eyes.

Jawahir had offered to have Malhadiev buried, but Kima had declined. The last thing he would allow was for the people of the place where his brother had died to handle his body. In the end, Malhadiev had destroyed his home and roamed Samhar. So he'd buried his brother in Samhar.

Kima rested his forearms on the front of the saddle. At the leisurely pace his camel walked, it would be at least two weeks before he reached Zalrabi. A black flicker passed across the whites of his eyes as he leaned on his arm and let himself sway back and forth to the camel's lazy gait. What was the rush?

GLOSSARY

Lancing/Streamdancing

The stream permeates through the world. It is wielded through the act of Lancing. A Lancer is one who has the ability to see the stream-flows (flow) in the air as pools or running streams. They are able to access that power by piercing (or lancing) the stream of power, forming it, molding it. Most Lancers use their fingers to draw the power from the air, but there are some very rare individuals who have the ability to lance not only with their fingers, but with their hands, a limb, or even a weapon.

In the land of Samhar, those who touch the stream are called Streamdancers. Whereas lancers—as is commonly known the world over—touch and pierce the stream to draw out the flow of power, streamdancers draw upon that power by dipping into it, spreading it, swirling it. The term "dancing the stream" or "dancing" refers to the method in which Samharans access and utilize the power of the stream.

Attributes

They type of stream wielder depends on their past actions. For simplicity, all will be referred to as Lancers.

Generally, a lancer leaves a light gold lance-resin. Any lance-resin that is not gold is discolored, and is an indication that the lancer has siphoned a life essence. Yellow indicates that the lancer has taken one life. The darker the color, the more lives siphoned. In order: Gold, yellow, pale orange, dark orange, black.

The art of lancing is limited only by the skill and imagination of the lancer. The feeling one has when lancing is that of euphoria and an inner power that can be heady. If a lancer ever siphons the life of another, the sense of power becomes as addictive as a narcotic, and the lancer develops an insatiable craving for more.

Effects

Lancing bears a cost in the life essence of the lancer. Simple lancing, such as creating a campfire or blowing away leaves from in front of a home take only seconds away from one's life, while greater amounts of the power, such as creating a force of nature, drain days to years from a lancer.

Degrees of lance resin taint

Gold - Pure, untainted lancer.

Darklancer
Yellow - Tainted lancer. Has syphoned one to three lifestreams.
Orange - Syphoned four to six lifestreams.
Red - Syphoned seven to ten lifestreams.
Crimson - Syphoned eleven to fifteen lifestreams.

Shadowlancer
Black - Beyond sixteen lifestreams syphoned.

Lancing Techniques

Defensive

Most adept at creating shields, masking sound, repelling outside aggressive forces.

Offensive

Aggressors. Adept at forming weapons from the flow.

Flowing

The most agile, and versatile. Adept at redirection and return of aggression. A tactic of avoidance and alteration of threat. Flow lancing is also a tactic whereby a lancer can draw from the stream and hold it, continuously moving it about one's self and draw from it until depleted. Healers use this method, and it draws the least amount of lifeprice.

Compounding:

When two lancers move in unison to create a larger desired effect over an extended amount of time to greatly diminish the lifeprice.

Lifeprice

The amount of one's lifestream drained due to use of the stream. Depending on the amount of power drawn, one might sacrifice a few seconds of their life, or years. In extreme cases, one might sacrifice their life to access as much of the stream as possible.

Shydon Hunter

(Samhari term known as Shadow Hunter in Dor'haighen)
Hunt and eliminate darklancers.
TEAM: Consists of Five Lancers: Two Offensive, Two Defensive, and One Flowing.
FORCE: Consists of eight hunters: Four Offensive, Two Defensive, and Two Flowing.

Swordlancer
Rare form of soldier able to lance in the midst of melee battle.

Seeker
Hunts and capture lancers to be used as living weapons. Exclusively flow lancers.

Terms:

The Stream - The power that permeates the entire world and everything in it. Can be drawn upon and used at the cost of one's personal lifestream.

The Flow - When one draws power from the stream, that power becomes the flow, that which can be utilized by the one who has drawn it.
Lancer - One who pierces the stream and uses the power from it.
Streamdancer - One from the land of Samhar who touches the stream and draws it forth through the act of bodily movement, such as dance.
Tokailan - Those from the land of Yuntai who touch the stream.

Dancecraft (Lancecraft) Artifact
Item created through the act of lancing a great deal of stream into the creation of an item to imbue it with a specific property. Such an item enacts a large amount of lifesprice.

Samhari Terms

Kivuli Dayasa – (Shadowlancer) Samharan translation: One who dances in shadow.
Uluma - Respectful term when addressing a female elder.
Niyima - Respectful term when addressing a female.
Dyenbe - Respectful term when addressing a male elder.

Osa - Respectful term when addressing a male.

Dakhiva - Protectors. Some of the most formidable warriors in all of Samhar.

Hara Dakhiva - Highest ranked among the Dakhiva forces.

Kha -Tribe.

ALSO BY RAMÓN TERRELL

<u>Saga of Ruination:</u>

Unleashed

Emergence

<u>World of a Broken Age:</u>

Echoes of a Shattered Age

Legends of a Shattered Age

Heroes of a Broken Age

<u>The Fairies:</u>

Out of Ordure

Revenge of the Nymph

<u>Hunter's Moon:</u>

Running from the Night

Hunter's Moon

Darkness of Day

Revenire

www.ingramcontent.com/pod-product-compliance
Lightning Source LLC
Chambersburg PA
CBHW061203190726
48288CB00001B/35